Cocky Lobin over Germany

This is a must read for those of us intrigued by the air battles of WWII, particularly those involving Bomber Command. This is the story of a crew participating in a terrifying mission over Germany, coupled with insight into their life on a bomber station, their fears, their hopes and their dreams. A group of young men barely out of their teens, bound together by war and comradeship ... the next flight may very well be their last. - Mike Hockin

Daryl again engages the reader with his unique style, mixing raw emotions with deft technical explanations to explore the milieu of men and women subjected to the horrors of the bomber war. 'Cocky Lobin' is a snapshot of one short period in the long and deadly struggle which was the Air War over Europe, brought to life by Daryl's gift for storytelling. A 'must read' for all of us who grew up knowing men and women who were part of that War, but most likely never spoke of it. Most are gone now, but 'Cocky Lobin' allows us a glimpse of their lives – John Bucknell

Cocky Lobin makes for a good read and is an action packed story appealing to all readers who enjoy a good war story backed up by history – the research and detail is excellent. Daryl has once again demonstrated his talent as a writer with this book which is every bit as exciting as his first two books. - Ian Livingstone-Blevins

Cocky Lobin quickly draws you into the storyline with well-paced narrative, convincing characters, and impressive and authentic detail that only comes from painstaking research. I loved it. - Jeremy Martineau

The noise, the vibration, the fear and the humour mixed with the smell of grease and 100-octane petrol make this book a captivating read. This is a fitting tribute to the thousands who fought and died in the skies over Europe. The characters and the stories of their lives bring this book to life in vivid detail, I felt part of it ... - Clive Cooke

Daryl Sahli was born in Bulawayo Zimbabwe (Rhodesia) and attended Hillside Junior School and Gifford High School ('Tech'). After completing A-levels, he, like all other young men at the time, was called up for national service. The bush war was raging as 163 intake arrived at Cranborne Barracks in Salisbury (Harare). After completing training he was posted to 4 Independent Company (RAR) based at Victoria Falls where he completed his national service.

Daryl completed a B.Comm LLB degree at the University of Natal (Pietermaritzburg) and worked at both Ernst & Whinney (Young) and Arthur Andersen in Johannesburg. After immigrating to Australia, Daryl completed an LLM degree at the University of Queensland. Today Daryl works as a management consultant in his own practice in Brisbane. Daryl is married to Karen (nee Young, born in Ndola, Zambia) with two children Megan and Jason.

Other Books by Daryl Sahli

Rhodesian Bush War Series

A Skirmish in Africa (2011)
Winner of the Bronze Award in the Military/Wartime
Fiction category in the 2012 Independent Publisher (IPPY)
Book Awards in the United States.

Steely-Eyed Killers (2012)

Victims of a Giant Hoax
(due for release in 2014)

COCKY LOBIN OVER GERMANY

DARYL SAHLI

MyStory
PUBLISHING

Northlands Business Consultants Pty Ltd
ABN 75 091 308 146 Trading As

MyStory Publishing
P.O. Box 5336, West End, QLD, 4101, Australia
www.mystorypublishing.com.au

National Library of Australia Cataloguing-in-Publication entry:

Sahli , Daryl , author.
Cocky Lobin over Germany / Daryl Sahli ;
photograph, Jason Sahli ; cover design, Despina Papamanolis.

ISBN: 9780987156457 (paperback.)

Great Britain. Royal Air Force. Bomber Command - - Fiction.
World War, 1939-1945 - - Aerial operations, British - - Fiction.
Bombing, Aerial - - Germany - - Fiction.

Dewey Number: A823.4

ISBN: 9780987156471 (Kindle)
ISBN: 9780987156488 (Epub)

Maps & Tables by Daryl Sahli
Cover design by Despina Papamanolis
Author photograph by Jason Sahli
Book design by Karen Sahli
Typeset in 11 / 13.2pt Palatino
85gsm creme

My grateful thanks to three outstanding English teachers, Mr R. T. (Rob) McGeoch, Mrs A. (Althea) Farren and Mr B P (Brian) Webb, and one brilliant history teacher, Mr A. L. (Andre) Van Heerden, Gifford High School, Bulawayo, Rhodesia (Zimbabwe).

It is the supreme art of the teacher to awaken joy in creative expression and knowledge.
Albert Einstein

As always, it is impossible to take on writing projects like this without tremendous support. My love and thanks to my wife Karen who has published this and my previous books, to my beautiful daughter Megan who has insight well beyond her years. Then to my long-suffering editorial panel who throw themselves headlong into these new projects: Ian Livingstone-Blevins, Bill Picken, Clive Cooke, Jeremy Martineau, James Knox, John Bucknell and Mike Hockin. My heartfelt thanks to you all.

This book is dedicated to the men and women of
44 (Rhodesia) Squadron, 5 Group, Bomber
Command, Royal Air Force. Not all in the squadron
were Rhodesians … they came to serve from the
four corners of the Empire.

Of the 2,409 Rhodesian airmen who served in World
War II 697 (29%) never returned. Most of them did
not reach their 22nd birthday.

The motto of 44 (Rhodesia) Squadron reads:

Fulmina Regis iusta,
'The King's Thunderbolts are Righteous'.

Appropriately, the badge shows an African
Elephant, the symbol of power and strength. In the
case of 44 (Rhodesia) Squadron, power and strength
came from the majestic Avro Lancaster that they
flew from 24 December 1941 till the end of the war.
They were the first squadron in the RAF to take
delivery of these magnificent aircraft.

The Squadron badge is reported to be based upon the elephant on the Royal Seal of King Lobengula Khumalo (1845–1894), second king of the great Matabele nation, son of Mzilikazi the first King of the Matabele, son of Matshobana, son of Mangete, son of Ngululu, son of Langa, son of Zimangele; all descendants of the Zulu Khumalo Dynasty. Mzilikazi's personal ambition and charisma had incurred the wrath of the powerful King of the Zulus, Shaka; he had been forced to flee his native land near the Black Mfolozi River in Zululand, South Africa, in 1821. Mzilikazi took his clan north, eventually settling in the area known as Matabeleland, north of the Limpopo River. The name Matabele means 'The men of the long shields', an appropriate metaphor for the Avro Lancaster's operational reach of over 2,500 miles.

The name of Lobengula means 'He That Drives Like the Wind'. King Lobengula's salute by his *m'bongo*, his praisemaker: 'Behold, the great elephant, he comes! When he walks, the earth trembles! When he opens his mouth, the heavens roar!' Listening to the ear-splitting throb of the four Merlin engines of the Lancaster, they indeed made the heavens roar making the earth of their enemies tremble under their onslaught.

The Squadron was created under the authority of King George VI, in October 1941, its two-letter RAF identification was KM and its radio call-sign was 'March Tune'.

Map 1: Empire Air Training Scheme locations in Southern Rhodesia

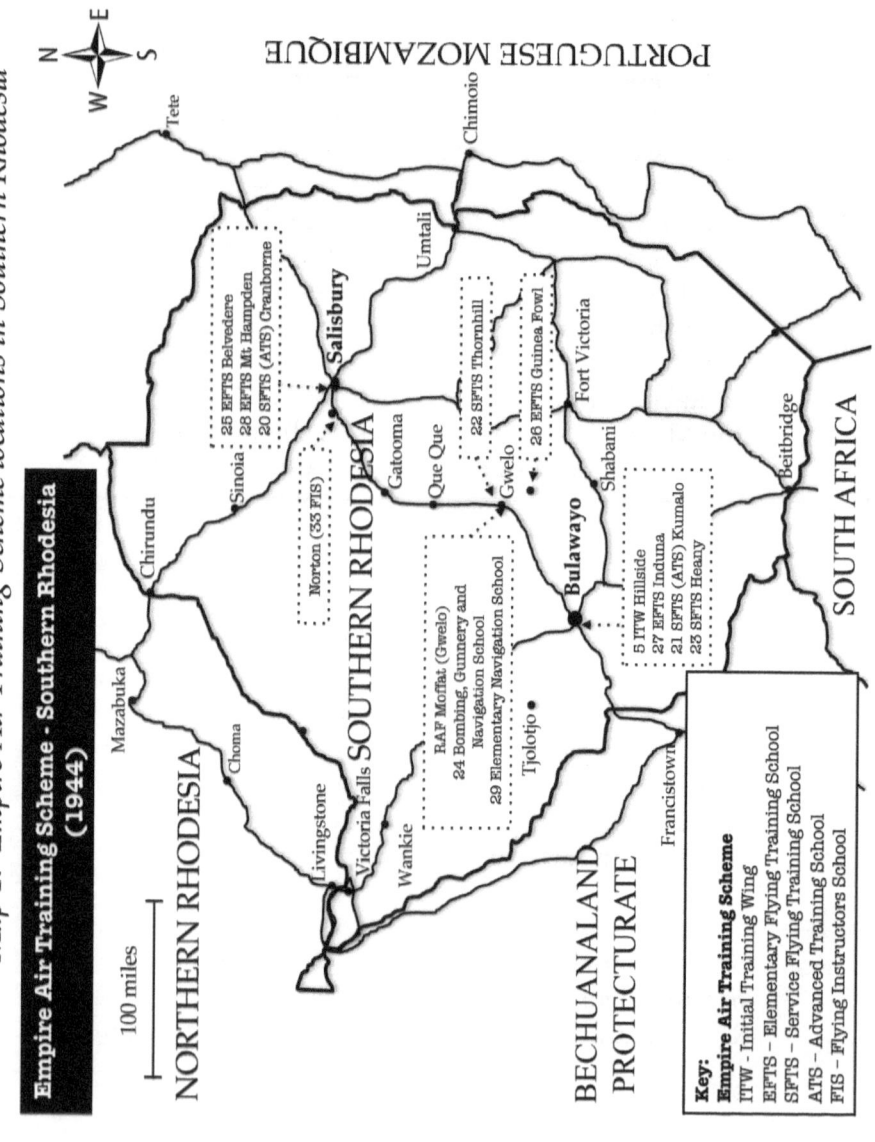

Empire Air Training Scheme - Southern Rhodesia (1944)

NORTHERN RHODESIA

SOUTHERN RHODESIA

PORTUGUESE MOZAMBIQUE

BECHUANALAND PROTECTORATE

SOUTH AFRICA

25 EFTS Belvedere
28 EFTS Mt. Hampden
20 SFTS (ATS) Cranborne

22 SFTS Thornhill

26 EFTS Guinea Fowl

Norton (33 FIS)

RAF Moffat (Gwelo)
24 Bombing, Gunnery and Navigation School
29 Elementary Navigation School

5 ITW Hillside
27 EFTS Induna
21 SFTS (ATS) Kumalo
23 SFTS Heany

Tete
Chimoio
Umtali
Salisbury
Sinoia
Chirundu
Mazabuka
Choma
Livingstone
Victoria Falls
Wankie
Gatooma
Que Que
Gwelo
Fort Victoria
Shabani
Bulawayo
Tjolotjo
Francistown
Beitbridge

100 miles

Key:
Empire Air Training Scheme
ITW - Initial Training Wing
EFTS - Elementary Flying Training School
SFTS - Service Flying Training School
ATS - Advanced Training School
FIS - Flying Instructors School

Map 2: RAF Stations mentioned in this story

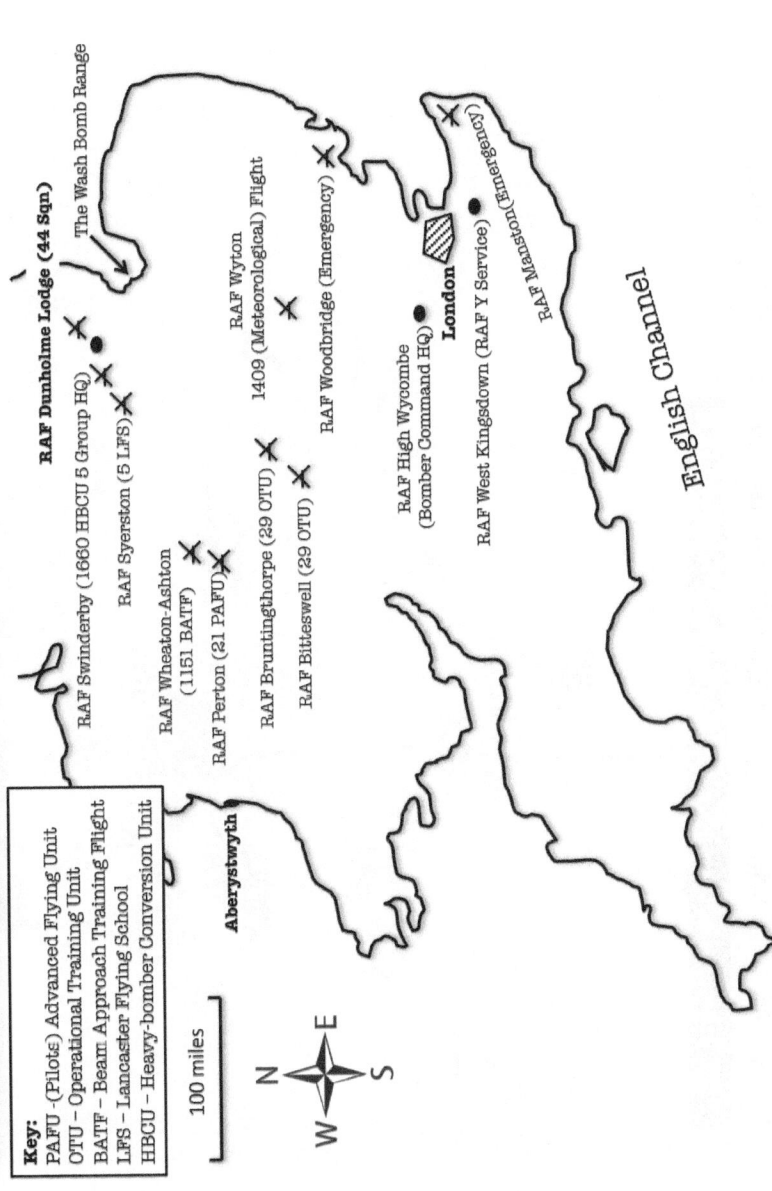

RAF Stations in England Mentioned in this Story
(Stations that PO Carter & crew attended during training)

Key:
PAFU – (Pilots) Advanced Flying Unit
OTU – Operational Training Unit
BATTF – Beam Approach Training Flight
LFS – Lancaster Flying School
HBCU – Heavy-bomber Conversion Unit

100 miles

N
W E
S

Aberystwyth

RAF Swinderby (1660 HBCU 5 Group HQ)
RAF Syerston (5 LFS)
RAF Dunholme Lodge (44 Sqn)
The Wash Bomb Range

RAF Wheaton-Ashton
(1151 BATTF)
RAF Perton (21 PAFU)

RAF Bruntingthorpe (29 OTU)
RAF Bitteswell (29 OTU)

RAF Wyton
1409 (Meteorological) Flight
RAF Woodbridge (Emergency)

RAF High Wycombe
(Bomber Command HQ)
London
RAF West Kingsdown (RAF Y Service)

RAF Manston (Emergency)

English Channel

Map 3: RAF Bomber Command Stations within 18 miles of Lincoln

RAF Stations within 18 miles of Lincoln – March 1944

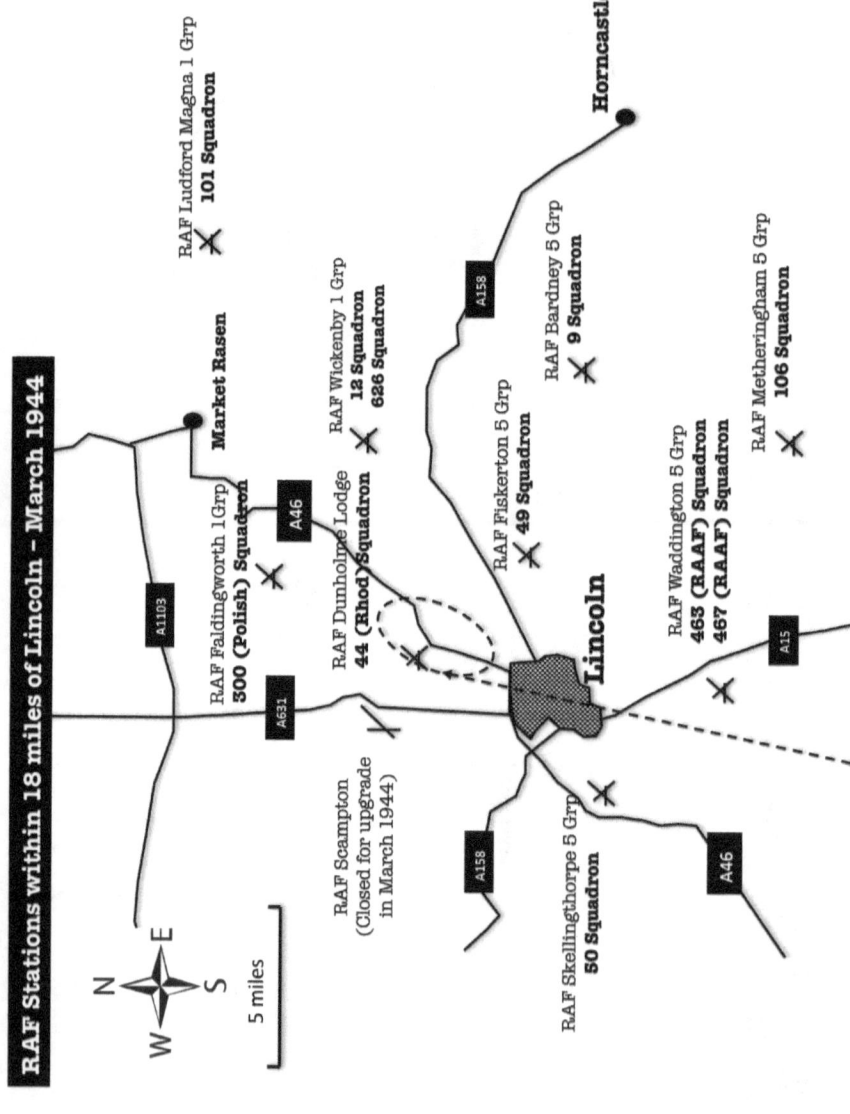

N
E
S
W

5 miles

RAF Ludford Magna 1 Grp
✕ **101 Squadron**

Market Rasen

RAF Wickenby 1 Grp
✕ **12 Squadron**
626 Squadron

A1103

RAF Faldingworth 1 Grp
✕ **300 (Polish) Squadron**

A46

RAF Dunholme Lodge
✕ **44 (Rhod) Squadron**

A631

RAF Scampton
(Closed for upgrade
in March 1944)

A158

RAF Bardney 5 Grp
✕ **9 Squadron**

RAF Fiskerton 5 Grp
✕ **49 Squadron**

RAF Metheringham 5 Grp
✕ **106 Squadron**

Lincoln

RAF Waddington 5 Grp
463 (RAAF) Squadron
467 (RAAF) Squadron
✕

A15

A158

RAF Skellingthorpe 5 Grp
✕ **50 Squadron**

A46

Horncastle

Map 4: German Nightfighter Defensive System over Western Europe

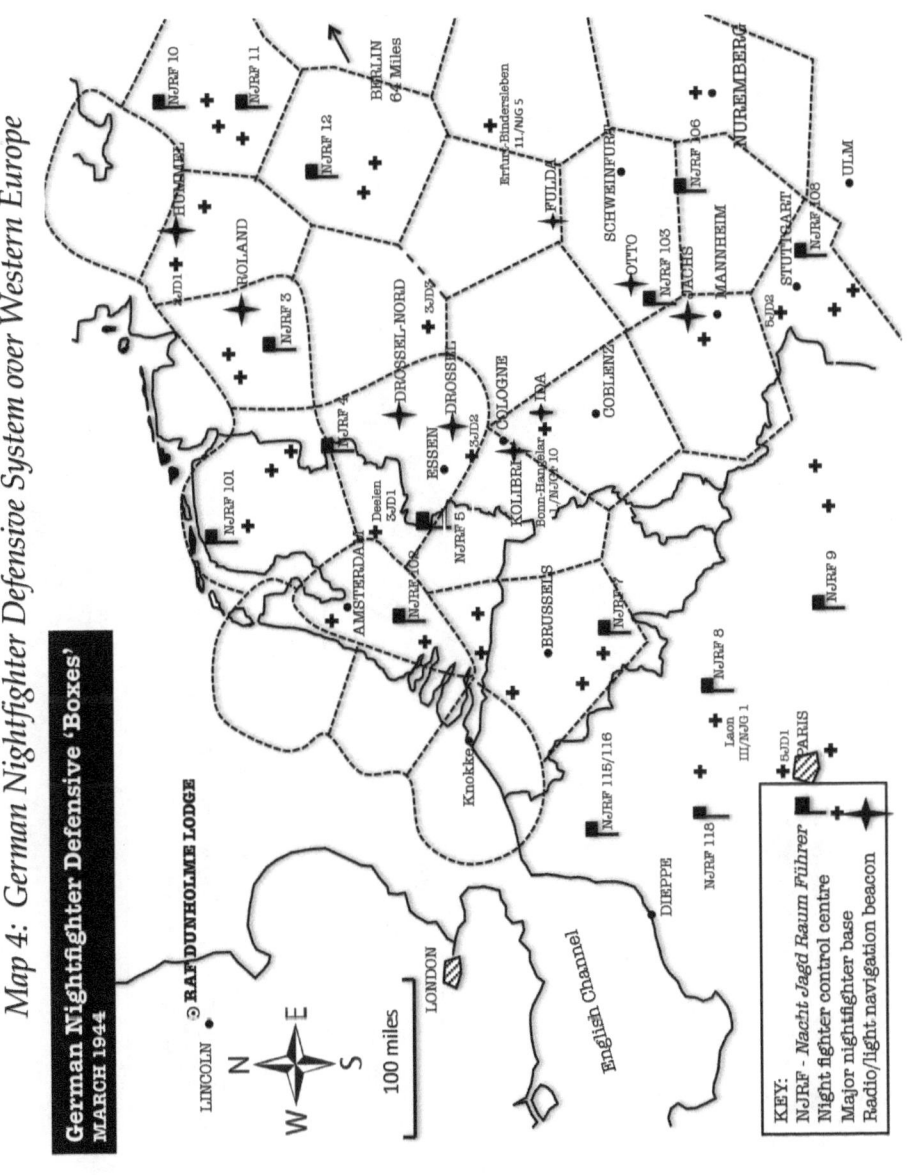

German Nightfighter Defensive 'Boxes'
MARCH 1944

KEY:
NJRF - *Nacht Jagd Raum Führer*
Night fighter control centre
Major nightfighter base
Radio/light navigation beacon

Map 5: RAF Dunholme Lodge, Lincolnshire, home to 44 (Rhodesia) Squadron from May 1943 to September 1944

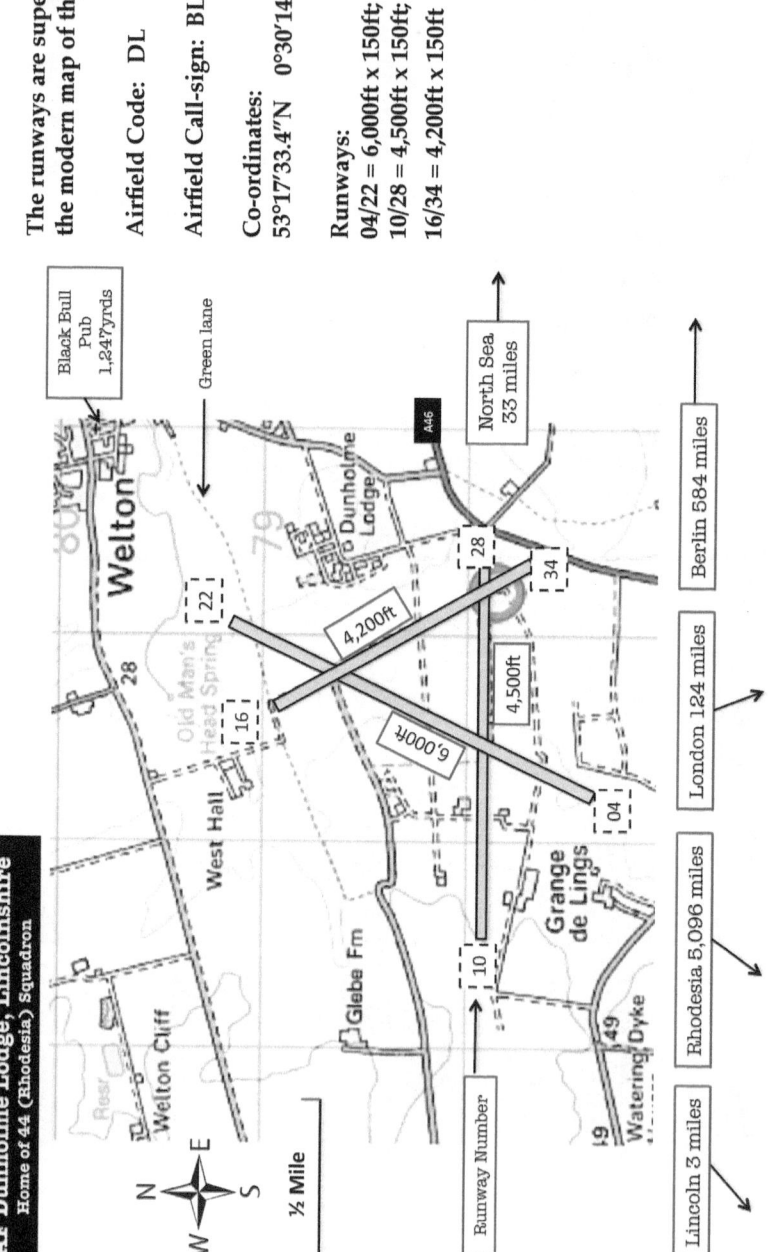

The runways are superimposed on the modern map of the area.

Airfield Code: DL

Airfield Call-sign: BLUESTRIPE

Co-ordinates:
53°17'33.4"N   0°30'14.0"W

Runways:
04/22 = 6,000ft x 150ft;
10/28 = 4,500ft x 150ft;
16/34 = 4,200ft x 150ft

RAF Dunholme Lodge, Lincolnshire
Home of 44 (Rhodesia) Squadron

Black Bull
Pub
1,247yrds

Green lane

Welton

Dunholme
Lodge

A46

North Sea
33 miles

22

28

4,200ft

16

4,500ft

6,000ft

West Hall

Old Man's
Head Spring

34

28

04

Grange
de Lings

10

Glebe Fm

Welton Cliff

Resr

½ Mile

Runway Number

Watering Dyke

49

Berlin 584 miles

London 124 miles

Rhodesia 5,096 miles

Lincoln 3 miles

Aircraft described in this story shown to approximate relative scale

Avro Lancaster B1

---------69ft 10in---------

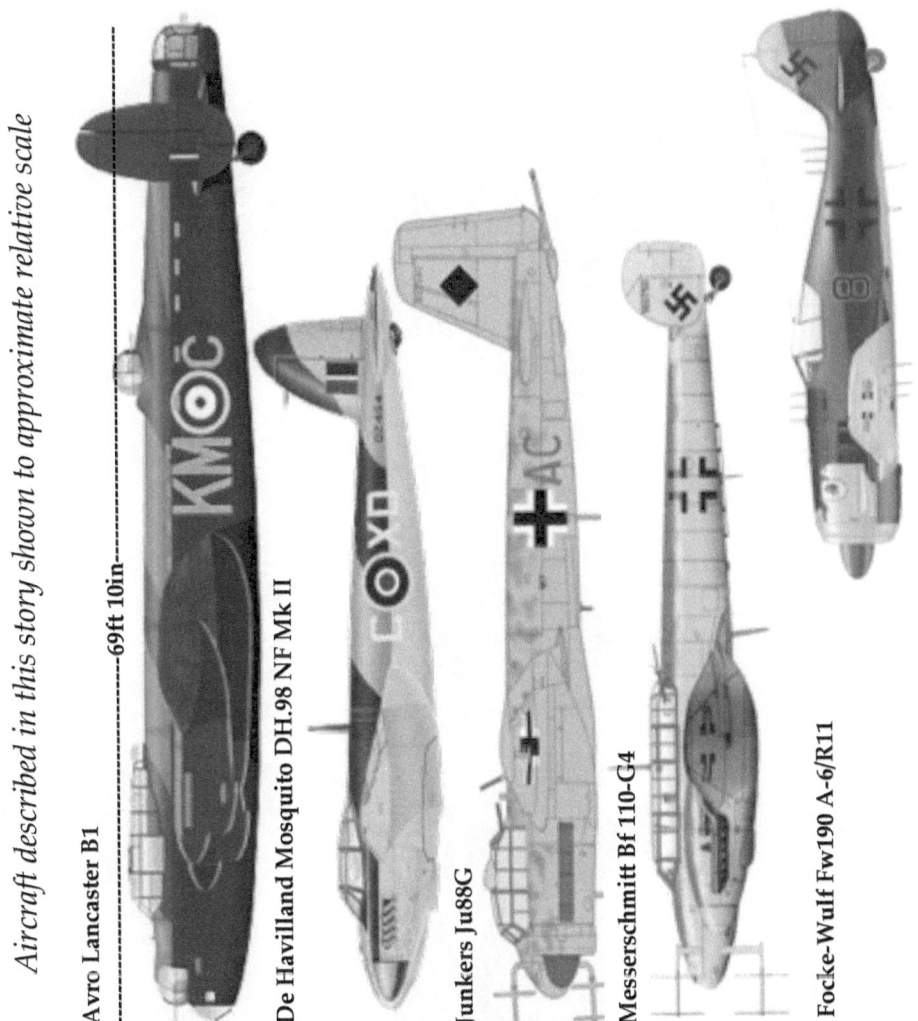

De Havilland Mosquito DH.98 NF Mk II

Junkers Ju88G

Messerschmitt Bf 110-G4

Focke-Wulf Fw190 A-6/R11

ROYAL AIR FORCE - PILOT'S FLYING LOG BOOK - W. J. CARTER 758367   FORM 414 (Summary)

YEAR		AIRCRAFT	PILOT, or 1st PILOT	2nd PILOT, PUPIL, PASSENGER	DUTY (Including Results and Remarks)	Hrs. Single/Multi-engined
MONTH	DATE	TYPE				
Dec 41 – Feb 1942	2 Dec 41 – 27 Feb 42	Tiger	SGT. Froud PO Arnold CFI Test: S/Ldr Boult	Self	27 EFTS, Induna, Bulawayo, Exercises 1 – 25 including night flying.	96
Mar – May 42	4th Mar – 23rd May	Harvard MKI	FO Whiffen FO wood CFI Test: F/Lt Amlot	Self	20 SFTS, Cranborne, Salisbury, repeat exercises 1 – 25	78 Sub-total: 174
June – Aug 42	2 June – 28th Aug	Harvard MKI	F/Lt Bentley F/Lt Drew SGT. Taylor ATS Flying Test: F/Lt Bentley	Self	ATS, 20 SFTS, Cranborne, Salisbury, Instrument Flying, bombing, formation flying.	75 Sub-total: 249
Nov 42 – Mar 1943	6th Nov – 25th Mar 43	Oxford	F/Sgt Prickett F/Sgt Wescomb	Self	21 PAFU, Perton (Wolverhampton), navigation, instruments, night flying	60 Sub-total: 309
Mar – Apr 43	3 Mar – 2 Apr.	Oxfords	Flt/Sgt Ellis FO Evans	Self	1511 BATF, Wheaton-Aston, Beam Approach, night flying, cross-country, Instruments.	10 Sub-total: 319

ROYAL AIR FORCE - PILOT'S FLYING LOG BOOK - W. J. CARTER 758367   FORM 414 (Summary)

YEAR		AIRCRAFT	PILOT, or 1st PILOT	2nd PILOT, PUPIL, PASSENGER	DUTY (Including Results and Remarks)	Hrs. Single/Multi-engined
MONTH	DATE	TYPE				
Apr – Jun 43	4th Apr – 24th Jun	Wellington	F/Sgt Rosser FO Hooper Flt/Lt Croskell	Crew	29 OTU, Bitteswell & Bruntingthorpe	60 Sub-total: 379
Aug – Nov 43	25th Aug – 3 Nov	Stirling	Flt/Lt Pilgrim Flt/Sgt Crowston	Crew	1660 HBCU, Swinderby	71 Sub-total: 450
Nov 43	8th – 23rd	Lancaster	Self	Crew	5 LFS Syerston	21 Sub-total: 461
Dec 43	16th	Lancaster	Self	Crew	Berlin	10.02
Dec 43	20th	Lancaster	Self	Crew	Frankfurt	8.10
Dec 43	23rd	Lancaster	Self	Crew	Berlin	9.35
Oct – Dec 43	1943	Lancaster	Self	Crew	H/LB, NFT and Cross Country Training 1943	42
Jan 1944	1st	Lancaster	Self	Crew	Berlin	9.45

ROYAL AIR FORCE - PILOT'S FLYING LOG BOOK - W. J. CARTER 758367 FORM 414 (Summary)

YEAR		AIRCRAFT		PILOT, or 1st PILOT	2nd PILOT, PUPIL, PASSENGER	DUTY (Including Results and Remarks)	Hrs. Single/Multi-engined
MONTH	DATE	TYPE					
Jan 44	12th	Lancaster		Self	Crew	Gardening Kiel Bay	7.25
Jan 44	14th	Lancaster		Self	Crew	Brunswick	6.20
Jan 44	21st	Lancaster		Self	Crew	Magdeburg	9.05
Jan 44	30th	Lancaster		Self	Crew	Berlin	10.25
Feb 44	23rd	Lancaster		Self	Crew	Gardening Terschelling	4.20
Feb 44	24th	Lancaster		Self	Crew	Schweinfurt	7.25
Feb 44	25th	Lancaster		Self	Crew	Augsburg	10.15
Feb 44	27th	Lancaster		Self	Crew	Gardening – Helgoland	4.50
March	1st	Lancaster		Self	Crew	Stuttgart	8.0

ROYAL AIR FORCE - PILOT'S FLYING LOG BOOK - W. J. CARTER 758367   FORM 414 (Summary)

YEAR		AIRCRAFT	PILOT, or 1st PILOT	2nd PILOT, PUPIL, PASSENGER	DUTY (Including Results and Remarks)	Hrs. Single/Multi-engined
MONTH	DATE	TYPE				
March	15th	Lancaster	Self	Crew	Stuttgart	7.55
March	22nd	Lancaster	Self	Crew	Frankfurt	7.25
March	24th	Lancaster	Self	Crew	Berlin	9.25
Jan – March	1944	Lancaster	Self	Crew	HLB, NFT and Cross Country Training 1944	15
March	30th					?

HLB, high level bombing. NFT, night flying training.

Lancaster B1

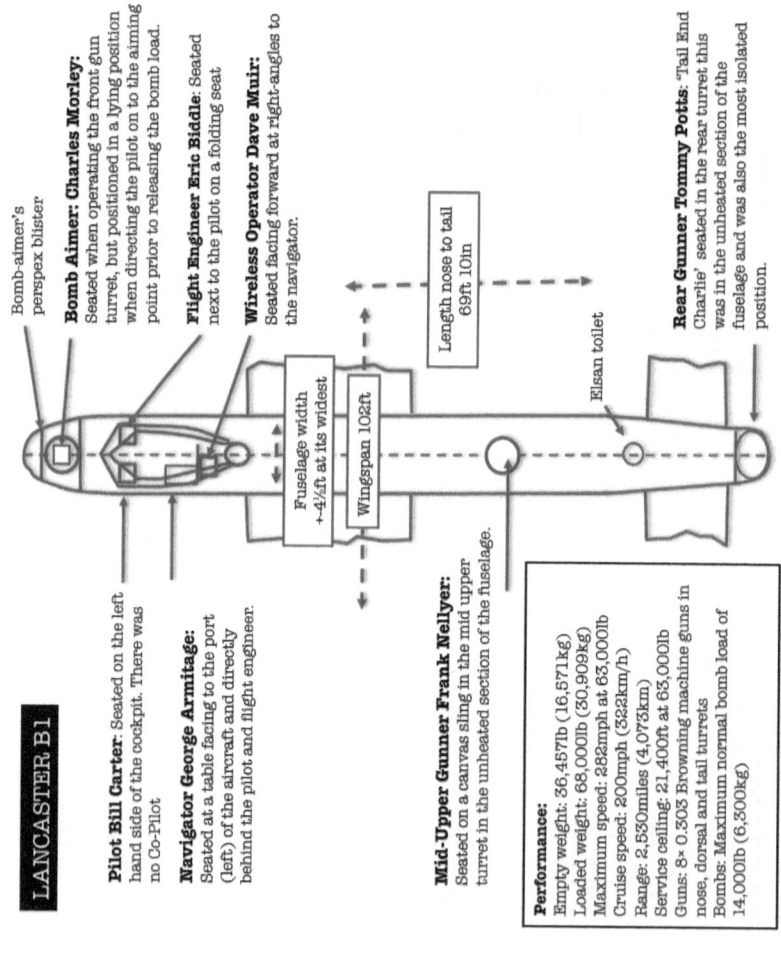

LANCASTER B1

Pilot Bill Carter: Seated on the left hand side of the cockpit. There was no Co-Pilot.

Navigator George Armitage: Seated at a table facing to the port (left) of the aircraft and directly behind the pilot and flight engineer.

Bomb-aimer's perspex blister

Bomb Aimer: Charles Morley: Seated when operating the front gun turret, but positioned in a lying position when directing the pilot on to the aiming point prior to releasing the bomb load.

Flight Engineer Eric Biddle: Seated next to the pilot on a folding seat

Wireless Operator Dave Muir: Seated facing forward at right-angles to the navigator.

Fuselage width +-4½ft at its widest

Wingspan 102ft

Length nose to tail 69ft 10in

Elsan toilet

Rear Gunner Tommy Potts: 'Tail End Charlie' seated in the rear turret this was in the unheated section of the fuselage and was also the most isolated position.

Mid-Upper Gunner Frank Nellyer: Seated on a canvas sling in the mid upper turret in the unheated section of the fuselage.

Performance:
Empty weight: 36,457lb (16,571kg)
Loaded weight: 68,000lb (30,909kg)
Maximum speed: 282mph at 63,000lb
Cruise speed: 200mph (323km/h)
Range: 2,530miles (4,073km)
Service ceiling: 21,400ft at 63,000lb
Guns: 8× 0.303 Browning machine guns in nose, dorsal and tail turrets
Bombs: Maximum normal bomb load of 14,000lb (6,300kg)

AIRCRAFT: LANCASTER ND796 – C-Charlie - 30/31st March 1944

CREW	NAME	HOMETOWN	OCCUPATION	AGE
Pilot	F/O William Carter	Bulawayo, Matabeleland, Rhodesia	Trainee Banker	20
Navigator	P/O George Armitage	Lincoln, Lincolnshire, England	Trainee Accountant	22
Bomb-Aimer	P/O Charles Morley	Mudgee, New South Wales, Australia	History Teacher	23
Flight Engineer	WO Eric Biddle	Preston, Lancashire, England	Policeman	30
Mid-Upper Gunner	Sgt Frank Nellyer	Clyde, Alberta, Canada	Farmhand	19
Wireless Operator	Sgt David Muir	Que Que, Midlands, Rhodesia	Junior District Officer, Dept. Internal Affairs	21
Rear Gunner	Sgt Tommy Potts	Mile End, London, England	Cleaner	18

Glossary

2IC	Second in Command
ACM	Air Chief-Marshall
AFS (RAF)	Advanced Flying School
AGL	Above ground level.
AI	Airborne Intercept radar.
AOC	Air Officer Commanding
AVM	Air Vice-Marshall
BATF (RAF)	Beam Approach Training Flight
Bf 110-G4 (German)	Messerschmitt twin-engined, radar equipped, nightfighter. Three-crew night fighter, FuG202/220 radar, optional *Schrage Musik* usually mounted midway down the cockpit with the cannon muzzles barely protruding above the canopy glazing. Speed: 370mph (595km/h). Range: 558miles (900km); 807miles (1,300km) with drop-tanks. Ceiling: 36,000ft (11,000m). Rate of Climb: 8 min to 20,000ft (6,000m). Guns: 2 × 20 mm MG 151 Cannons, 750rpg (rounds per gun), 4 × 7.92 mm MG 17 Machine guns with 1,000 rounds per gun. 1 × 7.92 mm MG 81 Z twin machine gun installation in rear cockpit, with 850rpg.
C-in-C	Commander in Chief
Chilapalapa	Hybrid language, developed by the earliest settlers, miners, traders, hunters and farmers to assist with communication with the African tribes of Southern Africa. Words were taken from seShona, siNdebele, Afrikaans and English. The language was in daily use and played a vital role in improving communication between the races.
DR	Dead reckoning - Also DED (for deduced reckoning) is the process of calculating one's current position by using a previously determined position, or fix, and advancing that position based upon known or estimated speeds over elapsed time, and course. Dead reckoning, using best estimates of speed and direction, is subject to cumulative errors particularly if estimates of wind speed and direction are inaccurate.
EFTS (RAF)	Elementary Flying Training School
F/O	Flying Officer. The second lowest officer rank in the RAF. The rank title did not imply that an officer in the rank of flying officer flew an aircraft. Some flying officers were aircrew, but many were ground branch officers.

Flak (German)	*Fliegerabwehrkanonen*, Flak or Ack-Ack. By 1942, 15,000 88mm guns formed the bulk of heavy flak defences for Germany. Large numbers of 37mm and 20mm guns filled the skies with shells during every air raid. Often arrayed in 'belts' around a city or target 88s could fire 22lb (10kg) shells up to 35,000 ft. (10,600 m) at a rate of 15-20 rounds per minute. The excellent 88mm gun proved very effective especially when radar was used to help with aiming. The shells exploding at a pre-set altitude sending metal splinters flying in all directions. Later groups of up to 40 heavy flak guns, *Grossbatterien,* fired rectangular patterns of shell bursts known as box barrages that proved very deadly to enemy bombers. German Flak accounted for 50 of the 72 RAF bombers lost over Berlin on the night of 24 March 1944.
Flt/Sgt	Flight Sergeant, 'Chiefy'
Fw190 A-6/ R11 (German)	Focke-Wulf single-engined fighter. Four MG151/20E 20 mm cannons. The wings were redesigned for the heavier cannon mount and had larger ammunition boxes. 2 x MG17 7.9mm machine guns. Speed 357mph (sea level) , 397mph (10,830ft) , 426mph (21,650ft) . Climb Rate Time to 6,560ft - 2.1mins . Time to 32,801ft - 16.8mins. Used as part of nightfighter tactics, fitted with small flame dampers and FuG217 "Neptun" radar. The Neptune aerials consisted of sets of three antennae arrays in four positions in the wings, forward and rear of the cockpit.
GEE (RAF)	A receiver for a navigation system of synchronized pulses transmitted from the UK - aircraft calculated their position from the time delay between pulses. The range of GEE was 300-400miles (483-644km). GEE used a whip aerial mounted on the top of the fuselage ahead of the mid-upper turret.
Grp/Capt	Group Captain
H2S (RAF)	Ground-looking navigation radar system, housed in a large blister under the rear fuselage. It could be homed in on by the German nightfighter's NAXOS receiver and had to be used with discretion.
HBCU (RAF)	Heavy Bomber Conversion Unit
IAS	Indicated Airspeed
ITW (RAF)	Initial Training Wing

Ju88G (German)	German Night fighter, speed 342miles/hr., ceiling 32,000ft, range 1,500 miles, endurance 4hours, aerodynamically improved conformal gun pod for a quartet of forward-firing 20mm, MG 151/20 autocannons below the former bomb bay. Electronic equipment, FuG 220 Lichtenstein SN-2 90 MHz, VHF radar, using eight-dipole *Hirschgeweih* antennas. Two, 1,750 PS Jumo 213A inline-V12 engines, enlarged fuel tanks and often one or two 20mm MG 151/20 autocannons in a *Schrage Musik* ('Jazz Music', i.e. slanted) installation. These guns were pointed obliquely upwards and forwards from the upper fuselage - usually at an angle of 70°.
Lancaster (RAF)	Avro Lancaster B1. This was Cocky Lobin. The original Lancasters were produced with Rolls-Royce Merlin XX engines with SU Carburettors. Minor details were changed throughout the production series - for example, the pitot head design was changed from being on a long mast at the front of the nose to a short fairing mounted on the side of the fuselage under the cockpit. Later production Lancasters had Merlin 22 and 24 engines. No designation change was made to denote these alterations.
LFS	Lancaster Flying School
MEW	Ministry for Economic Warfare.
MONICA (RAF)	A rearward-looking radar to warn of nightfighter approaches. However, it could not distinguish between attacking enemy fighters and nearby friendly bombers and served as a homing beacon for suitably equipped German nightfighters. Once this was realised, it was removed altogether.
Mosquito (RAF)	De Havilland Mosquito DH.98 NF Mk II. The first production nightfighter Mosquitos were designated NF Mk II. Wooden – twin-engined, fighter. Speed: 366mph (610 km/h) at 21,400ft (6,500 m). Range: 900 miles (1,500 km) with 410 gal (1,864 litre) fuel load at 20,000ft (6,100 m). Armament: 4 × 20 mm (.79 in) Hispano Mk II cannon (fuselage) and 4 × .303 in (7.7 mm) Browning machine guns (nose)
NAAFI	Navy, Army and Air Force Institutes. Organisation created by the British government in 1921 to run recreational establishments needed by the armed forces, and to sell goods to servicemen and their families. By April 1944, the NAAFI ran 7,000 canteens and had 96,000 personnel. At Dunholme Lodge, as with most other air stations, the NAAFI operated a truck for supplying tea and sandwiches.

Naxos (German)	The Telefunken FuG 350 Naxos radar-warning receiver, a German countermeasure to SHF band radar. Could pick up 10cm / 3GHz British H2S radar transmissions.
NJRF (German)	A belt of surveillance radars monitored access to Germany. Each sector was under the operational control of an *NJRF, Nachtjagdraumführung,* itself under the supervision of a *Nachtjagdgruppe (NJG)*. The radar installations formed a complete integrated system, grouped into three-dimensional areas called *Raum,* layered three deep from Denmark to the middle of France. The control centre of each of these sectors governed every detection station spread across the *Luftnachrichten* Regiments geographical area. Each Raum control centre was a three-dimensional zone, consisting of long-range and short-range radar. The achievement of a three-dimensional night air interception was based on the integration of the ground component and the air component. The radars detected targets, selected one, and then directed the interceptor towards that spot.
OBOE (RAF)	A very accurate navigation system consisting of a receiver/ transponder for two radar stations transmitting from widely separated locations in Southern England, which together, determined the range and the bearing of the aircraft. The system could only handle one aircraft at a time, and was fitted to a Pathfinder aircraft, usually a fast and manoeuvrable Mosquito that marked the target for the main force.
OTU	Operational Training Unit
P/O	Pilot Officer. The most junior officer rank for RAF officers. The rank title did not imply that an officer in the rank of pilot officer was a pilot. Some pilot officers were aircrew, whilst many were ground branch officers.
R/T	Radio telephone
Schrage Musik (German)	A German nickname given to the *Nachtjagd* 'Nightfighters' equipped with two MG FF's or MG 151/20s 20mm cannons mounted in the cabin or fuselage at a 70-80° angle which were aimed by a second Revi C 12/D or 16B gun sight mounted on the canopy roof. 'Schrage Musik' proved to be lethal and took a fearsome toll of heavy bombers in the night battles.
SFTS	Service Flying Training School
Sgt	Sergeant (NCO) non-commissioned officer.

SN-2 (Germany)	By late 1943, the *Luftwaffe* was starting to deploy the greatly improved FuG 220 Lichtenstein SN-2, operating on a longer-wavelength of 90MHz (lower end of the US VHF broadcast band) frequency, which was far less affected by electronic jamming, but this required the much larger *Hirschgeweih* (stag's antlers) antennas, with eight dipole elements. This aerial setup also produced tremendous drag and slowed the operating aircraft by up to 50 km/h (30 mph). The Lichtenstein FuG220 intercept radar had a relatively wide cone of search, around ±45°, direction finding for flying targets was good, being 1.65:1 for 10° off-centre at an operational frequency of 90MHz. The forward cover against flying targets was excellent and the ambiguities not serious. The Lichtenstein FuG220 had an instrumented range of 8 km, however the greatest practical range of the set was limited to the flight altitude, beyond ground clutter. The minimum detectable range of the set was limited by the T/R switch around 900 meters.
Sqn/Ldr	Squadron Leader
WAAF	Women's Auxiliary Air Force, whose members were invariably referred to as Waafs, was the female auxiliary of the Royal Air Force during the Second World War. They performed numerous tasks; radar, wireless, telephony, driving, packing parachutes, meteorology, air-traffic control, aircraft delivery (pilots), intelligence and administration to name a few.
WD	Women's Division, the Canadian equivalent of the WAAF.
Window (RAF)	Electronic Counter-measures (ECM) called chaff or Window, for jamming and spoofing radar and navigation signals. Strips of aluminium-foil, measured 6 inches long and 1 inch wide. They were packed in bundles of 2,200 held together with elastic bands. Each aircraft carried between 50 – 60 bundles on a long trip. By varying the dimensions of the Window, different radar wavelengths could be disrupted.
Wingco	Wing Commander
WO	Warrant Officer

Foreword

I am of the generation that made plastic Airfix aeroplane models and read *Boy's Own*, *Victor* and *Commando* comics. We played with plastic 'men', Waterloo Infantry, French Cavalry, 8th Army, Germans and Marines. As children we read, Enid Blyton's *Secret Seven* and *Famous Five*; as we got older we read Edward Stratemeyer's *Hardy Boys*, W. E. Johns' *Biggles*, Ryder Haggard's *Alan Quatermain* and *King Solomon's Mines* with set-books at school like Douglas Bader's *Reach for the Sky*, Guy Gibson's *Enemy Coast Ahead* and Nicolas Montserrat's *Cruel Sea* and *HMS Ulysses*. In class, we took turns reading the parts in the play *The Long and the Short and the Tall* by Willis Hall, and we were required to interpret the harrowing words of Siegfried Sassoon, Wilfred Owen and John McCrae.

A Spitfire, Messerschmitt Bf109, B17, B29, B24, Vickers Wellington and my favourite of all, the Avro Lancaster, hung from the ceiling above my bed ... all collecting dust to the chagrin of my mother.

I was brought up in the dry, dusty, heat of Matabeleland in Rhodesia (Zimbabwe). We shot catties, climbed trees, hunted termites and built 'forts' of thorn acacia in the surrounding bush. We listened to stories of the 'war', from parents, aunts, uncles, and family friends. I had a grandfather who fought in Abyssinia, North Africa and Italy.

We ended up with our own war to fight ...

Cocky Lobin over Germany is the fulfilment of a childhood dream to write a story about Bomber Command, but is, more importantly, meant as my personal tribute to the bomber crews who lost their lives over Germany, more specifically the men and women of 44 (Rhodesia) Squadron, Royal Air Force.

44 Squadron became 44 (Rhodesia) Squadron in November 1941 in recognition of that colony's support of the war effort. Southern Rhodesia, as it was called then, had been a self-governing colony from October 1923 and remained so throughout the war until 1965.

For all those from Southern Rhodesia, both black and white, who lost their lives fighting on the battlefields of the Empire, the Boer War, both World Wars, Korea, Suez and Malaya, alas, the vast majority of people of modern Zimbabwe have no knowledge or understanding of their sacrifice ... and may never have.

This story covers a short snapshot of time between 24 March and 31 March 1944 for the crew of C-Charlie, christened 'Cocky Lobin'. The crew, of course, are part of my own imagination and there would have been many C-Charlies during the war. The wonderfully poignant book, *A Bundu Boy in Bomber Command* by William Dives DFC, inspires the story. William Dives was a Rhodesian pilot in 44 Squadron and he describes, in a beautifully simple way, what it was like to travel from tiny, isolated, Rhodesia to war-torn England. There, to be thrust into a giant bomber and sent to Germany, night after night, with little prospect of survival. William joined 44 Squadron on 23 August 1944, after the period of this book, but his observations were enormously instructive.

I would like to thank my good friend Bill Picken for giving me a copy of his uncle's logbook (Form 414) from his time in Bomber Command. Bill's uncle William (also called Bill) went to Chaplin High School in Gwelo, then trained to fly in Bulawayo and Salisbury (Harare) before being sent to England. Bill (senior) finished training at 16 OTU Upper Heyford before being posted to 106 Squadron in October 1941. He flew Hampdens, Manchesters and Lancasters, his first operation being to Bremen on 20 October 1941. Bill (senior) and the other Rhodesian pilots of 106 Sqn are mentioned with great affection by Guy Gibson in his book *Enemy Coast Ahead*. Guy Gibson was the commander of 106 Sqn at the time and went on to the famous 617 Sqn and the dambuster's raid for which he was awarded the Victoria Cross. Bill Picken's logbook records poignantly on 5 March 1943, 'Operating Essen' ... 'Failed to Return' ... signed Guy Gibson, W/Cdr, Commanding 106 Squadron ...

A total of 55,573 men died in Bomber Command during the war.

I have made every effort to give the reader an accurate impression of conditions on a bomber station, flying Lancasters and participating in a historic operation ... as best an impression that research can possibly give for a person born fifteen years after the war ended.

Cocky Lobin is the Chilapalapa translation of the children's nursery rhyme, *Who Killed Cock Robin?* Chilapalapa is a hybrid language, developed by the earliest settlers, miners, traders, hunters and farmers to assist with communication with the African tribes of Southern Africa. Words were taken from seShona, siNdebele, Afrikaans and English. In the African accent, the English 'R' is often pronounced as 'L', hence 'Robin' becomes 'Lobin'.

The Chilapalapa language was in daily use and played a vital role in improving communication between the races. The Rhodesians in England at the time of the war would all have had a working knowledge of the language and many spoke to each other in the language as a sort of private code ... and of course as a reminder of home.

William Dives described how the bomber crews spoke to each

other in Chilapalapa on the R/T, and how they sang their version of Cocky Lobin in the mess, or during drink-ups in the surrounding bars in Lincolnshire. The song Cocky Lobin was made famous amongst the people of Southern Africa in the 1960s by the singer and comedian Wrexham Tarr, who applied, with his characteristic sense of humour, his own words[1].

Those who have read my other books will know that I enjoy detail and this book is no different. By the end, you will have a good working knowledge of the Lancaster and how she was flown, together with insight into bombing tactics and the complexity and sophistication of the German radar and air defence system.

Just as a note, the radio voice procedure used by the bomber crews and the ground flying control (air traffic control) was much less formal than modern military procedure. While flying on an operation the crew referred to each other by their respective positions, Navigator, Bomb Aimer, Rear Gunner etc., with the Captain of the aircraft regardless of rank 'Skipper' or 'Pilot'. To avoid slowing the pace of the story I have not stuck to the voice procedure of the time in all cases.

Finally, I would like to remember the men who provided such a powerful influence on my childhood; my grandfather Jack Sahli (RSM SA Artillery, Abyssinia, North Africa and Italy, my uncle Eric Sahli (Royal Navy and South African Navy), Keith Clements (B-24 Aircraft Electrician, 34 Squadron SAAF, North Africa and Italy), Robin Nicholson (Wellington Pilot, 26 Squadron SAAF, West Africa), Ray Pratt (21 SFTS, Bulawayo, Empire Air Training Scheme), my father-in-law Robbie Young (3rd Battalion RR, BSAP Police Reserve) and my father Des Sahli (Colour Sergeant, 9th Battalion RR, Rhodesian Corps of Engineers and Rhodesian Intelligence Corp).

The poem by Noel Coward, *Lie in the Dark and Listen,* is one of the most moving and poignant war poems I have read on the bomber war. A truly heartrending poem composed at night while contemplating the sounds of RAF bombers flying overhead on their way to Cologne.

---

1   See YouTube clip by typing in 'Cocky Lobin'.

Lie in the Dark and Listen

Lie in the dark and listen
It's clear tonight so they're flying high
Hundreds of them, thousands perhaps
Riding the icy, moonlit sky
Men, machinery, bombs and maps
Altimeters and guns and charts
Coffee, sandwiches, fleece-lined boots
Bones and muscles and minds and hearts
English saplings with English roots
Deep in the earth they've left below
Lie in the dark and let them go
Lie in the dark and listen.

Lie in the dark and listen
They're going over in waves and waves
High above villages, hills and streams
Country churches and little graves
And little citizens' worried dreams
Very soon they'll have reached the sea
And far below them will lie the bays
And cliffs and sands where they used to be
Taken for summer holidays
Lie in the dark and let them go
Theirs is a world we'll never know
Lie in the dark and listen.

Lie in the dark and listen
City magnates and steel contractors
Factory workers and politicians
Soft hysterical little actors
Ballet dancers, reserved musicians
Safe in your warm civilian beds
Count your profits and count your sheep
Life is passing over your heads
Just turn over and try to sleep
Lie in the dark and let them go
There's one debt you'll forever owe
Lie in the dark and listen.

I hope you enjoy reading this as much as I have enjoyed writing it ...

1

Ault, Channel Coast, German Occupied France
Saturday 25 March 1944, 5:45am

Jean-Claude Sueur had been up since 4am. He was pottering about in his small kitchen above the chalk cliffs of Ault, 20 miles northeast of Dieppe on the French channel coast. His small dairy farm had been in the family for a hundred years. As he stood looking out across the starlit pastures, he contemplated the chances of his family still farming the land in another hundred years. He felt exhausted, the bitter cold making his old war-wounded leg throb painfully. The pain brought back the hideous memories of the last time the Boche had invaded his country. He had cheated Death that fateful night on the 2nd day of June in 1916 at Hardecourt, the second day of the Battle of the Somme. He had been lucky to keep his leg after a German shell shredded it to pieces.

Closing his eyes against the pain and the dreadful memory, he rubbed his aching leg.

Jean-Claude had just celebrated his seventy-fourth birthday ... the way he was feeling, the seventy-fifth seemed like an insurmountable obstacle, a mountain rising up ahead of him that somehow he had to cross. The reality of his own mortality weighed heavily on the old man.

His gaze turned to the south, where the hulking, domed mass of a German heavy-gun emplacement stood silhouetted against the starry sky, part of Hitler's 'Atlantic Wall'. The sight made Jean-Claude sick to the stomach.

The old man cursed the Boche invaders under his breath.

The first light of morning lit the western horizon. The 6am curfew prevented him milking his tiny dairy herd any earlier. The Germans had expropriated most of his herd. *Für das Wohl*, for the greater good, as the German officer, who took them away, had explained.

Lifting his walking stick from the rack, Jean-Claude pushed open the back door.

If the Boche want to shoot an old man milking his cows ... well so be it.

The biting cold from the breeze off the channel struck him in the face, he pulled his coat tighter and dragged his beret down over his ears. The cattle were standing at the gate to the shed, waiting for the milking. Jean-Claude called to them softly; he knew them all by name. They stood silently, watching his approach.

Every morning Jean-Claude performed a short ritual before he

31

started milking. He limped past the shed, taking the narrow, well-trodden path towards the cliffs overlooking the channel. Approaching the edge, he slowly scanned the horizon. The sea shimmered in the starlight; waves thumped on the rocks below. He could smell the flying sea spray, tinged with rotting seaweed.

Rubbing his tired eyes, Jean-Claude looked again ... *Are they coming?*

Holding his breath, he listened for the faintest sound of boat engines. He twisted his head to make sure his old ears were not playing tricks ... *no, there is nothing ...*

Jean-Claude studied the horizon towards England, where all hope lay, he prayed, ... *Veuillez Dieu dans le ciel peuvent ils*[2], silently mouthing the words into the frigid breeze ... living every day in the hope the invasion would come, that France could be whole again. The thought brought a tear to his ancient eyes, his age and his pain put his melancholy emotions just below the surface.

A faint growl carried to Jean Claude on the wind.

It was a familiar sound, a sound that lifted the spirits, ... a sound confirming that France was not alone in her anguish and pain. He turned to the east, as the deep rumble grew louder.

Dark shadows crossed the sky. Not shadows of fear ... shadows of salvation!

There they are! ... Tommies and their bombers, one after another, at different heights, the engines howling their throaty, early morning welcome.

The old soldier lifted his hand in a lonely salute ... *God speed!* The sound was like nothing else, it filled the soul ... those powerful engines beating a message of hope ... *you are not alone* ... each beat a consolation ... *you are not alone ... we are coming ... you are not alone.*

A bomber, its engines on fire, burst overhead, so low that Jean-Claude fell to the ground. As it struggled out to sea one of the wings dropped, the sound of the engines strangely different, a wounded sound, of grating metal. Clambering back to his feet, Jean-Claude watched in horror as the mortally wounded bomber dived into the sea. The noise of the crunching splash sent a shiver down his spine; the spray lifted in a cloud above the churning waves ... then there was silence ... like nothing had happened ... as if no men had died.

Jean-Claude paused in shock at what he had seen. In the Great War, he had witnessed many men die in the most brutal and barbaric ways, he could never get used to it. The old man, crossed himself and bowed

2   Please God in Heaven can they come ...

his head ... *Veuillez Dieu ait pitié de leurs*[3]. *Such brave men* ...

A heavy machinegun from the German gun emplacement fired spitefully out into the night, the bright tracer chasing after the bombers struggling back to England.

The fading note of hundreds of engines ...

... You are not alone ... we are coming ... you are not alone.

*

C-Charlie, A Flight, 44 (Rhodesia) Squadron, 6,000ft above the coast of France
Saturday 25 March 1944, 6:00am

'Hello Skipper, Rear Gunner, someone's bought it ... port side low,' called the cockney Tommy Potts.

'Pilot to Navigator, please mark the position of that aircraft on your chart,' called the steady voice of P/O William (Bill) Carter the pilot of C-Charlie. Carter's accent was Rhodesian, from Bulawayo.

George Armitage the navigator, marked the rough position of the crash on his chart so the Air/Sea Rescue boys could look for survivors.

'Did you see any chutes Pottsy?' asked Armitage with his characteristic Lincolnshire accent.

'No ... the poor beggars just went straight in ... they were on fire,' replied Potts. The rear gunner's legs were numb from sitting in his confined, freezing cold, position for so long. No amount of rubbing or toe-wiggling could provide relief. It was the hamstrings that were the worst, they seemed to go into a sort of spasm that was impossible to release because he couldn't straighten his legs.

They had been on oxygen the whole way and he longed to breathe fresh air after the constant stink of the Elsan toilet[4] situated in the fuselage behind his turret. He hated the thing, he called it the 'devil's invention'. This loathsome creation invariably overflowed on long trips and in turbulence was always prone to slosh muck about the cabin, running down towards the bomb bay. Potts cursed the Elsan, if it wasn't an invention of the devil, it certainly must have been one foisted on them by the enemy.

This was Tommy Potts' life on the Lancaster, aching eyes, relentless

---

3   Please God have mercy on their souls ...

4   The Elsan was the portable metal toilet used in bomber aircraft and it was something that was hated by air crew and ground crew alike; the air crew because they had to use it, and the ground crew because they had to empty it. While flying in rough air, this 'devil's' convenience often shared its contents with the floor of the aircraft, the walls, the ceiling and, sometimes (rarely), a bit remained in the container itself.

stink, cramping legs and frigid cold amid the vibrating cacophony of roaring engines. The only comfort provided by the distant, muffled voices of his crewmates on the intercom.

'Hello Wireless Operator, Pilot here, can you send a signal with the approximate position of that kite in the drink.'

'Wilco Skipper', replied Sgt. David Muir, the wireless operator. He was already bashing away expertly on the morse-key fixed to his table situated amidships. Muir was also from Rhodesia, from Que Que.

'Nearly home lads,' called Charlie Morley from the bomb aimer's position in the nose. Morley was from Mudgee in New South Wales in Australia.

'Bloody marvellous,' replied Eric Biddle the flight engineer from Preston in Lancashire, sitting in the jump seat next to his skipper.

'Okay everyone, keep on the ball, we don't want to get jumped by a Hun so close to home,' added Carter. He knew he didn't have to say it, the boys were wide-awake, but sometimes it helped him with his own concentration. They had been in the air for close on ten hours. Nerves were jangled after the harrowing trip home from bombing Berlin.

The raid had been hopeless. They had not been able to bomb anywhere near the planned aiming point. A strong northerly wind had pushed them well south of the city. Pathfinders had dropped their marker flares as best they could but they were way off target. At least the flak south of the city had been lighter than it would have been close to the aiming point. The powerful northerly wind on the way home pushed them well to the south of the planned return track. The result was a heavy pounding from the Ruhr defences and then a string of German nightfighter cannon shells through the top of the fuselage that miraculously had not hit anything vital.

'Pilot to Mid-Upper, how are you Frank?' asked Carter, of his mid-upper gunner.

'I am okay Skipper,' lied Frank Nellyer, from Alberta Canada, his hands feeling like a thousand needles were being pushed in at once. The pain was so intense he had tears running down his ice-cold cheeks.

'Good man.'

A shell splinter had hit a magnesium flare in the flare-chute causing a fire inside the fuselage aft of the main spar, directly under Frank Nellyer's mid-upper gun position. Nellyer managed to get the fire out on his own using the hand extinguisher but despite his heavy gloves, he had burned his hands in the process. Dave Muir had helped him apply No. 9 Cream and wrap them in a bandage. He now sat back in his canvas sling inside his turret, his hands throbbing painfully, unable to hold the gun triggers.

Nellyer reported a gaping hole from flak aft of his turret and a huge chunk out of the starboard fin supporting the rudder. The inside of the fuselage reeked from the smell of burnt rubber and magnesium despite the many 'ventilation' holes created by the flak and the German nightfighter.

'Feel like a sandwich Skipper?' asked David Muir. He squeezed past the navigator's station to lift the sandwich up to his pilot in the cockpit.

'Thanks Dave … have you buggers drunk all the tea, my throat is parched?' replied Carter.

'Sorry Skipper, the thermos must have taken some flak, its kaput!' laughed Muir.

'We've heard that before, you people in the back always drink all the tea. I'm going to bring my own in future,' objected the bomb aimer Charles Morley with feigned indignation.

'Skipper, can I call H-Harry and M-Mother to see how they are?' asked Muir.

'Might as well,' agreed Carter.

All the men listened for the message, the Rhodesian crews sometimes called each other on the VHF R/T in Chilapalapa on the way home; it was their secret code, enjoyed by all.

'*Bwana Lobenson, Bwana Lobenson. Kanjan wena?*[5]' called Muir to Peter Robinson, the Skipper of H-Harry.

There was a short delay followed by a crackled reply. '*Mushe sterek*[6].'

'*Bwana Pallister, mangwanani, wena longile?*[7]' Muir called Gavin Pallister, the Skipper of M-Mother.

'*Aikona, lo port outer ka meena ena ifeele!*[8]' replied Pallister.

'*How! Meena solly maningi, hamba gashle!*[9]'

Nyamazaans! Basopa lo bandits![10]' called Carter from the cockpit of C-Charlie.

'*Bona zonke lo Bobojaans, pasi lo aerodrome pagati, hamba zavanaka!*[11]' signed off Muir.

Giggles could be heard from the crew. Those that were not from Rhodesia had learned the meaning of the playful banter, but most

5   Mr Robinson, Mr Robinson, how are you?
6   Very well.
7   Mr Pallister, good morning, how are you going?
8   Not well. My port outer engine is dead!
9   Oh! I am very sorry, go carefully!
10   Animals (term of endearment), watch out for bandits (German night fighters).
11   I will see all you Baboons (term of endearment) when we get down to the aerodrome, go well!

35

importantly, it was a great way of finding out how their fellow A Flight crews were faring. No amount of German effort would break that code.

As the bomber approached the English coast the German jamming of the GEE navigation beams faded and George Armitage was able to get an accurate fix on their position.

'Skipper, Nav … keep on two-nine-four degrees … I am estimating a hundred miles to West Wittering, speed one hundred and seventy miles per hour,' called Armitage. The wind had played havoc with his navigation; fortunately, the lack of cloud over northern France and Belgium had allowed him to get an approximate sextant-fix using the stars. They were at least 200miles south of the planned return track. They were not the only ones way off course.

Armitage's new plan was to make landfall as close to West Wittering as possible then turn due north to Reading, keeping well to the west of London with its skittish air defences … then onto their home airfield at Dunholme Lodge in the Lincolnshire countryside.

'Its going to be tight on the fuel skipper,' said Eric Biddle the flight engineer. Monitoring fuel status and moving fuel between tanks was one of his key tasks. The fuel system was managed by the flight engineer on a panel on the starboard side, below the cockpit. 'I'm getting a low pressure reading in port number one tank and the bloody fuel pressure warning light is on.'

The Lancaster had three wing tanks on each side plus long-range tanks in the fuselage aft of the front wing spar. The fuel in the long-range tanks had already been transferred. No. 3 tank on the Port side was empty. C-Charlie was flying on the proverbial 'smell of an oily rag'.

'Do you think the pressure gauge is faulty?' asked Carter, concentrating hard on maintaining his airspeed and bearing.

'I don't think so Skipper … blast! … The pressure's dropping in port number two as well. We may have sprung a leak. Frank, take a gander on the port side, can you see any fuel spray?' Biddle was speaking to the mid-upper gunner Frank Nellyer who had a good view of both wings in the starlight.

'Hang on a second Eric while I swing around,' replied Frank Nellyer. 'No I can't see anything.'

'You best throttle back a bit Skipper and drop the revs[12],' said Biddle, concern creeping into his voice.

'George, I'm dropping back to one fifty miles an hour indicated,'

---

12   Throttles for boost (power), propeller speed controls revolutions.

said Carter to his navigator.

'Roger Skipper.'

'George, I have a bank of clouds closing from the north, is that on the met report?' asked Carter, now trying to do fuel consumption arithmetic in his head.

'No, it isn't, we are supposed to have clear sky over England, only high cloud above twenty five thousand feet.'

'I can't climb above it with our fuel state, we are just going to have to plough through.'

'Skipper, I have the cross-feed cock open,' said Biddle. 'I have over three hundred gallons indicated in the starboard tanks ... if I can transfer fuel to the port number one, we may just make it all the way home. The problem is that I may not be able to transfer the fuel quicker than we are losing it. At one hundred and fifty miles an hour we are getting about one mile to the gallon.'

'Okay Eric, transfer the fuel ... you watch those gauges like a hawk,' said Carter encouragingly; he didn't want his crew to worry unnecessarily. Light as she was, the old girl could fly quite well on three engines. The crew could all hear the conversation on the intercom.

The fact that there was fuel in the starboard tanks and the port tanks would not pump quick enough, meant that he may lose both port engines from fuel starvation ... *that will be interesting,* thought Carter as he started playing emergency drills over in his mind. Biddle needed to pump fuel from the starboard to the port tanks to keep all four engines running.

The cloud ahead rolled towards them, Carter said a silent prayer ... *Please God ... just give me another forty-five minutes.* If the cloud base was too low, they may struggle to get into their home airfield and would likely run out of fuel before they could divert to another.

Before volunteering for the war, Bill Carter had not been a particularly religious man, but fourteen previous operations over Germany had changed all that. Flying at 20,000ft, surrounded by a glass canopy, with the stars cascaded above him, Carter had never felt closer to his God. He had taken to praying when the searchlights were probing, flak flying, running in on the target, or trying to dodge nightfighters.

It was his crew that he prayed for most; getting them all back safely, ... he couldn't bear the thought of letting them down.

I must get my chaps home ...

'Alright Skipper, one minute to the turn, if we could see through the cloud, good old Blighty should be coming up on the starboard beam,' called Armitage, his voice raised with the excitement of being so close to home.

'Nav lights on George?'

'Nav lights on Skipper.'

'Switch on the IFF[13] Dave.'

'IFF on Skipper,'

The Lancaster turned onto her new course; the cloud closed in. Carter started a slow descent hoping to fly out underneath the cloud.

'Skipper met reports cloud all the way home, down to two thousand feet,' called David Muir.

'Dave, contact Bluestripe and tell them we are about forty-five minutes out. Tell them we need landing priority,' called Carter to his radio operator. Bluestripe was the call-sign for Dunholme Lodge … *home!*

*

RAF Dunholme Lodge, 4 miles northeast of the City of Lincoln, Lincolnshire Saturday 25 March 1944, 6:32am

Corporal Ron Boswell, the fitter responsible for C-Charlie, had been awake since 5:30am. He had taken his bike and ridden from his mess to the dispersal hut situated close to the pan allocated to his aircraft. Despite it being early spring, it was bitterly cold outside with a stiff northeasterly wind blowing freezing air off the North Sea, only 33miles away. The bike squeaked annoyingly as Boswell pushed hard against the wind, his heavy coat made riding doubly difficult.

Dunholme Lodge was a desolate place. The only solidly constructed building was the control tower, the central focus of the air station. They said that all the towers on these new stations were identical in design, austere, practical, grey-green paintwork, two stories, with a rooftop observation deck. It was positioned to have a commanding view of all three runways. Numerous one story prefab huts were clustered behind the tower with rows of oval roofed Nissen huts huddled along the boundary fence on the eastern edge of the station. Everything was built to be temporary … 'built to Heath Robinson[14] standard', was the

---

13   Identification Friend or Foe, radio signal. To prevent being shot down by friendly night fighters and flak defenses.

14   The phrase 'It's a bit of a Heath Robinson', in British Empire English means a situation of apparent muddle, mess, over complication. It is named after a famous English cartoonist whose work was characterised by drawings of pieces of equipment, often very over-elaborate, designed to perform apparently simple, unnecessary tasks very badly.

way Boswell would have described it. By the time he got to the A Flight maintenance hut, Boswell was shivering violently despite the hard ride.

'Nice dare 'ut,' said Boswell in his broad, Wearside-Sunderland accent[15].

The other ground crew inside the hut all mumbled a welcome. They all stood crowded around the coke-burning iron stove trying to defrost. Everything on the base smelled of smoke from the heating stoves burning in the buildings. It was possible to tell RAF Bomber Command people on a train or in a crowded bar simply from the distinctive sulphur-coal smell that impregnated their clothing.

'Sorry to get yew up so early Rrronny me uld son,' laughed Flight Sergeant Joe Kennedy with his rough gritty Scouse accent from North Merseyside. Kennedy was the 2IC for engineering on A Flight.

'Any news on our kites Chiefy[16]?' asked Boswell.

There was a field telephone in the hut used by the control tower as soon as incoming aircraft joined the circuit.

'A-Able has called in, so has G-George and E-Easy, they should be coming in thick and fast in the next few minutes,' replied Kennedy.

'God willing!' groaned Boswell, always dreading the thought of losing more aircrew.

Boswell sneezed, taking a handkerchief from his trouser pocket. He blew his nose loudly. Ron knew all about the cold working on Hendon Dock in Sunderland harbour.

'Still got the flu Rrronny?' asked Kennedy. The ground crews were plagued by illness, working out in the elements, completely unprotected from the weather.

'Yes, I can't ruddy shake it … this job is going to be the death of me for sure,' replied Boswell smiling weakly. He felt like hell, sore throat, runny nose, aches and pains everywhere.

'Have a niice cup of tea son, that will make you feel better,' said Kennedy encouragingly, holding out a cup of steaming hot tea. Kennedy was twenty-nine, an old man by Bomber Command standards. He called everyone 'son', the vast majority of the ground crew were in their early twenties, Boswell was only twenty-two.

'Thanks Chiefy,' replied Boswell grateful for the tea, he sipped it, feeling the warm sweet liquid soothing his raw throat.

On cue, the first throaty roars of Merlin aero-engines could be heard in the distance.

'There come our little bundles of joy lads … off you go,' laughed

---

15   Tyne and Wear.
16   RAF slang, Flight Sergeant.

Kennedy encouragingly. The crew chiefs for the aircraft, now entering the circuit, filed out the door to get to the various dispersal points scattered around the perimeter of the airfield.

The phone rang and Kennedy picked up the receiver. He listened intently … nodding his understanding.

Replacing the receiver, he called to Boswell, 'Your lot have called in Ron, sounds like they are short of fuel, they have declared an emergency. They are expected in the next twenty minutes.'

Boswell did not answer. C-Charlie was almost new, only two operations old. Boswell had lost her two predecessors in quick succession with all the crew. He was beginning to think he was jinxed. It worried him a lot.

'Which runway are they using Chiefy?'

'Zero four.'

'Well I better get over there, let's hope Bill Carter doesn't prang my new kite,' added Boswell.

The dispersal hut for A Flight was situated between runway numbers 04 and 34. If C-Charlie was landing on 04, that was south to north meaning that Boswell had a two-mile uncomfortable ride on the Fordson N Airfield towing tractor to get to the end of number 04. If C-Charlie stopped on the runway, she would block the landing of all the other incoming aircraft, creating havoc. She would need to be towed off as soon as possible.

One extra task Ron Boswell had been asked to perform was to keep an eye on Tommy Potts' stray dog, Paddy, an Irish Red Setter.

'Come on Paddy,' Boswell called the dog sleeping in the corner of the hut. 'Your Tommy's on his way home lad.' The cold air bit into him as he opened the door to the hut, his hot breath forming a cloud in front of his face. In moments, he was shivering all over again.

Dogs were forbidden on the base but Paddy had ignored those rules and attached himself to Tommy Potts. The ground crew of C-Charlie allowed him to sleep in the dispersal hut when Tommy was on Ops and the cooks fed him with scraps from the kitchen. He normally slept under Tommy's bed in the crew Nissen hut. The Adjutant had caught Paddy on a few occasions and ordered the Station Police to 'dispose of' him to the local pound. It was just amazing how effective Paddy was as an escape artist. Paddy was the unofficial mascot of 44 (Rhodesia) Squadron. He lavished his affection on all the ground crew who loved having him around.

Paddy carried an old tennis ball somebody had given him. It was his prized possession. He would belt up to the ground crew working

40

on an aircraft, drop the ball and bark loudly until someone threw it for him, then tear off to the next pan. He shared the ball-throwing duties around. His favourite ground crew was C-Charlie. He had somehow figured out the connection between them and Tommy Potts. Ron swore blind that the dog could distinguish the engine note of C-Charlie against the others.

'Up on the tractor, come on lad,' called Boswell and the dog leapt up onto his lap, giving his freezing nose a slobbery lick.

Out to the west the first Lancaster came floating in over the perimeter fence, her engine revs up for the landing[17]. The distinctive throaty roar never ceased to lift Ron's spirits ... *ruddy beautiful thing!*

*

Standing at the end of runway 04, a small group of off-duty Waafs had gathered. They all wore their heavy overcoats with scarves wrapped tightly against the cold. This was their early morning ritual when their squadron was on Ops. They came from all sections of the squadron; Met, Fuel, Catering, Admin, Flying Control, Drivers, Maintenance ...

Maggie Smith worked in the Met office typing up forecasts, manning the radios, keeping in touch with Group Met and preparing briefing papers for the crews on Ops. She loved her job. She had only just turned eighteen, short at 5ft 3", with the creamy flawless complexion of youth. Wavy strawberry-blond hair, cut short, curled out from under her cap. Her cheeks were flushed against the biting early morning breeze, her gloved hands thrust into her greatcoat pockets.

The first of their kites roared its arrival, as the Waafs turned their faces to the south. There it was ... coming out from underneath the low cloud ... the faithful sound of powerful Merlin engines carrying across the runway.

A Lancaster touched down on the runway with a loud biting skid as its tyres struck the concrete. All the girls clapped and cheered, jumping up and down on the spot ... G-George was first home.

---

17   Whilst power would be on to overcome the drag of the undercarriage and flaps, it would not be at full boost as it would be for take off and climb out.

C-Charlie, A Flight, 44 (Rhodesia) Squadron, 2,000ft above Newark-on-Trent, 18 miles southwest of Dunholme Lodge
Saturday 25 March 1944, 6:40am

'We are bang on the beam,' called Bill Carter referring to the navigation radio Lorenz beam for the standard beam approach (SBA) to Dunholme Lodge. Carter could hear the steady monotone of the main beam in his earpiece confirming he was approaching the runway. The SBA system transmitted dots (left) and dashes (right) if the aircraft was off-centre; a steady sound meant he was lined up correctly.

They were flying blind in thick cloud … the SBA was vital … their only tenuous connection with the ground.

'Let me talk to the tower Dave,' asked William Carter of his radio operator.

'Go ahead Skipper,' replied Dave Muir as he flicked the switch to allow his Skipper to talk to the control tower.

Before Carter could respond, the port outer engine coughed, spluttered and stopped. The sudden loss of power affected the aircraft's trim and it slewed to port as the starboard engines pushed the aircraft around. He pulled back the throttles slightly on the starboard engines and advanced the remaining port engine. Leaning far over to his right, he pressed the feather button to feather the propeller on the dead engine, to stop it creating drag.

'I am going to need some help with the throttles Eric,' said Carter to his engineer. 'Set flaps to 20°.'

'Right Skipper,' replied Eric Biddle calmly.

Carter was feeling the pressure, sweat beaded on his forehead despite the cold. He appreciated the steady reassurance of his flight engineer.

'Hello Bluestripe this is March Tune C-Charlie, request immediate clearance for landing. We are at nine miles, two thousand feet. Over' called Carter on the R/T. March Tune was the call-sign for 44 (Rhodesia) Squadron.

The radio was a mass of static. Carter had to repeat his call, a sick feeling building in his stomach.

'Hello C-Charlie, this is Bluestripe, you are clear to land runway zero four, wind from northeast at ten miles an hour, cloud base 1,000ft, ground visibility three miles, QFE 1002[18] … Over[19],' came the distant calm female voice in reply.

'Wilco Bluestripe,' replied Carter, setting the air pressure on his altimeter. The stress of landing an aircraft without any second chances could be heard in his voice.

'I am going down to a thousand feet Eric. Okay … superchargers set at M … air intake cold … what have you got on brake pressure?'

'Two eighty pounds.'

Carter was now concentrating hard; going through the landing checklist, … it helped to have Eric to confirm.

'Right … good on brake pressure … flaps at 20° check … speed back to one hundred and ten.' Eric helped to pull back the throttles as the speed bled off.

They were still in cloud.

'Undercarriage down,' said Carter, pushing the lever to the right of his seat into the down position. The warning horn sounded as the wheels locked in place. 'I have two green lights.'

'Revs to 2,650rpm … booster pumps on port and starboard number one tanks. Right, lets get the speed down to a hundred … flaps to 25° …'

As they crossed the outer marker at 2 miles, there was an audio 'Onk, Onk, Onk' in the earpiece from the SBA system.

'Roger I have the outer marker, start the stopwatch, height … six hundred feet. Nose down slightly.'

They started to break out under the cloud … *thank God* breathed Carter. It was still misty and murky with spitting drizzle making forward vision difficult … out in the distance was a bright flashing light.

'I can see runway ident Skipper,' called Charles Morley the bomb aimer sitting in the front turret. Out ahead, Dunholme Lodge was flashing brightly in Morse code, — • •D, •—• •L, it's identification letters.

The runway flight path came into view. A three way, coloured flight path helped to show the correct rate of descent. It was flashing RED … he was too low.

'More power Eric,' the engines increased revs as Carter tried to lift

---

18   Atmospheric pressure at sea level, corrected for temperature and adjusted to a specified datum such as airfield elevation. When set on the altimeter it reads height above the airfield.

19   The controller told C-Charlie to land to the northeast, and the adjustments to the altimeter to ensure that it would read the aircraft's correct height above the aerodrome.

height. 'We are too fast … inner marker coming up … Full Flaps!'

'Bluestripe we can see the runway zero four,' called Carter to Flying Control.

'C-Charlie … you are clear to land. Over.'

As they crossed the inner marker an audio, 'Peep, Peep, Peep' sounded in Carter's earpiece. A green flare shot up from the airfield controller in a van beside the runway to show that the runway was clear.

The Lancaster had a tendency to float when it was lightly loaded. The only way to get her down was to lift the noise slightly and cut power so that her forward speed and, therefore, lift on those magnificent wings, dropped off. Coming in too fast made landing all the more difficult.

In they came over the boundary fence, the runway lights marked the path ahead. The drizzle made the surface shine slickly in the lights. Eric Biddle had both hands on the throttles, ready to pull back on the power at the right second.

They had no way of knowing that the starboard main wheel had taken a piece of flak, cutting it deeply but not enough to puncture the tyre.

'Come on old girl, gently does it,' said Carter as if trying to coax the aircraft onto the ground. He pulled back on the throttles as soon as he crossed the white markers at the entrance to the runway, the huge white '04' disappearing behind them.

He knew he was coming in too fast, it was going to be hard … C-Charlie touched … bounced up … touched again, the wheels skidding as they fought for grip.

As the weight came on, the starboard main wheel burst.

Before Carter could react, the tyre ripped itself to shreds, the wheel rim grinding on the concrete. The heat and friction was too much for the rim, it gave way, the undercarriage struts dug in, yanking the aircraft violently around onto the grass.

Carter snatched back on the throttles, moving mixture to idle cut off, shutting down the engines … the starboard undercarriage collapsed. The aircraft slewed around, still travelling at a hundred miles an hour, turf flying out behind it. Carter had no control, thrown viciously left and right, he held onto the control column for all he was worth. Eric Biddle wasn't strapped in; he was hurled off his seat, falling backwards into the fuselage, cutting himself horribly on Former D, one of the ribs of the aircraft airframe.

The port main wheel strut collapsed.

C-Charlie, now on her belly, ploughed towards the perimeter fence. The bomb-aimer's blister burst open throwing dirt into the fuselage, spraying mud all over Charles Morley in the nose and the prostrate Eric Biddle lying behind him. George Armitage, holding onto his navigator's table for dear life, was also splattered with mud and slosh. Poor Tommy Potts bashed his head on the roof of the rear turret leaving him unconscious slumped over his guns. Frank Nellyer, who could not hold onto anything with his painful hands, was thrown off his seat into the fuselage and lay senseless next to the burnt flare chute.

The aircraft swung around again, more savagely, hitting the boundary fence, punching through the hedge on the other side. Dirt sprayed up covering the wings and fuselage in muddy streaks.

Sliding on, the aircraft struck the earth embankment of a drainage ditch, ramping up over it. The crumpled nose dived down the other side into the muddy water at the bottom. The aircraft stopping with a brutal impact throwing Carter hard against his harness, the force flinging his head against the instrument panel, knocking him senseless.

Tottering in the vertical position, she collapsed back onto her belly, her nose buried deep in the bottom of the ditch. The crew inside tossed about like apples in a barrel.

C-Charlie came to rest with her tail standing up in the air, steam sizzled from the hot engines covered in soggy mud.

All was eerily silent … then the distant sound of another Lancaster crossing the threshold onto the runway.

Miraculously the intercom was still working.

'*Lo N'deke ka mina ene ifeele*[20],' said Dave Muir mournfully, his nose bleeding from a hard thump against the bank of radios.

---

20   My aeroplane has died

2

Ron Boswell had watched C-Charlie clear the threshold, gently glide onto the runway ... then all hell broke loose. Paddy the Irish Setter was off the tractor and running towards the wreck, his sleek coat shining in the early morning light. Boswell fired up the tractor and put his foot down, bouncing across the turf towards the crashed aircraft. Behind he could hear the ringing of bells as the ambulance and fire engines raced across the runway.

The first on the scene was Paddy, barking up at the rear turret sitting twenty feet off the ground. He could see Tommy Potts collapsed over his guns. As Boswell jerked to a stop, the hatch above the cockpit was slung open and Bill Carter stuck his head out.

'Ron ...'

'Help ... help me please,' came the muffled call from someone trapped inside.

Carter ducked back.

Boswell drove the tractor through the boundary fence and the flattened hedge, leaping off, then clambered up the muddy embankment sliding as his boots tried to get a grip. Eventually he dragged himself up on all fours holding onto the top of the bank. The nose was buried in the water; the front turret was just sticking up above the surface, while the bomb-aimer's blister was completely submerged.

'Its Charlie Morley, Ron,' called Carter from the cockpit hatch. 'He's trapped and the water is rising above his head, I can't pull him out on my own.' Carter got down into the bomb aimer's compartment, water filling his flying boots, holding Morley's head out of the water. 'Hang on Charlie, we'll get you out.'

Morley was dazed having cracked his head when the aircraft crashed.

Boswell slid back down the embankment and rushed back to the tractor. He lifted the lid of the toolbox and pulled out an axe. As he did so, the rear access door, on the starboard side of the fuselage, was flung open and Dave Muir appeared. Muir called out something that Boswell could not hear, the sound of returning Lancaster's landing and taxiing around the airfield drowned out all other noise.

The urgently ringing bells of the crash crew and fire engine carried on the wind.

Without hesitation, Boswell pulled himself up the embankment using the axe for grip, then slipped down into the ditch. The bitterly cold water was up to his chest, as he lifted the axe above his head and launched it at the front turret. The perspex shattered. The second blow bent the thin aluminium frame, the third split it open.

'Hang on Sir, give me a few more seconds,' called out Boswell, frantically smashing at the turret.

'Quickly Ron,' shouted Carter from inside, concern in his voice. The weight of the Lancaster was pushing it down into the mud at the bottom of the ditch.

The fire engine skidded to a halt, its crew jumping to the ground. Eric Biddle, his face covered in blood, joined Carter in the cockpit. A fireman appeared on the other side of the turret also carrying an axe.

'It's Pilot Officer Morley ... he's trapped in the water,' shouted Boswell. Both men took to the turret, desperately smashing their way through. As soon as a space was big enough, Boswell pulled himself up through the mangled metal and looked inside. Carter was waist deep in water, holding Morley around the shoulders to keep his face out of the water.

'I think his flying boots are stuck, I can't pull him any higher,' groaned Carter.

Boswell leaned down, stretching towards the leather flying helmet. It was no good he couldn't reach. More holes appeared on the other side as the firemen layed into the side of the fuselage.

'Steady on lads ... let me get inside,' shouted Boswell, using the two Browning machine guns as supports he lowered himself down. Morley's head went under, bubbles burst through the muddy water. Wedging his feet on either side of the fuselage, Boswell stretched down and grabbed Morley by the life vest.

'Okay Sir, on my count ... one ... two ... three.' Pushing as hard as he could with his legs, Boswell got Morley's head above the water. His flying suit was saturated making him doubly heavy.

'I've got him, but I can't pull him out on my own,' called Boswell.

'I'm sorry Ron I just don't have any strength left,' said Carter desperately. The freezing water was in his flying suit, his face was turning blue and his teeth were chattering.

The fuselage gave a violent lurch. Someone had the presence of mind to throw a hawser around the rear of the tail section and had attached it to the tractor. They were gently dragging the aircraft backwards out of the ditch. A fireman appeared behind Boswell, he had smashed his way threw the wreckage in the cockpit. Together they lifted Morley up as the aircraft settled back onto the ground. They had to go back for Carter who lay exhausted, soaking wet, in the nose of the aircraft.

The unhurt members of C-Charlie's crew sat on the grass wrapped in blankets, it was bitterly cold. Nurses and medical orderlies fussed about them, Tommy Potts was on a stretcher, moaning loudly. Paddy was darting in and out to lick at his face.

Frank Nellyer lay quietly on a stretcher covered in a thick blanket, looking up at the drizzly sky, blinking back tears of relief that they were home … and alive.

'Can somebody grab that blasted dog!' shouted the doctor.

An orderly was wrapping a bandage around Eric Biddle's head. He was complaining that it was just a scratch … *I've had worse.*

Hot tea was produced from the Naafi truck and the men sat in silence sipping at the relieving liquid, the elixir of the gods. Charles Morley was carried to the rear access door and gently lowered onto a stretcher. The doctor had given him a good thump on the chest and he was now throwing up convulsively. Muddy water and puke sprayed everywhere.

Too exhausted to speak, Carter, Armitage and Muir sat in muted shock watching as the three stretcher cases, Morley, Nellyer, Potts, and a complaining Biddle were loaded into the ambulance. Doors thudded closed, then it bounced off towards the perimeter track on the way to the Station Hospital.

Ron Boswell took a cup of tea from the Naafi truck and walked across to speak to the remainder of the crew sitting in the grass.

'Glad you made it back in one piece Sir,' said Boswell to Carter, with his characteristic smile.

'Sorry we pranged your kite Ron, she looks like a write off,' replied Carter apologetically, now shivering violently.

'Better to write it off than doing a half-baked job, Sir … at least I don't have to try and fix it,' replied Boswell with a laugh. 'Look on the bright side, you may be off flying duties for a few days while I order a replacement.'

'What a happy thought Ron, but I would rather get my thirty operations over as soon as possible,' smiled Carter thinly, his face grey with fatigue.

'Touché to that,' agreed Armitage.

A very young Waaf driver wearing overalls walked up to the men sitting in the grass.

'The gharrie's[21] ready to take you to debriefing Sir,' said Winnie Daly politely, blushing brightly when Dave Muir winked at her.

'Okay, let's be off then,' said Carter. 'Bloody good job this morning Ron, we owe you a few beers, that's for sure.'

'I'll hold you to that Sir,' replied Boswell, happy to know that his efforts were appreciated. He helped Carter to his feet supporting him as he struggled to walk the few yards to the truck.

'Thanks again Ron,' said Carter gratefully, his legs feeling like jelly from shock and fatigue. Then turning to the Waaf driver, he asked, 'Winnie, please pop past the crew room so I can get out of this wet clothing.' The young girl blushed again even more brightly ... *he called me by my first name!*

*

The war had taken Maggie Smith out of the rigidity of home and opened her life to a new and exhilarating world ... full of exciting young men. She had only been on the squadron for a few weeks and had already been chased by what seemed to her like hundreds of men.

There was one man that Maggie found intriguing, a young Rhodesian pilot named William Carter, Bill to his friends. He was two years older then her, shy and softly spoken. She had liked him from the first time they had been introduced, when he had visited the Met Office looking for a forecast.

They weren't stepping out or anything; they had only had a few beers together in the Black Bull pub in Welton, the village just to the northeast of the base. His accent was something new and different to the Lancashire accent from her hometown of Rochdale north of Manchester. He had endless stories about Africa that sounded so wild and romantic, exotic and exciting ... it had got her thinking ...

Maggie loved joining the other Waafs at the end of the runway when the men returned. She felt it was important for the crews to see that the girls cared about them, that they were supported; no matter how rude or obnoxious. Maggie had been shocked the first time one of them referred to her as an 'aircrew comfort.' Another asked her, 'What's the collective noun for Waafs Maggie?' She said she didn't know. 'It's a *mattress* of Waafs', he said, bursting into laughter with the rest of his crew. She had burst into tears in front of him. 'I am sorry' he had stuttered, blushing brightly, much to the delight of his crew. The other girls had a word to her about the stress and pressure

---

21   In service terms a covered Bedford 3 ton-truck.

the men were under, 'They don't really mean it Maggie, it's just their way', she had been told.

William Carter was different, like no man she had ever met … not that she had much experience with men, she had not had a real boyfriend before. Her father, the Vicar at St. Chads Parish Church, had discouraged his daughter at every opportunity … *the time will come for boys … all in good time*. Maggie was now convinced that her time had well and truly arrived. The boys at school were children compared with these men, the bomber crews. These gladiators of the sky were so grown up, so brave, so stimulating … exciting.

Maggie had found herself thinking about William Carter at different times of the day. While he and his crew were preparing for this Op, she had driven round to the dispersal point with the Naafi truck to say goodbye and wish him luck. She had no way of knowing that was the worst possible thing she could have done. The crews saw it as the worst possible omen for women to send them off at the dispersal point. It was an unwritten rule. William had been polite but distant. He had thanked her very kindly, but had made an excuse that he needed to check something in the aircraft. She had attributed his strange behaviour to nerves.

Maggie Smith had watched in horror as C-Charlie had veered off the runway, and crashed through the boundary fence. From where she and her fellow Waafs were standing, it was a good mile and a half to the crash site. Maggie had spontaneously broken into a run, screaming out, tears running down her cheeks … *this can't be happening!* The other girls had pulled her back.

Vera Johns, who also worked in Met, held onto Maggie tightly, 'There is nothing we can do Maggie … there's nothing anybody can do,' Vera had whispered. She knew what that meant. She had lost three boyfriends, lovers, future husbands, soul mates … lost somewhere over Germany. Vera threw her arm around Maggie's shoulders and led her across the turf to the control tower and administration offices, 'We should wait at the A Flight Office for news,' Vera had said.

*

'I estimate we were about four miles south of the aiming point when we dropped our load,' said the navigator George Armitage taking a big swig of tea, fortified with a tot of rum. He was talking to one of the squadron intelligence officers, a very attractive Waaf Section Officer[22], by the name of Jill Evans.

---

22   Equivalent to the RAF rank of Flying Officer.

Everyone guessed Jill was about 25, but nobody knew for sure. She had made it abundantly clear that she was not available but that did not dissuade the many who tried.

Bill Carter felt a sense of cosiness in the debriefing room, the heating stove had been given a good poke and the coal burned bright red. He was still shivering slightly from the dunking in the drainage ditch. A strong smell of damp, coal and cigarette smoke permeated the room, the smell familiar and strangely comforting. It was the smell of survival.

The station padre was there with words of welcome and encouragement, handing out rum and chocolate. The three unhurt crew of C-Charlie sat at a round table with a large bowl of currants and raisins in the middle, with packets of cigarettes scattered about. Thames Cigarettes, the cheapest on the market. A radio was on in the corner, turned down low, but the smooth sultry voice of Dinah Shore singing *Silver Wings* was clearly discernable above the rowdy discussion in the room.

> *And though it's pretty tough, the job he does above*
> *I wouldn't have him change it for a king*
> *An ordinary fellow in a uniform I love*
> *He wears a pair of silver wings*[23]

Feeling completely drained, Bill Carter sat back in his chair. He closed his eyes for a brief moment, allowing the sounds in the room to wash over him, the spirited chatter of those who got back.

> *... For I adore that crazy guy who taught my happy heart*
> *To wear a pair of silver wings ...*

He said a silent prayer ... *thank you for getting my boys back ... banged up a bit ... but safe.*

Opening his eyes, he was struck by a cloud of exhaled cigarette smoke. Looking across the table at his men smoking, Carter wished he could smoke; it seemed to relax them, to take the edge off. He'd tried smoking but it gave him a raking cough.

'Did you bomb on the skymarkers[24],' asked Jill Evans in her quiet business-like fashion.

'Yes, Charlie Morley said we did, but as it turns out the wind had

23   Dinah Shore, words by Eric Maschwitz and Music by Michael Carr (1942).
24   When a target was obscured by cloud or haze, skymarker flares (the Wanganui method) were used to show the position of the target above the clouds.

dragged them way south,' replied George Armitage.

Carter watched Jill Evans across the table, taking in every movement of her eyes, the careful flow of her hand as she wrote down her notes. She had deep brown eyes, a flawless English complexion, her auburn hair in the modern curled style beneath her air force cap. He couldn't help staring at her, studying her every detail. Her uniform only served to accentuate a perfect figure, with sleek long legs sheathed in nylon stockings.

Reflecting on the Waaf uniform, Carter and his fellow officers had discussed whether the RAF had deliberately designed the uniform to be so provocative. 'Its only because there's a woman inside ... they also look ruddy fantastic in overalls!' someone had said ... it made sense.

Jill Evans spoke in a soft gentle voice, with an English accent that would have been at home drinking champagne while stamping down divots at Cirencester Park Polo Club. Carter found her voice and accent captivating, he closed his eyes again, listening to her question George Armitage more closely on the route to the target.

'William, just a few more questions,' interjected Jill Evans, noticing that he had nodded off.

Carter's eyes flicked open when he heard his name. She was looking directly at him.

'Yes ... sorry.'

Jill's tie was held neatly in a small Windsor knot at her slender neck. Carter could not help but watch the tie move as she spoke. She was a Vision. Carter blushed and averted his eyes as Jill caught him staring. Each of her questions, delivered in a soft, captivating way, felt like an invitation.

She has to know the effect she has on me! Carter blushed again at the mere thought of her.

'The wind must have been double the forecast strength; in fact I don't remember the Met warning us about the wind. It was pretty hopeless really,' carried on Armitage, making sure everyone understood his opinion of poor weather forecasting.

'We didn't get any wind updates during the flight,' added Dave Muir.

'Light flak over the target, or what was not the target, we dropped at fourteen thousand feet, only a few fires seen, plenty of searchlights,' chipped in Carter wearily.

'Anything else?' asked Jill, in a voice that sounded to Carter like a dreamy invitation.

'Bags of flak on the way home, we saw some more of those massive aerial explosions. I counted three … any news on what those are?' asked Carter, suddenly more animated.

'The word is just heavy flak guns,' replied Jill abruptly.

These mysterious explosions were making the crews jumpy … everyone was reporting them. They had even been given a codename, 'Scarecrows'. Jill had been instructed by 5 Group HQ to play the subject down until they had more information.

'Tommy Potts reported a Lanc going into the drink about here …' added Armitage, showing a point marked on his mud soaked map.

Another crew shuffled into the debriefing room, waiting for their turn.

'Well, if that's all gentlemen, you can adjourn for breakfast and a good sleep,' said Jill in her Greta Garbo voice, with a smile that could launch ships.

The men pushed back their chairs, that squeaked loudly on the wooden floor.

'Please make sure that you've completed the 540[25] William,' said Jill. 'Sorry about the accident, I heard everyone got out alright.'

Jill Evans always called Carter by his first name, they were of the same rank, so it was perfectly acceptable, plus he and his crew were classified as veterans with fifteen operations now completed. There were only two other crews on the whole squadron with more operations. 44 Squadron had lost 11 aircraft in February and another 11 in March. Veterans were few and far between.

'Yes, thank you Jill, only a few bumps and scratches, should be right as rain in a few days,' replied Carter, returning the smile. The way she pronounced 'William' turned his insides into mush.

The crew of C-Charlie shuffled out of the debriefing room and began the short walk back to the mess and their long-awaited breakfast.

If there was a best part to all of this … it was this moment, thought Bill Carter, glancing at his crew.

The feeling of relief was palpable.

'Would you like a little shag, William?' mimicked Dave Muir, putting on Jill Evan's posh accent.

The three men burst into laughter, in that sometimes manic way soldiers laugh when the action is over and the guns are silent … With the pressure and stress released, they laughed together, holding their sides, tears running down their cheeks … like a massive valve opening

25   Form 540: pages of this form make up the Operations Record Books (ORB), which included columns for date, aircraft type and number, crew, duty, time up, time down, details of sortie or flight, plus references and summaries.

to let off steam ... *Would you like a little shag, William?*

*

Looking out of the Met Office window, Maggie Smith and Vera Johns watched Carter and his crew leave the debriefing room. Maggie turned and gave Vera another tight hug, tears again in her eyes ... *he's all right! Thank God, he's all right!*

... I sometimes wonder what tomorrow brings ...

RAF Dunholme Lodge, Lincolnshire
Saturday 25 March 1944, 6:15pm

'Bill, the runway is that long flat concrete thing, with lights along it,' shouted P/O Peter Robinson as Bill Carter walked into the officer's mess. Robinson laughed infectiously, much to the delight of the other officers that had collected to read the paper and have a beer. A few were playing darts, 301 … *open with a double, end with a double.*

'Yes, and you needn't drown poor old Charlie Morley if he's no bloody good at dropping bombs,' added P/O Gavin Pallister. All were in a lively mood, the typical reaction after a tough operation, but also happy in the knowledge that no new operations had been called.

The officer's mess was constructed from two large Nissen huts that had been joined by a passageway. One comprised a dining room and the other a lounge and bar. On the white, domed ceiling above the lounge were footprints leading from the floor right across the top down the other side. It was as if someone with sooty feet had walked upside down from one side to the other. Above the large fireplace at the end of the room was a huge print of one of Peter Fleming's paintings of ducks flying across the marches. The painting was hung inverted. Above the bar was a coloured drawing of the squadron crest with the words, 'The King's Thunderbolts are Righteous'. Some Rhodesian wag had provided a Chilapalapa translation, '*Lo n'Gozi ka lo n'Kos Zaka-Naka*!

Carter smiled broadly at the ribbing he was getting from his two close friends. He, Robinson and Pallister had been together since 21 EFTS[26] at Kumalo Airfield, at the Old Show Grounds in Bulawayo. All three were from Rhodesia, Pallister and Robinson were from Salisbury, *Bamba Zonke*[27], while Carter was from Bulawayo, thrown together through war and twist of fate. Robinson had attended Prince Edward High School while Pallister went to St George's College. This provided some additional rivalry as they had played high school rugby against each other.

'S-Sugar and H-Harry got the chop today,' added Robinson. 'I didn't know their names, the poor beggars in S-Sugar were only on

---

26   21 Elementary Flying Training School, one of 8 pilot training schools set up in Rhodesia in support of the Empire Air Training Scheme.

27   Chilapalapa, Take Everything. Salisbury was the capital of Rhodesia so the people from the other towns and cities referred to it as Bamba Zonke, in that the implication was that the capital city always took the best of everything.

their first operation.'

'I hope we have seen the last of Berlin for a while,' said Pallister, changing the subject. The men avoided talking about lost crews, particularly lost crews that nobody knew.

'Let's bloody hope so!' replied Robinson. What he didn't say, that was clear to all, was that at last count, 44 Squadron had lost thirteen aircraft over Berlin since November … *perish the thought of going back to the place.*

'The beautiful Jill Evans told me that they have got to the bottom of this scarecrow business,' added Pallister. 'At the moment the story is flak guns … doesn't sound right to me.'

George Armitage sauntered into the mess interrupting the conversation. He was dressed in a newly pressed uniform.

'Ah George, nice to see you in one piece after Bill tried to write you off this morning!' laughed Robinson, always the first with a witty comment.

'I'm still trying to get the mud out of my nose,' replied Armitage, in his characteristic Lincolnshire accent. His hometown was only four miles away.

'Bet it smells better than that Waaf mechanic you have been seeing,' said Robinson to a roar of laughter … 'You're looking all spivved up tonight George, are you going out to test your crankshaft?'

Another rumble of laughter … a few handclaps.

More officers were entering the mess all the time.

'Well in actual fact I am, there's a dance on at the Assembly Rooms[28] … The Squadronaires[29] are playing. I thought I would go along to show a few girls how to do it so to speak,' replied Armitage with a wink. 'Who wants to come along? What about you Bill?'

George Armitage looked across at his skipper, two years younger than he was, at just twenty. He had decided a long time before that he did not ever want to fly with any other pilot. Carter was not tall, maybe 5ft 9", light sandy coloured short-cropped hair, expressive light blue eyes, slimly built with a friendly compassionate face, unblemished by age. He had tried to grow a moustache but gave up after the numerous 'bum-fluff' comments he received from his friends.

---

28   The County Assembly Rooms were built on Bailgate, Lincoln, in 1745. The Assembly Rooms still host many functions, during the war it was used for dances.
29   In 1939, the Royal Air Force implemented a plan to raise morale and entertain the troops during wartime, and The Squadronaires was on of the bands organized as a result. The Squadronaires played at dances and concerts for service personnel and also broadcast on the BBC. The band was led by Jimmy Miller (singer) and the famous Ronny Aldrich played the piano.

Burdened with shyness, he struggled with people he did not know well. His shyness made him seem aloof, while his face displayed an expression of seriousness and determination, which some interpreted as being a bit 'stuck-up' or superior. Nothing could have been further from the truth. He was known as an attentive listener, concentrating intently on conversation but seldom spoke himself. When he did speak, he was animated and articulate. With his friends and crew, he could be the life and soul of the party. Quick to laugh, he revelled in the dry, understated English sense of humour that came so naturally to Biddle, Potts and Armitage.

The thing that Armitage liked most about Carter was his quietly spoken unassuming manner. Even though Carter was the captain of the aircraft, with the awesome responsibility that that entailed, he would always seek the advice of his crew. This was something that Armitage had not come across before, someone who listened to and respected his opinion.

Armitage remembered how Carter had approached him during their initial 'crew-up' at 29 OTU[30] at Bitteswell. He had been almost apologetic about needing a navigator.

Carter had approached Armitage relatively late in the piece, he had smiled and asked quietly, 'Excuse me … I need a navigator … are you taken? I can quite understand if you would rather fly with a fellow Englishman, I am from Rhodesia … but if you are available, I would very much like to have you …' Armitage had to lift his hand to stop the jabbered explanation by saying simply … 'I should be happy to join your crew.' He had liked Carter from the very start.

Armitage put Carter's attitude down to the fact that he came from the African colonies, where the burden of the stratified English class system had little place. The contrast between the Rhodesian, South African, Canadian, New Zealand and Australian crew was stark when compared with their English public school counterparts.

George had decided that he was going to Rhodesia after the war. If Bill Carter and Dave Muir were indicative of all the people in that country, that was the place for him. He would finish his chartered accountancy exams first, … *they were bound to need accountants in Rhodesia after the war.*

What impressed Armitage above all else was the deep sense of responsibility that Carter had for his crew. He did not talk about it, it was just his approach, his even-temper and self-control … *Amazing for such a young man!* He had proved to be cool and balanced under

---

30   Operational Training Unit

pressure ... *he had just saved all their lives*. While he was easy going, when the chips were down nobody disputed his orders. He was obeyed instantly and without question ... *such respect was not easily bestowed ... it had to be earned*. The result was that George Armitage would follow this young man to the ends of the earth ... he trusted Bill Carter with his life.

The story Armitage loved telling about his Skipper was when they were on their very first daylight cross-country exercise at 29 OTU. Armitage had got them hopelessly lost, in an attempted practice-bombing operation on the Welsh coast. The weather had been bad, with rain and low cloud with the added pressure of working with his new crew, trying desperately not to 'cock it up'. Carter, and the rest of the crew, had sensed the fact that they may be lost, but he did not say anything, simply dropped altitude coming out from under the cloud over the sea.

Carter called Armitage on the intercom, 'Navigator, can you take a squiz out the astrodome.'

Keeping low over the Welsh coastline, they passed over the village of Aberystwyth at wave-top level.

Looking out the cockpit as they passed overhead, Carter said conversationally, 'Navigator, that sign said Tipperary ... do we still have a long way to go?'

The aircraft had erupted with laughter, the nervous tension suddenly broken, it was as if that one simple remark instantly welded the crew together. Nobody could ever understand why at any sing-along involving, *It's a Long, Long Way to Tipperary*, Carter's crew would roll about laughing, pointing at Armitage ... *where the hell are we George?*

*

A senior officer marched purposefully into the mess. Sqn/Ldr Jack Haworth DFC, the CO of A Flight, was 26, tall, slimly built, with short blond hair and striking blue eyes. He could be described as the quintessential, dashing, good looking, intelligent, light-hearted RAF pilot with a wicked sense of humour. He had completed one tour of duty with 44 Squadron, and after a brief period as an instructor, returned to the Squadron as commander of A Flight.

Jack Haworth was the sort of bloke who had presence; he commanded attention. Women found him irresistible.

Haworth had the pick of the Waafs on the station, a challenge he was doing his best to accomplish. His ground crew on his beloved

A-Able had an unofficial record of his exploits painted on the inside of the bomb bay. The ground crews had given him the rather unflattering nickname, 'Pecker[31]' Haworth, in recognition of his exploits with the fairer sex.

Hailing from the great city of Birmingham, Haworth had attended Rugby School in Warwickshire where he had excelled both academically and on the rugby field, a very capable outside centre. He had been House Captain of Cotton House, something he was immensely proud of. His senior year house photograph was framed and hung in his office together with the 1st Rugby XV 'The Fifteen' of 1936. Jack won the school's Crick cross-country run in 1935 and 1936[32]. His father was a wealthy industrialist with factories making cutlery and buttons and a great interest in politics. The young Jack Haworth was the apple of his father's eye. Plans were being hatched for a seat in the House of Commons when the war was over. For the Conservative Party of course! His glittering career in Bomber Command would be a great stepping-stone to politics. If the war lasted beyond 1944, he was bound to be a Wing Commander or Group Captain. *Who knows … Jack could be Prime Minister!* Jack was just that sort of person … he made even the most difficult things seem possible.

Jack Haworth was greatly admired and respected by the young men of the squadron and A Flight in particular. He would never ask his men to do anything that he was not prepared to do himself. He led from the front. His wonderful sense of humour and his inclusive attitude endeared him to the ground crews as well. He always made a special effort every morning, regardless of the weather, to ride his bicycle along the boundary track to speak to the ground crews as they laboured to bring the aircraft up to the top line. He always had a moment to speak to the men, to enquire as to whether they had all they needed, often sitting in the grass under a wing with a mug of tea in his hand, having a good old natter, free with a joke and a smile.

'Well you motley bunch … I have some good news and some bad news,' announced Jack Haworth on the top of his voice.

'Let's have the bad news first, Sir,' returned Robinson.

'Very well … A Flight will do some daylight cross-country training tomorrow,' stated Haworth looking around the room. A few groans

---

31   English slang, n. penis, the word became a euphemism for 'penis' after the poet Catullus used it to refer to his love Lesbia's pet sparrow in a rather suggestive poem which drew some fairly blatant parallels. The phrase 'keep your pecker up' can be interpreted as both 'keep your chin up' or … something else.

32   Historical run of 10.4 miles begins in Crick and covers Barby and Kilsby villages before ending on the School's Close.

could be heard. 'Group[33] want us to get some practice at low level bombing.'

'Bloody hell Sir, what's the good news then?'

'All Ops are off for two nights at least, bad weather over Germany I'm afraid. We may get to go gardening[34] instead ... I don't know for sure,' added Haworth, hands on his hips.

This news was met with a roar of approval as men rushed to the bar for another pint ... *we can all have a few pints tonight!*

'Pilot Officer Carter?' called out Haworth.

'Sir!'

'You owe His Majesty's Government £50,000 for that Lancaster you so irresponsibly drove through the boundary fence today ... I am told a crossed check, account payee only will do!' demanded Haworth, with feigned seriousness.

The mess erupted once again with laughter.

'You may buy me a pint ... as a start,' smiled Haworth. 'Ah ... one more thing Carter ... we have a replacement crew for A Flight arriving tomorrow ... will you arrange to take them up on a Crew Check.'

'Yes Sir,' replied Carter, taken aback.

The request for Carter to do the Crew Check was pointed. Only accomplished pilots performed Check Flights. Carter had never seen himself as a particularly good pilot; he had not excelled in any of his training courses. After EFTS, 96 hours on Tiger Moths, he had been rated as 'average as a pilot'. The report regarding suitability for multi-engined aircraft had been marked emphatically 'No'. After training at 20 SFTS[35] at Cranborne in Salisbury, with 78 hours on Harvards, he was again rated 'Average on Harvards'. Finally, after ATS[36], also at Cranborne, as a fully-fledged pilot, he had been packed off to England with the rest of his class, with a total of 249 hours under the belt.

On the ship over to England from Cape Town, Peter Robinson had worked out a way of opening their wax-sealed Confidential Service Records that they had been given to take with them. To his horror, Carter had read his rating, 'Just Average – Not suited to night flying or multi-engined aircraft'. His overall score had been a princely 52%!

No reference was made to Carter's Confidential Service Record

---

33   Haworth is referring to 5 Group HQ, located at Morton Hall, Swinderby. 5 Group was commanded by Air Vice-Marshal the Hon. RA Cochrane in March 1944.

34   Code word for mine-laying.

35   Service Flying Training School

36   Advanced Training School, also on Harvards, included cross-country navigation, aircraft recovery, aerobatics, low level bombing, dive bombing, air to ground firing and instrument flying.

at the interview with the pilot selection board, at the Pilot Reception Centre at the requisitioned Pannel Ash School for Girls in Harrogate. He was convinced that they hadn't even read it. When he filled in the questionnaire, he circled his first choice as 'A – Single Engine Fighter' for obvious reasons. His interview had lasted twenty minutes, and the Wing Commander, with a DFC ribbon, had concluded expansively, 'We don't need fighter pilots, its all about attack … attack! We are taking the war to the Huns!' The stamp came down loudly, with a large, double-ringed inked circle around, 'Multi-engine Heavy Bomber Pilot'.

After fifteen completed operations, Carter had proved his ability as a pilot in his own mind, but it was with great satisfaction that this was recognised by Jack Haworth. He couldn't help smiling broadly, as he pushed his way to the bar to buy his 'Boss' a beer.

Haworth, obviously in high spirits, jumped on a chair, then holding his beer glass above his head he yelled out …

> Hitler, he's only got one ball
> The other, is in the Albert Hall
> With his mother, the dirty bugger
> She cut it off when he was four
> She threw it into a Chestnut tree
> And it rolled into the deep blue sea
> Where the fishes, rolled out the dishes
> And had bollocks, and scallops for tea[37].

'Hurrah! Hurrah!' shouted the crowd.
A group of Waaf officers took up in full voice …

> We've tried it once or twice
> And found it rather nice …

The rest of the mess spontaneously responded.

> Roll me over lay me down and do it again
> Roll me oooover in the cloooover,
> roll me over, lay me down, and do it again …[38]

---

37   *Hitler Has Only Got One Ball* was a British song that mocked Nazi leaders. Multiple variants of the lyrics exist, generally sung as four-line verses to the tune of the *Colonel Bogey March*, written in 1914 by Lieutenant F J Ricketts (1881-1945), a British army bandmaster.
38   According to *Shanties from the Seven Seas*, collected by Stan Hugill this song is a

Holding their beer glasses high, the Waafs continued …

Oh this is number one
And the fun has just begun

Roooll me over lay me down and do it again
Roooll me ooover in the cloooover,
roll me over, lay me down, and do it again …

By now the whole mess was in full voice, swinging their beer glasses from side to side, stamping their feet to, *roll me over, lay me down, and do it again …*

That's for the RAF for sure
Roooll me over lay me down and do it again
Roooll me ooover in the cloooover,
roll me over, lay me down, and do it again …

When the Spitfire's fire spits
We'll pull down Hitler's Messerschmitts
Roll me over, lay me down and do it again
Roooll me ooover in the cloooover,
roll me over, lay me down, and do it again …

… And so it went on with all the bawdy verses to much excitement and laughter. All the Waafs in the mess joined in with the same enthusiasm … taking it all in their stride.

After Haworth's song came to an end with a full-throated … *roooll me over, lay me down, and do it again* … someone shouted to Peter Robinson, 'Give us a song Pete, give us the one about Cocky Lobin.'

Beers were now being sunk in quick succession … the boys were in a great mood. The relief of knowing that Ops were off for a few nights had released pent up stress and pressure, replacing it with a wild uninhibited euphoria.

'Yes Robinson, get your Rhodesians together and give us a song,' agreed Haworth, always ready for a bit of sport. Men shouted their encouragement … 'come on Peter give us a song.'

'Oh, alright,' shouted Robinson waving his arms, '*Iwe … iwe lo*

soldiers' song, enormously popular during World War II. The rhyming, melody and rhythm probably have stayed the same over the years, but it lends itself to added words as the RAF had done.

mampara ka lo Rhodesia, buya lapa.[39']

The Rhodesian officers in the mess formed a group next to the bar that included Carter and Pallister to much banter and cheering.

'Maestro, *Tatenda,*' called out Robinson to George Armitage, who could tickle the ivories on the old, out of tune, piano. Armitage took up his place at the piano and nodded to Robinson that he was ready.

Robinson stood up on a chair and called out to his accompanist, '*Baas Armitage niga mina lo C.*[40']

Armitage followed the requirement for a 'C', plinking the piano while Robinson hummed loudly in an attempt to get to the correct pitch. The mess howled with laughter.

'*Aikona ... Baas Armitage niga mina lo E,*[41'] shouted Robinson above the noise, feigning unhappiness with the chosen pitch.

Plink ... plink ... plink ... hummm ... hummm ... hummm.

The laughter in the officer's mess carried to the NCO's mess close by, David Muir and some of his fellow NCOs went outside to listen to the hilarity.

'*Nyamazaans ... kuimba!*' instructed Robinson and the group of about fifteen Rhodesians sang the opening chorus to *Cocky Lobin.*

> *Zonke nyoni lapa moyo ena kala, ena kala*
> *Ena izwile ena ifile lo nyoni Cocky Lobin*
> *Ena izwile, ena ifile,*
> *ena izwile ena ifile Cocky Lobin*[42] *...*

They sang at the top of their voices, tears of laughter running down their cheeks. Robinson then sang the first verse, in a slow enquiring fashion.

> *Kubani ena bulalile Cocky Lobin?*
> *Meena kuluma lo Sparrow*
> *Na lo picannin 303 Browning kamina*
> *Meena bulalile Cocky Lobin!*[43]

---

39   You ... all you insane people from Rhodesia, come here.
40   Mr Armitage give me a C.
41   No ... Mr Armitage, give me an E.
42   All the birds in the sky cried and cried, when they heard of the death of the bird Cock Robin, when they heard of the death of Cock Robin.
43   Who was it that killed Cock Robin? It was I said the Sparrow, with my tiny .303 browning, it was I who killed Cock Robin.

Like a conductor in front of an orchestra, Robinson led the rest of the mess with the chorus. They all joined in with gusto including the NCOs outside.

> *Zonke nyoni lapa moyo ena kala, ena kala*
> *Ena izwile ena ifile lo nyoni Cocky Lobin*
> *Ena izwile, ena ifile,*
> *ena izwile ena ifile Cocky Lobin.*

Pallister was next with the second verse; he took up the pose of Sherlock Holmes, questioning the audience with …

> *Kubani ena bona ene ifile?*
> *Meena kuluma lo Mosweeto*
> *Na lo cleva bomb sight kamina*
> *Meena bona ene ifile …*[44]

The crowd inside and outside the mess enthusiastically sang the chorus once again. A different pilot sang each of the verses in turn, embellishing the words to give a Bomber Command flavour. The tension and stress of the past weeks momentarily melted away as the men and off-duty Waafs sang in full voice.

> *Zonke nyoni lapa moyo ena kala, ena kala*
> *Ena izwile ena ifile lo nyoni Cocky Lobin*
> *Ena izwile, ena ifile,*
> *ena izwile ena ifile Cocky Lobin.*

The song Cocky Lobin, the Chilapalapa incarnation of the English nursery rhyme, *Who Killed Cock Robin*, united the Dunholme Lodge air station like nothing else could … a tiny taste of Southern Africa, on the miserably cold windswept plains of Lincolnshire.

Ron Boswell knew the words, the song was sung by the Rhodesian fitters and electricians in the NCO's mess … it gave him an idea …

> *… Ena izwile, ena ifile,*
> *ena izwile ena ifile Cocky Lobin …*

---

44   Who saw him die? It was I said the Mosquito, through my clever bomb-sight, it was I that saw him die.

*

County Assembly Rooms, Bailgate Rd, Lincoln, Lincolnshire
Saturday 25 March 1944, 8:15pm

'Well, Bill, old chum, are you going to invite someone to dance?' enquired Peter Robinson mimicking a posh English accent.

The dance floor was full of servicemen and women from the many air stations within striking distance of Lincoln. Scampton, Fiskerton, Waddington, Skellingthorpe and Dunholme Lodge, were closest to the town. The heaving mass was doing an enthusiastic jitterbug to The Squadronaires' *South Rampart Street Parade.*

'No, I just can't get the steps, I'll look like a bloody fool,' replied Carter.

'That little Maggie Smith keeps looking over here,' added Gavin Pallister, 'Is it me or you she's looking at Pete?'

'Her mate is a bit of a looker, what's her name?' asked Robinson.

'Her name's Vera Johns but you'll want to keep your distance from her I'm afraid,' replied Pallister, gravely. 'She's a chop girl[45], word has it that she has dated three pilots on forty-four squadron, none of them have come back. She's bad luck ... poor show really ... she certainly is very attractive.'

'Here are the beers,' called David Muir, pushing through the crowd towards the table occupied by the Rhodesian pilots.

The neighbouring tables were full of 44 Squadron crews that were out for the night, together with their dates. Most of the girls were dressed in the fashionable dancing skirts, while the Waafs who had just knocked off duty, were still in uniform.

Muir had four beer tankards in his hands, followed by Eric Biddle with another four. Biddle's head was wrapped in a bandage from the cut he received in the crash. Despite a throbbing headache, he was determined to go out with his crew. Tommy Potts and Charles Morley were being kept in the Station Hospital under 'observation'.

The Rhodesians had an informal approach to rank, happy to be in company with the NCOs particularly those from the 'Colonies'.

Frank Nellyer, with hands still bandaged, had his arm around a girl he had met in the town. He had chatted her up in the post office.

---

45   Aircrews, on the whole, were superstitious, avoiding any possible hint of bad luck. Girls on the air bases who had dated men that had gone missing on operations unwittingly became, so called, 'chop girls'. Chop being slang for 'getting the chop' i.e. being killed or shot down. These unfortunate souls were avoided (shunned) by the aircrew, to avoid their perceived bad luck rubbing off.

His smooth Canadian accent had soon won her over. The nurses at the station hospital had refused to allow him out of the ward so they could change his dressings but he had escaped out of the toilet window, not wanting to miss a night out on the town.

George Armitage came screaming past on the dance floor, doing the jitterbug for all he was worth, he slowed in front of the table to throw the girl through his legs whipping her up onto her feet again, her skirt flying above her head. A great roar of appreciation followed from the servicemen sitting nearby.

Armitage loved dancing and always seemed to have a new girl on his arm. He would have been described as good looking in a George Sanders sort of way, 6ft 2", black hair with liberal use of Brylcream, a smooth voice, urbane manner and upper-class accent. Despite his Public School education and slightly ponsi-pretentious accent, he still described himself deprecatingly as the Grocer's son ... and proud of it.

While George loved a party and sing-along, coming across as frivolous and fun-loving, when it came to a his job, he was nothing short of fanatical. He studied maps, weather reports, phases of the moon, cloud formations, operating manuals for sextant, GEE, H2S, the SBA system, radio frequencies, fuel consumption and all other things navigational. He even wrote a little ditty he called: *Speed equals distance over time,* to the tune of *Hang out the washing on the Siegfried Line.* George's first thing every day was a trip to the Met Office where he would interrogate the poor duty-officer on the latest reports and wind speeds.

As he was from Lincoln, he was a great source of introductions to the local girls. This gave the men from 44 Squadron a great advantage over those from other squadrons in the surrounding area. George had a constant stream of requests from members of the squadron for introductions. On the other side of the coin the girls knew that George had an equally good supply of men. George Armitage also had a very attractive younger sister, Linda, who had caught the eye of Gavin Pallister.

George had a friendly open disposition and was a huge hit at a party because he could play the piano and sing very well indeed. He had a great repertoire of songs and was one of those people who could rattle off jokes one after the another for an hour without stopping. He and Dave Muir knew all the words to *We're off on the road to Morocco,* by Bing Crosby and Bob Hope from the film, *Road to Morocco.* At the drop of a hat, they would sing the song, one of them playing the piano.

Off on the road to Morocco
Hang on till the end of the line (I like your jockey. Quiet)
I hear this country's where they do the dance of the seven veils
We'd tell you more (uh-ah)
But we would have the censor on our tails (good boy)

It was one of George's funny stories that he had travelled a long way to get to the war ... all of 4 miles. His family offered a sort of open house for the crew of C-Charlie. Mister and Misses Armitage, as the crew knew them, were a jovial pair always ready with a quickly concocted meal or a pint with a weekly drop of scones at the main gate. They provided a home away from home for the crew, in a lovely old Tudor style house in Wordsworth Street close to Lincoln Castle on top of Castle Hill. The house was walking distance from the pubs and many a night was spent there after a few too many. As the house was so close to Lincoln Cathedral it was easy to see as they came into land, 'bombing' it with left over Window as they passed overhead ... *stand by to bomb the Armitage's!*

The music changed. The throbbing beat of *Boogie Woogie Bugle Boy Of Company B,* sung by Suzi Miller and Dorothy Squires filled the room. More couples pushed on to the dance floor, the girls singing at the top of their voices.

They made him blow a bugle for his Uncle Sam.
It really brought him down because he could not jam.
The captain seemed to understand,
Because the next day the cap' went out and drafted the band.
And now the company jumps when he plays reveille.
He's the boogie-woogie bugle boy of Company B ...

Bill Carter tapped his feet to the rhythm, the vibrant happy music seemed to clear the mind ... it was fantastic. For a few brief moments there was no war, just a crowd of young people having a great time, living for that single moment.

He reflected on this great adventure that he had embarked on since he had left Rhodesia after his pilot training. This was his first time outside of his tiny landlocked country, off to the 'Mother Country', to the glory and excitement of contributing to the war effort. He had been more concerned about being too late; on missing out, ... he needn't have worried. The reality fell far short of expectation ...

A root, a toot, a toodlie-a-da-toot.
He blows it eight to the bar in boogie rhythm.
He can't blow a note unless a bass and guitar
Is playin' with him.

Bill's family lived in a beautiful old home on an acre at the golf-course end of Duncan Road in 'Suburbs'. He had attended Bulawayo Technical School, later Gifford Technical High School. His father Walter, an electrical engineer on the Bulawayo City Council, believed that a technical education was the way of the future. Walter was a strict disciplinarian, born and raised in a tough neighbourhood in Manchester. He was mortified when his son informed him that he wanted to go banking. Walter Carter referred to all bankers as 'blood suckers'. While his father was a man of few words, Bill knew that he loved him and was very proud of him signing up for the RAF. Walter had served with the 2nd Salford Pals in the Great War, was secretly greatly relieved that his son was not in the infantry. As it turned out, Bill's chances of survival were considerably less than regimental subalterns in the Great War.

There was always a paragraph from his father at the bottom of all his mother's letters from home ... *keep your head down son* ... typical infantry!

Bill was very attached to his mother who had met his father after she had come out to Rhodesia from England as a nurse. His mother, Cynthia, came from Devon and still spoke with, what his father jokingly described, as a 'posh' English accent. Her accent contrasted with his father's Lancashire drawl. She wrote to him every week with all the news and goings-on in the town. Included were newspaper cuttings from the Bulawayo Chronicle, especially the cartoons that he loved ... the *Katzenjammer Kids*. Bill had a younger sister Edith who was in the Sixth Form at Eveline High School in Bulawayo. She also wrote every week with all of her news.

The Standard Bank had taken Bill in as a trainee straight from school, but he, and all his friends, had as their single ambition signing up as soon as possible. By way of coincidence, 5 Initial Training Wing RAF (5 ITW) was located across Hillside Road from Bulawayo Technical School, at the Bulawayo Show Grounds. As schoolboys, they had watched the airmen from the Empire Air Training Scheme using the school playing fields for their rugby matches and the RAF had built a gym and squash courts on the school grounds. Letters from home had said the RAF had built a swimming pool on the school grounds.

Carter wished it had been there when he had been at school.

On 10 January 1942, Bill Carter had presented himself at the gates to 5 ITW to begin his training as a pilot. He then went on to 21 EFTS at Kumalo airfield, also in Bulawayo, where he had met Pallister and Robinson.

Carter reflected on standing in front of the Lancaster for the first time, it had been an awe-inspiring experience. He was at No. 5 Lancaster Flying School (LFS) at Syerston, 5½ miles southwest of Newark-on-Trent, Nottinghamshire. There they were to be taught how to fly and manoeuvre that magnificent state-of-the-art machine. He remembered thinking how big the aircraft was with such an enormous wingspan … *how could I possibly fly this thing?*

Flying the Lancaster had been a pleasure from the start, she handled beautifully and George Armitage, using his GEE[46] and H2S[47] sets, bar his initial mishap, had always brought them safely home from their many cross-country flights. They flew mostly in weather that was described officially as poor but more accurately, atrocious. Incongruously, Carter's small hands were the greatest impediment. He could not get his little finger around the starboard outer engine lever, so he had to rely on Eric Biddle with his big hands to hang onto the four throttles, while he concentrated on getting the giant machine onto the ground. They had worked so well as a team from the very outset.

The seven of them, all complete strangers to each other, had been thrust together by pure circumstance. He still marvelled at the simple way the RAF put crews together, 'crewing up' as they called it.

At 29 OTU[48] at Bitteswell in Leicestershire, where Carter was sent to convert on to the twin engine Wellingtons, the pilots had been told to mill around with the airmen from the various disciplines and invite them to be members of their crews. There was one proviso stipulated by the instructors … *only two Rhodesians per crew*. The Southern Rhodesian Government had requested that no more than two of their

---

46 GEE was the code name given to a radio navigation system used by the RAF. It was the first hyperbolic navigation system to be used operationally, using a chain of radio towers transmitting on known frequencies, allowing the aircraft to fix its position. The transmitters had a power output of about 300kW and operated in four frequency bands between 20 and 85 MHz. On board the aircraft, the signals from at least three stations were received and sent to the oscilloscope display. At 10,000ft, the system had a range of 400 miles. Gee's greatest limitation was line of sight.
47 H2S was the first airborne, ground scanning radar system. Named after hydrogen sulphide, as the delay in its acceptance caused Lord Cherwell, the English physicist, to say that 'it stinks'.
48 Operational Training Unit

men be placed in each crew, as the tiny colony could not handle the loss of seven young men each time a Lancaster went down.

As Carter was naturally shy and reserved, asking people to join his crew had been no easy task. Fortunately, he had met Dave Muir, who was also Rhodesian, early on. He was much more outgoing, so between the two of them, they managed to get the crew together. The memory of crewing up still played on Carter's mind ... *would you like to join my crew? ... I know I have a strange accent ... you don't know me from a bar of soap ... I come from a country you may not have heard of ... in Africa ... I am asking you to put your life in my hands day after day for thirty operations ... you only have a few minutes to decide!*

The overwhelming responsibility of bringing these men back from a sortie, weighed heavily on his mind.

He's the boogie-woogie bugle boy of Company B.

The music changed again. Suzi Miller's lilting voice dreamily began, *When I Grow too Old to Dream*[49], changing the atmosphere in a moment. Couples needed no encouragement; they held each other tightly as they swayed to the familiar slow rhythm.

> *When I grow too old to dream*
> *I'll have you to remember*
> *When I grow too old to dream*
> *Your love will live in my heart ...*

This is more my speed, thought Carter as he watched the couples dancing. As he turned to talk to Peter Robinson, there in front of him was Maggie Smith, wearing her Waaf uniform.

'I'll dance with you Bill,' she said softly, blushing brightly.

> *... So kiss me my sweet*
> *And so let us part*
> *And when I grow too old to dream*
> *That kiss will live in my heart ...*

She held out her hand and Carter spontaneously took it. Her friend Vera stood on the edge of the dance floor, longingly watching the couples embracing to the slow tune. Peter Robinson saw her standing there, completely alone ... a truly beautiful girl, tall, long brown

49   Song by Vera Lynn, from the film *The Night Is Young* (1935), Sigmund Romberg and Oscar Hammerstein II.

shoulder length hair, her Waaf cap neatly in place.

'Ah, to hell with it … we all have to go sometime,' announced Robinson loudly. He walked over the few feet to where Vera was standing, 'Will you dance with me Vera?' he asked, a broad friendly smile on his face.

The girl looked up at him in complete surprise, blushing brightly, she knew what people were saying about her.

'I would very much like to dance with you Mr Robinson,' she replied quietly so only he could hear, looking up at him with flawless deep green eyes, like Sandawana Emeralds[50] he would say later.

As Bill Carter and Maggie Smith stepped onto the dance floor, she threw her arms around his neck and thrust her face into his chest. He could not see her face, but her eyes filled with tears and her body shook with a stifled sob. Carter was taken aback; he put his arms around her waist and held her, feeling her body trembling against his.

The music washed over him, and he felt an overpowering feeling of need … he held her tightly … closing his eyes.

> *… When I grow too old to dream*
> *I'll have you to remember*
> *When I grow too old to dream*
> *Your love will live in my heart …*

The crowd sang the lilting chorus, the sound filling the room, vibrating in the chest. It was one of the most wonderful moments Bill Carter could remember in his young life.

When the song finished, Maggie stayed in his arms, not wanting to let him go.

'I am so sorry, I didn't mean to cry,' she blurted out. 'Its just that I watched you crash today … I couldn't bear it … it was too awful … I thought you would be hurt.'

'We were lucky today Maggie,' replied Carter, not quite sure what to say. The young girl's reaction was totally unexpected, but lovely … very lovely indeed.

'I so wanted to talk to you … to find out, but I couldn't … you had to go to debrief I had to work … I couldn't come to the mess or your room … I just so wanted to speak to you,' said Maggie, the words tumbling out, her eyes again filling with tears, 'I feel so silly … I am sorry, please forgive me.'

'It's alright Maggie … please don't worry,' replied Carter, feeling

---

50   The famous Sandawana emeralds are mined in Southern Matabeleland.

awkward, very caught up in the girl's emotions

'All the girls have warned me not to get attached to you ... because ... well I don't care, I can't help it,' she said, looking up into his eyes. He saw his own need reflected there.

The Band Leader called 'time', breaking into Arthur Askey's *Kiss me goodnight Sergeant Major*[51]. The crowd joined in, everyone singing on the top of their voices.

> *Private Jones came in one night*
> *Full of cheer and very bright*
> *He'd been out all day upon the spree*
> *He bumped into Sergeant Smeck*
> *Put his arms around his neck*
> *And in his ear he whispered tenderly ...*

The sound of singing filled the room, flowing out into the surrounding streets.

> *Kiss me goodnight, Sergeant-Major*
> *Tuck me in my little wooden bed*
> *We all love you, Sergeant-Major,*
> *When we hear you bawling, 'Show a leg!'...*

Bill Carter and Maggie Smith stayed in each other's arms, singing for all they were worth, laughing and crying at the same time ... it didn't matter which.

> *Don't forget to wake me in the morning*
> *And bring me 'round a nice hot cup of tea*
> *Kiss me goodnight, Sergeant-Major*
> *Sergeant-Major, be a mother to me ...*

---

51   By Art Noell and Don Pelosi, sung by Arthur Askey (1939)

4

RAF Dunholme Lodge, Lincolnshire
Sunday 26 March 1944, 10:15am

Bill Carter arrived in good time to meet the new crew at the A Flight office. The office was located in a Nissen hut close to the control tower. He was already dressed in his flying kit holding his leather flying helmet and gloves in his hand. Sqn/Ldr Haworth was in his office going through the mountain of useless paperwork, 'bumph', that he constantly complained about.

'Ah, Carter my good man ... you will be happy to know that your replacement aircraft should be delivered tomorrow ... brand spanking new. Let's hope that you keep this one on the runway,' laughed Haworth buoyantly.

'Good news Sir, it will be interesting to see what new gadgets the boffins have added,' replied Carter. Haworth's easy going and friendly manner was infectious, Carter smiled back at him.

'I need to go to the briefing room to brief the rest of the flight on their cross country tour this afternoon ... they will be waiting for me. I have organised E-Easy for the Crew Check. You should find her in Pan F. Flight Sergeant Kennedy has reported all is in order ... where is that blasted new crew?' demanded Haworth, with his usual frustration when people were even a fraction of a minute late.

'Potter, go and see where they are,' shouted Haworth to Leading Aircraftswoman Linda Potter, A Flight's long-suffering clerk.

'They will be along shortly Sir, I spoke to Pilot Officer Fullerton only a few minutes ago. They are coming across from the parachute store,' replied Potter, who was used to her boss's lack of patience. She spoke with an accent that Carter had been told came from the south of England near Portsmouth.

Carter looked out the window and could see the new crew making their way towards the flight office. They had already clipped on their parachute harnesses, parachutes slung over their shoulders with yellow 'Mae West'[52] life jackets. They arrived at the door to the Nissen hut and stood outside, clearly unsure of what to do next.

The natural instinct was to feel some sort of attachment to these new members of the squadron, but Carter fought against it. They were all green and scared, as he had been, but full of the terrific romance of their uniform and their flying machines ... a romance that was quickly and often tragically dispelled. What was so irksome were the perfectly

---

52   Inflatable life jacket, named after a well-endowed film actress.

reasonable questions new men asked, a) How many have you done? b) What's it like? c) Do you get scared when nightfighters attack? To which the old lags answer; a) the truth, b) fucking awful, c) Yes ... but add the word shitless.

The odds were stacked so heavily against them ... *against all of us!* So many men had come and gone, their faces murky blurs, lost to life and to memory. Just young men, full of life one day, an empty bunk the next. Carter knew it was callous but his defence mechanism was to think only of his own crew and those of his close friends Robinson and Pallister. He refused to allow his mind to consider what might happen ... *live for the moment ... take one day and one operation at a time.*

'Potter, for goodness sake, get those men in here,' demanded Haworth. Potter huffed loudly to show her response to this unnecessary fuss, pushed her chair back with a squeak on the concrete floor, stood up, straightened her skirt and walked purposefully to the door.

'Pilot Officer Fullerton, please come in Sir,' announced Potter formally. 'His Lordship awaits,' she added softly with a wink.

The seven men shuffled in, standing in a tight group for mutual support, not knowing what to expect.

'Good morning Sir, Pilot Officer Fullerton Sir,' said the new man with a clear precise Rhodesian accent, throwing a very creditable salute despite the bulky flying suit.

'Welcome to A Flight Fullerton my good man,' replied Haworth, immediately clicking back to his affable self. 'Another man from the African colonies I see, well you will be quite at home here ... we have a good many of your lot already,' added Haworth with a smiling glance at Carter.

Haworth then delivered his usual welcome to new crews.

'Welcome to 44, I think you will be happy here with us. We are a happy squadron and a bloody good one. All I ask is that you do what you have been trained to do to the best of your ability and then, God willing, we will all come through this thing together. I wish you all the very best of luck,' smiled Haworth in his winning way. 'I can't stay for a chat, I have to deliver a briefing ... Fullerton please introduce me to your crew and then I will leave you in the capable hands of Pilot Officer Carter here for your Crew Check ... also one of your fellow countrymen,' said Haworth, getting to his feet.

Haworth introduced Fullerton to Carter, they shook hands, then he welcomed each man in the crew in turn. He wanted to know where they came from; all were from England except for their Skipper. As he shook each of their hands he gave them the name of the squadron officer responsible for each of their respective disciplines; navigation, radios, gunnery, bomb aiming and engineering. Carter marvelled at the effortless way that Haworth put the men at ease. His welcome was demonstrably genuine with a noticeable effect on the new men; they smiled back at him … after only a brief moment of introduction … ready to follow this man through the very gates of hell.

Haworth then placed his cap on his head, at its normal rakish angle, grabbed his maps and briefing material and marched out of the office, 'have a good flight gentlemen, should be a piece of cake,' he said. The new men stood watching him walk across to the briefing room, totally amazed at their reception.

Leading Aircraftswoman Potter also watched him go.

'Don't be too taken in by that carefree manner, if you are late again, he will happily tear a strip off you,' she said, going back to her desk.

'Right, we might as well get on with it,' said Carter. 'Where in Rhodesia are you from?' he asked Fullerton.

'Umtali,' replied Fullerton, 'we farm fruit trees, mainly peaches and plums in the Vumba Mountains.'

'I'm from Bulawayo, hot and dry as you know. How many hours have you got on Lancs?' asked Carter

'I've got four hundred and eighty-seven in total, and twenty-two on Lancasters,' replied Fullerton, trying to make the most of it.

Carter nodded, not wanting to comment on the low number of hours on Lancasters. The flying schools were pushing out pilots like sausages. The new crews just had to learn quickly … or die equally quickly.

'Don't forget to fill in Form 540 Mr Carter,' ordered Potter in her usual off-handed manner. She ran the flight like a well-oiled machine despite Haworth's best attempts at 'stuffing' it up.

'Yes, thank you Potter,' replied Carter, smiling at her. He really did like Potter, all the men did. She could be a bit abrupt and off-handed but her heart was in the right place.

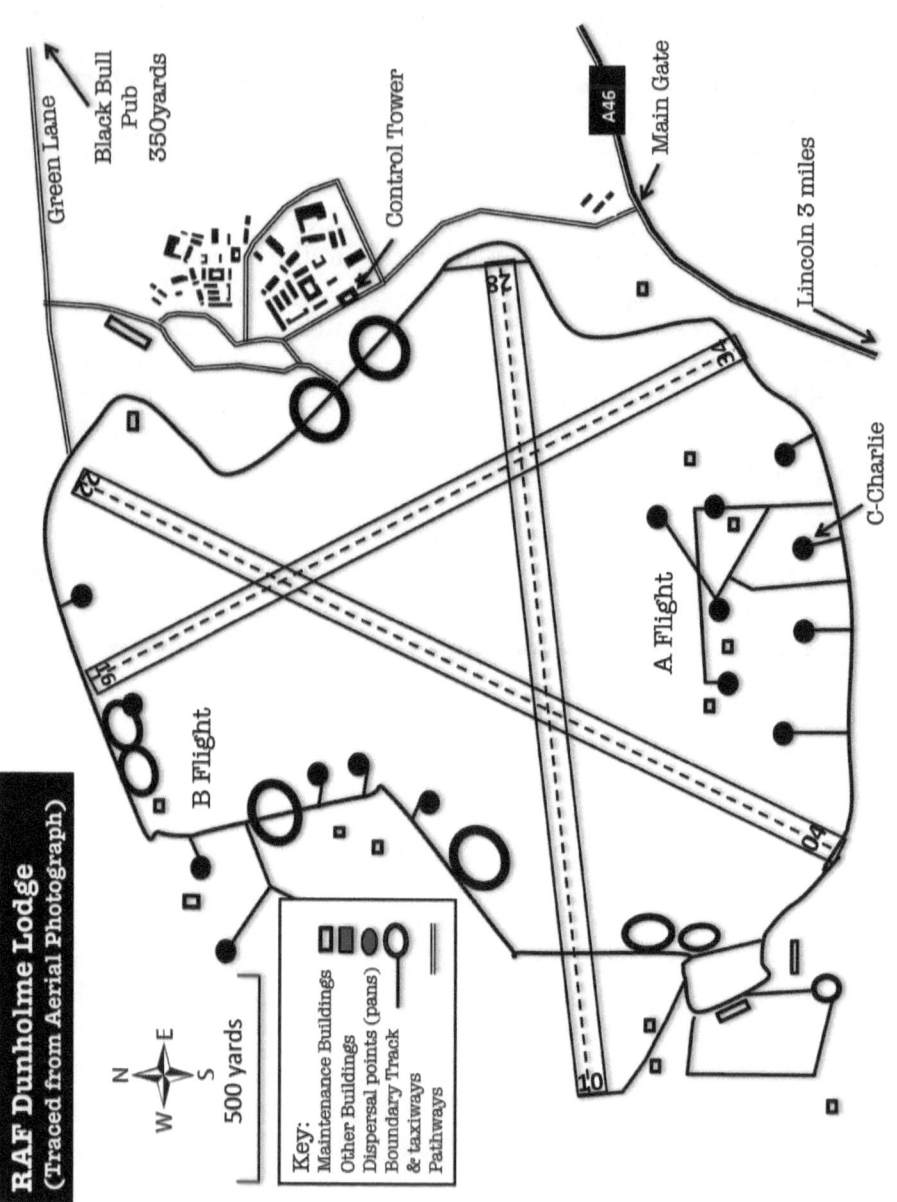

RAF Dunholme Lodge
(Traced from Aerial Photograph)

Green Lane

Black Bull
Pub
350yards

Control Tower

Main Gate

A46

Lincoln 3 miles

C-Charlie

A Flight

B Flight

32

34

22

19

04

10

Key:
Maintenance Buildings
Other Buildings
Dispersal points (pans)
Boundary Track
& taxiways
Pathways

N
E
S
W

500 yards

Leading the new crew out of the A Flight office, Carter pointed out the various parts of the air station; workshops, canteens, briefing rooms, the messes and the administration offices. He gave a brief rundown of the structure of the place, 44 Squadron was the only squadron at Dunholme Lodge, but they were expecting another squadron to join them at any time. Rumour had it that it might be 619 Squadron. 44 Squadron was divided into two flights, A and B, each with thirteen aircraft. A Flight had Lancasters A-Able to M-Mother, while B Flight had N-Nan to Z-Zebra all with the 44 Squadron 'KM' prefix.

They climbed into the back of the gharrie to be taken around the air station to Pan F, the dispersal point where E-Easy was parked. As they drove along Carter described other aspects of the air station, flying control and the location of neighbouring air stations. The men all listened intently, taking it all in. Carter pointed out the large country house that had given the air station its name, an impressive greyish-red, Victorian building with a slate roof, possibly the only permanent building on the station, now requisitioned for accommodation. Dispersed in the countryside, mainly to the east of the station, south of Welton, were domestic, communal and the sick quarters providing for a maximum 1,637 males and the 468 females in the 'Waafery'. The buildings were linked by black cinder paths that gave off a strong 'rotten eggs' sulphur smell, the by-product from the hundreds of coke and coal fired heating stoves around the base. A fifty-foot wide concrete track/taxiway ran around the perimeter of the station.

Pointing out the barbed wire perimeter fence, Carter explained that Station Police constantly patrolled it, just in case anybody had ideas of sneaking off the base for a beer or assignation. Having given the warning, Carter then pointed out the various half-concealed gaps in the barbed-wire created by the ground crews to link up with the extensive local network of footpaths through the surrounding fields. The most useful holes being in the SE towards the A46 and Lincoln, the other in the NE to the closest pub, The Black Bull, in Welton.

The three runways were hard surfaced with a homing system called Standard Beam Approach, or SBA, on the longest 6,000ft NE-SW runway, number 22 from the NE and number 04 from the SW. This runway 22/04 also had the airfield's light beacons with the main beacon near the station's domestic quarters. The three massive runways crossed over one another making a striking geometric pattern when seen from the air. The prevailing winds were southwesterly, which meant that the shorter east-west runway, 10-28 and 16-34 were seldom used. The prevailing wind resulted in most 44 Squadron aircraft taking off to the southwest directly towards the City of Lincoln, right over the top of Lincoln Cathedral Tower. Uncomfortably close when carrying a full load of bombs and fuel.

As they passed the empty pan 'C', Carter could not help but think about the impending arrival of his new kite. The truck stopped next to Pan F and the men all jumped onto the concrete apron. The pan was set back close to a stand of trees that added to the camouflage of the aircraft. E-Easy stood serenely in her parking. A fitter had a ladder up against No 1 engine, replacing an inspection cover.

The low drone of Merlin engines being run-up, carried across the windswept airfield. It has a comforting sound, powerful, warm and reliable … the distinct smell of high-octane aviation fuel mixed with coal smoke filled the air.

Flight Sergeant Kennedy saw the crew arrive, he and Corporal Ron Boswell walked over to meet them.

'Good morning Sir, good day for it,' said Kennedy addressing Carter in his usual friendly manner. It was mainly overcast, with high cloud but no rain forecast, a good day for flying.

'Morning Chiefy, let me introduce you to the new crew,' replied Carter.

Kennedy shook hands with each man in turn, smiling broadly as he did so.

'She's in good order Sir, nothing to report … but she is getting on a bit as you know,' added Kennedy after the introductions.

E-Easy was used for training purposes and was a rare example of a Lancaster fitted with dual controls. Like her sisters, her upper surfaces were painted in rich dark green and brown curves to break up her profile. Her lower surfaces were painted in matt black. An RAF roundel was painted on the top of each wing and on the side of the fuselage with her call-sign, KM-E, painted in large red letters on both sides of the fuselage aft of the wing. E-Easy, as with most of her 44 Squadron sisters, was a Lancaster B1, fitted with Rolls Royce Merlin 24 engines.

Turning to Fullerton, 'You should do your pre-flight checks, I will wait until you have finished,' instructed Carter. The pre-flight checklist was imprinted on Carter's brain, he could recite it word for word from the Operations Manual.

Fullerton's crew immediately went about their business; they were clearly very comfortable with each other. Fullerton and his flight engineer walked around the aircraft doing the external checks …

pitot head covers removed, all cowlings, inspection panels and leading edges secured. Check tyres for creep ...

Carter was impressed with their professional approach, while he didn't 'hover' he watched and listened to the new crew closely. After about twenty minutes, Fullerton slid back the cockpit window and gave Carter a thumb's up to show he was ready. The ground crew had the external battery attached and manned the fuel priming-pump to the port outer engine.

Carter walked around to the crew access door on the starboard side and climbed up the steps into the aircraft. Inside the aircraft, he was greeted with the familiar smell of cellulose, oil and 100-octane fuel. Casting an eye over the equipment in the fuselage as he went, he climbed the steep slope forward struggling over the main spar. Fullerton was settled into the left-hand pilot's seat. All the crew were in their positions and Carter took up his seat next to the pilot. Fullerton had his mask clipped over his mouth so he could speak into the intercom; Carter did the same, plugging his helmet mic into the socket next to his seat. It was about 50°F outside so the engines should fire after only seven strokes.

'Please sign this Sir,' asked Ron Boswell thrusting a clipboard between the two pilots with a greasy Form 700 stuck to it. This was the pilot's final agreement that the ground crew had handed him a serviceable aircraft. Fullerton cast his eye down the form and signed on the bottom, handing it back to Boswell.

'Thank you Sir ... pleasant flight,' said Boswell in his friendly way.

Fullerton switched on the intercom.

'Pilot to crew, check?'

Each of the seven crew members replied in turn.

'Rear gunner okay Skip.'

'Mid-upper okay.'

'Wireless Operator okay.'

'Navigator okay.

'Bomb aimer okay.'

'Okay Engineer we're ready to start up,' called Fullerton to the Flight Engineer sitting behind Carter.

'Roger Skip, ground/flight switch to Ground, Trolley AC is plugged in, engine controls set, fuel okay.'

'Throttles half-inch open, propeller controls up ... Tank selector cock to No. 2 tank ... master engine cock of port outer on ... booster pump on No 2 tank on ... booster coil on ... clear to start,' Fullerton called out the checklist, then signalled to Ron Boswell, standing in front of the aircraft looking up at him, that he was ready. Ron held up his hand, called to the men on the ground to stand clear … then gave thumbs up.

Fullerton pressed the starter button, the Merlin turned over, one … two … three, the big prop turned slowly with a whining noise … coughed … coughed again and roared. The sequence was followed until all four engines were running … all at 1,200 rpm until they were warmed up.

'Check hydraulics … flaps,' the gunners confirmed their turrets were working, 'radiator shutters over-ride switches open, rpm to 1,500, magnetos serviceable, superchargers to 4lb/sq.in,' listed Fullerton, calmly calling off each process on the checklist.

Fullerton turned and nodded back at Boswell, his oxygen mask still in place. Boswell then pushed past navigator's station and radio operator, climbing over the main spar, to exit the aircraft at the rear crew door. The mid-upper gunner rammed the door shut, locking it in place.

'Ready to taxi,' said Fullerton glancing at Carter.

Carter nodded, 'Off you go … call the tower to confirm.'

'Hello Bluestripe, good morning … this is March Tune E-Easy requesting clearance to taxi runway one-zero,' called Fullerton.

'Good morning to you March Tune E-Easy, clear to taxi runway one-zero, hold at approach,' came the sultry reply from the Waaf in Flying Control[53]. Carter made a mental note to find out who she was … she sounded like Rita Hayworth.

Fullerton advanced the throttles and the Lancaster trundled out of its pan onto the concrete perimeter track. 'Brake pressure 300lb/sq.in, nav lights on, altimeter set, DR compass normal, elevator slightly forward, flaps 20° down, rudder neutral, superchargers MOD.'

The Lancaster bumped along gently towards the approach to runway one-zero; take-off would be due east. They watched as a Lancaster ahead of them turned onto the runway and rapidly increased speed, she was B Flight Q-Queenie, another sprog crew on a crew check flight. While runway 10 was shorter than the others, it was perfectly adequate for a lightly loaded Lancaster.

'Bluestripe, this is March Tune E-Easy holding at runway one-zero.'

'March Tune, E-Easy you are clear to take off, wind east-northeast at five miles an hour, beware of crossing traffic above 5,000ft.'

'Bluestripe, cleared for take off, runway one-zero, wind east northeast at five miles an hour.'

---

53   Air traffic control in modern times.

Fullerton brought the Lancaster around onto the centre of the runway. Carter watched as Fullerton made a final scan of his instrument panel, checking the compass and direction indicator by tapping at their screens. When he was happy he glanced across at Carter who nodded that he should proceed.

'Okay chaps, here we go!' called Fullerton to his crew.

Opening the throttles with zero boost level against the brakes, he held the brake handle on the control column, similar to a bicycle brake. The Lancaster shivered as the engines increased their power. Testing that the engines responded evenly to the throttles, he throttled back. It was important to open the throttles again gently at the start of the take-off run as the enormous torque could swing the aircraft off line. The Lancaster had a tendency to swing to port once the tail came up, so the port throttles were advanced slightly ahead of the others.

Carter studied the pilot's actions, watching every tiny movement … saying nothing. His task was to provide the support that would have been given by Fullerton's flight engineer.

Left hand on the control column, feet on the rudder pedals …

The four big throttle levers in his right hand, Fullerton eased forward, leading with the left engines to counteract the swing.

Releasing the brakes, down the runway they went, rapidly increasing speed.

'Full Power!' called Fullerton

Carter took over the throttles and pushed them right forward.

'Full Power on.'

Keep her straight with the runway.

The deep-throated roar enveloped the cockpit. Carter could feel the rudder was beginning to respond as Fullerton tapped it to keep straight.

A bit of right rudder, that's it … Ease the stick forward, get the tail up, that's it!

The aircraft was throbbing, the roar from the four engines deafening.

Keep her straight, that's it! Throttles forward …

Airspeed was building.

Both hands on the control column now, keep her straight

'60 … 80 … 90mph,' called out Carter, his hands still holding the throttles through the gate.

Just before the main wheels lifted into flight, the plane gave the characteristic 'Lancaster-wag' of its tail, as if waving goodbye to *terra firma*. At 100mph, Fullerton gently eased back on the control column and E-Easy lifted off the ground, lightly loaded as she was.

All the rumbling and shaking stopped, they were airborne, just in time to see the end of the runway slide away underneath.

'Undercarriage up … airspeed 120mph, electric fuel pumps on number one tanks,' instructed Fullerton calm and assured.

Dunholme Lodge was built on the top of a hill, which made it saucer shaped; meaning that taking off was uphill. It took a bit of getting used to as the aircraft had to be lifted off the ground rather than flying off as would be the case on a flat runway.

'Right, let's do one circuit first then a bump and run,' instructed Carter.

Each aerodrome had a circuit shaped like an oval racetrack in the sky. This helped flying control manage each aircraft coming in to land. Fullerton gently brought E-Easy around onto the circuit and lined up once again on runway ten, lowered the flaps, pulled back the throttles, and dropped the undercarriage. She floated in over the boundary fence and Carter could see that Fullerton was a little perturbed by the fact that the hill made the runway drop away as the aircraft lost speed. He touched the runway with the main wheels, applied full power again and the aircraft lifted back into the sky.

Carter, speaking on the intercom so all the crew could hear, went through a process of pointing out all the major landmarks in the region, including the magnificent Lincoln Cathedral Tower. It was right on the approach to runway 04, uncomfortably close. Carter also pointed out the neighbouring air stations in particular Fiskerton, the home of 49 Squadron, whose circuit almost overlapped with Dunholme Lodge.

Carter then went through a detailed explanation of the procedure for returning from a sortie. Approaching an aerodrome at night, the crew would see a widespread circle of lights surrounding not only the runway but extending out over a mile. These lights, called DREM[54] lighting, would show up clearly on all but the worst nights. The pilot would follow this circle round at 1,000ft until he reached the downwind side of the aerodrome.

There could be as many as twenty aircraft queuing up to land in the space of half an hour. Those with casualties on board were given priority to land first. The first part of the process was to identify the

---

54   The DREM Lighting System consisted of dim-able and hooded lights to restrict the viewable angle. The lights were placed atop poles at a fixed radius in two circles around the airfield. In the middle, were two sets of lights running parallel either side of the runway in use, with a funnel type shape at either end making a shape similar to that of a bridge symbol used on ordinance survey maps. On the active runway, there was a red light at one end of the strip with a white light at the other to indicate the active end.

beacon, or outer marker, showing the approach to the runway. Once this was identified, the aircraft would call in and identify itself by its call-sign. The Flying Controller would acknowledge the call and give a number to land. The aircraft then entered the circuit. Each part of the circuit had a name like corners on a race track, the first was the base-leg, then the up-wind leg, the cross-wind leg, the down-wind leg and finally the last turn into the lead-in funnel of the circuit that would be lit up if it was dark. The lights were not put on during the day unless the weather closed in. As each aircraft called out its number to land, giving its position in the circuit, it gave the following aircraft an idea of how close behind it was.

After his explanation of local landmarks and the circuit, Carter instructed Fullerton to begin the flight plan for the crew check. This was a cross-country flight, finishing with a practice bomb drop at the bombing range in the tidal estuary on the east coast called The Wash.

The whole exercise was to last about four hours … a piece of cake!

*

RAF Bomber Command HQ, Code Name 'Southdown', Walters Ash, Buckinghamshire, 4 miles northwest of High Wycombe Sunday 26 March 1944, 12 noon

The overall objective of the bombing operation is to accomplish the progressive destruction and dislocation of the German military, industrial and economic system and the undermining of morale of the German people to a point where their capacity for armed resistance is fatally weakened –
Preamble to the Pointblank Directive, February 1943[55]

The staff at RAF Bomber Command HQ were still coming to terms with the disastrous attack on Berlin the night before. At last count, 73 aircraft had been lost, mainly, from what they could gather, because the adverse winds had pushed the force over the Ruhr flak defences on the way back. The loss of 73 aircraft meant 511 men dead, injured or captured by the Germans. Three quarters of the losses were being attributed to the flak. What was equally disturbing was the fact that the bomber force had virtually missed the city completely. The air photographs, recovered from the cameras in the bombers, showed that the concentration of bombs was five miles south of the city with

55   On 4 February 1943, the Combined Chiefs of Staff issued the Pointblank directive which created as the highest priority targets, the submarine yards and the fighter aircraft factories. the Western Allied invasion of France could not take place without fighter superiority. The 5,000 word directive was complex and ambiguous, allowing Harris a broad interpretation as the preamble indicates.

some bombers dropping as far away as ten miles.

The HQ for Bomber Command had been constructed in the late 1930s within the Chiltern Beechwoods near the village of Walters Ash, between High Wycombe and Princes Risborough. The buildings had been purpose-built with offices and accommodation including a modern underground Operations Room. The office of the AOC-in-C[56] Bomber Command, Air Chief Marshal Arthur Harris, was on the ground floor of the Air Staff Block; a stone's throw from the main entrance. The C-in-C's personal secretary, Section Officer Peggy Wherry, sat in an anteroom in front of her boss's office.

Group Captain Walter Inness, Operations Officer, sat hard at work in his small office down 'The Hole', the name given to the Bomber Command Operations Room. He had been composing a report for the Commander-in-Chief's conference the following morning and it did not make very good reading. The central problem was the fact that accurate target marking beyond the range of Oboe had not been solved.

Oboe was more of a blind bombing device than a navigational aid. Like GEE, it depended on signals transmitted from ground stations in England. It worked with radio beams that could be laid with great accuracy over targets as small as a single factory, where a receiver in the bomber guided it exactly to this point. The disadvantage of the system was that only one bomber could use the Oboe stations at any one time, so even with three pairs of stations only eighteen aircraft could use the system in an hour. Furthermore, the Pathfinder aircraft marking targets using Oboe had to fly straight and level for several minutes, making them very vulnerable to fighter attack and flak. The greatest limitation was the fact that its range was restricted by the curvature of the earth. For targets deep in Germany the marker aircraft had to fly above 30,000ft. Only the twin-engined Mosquito could do this with a full load of flares and markers.

As Group Captain Inness was tussling with the best way of couching his report, another officer knocked on the door of his office.

'Good afternoon Sir,' said Wing Commander Felix Fawssett, Intelligence Officer - Targeting, in his usual formal fashion. He had shoulder flashes showing that he was from Australia.

'Yes Felix, what can I do for you? I am struggling a bit with this Oboe business,' replied Inness, who came from Sevenoaks in Kent.

'Sir, it's this targeting directive we have got from the Air Ministry, the C-in-C is not going to like it one bit,' said Fawssett, concern in his

---

56   Air Officer Commander in Chief.

voice.

'What do you mean?'

'Well, as you know, the Point Blank Directive is still in force but the Air Ministry have added new target priorities. I just know Bert[57] is going to blow a fuse on this one,' replied Fawssett, his face flushed. He did not want to be the one to explain this to the C-in-C, who had a notorious short temper, particularly when issued with what he thought were ridiculous instructions from the Air Ministry.

'What are the targets then?' asked Inness, also not keen to be the harbinger of unacceptable news.

'They have added six towns. This is certainly coming from the MEW[58], targeting ball-bearings and the aircraft industry; Schweinfurt ...'

The 'experts' that Harris most distrusted were in the Ministry of Economic Warfare, these were the Penguins, who flew mahogany Spitfires[59].

'Schweinfurt! ... You have got to be joking. Bert has told them in no-uncertain terms what he thinks about that!' exclaimed Inness.

Harris's sole focus was on Area Bombing, intended to decimate German cities, destroy their infrastructure, homes and workplaces and undermine the morale of the German people. His plan was to systematically destroy each major city in turn, to wipe them off the face of the earth, as Harris said in a letter to Winston Churchill, ' ... every bomb that leaves the racks makes smoother the path of the armies of the United Nations as they close in to the kill.[60]'

'Let me have a look at that,' said Inness, referring to the orders marked 'TOP SECRET' in Fawssett's hand. Fawssett passed them over and Inness scanned the contents, passing his finger down the page. After he had finished, he sat back in his chair. The list of priority targets was clear; No 1 was Schweinfurt, 2 Leipzig, 3 Brunswick, 4 Regensburg, 5 Gotha and 6 Augsburg. At the bottom of the list was the explicit instruction, ' ...the foregoing priorities supersede all previous instructions on this subject.'

'You are right ... Bert will blow a fuse. This is the work of those

---

57 Nickname for Arthur Harris at HQ. He was also called 'Butch' by the aircrew and rank and file in Bomber Command. The name 'Bomber' Harris was a creation of the press; his staff did not refer to him by that name, they called him 'Bert'.

58 Minister of Economic Warfare.

59 Term for ground officers and autocrats without operation experience - ground officer with limited flying and operational experience - a bird with wings that cannot fly - or who flew wooden desks.

60 *Bomber Harris - His life and times*, Henry Probert, Greenhill books, at 263.

Panacea Merchants he refers to,' agreed Inness.

Arthur Harris had been ordered on a number of occasions to pursue, so-called, economic targets. The theory being that, if the rubber, oil and ball-bearing industries could be destroyed, the German armies in the field would grind to a halt. It all made perfect sense, the problem being, in Harris' opinion, that the Germans defended these targets to the hilt. These specialist industries were small, well-dispersed, targets making them difficult to hit effectively at night. More importantly, according to Harris, was the possibility of German morale remaining intact. Without Area Bombing to kill morale, they could fight on indefinitely. In a letter to Lord Trenchard, Harris had said bluntly, 'I do not believe in 'panacea targets' ... if the panacea fails all is lost. Finally I distrust experts and specialists on panacea commodities ... for example a fortnight after we were told Germany was nearly on the rocks for oil she staged the biggest campaign in history [Russia] using millions of gallons ...[61]'

The Americans had attacked Schweinfurt on two occasions with enormous losses and uncertain results; Harris did not want his resources squandered in this way.

'What do you suggest I do?' asked Fawssett.

'There's nothing for it but to go up to his office and request an audience,' replied Inness, holding back a smile at his fellow officer's obvious discomfort. 'Rather you than me old fruit, I am glad I am down here ... away from the stuff when it hits the fan.'

Both officers burst into laughter, the one relieved, the other nervous ... both would not deny that they were terrified of Bert Harris.

*

Ju88G-1, 25,000ft above North Sea, 83 miles northeast of RAF Dunholme Lodge on a bearing of 62° Sunday, 26 March 1944, 02:15pm

The cloud cover over the North Sea was 10/10ths above 18,000ft, in a bank rising above 25,000ft. Below this level visibility was at about 7miles. Down at sea level, it was hazy with a stiff northeasterly breeze whipping the waves into a disordered jumble of white water.

---

61   Letter to Lord Trenchard, former Chief of Air Staff and a great influence in government and in the RAF. He took it upon himself to act as an unofficial Inspector-General for the RAF, visiting deployed squadrons across Europe and North Africa on morale-raising visits. As a peer, a friend of Churchill's and with direct connections to the Air Staff, Trenchard championed the cause of the Air Force in the Lords, in the Press and with the Government. Arthur Harris had enormous respect for Trenchard and often sought his council and advice.

'Hauptmann, I am picking up a contact bearing two-eight-one, six kilometres,' snapped *Oberleutnant* Gustav Lau, navigator and radar operator. He was staring at the three scopes of the indicator on the FuG 220 Lichtenstein SN-2 90 MHz VHF radar. Each scope was about 2½ inches in diameter, arranged alongside each other; a circular range scope reading up to 8km, an azimuth scope with the pips on opposite sides of the vertical base-line, and an elevation scope with the pips on opposite sides of the horizontal baseline. By reading all three scopes, he could tell whether the contact was above, below and on what bearing.

'Good Gustav can you give me the direction they are flying in?' replied Hauptmann Helmut Schulte, the pilot of the Junkers Ju88G-1, nightfighter. He was deliberately flying inside the cloud layer. His operation was a reconnaissance along the east coast of England to test the effectiveness of the upgraded British radar installations. They were tasked to measure the time it would take for the enemy to attempt an intercept.

Schulte was the Commander of *Luftbeobachterstaffel* (Reconnaissance Squadron) 3 attached to the Luftwaffe 3rd *Jagddivision* (Fighter Division) HQ based at Deelen in Holland. He was an extremely experienced nightfighter pilot with 19 victories to his credit. It was now number 20 that he was hunting.

Schulte and his crew were part of an elite group of pilots who were trained to shadow and report on the size and strength of American and British bomber streams. In the case of USAAF daylight raids, one of their major tasks was to locate areas of weak escort strength, an extremely hazardous undertaking. The *Luftbeobachterstaffel 3*, however, operated mainly at night so it was rare for them to be out in daylight on such an operation.

As Schulte increased speed to intercept the contact, he instinctively felt for the Knight's Cross, *Ritterkreuz des Eisernen Kreuzes*at, at his neck. The award for bravery had been presented to Schulte by Herman Goering himself. Schulte felt it was a lucky charm, touching it before every battle.

The flight had originated at Deelen, then out over the North Sea at low level below the radar coverage. Once he had reached a designated point off the English Coast, he had rapidly gained altitude topping out at 25,000ft. The stripped down Ju88 was fast, at 25,000ft she could get close to 520km/hr. The German radar operators along the Dutch coast now watched him on their screens, waiting for the RAF fighters to react.

Schulte had not expected the presence of another aircraft at this position.

'Hans, keep your eyes peeled, we will be diving out under the cloud any second, we don't want any surprises,' said Schulte to his rear gunner and observer, *Oberveltwebel* Hans Weitz.

'Yes Sir, I am ready,' replied Weitz, deep in concentration. He had a very vivid and frightening memory of being jumped by a Spitfire over the English Channel, not an experience to be repeated.

'Range closing to four kilometres, contact speed two forty, bearing now one-nine-six,' called Lau. His voice was steady, a veteran of most of Schulte's victories. Schulte described him as an artist on the SN-2 radar.

'We are coming in behind the contact, when we break cloud it should be directly in front of us ... bearing one-nine-six, my speed is four nine zero,' replied Schulte, concentrating hard. His left thumb flipped the trigger guard on the control column into the Up position, caressing the button with his flying glove. Slung below the fuselage sat the gun pod with a quartet of forward-firing 20mm, MG 151/20 auto-cannons, they spelt instant death to the unwary.

'Any second now ...'

The Ju88 slipped out below the cloud ... there in front of them, at only three kilometres, just under two miles, was a lone Lancaster.

*

E-Easy, North Sea, 18,000ft, 70miles east of RAF Dunholme Lodge on a bearing of 85°
Sunday, 26 March 1944, 02:30pm

'Maintain eighteen thousand feet, we will bomb at this height,' said Bill Carter to the new man Fullerton.

'Roger ... Mike confirm our position?' said Fullerton, talking to his navigator.

'Skipper, according to GEE we are forty-nine miles from the target; we will turn onto bearing two-two-six degrees, in ... thirty seconds. Maintain your speed at one seventy indicated,' replied the navigator.

Carter was reasonably impressed. After their circuits of the airfield, their flight plan had taken them north along the English coast, then slightly inland over New Moor House on the edge of Thrunton Wood in Northumberland, back out over the North Sea to track back south to make the bomb run at The Wash bomb range. The navigator had been on the ball, but then the weather had been kind. Carter had made them fly inside the cloud base above 20,000ft for much of the way, to see how Fullerton handled instrument flying.

One of the manoeuvres that Carter had made Fullerton perform was the so-called corkscrew manoeuvre used to evade nightfighters. They would have been trained on this at LFS, but Carter wanted to make sure … it could be the difference between life and death …

The corkscrew manoeuvre was evolved as a defence against nightfighters and searchlights. This consisted of a series of steep diving and climbing turns in alternate directions. It was intended to make it difficult for a nightfighter to bring its fixed guns to bear or a searchlight to follow. A rapid change in direction made it difficult for the nightfighter to pick up quickly enough and so missed its aim. The manoeuvre, however, would be as good as useless during the day. It was physically demanding and required a fair amount of strength on the controls.

'Skipper turn onto two-two-six degrees now,' called the navigator.

The rear gunner had a quiet morning, the clear visibility had allowed him to watch parts of England disappear out behind the aircraft; he had been trying to pick out the landmarks as they were pinpointed by Mike the navigator. He felt nervous, as did the whole crew, at finally being posted to a squadron. They had all been so pleased that they had been sent to 5 Group, 'the glory boys', and especially 44 Squadron. They were all itching to get their first op behind them.

Is that an aircraft? The rear gunner squinted out into the cloud base a few thousand feet above them. He blinked … *are my eyes playing tricks on me?*

There was no time to hit the triggers on his four .303 Brownings. The first 20mm shell struck the top of the turret shattering the perspex; the second took the gunner's head off. More 20mm cannon shells walked their way along the top of the fuselage killing the mid-upper gunner who had his turret facing forward.

Bill Carter had been looking out the cockpit window at the starboard engine as a 20mm cannon round struck the wing. He knew instantly they were in trouble.

'Corkscrew … Dive … Dive,' screamed Carter, throwing both hands at the engine throttles, yanking them back, cutting power to make the fighter overshoot, at the same time reaching down to pull back the flap selector.

Fullerton pushed forward on the control column and E-Easy nosed over into a power dive. Carter swung his head around to see the Ju88 pass overhead, the distinctive black crosses on its fuselage, the radar dipole aerials protruding from its nose.

'Rolling left,' called Fullerton, the big aircraft rapidly gathered speed in the dive, by putting in aileron and rudder, he made it start to twist into a corkscrew action. The negative g-forces pushed Fullerton up against his harness, Carter holding on for dear life, the stomach lifting as if it was filled with a thousand agitated butterflies.

The aircraft shuddered from more cannon strikes, tracer rounds swept past the cockpit canopy, disappearing towards the grey/green sea below.

'The bastard's coming after us,' shouted Carter, twisting his head back to look for the German. 'Gunners shoot the bastard!'

There was no reply.

*

Hauptmann Helmut Schulte could not believe his luck. As he had eased out of the cloud layer, he had spotted the solitary Lancaster, out in front of him, about 3,000ft below. Immediately ducking back up into the cloud, he planned his attack.

Gustav Lau had tracked the bomber as it maintained the same height and course parallel to the English coast. The bomber had then changed course to fly back towards the mainland. Lau had brought them around on a parallel course until the bomber was almost directly below them.

Schulte pushed forward on the control column and dived out of the cloud, the Lancaster was below and slightly ahead. The tail section of the bomber filled the gun-sight as he opened with a deadly salvo from the four 20mm cannons. The tail section and the rear turret disintegrated, bits of the elevator tore off. He was so close he could see blood splattering the perspex.

Correcting the angle of dive, Schulte raked the rear fuselage, watching the mid-upper gunner thrown forward in his turret, then disappearing from view. The Ju88 had dived passed only a few feet above the cockpit canopy.

Now in a steep dive, the Lancaster twisted around in the corkscrew motion; Schulte pulled the Ju88 around to follow the dive, slamming down his dive brakes to slow his descent, to steady the gun platform. There was no return fire; both rear-facing defensive turrets were out of action.

Expert pilot as he was, Schulte matched the rate of turn of the Lancaster in its dive, kicking the rudder, making minor adjustments *... retract dive brakes slightly, more throttle ... around you come ... around you come ... Fire!*

More chunks of the Lancaster flew off as the cannon shells went home … an engine burst into flames, thick smoke now marking the aircraft's descent. Watching the altimeter unwind, like a spinning top, 15,000ft … 12,000ft … 10,000ft still the Lancaster dived … *maybe I have killed the pilot*, thought Schulte as the stricken bomber spun below him, it looked completely out of control … the damage to the elevators and rudder too great to regain level flight. More cannon shells were pumped at the Lancaster for good measure, it's rate of turn increasing.

'Multiple contacts bearing two-seven-eight,' called Lau calmly, still watching his instruments despite the violence of the aircraft's attacking manoeuvres.

'I think the Tommy has had it,' replied Schulte, correcting his dive to take his aircraft away towards the Dutch coast. The throttles were advanced to full power as the waves of the North Sea flew past only 2,000ft below. 'Give me a course for home Gustav,' said Schulte, the Ju88 accelerated away at over 500km/hr. … *nothing can catch us now …*

*

The starboard inner engine had burst into flames and the engine stopped. Carter shut the throttle then pressed the automatic fire extinguisher button located on the instrument panel directly in front of the co-pilot's seat, and flicked the propeller feathering switch just above that.

Watching in horror, Carter glanced at the altimeter passing through 8,000ft and still unwinding at ridiculous speed … the airspeed indicator showed 340mph. Fullerton was fighting the controls, the spiralling motion throwing their heads to the side, blood draining from behind the eyes, making everything change colour and blur. The twisting motion made Carter nauseous … pushed down into his seat by the positive –g … fighting the bile filling his throat …

'Pull out … we must pull out now!' called Carter, the g-forces pulling on his arms as he reached for the control column in front of him.

'She won't respond … I am pulling back … I have full starboard aileron and rudder.' The downward acceleration was forcing Fullerton back in his seat, reducing the amount of power he could exert on the controls.

'We must reduce speed.'

Carter pulled the throttles back further, deploying full flaps, then grabbed his control column. Both men, using all their strength, pulled for all they were worth … she was just too nose-heavy.

Roll wings level ... find the horizon!

The flaps were not responding, the pressure in the accumulator had fallen below the pressure required to operate the flaps, but not sufficient to cause the hydraulic pumps to cut in.

Shoving the flap selector to UP, Carter then immediately put it to fully DOWN ... the hydraulic pumps cut in.

The sea was coming up at them, the waves now clearly visible ... *6,000ft ...*

Come on ... Come on ... 5,000ft. ... 4,000ft ... Come on! ...

E-Easy began a slow tentative response, the two men heaving with all the strength they could muster

... 2,000ft ...

Then they had her ... at an increasing rate the aircraft crept back to unstable vibrating level flight

... 500ft.

Skimming now just above the waves, spray from the northerly gale splattering the windscreen.

Thank God, the vicious dive has blown out the fire in the starboard inner engine.

Carter looked across at Fullerton, his face covered in sweat, his eyes grey with the shock of what he had just experienced, his first introduction to abject, unadulterated terror ... *welcome to Bomber Command!*

'Skipper, Ken's been hit,' called the radio operator referring to the mid-upper gunner, '... there is no rear turret, I am looking at the sky outside ...'

'Where's Jimmy?' asked Fullerton.

'He's gone Skipper ... there is nothing left, just a gaping hole, even the guns have gone,' came the stilted reply.

'Jesus! ...'

'Yes, you will need to pray to Him ... you will not believe how often,' said Carter gently.

'We best jettison those practice bombs ... Nav give us a course for Bluestripe ... Radio Op, call to tell them we will need immediate clearance to land ... declare an emergency ... wounded on board,' called Carter, taking charge.

He could see that all Fullerton could do at the moment was fly the plane, his mind numbed from the trauma and horror of near-death ... of losing two men ... friends ... together almost constantly for the past year and a half ... now gone in the blink of an eye.

'Skipper ... I have put morphine into Ken but I think he's dead ...

Skipper … did you hear me?'

'Yes Eddie … I heard you,' replied Fullerton, his voice cracked with emotion.

Lancaster E-Easy flying at only 1,000ft, crossed the English coast at Wainfleet-All-Saints … limping the last 57 miles home.

RAF Dunholme Lodge, Lincolnshire
Sunday 26 March 1944, 5:15pm

'Bill, are you awake?' asked P/O Charles Morley, Bomb-Aimer, walking into the Nissen hut that he shared with Carter, Armitage, Robinson, Pallister and a few others. Carter was lying on his bunk fully clothed, his pillow pulled over his head. The twelve beds were arranged barrack-room style along the sides of the hut; each bed had a wooden cupboard and a bedside table. The weather had closed in outside so it was impossible to see without the lights on.

'Yes, I was just having a lie down before dinner,' replied Carter, removing the pillow from his face.

'I just came to see how you are. Another tough day at the office … E-Easy is almost a write-off,' added Morley, taking a seat on his bunk one over from Carter's. 'I have never seen the rear turret literally ripped out of an aircraft … the gunner had no chance at all.'

'You can say that again … we were incredibly lucky to get home today, those poor sods losing two crew members on their check flight, for goodness sake! I still can't believe our ground radar didn't pick up the bastard and warn us… we were only forty miles off the coast.'

Carter rolled onto his side, to talk to his friend and colleague, one arm propping up his head.

Charles Morley, his full name Charles Leslie Morley, was a schoolteacher from New South Wales in Australia. He was the only man in the crew that had any form of formal tertiary education. He was very proud of his school, The Kings School in Parramatta, to the west of the sprawling city of Sydney. He spoke about it often. His descriptions were so graphic that Carter could almost picture the buildings in his mind. Morley was average height, about 5ft 10", slightly built with dark, almost black, curly hair and a thin aristocratic moustache. When he wasn't on ops Morley had a pipe stuck in his mouth, it was his signature. He had brown, compassionate eyes, that would not fail to show what he was thinking or feeling. His early childhood had been on a farm in a small town called Mudgee in central New South Wales, where they farmed sheep and beef cattle. His father had been a very capable farmer despite the mental and physical ravages of being wounded during the ill-fated Gallipoli campaign in the Great War.

The family had packed Charles and his two sisters off to boarding school in Sydney, where Charles had attended the Kings School, following in the footsteps of his father and grandfather. History had been Charles' great passion from an early age. A voracious reader, he devoured books like others had hot dinners. Even now, his bedside table had three books on it. At present his interests were American history, *The Year of Decision - 1846* by Bernard De Voto, was on top of the pile. The crew were happy to be regaled by Morley on his latest insights from what he read, telling fascinating stories of the U.S. explorers who began the western march from the Mississippi to the Pacific, from Canada to the annexation of Texas, California, and the southwest lands from Mexico.

After finishing school, Charles attended the University of New South Wales where he completed a BA, majoring in history. He was delighted to be offered a post at his old school, where he taught both History and English and coached the 4th rugby team. Charles had signed up with the Royal Australian Air Force in 1942, where he had visions of being a pilot. His father had been very proud of his decision to sign up, following in the family's history of making sacrifices for the Empire. His grandfather had fought with the New South Wales Citizens' Bushmen in the Boer War.

A great coincidence, that appealed to Morley's sense of history, was contained in a letter received from his father. When his father had heard of Charles' posting to 44 (Rhodesia) Squadron, he wrote to remind him of the battle of Brakfontein on the Elands River where his grandfather, with 105 fellow New South Welshmen, and 190 other Australians, fought alongside 201 Rhodesian volunteers against General de la Rey's vastly superior force. Charles felt an incredible bond with his Rhodesian Skipper and the many Rhodesians on the squadron, fighting as they were against terrible odds over Germany, in the same way that their forefathers had fought, under constant bombardment, against over 3,000 Boers. They survived for eleven days before relief came.

History's inevitable contradiction was the many South African pilots and ground crew that were now spread through the squadrons of the RAF. These men now fought in the skies over Italy and Germany, in the same way that their fathers had fought in the fields of France in the Great War. The contradiction being that their grandfathers would have fought the British over the rolling hills of Natal and the flat grasslands of the Orange Free State and Transvaal during the Boer War.

Morley also appreciated the fact that Bomber Command's C-in-C, Arthur Harris, while born in England, considered himself a Rhodesian. He had settled there as a young man, farming tobacco, and serving with the 1st Rhodesia Regiment in the deserts of German South West Africa in the Great War.

From the very start of pilot training, Charles Morley had suffered terribly from airsickness and for some inexplicable reason, nosebleeds, with the result that he was washed out of pilot training. Determined to succeed, he looked for the shortest course that would qualify him for flying duties, in any capacity. The Nav/B course was only 14 weeks … that was just the ticket! As he had covered most of the navigation part of the course in his pilot training, he breezed through, while the bomb-aiming part could hardly be described as a stretch. As he passed out in the top three of the course, he was immediately commissioned and sent to England. He was proud of his bomb aimer's brevet, the single wing with a B surrounded by a laurel wreath.

The airsickness and nosebleeds had not in any way abated; Charles Morley suffered uncomplainingly through every flight, his oxygen mask slick with blood and the smell of vomit on his flying kit.

Morley was the second oldest member of the crew, well behind Eric Biddle who was thirty. His natural school-teaching skills of empathy and understanding made him a good reader of moods and emotions. In his own quiet way, he had taken it upon himself to look after the mental wellbeing of the crew, careful, however, not to overstep the mark. In his intelligent, but untrained way, he made a study of the reactions of the members of the crew to the enormous stress and pressure they were under … living with the constant and very real possibility of death … in the most awful and terrifying circumstances. As they all relied so completely on Bill Carter, Charles Morley made a special effort to ensure his skipper kept up his spirits. Strange as it seemed, Morley was convinced that the rest of crew appreciated the role he had taken on, unconsciously accepting his subtle enquiries and encouraging words. He used his story telling and summarized history lessons as a method of giving them all something else to think about.

Morley's own mental health was in an increasingly precarious state. He had analysed his own feelings as best he could; a combination of stress and pressure, the thought of imminent death, overlaying a sense of not wanting to let his crew down, contrasted with the disgrace of being branded as having a 'Lack of Moral Fibre'. The RAF had created this unique term to describe airmen who had lost the will to fight, those that were innately weak or cowardly, who cracked under pressure.

The threat of being classified LMF was almost a tactic created to terrify aircrew into continuing the fight, it was the Sword of Damocles hanging over their heads. The subject was completely taboo; airmen would not discuss their feelings with each other, much less the Medical Officers on the squadron. Even the slightest suggestion of going LMF was appalling, the fear of being regarded as inadequate, not measuring up to the pressures of war when your country needed you most.

The reality of the consequences of LMF was brought home to Morley when he saw the impact on one of his fellow bomb aimers. The man had confided in Morley about feeling totally exhausted after every operation, so tired that even taking a shower or walking to the mess was an effort. His skin had turned deathly pale, almost yellow, and he was violently sick after eating even the smallest amount. As the man had felt that his condition might impact on his crew, he presented himself to the Medical Officer. After a brief interview, the MO had said, 'I think you are frightened of flying and that's the reason why you are looking so pale, your nerves are causing a tummy upset. There's nothing else the matter with you.' The young man, only twenty, had crawled under a hedge on the edge of the airfield and shot himself ... Stamp! ... *Diagnosis LMF confirmed!*

Charles' intimate understanding of history was also a contributory factor to his own mental state. As the bomb aimer he was the one who 'pressed the tit', he was the one releasing the bombs to destroy centuries of art and culture, reducing magnificent medieval cities to smouldering ruin. The thought of creating firestorms that burnt thousands of civilians to death, incinerating priceless art, libraries, churches and cathedrals, haunted his every day ... *how are we to be judged by history?*

'How are you feeling Charles, after your little swim in the ditch?' asked Carter.

'I may have picked up a cold, that ditch water doesn't do much for the constitution,' replied Morley with a thin smile. 'I took in a bit too much, I can still taste it in my mouth, there must have been a dead cow or something in it.'

'It was pretty foul ... more than likely caused by that unique farming practice called muck-spreading. You've just had a taste of good old English cow shit,' laughed Carter.

'I thought the English's shit didn't stink, even their cows,' said Morley, the two colonial boys laughed together, having a go at their English counterparts.

There was a knock on the door of the hut.

'Come in,' called Carter.

'I have a message from Mr Haworth Sir,' stuttered Winnie Daly the

Waaf driver, opening the door only a few inches. 'He said to give you his compliments and asks for you to go to the A Flight Office, Sir.'

'Speaking of shit that doesn't stink,' said Carter to Morley with a wink, the latter nodding in agreement. 'Thank you Winnie, I will be along directly.' It was just Haworth's style to offer his compliments with the message, a nice Victorian touch.

*

'Ah, Carter my good man,' exclaimed Jack Haworth when William Carter entered the A Flight Offices. It never ceased to amaze Carter that Haworth had the knack of making everyone feel like a long lost friend.

'Good evening to you Sir,' replied Carter bracing up smartly, it was impossible not to smile in Haworth's company, he was irrepressible.

'Some good news I hope Carter, firstly, you are being promoted to Flying Officer … congratulations.'

'Thank you Sir,' replied Carter, blushing in surprise, not sure what to say.

'Secondly … you and your crew are being given a spot of leave … seventy-two hours to be exact,' added Haworth still smiling broadly. 'Butch Harris called to say that we don't have enough planes to go around with you writing off two in two days … we thought you should have a break … to protect our aeroplanes.'

Haworth threw his head back and laughed heartily, he loved his own jokes and witty comments.

'Thank you Sir, that is good news, the men will appreciate it,' said Carter, smiling back, politely ignoring his CO's comments.

'Go off to London, see the sights, take in a show … lighten up old man … you don't have to carry the world on your shoulders,' added Haworth encouragingly. 'I am letting a few other crews off as well, the weather over Germany is pretty awful, so the met boys are saying … should be fine again on the 29th.'

'Isn't the 29th nearly half-moon with no set, Sir?' asked Carter, who had made it his business to study the phases of the moon in minute detail.

'Quite right Carter, all the better to see the target with … ours is not to reason why and all that,' quipped Haworth flippantly. The impact of what Carter had said was not lost on him … *all the better for the nightfighters!* 'You can collect your leave passes from Potter.'

'Thank you once again Sir,' said Carter saluting smartly, turning on his heel to leave the office.

Leading Aircraftswoman Linda Potter was standing behind her desk, her horn-rimmed spectacles on the edge of her nose.

'Don't mind Lord Muck-on-Toast, Sir,' said Potter softly, with a wink and a smile. If the truth were known, Potter was really the one who ran A Flight. 'Here are your passes Sir. Congratulations on your promotion Sir,' she said, like a mother hen looking after her chicks, despite the fact that she was only twenty herself. 'Ah, by the way Sir, your new kite is at dispersal ... you can see her in the morning.'

'Thanks Potter, I appreciate it ... even if he doesn't,' replied Carter, winking back at her conspiratorially, pointing towards Haworth's office with his thumb.

'POTTER ... bring me some of that horrible tea you make ... God preserve us!' shouted Haworth from his office. 'This paperwork will defeat us long before the bloody Germans!'

'That man will be the death of me ...' clucked Potter, resetting her forage cap and straightening her skirt as she went off to make tea.

*

Officers Mess, RAF Dunholme Lodge, Lincolnshire
26 March 1944, 8:15pm

'Congratulations on your promotion Carter,' said Wing Commander Thompson DSO, DFC, the CO of 44 Squadron.

'Yes congratulations,' added the Dunholme Lodge Station Commander Grp/Cpt Tony Fitzroy standing next to Thompson.

'Thank you,' replied Carter formally, pronouncing his words slowly and precisely in an attempt to hide the effects of a large amount of beer. Fitzroy shook hands with Carter and moved off to speak to the other officers.

Carter was nervous around Wing Commander Thompson; he was a strict disciplinarian, who had chosen the RAF as a career. He could have been described as distant and aloof, aware of his rank and position, his nickname predictably, 'Stuffy' Thompson. He was an ex-schoolmaster from Chaplin High School in the Midlands of Rhodesia, before he had accepted a short service commission with the RAF in 1936. While Stuffy was a bit of a 'stick-in-the-mud', he was a veteran of over 45 operations, starting on Hampdens, then Wellingtons and finally Lancasters.

'Poor show at being jumped by that Ju88?' asked Thompson, in a tone that pointed towards an interrogation. While Carter had a few beers under the belt, he picked up the implication.

'Yes Sir ... very poor show,' replied Carter, equally precisely.

'Rear gunner asleep … eh?' This was more of a statement than a question.

Carter could see where he was going, he looked around the bar for help but his mates had retreated to a safe distance. Choosing not to answer, Carter took an interest in the bottom of his beer glass. He could feel his ears going red with indignation and embarrassment.

'The quality of people we are getting out of the OTUs and LFSs is hopeless, they are pushing them through too fast …' complained Thompson, ignoring the fact that two very young men had just lost their lives … inexperienced as they were.

Still refusing to be drawn, Carter asked, 'Can I buy you a beer Sir?' He couldn't think of anything else as a suitable diversion, he glimpsed Jack Haworth watching from across the room.

'No thank you Carter, maybe another time, work to do I am afraid,' said Thompson, turning to leave.

'Yes Sir,' replied Carter, dismayed that the obvious official view from the 'Powers That Be' was that the two young gunners on E-Easy were 'asleep at the wheel', not concentrating hard enough, leading to their deaths and severe damage to the aircraft. Carter watched as the OC made his way to the door, the path through the packed crowd of officers opening as if by magic.

'Old Stuffy giving you the third-degree[62],' asked Peter Robinson, followed by a pointed '… Sir!'

'You need to show more respect when speaking to your betters,' replied Carter, 'I order you to buy me another beer.' They laughed together, arms over shoulders. 'Another beer for Mister bloody Carter,' shouted Robinson to the duty barman.

A shout in Afrikaans came from across the room, 'Bok-Bok[63], staan styf. Hoeveel vingers op jou lyf?' The call had come from one of the B Flight pilots, Captain Gawie Louw, a South African from the tiny

62   The expression, which describes harsh questioning of a prisoner to elicit information or a confession, probably is related to the Freemasons, an international secret society. Achieving the third, or highest degree of Freemasonry requires that the applicant pass grueling tests of proficiency. Since the 1890s, the third degree has been broadened to include any intense questioning, according to the Henry Holt Enclyclopedia of Word and Phrase.

63   Bok-Bok is a very ancient game, played in Roman times, similar to the English Public School game called ... Jimmy Knacker up against the wall or High (Hey) Coackalorum. In England, they shout 'Stand rigid, how many fingers on your body'. Bok-bok involves two teams. The members of one team form a scrum bending over facing a wall, or a tree if outdoors (the boking team), while the other team jumps on their backs, trying to make them collapse. It has been known to deteriorate into a free-for-all. Injuries are common, mainly broken fingers, shoulder dislocations and sore backs.

farming town of Viljoenskroon in the Orange Free State. The OC of B Flight, Sqn/Ldr Andrew 'Chalky' White took up the call. Chalky, while a Pom from Hampshire, had learned the Afrikaans name for the English version of the game, *Jimmy Knacker up against the wall*.

This was a challenge to A Flight, that Haworth was not going to decline. The men knew the drill, spontaneously forming two teams on either end of the bar for a game of Bok-Bok.

There were rules to the game, the most important of which was that all rules were there to be broken. The Squadron Adjutant, Flt/Lt 'Dickie' Bird, a non-flying veteran of the Great War, was appointed as referee to adjudge misdemeanours such as ... eye-gouging, kidney-punching, rib-breaking, hair-pulling and rearranging of the 'goolies' with the skilful back-heel kick as ... foul play! The penalty suffered by the offending team was to endure the gruelling mauling that was the automatic consequence of being the team bending over (bokking).

The two team captains met in the centre of the mess with the referee, while chairs and tables were stacked out of the way. A half-crown was tossed in the air; it bounced loudly on the concrete floor ... heads! It was Haworth's call. A great cheer went up from A Flight; it was always best to be runners first, to weaken the opposition.

B Flight took up their position as the bokking or 'down' team against the wall of the mess, bound tightly as in a rugby scrum, bums facing their opposition. The two men at the back of the 'scrum' were tall, tough Scottish bomb aimers, who would have looked more at home in the Black Watch or Royal Marine Commandos. It was always important to have the toughest and tallest in the team at the back, as they took the brunt of the attack, while their height would disadvantage the smaller and less athletic runners. B Flight were practised players of the game. They put their heaviest and most sturdy chaps in the middle, as inevitably this was where most of the runners concentrated their forces, while keeping the smaller fellows up at the front, out of harm's way.

'Right lads,' said Haworth to his huddle of 'runners', 'I will go first, next you Armitage then Robinson, followed by Pallister, ... ' counting off all his men, the last, most agile men, who could jump the highest included Carter and Morley. A Flight did not really have any real heavyweights who would usually be sent first as part of a shock tactic, this was a real disadvantage. Armitage was their biggest by far at 6ft 2", although he was slimly built. Haworth was always going to lead from the front. The idea was that the first man should be athletic and nimble enough to be able to change direction on the run, make the initial big leap, then scramble across the scrum of backs to make room for his teammates.

A Flight lined up against the bar, for the maximum run up.

Off went Haworth sprinting for all he was worth … his team baying their support. Once a member of the running team was committed to and had started his run, he was not allowed to stop, restart or miss the target. Any of these was counted as falling off and, therefore, the running team were given 'out'. Haworth did not flinch, the Bokking team twisted to disturb his aim, leaping up into the air he landed fists first in the middle of the B Flight scrum. Armitage was already on his way, up he went next to Haworth the weight of two men putting pressure on the centre, then came Robinson and Pallister together. Up they went, the scrum swerved, Pallister missed his grip, his foot touching the floor as he tried to regain his position.

'OUT … OUT' came the appeal from B Flight. If any part of any runners' body touched the ground once aboard the Bokking team, that was counted as falling off. Up went the finger of the referee like an umpire at a cricket match … time to change positions.

This was the part Carter dreaded, he glanced in dismay at the two intimidating Scotsmen … *I'd rather fly to Germany* … poor Armitage was the man at the rear of the scrum. The smaller men took their position against the wall, their bigger teammates binding behind them, locking them against the wall. A crunching thump shook the Bokkers as the first Scotsman jumped on top, the scrum veered to stay bound. The Bokking team had to remain connected otherwise a break was counted as a collapse.

The big Scotsman crawled on the backs of the scrum, as A Flight tried desperately to dislodge him while staying bound at the same time.

'Hold tight lads,' shouted Haworth, loving every second, despite being in the middle, an obvious target for the opposition. Bok-bok was an opportunity to give a senior officer a good thump without any recriminations, he couldn't see anyway, with his head down in the scrum.

The weight came on as more and more B Flight runners climbed on top, issuing a few rabid punches to those below. Carter felt a hard thud on the back of his head, driving it hard into the wall, making him dizzy. The beer swilling in his gut did not help matters.

A Flight swerved to stay bound, the weight on their backs taking its toll. It was exhausting, increasingly difficult to stay connected, Armitage shouted instructions as the only man who could see what was going on. Try as they might, the men in the middle collapsed under the weight ... the B Flight team screamed victory.

B Flight 2 – A Flight 0 was the score.

The referee marked the score in chalk on the blackboard next to the billiard table.

'Let me go first Sir,' demanded Armitage, 'those two bloody Scots are a menace.' His nose was bleeding from a punch.

'We'll go together Armitage, you on the left, me on the right, we must land together, aim at Chalky White,' replied Haworth, his right eye starting to swell.

Away they went together, up and then crunching down fists flying. White could not hold the combined assault aimed at him, he dropped to his knees, 'DOWN ... DOWN.'

B Flight 2 - A Flight 1.

Both teams stood up to take a rest, huffing and puffing, hands on hips like rugby forwards waiting for a lineout. There was more than one blood-nose and a few thick ears. Carter gulped down his beer as he tried to clear his head, he was already getting a splitting headache.

A Flight went back to the wall, taking up their bind, Carter and Morley once again thrust against the wall.

'It can't go on much longer, Bill,' whispered Morley to Carter forlornly. Carter merely grunted a strained reply, bracing for the next assault.

'Come on lads, keep it together, we can hold back those blighters,' urged Haworth. 'Armitage can you hear me.'

'Yes Sir.'

'Time to execute Plan B.'

'Got it Sir,' replied Armitage.

Plan B what the hell is that, thought Carter, the top of his head hurting like hell as the weight from behind came on, he felt sure his hair was going to fall out from being rubbed against the wall. A hazy vision of a partly bald head entered his inebriated brain.

'AHHHHHHH ... ' screamed the Scottish attack, Carter imagined flying kilts and brandished claymores.

The first man approached at a sprint, as he was about to leap, Armitage lifted his foot and thrust it backwards, catching the unsuspecting Scotsman in the family jewels. Down he went, groaning loudly, clutching his nether region, rolling from side to side. His mate, seeing the obvious foul, swung his fist at Armitage's exposed kidney. Armitage let out a yelp as the pain shot through his body. He stood up, at the same time swinging wildly at his attacker, missing hopelessly as the Scotsman stood back out the way. The effect of too much beer made a telling blow near impossible. The two men stood in the middle of the mess, swinging wildly at each other.

'Fooking Haggis Eater!' shouted Armitage ... trying desperately to land the first punch.

'Fooking Sassenach!' came the screamed reply.

That was enough for the runners; they ran en masse at the A Flight Bokkers, screaming their rallying cry.

A Flight collapsed in disarray, fists flying in all directions, the referee shouting, 'STOP ... STOP'.

The squadron officers were too tired and too inebriated to make the fight last any time at all. Most just lay where they were, sucking in air and laughing at the same time. Carter saw Armitage, tears of laughter running down his cheeks, shaking hands with the two Scotsmen ... all was quickly forgotten.

'DRAW,' shouted Haworth, without receiving any opposition to the suggestion, the men now intent on getting another beer.

Haworth's high spirits continued unabated as he launched into another song.

> Old King Cole was a merry old soul
> And a merry old soul was he.
> He called for his pipe and he called for his bowl
> and he called for his Privates three

The airmen at the bar joined in on the chorus ...

> Beer, beer ... beer called the Privates
> Jolly old pals are we
> For there are none so fair as we can compare
> to the British Infantry!

> Old King Cole was a merry old soul,
> a merry old soul was he
> He called for his pipe and he called for his bowl
> and he called for his Corporals three.

Carter held his beer above his head as he sang on the top of his voice with the others ...

Left right, left right, left called the sergeants
Move to the left in threes called the Corporals
Beer, beer, beer, called the Privates
Jolly old pals are we
For there are none so fair as we can compare
to the British Infantry!

'SKY-WALKING,' demanded Haworth, clearly enjoying himself immensely. 'Time to get the new Flying Officer initiated.'

Being a Nissen hut, the ceiling of the mess was oval, painted white. All along the roof at different angles were black footprints marking the track of various officers who had 'sky-walked' in the past.

Bill Carter was grabbed by his mates, his shoes and trousers unceremoniously removed. A fire bucket with a mixture of soggy cinders from the coke stove was produced and Carter's feet stuck into it one by one, covering them in sticky black goo. He was beyond caring, offering no objection as he was upended, his feet thrust towards the ceiling.

'For he's a jolly good fellow, for he's a jolly good fellow,' rang out, as in his compromised state, Carter tried to 'walk' along the ceiling.

It was hard work, keeping his legs straight, fighting against gravity. In no time, he was huffing and puffing, starting to feel ill from the beer washing around in his tummy, gravity making him bilious. Brought down for his feet to be reapplied with the black gunk, up he went again, managing another five steps before his legs flopped down. He then threw up in a horribly undignified fashion into the fire bucket.

'… And so say all of us … and so say all of us … for he's a jolly good fellow … and so say all of us!'

*

'Snake Pit', Lincoln, Lincolnshire
Sunday 26 March 1944, 10:02pm

'Have another beer Bill,' slurred Pete Robinson, sprawled on a bench seat. Squashed next to him were George Armitage, Charles Morley, Eric Biddle, Dave Muir, Tommy Potts and Frank Nellyer on the end. All looked much the worse for wear. Tommy had his head in his arms and looked like he was fast asleep although he periodically hiccupped loudly. He had very little tolerance for beer, two pints of bitter and it was normally all over for him.

The 'Snake-pit', was really the nickname of the Saracen's Head Pub in High Street Lincoln[64]. It was a popular haunt for airmen because it attracted a particular type of local girl, those that drank too much, asked very few questions … and could be 'persuaded' under the right circumstances. These girls also had a bite that could kill … the clap[65]!

It was a dark, noisy, smelly, crowded, boisterous place, full of men and women from surrounding air stations letting off steam. Clearly, the bad weather over Germany had affected most of the air stations surrounding Lincoln.

Carter had decided that he wanted to celebrate his promotion with his own crew and had asked the duty driver, Winnie Daly, to give them a lift into town. Sqn/Ldr Haworth had given vague permission, as it was not normally allowed to use air force transport for a trip to the pub. Carter felt the top of his head where a hard bump had risen from being smashed against the wall during Bok-Bok. It hurt to the touch. He felt like he needed to throw up again, as he had been doing periodically after 'walking' along the ceiling in the mess.

'I heard this ish where 617 the Dambushters drank the night before their operation,' stated Charlie Morley, authoritatively, with a slight slur, his pipe clamped between his teeth.

'How could you possibly know that?' asked Muir, equally drunk.

'The barmaid told me … they were based at Scampton just up the road … you know,' replied Morley shaking his finger as if instructing a child at school.

'Well the barmaid! Who could hope for a more reliable source of information?' added Muir sardonically, '… did she tell you where we are going on our next operation?'

'Where is bloody Pallister,' asked Robinson, virtually on the top of his voice.

'He went off with a tallish blonde in a cream and black dress, I tried to stop him,' replied Eric Biddle. 'He will get a dose of something sure as God made little apples.'

'Ullo … Ullo Eric,' laughed Muir, 'always on the job … did you get the colour of her nickers as well?'

'Didn't need to, she didn't have any on,' replied Biddle confidently.

The boys laughed, in the way men laugh after too many beers, where even the slightest thing is absolutely hilarious … there was no stopping them … *she wasn't wearing nickers!*

Biddle took his status as the oldest man in the crew, in fact in all of A Flight, seriously. He kept an eye on the youngsters even if some of

64   297a High Street, Lincoln, now occupied by Waterstones Bookshop.
65   Venereal disease.

them were officers. The fact he had been a policeman in his hometown of Preston before he signed up gave him a good nose for potential trouble. More importantly, it gave him an air of authority that rubbed off on everyone including the most senior officers. He had a great eye for detail that made him an excellent flight engineer.

Eric was a few inches taller than Bill Carter, maybe just 6ft, but he was thicker set, with strong arms and upper body. He had dark, almost black hair, with striking green eyes that he said he got from his mother who was from Limerick in Ireland. He had a broad friendly face which some might say had character, added to by the broken nose he got from an unruly fan at a Preston North End football game. Eric had a happy-go-lucky disposition and enjoyed a laugh and a joke. He was the sort of person who could strike up a conversation with anyone, making them feel, in no time at all, that they might have known him their whole life.

Eric's father ran a small motorcar repair shop on Deepdale Road. This is where Eric learnt his mechanical skills. As young as 12, he could be found covered in grease, tinkering with some part of a car or truck. Old Man Biddle, as he was called by his friends and neighbours, had been married very late in life after twenty years in the Navy as a Yeoman of Signals. He had been aboard the battlecruiser HMS Invincible when she blew in half at the Battle of Jutland on 31 May 1916. The only reason Old Man Biddle had survived was because he was stationed in the fire control top located at the top of the tripod foremast.

When Eric had announced to his father that he wanted to be a policeman, Old Man Biddle had been mortified. He had spent most of his life avoiding Coppers, being thrown out of pubs, fallen foul of the law, most notably caught for receiving stolen property. A load of truck tyres had 'fallen off the back of a lorry'. Due to his long service in the navy, Old Man Biddle was given a suspended sentence.

After five years in the police, the war broke out and Eric signed up for the air force. This was another disappointment for his father who wanted him to join the navy. The thought of working on aero-engines had attracted Eric who had always enjoyed working with 'the tools'. In 1942, he passed out of RAF Halton as a Fitter 2E and very quickly developed the itch to fly. The increasing number of four-engined bombers created the new aircrew category of flight engineer and Eric volunteered.

They sent him to St Althan in South Wales on a six-week ground course on the duties of a flight engineer, then to RAF Pembrey on an air gunnery course. Bizarrely, none of his training up to that point took place in the air! His very first flight in an aircraft took place with Bill Carter at 1660 HBCU, Swinderby.

Eric enjoyed telling the story of how Bill Carter had invited him to join his crew.

The rest of the crew had been together since OTU, but their conversion onto four-engined Stirlings created the requirement to add an engineer. Eric had been milling about with all the other newly posted flight engineers, feeling a bit like a lost fart in a perfume factory, when a call was made for the first orientation flight. Bill Carter had not realised that he actually needed a flight engineer at that point. The crew went out to the aircraft, climbed into their positions and waited. The instructor arrived and asked incredulously where their flight engineer was. Everyone sat in the aircraft in dismay not knowing what to do next.

The instructor had turned to Carter and said indignantly, 'You better get down to the flight office and get a bloody engineer!'

Bill had squeezed out his seat and jogged the half-mile to the flight office where only Eric Biddle was left sitting, all kitted up, but with nowhere to go.

'Excuse me?' Carter asked politely, out of breath from the run in full kit, '… have you any idea what a flight engineer looks like?' Meaning, of course, what brevet they wore.

Eric in his dry north country drawl replied, 'I heard they are bluudy ugly.'

Carter had looked him in the eyes and with a perfectly straight face, replied, '… well, you must be a *bluudy* good one then,' mimicking Eric's accent.

Eric laughed till he cried every time he told the story … *you must be a bluudy good one then!*

'I need to throw up again,' groaned Carter, standing up shakily.

'Not to worry Skipper,' said Biddle getting up to help him. The two tottered off to the toilet, Biddle supporting Carter. Eric took his job looking after the Skipper very seriously.

'I like the look of that bunch over there,' said Frank Nellyer pointing at a group of uniformed Waafs in the next booth. 'Some of them are from Canada.' Nellyer was the second youngest man in the crew after Tommy Potts at only nineteen, and he looked it too.

'They look a bit old for you Frank … me on the other hand,' added Muir, '… might be worth a bit of a flutter.'

'Well it's your round Davey boy,' chipped in Robinson, 'mine's a pint of bitter … with a dash of speed please. You better get one for your Skipper while you are there.'

Eric Biddle came back weaving through the crowd, 'Well the Skipper's got a few things off his chest,' he laughed. 'He's just cleaning himself up a bit.'

'Help me with the beers please Eric,' asked Muir moving towards the bar, pushing through the crowd that was three deep.

Tommy Potts didn't move. His head in his arms, just a sporadic groan was his only hopeless attempt at contributing to the conversation.

Carter came back through the crowd, wavering on unsteady legs. As he approached, someone in front of him inadvertently bumped into him, knocking him in the direction of the table full of Waafs. He tried to correct, legs wobbled, he swung his arms to keep balance, falling helplessly onto the lap of the girl on the end. Beer spilled all over the table. She screamed in surprise, pushed Carter away and leapt to her feet to avoid the beer dripping onto her skirt. All the others were forced to stand as well as the beer inched ominously towards the edge of the table.

'I am sho shorry,' apologised Carter, trying to brush the splatters of beer off the girl's skirt.

'Leave me alone!' she shouted, smacking his hand away.

Putting his hand in his pocket, Carter pulled out a scrunched up handkerchief that he attempted to use to delicately dab at her blouse.

'Leave me alone!' she shouted again, more urgently, backing away from the shaky hand holding the grubby looking handkerchief.

Frank Nellyer came to the rescue with a towel from the bar, quickly wiping the table, 'Not to worry girls … we are just celebrating our Skipper's promotion,' he said brightly, his Canadian accent clearly having a calming effect on his countrywomen. 'There you go, no harm done.'

'Pleash may I buy you all a drink?' pleaded Carter, now blushing with embarrassment. His offer was duly accepted with a few smiles of encouragement.

'Would you like to join us?' asked one of the Waafs. She had bright red hair and a broad smile, her shoulder flash read 'Canada'. As it turned out, they were all from Canada, from RCAF Fighter Station Digby.

Carter pushed in next to the red headed girl, 'You have a gong,' he said pointing at the ribbon on her uniform, his finger inappropriately close to her left breast. As he looked around the table, a few of the girls had the same medal.

'That's the Spam Eaters ribbon,' said the girl that Carter had spilled beer over. 'We also call it the EBGO, Every Bastard's Got One.'

The boys were now crowding around the Waaf's booth, having a good look at the girls ... taking it all in.

'How do you get it then?' asked Carter, trying to appear coherent. He noticed through the haze that the girl was very attractive, with full lips, flawless complexion, brown eyes and shiny curly hair.

'It's for eighteen month's service ... a bit embarrassing really, bearing in mind you lot have to do three years to get a medal,' replied the girl now with a smile. Her soft Canadian accent becoming quite captivating ... *those lips* ...

The sound of Benny Goodman's *Sing Sing Sing*, carried to the bar from the small dance floor in a neighbouring room.

'Would you like to dance?' asked Carter, instantly regretting the offer, his legs feeling like jelly, not in good shape for dancing the jitterbug.

'Yes I would,' she replied instantly, jumping to her feet, giving him her hand.

The boys took their Skipper's lead and in no time the whole crew were on the dance floor except for poor Tommy Potts who slept soundly under the drooping eye of Pete Robinson, who was now totally smashed.

'What's your name?' asked Carter, over the sound of the gramophone speakers.

'Ann ... Ann Woodcroft, from Winnipeg.'

'I'm William Carter, from Rhodesia, everyone calls me Bill,' then with totally uncharacteristic, alcohol induced, bravado, '... you are very attractive Ann Woodcroft.'

The girl threw her head back and laughed ... 'thank you William Carter from Rhodesia,' she said graciously.

After only a few hesitant steps Carter gave up the wild jitterbug, choosing instead to take the captivating Ann in his arms, she made no objection.

The music washed over him, his head already swimming from too much beer and the inevitable delayed reaction from a near-death experience. The combination was the type of inebriation that hopelessly numbs the mind, drops the defences, where all words that need to be said, tumble out spontaneously.

The music changed to *Always in My Heart*[66] sung by Ann Shelton.

---

66   Written by Glen Miller

You are always in my heart
Even though you're far away
I can hear the music of
The song of love
I sang with you
You are always in my heart ...

Carter held Ann tighter burying his face in her hair ... it smelt like apple ... he felt her react, her arms tightened around his neck, holding him close.

And when skies above are grey
I remember that you care
And then and there
The sun breaks through ...

'I could have died today Ann ...' he whispered in her ear. 'I could be at the bottom of the North Sea at this very minute.'
    She didn't answer him, just held his head in her hands.

Just before I go to sleep
there's a rendezvous I keep
And a dream I always meet
Helps me forget we're far apart ...

'I don't want to die Ann ...' he whispered with the morbidity of the despairingly drunk.

I don't know exactly when, dear,
But I'm sure we'll meet again, dear,
And my darling, till we do
You are always in my heart!

'You are not going to die ...' she said, looking up into his eyes. Then she kissed him full on the lips. 'Bill Carter from Rhodesia, you are not going to die.'
    A commotion broke out in the main bar. Through his melancholy drunkenness, Carter was sure he heard Robinson shouting.
    Eric Biddle disentangled himself from the Canadian Waaf with

111

flowing red hair and ran towards the door. Just as he did so, a man appeared in the dim light at the door to the dancehall, carrying what looked like his trousers.

'Eric ... Bill ... you have got to help me, my life is in danger,' shouted Gavin Pallister. He was holding his trousers in one hand and his shoes in the other.

The crowd started to laugh ... he looked ridiculous.

'They will kill me for sure!'

'Who is going to kill you?' asked Biddle, the rest of Carter's crew now standing behind him. Carter was not letting go of Ann unless there was an earthquake.

'Its Mavis's husband from the 6[67] Battalion ... he's home on leave, he's fetching his mates ...'

The crowd were now really enjoying this sudden intrusion. Advice was being issued left, right and centre.

A man shouted from the bar on the top of his voice, ' ... where is he?'

Loud stomping of heavy boots could be heard thumping on the wooden floor in the passage outside. 'There he is ... get him lads.'

Pallister took off into the crowded dance floor, a gap opened and closed behind him. Three giant men arrived at the door, virtually shutting the light out from outside. They were dressed in khaki uniforms with neat berets; their skins darkly tanned having just left Italy for refitting.

Dodging through the crowd, Pallister headed for the small stage. Biddle tried to do his best policeman routine by stepping in front of the leading soldier.

'We don't want any trouble ... let's go outside and talk about it,' said Biddle, trying to sound as reasonable as possible.

'Piss off, that bastard was shagging my wife!' shouted the big man, not in a mood to be placated. He moved to push past Biddle, but Eric sidestepped in front of him again.

'Get out of my way, you Brylcream Boy,' demanded the big man, now obviously very agitated. He swung his hand and knocked off Eric's side-cap.

Biddle, not a man quick to temper, nor violent by nature, punched the big man squarely on the nose.

It was on for young and old.

The big soldier gave out a howl that Johnny Weissmuller[68] would

---

67   Lincolnshire Regiment.
68   The lead actor in *Tarzan the Apeman* (1932), Metro-Goldwyn-Meyer.

have been proud of, taking an almighty swing at Biddle's head. A woman screamed, as the blow sailed past Biddle's ducking head. Muir and Nellyer tried to pin the Giant's arms, grabbing and holding on for dear life. The Giant's mates took off through the crowd determined to get at Pallister who had now reached the stage, shouting back loudly at his pursuers, 'It's all a simple misunderstanding … I can explain.'

His credibility was somewhat compromised with no pants on.

Morley tried his best at a rugby tackle around the Giant's ankles, not budging the man an inch. The man swung around with the two airmen still on his arms, lifting them off the ground, trying to hit Biddle and move towards the stage at the same time, dragging Morley behind him, still clinging to one leg.

Carter blinked, his numbed mind trying to comprehend what was going on in the half-light of the dancehall. He held Ann more tightly.

Pallister got to the stage before his two pursuers, leaping up onto it.

'Get your bloody trousers on Gavin,' urged George Armitage as he tried to block the short flight of stairs up onto the stage.

The crowd were loving it, clapping and shouting at the two airmen on the stage next to the gramophone.

'Give us a song … Give us a dance,' called the crowd, the vast majority of which were air force personnel and their partners.

Somehow, someone turned on the stage lights that suddenly bathed the men on the stage in bright white light, as clear as being coned[69] by German searchlights.

'Get out of the way,' demanded the soldiers, pointing menacingly at Armitage on the stairs. Pallister had one leg in his trousers, hopping frantically to get the other one in. The crowd clapping their excitement.

The two men were too much for Armitage. He managed to get a deflected punch on the first man but the second got him with a hearty blow to the solar plexus.

'Ooooooo,' the crowd responded. Armitage doubled over with pain as his insides turned into mush, he threw up all over the stage. 'Ahhhhhh,' from the crowd.

'It's all a simple misunderstanding … I can explain,' pleaded Pallister on the top of his voice as the two soldiers grabbed him by the arms. His trousers fell down again to shrieks of laugher from the crowd.

'We've got him Tiny,' shouted one of the soldiers in triumph.

Tiny, who was still trying to pry the three airmen off him, bellowed

---

69   When one searchlight, often radar controlled, picked up an aircraft all of the other searchlights in the target area would swing onto that aircraft, thus 'coning' it - then the flak would be 'poured into the cone'.

back, 'Kill the bastard.'

Perplexed by the violence of the suggestion, the two soldiers on the stage looked at each other, clearly they too had had a skin-full, but not sure whether murder was on the agenda.

'Don't kill him,' called a woman from the crowd, supported instantly by another. The others took up the call.

'Don't kill him ... don't kill him ... don't kill him,' they chanted, stamping their feet. The dancehall was transformed into a loud stomping mass, like at a football match. The sound reverberated through the whole building as the wooden floor was pounded, 'Don't kill him ... don't kill him.' The crowd took to pointing at the men on the stage in time with their chant, now just like a football match, 'Don't kill him ... don't kill him.'

The two soldiers, overwhelmed by the support Pallister was getting from the crowd, looked confused, gently lowering Pallister back onto the stage.

'He was sleeping with our mate's wife,' explained one of the soldiers, appealing to the crowd.

'Mavis's been sleeping with half of the RAF mate!' shouted someone from the crowd, to much clapping and shouts of agreement.

A screeching whistle, repeated again even more loudly, could be heard from the direction of the pub.

'It's the SPs!' someone shouted.

The airmen holding Tiny the Giant let him go and ran for the door. Poor George Armitage, still doubled over, was stuck on the stage. The two soldiers dropped Pallister and headed for the door. The whistles became more urgent; the pub manager must have called the Station Police who had arrived supported by the local Bobbies.

William Carter didn't budge, he held onto Ann Woodcroft.

'Come on Skipper,' called Biddle who had retrieved Armitage and Pallister from the stage,' we better get out of here ... we don't want our leave cancelled.'

Reluctantly Carter let Ann go. 'Will I ever see you again?' he pleaded.

'Where are you stationed?' she asked.

'Forty-four squadron ... at Dunholme Lodge,' he called back to her as Biddle pushed him through the crowd. 'Where are you?' he called desperately.

The whistles were louder, she called out a reply but it was lost in the hubbub and commotion.

... *Will I ever see her again?*

I don't know exactly when, dear,
But I'm sure we'll meet again, dear,
And my darling, till we do
You are always in my heart!

6

RAF Dunholme Lodge, Lincolnshire
Monday 27 March 1944, 8:15am

'Wakey Wakey, rise and shine,' called George Armitage, to his fellow officers Morley and Carter. Both moaned in agony from the aftereffects of the night before.

'Bugger off George,' complained Charles Morley, 'I am never having another drink.'

'Ron Boswell has a surprise, our new kite is in Pan C. He's asked for us to call around,' said Armitage. He was right as rain, no hangover from the heavy night at all, besides the black-eye and swollen cheek from the game of Bok-Bok.

Carter's head throbbed mercilessly, not sure if it was from the beer or from the hard bump on his head from Bok-Bok. He felt it with his hand; it seemed to have grown larger, a hard knob, still painful to the touch.

'I need a plate of eggs and bacon ... really badly,' groaned Carter.

'Did you get the name of that Canadian Waaf Skipper? She was a nice piece of work ... You were holding on to her so tightly she nearly died of suffocation,' laughed Armitage.

The vision of the magnificent Ann Woodcroft floated into focus.

'I am in love ... there's no doubt about it,' said Carter emphatically.

'Skipper, you were three sheets to the wind. She could have had one eye and a moustache and you still would have fallen in love with her.'

'Did she tell you which station she was on?' asked Carter, trying to get some glimpses of the night before back into his mind.

'No ... didn't she tell you?'

'She might have but I can't remember,' replied Carter ... *how will I find her again?* 'Maybe Frank will know,' added Armitage unconvincingly.

The noise of a Lancaster running up nearby drowned out the conversation, the deep guttural roar, vibrated in the chest. The engine reached a crescendo and then was throttled back.

'There's the test of a real woman, throw a pint of beer over her and she still dances with you afterwards,' quipped Armitage, then getting a little impatient, 'Come on you lot, up you get, you don't want to miss out on your leave. I'm off home to see my parents before I visit the captivating Mollie Jones,' said Armitage brightly.

The door to the Nissen hut flew open and in walked Ethel Greaves,

116

Carter and Pallister's Waaf batwoman. She was of indeterminate age, large about the waist, and cantankerous as all hell. 'Mr Greaves', as she referred to her husband, was an aircraft fitter on the squadron. Ethel's job, as was the case with her fellow batwomen, was to look after two junior officers, to take care of their domestic welfare. She was carrying a pile of neatly ironed clothing.

'Mr Carter ... I have a bone to pick with you,' she announced loudly.

'Please Ethel I have a terrible hangover ...' appealed Carter, pulling his pillow over his head.

'It's a disgrace the things you do to your uniform!' stated Ethel disgustedly. 'There was vomit over your shirt and mud all over your pants ... I have had to darn a hole in the leg ... what have you been doing?'

'Please Ethel ...'

'I'll have no more of it I tell you ... you need to behave like an officer,' she said, pointing her finger at him like a disappointed mother.

'Come on Ethel, the chaps have just been letting off a bit of steam,' chipped in Armitage, coming to Carter's defence.

'Mr Armitage, don't you play the innocent with me ... if anything, you are worse,' said Ethel, now pointing her accusing finger at him.

She walked up to the edge of Carter's bed and saw the new pile of soiled clothing from the night before.

'Well I never ... you've done it again. That's it ... I am reporting you to Mrs Malsen. I am not going to be treated like this.'

Muttering loudly, Ethel opened Carter's cupboard, neatly packed away his clothing, hung up his tunic and banged the door shut. Then without another word, she stormed out of the room to complain to Mrs Malsen the Waaf in charge of all the batwomen.

'Has she gone?' croaked Carter.

'Yes she has ... now shake a leg Bill, come on Charlie me boy. It's a beautiful day.'

'Now we know why they call them BAT-women,' groaned Morley.

Carter and Morley dragged themselves out of bed and struggled off to the ablution blocks for a shower, they both smelled to high heaven, a combination of cigarette smoke, beer and puke ... horrible!

Shovelling down a quick breakfast Carter noticed the newspaper headline, *Soviets Block Breakout Path, Kamenets-Podolski, on the Dnestr River and Gorodenka has been captured by forces of the Soviet 1st Ukrainian Front (Zhukov). This movement is intended to block the breakout of the forces of the German 1st Panzer Army (Hube). Meanwhile, during the night, all units trapped in Hube's Pocket receive the following signal: '1st Panzer*

Army will fight its way through the enemy and defeat him wherever he is encountered.'

Carter reflected on how surreal it was to think about allied armies fighting in the Pacific, Burma, Italy and Russia, so many people spread throughout the world, and here he was eating eggs and bacon on a bomber station in England. While Germany had been thrown out of North Africa, it was far from defeated.

Once everyone in the crew had been assembled, they set off for Pan C. All looked much worse for wear, other than Armitage and Biddle who seemed to be able to drink vast quantities without ill effect. Pan C was about half a mile from the A Flight offices, a nice brisk walk in the morning which was overcast, with very light intermittent drizzle, temperature a comparatively warm 45°F.

It's a beautiful day ... Carter couldn't believe that this was actually Spring, Bulawayo would have Spring temperatures over 85°F.

The biting wind was from the northeast at 12mph, due to a build up of high pressure over Scandinavia according to George Armitage, who had been off to the Met Office already that morning. Coming from Lincoln, George thought this was a beautiful day!

Paddy the Irish Setter was with them, barking at Tommy Potts to throw the tennis ball, dropping it invitingly in front of him. The crew took turns throwing the ball, watching the dog race at full speed, sometimes catching the ball on the first bounce.

Lancasters filled all the dispersal points, ground crews taking the lull in operations as an opportunity to do much needed maintenance. Blocks and tackle were being used to swop out engines The air was filled with the sound of hissing compressors and air hammers driving rivets against bucking bars. Some aircraft had been jacked clear of the ground so that crews could work on the undercarriage or replace damaged tyres. Hammers were banging on stubborn wheel bolts, metal-cutters cutting metal patches for holes in the aircraft skin. It was all pulsating noise, a hive of activity, with the sound of Merlin engines ticking over everywhere as crews tuned them to perfection.

The NAAFI truck was making its way around the boundary track, stopping off in places to hand over tea and sandwiches. Some ground crew sat in the grass under the wings of their kites having a chat.

As Carter and his crew approached Pan C, their brand new Lancaster came into view, her paintwork shining and bright. From what Carter could see, they had a small reception committee.

'They have got a surprise for you Skipper,' said David Muir, smiling knowingly.

'Good morning Ron,' called Carter as they approached the new C-Charlie, the 'C' painted in red on the port and starboard sides of her nose. A huge canvas tarpaulin covered most of the cockpit and nose.

'Good Morning Mr Carter,' said a smiling Maggie Smith who was standing next to Ron Boswell, her friend Vera Johns beside her.

'Well what's all this about then?' asked Carter smiling back at her.

'Da Daaaaa!' shouted Ron Boswell waving his arm at the nose of the Lancaster. The tarpaulin was released to reveal a colourful painting below the cockpit.

The crew stood in complete surprise, above them was a bright mural of a cartoon bird, wings outstretched, a broad mischievous smile, sitting astride a large bomb. Above the bird, in big yellows letters read the words, *Cocky Lobin*.

'We were up half the night Mr Carter,' said Boswell excitedly. 'Maggie and Vera helped with the painting, they have done a great job haven't they?'

'I like it,' said Tommy Potts.

'So do I,' added Frank Nellyer.

'We've heard you sing the song so many times in the mess, we thought it's time that Cocky Lobin flew again,' added Boswell, clearly delighted with his handy-work.

'Well done Ron,' said Charles Morley, '... she's great.'

'My brother is in the Long Range Desert Group[70], they named his truck Cocky Lobin. They also sing the song in Chilapalapa ... he told me in a letter,' announced Muir proudly.

'Do we know whether Cock Robin was male or female?' asked George Armitage, always interested in the detail.

'I never thought about it. I assumed that Cock Robin was a he. Who would want to kill a girl robin?' replied Muir. 'When Ron asked me about naming the kite Cocky Lobin it didn't occur to me.'

Carter didn't know quite what to say.

'Dave, is this a good omen ... you know ... Cocky Lobin has been killed?' asked Carter gently; not wanting to dampen everyone's enthusiasm.

The crew and the artists all stood looking at him ... the expression on their faces a combination of confusion and puzzlement; he'd thrown the cat amongst the pigeons.

'Well Cocky Lobin was very well liked, why else would all the birds cry and cry at his death?' volunteered Dave Muir, worried that this excellent idea may be undone.

70   A deep roconnaissance unit formed during the North Africa campaign made of British, New Zealand and Southern Rhodesian volunteers.

'If my memory serves me correctly, the song *Who killed Cock Robin?* refers to the death of Robin Hood and not that of a bird,' said Morley, ever the teacher and the fount of all knowledge. 'The legend of Robin Hood is about stealing from the rich to give to the poor. The words of *Who killed Cock Robin?* describe how help was offered from all quarters following the death of Robin Hood reflecting the high esteem in which he was held by the common folk.' Morley ended his explanation with a satisfied smile.

'There you go then,' said Muir, relief in his voice. 'He was a good bloke and everybody liked him.'

'I also think 'Cock' gives the game away. Cock Robin is male, as in rooster,' added Morley authoritatively.

'Yes, but he died,' groaned Carter, now very worried that he had put his foot in it, there was no going back. Nobody had even thought of the fact that poor Cock Robin had been killed, and nobody appeared to be at all bothered at the implication. All Carter had succeeded in doing was casting himself as a wet blanket.

Everyone stood looking at the excellent cartoon of the bird delivering its bomb to Germany ... grasping for some inspiration to retrieve the situation. The little bird did look more like a girl than a boy ... it was in the large determined eyes, long eyelashes and the mischievous smile.

After a moment of collective reflection, Eric Biddle chipped in, 'Cocky, can also refer to someone with a bit of an attitude'.

'Well, if Cocky Lobin is dead ... but he was a good bloke with a bit of an attitude ... and everyone remembered him for doing good things for the poor people, why don't we call it *Spirit of Cocky Lobin*?' explained Ron Boswell, searching the faces of the crew for support.

Everyone looked at Carter to gauge his reaction; he had cast himself as the one who needed to be placated.

'Excellent idea Ron! ... That's it! ... *Spirit of Cocky Lobin* ... Cocky Lobin is the spirit of a bird ... the brave little girl bird that flew out to bomb Germany,' said Carter breaking into applause. They all stood and clapped, the artists were all smiles, their project now retrieved ... a resounding success.

The happy group were interrupted by a hoot from an Austin 8 'Tilly' racing along the perimeter track. When the driver saw the crew standing next to the new C-Charlie, she pulled up. Leading Aircraftswoman Linda Potter stuck her head out the passenger side window.

'Thank goodness you're still here. He-who-shall-be-obeyed wants to see you in the A Flight Office Mr Carter … we're working tonight … your crew have been asked to standby,' clipped Potter in her business-like, efficient manner. 'I can give you a lift if you like … Pre-Briefing is at twelve.'

Carter did not think to complain, the shock of the instructions like a punch in the gut. He and Armitage reluctantly climbed into the Tilly load box at the back, watched by the rest of the crew. The looks on their faces said it all, bewilderment … *we are supposed to be on leave!*

As the driver slammed the Austin into gear, Carter called out, 'Ron you better get that kite ready for a NFT[71],' he glanced at his watch it was 10am. 'Take-off at eleven,' he shouted.

The Tilly raced off to the next dispersal point to warn the crew.

An AEC 6x6 2,500gal bowser, refueller truck, came grinding along the track and pulled up next to Pan C. The truck had a Matabele war shield painted on the side above the white-painted words, 'Presented by the African workers of Shabani Mine, S. Rhodesia'.

The driver, a young Waaf who was keen on Ron Boswell, leaned out the window and announced in a broad Yorkshire accent, 'There's a flap on Ron. They're going gardening tonight.'

The tight RAF security, coming down from High Wycombe, through 5 Group HQ to the Squadron Intelligence Officer, was no match for the Waaf grapevine, she probably knew what Butch Harris had for breakfast.

*

'What new gizmos have they got in this kite Ron?' asked Dave Muir, watching as the driver of the refueller truck, who had a tight little bum under her overalls, began to unroll the hoses.

Dave Muir was about the same height as Carter but with blond curly hair that he refused to cut short. He was thin and wiry with a pointy mischievous face that accurately reflected his personality. If he had been Australian, he would have been described as a larrikin, 'irreverent, mocking of authority with a healthy disregard for rigid norms of propriety'. His attitude to haircuts was a typical example of challenging the system, constantly picked out by the senior officers on the station for having hair that was too long. It curled out from under his side cap making it all the more obvious. When questioned by Sqn/Ldr Haworth on the subject he had replied,' … well Sir, will my hair prevent my Lancaster from flying?' Haworth had accepted the argument as reasonable and left it at that.

---

71   Night Flying Test.

For Muir, his longish hair was a form of rebellion, something he had done since he could walk. His fierce independence and feisty character may have been a result of being the second youngest of four brothers, with all the rough and tough treatment that entailed. The family came from the town of Que Que in the Midlands of Rhodesia where Muir's father James was a Native Commissioner, later called a District Commissioner. James Muir's area of responsibility stretched from Que Que to Gokwe an area of over 2,000 square miles. Managing such a large area took him away from his family a great deal. As his sons grew older, he took them along on his trips that were all on horseback with pack mules carrying tents and supplies.

The family home was on the banks of the Kwe Kwe River about 10-miles south of Que Que. It was built of burnt mud bricks with hardwood window and doorframes, not far from the main north-south railway line between Bulawayo and Salisbury. Living in the bush with his brothers and the local boys from the native villages, Dave learned to speak seShona fluently as well as the simplified and more white-man-friendly, Chilapalapa. Dave's mother Frances was a schoolteacher from Maidstone in Kent. She had come out to Rhodesia as part of the expansion that took place between the wars. She had met James Muir at a farmer's dance at the Golden Saloon Bar in Main Street Que Que.

At the age of 13, Dave was sent to Chaplin High School in Gwelo 20-miles to the south. Dave's eldest brothers Robert and Mark had created a family reputation and Dave was expected to live up to expectations, smoking, drinking and scaring the living daylights out of the girls. Dave played an excellent game of hockey at centre forward, learned to play the piano, which he did very well, and was in every school play from the age of 14. He was the song and dance man in the family and had told his father that he was going to join the RBC[72] when he left school. The old man had put that idea on the backburner as he signed his son up as a Junior District Officer on his last day of school.

Dave's oldest brother, Robert was a pilot on 266 (Rhodesia) Squadron at RAF Duxford, while Mark had been in the Long Range Desert Group in North Africa which, judging by the letters from his brother, was now somewhere in Italy. His youngest brother, Ian had just been commissioned into the 1st Battalion, Rhodesian African Rifles, recently deployed to Moshi in Kenya near Mount Kilimanjaro. Ian's latest letter indicated that he thought that they were likely to be

---

72   Rhodesian Broadcasting Corporation.

sent to Burma or somewhere in South East Asia as part of the 22nd East African Infantry Brigade. Dave was immensely proud of his brothers and talked about them to anyone who would listen.

When Dave signed up for the air force it soon became apparent that training as a pilot was out of the question. He refused to study the textbooks or concentrate in lectures with the result that he was washed out almost immediately. In desperation, his instructors sent him to wireless school where his long, bony fingers proved a major asset. Morse code was a breeze for Muir, quickly reaching the required 22 words per minute. The technical nature of the training, plus Dave's carnal knowledge of the school CO's daughter, resulted in an immediate posting to England to No.1 Signals School at Compton Bassett, near Calne in Wiltshire. Here he learned navigation, beam approach, aircraft recognition and radar. His interest in flying had him posted to No.4 Radio Flying School at Madley in Herefordshire where he was finally awarded his 'S' brevet. He was then posted to 29 OTU at Bitteswell where he met Bill Carter who he immediately cottoned on to as a fellow Rhodesian.

Radio silence was not a strength of Dave Muir's. He insisted on calling up other aircraft while on training exercises which resulted in a severe reprimand for Bill Carter. The solution devised by Muir, was the use of Chilapalapa with his fellow Rhodesian pilots and wireless operators that the Poms had thus far not managed to figure out. 'Stuffy' Thompson being from Rhodesia, of course, knew all about it but cast a blind eye. When the matter was raised with him by 5 Group, he was happy to blame the strange language on the nearby Polish squadrons.

Dave was the 'go-to' man in the crew. He could source cigarettes, whisky, transport, in fact anything that required even the slightest deviancy or initiative. His wicked sense of humour and childish pranks earned him great affection, with his crew, ground crew, and the sergeant's mess for whom he had purloined a piano.

*

The A Flight Office was crowded with pilots and navigators for six aircraft, most of whom were supposed to be on a '48[73]'. Some of the early risers had been rounded up by the SPs at the Lincoln railway station while they waited for the London train. The worst part was that, after being told that they were on a leave pass, they were not as mentally prepared as they would have been if on standby. Now everyone had to get their minds off the excitement of London or seeing

---

73   48 hour leave pass.

their families, back into the concentration and pressure of planning an operation. Carter noticed the new man Fullerton with two other 'sprogs[74]'.

'Well lads … I am sorry about the delay to your holiday plans but there is a war on,' announced Haworth buoyantly. 'We are going to sow a few Daffodils in the Baltic gentleman, at Gydinia in Poland to be exact.' Haworth stopped to check that he had everyone's undivided attention. 'I know it is a bit unorthodox to tell you this so early but I thought it only fair in light of the need to get ready.'

The men looked on glumly, all trying to come to terms with the sudden change to their plans.

'Come on lads, stiffen the sinews, summon up the blood[75] … we have a job to do,' said Haworth encouragingly, quoting Shakespeare as he was wont to do from time to time. 'Don't tell anybody about the operation outside of your crews until final briefing. Any questions?'

The men all looked at him blankly, most doing the mental arithmetic of the flight time to Gyninia via the Kattegat between northern Denmark and Sweden.

'Well, off you go then … plenty to do. See you at pre-briefing at twelve, final briefing at fifteen hundred, take-off is at eighteen hundred.'

The men filed out of the office. Carter had to get his half-hour flight test in before the pre-briefing. As C-Charlie was brand new there were bound to be a few teething problems and gremlins in the works.

*

RAF Bomber Command HQ, Code name 'Southdown', Walters Ash, Buckinghamshire, 4 miles northwest of High Wycombe Monday 27 March 1944, 10:45am

War. The only thing that matters is you win. You bloody well win! And then to hell with it.
AOC Bomber Command, Air Marshall Arthur Harris

Grp/Capt Walter Inness, Operations Officer, Bomber Command HQ had submitted his report to the C-in-C on the operational effectiveness of the Oboe target marking and navigation system. He was happy that he had adequately encapsulated the problem; the question now was whether the 'boffins' could refine a solution.

---

74   New inexperienced crews.
75   The 'Cry God for Harry, England, and Saint George!' speech of Shakespeare's Henry V, Act III, 1598.

The gist of his report was that Oboe[76] was extremely accurate, with an error radius of about 120yrds at a range of 250miles, about as good as an optical bombsight. What was now almost beyond doubt was that the Germans were trying, and in some cases succeeding, in jamming 1.5metre (200MHz) Oboe signals. This was the only frequency that the existing system used. It was imperative that the system move to the 10cm (3GHz) frequency as soon as possible, but to retain the old frequency as a ruse. Along with the range restriction, Oboe had another limitation: it could only really be used by one aircraft at a time. Doctor Denis Stops, University College London, a secret member of the development team, had suggested a simple and ingenious idea. The solution was that the aircraft carried the transmitter and the ground stations were fitted with the transponder instead of the other way around. That way, multiple aircraft could use the system at the same time … *brilliant!*

Now another problem had been added to the growing pile on Grp/ Capt Inness's desk. He looked at the file that was remarkably thin compared with other 'problem' files. Printed in black-stencilled letters horizontally across the page, read the word 'Scarecrow'. The top of the file in big red letters read TOP SECRET.

The summary page in the front of the file was as brief as it was alarming. Intelligence reports included a total of 500 sightings by bomber crews of massive mid-air explosions. The mysterious explosions were reported at various heights, over known flak areas and over open country, inward and outward bound, over the target, approaching the target and after leaving the target. There was no discernable pattern to the reports, just a massive bright yellow and orange explosion, above, in front or below the bomber stream. The sightings were first reported in December 1943, but had increased significantly since then. Twenty were reported during the last raid on Berlin on 25 March.

As he cast his eye down the summary page, Inness discovered why the file was so thin. The actual crew reports were in fifteen bulging lever-arch files in the Intelligence Section. Only a few of the more informative reports were included in the summary file.

Inness turned to a report by a pilot from 169 Squadron flying the De Havilland Mosquito. 169 Squadron's principal task was to fly intruder operations over Germany, attacking German nightfighters and supporting the heavy bomber force. The pilot of the Mosquito reported his position near Neubrandenburg over the Neubrandenburg-

---

76   AMES Type 9000

Trollenhagen Luftwaffe airbase, home to a flight training school. According to the report, the bomber stream was approaching Berlin from the north, about 10miles to the east of Neubrandenberg. The Mosquito had been hoping to jump a German nightfighter taking off from Neubrandenburg-Trollenhagen airbase, as it gained altitude up towards the bomber stream. The 169 Squadron pilot was at 18,000ft when approximately 2 miles ahead of him, and 5,000ft below him, a massive fireball exploded. The pilot expressed the view that the explosion looked like a fully laden bomber exploding. The huge flash was followed by debris falling to earth in exactly the same way that an aircraft would blow up. The conundrum was that there was no preliminary combat, tracer shells or tracer from defensive weapons. There was also no sign of any other flak explosions anywhere near the giant explosion.

Noted on the file was a rudimentary explanation: a new flak shell, designed to break the morale of bomber crews. *Massive explosions designed to simulate a bomber exploding without any hope of survival.*

Inness flicked through the rest of the file to see if there was any mention of the sighting of a gun that could fire such a shell. There was nothing. None of the existing German flak guns were capable of firing such a shell. The only explanation was that these new guns were in open country, well hidden, probably underground, or in railway tunnels.

The whole thing struck Inness as a bit strange ... *why would the Germans go to such effort to build a weapon that was only to be used to frighten bomber crews? Why had nobody, including the Americans, reported seeing such a gun? Plus the spooks at SIS[77] had not reported anything ... or had they!*

Deciding his course of action, Inness drafted a memo to RAF Central Intelligence Unit (Imagery Intelligence) staff at RAF Medmenham[78]. His request would then be forwarded to the boys at 140 Squadron, to send one of their photoreconnaissance Mosquito PR Mk XVIs over the Neubrandenburg-Trollenhagen area to look for this gun. He took a map out of his drawer and marked a square box over the area that the 169 Squadron crew had identified. He then drafted another memo to Wingco Fred Winterbotham at SIS Section IV (Air Section) requesting information on any mysterious guns their agents may have reported.

Inness marvelled at the red tape and protocol, war or no war ... the

77   Secret Intelligence Service. It is frequently referred to by the name MI6, a name used as a flag of convenience during the Second World War when it was known by many names. The existence of MI6 was not officially acknowledged until 1992.
78   Danesfield House, Medmenham, Buckinghamshire.

desk-jockeys had to have their process.

*

Bonn-Hangelar Forward Airfield, Luftwaffe *Nachtjagdgruppe 10*, 3.8 miles northeast of Bonn
Monday, 27 March 1944, 10:40am

The sleek lines of a Focke-Wulf Fw190 A-6/R11 broke cloud into bright sunshine above 10,500ft. The dark blue/grey upper surfaces of the aircraft contrasted starkly against the white cloud-base below. This was no ordinary Fw190, it was being flown by Hauptmann Friedrich-Karl Müller, the *Gruppenkommandeur* of 1./*Nachtjagdgruppe* 10[79]. Friedrich-Karl was known as *Nasen*-Müller, or Nose-Müller, to his friends and colleagues because of his distinctive protruding nose. His was an elite nightfighter unit charged with evaluating all aspects of technical and tactical experimentation concerning single-engine night fighting.

Accelerating to just under 550km/hr. (340miles/hr.), Müller levelled out, jinking left and right as he studied the sky above and below him, always aware of the danger of marauding enemy fighters. As he studied the sky, Müller felt exposed, unaccustomed to flying during the day. He felt slightly heady, the feeling a little like vertigo. Müller's rear-view mirror, mounted above his head on the canopy, reflected his wingman Hans Zimmerman, pulling in a kilometre behind, 200m above. Flying with a wingman was also a novelty nightfighters were not used to.

The distinctive wild boar's head, painted in black on a yellow shield on the nose, identified the squadron, 1./NJGr.10, while the '8' painted in black on the side of the fuselage, identified Müller. Clusters of antennas in groups of three vertical elements were installed in rows over the top centreline of the fuselage, in front and behind the canopy, together with three rows, set at 45° angle in the upper surface of the middle part of both wings. This was the distinctive configuration of the brand new FuG 217 *Neptun* (Neptune) J2[80] air-to-air tracking radar. The typical arrangements of three vertical antennas gave the FuG217 the name of Neptune. This version of the Fw190 had two 7.92mm MG17 fuselage-mounted machine guns in front of the cockpit, firing through the propeller blades, and four 20 mm MG151/20E wing-root and outer-wing cannon with larger ammunition boxes.

This Fw190 was the ultimate night fighting machine. In the hands

---

79   1 Squadron, Nightfighter Group 10.
80   Designed for single-engine nightfighters.

of a man with the skills of Friedrich-Karl Müller, it became a merciless bomber-killing weapon. The *Deutsches Kreuz in Gold*[81] hung at his neck, twenty-two British roundels set in two neat rows below his cockpit canopy.

The final installation of the new version of the FuG217 radar had been completed in the early hours that morning. It was now on its first test flight. Müller had decided that there was no time to lose in testing new equipment.

Flying high above the cloud in clear blue sky, it was difficult to believe that below 10,000ft it was 10/10ths cloud down to virtually ground level, with strong northerly winds and intermittent rain.

Testing new radar during the day was preferable as the test pilot could confirm the technical range and bearing information from the suppliers of the equipment with what he could see with the naked eye. The briefing Müller had been given by the scientists from *Flugfunkforschungsinstitut Oberpfaffenhofen* (FFO, Airborne Radio Research Institute), had indicated that the Neptune operated with two fixed frequencies, 158 and 187 MHz with a range of 400m to 4,000m at a 120° vision range.

A Ju88G from 1./NJGr.10 was to play the 'prey' while he the 'hunter'. The test was to be based on the practised Luftwaffe nightfighter method for single-engine fighters.

The method, called *Wilde Sau*, or Wild Boar, had been developed by the Luftwaffe as a reaction to the RAF ground-based radar jamming techniques, in particular the simple but extremely effective 'Window', strips of aluminium foil. Hauptmann Müller was one of the leading exponents of the *Wilde Sau* method. He had a sixth sense about the presence of the bomber stream at night, the distinctive buffeting of disturbed air created by thousands of propellers, fleeting shadows against the stars, reflections from exploding flak or star-shells. He was a master at estimating range and bearing, now hopefully made even more deadly with the use of this on-board radar equipment.

'*Ein L Acht, Drossel-Nord, lesien sie?* One-L-Eight this is Drossel-North, do you read?' called the Fighter Controller.

The controller belonged to *Flugmelde-Leit Kompanie, Stellung* (radar), a division of *Luftnachrichten-Regiment 201*[82]. The control room was located at the station called *Drossel-Nord* outside the village of

---

81   The German Cross in Gold was awarded for bravery and outstanding achievements in combat.

82   The Controller was in the Flight Reporting Company positioned at a point called Drossel-North situated between the towns of Velen and Coesfeld, part of the Night Fighting Reporting Regiment 201.

Velen, 30miles north of Essen, in the Ruhr industrial region.

The Fighter Controller had called Müller on the VHF radio.

'Drossel-Nord, Ein-L-Acht ... bitte beginnen Sie die Üebung ... please commence the exercise,' replied Müller.

Drossel-North was a *Nachtjagdraumführung (NJRF)*, Nightfighter control centre, part of the network of radar-guided fighter control stations, shielding the Reich from attacks from Britain. The fortress-like NJRF control centres were built of thick reinforced concrete, nicknamed opera houses for their sheer scale.

Northern France, the Low Countries and Germany were divided into radar control boxes (Raum) each commanded by a NJRF. The system relied on early detection of the bomber stream using long-range radar and airborne reconnaissance aircraft. Once the stream was located, the fighter controllers would guide the nightfighters to the closest radio and light beacons in the path of the enemy, from there they were 'talked' onto the target as the bomber stream passed through.

As the attack unfolded, the Fighter Controller began a running commentary to all fighters directed at the bomber stream, updating them with new information regarding the possible target as it came to hand. Once the fighters were directed at the stream they still had to find their respective targets either using their own on-board radar, as was the case with twin-engined nightfighters, or by visual sightings as was the case with single-engined nightfighters.

The radar control boxes included one *Freya* and two *Wurzburg-Riese* (Würzburg-Giant) radars. *Freya* was a long-range early warning radar to track the course of incoming streams of bombers at up to 120miles. The short-range *Wurzburg-Riese* radar was used for aircraft tracking at a range of 20miles. One *Wurzburg-Riese* was used to track bomber formations, while the other was used to track friendly Luftwaffe interceptors. Each German aircraft was fitted with an Identification Friend or Foe (IFF) device called FuG25. It worked by responding to the *Freya* and *Wurzburg-Riese* ground control radars through the transmission of identifying pulses. This IFF signal prevented German fighters being shot down by their own aircraft or flak batteries.

The system was a sophisticated, co-ordinated effort combining long-range radar, short-range radar, with nightfighters circling radio and light beacons ready to pounce on the incoming bomber streams.

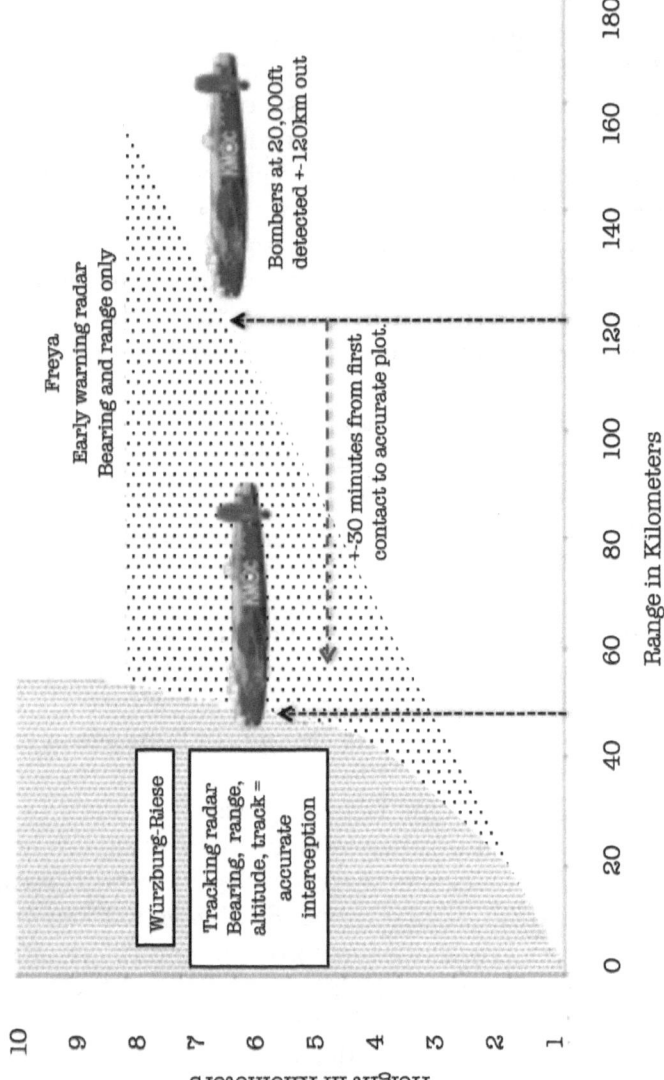

German Ground-based Radar capability March 1944

Height in Kilometers (vertical axis): 1, 2, 3, 4, 5, 6, 7, 8, 9, 10

Range in Kilometers (horizontal axis): 0, 20, 40, 60, 80, 100, 120, 140, 160, 180

Freya.
Early warning radar
Bearing and range only

Bombers at 20,000ft
detected +120km out

+30 minutes from first
contact to accurate plot.

Würzburg-Riese

Tracking radar
Bearing, range,
altitude, track =
accurate
interception

130

NJRF Nightfighter Control System March 1944

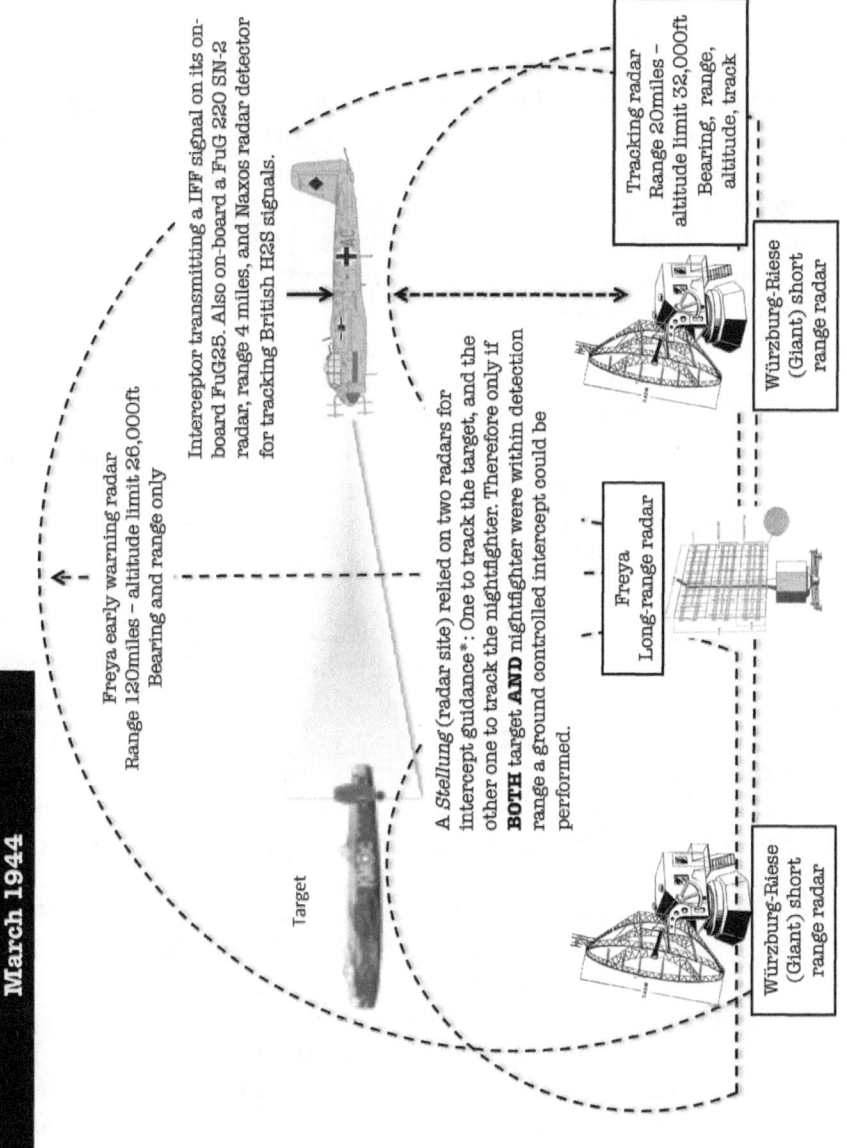

Freya early warning radar
Range 120miles – altitude limit 26,000ft
Bearing and range only

Interceptor transmitting a IFF signal on its on-board FuG25. Also on-board a FuG 220 SN-2 radar, range 4 miles, and Naxos radar detector for tracking British H2S signals.

Tracking radar
Range 20miles – altitude limit 32,000ft
Bearing, range, altitude, track

Würzburg-Riese (Giant) short range radar

Freya
Long range radar

A *Stellung* (radar site) relied on two radars for intercept guidance*: One to track the target, and the other one to track the nightfighter. Therefore only if **BOTH** target **AND** nightfighter were within detection range a ground controlled intercept could be performed.

Target

Würzburg-Riese (Giant) short range radar

The Fighter Controller at NJRF Drossel-North was tracking Hauptmann Müller (call-sign 1L8) from the top row of seats in the huge concrete fighter control centre. Below him were staggered rows of seats in front of a huge frosted-glass, horizontal rear-projection, Seeburg plotting table, which had a 1:50,000 scale map of the designated control area pasted over it.

The layout resembled that of a film theatre but with tiered seating on all four sides, while the 'screen' was on the flat glass Seeburg table situated in the middle. Operators on each tier of seating performed different tasks, but the layout allowed all to see the situation on the plotting table developing in real time. On the highest tier were the fighter controllers, below them were operators manning banks of telephones and radios, to take in reports from the ground radar operators and nightfighter crews. Below them were operators in touch with fighter bases, while operators in the lower tiered seats shone lights onto the underside of the plotting table to track the movement of aircraft. The aircraft co-ordinates were entered into the plotting machine that then translated the information into a light beam shining on the underside of the table. Blue lights meant friendly interceptors; red lights meant hostile bombers, making the effect similar to a lighted aquarium with brightly coloured water beetles scuttling underneath the glass-topped table[83].

A blue light, representing Hauptmann Müller, blinked on the otherwise blank Seeburg plotting table below the Fighter Controller. The lighting inside the 'Opera House' was subdued, making the lights on the plotting table shine brightly.

'One-L-Eight maintain your height, heading three-five-one degrees to beacon ACHMET, thirty two kilometres,' called the Fighter Controller. 'The exercise will commence in approximately five minutes … Over.'

Müller was being directed to a beacon codenamed ACHMET, located 30miles north of Bonn-Hangelar airfield. The nightfighters were expected to navigate autonomously utilizing the *Funk Feuer* (radio beacons) established throughout Germany and occupied countries. Many of these beacons had been established before the war to serve civilian air traffic and the *Luftwaffe* alike. The radio beacon would give the crew a bearing on the radio compass, but the crew had to take bearings from at least two beacons in order to get a fix. The position thus obtained was not very accurate, but it would give

---

83   This description was given by German fighter ace Adolf Galland.

the nightfighter crew a good idea of what course to fly, in order to intercept some part of the bomber stream.

In the case of the single seat fighters, they were directed to bright flashing light beacons that could be seen from the air.

Once above the beacon ACHMET, Müller was to orbit until a Fighter Controller called him and directed him to the vicinity of the target. He would then turn on his new radar, acquire the target, and perform the attack.

To the west of Müller's position, a Ju88G, 'the target', was flying on a reciprocal course. It also flashed up on the Seeburg plotting table as a blue light.

In this case, there were no other aircraft in the vicinity to make the test easier to manage and to adjudge the results.

'*Ein-L-Acht, Achtung Kontakt!* Attention Contact! Turn onto heading two-seven-six degrees, range forty kilometres. Maintain your height.'

The Controller's voice was clipped and precise, confirming him as a seasoned professional. The experienced controllers could rapidly form a 3D image of the airspace in their minds, picturing the approaching aircraft, its bearing, speed and altitude, matching it with that of the nightfighter. He was vectoring Müller's aircraft into a position to attack the target from behind, the only real option for single-seat nightfighters.

The 'target' Ju88 turned onto a course taking it directly to the east, reducing its speed to 170mph. (273km/hr.) to match that of a fully loaded Lancaster.

Hauptmann Müller flicked the Fw190 over onto the new course, his wingman closing in behind him. The Fw190 accelerated effortlessly as Müller thrust the throttle to full power.

'One-L-Eight, climb to altitude four five (15,000ft)[84].'

It was not necessary for Müller to respond; the Fighter Controller was watching his aircraft streak across the sky at over 600km/hr.

Running the mathematics in his head, Müller figured five minutes to the turn, then another five minutes for the attack.

'One-L-Eight, make your turn to two-zero-three, target bearing one-two-four, speed two five zero, height level three … range five kilometres.'

Müller flicked on the radarscope mounted in the top left corner of the instrument panel, it flashed green as it warmed up. Almost immediately a blurred green image appeared, two parallel vertical lines with a green flicker on the left of the scope. He looked forward,

---

84   The Germans used the metric system, in this case 4,500 metres

searching the sector where the scope said the contact was positioned, 60° to the left of the direction he was flying. As he flicked the aircraft to the left, the image on the scope brightened and moved more to the centre. *This is amazing* … he could not see the target but the scope confirmed it was ahead of him, now at an angle of 10°.

'One-L-Eight, target range three kilometres.'

Out in the distance the Ju88G came into view flying at 250km/hr straight and level … the scope had picked it up at over 5km, with a search angle of 120° … *just as the scientists had said!*

Müller tapped the rudder left and right watching as the scope tracked the contact … *now we have a truly devastating weapon, no more creeping around in the dark!*

*

Two De Havilland Mosquito NF.II Intruders from 141 Squadron RAF, raced across the English Channel, literally skimming the waves. They had taken off only minutes before from their base at West Raynham, Norfolk. The cloud base was right on the deck only just high enough to give the Mosquitos visibility to fly in. The Mosquitos were fitted with the new Serrate Mk. II radar in the nose. Four nose-mounted 20mm cannons made the Mosquito a formidable fighting machine.

This operation was as much a test of the aircraft as it was an intruder operation. The crews from 141 Squadron had only been part of the newly created 100 Group RAF for a few months and they were still learning new skills and adapting to the Mosquito after converting from Bristol Beaufighters. Both Mosquitos had new engines, upgraded Merlin 22s. This their first long-range test flight.

At 500ft, over 300miles/hr, the Mosquitos were flying below German radar coverage.

Crossing the Dutch coast near Leiden, the Mosquitos altered course onto 095° to the east, aiming directly for the Luftwaffe 3rd Fighter Division base at Deelen. Their plan was to pick off German fighters sitting on the ground or on training circuits.

As the aircraft approached Deelen, the weather deteriorated even further with heavy rain and cloud. The leader of the section called his wingman on the R/T to abort the operation … to climb out above the cloud that was believed to be at 10,000ft.

Both aircraft rapidly gained altitude, their new Merlins driving them upwards at 1,700ft/min.

The Navigator in the lead aircraft instinctively switched on the

Serrate radar, not expecting any result. The cathode-ray screen sprang to life; Serrate could detect the 490MHz Lichtenstein B/C Air Intercept (AI) radar aboard German nightfighters. That was what was lighting up the screen. The Navigator could hardly believe his eyes.

'Trev, you're not going to believe this, I have a contact dead ahead,' called the navigator to his pilot.

Before the pilot could reply, they broke through the cloud layer. There above them, shining in the bright sunlight was a Ju88G.

'T-Tommy, can you see that Ju88,' called the pilot to his wingman.

'Tally-ho Trev, I have your back,' replied the wingman.

The two Mosquitos continued their climb. The Ju88G maintained its course, the crew oblivious to the desperate danger they were in. This model was built as a specialist nightfighter with the rear facing ventral gondola removed, creating a blind spot beneath it.

The Mosquito pilot could not believe his luck, a single aircraft, flying at 170miles/hr, straight and level. Without deviating, he aimed the nose of his Mosquito at the middle of the aircraft above him, the gun-sight centred between the wing roots. He caressed the firing button on the control column.

*

Hauptmann Friedrich-Karl Müller in his Fw190 continued to test the FuG 217, changing the bearing of his aircraft to establish the extreme angle for the search radar. He backed off his speed to test the range, impressed that he was getting a faint signal from 6,000m directly from the rear. Next, he tested the downward scanning capability of the radar, pulling the nose up to gain altitude.

The green parallel lines on the radarscope flickered. Müller leaned forward to adjust the tuning … *why am I getting interference?* Accelerating the Focke Wulf back to 500km/hr, the screen continued to flicker.

Have they sent up another test aircraft to confuse me? …

Thinking that the problem was the fact that he was climbing, thereby creating a shadow for the radar, he levelled out.

Rapidly closing on the Ju88 … 1,500ft below him … he glanced down …

It exploded … a bright orange fireball, giving way to thick black smoke.

In stunned shock, Müller watched a wing break off. Churning smoke filled the sky in front of him. Pieces of burning aircraft tumbled away, an engine, its propeller still turning, was thrown up and away from the explosion. Trying to comprehend what was happening, Müller flicked his aircraft onto its wing … a Mosquito passed 1,000m ahead of him … climbing away.

Glancing in his rear-view mirror, Müller spun his head through 180°, above and below … *are there others?* The second Mosquito flew up in front of him, following its leader.

Smashing the throttle through the gate, full boost, Müller's instincts took over, the automatic reaction to combat … the man and the machine acting as one … pure hunter.

The distance narrowed rapidly as the second Mosquito was still in a climb, its speed draining off. Müller selected the four cannons in his wings.

The whole fuselage of the Focke Wulf vibrated from the recoil as he fired, THUD … THUD … THUD.

Cannon shells punched through the sky, the power from the recoil smashing Müller in the chest, he could feel the shudder of the tremor through his seat, like a horse jumping a fence.

Range closing every split second, the Mosquito filled the windscreen. His thumb flickered to the nose-mounted machine guns, the sound of their rattle pulsated in his ears … KIT … KIT … KIT … KIT … deafening, chattering … the smell of cordite filled the cockpit.

Two cannon shells impacted the Mosquito's tail, tearing off a horizontal stabilizer. The machine gun strikes entered the wooden fuselage just aft of the cockpit canopy, killing the navigator instantly. The pilot of the Mosquito spun the aircraft over onto its back, diving away to starboard.

Müller anticipated him perfectly, his aircraft already inverted. More cannon shells struck the Mosquito. An engine burst into flames … it was done … the roof panel flew off … the pilot stood on his seat, pulling himself up through the canopy … the Mosquito spinning violently out of the sky, centrifugal force throwing the pilot out and clear of the aircraft.

Hauptmann Müller scanned the sky looking for the lead Mosquito. He saw its canopy glint in the sunlight as it banked and dived towards him.

Faintly aware of his wingman screaming a warning in his ears, Müller grimly turned towards his enemy.

Flying suit soaked with perspiration, Müller's hands were slick inside his flying gloves; sweat pouring into his eyes behind his flying goggles nearly blinding him. He shook his head, thrust the stick forward, pulling negative-g, blood flying into his head, eyes bulging

... full left aileron ... then full right aileron ... following with the rudder, dragging the Fw190 into a turn ... positive-g now drained blood from his head ... pulling back on the throttle ... *overshoot! Bitte Überschwingen!* Tiny streaks of vapour poured off the Focke-Wulf's wingtips as the aircraft jinked and turned, constantly changing direction.

The diving Mosquito opened up at Müller with its own 20mm Hispano cannons; he could see the muzzle flashes. Shells blew past the canopy, missing by inches. As his aircraft tightened the turn he pulled the control column into his gut, the g-force almost made him black out, the black g-veil descending over his eyes. Bending his head between his knees to bring the blood back, he prayed nothing would ram him while he was striving to regain total consciousness. As his head cleared, he saw the Mosquito making another turn towards him, head to head now, becoming larger every second until it filled his vision and his gun sights.

Guns firing ... THUD THUD ... from the cannon ... staccato rattle from the machineguns TAKKA ... TAKKA ... TAK.

The Focke Wulf felt like a living thing, its racing heart beating against his back. The two aircraft screamed past each other, missing by only a few feet. Müller glimpsed the pilot looking at him through the canopy, before the Mosquito plunged away vertically, chased by Müller's wingman, puffs of smoke above the wings as he fired his cannons.

Two columns of smoke were left hanging in the air. A single parachute floated gently towards the top of the cloud layer ... then disappeared ... thirty seconds of mayhem ... four men dead ... the RAF navigator and the three crewmen in the Ju88.

Pan C, RAF Dunholme Lodge, Lincolnshire
Monday 27 March 1944, 07:00pm

The new C-Charlie, christened 'Spirit of Cocky Lobin', smelled like new paint, mixed with 100-octane aviation spirit. It was a delicious smell of factory goodness, the freshness of a pretty girl at a dance, the scent of her newly washed hair.

Inside the fuselage was painted in a puke-green, as the crews referred to it. Not an inch of perspex or a single dial had a scratch, smear or speck of dust. The engines had been run up a short while earlier so that when the time came to go they were already warm. Bill Carter was methodically working through the take-off checklist, calling to the crew on the intercom with respect to the status of their equipment. Eric Biddle was helping by repeating and confirming each aspect of the checklist carefully and precisely.

C-Charlie had passed her test flight with flying colours to the great relief of all. It was testimony to the efficiency of Ron Boswell and his crew who had gone over her with a fine-tooth comb. She was taut and responsive ... Bill Carter was delighted with her, he could not ask for more ... *except that she should be lucky*. Outside, flickering torchlights marked the positions of the ground crew as they went about the final preparations before sending their kite off to war.

Hanging back, next to the flight engineer's station, Boswell waited for the checks to be completed so he could clear the aircraft. George Armitage was at his desk, his maps unfolded in front of him, rereading his hand-written notes, memorizing each aspect of the flight ... distances, bearings, turns, the run in on the target ... the way back.

Gydinia was a long, long, way from home. Armitage's stomach tightened as he recalled the briefing from earlier in the day. A piece of ribbon stretching from Lincoln out over the North Sea to the top of Denmark, then onto Sweden where the last turning point was to be made. They were to cross the Swedish coast near Gothenburg, across to the Swedish east coast, turning south on the last leg over the Baltic Sea towards Gydinia. The run-in to the 'vegetable patch' was from the east into the neck of the port entrance, protected by flak batteries all the way. The return flight was north to Sweden then following the same route home, about 1,800miles in all.

The problem was the weather. A front was sitting over Sweden, moving slowly to the south. The forecast expected thick cloud and mist all the way down to 2,000ft. That was going to make finding the target difficult, GEE was no good at a range of 750 miles at low level.

Ron Boswell could hear the hydraulic turrets gently humming as the gunners swung them left and tight. He had loaded full tanks, 2,140gal to give the Lanc 11hrs endurance. He had discussed the fuel load with Eric Biddle. It was going to be tight if they struck headwinds. Taking into account the forecast winds, they should have an hour to find their home airfield, join the queue for landing, and make the final approach. George Armitage and Bill Carter were going to have to be on the ball, there was no cushion of extra fuel for getting lost or going around again after a ropey landing attempt!

Charles Morley had watched the loading of the mines. C-Charlie carried six 1,500lb Type A sea mines in her belly, the 'vegetables' in this 'gardening' operation. He marvelled at the new Stabilizing Automatic Bombsight (SABS) that C-Charlie was fitted with. The SABS worked by computing various bits of information, height, aircraft speed, allowing for wind, temperature and the flying characteristics of the bomb load. A disc was inserted into the bombsight that worked electrically. Once the target was in sight, the SABS was switched on and it pointed to the target, releasing the bombs automatically. The bomb aimer's job was to instruct the pilot to stay on the track by calling left or right corrections.

The bombsight was of no consequence to this flight, as the mines had to be dropped from a much lower level, where height, speed and heading were vital. The mines were fitted with parachutes to prevent them from breaking up when they hit the water. It was all up to George Armitage to navigate them to the right place.

The bomb doors were still open, as the electrician had found a fault with the bomb release system that required the replacement of a fuse.

Everyone listened to their Skipper finishing his checks. The confidence and authority in his voice was a source of reassurance ... *we are in good hands*.

Tommy Potts could be heard having a natter to his mate Frank Nellyer about some inconsequential subject, anything to settle the nerves. The two gunners being of similar age had a great deal in common, both had very tough and difficult times growing up. It was this shared experience that bound the two youngest members of the crew together. They were inseparable.

Tommy Potts stood having a last smoke at the foot of the ladder leading up to the rear door with his best mate Frank Nellyer.

'You got your brick Tom?' asked Frank with a smile. Tommy took a brick along on operations, lobbing them out of his 'clear vision panel' (a panel open to the elements) when over the target. It was his personal piece of revenge for the German bombing of his home in London.

'Nah, I stopped doing that, I don't want to kill any innocent people or animals like Paddy,' replied Tommy.

Frank nodded his agreement.

'How are you getting on with that Waaf driver Tom?' asked Nellyer, changing the subject, referring to the girl that Potts was keen on. His soft Canadian accent was a stark contrast to Potts' cockney.

'Ah, she's playin 'ard to get ...' replied Potts, blowing smoke into the breeze. Then changing the subject, 'This is number sixteen for us Frank, only fourteen to go.'

'Only fourteen to go Tom ... it will be over before you know it,' laughed Nellyer. 'You won't have to worry about the Skipper driving us through any hedges ... or George getting us lost ... or Dave speaking in his strange language ... or Eric trying to boss us about ... or Charlie trying to educate us on the Crimean War.'

'Yea, you wouldn't be dead for quids,' smiled Potts, mimicking the Aussie phrase used by Charlie Morley.

Frank's comment made Tom Potts pause for thought. Before he had joined the air force, he had been trapped in the depression and squalor of East London cleaning windows for the 'rich' with no education and no prospects.

Tom was tough and nuggety with a 'devil may care' attitude so typical of a teenager. His cockney accent was delivered at speed coupled with a lightning-fast sense of humour. He was short, no more than 5ft 5', with short sandy coloured hair and an open smiling face. While he had just turned 18, he looked much younger. Being brought up on the streets of Tower Hamlets in the East End of London, he had learned how to look after himself.

An only child, Tom was brought up by his single mother who worked as a housemaid for a wealthy family in Kensington. He never knew his father who left before he was born. At the age of 16, Tom's mother helped him get a job as a cleaner working in the houses along the street she worked in. Between the two of them, they scraped together a living.

Tom's mother had lived for twenty years in a terraced house on the corner of Regents Road and Park Road in Mile End in the East End. That was until October 1941 when a string of German bombs obliterated the house and all the surrounding streets. The Andersen Shelter that Tom had helped construct in the backyard had not been enough to save Tom's mother and her two closest neighbours. The emergency crews took over a week to dig through the rubble; four streets and hundreds of people had been wiped out[85].

Tom had been drinking at the Wentworth Arms up on Eric Street when the air-raid sirens had gone off. His mate's older brother worked behind the bar and smuggled a few beers to the underage drinkers. Tom had thought of running the 300yrds to get home. He had a full pint in front of him so decided instead to use the air-raid shelter across the road. That extra pint saved his life.

Losing his mother felt like life had come to an end for Tom. It had only been the two of them. They had battled through together, living from hand to mouth. Those German bombs destroyed what little Tom had in the world, there was nothing left except the clothes he stood up in.

The only church that wasn't bomb-damaged was St Dunstan & All Saints on Stepney High Street. That was where Tom's mother's remains were taken along with hundreds of others. The joint funeral was well attended by the local community but only Tom was there for his mother. All the bodies were taken away for cremation, to be replaced by more as the German bombing intensified.

As Tom stood at the entrance to the church after the funeral, an elderly fire warden wearing his steel helmet, with gas mask hanging on his shoulder, had said to him, 'Well son, there's nothing for it … you need to join the army … go and give the Huns some of their own back!'

It had not occurred to Tom that he could join the army; his mother had been totally against it. He was too young, she had said. Seeing his home and the surrounding suburb reduced to rubble, with barely one brick standing upon another, had built a deep-seated hatred in Tom. He wanted to hurt the Germans for what they had done, with all the outrage, power and urgency of his youth.

The nearest recruitment office was a requisitioned house next to the Blind Beggar public house in Whitechapel Road. The recruitment officer, a neatly dressed sergeant in his sixties, took one look at Tom and said, 'The army's no place for you lad … at your size, you need to be an air gunner!'

'How long will I have to wait?' Tom had asked, as he couldn't continue sleeping on the floor in his mate's council flat.

---

85   Regents Road and Park Road exist today only as walking tracks in the Mile End Park. The damage to the area had been so great that it was decided not to reconstruct but instead to turn the area into a park. If Tom's house were still standing today, it would be overlooking the last bend of the Mile End Athletics Stadium.

'Immediate acceptance ... lad,' the sergeant had replied.

'How long will the training take?'

'Six weeks.'

'That's the thing for me!' said Tom, signing the form thrust in front of him by the sergeant. Tom had no papers to present and no birth certificate but the sergeant signed him up anyway, packing him off to air force selection, thence to A.B. Initial Gunnery course at No. 2 AGS Dalcross[86] in Scotland. Tom had the romantic view in his mind that he would be shooting Huns out of the sky in only six weeks.

Gunnery school had opened a whole new world for Tom. It was exciting and stimulating, made all the better for meeting men from all over the Empire. They flew Faithful Annies, Avro Ansons, fitted with turrets, blasting away at sausage-shaped drogues made from canvas. He was taught the science of deflection shooting, how to strip and assemble the .303 Browning until he could do it blindfolded. Sitting in turrets mounted on trailers they were dragged around firing ranges, shooting at targets. At night they were shown film footage of enemy aircraft, models were flown at them from all angles until he knew every shape perfectly.

Tom remembered the instructor holding up a model of the Ju88, 'Make sure you remember this one lads ... if you miss him he will surely kill you!'

After six weeks of intensive training, Tom Potts qualified in February 1942. The official remarks on his assessment were: 'Average intelligence, has worked hard, should be an asset to his crew.' He was issued his new air gunner's brevet that he sewed on just above his left breast pocket, a single silvery-white wing with the letters AG surrounded by a laurel wreath. It had been the proudest moment of his life and he wished that his beloved mother had been there to see it.

Tom was posted to 15 OTU at Harwell in Oxfordshire, where he was crewed up for the first time. Tragedy was to prevent Tom getting to know his first crew. They were on a night cross-country exercise; Tom was in the rear turret of the Vickers Wellington[87]. The aircraft inexplicably began to lose height, the pilot called the bomb aimer up to help him and the two of them wrestled the control column using all their strength to pull the nose up. The weather was deteriorating and the pilot began calling on the R/T to any airfields nearby. There was no response, but to their relief they spotted an airfield through the murk. Someone on the ground was flashing an Aldis signal lamp.

---

86   Air gunnery school, Inverness Airport, Scotland.
87   Twin-engined bomber.

As they watched, it turned from red to green. This was the signal that they were clear to land. The pilot immediately banked the Wellington, to line up with the runway.

The runway they were lining up on was used for training pilots for clandestine operations into occupied France. Here they learned to land Westland Lysanders on darkened fields with only the light of a single lamp as guidance. Invisible, without landing lights, a pitch black Lysander was coming in to land at that precise moment. The green light was flashing as a signal for its benefit.

The pilot of Tom's Wellington, dropped the flaps, and slowed the engines. As he released the undercarriage, at a height of 500ft they struck the Lysander that was immediately below them. The Wellington's light duralumin structure was no match for the Lysander's steel propeller. Slicing through the underside of the Wellington, it cut the wireless operator and navigator to pieces. The Lysander nosed over straight into the ground on the approach to the runway while the Wellington flew on, its undercarriage ripped off and its airframe fatally weakened. The Wellington hit the concrete runway with tremendous force, the aircraft instantly disintegrated, the bomb aimer was killed as the impact threw him violently against the bombsight.

Continuing to slide across the runway the fuel tanks ignited, in seconds, the aircraft was a mass of fire. As Tom was facing backwards in his turret, he was shielded from the heat and flames. The rear tail section broke off as the aircraft spun viciously, saving Tom's life but only after a horribly broken arm and severe concussion. All except Tom died, including the Lysander pilot and his observer.

Tom spent three months in hospital and another three in rehabilitation before he was returned to flying duties in December 1942. This time he was sent to 29 OTU at Bitteswell where he met and befriended Charles Morley. That was how he ended up in Bill Carter's crew and that was how he eventually met his best friend in the world, Frank Nellyer.

'What are you going to do after the war Frank?' asked Tom.

'Oh, I don't know. After this lot it will be hard to go back to driving a tractor all day,' replied Frank, looking out into the watery darkness. 'What have you got in mind Tom?'

'Well, George says he is going out to Rhodesia to be an accountant … I might go with him … There's nobody left for me in England,' said Tom quietly, the enormity of being alone in the world weighing heavily upon him.

'I might come with you Tom, or we could go back to Canada,' said

Frank encouragingly, sensing the pain in Tom's voice.

This gesture from his friend and crewmate struck Tom hard … he wasn't alone … he was amongst mates, closer than any family, forged together by this great common purpose.

'Now that's something to think about,' replied Tom. 'Beautiful women in Canada judging by that bunch we met at the Snake Pit the other night.'

'Tom, you were completely shot to ribbons[88], I'm surprised you remember.'

Both men laughed loudly thinking about the antics of Gavin Pallister and the Skipper throwing beer all over the Canadian Waaf.

Frank respected Tommy for taking the rear gunner's job. The thought of sitting in the freezing cold, cooped up, completely isolated for the whole flight, the first target of nightfighters, terrified him. Frank enjoyed his job as mid-upper gunner. He could spin in all directions, scanning the sky, like being on the top of the world with everything else beneath him.

Frank Nellyer was the second youngest member of the crew, after Tommy Potts, at 19. While Frank was 19 he looked 14, only an inch taller than Potts, with a pale white skin made to look whiter against his dark brown eyes. It was Frank's hands that hinted at his past. They were hard and calloused, the hands of a man who had worked on the land, the hands of a man twice his age, in total contrast to his youthful appearance. He came from the tiny farming village of Clyde, 43 miles north of Edmonton in Alberta, population 302. He was the only child of Paul and Betty Nellyer, Paul had served with the 19th Alberta Dragoons (A Squadron, Canadian Light Horse) during the Great War. Betty was ten years younger than her husband, the third daughter of another poor farming family.

Frank came from a harsh part of the world and his life could only be described in one word, tough. After the stock market crashed at the end of 1929, the price of wheat fell to below the cost of seed and the Great Depression smothered the Prairies with poverty and unemployment. On top of that, 1930 was the start of a 10-year period of drought and dust storms. The land turned to dust, sweeping away the rich prairie soil and, with it, the hopes and dreams of many farmers including Frank's father Paul. Despite the stress and hardship, Paul Nellyer stayed on the land during the depression, facing down the environmental disaster and the nightmares that he carried with him from France.

---

88 Drunk; totally incapably drunk.

The young Frank had no chance of an education beyond the 7ᵗʰ Grade. He worked long and hard alongside his father who grew increasingly depressed and despondent. His mother never complained, certainly not that he could hear, but she became progressively quiet and introspective. The dust storms came in spring and summer when farmers had to be out on the land planting seed. After a hard day's work, the dust would have sifted under their goggles and through their clothes, blackening their skin. Often, the wind would lift the soil and the newly planted seed, reversing all of the day's hard work.

They also faced an infestation of grasshoppers and a weed called Russian thistle. The grasshoppers were so thick that they often clogged the radiators of cars and made the roads slippery. Chickens and turkeys ate the insects, giving a foul taste to the meat and eggs. There was no pesticide, and no way to control them. The Russian thistle piled up against fences and barns, often up to 20ft deep. By 1937, these conditions had reached their peak, and there was not even any hay to feed starving livestock, causing the price of cattle to drop to 3½ to 4 cents per animal. The situation was sole destroying.

One cold night Paul Nellyer, put on his coat, kissed his wife on the cheek, said goodnight to his son, picked up his rifle and went out into the night. He never came back. They found his body on the banks of the Tawatinaw River three weeks later. He had shot his head off.

Losing his father two weeks before his thirteenth birthday was a blow that the young Frank had never recovered from. The bank repossessed the farm and Frank and his mother were thrown out onto the street. They moved to a tiny room in a boarding house in Edmonton, Frank looking for work as a farm hand and his mother waiting tables at a rundown diner in Strathcona. When war broke out in 1939, Frank's mother took up with a travelling John Deere salesman, leaving Frank to fend for himself. He tried to join the army but no amount of persuasion could convince the recruitment officer that he was sixteen.

Frank drifted from job to job until one day a Tiger Moth flew low over his head while he was working at a farm outside Lethbridge Alberta. Seeing the aircraft hanging in the sky, free as a bird, fired the young man's imagination, promising an escape from the filth and desperation of his tragic life. He duly presented himself at the gates of RCAF Station Lethbridge, an airfield part of the British Commonwealth Air Training Plan. The Sergeant at the gatehouse took one look at the street urchin and told him to 'get lost.' Frank had stood his ground, refusing to budge explaining that he had nowhere else to go. The Sergeant took pity on the boy and arranged a job for him as a cleaner on the base, the home of No. 5 Elementary Flying Training School (EFTS). Frank worked hard and badgered the staff constantly to be allowed to join up. After a year, he was enrolled with No. 8 Bombing and Gunnery School, to be trained as an air gunner. As Frank had been around guns his whole life, he took to air gunnery like a duck to water.

He passed out of gunnery school, with his AG brevet and a report card which said 'Above average'. Like all of his classmates, he was sent to England, to what they all hoped would be one of the Canadian Squadrons in Bomber Command. Unfortunately, the way things turned out poor Frank was sent to 30 OTU at Hixon in Staffordshire. As the course ahead of him had already crewed up, he became what was known as a 'spare-bod', filling in for gunners who were sick or otherwise indisposed. Being so young and from Canada, Frank felt out of place with the other crews, most of whom were from England. He could not make any friends and became deeply listless and unhappy which inevitably impacted on his performance. His poor attitude drew the attention of the head of gunnery at the OTU who arranged to transfer him out as a man with few prospects. There, by a stroke of pure providence, as far as Frank was concerned, he was posted to 1660 HBCU Swinderby where he met Tommy Potts. 1660 HBCU was where the crew converted onto the four-engined Stirling that required, for the first time, a mid-upper gunner. Through Tommy, he had been invited to join Bill Carter's crew.

Frank had never felt a greater feeling of belonging than he did with his crew. The kindness, friendship and respect they offered was so totally new to the young man, he could hardly believe it. They were literally the only family he had. His mother had not written for months. In her last letter, she said that she had married the tractor salesman and had a kid with him. She had started a whole new life, a life from which Frank was excluded.

Finishing his cigarette, Frank dropped the end and twisted it hard into the ground.

Silence returned as Tom's and Frank's thoughts shifted to the operation at hand ... the charged tension of waiting ... apprehension ... churning in the stomach.

'I hate this waiting,' said Tom. 'It's the worst part ...'

Their thoughts were interrupted by the loud humming sound of the bomb-bay doors closing.

The instruction to start engines had not been given by the control tower. This would be with a green flare shot from a Very Pistol. The final decision to go had not come down from 5 Group HQ.

'Okay chaps, we are ready to go. Anyone who feels like a final pee, do so now,' called Bill Carter to his crew. Carter's stomach felt queasy and he was slightly lightheaded. It was always the same; the last minutes before take-off were the worst ... *come on, come on ... what's the bloody hold up?*

Outside a light drizzle had covered the canopy in thousands of water droplets that reflected the torchlight. The visibility was good despite the scudding low cloud. Carter watched a tractor dragging empty bomb trolleys race past on the perimeter track.

It was expectantly silent, possible to hear a pin drop.

Each man was alone with his thoughts, fighting his own fears, the realisation that in only a few minutes they were going to be on their way, at the mercy of the weather, flak and nightfighters, the deadly triumvirate.

The worst fears crept into Carter's mind, no matter how hard he fought against them. He could imagine being caught in a burning aircraft, plummeting from the sky ... screaming in death. He shut his eyes tightly against the nightmarish thoughts ... *pull yourself together ...*

A fitter appeared in front of where Tom and Frank were standing next to the rear door. He climbed the ladder up to the door, stuck his head inside and yelled out on the top of his voice, 'Ron, bomb bay's done, she's all tiggerty-boo[89].'

'Good show Sparks[90],' shouted back Ron. 'Okay Mister Carter, she's all yours ... break a leg.' Ron collected his Form 700 and climbed back through the aircraft, making comments to the crew as he passed. 'Give the bastards what for ... '

The aircraft returned to silent anticipation.

The rain outside got harder, Bill Carter could hear it pelting down onto the canopy ... *I hope its not like this over the target.*

He looked at his watch ... 7:30pm ... *I wonder what the wonderful Ann Woodcroft is doing.* Bill tried to picture her face in his mind, the smell of her hair ... *blast this waiting!*

As he sat in his seat in the darkness, Carter morbidly ticked off in his mind all the arrangements in the event of his death. He had drafted a will which really only said that everything should be given to his parents, *'everything' won't even fill a suitcase ...*

---

89   All is in order. Tiggerty from the Hindustani *teega*.
90   Aircraft electrician.

He had written his 'goodbye letter' to his family, as he always did before an operation, but this letter had been short and very hurried.

RAF Dunholme Lodge
27th March 1944

Dear Mom, Dad and Edith

Thank you very much indeed for all that you have done for me. No man could ever have had better parents and thank you too Edith for all your love and your wonderful letters. My only regret is that this letter will ever be read by you. You are my life. Cheerio for now and thank you all for everything. I hope I have done my part for Rhodesia ...

Your loving Son and brother

William Carter (Flying Officer)

Carter thought about the words he had written cursing himself for such a poor attempt ... *I hope they understand.* It was so hard not to be fatalistic ...

Come on, Come on for goodness sake!

*

In the shelter of the control tower, a small group of Waafs had gathered to see off the group of bombers being sent to Gydinia. The rain had increased in intensity as they huddled under their umbrellas. Maggie Smith was standing next to Vera Johns. They had planned to go along to the Black Bull in Welton for a drink after the boys had left. The delay in their departure was unnerving. They could hear the flying control staff talking about the weather. All were waiting for the signal to come down from Group to send them on their way. Maggie had studied the weather reports as they had come in and it did not look good at all. She had learned a lot about the weather in the six months she had been operational. She knew the good news from the bad news.

The 'Old Man' Stuffy Thompson had arrived a short while earlier and was complaining bitterly about the delay. Everyone had heard him ring up Group and ask them what the problem was. From what Maggie could determine, Group was waiting for Southdown (High

Wycombe).

The waiting was horrible ... the Waafs folded their umbrellas and went inside the tower as the ground outside turned to mud.

The phone rang ... the duty officer had it up in a flash.

'Yes ... yes ... I understand ... Thank you.' He put down the phone.

'Southdown have scrubbed the operation to Gydinia ... hopeless weather over the target ... a waste of time.'

'Blast,' was all Wingco Thompson said as he stormed out of the tower to return to his office.

The duty officer loaded his Very pistol and standing on the balcony next to the control room, he aimed it into sky. The flare popped out shooting a bright red streak of magnesium light. The flare arced over to bounce onto the concrete of runway 04 and fizzed out.

*

'Did you see that Skipper?' exclaimed Eric Biddle pointing out through the wet windshield.

'That Eric, was a red flare. The operation's been scrubbed,' said Bill Carter. 'Damn, I hate it when this happens, we just want to get this blasted thing over with!'

'Well we live to fight another day Skipper,' called George Armitage. 'It's off chaps,' shouted Armitage to the gunners in the back. Nellyer, Potts and Muir all swore loudly.

'Drinks in the Black Bull, last man in buys the first round,' called Carter to a great shout of excitement from the crew.

'Hurrah!'

*

Black Bull pub, Welton Lincolnshire
Monday 27 March 1944, 8:45pm

'It's haunted you know,' stated George Armitage, always ready to educate the Philistines from the colonies about his home county of Lincolnshire.

They were all still a little out of breath after the fast walk across from the airfield. The well-worn path was off the main 04/22 runway, through the hole in the security fence, between cultivated fields to Green Lane, then left up the road to the Black Bull. This was a total distance of just under a mile. The last 100yrds had to be at a sprint to avoid the first round, 'granddad' Eric Biddle, feeling every bit of his 30 years.

'How do you know that?' asked Charlie Morley, always interested

149

in a bit of local knowledge and history.

'My cousin Dorothy used to work here before the war … she said she heard strange sounds after closing-up time upstairs in the restaurant.'

'How would she know that, if it was after closing time?' pressed Morley, now very interested.

'Dorothy used to be given a room upstairs so she didn't have to catch the last bus. Eddie Wood, the publican, told her there was a ghost,' replied Armitage.

'What did the ghost sound like?' asked Dave Muir mischievously, intrigued by the story.

'Moaning and groaning, I bet!' chipped in Potts, digging his elbow into Frank Nellyer standing next to him. 'Wink … wink,' he added with two very deliberate winks, his finger held next to his nose in that distinctly English way of intimating a conspiracy.

'Your cousin a bit of a go'er then George,' giggled Tommy Potts who was already feeling the effects of his first pint.

The boys started to laugh.

'That's enough of that Pottsy my lad … casting aspersions on the honour of our Dorothy,' demanded Armitage, with feigned indignance. 'If you will know … it was like someone slowly walking up the eighteen stairs to the restaurant,' said Armitage to his now very attentive audience.

'That ghost knew his way up to Dorothy's room then, George?' said Biddle straight-faced. That brought the house down. The lads laughed, arms around shoulders, as close friends with shared experience.

Tears were running down Potts' cheeks, 'Dorothy was getting shagged by a ghost then, … George!'

Roars of laughter.

'Go and buy us all a pint Pottsy you little clot!' ordered Armitage, laughing with the rest of them. 'That's the last time I try to educate you lot!'

Potts shuffled off through the crowded bar to buy beers, shaking his head with laughter, helped along by his mate Frank Nellyer.

'We still on leave then Bill?' asked Morley through the laughter.

'I suppose so … they haven't said anything to the contrary,' replied Carter.

'Well I think we should make sure we are out of that place first thing in the morning, so they couldn't find us if they wanted to,' stated Armitage. 'I need to see my Edwina.'

'Ruddy good idea George, I think I am going to head off into

London. Even if it's for only one night,' agreed Carter.

'I'll come with you,' said Muir excitedly.

The sound of Vera Lynn's *White Cliffs of Dover* carried to the bar from the 'snug' next door.

> *There'll be bluebirds over*
> *The white cliffs of Dover*
> *Tomorrow …*
> *Just you wait and see …*

Bill Carter couldn't help pausing to listen to the words … they gave such a strong feeling of home. The picture in his mind of returning after a raid, those white cliffs standing out in the starlight, a beacon of hope … the relief of surviving another operation.

Thoughts of home inevitably turned to Rhodesia, the dusty, horribly corrugated dirt roads, the sound of the birds in the jacaranda trees in the early morning, his mother working in the kitchen, the smell of the wood stove … the long-drop!

'Would you like to dance Bill?' asked Maggie Smith, pulling at his sleeve.

'I … I didn't see you come in Maggie,' spluttered Carter, surprised to see her.

The other men smiled encouragingly at Maggie. It was painfully obvious to all except Carter how she felt. The tall, beautiful Vera Johns stood behind, not wanting to impose.

'Go on Skipper, dance with the lady,' said Eric Biddle, giving him a gentle push on the shoulder. Carter felt torn, he was enjoying having a good laugh with his crew. 'Come on Skipper, one dance won't kill you,' urged Biddle.

Biddle smiled at Vera who did not move, aware of her status as the 'chop girl'. None of the men were game enough to risk asking Vera to dance; instead, they stared at their beers uncomfortably.

'Hey Vera, would you like to dance?' called out Morley, she was such a stunning girl, he hated the fact that she was treated as some sort of pariah … *what could possibly be wrong with simply dancing with this girl?*

Vera smiled broadly, the relief on her face, at the passing of the awkward moment. She stepped forward. 'Thank you Charlie I would love to have a dance with you,' she said. The expression on the faces of the men said it all … *my, my, she is truly a magnificently beautiful woman … such a pity …*

... There'll be love and laughter
And peace ever after
Tomorrow
When the world is free ...

The snug next to the main bar had a small dance floor that could only hold ten or so couples. That did not matter as those already there were holding each other tightly, gently swaying to the music. Maggie threw her arms around Bill Carter's neck and buried her face in his chest.

'I was so relieved when they cancelled your Op tonight,' said Maggie softly. 'The weather reports were just awful.'

'To be honest, I wasn't happy at all ... ' said Carter, frustration clear in his voice.

'But you are safe?' she said, looking up into his eyes.

'Maggie, I have another fifteen Ops to go ... the quicker they are over the better ... delaying or cancelling a trip makes no difference at all ... they still have to be done. It's like running a race without knowing where the finish line is,' replied Carter irritably.

Maggie did not expect such a strong response to her comment, her youth, inexperience and naivety placing her at a disadvantage. She had not been around long enough to get a full understanding of the psyche of the bomber crews.

... There'll be bluebirds over
The white cliffs of Dover
Tomorrow ...
Just you wait and see ...

The song came to an end. Bill made to move back to the bar.

'I'm sorry if I've upset you,' said Maggie holding his arm, her eyes filing with tears.

'It's not your fault ... it's the blasted war ... it plays with the mind ... like waiting for something to happen, without having any idea what that something is,' said Carter, exasperation in his voice. 'I am sorry Maggie, but I won't be very good company tonight.'

With that, he pushed his way through the crowd to where his crew were standing; now chatting happily with a few other Waafs that had entered the bar.

Maggie watched him go, tears in her eyes, upset with herself that she had unwittingly made such a hash of things.

> *... There'll be bluebirds over*
> *The white cliffs of Dover*
> *Tomorrow ...*
> *Just you wait and see ...*

8

**Village of Schönberg, Middle Franconia District, Bavaria, 10 miles
(16.7km) northeast of Nuremberg
Tuesday 28 March 1944, 9:10am**

Frau Hanna Gregori was tired of the war. The endless rationing of basic foodstuffs was frustrating. The farm she worked with her husband Otto provided milk, eggs and pork, all of which were in short supply. Most of their produce was expropriated by the army at discount prices. They were left with the same meagre rations as the rest of the inhabitants of the tiny village of Schönberg, situated 3km southeast of the larger town of *Lauf an der Pegnitz* (Lauf on the Pegnitz river) through the *Spitalwald* forest. The farm was on the edge of the *Spitalwald* overlooking the walled church grounds of the magnificent *Kirche St. Jakobus* (Church of St James).

The Gregori family had lived in Schönberg for a hundred years according to the Parish records. Otto had fought in the mud in Flanders. At the age of 51, he was too old for the army. He now served with the local fire fighters and civil defence organisation. The village had no strategic value; there was no industry except for Herr Walter Zimmermann's small boot factory on the outskirts of town. Hanna had discussed this with her neighbours and all agreed that the British *Terrorfliegers*[91], as Reich Minister Goebbels called them, had no reason to bomb their town. This provided Frau Gregori with great comfort.

What occupied her mind most of all was the safety of her two children. All she knew was that her son was with the Luftwaffe NJRF 102[92] in the small town of Rijen in Holland. He had told her that he was just a radar operator sitting in a big concrete box completely protected. As he said in his letters, he was in the safest place in Europe.

Frau Gregori's daughter Klara was on the staff of Admiral Hermann von Fischel, the *Admiral Kanalküste* (Admiral Commanding the Channel Coast), at his HQ in Calais. Klara wrote to her mother every week with news of her exciting life in France, and the handsome naval officers she worked with. Her letters did not speak of the war, but instead dwelt on the many social events and parties she attended and the people she met. It all sounded wonderful. Frau Gregori was very proud of her daughter. If she continued on this path, she was bound to marry a senior officer, with all the status and benefits that would follow.

---

91   Terror Flyers (bombers)
92   *Nacht Jagd Raum Führer* Night fighter control center.

These were the thoughts that occupied Hanna Gregori as she walked down the snow-covered lane *Am Budbrunnen* towards the main street of Schönberg, Schönberger Marktplatz. She passed by the gate to her neighbour Heinz Bongart's farmstead. As she did so, Heinz's 12-year old daughter Rosemarie saw her and called out. The young girl came running down the path, her skirts held up out of the mud. She flew into Hanna's arms and the two hugged each other tightly. Rosemarie's mother Agnetha had died in childbirth and Heinz had not remarried. Hanna treated the girl as she would her own daughter and the two spent many happy hours together. Looking after the child was one of Hanna's great pleasures. She knew Heinz appreciated her attention to the child. He was a hardworking man of few words, also having served on the western front in the Great War.

'Where are you going Frau Gregori?' asked Rosemarie excitedly.

'I am going into the village to shop and visit Frau Neumeyer, you must come with me,' smiled Hanna.

The two walked hand in hand towards the main street. As they past the firehouse on the way, the volunteers on duty were busy checking their equipment and polishing their old fire-truck … Hanna smiled to herself … *they play with their toys, they will never be needed, the worst thing in Schönberg is a burning haystack.*

As they passed the gate to *Kirche St. Jakobus,* the two women crossed themselves, Hanna said a silent prayer for her family, as she did often each day.

'*Guten Morgen*, Hanna,' said Frau Neumeyer as Hanna entered her bakery.

'Good morning Magda,' smiled Hanna. She looked around her, shocked to see the shelves were empty. 'Have you fresh bread?'

'I have hidden some loaves, we had an army convoy through this morning and they took everything I had,' stated Magda Neumeyer resignedly. 'I have a letter from Angelika in Berlin … it does not sound good.'

'What does she say?' asked Hanna referring to Magda's daughter who lived in Berlin with her husband and three children.

'The Britishers have been bombing for weeks, almost every night, part of their roof has collapsed. She says she is very worried,' said Magda, concern in her voice. 'I told her she should bring the children to me, she cannot stay there if this continues.'

'The radio said that they were bombing Berlin but that the air force had shot them all down,' said Hanna. 'How can they keep coming?'

'I don't think we can believe the radio anymore Hanna. My Fredrik says that we are losing the war. He said that Hamburg, Cologne and Essen have been destroyed, barely one brick is standing upon another,' whispered Magda repeating her husband's words, looking about her … *the walls have ears!*

'You mustn't speak like this Magda, you never know who is listening. You know the Bürgermeister is a Nazi, I am sure he has spies all over the town,' hissed Hanna, anxious to protect her friend. She glanced at Rosemarie who was listening to the conversation attentively, she lifted he finger to her lips with stern eyes so the child understood what she meant.

'I wish it was all over … I hate living in fear … from our own people,' murmured Magda, tears filling her eyes. 'I worry for my children so much.'

'Well you must send for Angelika and the children … we are safe out here in the country, no bombs will come here,' said Hanna emphatically, taking eggs out of her basket and giving them to Magda, then replacing them with the loaf of bread. She smiled conspiratorially at her lifelong friend, 'Otto has hidden a chicken hock in the *Spitalwald*, we will always have eggs.'

'*Danke* Hanna, you are such a good friend … we will be all right won't we? Here Rosemarie … I have saved a bun!'

'Thank you Frau Neumeyer,' squealed the child. Both women smiled at the obvious delight on the young girl's face.

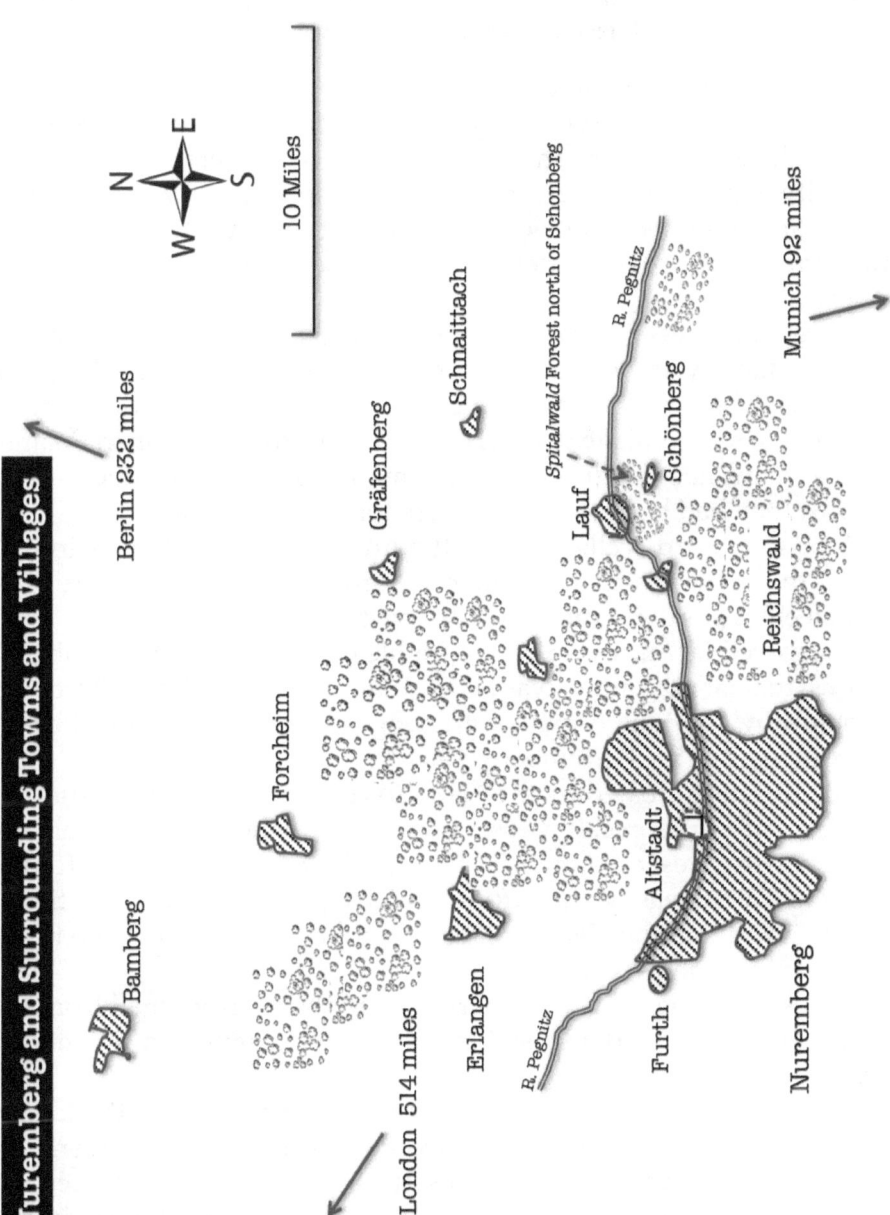

Nuremberg and Surrounding Towns and Villages

Bamberg

Berlin 232 miles

Forcheim

Gräfenberg

Schmaittach

London 514 miles

Erlangen

R. Pegnitz

Furth

Altstadt

Lauf

Spitalwald Forest north of Schornberg

R. Pegnitz

Schönberg

Reichswald

Munich 92 miles

Nuremberg

N
W E
S

10 Miles

*

Kraft durch Freude[93] camp, 2.3 miles southeast of Nuremberg Altstadt[94]
Tuesday 28 March 1944, 10:20am

Aurek Dabrowski shivered in the cold breeze as he took his spot in the long line of workers ready to take their place for the afternoon shift at the MAN factory in Frankenstrabe. In the inevitable German necessity for organisation and classification, Aurek was classified as a *Zwangsarbeiter* (forced worker), within the subcategory of *Militärinternierte* (military detainees) because he was a Polish prisoner of war.

Aurek knew every step of the 3.8km walk. He was sure he could find the factory if he was blindfolded. He was comforted by the presence of his two friends, Heniek in front of him and Iwan behind, all from the same village of Oborniki 30km north of Poznan in Poland. The Germans had captured the three men when they invaded Poland in 1939; they had been slave labourers for over four years.

A prison guard walked down the line, yanking on the chain that joined the manacles on their hands to make sure it was secure. The cold steel bit painfully into Aurek's wrists.

The forced labour camp was a jumble of Franconian half-timbered houses that at one time was a *Kraft durch Freude (KdF)*, 'Strength through Joy', holiday camp, on the edge of the Reichswald forest to the southeast of the Nuremberg *Altstadt*.

The KdF was created by the Nazis to provide organised leisure for the German work force. It was set up to bring to the 'common man' the pleasures once reserved only for the rich. By opening the door for the working class to easily and affordably take part in leisure activities, it was believed that the German labour force could be lulled into being more flexible and productive.

Aurek had long since been hardened to the horrific smell from the poor sanitation and damp staleness of men cramped in a confined place.

Prisoners from Poland, the Ukraine and Russia shared the labour camp; some had been brought in from the Dachau and Flossenburg concentration camps. The conditions in the huts were overcrowded but no one was complaining too much after hearing about the conditions

---

93   The NS *Gemeinschaft Kraft durch Freude*, the National Socialist Organisation 'Strength through Joy'.
94   Old City.

in the concentration camps ... they were on holiday by comparison. It was still a joke amongst the prisoners; they were living in a holiday camp ... *we should be happy to be on holiday! ... a holiday with only death at the end!*

Aurek's stomach growled from hunger as the long column of men set off. All the men were skin and bone, with only one meal served at the factory each day, normally a thin vegetable soup with a slice of black bread. The chains made a clicking sound in time with the shuffled footsteps. The Germans mounted only a small guard of five soldiers, armed with Schmeisser MP-40 machine pistols, on the column of a hundred and fifty prisoners.

Nuremberg was the site of the giant SS-Kaserne, barracks, built on the western outskirts of the Nazi Party Rally Grounds. They were the largest barracks erected by the National Socialists, housing thousands of SS troops and their families.

The column of labourers moved slowly as it was difficult in single file with arms manacled together. Shuffling down Valznerweilherstrabe in strictly enforced silence, they crossed over Regensburgerstrabe towards Zeppelinstrabe, the road that backed onto the Nazi complex. As they turned the corner, the giant *Zepplintribüne* reviewing stand came into view, the symbol of the might of the German Empire. This was the enormous arena designed by Albert Speer, with its massive colonnaded grandstand, where German athletes performed for Hitler.

Giant red Nazi swastika flags hung from flagpoles along the entire perimeter. When Aurek looked at the forbidding concrete buildings of the party grounds he was always overcome by the hopelessness of his situation. It seemed impossible that he would ever see his home in Poland again, he had no idea what had happened to his family, his parents and his three sisters. While he had only lived 20yrs, Aurek felt old, ... very, very old ... he was trapped in the 1,000-year Reich ... the chances of his surviving seemed remote[95].

The route to the MAN factory took the prisoners through the middle of the Nazi buildings. They passed the Nazi Kongresshalle on the left, still under construction, standing 39m high and 70m long in a giant horseshoe shape. Iwan had been on a work detail in the building and he said that the auditorium would provide seating for more than 50,000 people and would be nearly twice as large as the Coliseum in Rome.

On the right was the Luitpold Arena that could hold over 150,000

95   On 22 August 1939, on the invasion of Poland, Hitler gave explicit permission to his commanders to kill 'without pity or mercy, men, women and children of Polish descent or language.'

Nazis, the scene of SS[96] and SA[97] (*Sturmabteilung*) gatherings. At one end was the *Ehrenhalle*, a war memorial built in 1929. As the column shuffled past the war memorial, the guards raced down the line of men to make sure that none of them cast their eyes at the building. This was sacred German ground; the *Untermenschen*[98] could not be allowed to soil this place, which they would do, simply by looking at it. A guard slapped Aurek hard on the side of the face as he passed, making sure he was looking the other way.

After the *Kongresshalle* and *Luitpoldhain* was the old abandoned *Tiergarten* (zoo) that now housed two of Nuremberg's fire brigades. Then came the most haunting buildings of all, the SS-Kaserne. The entire entrance to the complex consisted of the sinister central main building with a *Portal der Ehre* 'Portal of Honour', with two side wings, both built around a courtyard. Above the portal was an eagle, the national symbol, *Hoheitszeich*, of the Third Reich. The eagle's head faced to its left as a symbol of the Nazi Party; if it had faced right, it would have been a symbol of the nation. The eagle's claws grasped a wreath of oak leaves surrounding a swastika.

Just the sight of the eagle over the forbidding portal sent shivers down the spine. As a prisoner, that portal spelt the gates of unspeakable hell … purgatory from which there was no return.

In front of Aurek his friend Heniek began to recite The Lord's Prayer in his native Polish.

> *Ojcze nasz, któryś jest w Niebie, święć się imię Twoje;*
> *przyjdź Królestwo Twoje;*
> *bądź wola Twoja,*
> *jako w niebie, tak i na ziemi.*

The other men took up the whispered chant.

> *… Give us this day our daily bread,*
> *… and forgive us our trespasses as we forgive those who trespass against us,*
> *and lead us not into temptation,*
> *but deliver us from evil …*

---

96   The *Schutzstaffel* translated to Protection Squadron or defense corps, abbreviated SS.

97   Paramilitary wing of the Nazi party in the 1930s. The SA was effectively superseded by the SS, although it was not formally dissolved and banned until after the Third Reich's final capitulation in 1945.

98   German for under man, sub-man, sub-human; used to describe 'inferior people', especially 'the masses from the East', that included the Slavic people, Poles, Russians and Ukrainians.

Aurek Dabrowski wept for his friends, for his family, for his country … for his own wretched existence …

The guards screamed at the men to be quiet … running down the shackled column, lashing out with truncheons until the prisoners returned to silence …

… deliver us from evil …

*

London, England
Tuesday 28 March 1944, 11:00am

Flying Officer William Carter and his wireless operator Sergeant David Muir arrived at Kings Cross Station at 11am, having caught the first train from Lincoln. They had escaped on their '48'.

The other members of their crew had dispersed to various parts of England. George Armitage went to his home in Lincoln, Eric Biddle to Preston, Frank Nellyer and Tommy Potts had gone off to Scotland to visit a family Tommy had met when he was on gunnery course, while Charles Morley was visiting his mother's younger brother in the Cotswolds.

Both men were sporting reasonable hangovers from the night before but nothing too debilitating. Their first port of call was to be Rhodesia House on The Strand. Carter's father knew the High Commissioner for Southern Rhodesia, Terence 'Tickey' Baggott. He had suggested that Bill introduce himself to the High Commissioner if he got the chance. Rhodesia House was also the base for the Rhodesian Comforts Committee set up for the dispatch of parcels to Rhodesian soldiers and airmen and providing hospitality and help for those visiting London. Rhodesia House was also the repository for all mail sent to service personnel from the colony from where it was dispatched to the UK army bases and air stations.

After a few false starts, the two servicemen made their way to Charing Cross on the 'tube'. From there, it was only a short walk to 429 The Strand. They arrived at Rhodesia House on the chime for lunchtime. Bill Carter passed on his father's compliments to the High Commissioner and in no time he and Muir were ushered into the High Commissioner's Office. 'Tickey' Baggott shook their hands enthusiastically, spontaneously offering lunch at the Curb Cafe. Mr Frank Cox, who ran the Rhodesian Comforts Committee, made a special point of saying hello and produced two letters for each of the young men.

161

Tickey Baggott was a short stocky man with a beaming smile and boundless energy and enthusiasm. He showered the two young men with questions about their squadron and their experiences. It was impossible to give an answer, as each question was fired off before the previous one could be answered.

The airmen were led out the main entrance of Rhodesian House, turning right into Agar Street. On the side of the embassy, at street level, were two red wooden doors. Both stood open and Mr Baggott led his visitors down a sharply descending staircase into the basement beneath Rhodesia House. Having descended the steep staircase, they turned left where they were confronted by a tall wooden sentry box serving as a reception desk. There stood Agatha, one of two elderly Victorian spinster sisters, the co-founders of the Curb Cafe. The High Commissioner and the two handsome young men were greeted with great excitement by Agatha, who, despite her advancing years, still had an eye for men in uniform. She led her guests along the passage which was an emporium of various exotic colonial tropical fruits stacked high on long wide tables either side. The two airmen could not remember when last they had seen fresh fruit. The air was enthused with an intoxicating fruit aroma. Agatha selected two items and handed them to the young men as a little welcome gift. They held the oranges in their hands as if they were precious jewels.

At the end of the underground passage, which acted as a foyer, were a series of alcoves leading off left and right like catacombs, inside of which were an assortment of odd tables with settees and ottomans. The High Commissioner was shown to a table that clearly was treated as 'his' when he visited. The ancient chairs were somewhat delicate and creaked loudly as they sat down.

There were no menus. Agatha merely enquired whether they ate fish to which they all consented, nodding their heads enthusiastically. The other sister, Lucinda was confined to the kitchen as the cook and preparer of the savoir-faire. In what seemed like no time at all, less than the time needed to drink a pint of bitter, three plates of sole were produced. It had been delicately and lightly cooked whole with a lemon slice on the side. Agatha returned with a big bowl of new potatoes and a mixed salad. Bill Carter had never eaten sole before and it tasted like heaven.

Tickey Baggott wanted to know all the news of 44 Squadron, all that wasn't censored of course. He was preparing for a visit from the Rhodesian Prime Minister Godfrey Huggins who had expressed a special interest in visiting the squadron. The empty plates were whisked away to be replaced almost immediately by melon and pineapple, served with a small bowl of caster sugar. After an hour of friendly banter and another two beers, the airmen excused themselves with the promise to visit again when they had the chance.

Frank Cox had suggested that the men stay at the Victoria League Club at 55 Leinster Square in Bayswater. He offered to call Gina Murphy, the Canadian manager to make arrangements, an offer gratefully accepted.

Both Peter Robinson and Gavin Pallister had recommended visiting The Finals Pub in St Martins Lane leading off Trafalgar Square. It was only a short walk from Rhodesia House along William IV Street. The noise from the pub could be heard from down the street despite the fact that it was heavily disguised for the 'black out' with canvas tarpaulins. It was only 3pm in the afternoon but the place was full of servicemen and women with shoulder flashes from Canada, Australia, New Zealand, as well as Rhodesia and the other colonies.

It didn't take long for the men to gravitate to a group of Rhodesians huddled around a table near the bar. They all introduced themselves. One was Sqn/Ldr Charles Green the CO of 266 (Rhodesia) Typhoon Squadron. Another was a young aircraft electrician, Tony Blackman, who had only just been posted to 44 Squadron. He was delighted and somewhat relieved to meet men from his new squadron. Dave Muir promised to show him around and maybe get him assigned to Ron Boswell and Cocky Lobin. Everyone had a good laugh as Dave related the story of the birth of C-Charlie 'Cocky Lobin'.

The beer flowed freely and discussion soon focused on home. Green was from a tobacco farming family in the Marandellas district and he talked about the crop that had just been harvested. Blackman was from the Centenary District where they farmed maize and a little tobacco. Bill Carter found it a relief to be able to talk about things that had nothing to do with the war. Everybody was friendly and relaxed as if they were having a beer at a sports club in Rhodesia. Rank did not seem to matter; they were just a bunch of colonial boys having a drink together. The smoke in the pub and the beers started to take their toll on Carter and he could feel the early onset of 'too much.'

Carter had hoped to see a film at one of the Leicester Square cinemas. The latest Rita Hayworth musical *Cover Girl*, had just been released and he was keen to see it. He had heard one of the songs from the musical, *Long ago and Far Away*, on the radio. Looking at his watch it was already 6 o'clock. If he was going to go, now was the time. Leicester Square was only two blocks away. Dave was on a roll, entertaining the crowd with his endless funny stories as a Junior District Officer in Que Que. Carter excused himself to much attempted persuasion to stay, but he was determined to see a film before he had to go back to the air station. It was now or never.

It was dark outside with a nip in the air. Carter had his heavy RAF greatcoat on which he buttoned up and thrust his hands deep in the pockets. He set off, crossing Charing Cross Road into Irving Street. The fresh air was a relief after the smoky pub. There was still a fair bit of traffic in the streets with taxis racing too and fro.

As he reached the end of Irving Street, a door opened onto the pavement and a tall Waaf stepped out, also dressed in a heavy coat. She had not seen him in the dark, forcing him to stop abruptly to avoid bumping into her.

'Oh, I am sorry I didn't see you there,' she said politely. The light from the doorway caught the colour of her hair under her cap

The voice was instantly recognisable. It was the voice that seemed to dissolve Carter's brain.

'My goodness, is that you Jill?' asked Carter in total surprise, squinting in the dark at the WAAF Intelligence Officer.

'William? Yes it is. I knew you were on leave. Fancy bumping into you in London,' she replied with a smile.

'What are you doing in London, are you also on leave?' asked Carter trying to contain his delight at seeing Jill Evans.

'No, unfortunately I am on a short three-day training course. I am staying here in my uncle's flat. Where are you off to?'

Carter was feeling the effects of an afternoon of beer drinking that overcame his shyness.

'I am off to see a film, I was going to see what was on at the Odeon around the corner. What are you doing?' asked Carter, not sure where he was going with this.

'I had a late lunch so I am not hungry … maybe I should join you. What shall we see?' replied Jill lightly. She seemed so much more relaxed than she was while on duty at the station. Her business-like abrupt manner seemed to have given way to a smiling friendly companionship. Carter was completely taken aback.

'That … that, would be wonderful. I am not sure what's on … we will have to go and have a look. The seven o'clock show will be starting soon,' replied Carter falteringly, trying to hide his astonishment.

'Well, we better be off then. What a pleasant surprise,' smiled Jill, thrusting her arm into his, as they stepped off in the direction of the Odeon. Carter felt like he had been struck by an electric shock, simply with the light touch of Jill Evans on his arm. He did everything in his power to prevent it shaking.

What an amazing surprise!

Carter could hardly believe this sudden turn of events, stealing a glance at Jill as if to satisfy himself that it wasn't his imagination.

The city was bustling in the early evening with people rushing home after work or going out to bars or restaurants. There was an air of excitement, the devil-may-care, of wartime London.

'Oh look, it's Girl Crazy with Judy Garland!' exclaimed Jill when they reached the theatre. 'I have heard all about it. They say it's every bit as good as the play.'

William Carter had not heard a word about the film, but he liked Judy Garland. He said simply, 'Yes.' He would have watched paint dry if it meant sitting next to Jill Evans.

A queue had formed at the ticket office and Carter took his place with Jill still on his arm. With the blackout, there were no ticket offices in the street, they were all on the inside of the theatre in the foyer. The lighting was subdued but Carter could see other patrons stealing glances at the handsome couple in RAF uniform. Jill was as tall as he was in her low practical heels.

The mere thought of having Jill as his girl made Carter flush. Standing in the queue, his mind raced for a suitable subject of conversation just so that he could look at her.

How to start ... what can I say that won't sound stupid?

An older fellow with his wife on his arm, turned around and smiled at the RAF couple.

'Bloody good show my lad ... giving the Hun what for,' he said in his strong cockney accent. He sounded just like Tommy Potts. 'Thank you for what you are doing ...'

Carter smiled back,' Thank you ... it's kind of you to say.'

'We appreciate you lads from the colonies coming over here to help,' added the man. 'Rhodesia 'ay?'

'Yes,' replied Carter smiling back.

'It is so nice to see a young couple in love,' said the wife with a wink to her husband.

Carter blushed brightly, spinning his head to judge Jill's reaction. She burst out laughing at his obvious discomfort. He was not sure whether he should try to correct the misapprehension.

'We work together at the station,' stammered Carter, making it worse.

'I am sure you do my lad,' laughed the cockney, winking at Jill.

Jill just laughed louder, causing other people in the queue to smile at her amusement. Carter could feel his ears turning red with embarrassment.

'You blush beautifully William,' she whispered into his ear, squeezing his arm a little tighter. He couldn't trust himself to reply, but he could feel the heat on his face as he blushed even more brightly.

Carter produced 2/10d[99] for the tickets, refusing to take a contribution from Jill.

They took their seats in a row ten from the back; the theatre was already almost full. A piano was playing a piece of music from the film, *But not for me.*

The lights flickered and the strong strident cords of *Land of Hope and Glory*[100] rung out.

> *Land of hope and glory, mother of the free,*
> *How shall we extol thee, who are born of thee?*
> *Wider still and wider shall thy bounds be set.*

The audience stood to their feet and sang the song at the top of their voices.

> *God, who made thee mighty, make thee mightier yet.*
> *God, who made thee mighty, make thee mightier yet.*

The crowd were in full voice thumping out the chorus. Jill stood resolutely next to him singing for all she was worth. Carter found himself caught up in the moment.

> *Land of hope and glory, mother of the free,*
> *How shall we extol thee, who are born of thee?*
> *Wider still and wider shall thy bounds be set.*

It was a stirring sight watching these people of London, singing their defiance at their enemies. William Carter couldn't help but feel that what he was doing in the war was all worthwhile.

> *God, who made thee mighty, make thee mightier yet,*
> *God, who made thee mighty, make thee mightier yet.*

---

99   2 shillings and 10 pence.
100 *Land of Hope and Glory* is a British song, with music by Edward Elgar and lyrics by A C Benson, written in 1902

The film began ... a story about a wealthy New York playboy whose father sends him West to get him away from bad influences. However, the city slicker brings his friends with him and they clash hilariously with the locals as the tenderfeet try to convert a rundown lodge into a moneymaking dude ranch.

The songs were fantastic; Judy Garland was wonderful, *I Got Rhythm* and *Could You Use Me?*, his favourites. Jill seemed to be enjoying the film immensely, giggling at the funny bits. Carter's mind wandered at the thought of what it would be like to court Jill ... he dismissed it as impossible ... *she was way too mature, what could I offer her as a twenty year old*. His mind clutched for a way to ask Jill out for a drink after the film without sounding presumptuous ... worse, ridiculous.

The film ended all too soon and the audience filed out of the theatre into the cold night air. Carter's mind was a jumble as he desperately searched for a way to interest Jill in a drink before they went their separate ways. She pre-empted him.

'I know a little pub around the corner, fancy a drink before we go home William?' she asked with another of her melting smiles.

He nodded enthusiastically, 'Yes I could do with a drink. Maybe they will serve sandwiches, I'm hungry now.' It was as if she could read his mind.

The bar was crammed full with standing room only. They pushed through the crowd to the bar where Carter ordered two pints of bitter.

'Thank you for coming with me Jill, it was a smashing film, don't you think?' said Carter over the hubbub.

'I should thank you ... it's no fun going to films on your own. I have seen so few films since ... since.' She broke off, as some sort of memory seemed to cloud her face.

Carter with his youthful lack of tact asked,' Since what Jill?'

A small table cleared and Carter grabbed one of the chairs, beating a large sergeant in army uniform.

'Not to worry Sir,' said the Sergeant smiling at him, ' ... you lot are doing a great job.'

Jill flashed the sergeant a dazzling smile as they sat down at the table.

There was an awkward silence as Carter waited for Jill to give an answer to his question, realising too late that it was not something she really wanted to discuss. She looked at him, their faces no more than a foot apart in the crowded noisy bar.

'I am sorry Jill, I didn't mean to pry.'

'No it's alright ... but you have to promise me that this is not information to be spread around the squadron,' she said, her eyes fixed on his.

'Of course not Jill, but you really don't have to say anything ... I am sorry.'

She continued to study him across the table; her brown eyes seemed to have a depth that he could drown in.

'I was married once, William. His name was Arthur Evans, his father was Sir Walter Evans of Truscott in Devon. I was twenty and he was thirty ... I was madly in love ... he died in Sicily last year. He was a captain in the Devonshire Regiment,' said Jill, ticking off the information almost mechanically. It was obvious that she was deeply hurt, her eyes glistened with tears

'You don't have to say anymore Jill. I should not have asked,' whispered Carter, now feeling awful about his insensitive question.

'You were not to know ... I normally never discuss Arthur ... it is like a part of my life that has simply evaporated. Almost like it never happened at all. Does that sound terrible ... that I can't talk about my husband?'

Carter was now completely out of his depth. His experience with females limited to his mother and his sister, a few girls at dances and the odd kiss.

'No, its not terrible ... you have had a dreadful loss ... I can't imagine how that must feel,' he ventured, trying to make sense of what to say. He took a long drink of beer to buy some time.

Jill smiled back, her eyes examining him, completely aware that this was way beyond his experience ... He looked so young ... like a schoolboy really ... despite his officer's uniform and pilot's wings. Jill had liked William from the first time they had met over the de-briefing table. It was his shyness and reserve that were so appealing and the way he stared at her, averting his eyes when she caught him. It was amusing, like a schoolboy crush. There was no shortage of admirers on the squadron. She had been pursued by a great many including Jack Haworth. The pain at the loss of Arthur had made her insular and distant, enough to put off even the most ardent suitor.

As she studied his face, the contradiction between man and boy was so evident. He was so balanced and mature in some respects, blooded in the most deadly battle of the war. She had seen how his crew respected him, how professional he was as a leader and the pilot of a heavy bomber ... Yet, despite all of this, he was still a teenage boy emotionally. She had overheard Jack Haworth speak of him in glowing terms, 'a future squadron leader', he had said. Yet the young man she saw in front of her still lacked the empathy and the emotional insight that age provided.

The similarities between William Carter and her husband Arthur were clear. They were both shy, sensitive and thoughtful. The sort of men that stimulated the maternal instinct in her ... to look after them ... to make them strong ... to support them in whatever way she could ...

A group of American airmen on the far side of the bar began to sing Kay Kyser's *Praise the Lord and pass the Ammunition*.

> *Praise the Lord and pass the ammunition*
> *Praise the Lord and pass the ammunition*
> *Praise the Lord and pass the ammunition*
> *And we'll all stay free .*

The crowd in the bar took up the song ...

> *Praise the Lord and swing into position*
> *Can't afford to be a politician*
> *Praise the Lord, we're all between perdition*
> *And the deep blue sea.*

The chorus rang out as the pub erupted with sound. Bill Carter and Jill Evans sang with the rest of them. He did not take his eyes off her for a second, watching her mouth crinkle at the corners as she smiled.

> *Shouting Praise the Lord, we're on a mighty operation*
> *All aboard, we ain't a-goin' fishin'*
> *Praise the Lord and pass the ammunition*
> *And we'll all stay free.*

They laughed together as one of the Americans stood up on a chair to conduct the choir, as if he was at the Albert Hall. Tears ran down their cheeks from the sheer delight of it all ... *we are all in this together ... we'll all stay free ...*

'My goodness, look at the time! I must be getting back ... I have an early start tomorrow,' said Jill, looking at her watch.

As she stood up to go, the distant wailing Carter Gents air raid sirens entered the noisy pub, instantly killing the party atmosphere, sending shockwaves through the spine.

The siren was instantly taken up by others, getting closer and closer until the mournful sound pervaded everything, beating in the chest. The sirens wailed in harmony, the one taken up after the other in sorrowful waves as if the city itself was moaning in dreaded anguish. The dreadful warning was so familiar yet still made the hair stand up on the back of the neck and the skin crawl.

'Everybody out … no need to panic, the air raid shelter is on the northeast corner of the square … you have plenty of time … off you go now,' shouted the publican.

The crowd sank the drinks in their hands and all left the pub in a very dignified and orderly fashion. Carter had not experienced a London air raid before but Jill seemed very relaxed about it all.

She took him by the hand, 'Come on, I know where the shelter is,' she said confidently. The street outside was full of people leaving the various pubs and restaurants. Everyone seemed remarkably calm about it all as the sirens continued their haunting howl. As Carter looked up at the sky searchlights were already sweeping back and forth. There was no sound of bomber engines above the sirens.

Carter followed Jill through the dilapidated park in Leicester Square. There was a queue forming at the entrance to the shelter. Looking up into the sky, Carter couldn't help anticipating the arrival of the German bombers. In January 1944, substantial German air raids resumed on London in the so-called 'Little Blitz' (or 'Baby Blitz'). Greater London and southeast England were singled out for attack again in retaliation for British saturation bombing of major German cities, particularly Berlin.

The sirens stopped.

A droning sound took their place coming from the east. Ack-Ack sites spread over a wide area, all opened up together. The sound drowned out everything, Jill had to scream at him to be heard. The 4.5s, the 3.7s and the Bofors Guns were all in action and the sky was filled with bursting shells, tracers, rocket projectiles and the brightness of numerous searchlights. On the eastern horizon fires glowed from enemy bombs.

'Come on, we will go back to the flat, we can't stay in the open,' called Jill over the scream of AA shells. They both took off back through the square as fast as their legs would carry them. The bombers had arrived much quicker than everyone had expected. As he ran for cover, for the first time William Carter understood the fear of what it was like to be on the receiving end. This was only a handful of German bombers … he could only imagine what it must be like under 800 or 1,000!

They reached the door to the block of flats on Irving Street and raced up to the second floor.

CRUMP ... CRUMP ... CRUMP.

Bombs were falling somewhere to the east, steadily closer. Jill struggled with the key in the door, it burst open and they stumbled into the flat, breathlessly laughing from the breakneck run. It was pitch dark inside.

Jill lit a match to help look for the candle ... it was on the dining room table.

Taking off his cap and greatcoat Carter dropped them onto one of the chairs in the lounge. He glanced at Jill, standing in the flickering light of the candle. She was looking back at him, still breathing hard, her chest rising and falling from their sprint across Leicester Square.

CRUMP ... CRUMP ... CRUMP.

She was in his arms, her lips thrust against his, an urgency that William could not believe was possible. The world stopped turning ... the sound of the bombing seemed to fade ... passionate instinct took over ... nothing else mattered ...

CRUMP ... CRUMP ... CRUMP ... CRUMP

9

Luftwaffe 3rd Jagddivision (Fighter) (3 JD 1) Division HQ, Deelen in Holland
Wednesday 29 March 1944, 8:58am

Generalmajor Walter Grabmann, the commander of 3 JD 1, strode into his operations room on the southern boundary of the airfield at Deelen, in the Dutch countryside about 4miles north of the town of Arnhem. The men and women in the room leapt to their feet and saluted their commander, *Heil Hitler*, in unison. He flicked his hand up acknowledging their salute.

'*Guten Morgen … bitte weitermachen*, please carry on,' he called out in reply.

Grabmann was slimly built, 5'11" with light brown hair and striking blue eyes. His skin showed the scars of teenage acne that made him appear forbidding. He was a career Luftwaffe Officer, starting with the Air Police in 1934. The Knight's Cross of the Iron Cross hung at his neck, awarded in 1940 for bravery. He was credited with 7 aerial victories during the Spanish Civil War and another 6 during the Battle of Britain. He had survived being shot down over France by RAF Hurricanes and had completed 110 combat operations.

Across the length of one wall was a large-scale map of the area the Luftwaffe 3rd Fighter Division covered. The map showed the boundary marked with large red dotted lines stretching inland from Brugge in Belgium in a straight line down to Luxembourg, looped across to Frankfurt and then north to Dokkum on the north Dutch coast. The area included nearly all of Holland and Belgium, but most importantly, the industrial heartland of the Ruhr. Grabmann had the enormous task of defending the engine room of the Reich, centred on the cities of Duisburg, Essen, Dusseldorf and Cologne.

There were 13 air bases marked on the map divided amongst four night fighting wings or *Nachtjagdgeschwader*, in turn divided into 9 *Gruppen*, making a total of about 374 aircraft including attached units.

Inside the operation's room was a bank of telephones. The walls were covered in blackboards marking the number of aircraft in each sub-unit and their state of readiness. The operations room was connected by radio and telephone to the fighter control NJRF and to each airfield to ensure the quickest possible response to a threat.

Walter Grabmann had a small office with glass windows off the operations room, keeping him in constant touch with the activity outside. The responsibility weighed heavily on his shoulders, his division bore the brunt of the defence against bombing raids from England. Many of the cities he was tasked to protect already lay in ruins. The accursed American P-51s, P-47s and British Typhoons and Mosquitos subjected his Dutch airfields to continual raids, day and night.

The Generalmajor was in a filthy mood. He was late to his office because American P-47s had flown a sweep over the Deelen airfield that very morning, destroying two aircraft on the ground. The low cloud and light drizzle had saved the base from greater damage. The Generalmajor was forced to return to his mess for a clean uniform as he had dived into a drainage ditch when the first enemy aircraft flew low over the base.

Instead of going into his office, Grabmann took his seat at the head of a large table set against the wall. The members of his staff, each carrying a pile of briefing papers, quickly joined him. Each member of the staff had been in touch with his opposite number at the 1 Fighter Corps (*Fliegerkorps*) HQ at Zeist in Holland[101]. This was not exactly true, as the 1 Fighter Corps was in the middle of transferring their headquarters from Zeist to Brunswick-Querum in Germany, a move that was causing considerable disruption.

Grabmann reflected on the move of the headquarters 320km inland *... a sign of the times ... the general staff no longer felt safe in Holland ...*

Not waiting for his commander, the intelligence officer stood up and nodded respectfully. He immediately began his morning update.

'Generalmajor the Americans have launched an attack which we believe is on Brunswick. It is probably the aircraft assembly factory of the Mühlenbau Industries at Waggum north of Brunswick. *Luftbeobachterstaffel* 3 report a low box of the 94th Combat Wing, they counted well over 200 aircraft. Other attacks are on Unterluss and Stedorf. Our aircraft have reported 9 enemy aircraft shot down so far. The Americans are still in the air.'

The intelligence officer watched his commander's reaction.

'That should upset the Generalleutnant Schmidt, being attacked in his new HQ in Brunswick before he has moved in,' replied Grabmann caustically.

The intelligence officer continued, 'There is heavy cloud over most of the continent north of Frankfurt so the bombing has been inaccurate. The cloud base is at 1,000 metres, broken cloud to the south, winds are southwesterly at 40km/hr.'

---

101 3rd *Jagddivision* (Fighter) (3 JD 1) Division formed part of 1 Fighter Corps. Other units within 1 Fighter Corps included, 1st Fighter Division - Döberitz (Berlin), 2nd Fighter Division - Stade (Hamburg), 7th Fighter Division - Schleissheim (Munich).

Grabmann grunted and waved his arm for the officer to continue, 'Talk to me about the British. What can we expect tonight?'

'The moon is approaching the first quarter, weather is reported as heavy cloud over the north of the continent above 2,000 metres, winds are from southwest. Our cities north of Munich will be protected by cloud, plus the moon will not set. Our assessment is that a raid tonight over Germany is unlikely. We can expect raids over France where the weather will be more favourable.'

'Good, what is the status of radio traffic?' asked Grabmann.

The officer responsible for communications and radio monitoring stood up,' Herr Generalmajor, traffic is low. We have much traffic from the Americans as their raid is still in progress but very little coming from the English bases. I agree with the intelligence assessment ... a large raid over Germany tonight seems unlikely.'

'Very good, let's keep alert. If anything changes call me immediately. We will update the status at four pm as usual,' ordered Grabmann who stood up and walked across to his office.

... If only the moon was always full ... and our skies blocked with cloud ...

*

RAF Bomber Command HQ, Code Name 'Southdown', Walters Ash, Buckinghamshire, 4 miles northwest of High Wycombe Wednesday 29 March 1944, 8:59am

The Nazis entered this war under the rather childish delusion that they were going to bomb everyone else, and nobody was going to bomb them. At Rotterdam, London, Warsaw and half a hundred other places, they put their rather naive theory into operation. They sowed the wind, and now they are going to reap the whirlwind[102].
AOC-in-C Bomber Command, Air Marshall Arthur Harris

'Burt is on his way,' whispered Grp/Capt Walter Inness, Operations Officer, Bomber Command HQ, standing at the bottom of the stairs leading to the 'hole'.

Each of the senior officers at Bomber Command HQ took up his place in a half circle in front of a small desk set up squarely in the middle of the underground operations room. The room was oblong shape with a rubber floor. Across the walls were large quarter-inch scale maps of Europe, orders of battle, target lists, weather charts and

---

102 The statement 'They sowed the wind, and now they are going to reap the whirlwind' was taken from the Old Testament (Hosea 8-7), first used by Arthur Harris during the London Blitz in 1940.

phases of the moon.

'High Mass', as the less reverent referred to the daily briefing, was about to commence.

The sound of someone coming down the stairs in quick succession carried into the room. They all took an involuntary breath, always anticipating a potential storm.

The brilliant shining shoes of the AOC-in-C were the first to appear on the staircase.

At 9am precisely, the AOC-in-C Bomber Command, Air Marshall Arthur Harris walked purposefully into the room. He was a man of 52, but looked considerably older, with thinning grey, almost white hair, glinting blue eyes that missed nothing, and a small grey moustache. Harris strode to the centre of the room followed by his PA, Flt/Lt Etienne Maze, his personal staff officer Grp/Capt Harry Weldon and the Bomber Command Deputy AOC-in-C Air Vice Marshall Robert 'Sandy' Saundby.

The room was in hushed silence. This was the standard early morning ritual, with no deviation.

'Good morning gentlemen,' said Harris in his usual clipped fashion. There was a murmured response. Arthur Harris was not a man given to shouting, his speech was delivered quietly, almost restrained, and never showed signs of irritability in front of his staff.

Harris removed his hat and placed it carefully on the desk in front of him. He then sat down, reached into his left-hand breast pocket and removed a packet of American Camel cigarettes. He lit up and asked the first question.

'Did the Hun do anything last night?' enquired Harris in a brusque but steady voice. Harris did not pretend at popularity, never wasting words nor time on civilities, his mere presence seemed to fill the room to bursting.

'Ju88 raids over London and the Thames estuary. We estimate no more than sixty aircraft. Results were mixed. Phosphorous incendiaries and high explosives in Westminster, Hyde Park, Knightsbridge, Monck Street, Cliveden Place and a church in Medway Street and Flask Lane SW1 were all hit, set alight or damaged. Paddington Railway Station took one 250kilogam bomb. Reports say five enemy aircraft shot down by Ack-Ack, none by nightfighters,' announced the Senior Intelligence Officer formally, reading from carefully prepared notes.

'How did we go?' asked Harris, dismissing the German raid.

Wng/Cmdr Felix Fawssett, Intelligence Officer – Targeting, lifted his notes and replied crisply, 'Poor weather limited operations overnight. Fourteen Mosquitos to Duisburg and thirty-two to Krefeld. No losses. Bombing results still coming in but likely to be ineffective.'

The limited Bomber Command activity the night before meant the report was short, after a big raid the report could have run to half an hour.

'What are our options for tonight?' asked Harris with the faintest hint of excitement.

Fawssett took a deep breath, 'the quarter moon will not set. Poor weather north of latitude 43° 23' limits targets deep in Germany. A Pointblank[103] target in France is the aero-engine factory in Lyons. The MEW list includes railway yards at Vaires. In Germany, weather permitting, Kiel, Krefeld, Aachen maybe Cologne.'

'Where are Met on all of this, Spence?' clipped Harris, turning to his Chief Meteorological Officer, Doctor Magnus Spence.

Dr Spence had a roll of synoptic charts under his arm. He removed one and placed it on the desk. He unrolled it and began a detailed weather summary confirming that the weather was not favourable for any heavy bomber raids beyond the German border. He also gave a detailed report on the weather over England that showed that heavy low cloud and rain over Lincolnshire would hamper returning bombers from 1 and 5 Groups. This eliminated these two groups from any attack.

Harris questioned Spence closely, some would have described the questioning as more of a grilling. Harris would not be put off with simple statements, he probed and pushed, trying to nudge the weather forecast in the direction he wanted, like a prosecutor in a courtroom. Despite the torrid questioning, Dr Spence stood firm, drawing a faint smile from Harris who eventually conceded defeat.

Harris' displeasure at the realisation of not being able to mount a large area raid seemed to pervade the room like an unpleasant smell … he made a decision.

'Target Vaires and Lyons with the heavies. Draw from 4, 6 and 8 Groups. Send Mosquitos to Kiel and Krefeld. Any questions?' he said sharply.

The decision on the targets for the night, like so many such decisions, was taken in the blink of an eye.

Despite his aloofness and abruptness that bordered on rudeness, Harris exuded such unbridled confidence that it couldn't help but rub off on his staff. Once his decision was made it seldom elicited any comment.

---

103 The Pointblank Directive of targets.

There were no questions.

'Anything else?'

Grp/Capt Walter Inness, Operations Officer, cleared his throat. 'Sir, we are getting an increasing number of German nightfighters flying out over the North Sea to intercept the bombers. They seem to be getting better at anticipating our attacks. We cannot give an explanation for this as yet but it does mean the number of spoof raids before major attacks need to be increased. I have a report on Oboe and our decreased bombing accuracy.' He placed the report gently onto the desk in front of Harris. Not waiting for a question he continued, 'The boffins have come up with an answer which I recommend we investigate urgently.'

'I will read it,' replied Harris, which meant in reality that he would study every word and dissect every suggestion.

'Finally Sir, we have found nothing on this Scarecrow business. I have instructed 140 Squadron to carry out a reconnaissance but they have not been able to fly as yet,' added Inness, expecting to be put through the hoop on this one.

'Very good, keep me informed. This thing is a worry,' said Harris standing up from his chair. Without any further comment, he turned on his heel and left the room.

Bomber Command's day had begun in earnest …

*

Irving Street, London
Wednesday 29 March 1944, 10:01am

F/O William 'Bill' Carter was still coming to terms with the events of the night before. He was alone in the small flat; a note had been placed on the dressing table that said simply 'Thank you for a wonderful evening – see you back at the Station. PS set the latch on the way out.'

He could not remember when last he had slept so deeply. For the first time in months, his mind felt clear, as if released from an intangible constraint. He showered and dressed, taking the stairs down to the street two at a time, now in search of a late breakfast.

Out in the hustle and bustle of the street, there was a slight nip in the air, a freshness that tasted faintly of apple. It was not cool enough for the greatcoat that Carter had hung over his arm. He looked up into the milky blue sky and took a deep breath, the unique smell of London filling his senses … *look at me now! From tiny Rhodesia to this! … God, it's great to be alive!*

Deciding upon a walk, Carter turned right down Irving Street, into Martin Place towards Trafalgar Square. He had in his mind to walk down the Mall towards Buckingham Palace, then along Constitution Hill past Wellington's Arch to the tube station at Knightsbridge, a distance of about a mile and a half. The train to Lincoln left at 12:30pm, so he hoped to squeeze in a cup of coffee and a sandwich at one of the tearooms near Hyde Park Corner.

The sun came out as he passed through Trafalgar Square, walking briskly on his way. It was impossible not to think of Jill Evans, she seemed to fill his mind as if nothing else existed. No matter how hard he tried to rationalise what had happened, it all came back to the same thing, he was head over heals in love with her. While that seemed impossible, a completely impractical and unobtainable idea, there it was … he was in love for the first time in his life … he was convinced of it.

The feeling of freedom walking down the Mall was wonderful, his uniform attracting smiles from passers by, many calling out 'Good Luck' … 'Good Show' …

'Thank you' … the enormity of what he and his fellow airmen were doing sank in. *This is what it is all about … right here, walking down a sunny street, to go anywhere and do anything I please … fighting so that everyone can live in freedom, released from fear.*

For a brief moment, Carter's own fears for his future, the dangers he still had to face, faded … happily replaced by thoughts of Jill Evans and the people of London.

Cockney feet mark the beat of history.
Every street pins a memory down.
Nothing ever can quite replace
The grace of London Town.

London Pride has been handed down to us.
London Pride is a flower that's free.
London Pride means our own dear town to us,
And our pride it for ever will be.

Every Blitz your resistance toughening,
From the Ritz to the Anchor and Crown,
Nothing ever could override
The pride of London Town[104].

104 Noel Coward, This song was inspired by an air raid on London in the Spring of 1941. Coward says he was at a railway station where 'Most of the glass in the roof

RAF Bomber Command HQ, Code Name 'Southdown', Walters Ash, Buckinghamshire, 4 miles northwest of High Wycombe
Thursday 30 March 1944, 8:59am

... the aim of the Combined Bomber Offensive ... should be unambiguously stated [as] the destruction of German cities, the killing of German workers, and the disruption of civilised life throughout Germany[105].
AOC-in-C Bomber Command, Air Marshall Arthur Harris

The early morning ritual at Bomber Command HQ was about to unfold. Once again, the staff officers and the support staff were assembled. They already had an informal discussion on the poor prospects for a raid that evening. A number of unfavourable circumstances existed.

Hushed conversation stopped as the familiar clumping sound on the staircase leading to 'the hole' carried into the room. The AOC-in-C Bomber Command entered, his face looked drawn, he was obviously irritate. The reason for his displeasure was unknown to his staff.

In addition to his staff, Harris was accompanied by an officer representing the American Eighth Army Air Force, that had just taken up residence at the requisitioned Wycombe Abbey School for Girls nearby.

Without any greeting, which was not unusual, Harris asked his trademark question, 'Did the Hun do anything last night?'

Each staff officer concerned took his turn at updating the AOC-in-C on the previous night's activities.

Wng/Co Felix Fawssett, Intelligence Officer – Targeting, gave his short report, 'Seventy-six Halifaxes and eight Mosquitos of Numbers 4, 6 and 8 Groups attacked the railway yards at Vaires, near Paris, in bright moonlight. Oboe Mosquitos provided effective target marking, the bombing was very accurate and two ammunition trains that were present blew up[106]. One Halifax lost. Nineteen Lancasters of 617

---

had been blown out and there was dust in the air and the smell of burning'. People were undeterred, and this moved him to write a song that captured the spirit of the Blitz. It took him a couple of days to finish; he based it on 'Won't You Buy My Sweet Blooming Lavender'.

105 Garret, Stephen A. Ethics and Air Power in World War II: The British Bombing of German Cities. London: Palgrave Macmillan, 1993, at 32-33.

106 Unknown to Bomber Command there were 13 German troop trains at Vaires, carrying the 10th S.S. Panzer Division. French rail workers knew of the raid and had placed a wagon full of sea mines in the siding. The mines exploded, killing

Squadron to the aero-engine factory at Lyons, which was bombed accurately. Oboe Mosquitos: thirty-two to Kiel, eleven to Krefeld, five to Aachen and four to Cologne. No losses.'

'Spence what have you got for us tonight?' asked Harris turning to his Chief Meteorological Officer.

Dr Spence cleared his throat, knowing he was the harbinger of bad news. His job was subject to so many mind-boggling parameters; suitable weather for take-off, no heavy convective cloud that could cause icing en-route, good visibility over the target to allow for accurate marking, and then no fog or low cloud for landing.

'Well, as you are aware the moon is a quarter through its cycle, therefore, we will have a half-moon which will be at its maximum elevation an hour before sunset, and will not set before one o'clock in the morning.' Dr Spence took a breath to gauge the reaction from Harris and his staff. Harris' face remained impassive, this was knowledge he already had.

Spence carried on,' ... I have the latest information from Dunstable[107]. A low-pressure area over Norway is causing cumulus cloud over the North Sea with the risk of icing. A complex cold front stretches from Ireland through northern France, southern Germany into the Balkans, swinging north to its source, a deep depression in Russia. The front is slow moving. We have been watching it for three days.'

'Yes, yes Magnus, what does it mean?' demanded Harris expectantly.

Spence had learned to be patient with his boss. He knew that he couldn't sugarcoat unfavourable news ... a huge number of lives were at stake. The responsibility weighed heavily on him.

'Well ... there are three implications for the cold front. Its leading southerly edge will probably contain low cloud that will most likely cover any target. The northerly edge will possibly contain high, layered cloud and there will be steady northerly winds. Elsewhere over Germany there will be shallow troughs of low pressure with little cloud,' replied Spence keeping his voice steady.

'Yes, come on now ... what can we do?' coached Harris, trying to pry the information out of his met officer.

'Well ... the cloud coming down from the North Sea will obscure all targets in northern Germany. South of the front, the moonlight will illuminate our aircraft. It does not look promising,' said Spence in trepidation.

1,200 S.S. men. Fourteen French railway workers were also killed by the massive explosion.
107 Central Meteorological Office at Dunstable, Bedfordshire.

'If we don't attack tonight, we will not get another chance for a major raid for another two weeks,' groaned Harris.

What Harris did not mention to his staff was two days before he had his first major briefing on Operation Overlord for the invasion of Europe. His command was about to be placed at the disposal of the Supreme Allied Commander for the invasion, where all targeting decisions would vest. This irked Harris beyond measure and was the reason for his present ill-temper. The decision, which Harris vehemently disagreed with, meant that all raids on German cities would be suspended in favour of clearing the invasion beaches and pounding infrastructure in France. Harris was appalled at the consequences of letting the German cities off the hook for months; they would rapidly rebuild their industry with terrible consequences.

He had the Germans on the rack; he needed to drive his advantage home!

'Spence, the high cloud behind the front will conceal our bombers, won't it?' asked Harris pointedly.

'Possibly ...'

'That's it then, high cloud on the way in will protect the bombers from the moon, the moon will have set by the time they bomb and start on the way home. We need a target in southern Germany outside of the line of the weather front,' stated Harris, the decision was made. 'Fawssett, what have you got on your priority list ... don't give me any of that MEW rubbish, give me an Area Target.'

Felix Fawssett was taken aback by the decision to mount a raid. It had seemed to him that the situation was too unfavourable. *It was obvious* ... A little flustered, he shuffled through his file for the targeting list.

'Sir ... south of the line we have ... Schweinfurt and Regensburg. Augsburg may be too far south because of the low cloud Doctor Spence mentioned,' said Fawssett quietly.

Harris stood up and walked to the large map of Germany on the wall. It had a number of pins in it with dates and tonnages marked, showing which cities and economic targets had been hit over the past year. The mere mention of Schweinfurt upset Harris, which he disdainfully saw as one of the MEW 'panacea' targets. He had attacked it already, albeit ineffectively, under huge duress. Regensburg was the site of a major Messerschmitt factory, he would leave it for the Americans, the Luftwaffe was their priority.

Arthur Harris scanned the map on the wall ... 'Magnus, show me the line of the weather front on this map,' he instructed, his arm outstretched.

The Nazis saw Nürnberg (Nuremberg) as a classic example of a city rich in Germanic and imperial history; indeed, Hitler agreed with the mayor who once called it the 'most German of German cities'. Wishing to capitalize on this, the Nazi hierarchy turned Nürnberg into *the* city for Nazi Party rallies, and every September from 1933 to 1938, the NSDAP[108] held its annual rallies in Nürnberg. These huge weeklong gatherings brought hundreds of thousands of people to the city to view the nationalistic and militaristic extravaganza.

To better accommodate these massive rallies, Hitler turned to his favourite architect Albert Speer (designer of the New Reich's Chancellery in Berlin, and later the Nazi Minister of Armaments) to design and build a suitable site, which became the Nazi Party Rally Grounds (the *Parteitagsgelände),* southeast of the city centre. This site eventually featured some of Speer's largest and most monumental works, with plans for an immense Olympic-style stadium with seating for 405,000 that would have dwarfed all else[109]. The Party Rallies featured large numbers of the SS, SA, Labour Service, Hitler Jugend, and the Wehrmacht, parading through the old walled town of Nürnberg and standing in mass formations on the several parade grounds, paying homage to their Führer and deceased Nazi heroes. Hitler made several speeches during the week, and viewed military demonstrations on the large exercise grounds, the *Zeppelinfeld.*

… Harris' eyes fixed on Nuremberg situated almost halfway between Schweinfurt and Regensburg. His photographic memory recalled a Bomber Command document that described Nuremberg as 'one of the sacred cities of the Nazi creed and a political target of the first importance'.

'Fawssett, remind me, when last did we go to Nuremberg?' asked Harris with the faintest hint of excitement.

Fawssett consulted his Area Target list.

'Seven months ago, Sir … limited damage.'

'It's the bloody heart of the Nazi regime, its untouched. It's the Huns' Holy Grail. What's there?'

'If you will excuse me Sir, I need to get my file,' said Fawssett,

---

108 *Nationalsozialistische Deutsche Arbeiterpartei* (NSDAP, Nazi Party)
109 This building never progressed much beyond the ground-breaking stage. Wartime necessities brought a halt to the building of the Party Grounds, which were never finished, but most of what was built is still there, in a somewhat ruined condition.

rushing across the room to his tiny office where he kept a file on every major city and target in Germany. He fetched the file and upon returning, he found himself the attention of every person in the room, waiting expectantly for his next words.

'Population about 426,000, 200,000 industrial workers, fifty factories, twenty-eight for military use … A huge S.S. barracks, the Nazi Party show grounds … the M.A.N[110] heavy engineering works … two Siemens-Schuckertwerke electrical factories, a few small factories making aircraft parts,' listed Fawssett in a steady voice, doing his best not to contribute to his boss's obvious enthusiasm.

'That's it then … the target is Nuremberg. Sandy I will leave you to build the plan. Call me when it is finished … Maximum Effort[111], people … that will be all,' ordered Harris; clearly happy with his decision … he had an Area Target to go for.

Air Vice Marshall Robert 'Sandy' Saundby stepped forward as his boss left the room, taking the stairs two at a time.

'Right, let's get on with it. We should start with the route options … any ideas?' said Saundby in his affable friendly fashion. He was the perfect foil for the C-in-C's abrupt, distant and aloof style.

Saundby's job was to oil the wheels, he was a tall, broad, stout man with a jolly red face and a twinkle in his eye, interested in everything and everyone. He never imposed his authority and never condescended. He loved a party and enjoyed entertaining his junior officers with hilarious stories over a drink in the mess. His abiding weakness, however, was that he seldom stood up to his boss when he needed to be told he was wrong. Striving for the middle ground, Saundby avoided confrontation of any kind, particularly with Arthur Harris, giving the benefit of the doubt at every turn.

The phones began ringing, teleprinters rattled, in each of the Bomber Command Group HQs spread around eastern England. At 5 Group HQ Morton Hall, a mile north of RAF Swinderby, the orders arrived *… we are working tonight … full fuel load … bomb loads are designated code-word 'Arson[112]' … briefing to follow … Maximum Effort!*

---

110 *Maschinen Augsburg - Nürnberg.*

111 The words 'Maximum Effort' had enormous connotations. What it meant was every available bomber!

112 Bomber Command Executive Codeword: 'ARSON'. Target Type: General. 7 Small Bomb containers (SBC), each loaded with 236 x 4 lb No. 15 Incendiary and No. 15 Explosive Incendiary (1 in 10 mix) bombs. Total bomb load: 7,000 lbs.

Village of Schönberg, Middle Franconia District, Bavaria, 10 miles (16.7km) northeast of Nuremberg, Thursday 30 March 1944, 9:25am

Otto Gregori picked his way along the rough path he had created through the Spitalwald forest that stretched for nearly 4 uninterrupted miles north of his farm. Berta the German wirehaired pointer walked at Otto's heel. She was a muscular hunting dog with her grey wiry all-weather coat. Not as energetic as she once was, she still loved the outdoors and her daily walks into the forest. She had hunted boar and pheasant in her youth and was Otto's constant companion. She never left his side for a moment, no matter what work he was doing on the farm.

Otto knew this forest like the back of his hand. He had played in the woods with his friends as children, hunted wild boar with his father and made love to Hanna the very first time. He made a point of carrying his rifle whenever he was in the forest. It was an old bolt-action 7.92 mm *Mauser Gewehr* 98, the same rifle he had carried in the Great War. He had heard stories of the forests being full of escaped prisoners from the east, who brutally killed any Germans they found. Other stories talked about British commandos who had been hiding in Germany's forests for years, attacking the local population. Then there were the thousands of British airmen shot down by the Luftwaffe, who were reportedly equally violent and desperate.

Otto Gregori did not believe a word of these rumours. He had never seen any sign of footprints in the forest that he had not seen before … *still it was better to take precautions*. Otto had hidden a wire henhouse in the forest to keep his chickens away from the thieves and autocrats in the town. The Bürgermeister was a devout Nazi who paraded around the town in his ridiculous uniform, followed by his two thugs. They would patrol from farm to farm making sure that all surplus produce was sold to the State. Nothing could be stored without permission.

Berta went rigid, her head pointed forward, one paw poised, tail outstretched in the classic gundog posture.

'Is it a boar girl?' whispered Otto, scanning the brush ahead.

As he approached the henhouse, which was hidden in thick undergrowth, he stopped suddenly. There was a distinctive smell of cigarette smoke in the air … *strange this deep in the forest*. Otto did not carry his rifle with a round in the chamber. He knelt down, eased the bolt out of its position, and rammed a round out of the five-round magazine into the chamber. The sound of the loud click was impossible to disguise.

He waited ... gently moving his head from side to side to listen for any noise, as he would if he were hunting boar. The dog took a few careful steps forward, remaining perfectly silent as her instinct told her.

Otto was not sure what to do ... the thought of retreating down the path crossed his mind. The cigarette smoke may mean that someone had found his chickens. He decided to push forward, reaching down to hold the dog's collar.

A chicken squawked loudly ... *there is somebody in the henhouse!*

Rushing forward, his rifle at the ready Otto burst through the thick undergrowth, a man was standing in the middle of the henhouse, a chicken held under his arm.

'Halt!' ... shouted Otto, lifting his rifle.

The man turned around. As Otto got closer, he could see it was one of the Bürgermeister's bullies.

He was a huge man in his mid-forties who went by the name of Drexler; he wore the uniform of a *Scharführer* or squad leader in the *Sturmabteilung* (SA). Drexler had been a wrestler in his youth, and his lack of intellect and penchant for violence made him a perfect SA enforcer.

'Ah, Herr Gregori, it seems that you have been keeping a little secret!' called out Drexler on the top of his sneering voice. He was wearing the standard brown coat worn over the basic brown shirt uniform and kepi cap. A 9mm Luger pistol hung in a holster at his waist.

'Put that chicken down!' demanded Otto.

'You have been hoarding food, Herr Gregori ... you know that is against the law. But I am sure we can reach some sort of arrangement,' laughed the thug, holding the chicken by the legs, swinging it in front of him.

'What arrangement?' demanded Otto, still covering the man with his rifle.

'You pay me a few Reichsmark to stay quiet and you supply me with hens and eggs ... or ... you can have a discussion with the Gestapo. Which will it be Herr Gregori?' smiled Drexler, his face twisted in a sinister smirk, he was enjoying himself.

'Put the chicken down ... I am not going to ask you again,' demanded Otto, feeling his temper rising, he hated these Nazi pigs with all his being. They were destroying his country and all he held dear.

Drexler ignored him completely, opening the wire-mesh gate to the henhouse, still holding the chicken in his free hand.

'Maybe we should include one night a week with the fetching Hanna. She is still a good-looking woman ...' retorted Drexler, now unhappy with the demands of this farming peasant, who clearly did not know his place.

This threat, Otto knew was not an idle one. These pigs had been raping women in the village for years with total impunity. They prayed on the women who had husbands and boyfriends in the army, they were at home helpless and unprotected.

Something snapped in Otto's brain, he fired a shot at the feet of the SA thug. The rifle rang out through the forest, like a thunderclap in the silence. Drexler blinked in shock ... trying to comprehend what had just happened. He threw the chicken down and reached for the holster.

'Stop ... Stop or I will shoot!' shouted Otto, pumping another round into the chamber.

The SA man still ignored him ... he had the holster open ... lifting out the Luger ... cocking the weapon ...

'Stop!'

The Luger was coming up, Otto saw the man's hand shake slightly from the rush of adrenaline bursting in his brain. The dog barked and leapt forward, her teeth bared.

Diving into the brush, Otto rolled ... the first pistol shot rang out, burying the 9mm bullet in the tree behind where Otto had been standing. Another shot rang out as the big man corrected his aim.

Berta leapt at the man, growling loudly. He fended her off with his giant forearm swatting her away like a fly.

Otto rolled again, bringing the rifle up into his shoulder, taking aim in an instant, his survival instincts taking over ... the rifle bucked in his shoulder ... he saw the man stagger slightly ...

Flicking the bolt expertly the cartridge was ejected, another took its place ... BANG ... another round entered the man's chest knocking him over backwards against a tree ... sliding down.

Up on his feet, Otto raced forward is if ready to bayonet his victim. The man toppled onto his back, his feet kicking spasmodically, blood at his mouth, his eyes wide with shock. Otto kicked the pistol out of the quivering hand, holding the rifle inches from the man's nose.

'Die you bastard ... may you rot in hell!' hissed Otto, spit flying from his mouth ... all the pent up hate and frustration flowing out of him like a raging river ... unstoppable.

The man died … Otto staggered back, the enormity of what had just happened too terrible to contemplate … the face of his beloved Hanna flashed before his eyes. He slumped onto the ground next to his victim, his chest heaving from the trauma and exertion … the storm in his mind slowly abated leaving an empty feeling of fear and dread.

*

In the village of Schönberg, Hanna Gregori did not hear the gunshots in the forest. She was having coffee with her very excited friend, Frau Magda Neumeyer. Magda was delighted; her eldest daughter Angelika had just arrived from Berlin with the children. She had been praying that this day would come, when she could look after her grandchildren in the safety of the countryside.

Angelika was a tall beautiful young woman with long jet-black hair that hung over her shoulders. She sat on the settee with her youngest child on her knee. The other two were playing in the backyard climbing trees, screaming excitedly.

'It was terrible … I cannot describe the fear. The British *Terrorfliegers* hit Mariendorf on the twenty-sixth. Many houses were destroyed. They have been coming since November, sometimes night after night. The Americans come during the day … they can be seen for many kilometres stretched across the sky. It seems they cannot be stopped,' wept Angelika, tears running down her cheeks.

'Now … Now Ange,' said Magda soothingly. 'You are safe now. There is nothing for them to bomb here in the country. Magda stood up to take the baby from Angelika's arms. The young woman's voice was quavering with fear and shock.

'On the train we came through Leipzig … the railway station was in rubble as were all the surrounding streets. It is not only Berlin that has been attacked,' sobbed Angelika, wiping her eyes with a handkerchief. Her hands were visibly shaking.

'I am sure it is only a matter of time before the bombers are stopped. They say so on the radio,' said Magda comfortingly.

'If we lose the war, what will become of us?' pleaded Angelika. 'What will happen to the children?' She was distraught, her face awash in tears.

Magda's husband Fredrik was convinced the war could not be won … it was only a matter of time. This was not the moment to discuss his opinions with her daughter. Angelika's husband Gustav worked in some secret government department. Nobody in the family trusted him.

'What does Gustav say?' asked Hanna Gregori quietly.

'He says that there are new weapons that we will unleash on the British and that the Atlantic Wall built by Rommel will throw them back into the sea if they try to invade,' said Angelika.

'Well, there you go then ... there is nothing to worry about,' said Magda lightly, steeling a glance at her friend across the room.

'Yes Angelika, Gustav must know the truth. It will all sort itself out,' added Hanna supportively.

'But the bombers keep coming ... night after night ... why can't we stop them ... where is the Luftwaffe?' pleaded Angelika. It was clear to the older women that she was at the end of her tether. She was quaking with fear. It was dreadful to see her in this terrible state.

Hanna watched the traumatised girl ... *how many other women in German cities have been reduced to this ... she is a gibbering wreck!*

*

RAF Dunholme Lodge, Lincolnshire
Thursday 30 March 1944, 9:45am

The gates were shut, the public telephones disconnected and all personnel on RAF Dunholme Lodge confined to the base. All outgoing phone calls were blocked and those incoming were intercepted, cutting the station off from the outside world as preparations for the raid began.

In the A-Flight offices, Leading Aircraftswoman Linda Potter had a group of expectant pilots in front of her, all eager to get the most information possible on the coming night's raid.

'It's a maximum effort but we only have six serviceable aircraft so far in A-Flight,' said Potter looking up into the faces of the men surrounding her.

'Who's going?' asked one of the men.

Bill Carter stood back, he knew he had a serviceable aircraft plus he had just returned from a break.

'Squadron Leader Haworth, Carter, Pallister, Robinson, Charlesworth and Hughes. If more aircraft get through their night-flying test, more crews will be added,' replied Potter.

Under normal circumstances, the response by those excluded would have been disappointment; instead, there was palpable relief. Everyone was fully aware of the state of the moon ... *this operation was dicey!*

'How long is it going to be?' asked Pallister, the question on everyone's lips.

'I have been told, maximum fuel load, … so it's going to be about nine hours,' responded Potter. 'Those pilots, navigators and bomb aimers on the roster are to report for pre-briefing at three pm, main briefing at six pm. That's all I have gentlemen,' said Potter, going back to her file and the other piles of paper on her desk.

The airmen slowly shuffled out of the office, there was nothing to say. The atmosphere was suddenly tense everyone alone with his own thoughts … *I should write a letter home … I hope this is not my night for the chop* …

Bill Carter took some time checking over the status of his aircraft C-Charlie on Form 78, as reported by Ron Boswell. The ground crew were required to notify the flight office of any 'gremlins[113]' that may have crept into their aircraft. The sheet was clean; with Ron's careful handwriting reading, 'aircraft is fully serviceable'.

Potter looked up from her papers and saw that Carter was still in the office.

'Ah, Mister Carter, thank goodness you are still here. I have a note here from He-who-must-be-obeyed that you are to take a second-dicky[114] with you tonight, Mr Fullerton,' said Potter, holding up a hand scribbled note.

Not knowing what to think, Carter merely grunted an acknowledgement. It was another endorsement by Haworth of his ability. The recent memory of his flight with Fullerton sent a shiver down his spine … *I hope this bloke isn't jinxed.*

As Bill Carter walked over to the Officer's Mess for a cup of tea he saw George Armitage come out of the Met Office. When he saw Carter, he came hurrying across.

'Bill, have you heard? We have ops on tonight! Can you believe it?' he asked earnestly.

'Yes, I have just had the word from Potter, we are on the roster. What's the problem?' asked Carter, his mind a jumble of thoughts and emotions, as the enormity of another operation deep into Germany sank in.

'It's going to be like daylight up there tonight, there's a half-moon,' stated Armitage incredulously.

'What does Met say?' asked Carter, knowing that Armitage made it his business to study every aspect of the developing weather situation.

---

113 A mythical creature that lived on certain aircraft and caused it to go 'US' at the most inconvenient times and then remained well hidden so as not to be located as the source of the problem.

114 A training flight where an inexperienced operational pilot would go with an experienced pilot on a real op.

'A cold front has most of northern Germany clouded over. We won't be able to see a bloody thing,' lamented Armitage. 'I just can't believe it. Nobody saw this one coming. Met are more surprised than anyone.'

'Well, we may not be going to Germany,' replied Carter helpfully.

'With a full fuel load, where could we be going, Italy?' asked Armitage sensing that Carter may know more than he was letting on. 'With the moon we will be sitting ducks flying to Italy silhouetted against the snow covered Alps!'

'Not much we can do about it. We will just have to wait and see. Anyway, if its unfavourable, I am sure they will scrub,' added Carter, trying to put a positive view on the situation.

George Armitage was clearly unconvinced; shaking his head and muttering under his breath, ... *Penguins at HQ ... no bloody idea at all ... decisions based on duff gen!*

Looking up at the sky, Carter concluded that there was no chance of the sun appearing. The weather was cold, overcast and misty, with low hanging clouds and virtually no wind. The windsock on top of the control tower hung limply from its rope.

Out in the dispersal points there was a hive of activity as the ground crews tried to respond to the call for 'maximum effort'. The 2-6 call had gone out, the general base call 'down the flights' putting all personnel on duty. Men in overalls were dashing about on foot, on bicycles, driving vans madly around the perimeter track. Some aircraft looked like they had been attacked by a swarm of ants. Ladders were up against wings, wheeled scaffolding was pushed against engines and inspection hatches gaped open. Fitters, riggers, mechanics and electricians, each had their tasks to perform. All seemed to be talking at once. Engines were running-up across the airfield, adding to the din. The air was full of the smell of grease and 100-octane aviation spirit. It was all a mad scramble to get as many aircraft serviceable as possible. Inside the aircraft, the frenetic activity was confined to the cramped working space, hands flying between tools, loose wires and electrical equipment.

As Carter walked slowly across to the mess with Armitage, the air filled with sound as K-King raced down the runway on her night flying test. Other aircraft were in the circuit doing the same thing. Those aircraft that were already passed fit were being bombed up and refuelled.

All was shouting ... banging ... crashing ... pulsating activity ...

8 (Pathfinder Force) Group RAF HQ at Castle Hill House, St Mary Street, Huntingdon
Thursday 30 March 1944, 10:30am

While there may not have been a storm over Southern Europe, there was a storm brewing at 8 (Pathfinder Force) Group HQ at Castle Hill House.

Air Vice-Marshal Donald Bennett, AOC 8 (PFF) Group, was not happy. He had been called by Sandy Saundby to ask his opinion on the planned route for the attack on Nuremberg. His staff had plotted the route on his map and he did not like what he saw.

Bennett was a thin-lipped Australian from a farming family near Toowoomba in Queensland. He was accustomed to being about people who called 'a spade a spade'. He was possessed of an impatient, dictatorial and pedantic style of command that, while sometimes most effective, inevitably made him enemies. Bennett would have been described as a 'press-on type', with 10,000 hours, and an unstinting keenness to get the job done … to press on regardless. He famously said that there would only be posthumous VCs issued in the Pathfinder Force. A difficult and naturally aloof man, Bennett earned a great deal of respect from his crews but little affection. As Arthur Harris described him, 'he did not suffer fools gladly, and by his own high standards there were many fools'. His greatest detractor was Air Vice-Marshal Ralph Cochrane, who commanded 5 Group, a rival in pioneering marking techniques for the main bomber force.

With the exception of the New Zealander, Air Vice-Marshall Roderick Carr of 4 Group, Bennett did not get on well with the other RAF Group Commanders: not only was he 15 years younger, he was an Australian! Indeed, Bennett saw his own appointment in those terms: it was, he believed, a victory for the 'players' over the 'gentlemen'[115]. A player, in this case, was a professional airman, with a full command of all tactics and technical developments, which by definition, eluded the 'gentlemen'. Bennett tackled the complex and technical problems of intricate bombing tactics with great energy and

---

115   The Gentlemen v Players game was a cricket match that was generally played on an annual basis between one team consisting of amateurs (the Gentlemen) and one of professionals (the Players). The first two games took place in 1806 but the fixture was not revived until 1819. It was more or less annual thereafter till 1962 and there were usually two or more games each season. After 1962, the concept of amateurism was abolished and so all first-class players became, in theory at least, professional.

ability. He had a most unusual memory and could pick up a book on some highly technical subject and in a very short time understand the whole thing intimately. He was an intellectual and, as Harris said, 'being still a young man, had at times the young intellectual's habit of underrating experience and overrating knowledge'.

Bennett called his secretary to get Air Vice Marshall Saundby on the phone. It rang on the other side and was picked up almost immediately.

'Saundby here,' came the voice from the Bomber Command Deputy after being put through by his secretary.

'Sandy, Don here, I am calling about this route planning for tonight,' said Bennett earnestly.

'Yes ...'

'It's just not on ... this long leg is a real problem. We are dead against it,' stated Bennett flatly with his characteristic directness.

The route, as it had come down from HQ, had adopted a predominantly straight-in straight-out approach. The plan required the bomber force to thread its way between the defences of the Ruhr and Frankfurt after crossing the German border south of Aachen. This gap between the Ruhr and Frankfurt was known colloquially as the Cologne Gap. This so-labelled 'long leg' was 265miles long in a dead straight line. At the end of the long leg, the track turned 90° south to Nuremberg. It was very unusual to have a leg of the route to the target so long and straight, as it gave the enemy fighters an easier and longer opportunity to attack the bomber stream on a consistently straight heading.

'We estimate that it's only sixty-two minutes flying time, because of the forecast tail wind,' replied Saundby.

'Yes, but there is no margin for error. The route bisects the German OTTO and IDA fighter beacons and is very close to the Ruhr ... we estimate only twenty-seven miles,' said Bennett, biting his tongue ... *it is so bloody obvious!*

'The time from the Belgian coast to the turn for Nuremberg is only a hundred minutes Don. You have seen the predicted tail wind. Surely, speed through the defences is most important? In addition, there is forecast high cloud along the route,' replied Saundby, keeping his voice passive; he did not want to inflame the 8 Group commander who was often quick to anger and frustration.

'We have considered all those factors but we still think the risk is too high. We have prepared an alternative route to add a dogleg well south of Frankfurt and the Ruhr. This will confuse the Germans by adding at least another four major cities to their calculations and avoid those fighter beacons. Sandy, I cannot emphasise more strongly our concern. Will you consider our suggestions?' asked Bennett respectfully.

Eternally the diplomat, Saundby took the consultative track.

'Send your suggestions through and I will discuss them with the C-in-C and the other Group commanders,' replied Saundby, hedging his bets.

'That's not necessary Sandy,' blurted Bennett, his temper rising. 'Our job is to get the bombers to the target and mark it. We are the experts in navigation, surely our recommendations should carry the day?'

'Yes, there is no disputing your skills and experience Don, but I have to keep the others informed. We are all in this together after all,' interjected Saundby before the younger man could go any further.

There was a grunt on the line with a mumbled goodbye before the phone went dead.

Bennett was fuming mad, he knew that when Cochrane heard of his suggestion he would seek to block it. Bennett had made his opinion of Cochrane abundantly clear, *a disaster lacking in both experience and understanding of operational matters.* He picked up the phone to speak to his only supporter, other than Butch Harris, Roddy Carr at 4 Group.

*

Luftwaffe 3rd *Jagddivision* (Fighter) (3 JD 1) Division HQ, Deelen in Holland
Thursday 30 March 1944, 10:48am

It was as if someone flicked a light switch, from about 10:30am on Thursday morning the German radarscopes and radio monitoring stations lit up. The reports were flowing into 3 JD 1 thick and fast. The message was clear … the British were coming that night.

Generalmajor Walter Grabmann the commander of 3 JD 1, sat at his desk watching the activity in the Operations Room. He had studied the weather reports, he already knew the moon phases off by heart. It was a surprise to him and his staff that, despite the moon and adverse weather, *Tommi* seemed to be planning an attack. It was too early for the codeword for an attack, FASAN (pheasant), to be signalled to the fighter stations but it certainly looked likely.

The listening stations had reported a significant increase in traffic. While it was all in code, the volume, together with source and destination, frequently revealed preparations for a major raid. The

British did not know that the Germans had recovered and dissected one of their H2S ground scanning radars from a downed aircraft. As a result, equipment was installed on the German coastal radar sites that were capable of monitoring H2S transmissions, even while it was being tested on the ground at bomber stations.

All the radar stations along the coast of Holland were reporting increased H2S traffic as aircraft were being prepared for a mission. Grabmann had only one course of action. He lifted the receiver of the telephone on his desk and gave an instruction.

'Befehl an alle Staffeln! In Alarmbereitschat gehen![116]'

*

RAF Wyton, 58 miles due north of London
Thursday 30 March 1944, 11:06am

A De Havilland Mosquito P.R.XVI of 1409 (Meteorological) Flight, RAF Wyton, waited at the threshold of runway 09 for final clearance to take off. This was the photoreconnaissance version of the Mosquito, with cameras in the bomb bay and additional fuel. The aircraft had a pressurised cockpit with Merlin 70 series engines, capable of 422mph at 30,000ft, with a range of 2,050 miles, which allowed the aircraft to operate at will over all of Europe.

The two-man crew had been briefed to fly out over the North Sea to inspect the weather on the route planned for a diversionary mining force. These flights were code-named PAMPA (Photorecce And Meteorological Photography Aircraft). PAMPA flights were responsible for long-range weather reconnaissance sorties deep into enemy territory to ascertain conditions prior to planned Bomber Command raids. Unlike the regular synoptic flights of most met operations, PAMPA flights were dispatched at short notice to specific targets to establish the exact weather conditions just before a raid. The aircraft were unarmed and the navigator/observer was responsible for taking the photographs by hand or with belly-mounted cameras.

The aircraft taxied onto the runway. The pilot opened the twin Merlins to full take-off power and the aircraft effortlessly lifted off towards the east. They flew out over the North Sea, keeping a mostly easterly heading towards the tiny island of Heligoland off the northern Dutch coast. The island guarded the entrance to the great German port of Hamburg. The crew found broken cumulus cloud mostly 9,000ft increasing as they flew east, but a bank of thick cloud was encountered further to the north creating a high risk of icing. This

---

116 'Send a signal to all fighter groups to go on alert!'

meant that the diversionary force would need to leave early to avoid this cloudbank as it moved south.

The German radar station (*Stellung 1'ord*) code-name SALZHERING situated near the village of Kleine Sluis in North Holland had monitored the 1409 (Meteorological) Flight from the moment it reached an altitude of 1,000ft, along the entire route of its flight across the North Sea, carefully marking each course change. The information was sent through to 3 JD 1 at Deelen via the intelligence chain.

The experienced Generalmajor Walter Grabmann, the commander of 3 JD 1, took one look at the information and said, 'we have two possibilities, mining operations, or Hamburg. Alert fighter stations in the northern sector.'

What Grabmann did not say was that it was highly unlikely, with the 10/10ths cloud cover over north Germany, that Hamburg was the target. It was still too early to make a decision, but in his mind everything screamed ... *diversion!* As the English called them, *spoof* raids.

11

RAF Bomber Command HQ, Code Name 'Southdown', Walters Ash, Buckinghamshire, 4 miles northwest of High Wycombe
Thursday 30 March 1944, 11:45am

We are going to scourge the Third Reich from end to end. We are bombing Germany city by city and ever more terribly in order to make it impossible for her to go on with the war. That is our object, and we shall pursue it relentlessly.
AOC-in-C Bomber Command, Air Marshall Arthur Harris

The debate was over ... the strongly held opinions mitigated ... the plan was complete. AVM Saundby held the operational plan for the attack on Nuremberg in his hand. Since 11:30am, the teleprinter operators had been bashing out the plan and detailed instructions to the Group HQs spread around eastern England.

Nuremberg was not mentioned by name but instead by its codeword, *'Grayling'*[117]. The orders stated very specifically, 'to cause maximum damage at the Aiming Point'.

The plan included the so-called 'Long Leg' as originally proposed. All the other Group Commanders with the exception of AVM Roddy Carr had disagreed with AVM Bennett's objections. This was to be expected in light of the personality differences and the fact that the Canadian 6 Group Halifaxes wanted the shortest possible route as they had the longest distance to cover. AVM Carr, who also fielded Halifaxes, had deferred to the majority.

The final decision had been made by Arthur Harris himself after much consideration of the arguments raised by Bennett.

The consummate professional, Bennett swallowed his pride and got on with his planning. He had no sooner sat down at his desk than his phone began to ring. One after the other the 8 Group squadron and station commanders phoned in to query the route for the operation.

Wng/Co Geoffrey Womersley DSO, DFC, the commander of 139 (Jamaica) Squadron phoned from RAF Upwood. He was one of Bennett's most trusted and reliable commanders.

'Sir, did you know that this route for tonight goes within a few miles of one of those visual beacons used by the Germans to direct single-seat fighters?' asked Womersley politely.

'Yes,' was Bennett's measured response.

---

117 The code word for Nuremberg. Saundby was a keen fisherman, all German targets were named after fish.

'Can't we change the route Sir?' continued Womersley.

'No, I am afraid not,' replied Bennett, trying his best to remain calm at the obviously relevant question being asked by his commander. 'Southdown have made their decision … it's final I am afraid.'

'Well, can't we get some of those 100 Group Serrate Mosquitos out ahead of the stream to try shoot down a few Hun at these beacons … or at least disrupt them?' pressed Womersley, clear concern in his voice.

'That suggestion has been made but I am under the impression it has been turned down,' said Bennett, now very frustrated, trying his best to keep his voice under control. This was the third time he had to answer this question. 'The argument is that the spoof raids will be enough to divert and confuse the Germans before we arrive … there's nothing more to be said.'

The die was cast …

*

RAF Wyton, 58 miles due north of London
Thursday 30 March 1944, 12:19pm

At 12:20pm another Mosquito from 1409 (Meteorological) Flight took off from Wyton, this time directly towards the Dutch coast. Their operation was to check the entire route planned for the attack on Nuremberg including the weather over the target. The aircraft rapidly gained altitude, topping out at 25,000ft and accelerating to just over 400mph.

Once again, the radar network along the Dutch and Belgian coast picked up the aircraft streaking towards the mainland. There was no point scrambling an interceptor aircraft, as the Germans had nothing that could operate at high altitude at the speed of a Mosquito. They were powerless to prevent the aircraft's over-flight, but instead watched and recorded its every move.

The Mosquito crossed the Dutch coast just north of Leiden, continued on a course directly east, passing only 20 miles north of 3 JD 1 at Deelen to cross the German border near Osnabrück. The aircraft maintained a course along the line of the cold front coming down from Scandinavia, then began a wide circular loop to the south around the Ruhr, then out again over the Channel near Oostende in Belgium.

The crew found the weather much the same throughout its flight. Flying between 25,000ft and 30,000ft the Mosquito left a long streaking white vapour trail in the still clear air. Well below them, at no more than 10,000ft, they could see between 6/10ths and 8/10ths of cumulus-humilis[118] cloud. As the Mosquito turned for home, the crew studied the weather over Nuremberg, 100miles away to the southeast. They could see large banks of what they thought was strato-cumulus[119] and some thinner cloud higher up. Other than this, no high cloud was observed.

---

118 *Cumulus humilis* is a puffy low to middle cloud with small vertical extent. In cold climates it occurs between 1,500ft - 10,000ft. If these clouds are present in the morning, it is a sign of an unstable atmosphere. Larger clouds and possibly thunderstorms could form throughout the day to cause storms in the afternoon or evening.
119 *Strato-cumulus* belongs to a class of clouds characterized by large dark, rounded masses, usually in groups, lines, or waves, at no more than 8,000ft. These clouds are often seen at either the front or tail end of worse weather, so may indicate storms to come.

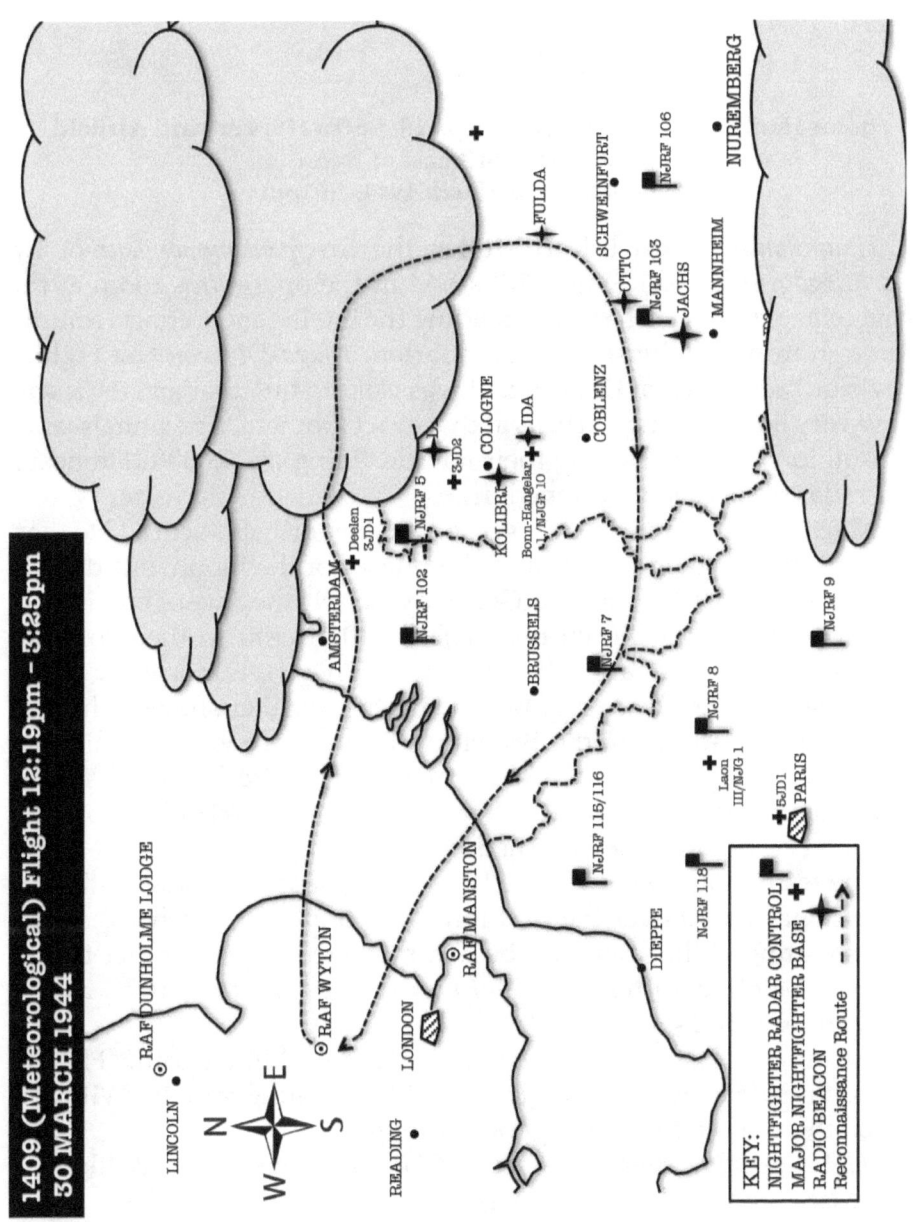

1409 (Meteorological) Flight 12:19pm - 3:25pm
30 MARCH 1944

KEY:
NIGHTFIGHTER RADAR CONTROL
MAJOR NIGHTFIGHTER BASE
RADIO BEACON
Reconnaissance Route

*

Bonn-Hangelar, 1. /*Nachtjagdgruppe 10*, Luftwaffe Forward Airfield,
3.8miles northeast of Bonn
Thursday 30 March 1944, 1:03pm

Hauptmann Friedrich-Karl Müller, the *Gruppenkommandeur* of 1./ *Nachtjagdgruppe* 10 (1./NJGr 10) stood in the operations room at the Hangelar air base. He had been reading the intelligence reports coming through from the divisional headquarters *1.Jagd-Division* (1st Fighter Division), stationed at Döberitz. It was clear to him that an attack was now very likely, particularly as at that exact moment, a reconnaissance Mosquito was approaching their airfield flying at 25,000ft. He heard the radar reports being phoned in.

Nasen-Müller had a sixth sense for the British tactics. He had studied the weather reports and the phases of the moon, but despite the poor forecast for most of Germany he felt they were coming. In anticipation, he had flown his *Staffel* of 10 aircraft to their forward airfield at Hangelar earlier that morning. They were normally based at Werneuchen to the east of Berlin, but the weather showed that the chances of an attack by the British on Berlin were virtually nil and, therefore, a target in southern Germany was more likely. They had flown above 10/10ths cloud virtually the entire 311mile trip, only breaking cloud once they reached Hangelar.

The testing of the new FuG 217 *Neptun* (Neptune) radar had gone exceptionally well over the past few days, and after much screaming and shouting at the scientists, he had managed to get another two of his Fw190s fitted with it. His *Staffel* was made up of 6 Bf109G-2s and 4 Fw190 A-6/R11s.

Turning to his second in command Nasen-Müller said, 'Hans, I think it is safe to assume that *Tommi* will be visiting tonight. With this moon there should be some good hunting.'

'*Ja*, I agree. The moon will set at about one am so they are likely to come late,' replied Hans Zimmerman.

Village of Schönberg, Middle Franconia District, Bavaria, 10 miles (16.7km) northeast of Nuremberg
Thursday 30 March 1944, 1:30pm

There was a loud knock on the front door of the Gregori farmhouse. Frau Hanna Gregori was jolted out of her reverie by the persistent banging and walked through from the kitchen. She opened the door, which was not locked, and her breath caught in her throat. Standing in front of her were three men in uniform. One was the Bürgermeister in his brown SA uniform, with his henchman Becker standing behind him and a third man in a black uniform holding a leather satchel.

'Is Herr Gregori here?' sneered the Bürgermeister without any attempt at pleasantries. He was a short ugly man with a moustache similar to that worn by the Fuhrer. His face reminded Hanna of a pig, with a flat nose and little piggy eyes. In fact, his unflattering nickname amongst the community was *Schweinchen* or Piggy. His nickname described both his looks and his behaviour.

'What do you want?' spat Hanna. She had made her opinion of the ugly man very clear.

'That is no business of yours ... where is he?' insisted the Bürgermeister, pushing past Hanna into the living room. The other two men hesitated at the door.

She was a strong sturdy woman. Hanna stepped in front of him, her hands on her hips.

He lifted his hands, as if to move her out of his way.

'Don't raise your hands to me *Schweinchen!*' warned Hanna, losing her temper, instantly regretting calling him by his nickname.

The little man blinked, shocked at what she had called him. He knew of his derogatory name, but nobody had ever dared to call him that to his face.

'Who do you think you are ... pe ... peasant?' screamed the man. His face flushed red, his fists clenched; he looked as if he was about to spring up at her.

'What is this?' demanded Otto Gregori, marching into the room with Berta at his heel. The dog started a deep-throated growl.

'Ah, Herr Gregori,' said the Bürgermeister, his temper instantly in check. His voice took on a sinister timbre. 'I have Herr Kalb with me from the Ministry of Food and Agriculture. He has a few questions for you.'

The Bürgermeister gestured to the man in the black uniform standing at the door to enter. The man wore a heavy overcoat that looked two sizes too big for him. He had a thin pointy face, a little like a rat. His nose seemed to twitch when he spoke. The man stepped forward shyly.

'Herr Gregori, I am sorry for the intrusion, but it seems your quota for the supply of eggs and chickens has dropped,' whispered the man apologetically, clearly embarrassed by the behaviour of the Bürgermeister.

'We have had a harsh winter,' replied Otto dismissively. Having these people in his house disgusted him.

'Yes, that is true but your production has dropped more than the average. As you know, we have been issued a directive by Herr Herbert Backe, the Minister of Food and Agriculture, to check on these circumstances,' replied the rat-faced man, more confidently. His eyes scanned the room and his nose twitched as if smelling for eggs and chickens.

'So what?' asked Otto contemptuously.

The Bürgermeister leapt in. 'You must come with us for questioning Gregori,' smirked the little man officiously. A sick, menacing grin spread across his face.

'Under whose authority?' shouted Hanna, starting to get very upset.

'Under the authority of the Ministry of Food and Agriculture,' said Kalb. 'I have an order here to investigate this matter.'

He undid the flap on his satchel and took out a single piece of paper with the crest of the German government on top. Handing it to Otto, he pointed to the part requiring 'investigation'.

'Please will you come with us Herr Gregori? We will not take up much of your time,' said Kalb disarmingly.

'He will not go!' demanded Hanna.

'It's all right, my dear. I will go with these *Schreibtischtater*[120],' said Otto, putting his hand on her shoulder. Hanna wanted to cry but she refused to give these animals the satisfaction.

Otto took his coat from behind the door and the men stepped out into a light drizzle. A black Mercedes Benz was parked in the road.

'Have you seen Drexler today?' asked the Bürgermeister disarmingly as they walked to the car.

The question hit Otto in the chest like a hammer. He flushed involuntarily.

'No.'

'We sent him into the forest this morning. There have been reports

---

120 Writing desk operator. Derogatory term for civil servants.

of farmers hiding food. We sent him to investigate. You know nothing of this?' enquired the Bürgermeister as they reached the car. The question could not have been more pointed.

'No … Nothing,' replied Otto, keeping his voice even, taking the back seat of the car.

His mind raced through the events of the morning. Drexler's body had been too heavy to carry so Otto had dragged it as far as he could away from the henhouse, then covered it with leaves and branches. He planned to return with a shovel to bury the body properly. Suddenly visions of stormtroopers with sniffer dogs scouring the forest entered his mind. The thought made him shiver in fear …

*

RAF Dunholme Lodge, Lincolnshire
Thursday 30 March 1944, 3:00pm

The navigators, bomb aimers and pilots of the thirteen serviceable 44 Sqn aircraft stood outside the door of the briefing room waiting to be called in. Bill Carter had asked his second-dicky, PO Ian Fullerton, to join them at the pre-briefing. As this was his first operational operation, it was important that he saw the whole thing unfolding.

Earlier, Carter had taken a stroll across the half-mile to the pan where C-Charlie, Cocky Lobin, was being prepared by the ground crew. Corporal Ron Boswell had greeted him with his usual friendly smile.

'How about a cup of tea Mister Carter?' Ron had asked. Waving at the Naafi truck as it trundled past.

Cocky Lobin stood with the bomb bay doors hanging open waiting for her load of 'taters'.

'Thanks Ron. What load are we taking tonight?' he asked as they strolled across to where the truck had stopped. Just as he asked the question, a tractor came bumping down the perimeter track with the bomb trailers in tow.

'As you can see Sir, it's a Cookie load[121],' replied Boswell pointing to the tractor as it stopped under the nose of the Lancaster. The tractor had been pulling 1 x 4,000lb impact-fused HC bomb, 2 x 1,000lb GP/HE bombs, and 4 SBCs (Small Bomb Containers) that held 24 30lb incendiary and explosive incendiary bomblets.

The two men took their mug of tea and walked back to where

---

121 The 4,000 pound bomb was called a Cookie. Taken together, this type of load was also called 'Plumduff'.

the ground crew were unhitching the trailers and pushing the large 4,000lb in under the centre of the bomb bay. The loading of the bombs had to be done in a fixed sequence with the heaviest bombs first. Once the bombs were winched into position and crutched, the fuses were connected.

Ron was holding the operation manual (Air Publication 2062A & C, Vol.1, Sec.4) in his hand. These held the instructions for calculating the aircraft centre of gravity (CG). The centre-of-gravity was crucial to the aircraft's stability in flight. To ensure the aircraft was safe to fly, the centre-of-gravity must fall within specified limits established by the manufacturer. As Cocky Lobin was new, with some additional equipment like the H2S bubble, the CG had to be calculated by taking the weight and location of all the equipment and the bomb load. As this was the aircraft's first operation fully loaded, Ron had to do the whole procedure from scratch using tables that specified the weight of each piece of equipment. It was a job he hated with a passion.

'Do you want me to give you a hand with that Ron?' asked Carter seeing the look on Boswell's face.

'Ah, that would be appreciated … thank you Sir. Here are the tables I will call out the equipment list, you just write in the weight on this chart and we will add it up afterwards,' replied Boswell delightedly, with obvious relief, this was a tedious job.

The table had a column for Arm (ft.) Weight (lb.), distance from the datum point, and Moment (ft./lb.) force exerted. Carter had a vested interest in getting this calculation right, as flying a Lancaster with CG out of limits was almost impossible.

'You have got the upgraded version of the H2S Sir. That should help Mister Armitage to get you to the right spot,' commented Boswell as they walked under the wing to begin the CG calculation process.

'Good news Ron, every little bit helps,' replied Carter looking at the new blister underneath the fuselage behind the bomb bay.

The doors opened and the crews filed into the briefing room. There was some friendly banter between the navigators who had a sort of club camaraderie between them. It was their job to get the boys there and back … an awesome responsibility under the most difficult circumstances.

Standing on the stage at one end of the briefing room was Sqn/Ldr Garth Cowling the Department Head for Navigation on the squadron.

' Good afternoon Gentlemen … the target for tonight is Nuremberg …' he began.

The men sat in silence absorbing the enormity of the news …

*

RAF Wyton, 58 miles due north of London
Thursday 30 March 1944, 3:24pm

Crossing the threshold to runway 09 at RAF Wyton at 3:25pm, the PR Mosquito taxied rapidly towards dispersal. The engines had not been shut down before the navigator jumped out of the hatch and ran straight to the telephone at Flying Control. Dr. Spence at Bomber Command HQ, on the other side of the shared line, had been waiting for the call, watching the clock for the entire 3hrs of the flight.

The weather reports and the information provided by the Mosquito crew were now all in. It was up to Magnus Spence to deliver the final verdict …

12

The night shift at the M.A.N. factory in Frankenstrabe Nuremberg waited patiently in a long line outside the gate. The guards had their faces pushed up against the boundary wall that ran along Frankenstrabe. It was cold with a strong westerly breeze adding to the wind chill.

Aurek Dabrowski looked up into the grey sky; his mind was blank, as if numbed by anaesthetic. His body felt distant from him. He had long since given up trying to manage the emotional impact of his confinement and forced labour. His life now was purely mechanical, where every movement required a kind of anticipation … *lift my hand … hold the wrench … tighten the bolt* … everything done in slow motion. He, Heniek and Iwan had created an emotional bubble where mutual support was their only focus. Nothing else mattered, nobody else mattered!

When they had first been imprisoned, a Polish doctor had explained the German strategy of hunger; how the German's understood the absolute minimum number of calories required for a person to remain alive and work. The key, he had explained, was hydration. The water they were given to drink prevented their bodies shutting down completely, with death from low blood pressure and multiple organ failure. The plate of vegetable soup made with copious quantities of pig fat and a slice of black bread was the formula for keeping these men alive and working. The theory did not work with all people and body types. The doctor had long since died, as had countless others.

The German factory workers had trained the forced labourers to perform simple tasks as befitted their physical and mental state. Aurek, Heniek and Iwan were responsible for fitting and bolting on truck tyres. That was all they did, lifting large heavy truck tyres and bolting them on, day after day, for twelve hours at a time. Their other meal each day was a single slice of bread and water was served at the beginning of the shift to build up the tiny amount of energy that they could muster.

The foreman on the truck line was a kindly man who did his best to smuggle more food to the workers in his section. If it was not for this man, Aurek was convinced that he would have given up and died long before. This man, who went by the name of Herr Scholtz, offered the only glimmer of hope that there was still some humanity in this world. If Herr Scholtz had been caught, his punishment would have been severe, possibly imprisonment and torture.

Each of the heavy six wheeled trucks had a large steel toolbox or storage box under the chassis. This was where Herr Scholtz would hide the extra food. As the new shift arrived, the men would take turns slowly lifting the lid to these boxes while the guards were distracted so that they might take a bite out of what was there.

Herr Scholtz did not ever talk to the men other than to give instructions, which he did with many insults and profanities as a convincing display for the factory supervisor and the prison guards.

A siren blew loudly as the previous shift appeared on the other side of the gate. They were slowly counted out of the factory, each person's number ticked off a list. Then Aurek's shift was ordered to enter, their numbers were re-checked against a list by the guards on the gate. They were not known by their names but by the number stitched to the back of their coats.

'*Guten Abend Sie hässlich Polnische Schweine*[122],' shouted Herr Scholtz as Aurek and his friends arrived at their section of the production line.

Herr Scholtz blew a whistle for the production line to start ... the night of work began.

'*Nummer sechsundfünfzig, wenn Sie diese schrauben festziehen nicht Sie fühlen sich die peitsche*[123],' screamed Herr Scholtz at Aurek as he picked up the torque wrench.

*

RAF Bomber Command HQ, Code Name 'Southdown', Walters Ash, Buckinghamshire, 4 miles northwest of High Wycombe
Thursday 30 March 1944, 04:05pm

... when I look round to see how we can win the war I see that there is only one sure path . . . and that is absolutely devastating, exterminating attack by very heavy bombers from this country upon the Nazi homeland. We must be able to overwhelm them by this means, without which I do not see a way through.
British Prime Minister Winston Churchill in a letter to Minister of Aircraft Production Lord Beaverbrook, July 1940.

Magnus Spence had studied the weather reports carefully. He had spoken to members of his staff and they too had confirmed his

---

122 Good evening you ugly Polish pigs.
123 Number Fifty-six, if you don't tighten those bolts properly you will feel the whip.

conclusions. The results of the second 1409 (Meteorological) Mosquito flight were of the utmost importance. It was now clear to Spence that the outward flight in the bright moonlight had little chance of cloud cover. Added to this, it now appeared that the target at Nuremberg was going to be obscured by cloud.

The main source of redemption on an otherwise irredeemable operation appeared to have been lost.

Spence walked across to his Waaf typist and handed her his handwritten forecast. It was only two lines long.

Nuremberg: Large amount of strato-cumulus with tops to about 8,000ft and risk of some patchy cloud at about 15,000 to 16,000ft.

At 4:40pm, this short note was handed to AVM Robert 'Sandy' Saundby. He read it, then turned to his Intelligence Officer, Wng/Co Felix Fawssett.

'Well, that should be that then, the target will be clouded in, looks like the operation will be scrubbed,' said Saundby with a look of relief on his face. It was a 50:50 decision, but on balance, the circumstances were unfavourable. 'I will take this through to the C-in-C.'

Leaving his office, Saundby walked down the passage to Arthur Harris' office. The door was closed and Harris's secretary Section Officer Peggy Wherry was at her desk.

'Peggy, this is the final weather forecast for tonight. Can I see the C-in-C?' asked Saundby softly.

'He's on the phone to the Chief[124], its not going well I am afraid,' replied Peggy, tilting her head towards the door. The sound of Arthur Harris' raised voice could be heard through the door. 'He has placed a call to the Deputy Chief[125] as well … he is waiting on the line. It could be a while.'

'Well he needs to see this weather forecast for tonight as soon as possible, will you ensure he gets it?' said Saundby earnestly; he was not game to interrupt his boss when he was in full stride.

'Yes,' replied Peggy taking the single sheet of paper.

Turning on his heel, Saundby returned to his office. There was a small delegation waiting outside his office to discuss the new OBOE technology. His mind was soon in a very different place.

Peggy Wherry cast her eye down the few lines on the weather forecast for Nuremberg. There was no summary of the whole weather

---

124 Chief of Air Staff, Air Chief-Marshall Sir Charles Portal, Arthur Harris' direct report.
125 Deputy Chief of Air Staff (Operations), AVM Norman Bottomley.

or tactical situation and there was no stated recommendation or specific request for a decision, just a simple statement of fact.

Nuremberg: Large amount of strato-cumulus with tops to about 8,000ft and risk of some patchy cloud at about 15,000 to 16,000ft.

*

RAF Dunholme Lodge, Lincolnshire
Thursday 30 March 1944, 6:00pm

The crews for the raid on Nuremberg were assembled in the briefing room. A total of 114 men were rostered to fly that night, including a few apprehensive second-dickys on their first flight. Men were smoking heavily, making the room stink of a combination of stale smoke and nervous humanity.

Every man in the room had his own fears ... his own worst nightmare.

Charles Morley sat chewing on his pipe next to his Skipper in the second row of folding chairs. He had a gippy tummy with a feeling of impending doom ... There was nothing new in this feeling; he had lived with it for over a year on every operation. It was as if his stomach knew an operation was on ... bringing on the trots and the shivers. He studied the faces of the men around him, as he would schoolboys waiting for the beginning of an exam. The difference was, while these men were not much older than schoolboys, they had a common 'mask of age' about them. They shared a pale, almost translucent pallor accentuated by hollows in their cheeks and black rings beneath their eyes. When sitting down in the mess they all seemed to assume a similar posture, lolling listlessly in chairs, unable to concentrate on more than a dozen lines in a newspaper at a time.

Charles Morley, like so many others, was in his own, very personal hell ...

The thought that haunted Morley most, was the fear of being blinded. He had recurring nightmares of being hit by flak in the eyes.

How can I teach if I am blind?

The worst thing would be that he could no longer read.

If I lost a leg or an arm, I could still teach ... couldn't I?

He had decided that if it happened, he would try to open the escape hatch in the nose and drop out for a quick death rather than spend the rest of his life blind. All those beautiful things that he would no longer be able to see ... *doesn't bear thinking about ...*

Frank Nellyer had confided in Morley about his dread of being

209

burned. The recent experience where his hands had been burned by the magnesium flare had created an even greater fear. Frank had seen the faces of men disfigured by burns in the hospital in Lincoln where the nurse sent him. Their smiles were twisted, swollen lips, raw-scarred skin, gimlet eyes, stumps of ears. Morley had done his best to reassure the young man, but there was no getting away from it … horrible burn injuries were a real possibility.

A large table, littered with writing pads, maps and radio scheds, separated each row of chairs. Carter sat in exactly the same spot for each main briefing; it was part of his own mental preparation. That seat had got him through 15 operations, it should get him through another 15. There was a general hubbub as the men talked to each other and laughed at a few jokes flying around.

The men had all eaten the pre-operation meal, the reliable and dependable bacon and eggs.

Carter found it difficult to be light-hearted and jovial before an operation, he preferred to sit quietly on his own. Dave Muir was quite the opposite. He continued to jabber away to anyone who would listen. He was at present in PO Fullerton's ear about Tsetse flies.

George Armitage was slowly flicking through his notes from the pre-briefing and he had his map spread on the table in front of him. He was a picture of concentration.

Tommy Potts was talking earnestly to Frank Nellyer about a girl he had met in Scotland. Frank in turn was talking about the girl he met at the post office. The two gunners were not required to concentrate too hard in a briefing; their job was all about vigilance on the job.

Eric Biddle sat leaning back in his chair, hands in his pockets, a cigarette trapped between his lips, studying the ceiling. His blank writing pad was in front of him, a pencil lying across it. He closed his eyes to think about a girl he had met while on leave in Preston … *I must write her a letter*. She lived with her parents three doors down, she had always seemed too young, he had never really noticed her before … *Judith … what a lovely name … Judith.* They had a pint together down at the Horse and Farrier, 'Scragg's', in Kilshaw Street. The thought of getting married had never crossed his mind … *there's never been anybody … maybe Judith? … just maybe …*

The Squadron Adjutant, Flt/Lt Walter 'Dicky' Bird entered the briefing room through a side door.

'Attention!' he shouted.

The men stood briskly to their feet as Wingco 'Stuffy' Thompson walked purposefully into the room flanked by his two flight commanders. It was Sqn/Ldr 'Pecker' Haworth's turn to be the Briefing Officer; they took it in turns between himself and the B-Flight commander, Sqn/Ldr 'Chalky' White.

As Carter watched, Jill Evans slipped into the room through the side door and sat down in a spare chair. He tried to catch her eye, but she sat perfectly straight concentrating on the officers on the stage. She crossed her legs revealing an exquisitely stockinged calf. Carter stared at her, willing her to turn around, taking in every detail, the whole episode in London was still a dream … *please look up.*

All the officers on the stage sat down except for Thompson who stepped forward. He picked up a billiard cue leaning against the lectern and turned towards the curtained wall behind him. He waved at two Waafs standing by and they pulled the curtains open to reveal a large map of Europe, with a bright red piece of string strung across it marking the track to and from the target.

'Jeeezus!' someone exclaimed loudly.

There was a general intake of breath as the significance of the planned route sunk in.

Thompson turned solemnly to his audience and spoke loudly and clearly.

'Gentlemen, your target tonight is Nuremberg on the river Pegnitz, some ninety miles to the north of Munich. Very shortly, Bomber Command will be called upon to support the invasion of Europe and the C-in-C is anxious to strike at one last major target before this happens. It is a target he knows is very dear to Prime Minister Churchill's heart. Now you'll have an opportunity to dissuade the Nazis from holding further mass rallies in the city most favoured for these,' said Thompson in his firm schoolmasterly fashion. 'I call upon Squadron Leader Haworth to manage the detailed briefing.'

Haworth stood to his feet and walked briskly across the platform to his commanding officer, taking the billiard cue offered to him.

'Good evening to you chaps … As a military target, Nuremberg is an important industrial city with a population of 350,000, a little larger than Leeds, and a centre for general and electrical engineering.'

Haworth waved the billiard cue over a detailed map of Nuremburg next to the map of Europe behind him and continued, 'As you can see, the target area is roughly the shape of an axe.'

'Yes! Chop! Chop!' shouted some wag from the back of the room to a terrific roar of laughter.

Haworth smiled at the sick joke, waving his hand for the men to be quiet.

'Alright chaps … settle down … let's get on … The city is home to the famous M.A.N. works that produce armaments of all kinds, and, since their large factory in Berlin was bombed, the Siemens plant in Nuremberg has stepped up production of its electric motors, searchlights and firing devices for mines. Nuremberg deserves a maximum effort and that is what it will now get. Ten squadrons in No. 1 Group, eight squadrons from No. 3 Group, seven squadrons from No. 4, twelve from us, nine from No. 6 and 12 squadrons from No. 8 Pathfinder Force will participate. Altogether 820 Lancasters and Halifaxes will take part. In addition, 15 Mosquitoes will adopt an intruder role to seek out nightfighters and destroy them. So, you'll have plenty of company, and it means everyone must keep a good look-out at the turning points to avoid collisions,' announced Haworth boldly and confidently. His voice was calm and professional but with the inimitable hint of excitement. As he scanned the faces in front of him, it was possible to hear a pin drop.

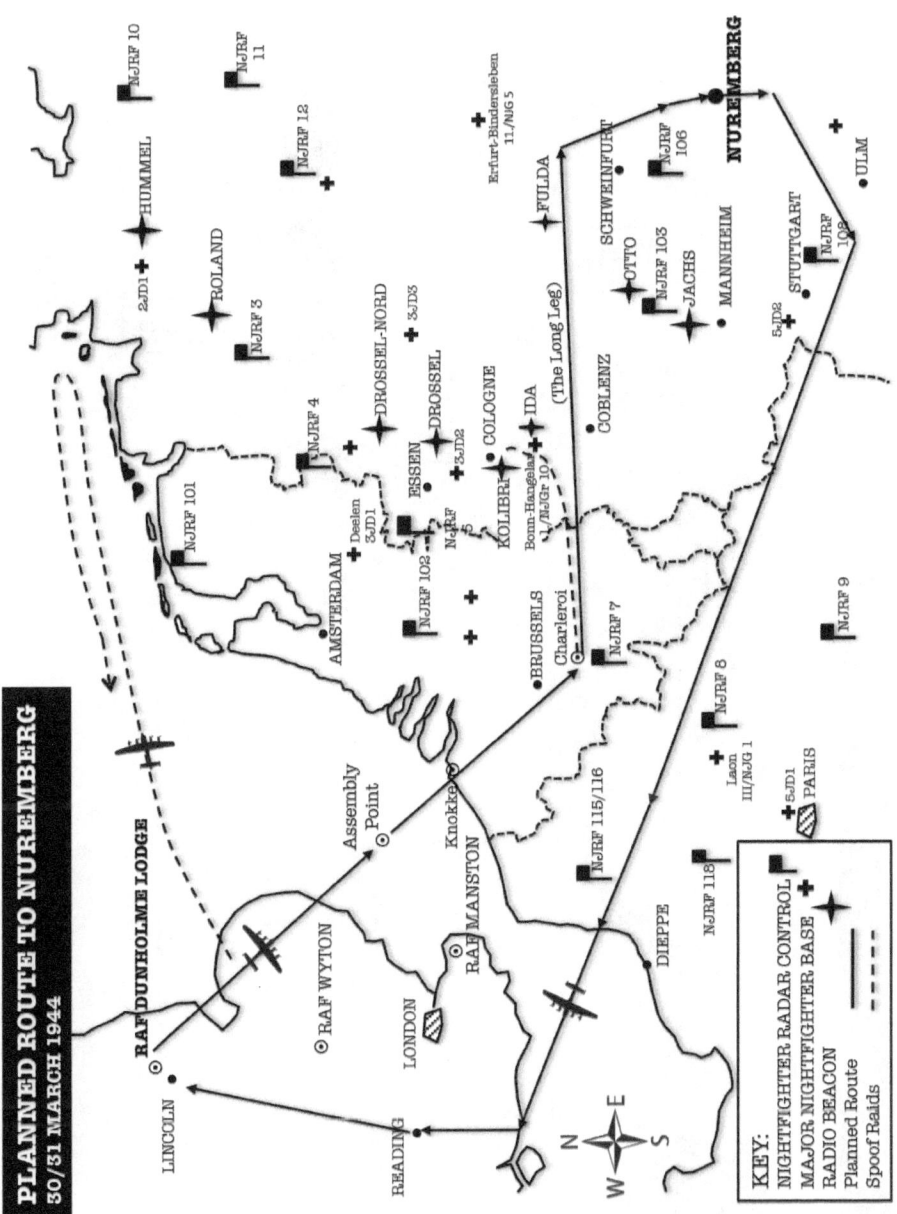

PLANNED ROUTE TO NUREMBERG
30/31 MARCH 1944

KEY:
NIGHTFIGHTER RADAR CONTROL
MAJOR NIGHTFIGHTER BASE
RADIO BEACON
Planned Route
Spoof Raids

NjRF 10
NjRF 11
NjRF 12
HUMMEL
2JD1
ROLAND
NjRF 3
DROSSEL-NORD
5JD5
DROSSEL
NjRF 4
ESSEN
5JD1
NjRF 5
Deelen
NjRF 101
NjRF 102
AMSTERDAM
COLOGNE
KOLIBRI
Bonn-Hangelar
III/NjGr 101
5JD2
IDA
(The Long Leg)
BRUSSELS
Charleroi
NjRF 7
COBLENZ
Erfurt-Bindersleben
11/NrG 5
FULDA
SCHWEINFURT
NjRF 106
NUREMBERG
OTTO
NjRF 103
JACHS
MANNHEIM
5JD8
STUTTGART
NjRF 108
ULM
NjRF 9
NjRF 8
Laon
III/NjG 1
5JD1
PARIS
NjRF 115/116
DIEPPE
NjRF 118
Knokke
Assembly Point
RAF MANSTON
RAF WYTON
LONDON
RAF DUNHOLME LODGE
LINCOLN
READING
N
E
S
W

City of Nuremberg – Attack 30/31 March 1944

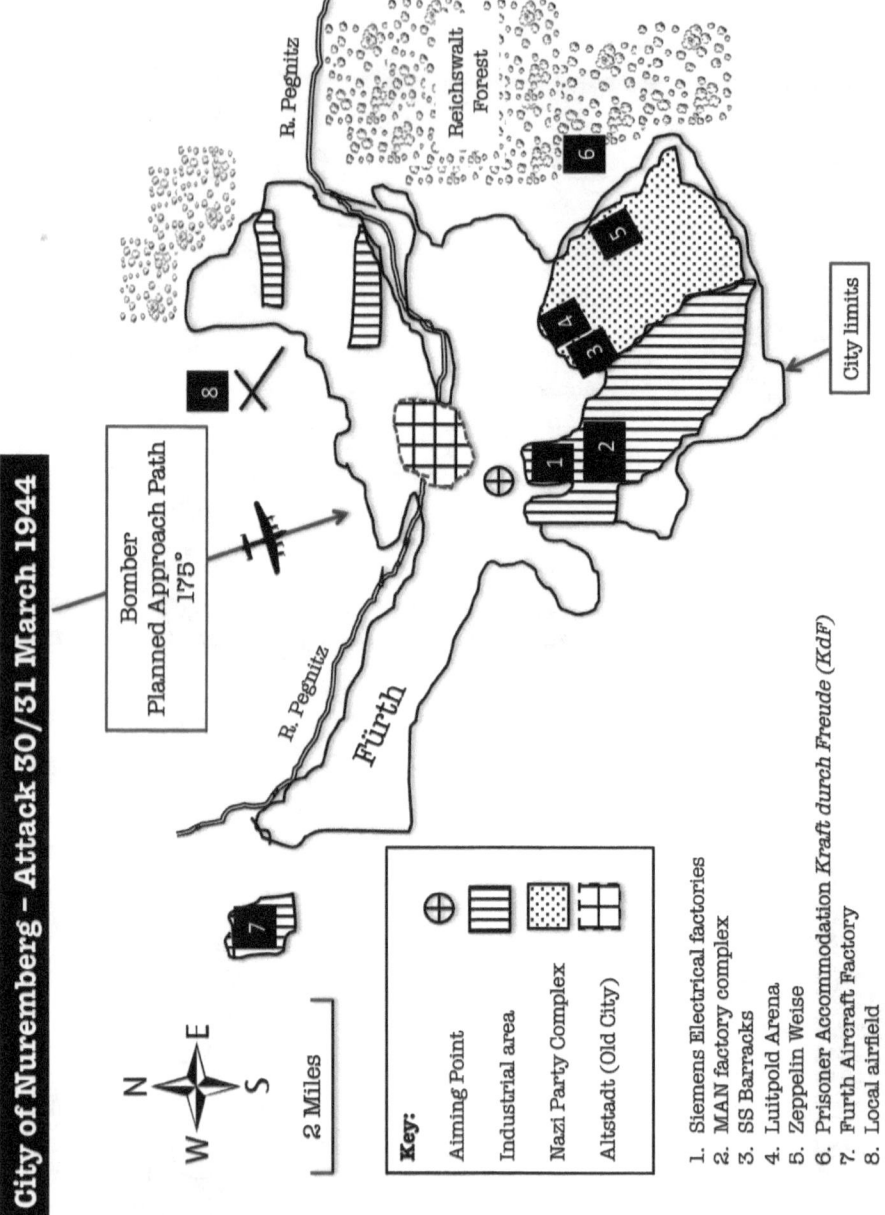

Bomber
Planned Approach Path
175°

R. Pegnitz

Reichswalt
Forest

City limits

R. Pegnitz

Fürth

N
W — E
S

2 Miles

Key:

⊕ Aiming Point

▤ Industrial area

▨ Nazi Party Complex

⊞ Altstadt (Old City)

1. Siemens Electrical factories
2. MAN factory complex
3. SS Barracks
4. Luitpold Arena
5. Zeppelin Weise
6. Prisoner Accommodation *Kraft durch Freude (KdF)*
7. Furth Aircraft Factory
8. Local airfield

Haworth continued in the same clear confident voice, 'You have six tanks of petrol, altogether 2,154 gallons, more than sufficient for the trip tonight which all up is approximately 1,580 miles including our climb out. Take-off time is 21:47hrs for us. If all goes well we should all be arriving home starting at approximately 05:40hrs ... just in time for breakfast. H-hour is 01:05 through to 01:22, seventeen minutes. After the PFF have marked the target, the main force will bomb from H-hour+5 minutes for the remaining 12 minutes. Our time on target is set for H-hour + 8 minutes between the band of 20,000 to 20,500 feet. Don't get out of this height band or you will run into other aircraft. Wing Commander Thompson will be first to take-off, followed by A-Flight and then B-Flight.'

Bill Carter rechecked his rough workings ... *seven hours and fifty-two minutes flying time.*

The audience of men made some whispered comments to each other; there were some shrugging of shoulders and a few weak smiles.

'I now call upon Squadron Leader Cowling to address you on navigation,' finished Haworth, passing the snooker cue to Garth Cowling, the squadron head of navigation, who stepped forward.

Cowling cleared his throat. He was always nervous giving briefings and it showed with his hesitant delivery.

'Navigators have already been briefed and have prepared their charts. You will climb to 10,000 feet before setting course across country on the first leg to the Assembly Point. You will set your standard climb rate of 100ft per minute and fly with navigation lights on to the Assembly point at 51° 50′ North 2° 30′ East. Please keep a very sharp lookout at this point, captains and gunners.'

Cowling marked the point he was referring to with the billiard cue, tracing the route to the point along the red piece of string. The cue ended at a point marked with a flag in the North Sea equidistant between the Continent and Britain. This was the Assembly Point.

'At the Assembly Point you will start a steady climb, switching off all lights when the turn is completed on to your south-easterly course of 130°. The Belgian Coast will be crossed at 15,000 feet just to the north of Knokke-Heist to the next turning point at 50° 30′ North 4°36′ East, just short of Charleroi; there you will alter course to port, gradually climb to your bombing height of 20,000ft and reach your last turning point at Fulda, 50° 32′ North 10° 36′ East ... and then on to the target.'

There was a grumbling murmur from the audience as the significance of the Long Leg sank in. George Armitage already had a heated discussion with Cowling on this exact subject during the pre-briefing.

Cowling barrelled on, '… after leaving the target, continue for a short distance to 49° North 11° 5′ East; then to 48° 30′ North 9° 20′ East and on to 50° North 3° East to cross the French coast at 50° 40′ North 2° East, at a height of 4,000 feet.'

This was information the navigators already had so there were no questions. That did not stop a few loud grumbles from the others.

'Indicated air speeds will be 172mph to the Assembly Point. Then climbing at 150mph across the Belgian coast to the next turning point where airspeed will be increased to 162mph and held to the target. If it is necessary to make a second run on the target, orbit left to avoid others in the main force coming up behind you.'

William Carter was checking his notes as the navigation officer was speaking, thinking through the speed changes and fuel consumption … *estimated 1,700gallons … 400gallon buffer … one and a half hours flying time.* The prospect of not finding the target, having to turn to go around through the flak again, sent a tremor down his spine.

'On leaving the target, increase speed to 182mph and hold this, gradually losing height to cross the coast at 4,000 ft. Corrected winds will be broadcast to the main force every half hour between 23:40 and 03:40. Are there any questions?' asked Cowling hoping that there wouldn't be any.

George Armitage thought about making a scene about the Long Leg but decided against it … there was no point … *ours is not to reason why … ours is but to do and die …*

'Very well then, Squadron Leader Lund, would you like to take us through the bombing information?' asked Haworth, as Cowling returned to his seat.

Mark 'Shorty' Lund took his place at the lectern. He was a very tall slim man with a thin moustache who came from the tiny town of Emerald in central Queensland. Carter had always liked Shorty Lund; they had had many a beer together in the mess. Lund had a strong booming voice with the characteristic Australian accent.

'Your all-up weight tonight is just short of 65,000lbs. Bomb load is just over 7,000 pounds with high explosive loads as stipulated by Group. The purpose is to cause maximum damage to the Aiming Point which is just south of the Old City, in a railway yard.'

Lund pointed to the more detailed map of Nuremberg next to the large map of Europe. The Aiming Point was marked with a red cross almost exactly in the middle of the built up area of the city, south of the Pegnitz River.

'If there is some creep-back[126] from the Aiming Point the wooden medieval buildings of the Old City will get some good fires going early. We will be in the first 25 miles of the bomber stream immediately behind the PFF force. Our high explosive loads are intended to intensify the marking. PFF will sky-mark the lane to the target with red flares that will change green after 120 seconds. At this time they will mark a point on the ground with yellow flares exactly 15 miles short of the Aiming Point. With the ground speed of estimated 245mph, this should give three and three-quarter minutes to get to the target. The red target indicator marker at the Aiming Point will go down at exactly H-Hour minus one. Depending on what cloud cover there may be, PFF will employ green sky flares if the target is obscured by cloud. As Met will tell you, we are not expecting much cloud over the target. PFF will continue marking the Aiming Point with red target illuminator markers from 01.09 to 01.22. Any questions so far?'

The men remained in silence; this was all very familiar for most of them.

'Met will tell you that a fairly stiff crosswind can be expected at the target, so bomb-aimers will need to be pretty snappy with their bombing and watch for creep-back! Make a good job of it, chaps. We don't want to go back again,' said Lund, taking a moment to scan the room for questions.

He continued, 'Right, bomb aimers, your instructions for window: one parcel a minute over the coast and up to the first turning point, over Charleroi in Belgium. At your next turning-point, at Fulda, release window at the rate of two parcels a minute for five minutes and at the rate of one a minute at designated points after leaving the target.'

Window was Charlie Morley's job on the flight. Carter leaned forward to see whether Morley was taking notes. Morley saw his Skipper and gave a weak smile and a thumb's up.

Once again Haworth got to his feet, 'Vernon, would you give us the Met report please.'

The Meteorological Officer, F/O Vernon Dalling, the youngest of all the staff officers stood up.

'At the line LW,' pointing to the chart, 'warm air is overtaking the cold air forming a warm front which is moving northward over NE Yorkshire and SW Scotland. The line LC marks a cold front now over Ireland and approaching the western side of England. It may lead to cumulo-nimbus, although we do not expect this to be continuous.

126 Bombers needed to avoid the tendency to 'creep-back' by dropping their bombs slightly too early and miss the vital areas.

What is forecast is broken, but fairly good, cloud cover for you all the way to the target and back, with some low cloud and precipitation in coastal areas. Winds over the Continent, moderate 40/50mph at 18,000ft, and generally blowing from SW or W. There may be some low cloud and poor visibility down to 2,000yds at base on return.'

Carter breathed a sigh of relief … *the weather report was all very positive. Despite the moon, we will have the benefit of high cloud to protect us from fighters.*

The Met Officer continued, '… To sum up then, for the outward flight, broken cloud can be expected everywhere except Southern Germany where it is expected to be layered. Winds WSW 40/50mph, veering WNW 50/60mph over target. May be some low cloud upon return but no fog is forecast. The usual wind updates will be transmitted by Group each half hour.'

Dalling returned to his seat and Haworth called the Squadron Intelligence Officer Sqn/Ldr Laurence Baxter to give his briefing. Baxter was Jill Evans' boss; Carter did not know him very well. He was a quiet aloof man in his mid-twenties, who had suffered a terrible leg injury in an aircraft crash during his training at an OTU. He walked with the help of a stick. He levered himself up off his seat, refusing a helping hand offered by Haworth, then shuffled painfully towards the lectern, his stick clicked loudly on the wooden platform.

Baxter reached the lectern and unfolded his notes that he had written in a school exercise book. He looked up at the sea of expectant faces and began his briefing.

'Well chaps, I don't have to tell you that the very direct nature of the route to the target tonight has been the subject of weighty discussion both here and at Group. The view has been expressed that the straight-in straight-out approach is too risky and should be broken up into different legs. Our C-in-C at 5 Group has supported the direct approach on the following grounds: one, that the distance involved precludes wasting time and fuel on too many doglegs; two, that the present route suggests a number of perhaps more vulnerable targets to the German defences, thus persuading them to disperse and thin-out fighter concentrations, three; that the sheer simplicity of this route will surprise the Germans and keep them off-balance long enough for you to complete the operation without too much trouble, and, finally, you will have a tail wind over the entire outward journey increasing your speed through the dangerous areas. I think you deserve this explanation and it may help to dispel any misgivings you have about the direct route as laid down.'

There was a shuffling of feet and a general murmured response from the men. It all made perfect sense … *nothing to worry about.*

Baxter shifted his weight on his feet; he was clearly in some pain.

'As a further encouragement, I can tell you that just ahead of you when you cross the coast, Mosquitoes will open the night's proceedings with low-level attacks on the known nightfighter fields in Holland at Leeuwarden, Twente, Deelen and Venlo in a bid to keep them on the ground until you're well past. At the same time, off Texel and the Heligoland Bight, a force of 50 Halifaxes will start dropping mines as a diversionary move to keep German ground controllers confused. In addition to this, and a while before the main force reaches the target, Mosquitoes will make a feint attack on Cologne between 23.55 and 7 minutes after midnight. A further force of twenty Mosquitoes will also drop fighter flares, markers and 'window' on Kassel between 26 and 28 minutes after midnight in an attempt to spoof the German controllers into believing the main attack is to be the Ruhr, and thus lead them to send the bulk of the fighters there.'

A man put his hand up. It was PO Gavin Pallister. Everyone turned to look at the man with a solitary hand in the air.

'Yes?' asked Baxter, pointing in Pallister's direction.

Pallister stood to his feet, he spoke out in a clear confident voice, 'I understand the thought behind the direct route that has been set, but why is it so close to the Ruhr defences, it is only a few miles.'

As Carter glanced up from his notes, he could see Jill Evans looking straight at him, her face expressionless except for her eyes that seemed to be trying to tell him something. He smiled at her … she immediately looked away.

Clearing his throat, Baxter took up the billiard cue leaning against the lectern and pointed at the map behind him.

'I agree the route takes you close to the southerly end of the heavily defended Ruhr area. So far as ground defences are concerned, we've tried to route you over areas both going and coming back where flak and searchlights are believed to be thin and the use of 'window' here will help to blur the picture from the ground. It goes without saying that much depends on your speed and the accuracy of your course-keeping, as well as your ability to maintain a well bunched-together pattern with no straying away from the main stream … Is that clear?' asked Baxter addressing Pallister.

Pallister waved his acceptance of Baxter's explanation, but in his heart, as with many others, the reality of navigating at night over hostile enemy territory was not always accurate.

219

Baxter nodded and continued, 'Nightfighters can as usual be expected, but with cloud-cover and the Mosquito attacks to keep them grounded, the danger from these, we believe, will be minimised. Keep a sharp lookout for them, however, and wireless operators with 'fishpond[127]', make sure it is working at all times.'

We don't have bloody fishpond on our aircraft, thought Carter.

There were not further questions for Baxter and he made his slow painful way back to his seat.

Stuffy Thompson stood up to give his last few words.

'Now, don't forget chaps,' he began, 'once you have reached the point marked by the PFF and the preliminary target indicator, you have three and three-quarter minutes to get to the target. The bearing will be 175° magnetic and you are to take no evasive action, but to keep straight on to the target. Once you have dropped your bombs, you may weave about slightly and gain speed by going into a gentle dive. The Pathfinders will drop a cluster of red and green flares 25 miles beyond Nuremberg, concentrate on these as you turn for home. Now don't forget, no straggling. Twist your tails a bit to keep an eye out for fighters coming up below … I think that is about all. Don't forget your landing discipline when you come in to base. I will see you down at the crew room before take-off.'

Thompson stood straight-backed … studying the faces of the men looking up at him …

'One final thing, navigators do not … I repeat do not … leave your H2S sets on for more than a few minutes at a time. We believe the new German radar can pick them up. Okay, let's go and give the Hun what for!'

The officers stood to leave, Jill slipped silently out the door.

There was not the usual noisy exit from the briefing room. In fact, other than the sound of shoes and the squeaking of chairs being pushed back on the wooden floor, there was very little noise at all. As the crews filed out of the room the station doctor was at the door handing out pills for staying awake, airsickness and anxiety. The so-called pep pills.

Carter studied the faces of his fellow pilots, particularly Pallister and Robinson; nothing much had to be said. Their expressions said it all. The more experienced crews had developed a far more sensitive collective 'nose' for the dangerous raids …

---

127 British fighter warning radar add-on to H2S, fitted in early 1944 to some bombers. It was designed to give early warning of night fighters approaching in the hemisphere below the carrying aircraft out to a range of 30 miles. Cocky Lobin had this modification.

They knew this was going to be a tough one ...

PO Fullerton, Carter's second-dicky for this operation made his way through the crowd of men pushing through the door of the briefing room.

'Is there anything I can do?' he asked Carter, the look of apprehension all over his face. The trauma of the check flight was still present.

'No ... we just have to wait until eight o'clock before we get kitted up and go out to the kite. I am going to have a lie down, maybe write a letter home. You should probably do the same,' smiled Carter, he remembered the terror and uncertainty of his own 'dicky' flights, being the spare-bod on an aircraft without a particular purpose, was unpleasant to say the least.

'What did you think of the briefing?' asked Fullerton.

'I am not sure quite what to think. The moon is my main worry. It will be like standing in the middle of a squash court up there if there is no high cloud cover. Anyway, there is no point worrying about it ... we're going and that's that,' replied Carter encouragingly, disguising his own feelings of nervous anticipation.

'Thanks for being so good about this. I know people don't like carrying second-dickys. I really appreciate it. I am very pleased that I will be flying with your crew ... My replacement gunners have still not arrived. God knows how long that will take,' added Fullerton. He needed to talk, to feel part of it.

'We all have to start somewhere, it's all part of our great adventure. It'll be fine, you'll see,' lied Carter trying to sound positive. The memories of his first dicky flight over Berlin on 2nd December 1943 still haunted him. They had to spray the inside of his aircraft out with hoses after the mid-upper gunner and wireless operator had been chopped to pieces by cannon shells.

The sun had set, the briefing had taken just over an hour. Bill Carter walked across to his Nissen hut. On his bed was a neatly folded clean towel and a hand written note. He picked it up to read.

Good luck tonight Sir ... I will be praying for you ... God Bless, Mrs Ethel Greaves.

**RAF Bomber Command HQ, Code Name 'Southdown', Walters Ash,
Buckinghamshire, 4 miles northwest of High Wycombe
Thursday 30 March 1944, 07:35pm**

*There are no words with which I can do justice to the aircrew who fought
under my command. There is no parallel in warfare to such courage and
determination in the face of danger over so prolonged a period, of danger
that at times was so great that scarcely one man in three could expect to
survive his tour of thirty operations... It was, furthermore, the courage of
the small hours, of men virtually alone, for at his battle station the airman is
virtually alone. It was the courage of men with long-drawn apprehensions
of daily 'going over the top'.*
AOC-in-C Bomber Command, Air Marshall Arthur Harris

'Blast, look at the time,' exclaimed AVM Robert Saundby looking at
his watch. He jumped to his feet and walked briskly down the passage
to the C-in-C's office. Peggy Wherry was just packing up her desk to
go home.

'Peggy, did the C-in-C look at that weather forecast?' asked
Saundby with urgency in his voice.

'Yes, I gave it to him at least an hour ago,' she replied.

The door to the office was still closed.

'Well, did he say anything? Did he leave any instructions?' pressed
Saundby, a slight feeling of uncertainty washed over him.

'No.'

'Is he still here, can I see him?'

'No I am afraid, he has left, he is entertaining some Americans at
his home this evening,' replied Peggy, now worried that she had done
the wrong thing.

'Are you absolutely sure he saw it? He definitely left no message
for me?' stressed Saundby, now feeling quite agitated.

'Is there a problem Sir? You didn't mention anything to me, you
just said to make sure he got it. I gave it to him in his hands, I watched
him read it,' replied Peggy, her face flushed with the concern that she
may have made a mistake.

'Yes quite right ... not to worry ... you have done what I asked,'
said Saundby, realising that Peggy was getting upset. 'Thank you ...
have a good evening ... I'll see you tomorrow.'

Saundby stood perfectly still, his mind racing ... *Surely this operation
should have been scrubbed? The target will be clouded over!*

Nuremberg: Large amount of strato-cumulus with tops to about 8,000ft and risk of some patchy cloud at about 15,000 to 16,000ft.

Robert Saundby walked slowly back to his office, the thought crossed his mind that he should phone Bert Harris at his home.

If Harris was entertaining that may be a bit of an intrusion. Peggy had said that Harris had read the forecast, he was aware of all the other conditions and circumstances, he had not left any instructions or asked any questions … he must be happy to continue with the raid.

It occurred to Saundby that there might have been some broader top-secret reason why the C-in-C had decided to continue. Harris did not share top-secret information, particularly concerning his talks with the Prime Minister.

There must be some political imperative … Nuremberg is the centre of Nazi power … Ah well … in for a penny, in for a pound!

The crucial mistake was that the weather report was not accompanied by a recommendation either by Spence or Saundby … they assumed that the C-in-C would have all the information present to his mind when he read the forecast … an incorrect assumption with horrific consequences.

The decisive updated weather information gathered by the PR Mosquito was never transmitted to the bomber stations …

*

RAF Dunholme Lodge, Lincolnshire
Thursday 30 March 1944, 8:30pm

Bill Carter stood in the A-Flight crew room in his full flying kit. The time had passed slowly, minutes seemed like hours. It was by far the worst part of the whole operation. At least when it came time to kit up, it gave him something to do. He had read and re-read his briefing notes and written a summarised operation profile on a single piece of paper that he would keep in his jacket pocket.

Summary of Bill Carter's Route Planning and Fuel Consumption to Nuremberg

AS PLANNED			DIS-TANCE	TIME		SPEED				ALTI-TUDE	FUEL BURN		
LEG	TURNING POINT	TRACK-TRUE (degrees)	LENGTH (miles)	TIME TO (mins:sees)	ETA (time)	Indicated Air-speed miles/hr	True Air-speed miles/hr	Wind Speed miles/hr	Ground Speed miles/hr	Height Indicated	Gallons/hr	Air miles/gal	Total Gallons
	Take-off				9:50:00								
	Gaining altitude		125	42:24	10:32:24	150	177	0	177	10,000	270	0.66	191
1st	Southwold	131	165	37:36	11:10:00	172	213	50	263	13,000	204	1.29	128
2nd	Assembly Point	134	49	11:30	11:21:30	172	217	40	257	14,000	204	1.26	39
3rd	Knokke-Heist	135	47	12:12	11:33:42	150	192	40	232	15,000	180	1.29	37
4th	Charleroi	135	82	20:24	11:54:06	150	201	40	241	18,000	180	1.34	61
5th	Long Leg (Fulda)	087	264	59:48	12:53:54	162	225	40	265	20,500	164	1.62	164
6th	Nuremberg	164	78	19:06	1:13:00	162	225	20	245	20,500	164	1.50	52
7th	Raitenbuch	179	31	7:00	1:20:00	182	244	20	2264	18,000	164	1.61	19
8th	Metzingen	247	87	26:48	1:46:48	182	240	-45	195	17,000	200	0.98	89

9th	Molslains	292	305	100:36	3:26:24	182	237	-55	182	16,000	200	0.91	335
10th	Rue	292	68	28:12	3:54:36	182	200	-55	145	6,000	196	0.74	92
11th	West Wittering	292	113	49:54	4:33:30	170	180	-30	150	4,000	196	0.69	163
12th	Reading	354	47	18:36	4:51:06	170	180	-30	150	4,000	196	0.77	61
13th	Home	09	129	51:18	**5:42:24**	150	159	-10	149	4,000	196	0.76	169
	Total miles	1,589		472:24						Average	203	0.99	1,600
	Total Time Hours				**7hrs 52 minutes**		Rule of Thumb check		(Overall Track miles + 200 gallons)				1,700

Carter's flying kit consisted of a C-type leather flying helmet, G-type oxygen mask, 41 pattern Mae West, observer type parachute harness, a leather sheepskin-lined Irving flying jacket made by Irving Air Chute of Great Britain, leather sheepskin-lined trousers over a battle dress tunic and trousers, long johns, a few pairs of socks, 43 pattern flying boots and a pair of lined leather gloves.

The gunners had to put on heavier, warmer gear, it was colder in their part of the aircraft.

Pockets were emptied of letters, bus tickets, cinema tickets and anything that could be of use to enemy intelligence in the event of being shot down. Carter noticed Tommy Potts slip his 'lucky' wishbone into his top pocket before he struggled into his thick, yellow, electrically heated suit. He caught Carter's eye with a shy grin on his face.

I hope it works! I mean, the wishbone.

The Waafs waiting outside the crew room had prepared flying rations of coffee, sandwiches, boiled sweets and chocolate. Next to their tables, chest-type parachute packs were piled ready for collection. The standard line was, 'If it doesn't work bring it back and I will exchange it for another.' Then there were the escape kits with sturdy, silk escape maps for the area they would be flying over.

With all the kit on, Carter felt a bit like Humpty-Dumpty ... *although he had no intention of having a great fall!* The thought made him smile to himself ... *all the King's horses and all the King's men would have to put me together again.* The strangest things entered the mind before an operation.

The one thing that he could not get out of his mind was his vision of Jill Evans in the flat in London, just the thought of her made his heart skip a beat and his face flush.

'Penny for your thoughts Skipper?' asked Charles Morley who was zipping up his flying jacket.

'Just thinking of home Charlie,' lied Carter, there was no way he was going to tell anyone about his evening with Jill. He had written a new farewell letter home to his parents in Bulawayo. He had tucked it into his clothing cupboard. If he were to be killed it would be collected with his other belongings and sent home ... *doesn't bear thinking about ...*

The letter he had spent most time over was to Jill Evans. He knew that there was probably no future with her, she was older than him for a start, but still the thought of her, her smell, the softness of her skin, her voice ... she filled his senses. He had taken ages over composing it, thinking about each word and her likely reaction ... trying to be light-hearted without sounding flippant, to be direct without sounding presumptuous. He cursed his lack of vocabulary. In the end, he was left thinking that Jill would laugh at his ridiculous attempt at describing his feelings ... his hopes ... his dreams. He had finished the letter and placed it in an envelope with Jill's name on it on his bedside table. As he stood waiting in the crew room, he was relieved that he had not sent it ... *she will think I am an immature schoolboy writing stupid love letters!* He cringed at the thought.

'Mister Carter, you have a visitor in the Orderly Room,' announced a young Waaf clerk sticking her head through the door. He glanced at his watch, *who could possibly be here to see me at this late hour?* They would be taking the bus out to the aircraft any minute.

The Orderly Room was over towards the road into the station. Carter shuffled across the hundred yards to the building that had a hooded red light shining on the covered veranda. He walked up the steps and pushed the door open.

There in front of him was Ann Woodcroft, from Winnipeg, Manitoba. She was dressed in her uniform, holding her cap in her hand. Her curly hair shone in the bright light of the Orderly Room. The Waafs on duty looked at the couple, sharing knowing glances.

'My goodness ... Ann ... I can hardly believe it,' blurted out Carter, momentarily forgetting her name.

'I know you are on an operation tonight. Some other girls and I were in Lincoln for dinner and I though it might be nice to drive over and say hello,' said Ann with her soft Canadian accent, smiling broadly at him. She was truly stunning. 'Can we speak outside?' she added, glancing at the two Waafs taking in every word.

They went out onto the veranda where the soft light made it hard to see her face.

'How did you get in, they normally shut all visitors out when there's an operation on?' asked Carter, still trying to come to terms with this unexpected visit.

'I have two things to confess, first that I have had a few drinks and, second, I told the Guard Commander that we were engaged. I hope that doesn't create a problem,' she laughed mischievously, a loud infectious throaty laugh. 'Once I told him that, he allowed me to come to the Orderly Room, but no further.'

'Well I never ... I am engaged!' laughed Carter, both giggling together at the incongruity of the situation. For that brief moment, his mind cleared ... *hope for the future.*

'Yes ... Congratulations!'

'Have we set a date?'

'Next spring I believe, when the flowers are out,' she said, quick as a flash.

'Well I look forward to that,' he said, with the overwhelming urge to take her in his arms. With all this kit on, he would likely crush her to death.

'Skipper!' came a call from the darkness, Frank Nellyer appeared.

'Yes Frank, give me a minute. I will be along directly.'

'I must go Ann, we take off in less than an hour,' said Carter, with the sudden urge to run away with this girl and never come back. He could smell her perfume, it was like lavender, intoxicating.

'I just wanted to see you again ... to tell you ...'

'I am very pleased you did, what a wonderful surprise, it will give me something to think about during my boring old flight.'

'Skipper!'

'Yes Frank ... in a minute!' replied Carter shouting out into the dark.

'I will be thinking of you ... I want to see you ... maybe we can go to a dance, the Marina Number One Dance Orchestra is playing at the Assembly Rooms tomorrow night,' said Ann, she was weeping, tears running down her cheeks.

He threw his arms around her and kissed her.

'Yes we will do that ... to celebrate our engagement,' he laughed. 'Don't worry I'll be fine, I have a great bunch of lads in my crew, we'll be fine.'

'Carter, if you don't get over here now, you will be in for the high jump,' shouted Jack Haworth.

'Goodbye Ann.'

He ran in his bulky flight suit to the waiting crew bus.

Ann stood on the veranda watching him run into the night ... the fear that this might be the last time she saw him made her shiver ... *please God bring him back.*

'Bloody hell Carter ... there's a war on. Sorry that a trip to Germany has to interrupt your love life ... but there it is,' smiled Haworth in mock indignation. The boys had a good chuckle.

'Is that the Canadian Waaf you threw beer over Skipper?' laughed Frank Nellyer.

'Yes it was,' smiled Carter who was having his leg pulled left, right and centre.

'Well Carter you must have made quite an impression. You will have to buy me a pint to tell me all about it,' called Haworth from the front of the bus.

Carter contemplated how funny it was to feel chilly and a little shivery at this point, regardless of the temperature. It was the same every time, snapped back into frightening reality, Carter's nerves were now stretched to breaking point.

It will be all right when we get on board the aircraft.

The bus jerked to a stop next to A-Able and Haworth's crew tumbled out.

'*Ufamba zakanaka*, Sir[128]' shouted Dave Muir to Haworth and his crew as the bus pulled away.

'You better not be bloody swearing at me, Muir,' shouted back Haworth with a wave. 'Good luck, we will see you in the morning!'

Dave Muir, sitting in the front of the bus turned to his crew and chanted.

> *Zonke nyoni lapa moyo ena kala, ena kala*
> *Ena izwile ena ifile lo nyoni Cocky Lobin*
> *Ena izwile, ena ifile, ena izwile ena ifile Cocky Lobin.*

They all joined in together … Carter was filled with overwhelming emotion of being so far from home … from Rhodesia … from Matabeleland … from his family, the Thorn-acacia and Mopani trees, the heat and the dust, the granite koppies, the bark of the baboon … the smell of the bush in the early morning … orange and purple sunsets …

> *Ena izwile, ena ifile, ena izwile ena ifile Cocky Lobin.*

William Carter sang at the top of his voice. He turned his face to the window, fighting back the emotion …

> *Ena izwile, ena ifile, ena izwile ena ifile Cocky Lobin.*

All across the air station the sound of Merlin engines being run-up filled the air. When all were running, 64 engines drowned out all other sound.

Sixteen 44 Squadron aircraft had been brought up to the top line.

As the bus pulled to a stop next to pan C, Cocky Lobin stood silhouetted in the moonlight. She was an awesome sight. Torch flashes showed the position of the ground crew as they made their

---

128 Travel safely. Go well.

final preparations for engine start.

'Give 'em 'ell Sir,' called Winnie Daly the driver, as they all struggled out of their seats and through the door.

'We will Winnie,' replied Carter giving her a tap on the shoulder as he climbed past her.

Touch for luck …

'You make sure you bring the bus around as soon as we get back Winnie me lass,' said Eric Biddle also tapping her on the shoulder.

All the others did exactly the same thing … *touch for luck*, Frank Nellyer the last out, gave her shoulder a bit of squeeze as he passed.

'We should have a drink Winnie,' he said with a smile.

'You'll be lucky!' she laughed.

He couldn't see her blush in the darkness. Winnie Daly shoved the bus back into first gear and pulled away. She began to cry … it happened every time … she couldn't help it …

Good luck, we will see you in the morning …

Mrs Ethel Greaves, Batwoman, had not gone home, she was waiting for her husband to knock off after the aircraft left. She had been ironing clothing before returning to the hut to put it away. She placed Bill Carter's shirts carefully in his cupboard, hanging his jacket up on a wire hanger. Scanning the room, she satisfied herself that all was in order, everything neatly in place. As she closed the cupboard, she touched Bill Carter's spare uniform jacket. Running her finger over the 'Rhodesia' flash on the shoulder … *So far from home …* tears pricked at her eyes …

As she turned to leave, she noticed the letter on the bedside table. She picked it up and read the name on the front, 'Section Officer Jill Evans'. Ethel slipped it into her skirt pocket, she would deliver it to the Intelligence Section herself.

Luftwaffe 3rd Jagddivision (Fighter) (3 JD 1) Division HQ, Deelen in Holland.
Thursday 30 March 1944, 9:00pm

Hauptmann Helmut Schulte Commander of *Luftbeobachterstaffel* (Reconnaissance Squadron) 3 attached to the Luftwaffe 3 JD 1 had been called to the Operations Room. His navigator, *Oberleutnant* Gustav Lau, followed him as they entered the brightly lit room. All the work stations in the room were occupied, telephones were ringing and the map plotters stood with their 'brooms' next to the giant map table waiting to move the various symbols that marked friend and foe as the approaching battle unfolded.

Generalmajor Walter Grabmann, the commander of 3 JD 1, was standing next to the radar communications officer who was in contact with each radar station in his sector.

'Ah Schulte, good evening to you,' called Grabmann with a smile.

Schulte and Lau came smartly to attention and saluted their commander in the military way, not the Nazi way.

'Good evening Herr Generalmajor,' replied Schulte formally, it was clear he had great respect for the man. While Schulte was only a *Staffel* (Squadron) commander, his specialist operational capability put him under the direct command of the fighter division leader.

'We have issued the signal FASAN. We expect an attack in the next two hours, maybe sooner,' said Grabmann confidently. 'I want you to fly out over England to this assembly point.' He showed a point on the map. 'This is where they would normally circle to gain height. You should be able to give us an indication of numbers, they will also still have their running lights on. I need to know whether this is a major raid as soon as possible.'

Lau took a few moments to write notes on the orders and marked the route they would take on his own charts.

'Good luck Schulte,' said Grabmann.

'Thank you Sir ... if they are there, we will find them,' replied Schulte saluting again, turning on his heel and leaving the room. Outside the sky was clear but a cold westerly wind was blowing off the North Sea. The Junkers Ju88G-1, nightfighter was parked in a bay not far from the Operations Room. As they approached the aircraft, the rear gunner and observer, *Oberfeltwebel* Hans Weitz greeted them in his usual jovial fashion.

'Nice night for hunting Sir,' called Weitz looking up into the bright moonlight. 'Are we to have company?'

'Yes, it appears we will be entertaining the British again tonight. Is all in order?' asked Schulte anxious to get on with it.

'Ready to go Sir.'

'Good let's be off.'

The Junkers Ju88G-1, nightfighter had a range of electronic equipment. Gustav Lau lit up the FuG 220 Lichtenstein SN-2 90 MHz VHF radar using eight-dipole *Hirschgeweih* antennas, plus the additional FuG 350 Naxos with its antenna in a teardrop-shaped fairing above the canopy. The FuG Naxos was designed to track the British H2S radar navigation system and that it did with amazing precision.

The engines were started effortlessly and the sleek menacing aircraft taxied onto the runway facing to the west. They then took off on the short flight of 266km to the point above the town of Horncastle in Lincolnshire where they would wait for the assembling bombers. It would take about 45 minutes flying time.

14

Cocky Lobin's engines had been run-up, to test for magneto drop[129] before taking off. The crew now stood outside the aircraft for the final few minutes before it was time to go. It was still possible that the raid could be scrubbed.

Tommy Potts was throwing the ball for Paddy the Red Setter. Paddy did not drop the ball, preferring it to be wrestled out of his jaw. He barked excitedly leaping about in the torchlight.

The flying rations, escape kits and parachutes had been stowed within easy reach, except for Tommy Potts who had to hang his parachute on a hook outside his turret. Carter would sit on his parachute clipped to his harness.

Ron Boswell stood next to Carter with the Form 700 ready for signing. It was always a time for contemplation; even the irrepressible Dave Muir was quiet. Most men had a last smoke; Charlie Morley chewed on his unlit pipe, moving it from one corner of his mouth to the other.

An eerie silence descended on the airfield, a faint smell of burning coal drifted on the light breeze. Bill Carter stood in the darkness, contemplating the eve of battle, as so many men in history had experienced before him, as his father had done in the trenches of France. It was the ominous quiet before the guns roar. This was his battleground.

'Last pee chaps,' called Carter looking at the luminous dial on his watch.

They all trudged around the back of the aircraft to take aim at the tail wheel. This was the final ritual before take-off.

One by one, the men climbed up the ladder through the rear door in strict order, Morley, Carter, Fullerton, Biddle, Armitage, Muir, Nellyer and Potts. Tommy gave Paddy a final rub on the head as he climbed the ladder.

---

129 A reciprocating internal combustion aircraft engine, gets electricity to the spark plugs through a magneto. Each cylinder has two spark plugs instead of just one like a motorcar. The left magneto fires one plug in each clylinder, and the right side magneto fires each cylinder's other plug. During the engine run-up, at the engine rpm called for in the aircraft's pre-takeoff engine procedures, 2,500 rpm, each mag is turned off with a toggle switch and the amount of engine rpm loss is noted. The loss of rpm occurs because one plug firing can't burn the fuel mixture as thoroughly as two, resulting in a slight loss of power. That is what is meant by 'mag drop'.

'Now you be a good boy.'

The dog knew that Tommy was in the rear turret; he raced around the back of the aircraft where the turret was only a few feet off the ground. He gave a yelp as he sat down and looked up at Tommy taking his position.

Settling into the pilot's seat on his parachute, Carter buckled on the seatbelt. His hands were shaking, none of the buckles would go together easily. The seat felt a bit hard and a bit too low. He adjusted it to make it more comfortable. He slipped his helmet on, plugged into the intercom, connected the oxygen, checked the instrument panel, switched on the radio and checked the intercom.

'Intercom check', called Carter.

'Rear gunner okay Skipper.'

'Mid upper gunner okay.'

'Wireless Op *Zvakanaka*.'

'Nav okay Skipper.'

'Bomb aimer okay.'

'Engineer okay.'

'Alright chaps do your final checks of your equipment,' replied Carter. Listening to the voices of his crew brought into sharp focus the reality of the dangers ahead.

Please bring us all through …

Ron preferred to get his Form 700 signed once the pilot was strapped in at his controls, it was his last gesture, his way of showing respect for what they were about to do. It also gave him the opportunity to say his own personal gentle encouraging goodbyes to the crew … *show them a thing or two … drop a bomb for me … teach the bastards a lesson!*

'Here you go Ron,' said Carter handing back his clipboard. 'See you tomorrow morning.'

'Break a leg Sir,' said Ron over his shoulder, squeezing past Armitage, sliding over the main spar, out the door.

There was a loud bang as Frank Nellyer rammed the door shut and locked in in place. The slamming of the door was their final severed link with the outside world. They all felt it … the sound of Frank locking the door had an ominous finality to it. They were now encased in their steel and aluminium cocoon for eight hours … their fate, uncertain.

Out in the distance, at the control tower, a green flare shot up into the darkness.

'Standby for start,' called Carter.

Each crewmember re-confirmed that they were ready in position and their intercom was working ... *rear gunner okay* ... *mid-upper gunner okay* ... *wireless operator okay Skipper* ...

As Fullerton was sitting in the jump seat where Eric Biddle would have sat for take-off, he was given the task of the take-off checklist. Eric stood behind checking the flight engineers panel.

Ron Boswell stood on the pad outside facing Carter's open cockpit window. He swung his torch in a circle to show that he was ready.

Outside, the noise of Merlin engines starting up around the air station could be heard clearly through the flying helmet. Inside, the smell of 100-octane was stronger as the ground crew in the undercarriage bay primed the pump for fuel to No. 3 Engine.

'Outer tank fuel pump is set to on,' called Biddle.

'Number 3 engine magneto switches on,' called Fullerton.

Carter lifted the guard over the No.3 Engine start button and pressed it. She fired instantly. The airframe vibrated as the engine was brought to 1,000 rpm. All the other engines were started in turn. The whole aircraft shook and trembled like a huge animal coming to life.

Wingco Thompson was already approaching the threshold for runway 04 which would allow a take-off into the light northwesterly breeze. As Carter looked out the left of the aircraft, he could see B-Bravo pulling out of its pan onto the taxiway. His two friends, Pallister M-Mother and Robinson H-Harry would be behind him.

He waved out the window for 'chocks away' and Ron and the ground crew pulled them from the wheels. Carter released the brake on the control column and throttled up both inboard engines to 2,500rpm and the aircraft eased forward, tapping the brake to get the aircraft to swing around onto the taxiway behind B-Bravo. The inner engines were throttled back to 1,000rpm once the taxi speed was achieved.

The aircraft bumping down the taxiway looked like a long string of ducks with their control surfaces waggled up and down and side-to-side as the pilots made sure everything was moving freely. A large group of Waafs and support staff had gathered at the entrance to runway 04, to see them off.

At precisely 9:46pm (21:46hrs), another green flare shot up from the tower, Thompson released his brakes and slowly gathered speed down the flare-lit runway. One after the other the giant bombers turned onto the runway racing away into the night. The noise was tremendous; the earth shook with the vibration from the powerful engines.

Cocky Lobin's turn came, fourth in line. As Carter made a final visual sweep of the runway in front of him with the bright flare path lighting the way, he caught a glimpse of the crowd of well-wishers.

Their faces could be seen quite distinctly in the burning light. All were waving and calling out, drowned by the roar of engines, Waafs, ground crews, clerks ... all were there.

A familiar face ... *is that Jill?* Carter leaned forward to make sure ... *yes there she is* ... he waved out the cockpit window excitedly ... she waved back smiling her encouragement.

She came to see me off!

Cocky Lobin swung neatly onto the centre line, her wheels squealing on the concrete. They waited a few seconds, then the cockpit was flooded with the green light from the signal hut's Aldis lamp.

It was their turn ... no going back now.

'Okay chaps, ready to go!'

Carter looked across at Fullerton who nodded ... he pushed forward the throttles to full boost, holding the aircraft on the brakes. She strained, shaking with anticipation, the intense vibration making the teeth rattle.

He slammed his window shut and released the brakes.

Anticipating the swing to the left, he applied right rudder, holding the aircraft on the centre line, runway lights racing past. She began to ease left, so he applied a tiny bit of right brake to keep her straight. As the speed came up he could feel the rudders biting, he pushed the column forward to lift the tail off the ground ... greater rudder authority came on as the speed and airflow over the wings increased. Fullerton had both hands on the throttles, holding them in position.

Fullerton, holding the throttles through the gate, called out the indicated air speed, '70mph ... 80mph ... 90mph ... 100mph ... 110mph rotate!'

Carter pulled back on the control column and 29 tonnes of Cocky Lobin took to the air. Keeping at a gentle climb-angle, ... he could feel her immense weight on the controls ... engines straining at full power.

Cocky Lobin left English soil at exactly 9:50pm.

'Airborne 21:50hrs George.'

'21:50hrs Skip.'

Carter touched on the brakes to stop the wheels spinning.

'Undercarriage up.'

'Undercarriage Up,' responded Fullerton. He selected the gear lever to the up position and two red lights appeared on the panel. With the noise of the engines, it was not possible to hear the wheels coming up into their bays under the inboard engines.

The heavy aircraft slowly gathered speed and height.

Below, on Heath Lane on the northern perimeter of the airfield, a car sat pulled off the road. A group of four Canadian Waafs waved and screamed as each of the lumbering Lancasters roared overhead at no more than 100ft. Ann Woodcroft said another silent prayer as she waved for all she was worth as each Lancaster burst overhead, it was exhilarating, the sound beating in her chest ... *please be well.*

'Flaps up to 10 degrees.'

Cocky Lobin gained a bit more speed.

'Flaps all the way up.'

'Flaps right up Skipper,' replied Fullerton. Calling Carter 'Skipper' gave him a feeling of belonging, he was now part of it all ... *this great adventure ... this noble calling ...*

Carter trimmed her nose up, now she was 'flying' as the airspeed slowly built to climbing speed of 175mph.

One thousand feet ...

'Reduce power to 2850, +9 boost.'

'2850, +9,' repeated Fullerton.

The higher they climbed the brighter it got, the moon and stars glistening on the Perspex.

Lancasters gathered around Cocky Lobin, shadows in the moonlit night, ... a formation of giant nocturnal birds of war churning noisily through the sky ...

The aircraft continued to accelerate. In the distance, Carter could see the nav lights of the aircraft in front of him. As they pushed through 2,000ft, he throttled back to standard climbing power as they began the half hour orbit to gain the required 10,000ft before setting course.

In the clear moonlight, it was possible to see the other aircraft above them and below, all in a long, graceful, sweeping turn slowly gaining altitude.

As soon as the altimeter hit 10,000ft, George Armitage called Carter.

'Hello Skipper, Nav here, turn left onto one-three-five degrees, maintain speed at one-seven-two,' called George already hard at work.

At 10:29pm, Cocky Lobin turned her nose towards Germany.

Luftwaffe 3rd Jagddivision (Fighter) (3 JD 1) Division HQ, Deelen in Holland.
Thursday 30 March 1944, 10:15pm

The German 'Naxburg' direction-finding receivers designed to pick up H2S signals could attain a range of 400km if optimally placed. Using cross bearings, accuracy was ¼°, the distance could be established with an accuracy of 10%. This monitoring equipment in each radar station along the Dutch coast was literally off the dial with the number of contacts.

'Generalmajor, Texel radar report multiple contacts flying on bearing 77.4° range 168km ground speed approximately 220km/hr,' called the radar liaison officer.

Walter Grabmann looked at the map. It could be Hamburg, or even Berlin, if they were taking the route over Denmark ... *but both those cities were clouded over.*

'How many aircraft?' snapped Grabmann.

'We estimate no more than 100 but of course they are dropping *Fenster*, window.'

'This is not the main attack. This is a diversion. Alert 2 JD 1 at Hamburg, they may be able to intercept them before they turn back,' called Grabmann decisively.

'Herr Generalmajor, *Hauptmann* Schulte of *Luftbeobachterstaffel* 3 reports multiple contacts at below 5,000m assembling in the Norwich area.'

'Does he have an estimate of numbers?'

'He says many hundreds Generalmajor.'

'Listen to me people!' shouted Grabmann to the staff in the Operations Room. The room was instantly silent, faces turned to their leader as he walked in the middle of the room. 'They are coming any minute, as you can see they are still assembling but based on the usual time it takes them to climb, we can expect the first of them at the coast between 23:30 and 24:00. We must be ready to give of our best. Put *Nachtjagdgeschwader* 1 and 2 on immediate cockpit alert! All other nightfighter units on five-minute standby. Carry On!'

The room filled with noise again as Grabmann's orders were carried out.

Grabmann turned to his operations officer, 'Wilhelm, call *Behelfsbeleuchterstaffel* 3 at Münster/Handorf put them in the air, bring them forward to KOLIBRI beacon.'

Behelfsbeleuchterstaffel 3 was a highly specialised squadron of Ju88s that were trained to drop illuminator flares above the British bomber steam so that night fighters and flak batteries could see them in the reflected light. KOLIBRI was a fighter control station and beacon located near the city of Cologne. Grabmann had figured that the British target had to be somewhere in the south. He needed to concentrate his forces for that eventuality.

*

C-Charlie, Cocky Lobin, 14,000ft above Hunstanton, Norfolk
Thursday 30 March 1944, 10:35pm

As Cocky Lobin and the other 44 Squadron aircraft left their orbit over Lincolnshire and turned to the south for the Assembly Point, so too were more than 800 others from all over the east of England. They still had their navigation lights on and most navigators were checking their positions using GEE and H2S to establish whether the forecast wind speeds were accurate.

With a steady drone, they climbed into the darkness, the outside world fading away with the cold, now invisible, Norfolk countryside two and a half miles below. Carter sat in quiet contemplation. As it was warm in his part of the aircraft it was easy to feel that the rest of the world didn't exist, just the cocoon of metal with the instruments glowing comfortably on the instrument panel.

With this false sense of security and with the steady drone of the engines one could easily be lulled off to sleep.

'Lancaster, starboard bow, same level Skip,' called Charlie Morley from his bomb aimer's position.

'Okay Charlie I see him.'

The call shook Carter out of his reverie, he made some minor adjustments to avoid the other aircraft.

It's not healthy to creep up behind another aircraft, a twitchy rear gunner is likely to think we are an enemy fighter and give us the benefit of his four Brownings ... it would seem such a waste to be shot down by a friendly aircraft ...

George Armitage watched the cathode screen on his H2S set, the radar clearly showed the outline of The Wash estuary as they crossed over Hunstanton, he was pleased that the winds were close to forecast, he was only half a mile or so south of the planned track.

'Hello Skipper, Navigator, maintain course one-two-nine degrees, speed one seven two. We will cross the Suffolk coast in twenty-three minutes,' called Armitage. The rest of the crew were always heartened to hear George giving his navigation instructions ... *as long as he knows where we are ...* he recalculated his position every twelve minutes throughout the flight.

As part of the detailed planning for the operation, the exact speed, height and position of every aircraft was pre-determined for the whole flight. If it all went well there would be no collisions, a tight bomber stream and concentrated bombing on the target.

In theory, the bomber stream was to be 68 miles long, so that it could pass over Nuremberg in the planned 17 minutes. In the first 20 miles of the stream were the Pathfinders made up of 97 aircraft. They were the 'openers', marker-illuminators and visual markers. The next 67 aircraft, included 44 Squadron and the rest of the 5 and 8 Group aircraft, carrying high explosive loads which would act as supporters to the marker aircraft. Following these would be 5 waves of the Main Force, each occupying just under 10 miles of the bomber stream The term wave is a bit misleading as they were not separated in any way and many overlapped. The average wave contained 138 bombers including additional Pathfinder 'backers-up', aircraft with the task of remarking the target as flares died out.

In the cockpit, William Carter had the aircraft in a steady climb at 100ft per minute, planning to cross the North Sea at 14,500ft. He flicked the switch to engage the automatic pilot 'George'. It always amused Carter that he had two George's on board, one to fly the plane and the other to tell him where to go.

The deadly game was on ...

*

Luftwaffe 3rd Jagddivision (Fighter) (3 JD 1) Division HQ, Deelen in Holland.
Thursday 30 March 1944, 10:45pm

'Hello, *Herr Generalleutnant,* we have a major attack on its way. The first wave of aircraft are crossing the English coast as we speak. They are maintaining a heading of between 120 and 130 degrees, if this is continued the front of the stream should cross the Belgian coast between Zeebrugge and Knokke at 23:22,' said *Generalmajor* Grabmann on the phone. He was talking to his direct boss, the commander of 1 Fighter Corps, *Generalleutnant* Joseph Schmidt.

'What is your appreciation Walter?' asked Schmidt who was also not a man for pleasantries when the pressure was on.

'The aircraft over the North Sea towards Heligoland are a diversion. Our reconnaissance aircraft report many hundreds forming up over England. I am convinced that the main attack is coming through my sector. I am giving instructions to launch all my aircraft in two minutes. I will place them around the fighter beacons BRUNO and IDA to block an attack on the Ruhr,' replied Grabmann.

'I approve of your decision Walter. I will launch all First Fighter Division aircraft and contact II Corps for more. Those that cannot get to IDA in time will be sent to FULDA and OTTO. Is there anything else?' asked Schmidt.

'I will keep you informed Sir,' replied Grabmann, replacing the receiver.

The staff officers were outside Grabmann's office waiting for their instructions.

'Launch all aircraft, send them to the fighter beacons,' said Grabmann quietly. Over 200 German aircraft would soon be converging on the navigation beacons.

The radar stations along the coast now had the mass of aircraft on their scopes, added to by the clouds of clutter as the bombers started to drop window in massive quantities.

As the nightfighter aircraft started their engines at Deelen, a loud explosion shook the Operations Room.

A flight of British Mosquitos from 105 Squadron RAF swept over the airfield strafing the runway and the parked aircraft. The noise of the anti-aircraft guns filled the air, another huge explosion as a 4,000 pounder hit a hanger. There was no time for the ground crew to run to the air-raid shelters. Flames leapt into the air as the aircraft trying to take off dodged through the debris to find a clear path along the runway. Three aircraft lay burning, their fuel and ammunition exploding, their crews incinerated where they sat.

*

Luftwaffe *10 Nachtjagdgruppe* **(Müller), Bonn-Hangelar Forward Airfield,**
3.8miles northeast of Bonn.
10:56pm

All 1 Fighter Corps fighter stations had received the alert, FASAN. *Hauptmann* Friedrich-Karl Müller, the *Gruppenkommandeur* of 1./ *Nachtjagdgruppe* lined his sleek Focke-Wulf Fw190 A-6/R11 up at the end of the runway. All of the planes of the NJG 10 were painted with distinctive grey/green and grey/violet on the topside of the aircraft, and either black or light grey on the underside.

Nasen-Müller smiled to himself. His decision to bring his *staffel* forward to Bonn-Hangelar was vindicated. The runway lights were on, this was the most dangerous time, the deadly British Mosquitos could be above waiting for him to start his take-off run. It was too dangerous to hesitate. Next to him, his faithful and dedicated wingman Hans Zimmerman sat in his cockpit watching for his leader's take-off roll. This was the last time they would see each other until they returned to refuel, which would be in more than 2 ½ hours with their drop tanks.

Müller thrust the throttle forward, the Focke-Wulf's powerful BMW 801 D-2 engine growled into life, and like a leopard on the hunt, the 'Black 8' *Wilde Sau* leapt into the night sky. The rest of the *Staffel* followed in quick succession.

At a climb rate of 2,650ft/min and 290miles/hr ground speed, it would take Müller about 30 minutes to get to altitude above navigation beacon IDA. It was important for him to climb above the approaching bomber stream. What he did not know at that moment was that Bonn-Hangelar was only 15 miles north of the planned track of the bomber stream. The flashing light of beacon IDA was situated on the northern boundary of the Bonn-Hangelar airfield while the radio beacon was only a further mile to the west.

*

Luftwaffe 11./NJG 5 (Schreiber), Erfurt-Bindersleben, 106 miles due north of Nuremberg.
10:57pm

The message to go to cockpit alert for the whole of 11./NJG 5 had been received at 11pm exactly. The decision to launch towards the bomber stream had not yet been taken because the target was still uncertain.

Leutnant Wilhelm Schreiber of *IV Gruppe*, 11./NJG 5, sat on the wing of his Messerschmitt Bf110 G-4 twin-engine night fighter. He was a short man with blond hair and bright blue eyes. His hometown was the tiny Bavarian village of Bad Tölz on the Isar River. Schreiber's rear gunner, *Oberfeldwebel* Gunther Mahle was making a few minor adjustments to the gun sight of his twin 7.92mm MG81Z machine guns. The ground control radio was turned up so it was possible to hear the instructions being issued to nearby fighter squadrons. The battle had not yet begun, just the careful positioning of the pieces like the opening of a game of chess.

Schreiber's navigator/radar operator, *Leutnant* Frederich Dohle, was in his seat behind the pilot testing the radar system. The Bf 110G-

4, equipped with Lichtenstein SN-2 (FuG220)[130]radar, bore the brunt of *Luftflotte Reich's* nightfighter commitment. The introduction of the Lichtenstein SN-2 had succeeded in negating the effect of the British 'Window'. The air-to-air radar could literally 'see' through the clouds of window dispensed by the bomber stream. Bomber Command had no idea that this was the case.

The SN-2, however, had its failings. The speed of a nightfighter carrying this system was compromised by 30mph because of the size of the radar antennae carried on the nose of the aircraft. The other problem was that the British Mosquito night fighters were equipped with 'Serrate' radar detection that allowed them to track German nightfighters by following the emissions from their SN-2 sets. Despite the Bf 110 G-4's slowness and lack of manoeuvrability in daylight, that was no problem after dark against the lumbering, unescorted, British bomber formations. Its large airframe easily handled the heavy, bulky radar arrays and electronics equipment needed to hunt prey in the dark. As a gun platform, the Bf110 was second to none, with 2 × 20mm MG 151 cannons and 4 × 7.92mm MG17 machine guns mounted in the nose.

The most deadly aspect of the Bf110 G-4, however, was the upward-firing cannon. The nightfighter merely had to keep station below the target and open fire. The British had no idea that such a weapon existed. The twin 30mm MK108 cannon, was installed in the aft cockpit to fire at an angle of 60-70° from the horizontal. The modification, known as *Schräge Musik* (slanting music, or jazz music), was aimed by a second Revi 16B gun-sight mounted on the canopy roof.

Wilhelm Schreiber had never used the *Schräge Musik* modification. His squadron had only received the equipment in the past month and his own aircraft was presently in the hanger having the guns mounted. He had no idea what to expect and only had very rudimentary instruction from his *Gruppen Commander*.

With only one previous victory, Schreiber was still very inexperienced as a nightfighter pilot. He was nervous, staying out of the friendly banter going on between Mahle and Dohle. The other crews waiting on the edge of the runway were smoking, some talking

130 The Lichtenstein SN-2 intercept radar was the state of the art, with a relatively wide cone of search, around ± 45°. Direction finding for flying targets was good, being 1.65:1 for 10° off-centre at an operational frequency of 90MHz. While the instrumented range was 8km, the greatest practical range of the set was limited to altitudes above 2,000m, beyond ground clutter. the minimum detectable range of the set was limited to around 900m. The scope unit contained an Azimut CRT-Display (cathode ray tube) as well as an Elevation CRT-display tube; both displays provided simultaneous range indication.

loudly, planning their next foray into the town of Erfurt 5km to the east. All things considered, this was a pleasant part of Germany to be based in, far from the bombing of the large cities. Erfurt was too small for any real attention. It was also tucked away from the attention of Mosquito intruders.

Schreiber was unaware that the planned route for the attack on Nuremberg was a mere 56km southwest of where he was sitting.

15

Cocky Lobin, 13,300ft above Southwold, Suffolk.
Thursday 30 March 1944, 11:13pm

'I can see the searchlight beacon at Southwold, Skipper,' called Charlie Morley from his bomb-aimer's blister. Part of his job was to help his pilot and navigator pick up landmarks.

George Armitage got up from his navigation table and went forward to get a bearing on the search light beacon.

'We are a bit late and we are tracking to the north. That means that the tail wind must be lighter than forecast and more south-westerly,' he said to Morley before ducking back to his table and plugging his mask back into the oxygen supply. He then called Carter again on the intercom.

'Skipper, Nav, give me a sec to give you a new bearing and speed.'

A single pillar of light stood out in the darkness, almost as a farewell to the bombers rumbling overhead on their way to the Assembly Point. As Carter scanned the sky in front of him, it seemed to be one solid mass of aircraft, all with their blinking bright navigation lights shining.

Out in the distance, the forbidding North Sea reflected the moonlight.

'Skipper, Nav, come right to one-three-five degrees, increase speed to one-seven-two miles per hour indicated.'

'Okay George,' replied Carter. 'Everyone make sure you have your oxygen on. Gunners, time to keep an eye out … long way to go. Charlie, are you pushing out window?'

'Yes Skipper it's a bugger of a job, the stuff is flying around in here.'

The Lancaster made a gentle turn to the right as Carter followed Armitage's instructions.

In the navigator's position the GEE system was still giving accurate positional information that Armitage double checked using dead reckoning and the H2S set. As he watched, the English coastline appeared on the H2S scope. He marked the position on his chart … *11 minutes to the Assembly Point and then another 12 minutes to Belgium … we will be over enemy territory at 11:40pm three minutes behind schedule … then …*

Out over the North Sea they flew, still climbing slowly.

The IFF (identification friend-or-foe) signal was still being transmitted by each bomber to keep them safe from RAF nightfighters. Dave Muir, the radio operator, had wound out his trailing dipole aerials that floated in the aircraft slipstream.

'Permission to test guns Skipper?' called Tommy Potts from the rear turret.

'Gunners test your guns,' replied Carter.

It was not possible to hear or feel the quadruple mounted .303 Brownings in the rear turret being tested. Tommy let off a short burst mindful of conserving ammunition. Then it was Frank Nellyer's turn in the mid-upper turret. His firing could be heard in the cockpit. The nose turret guns were tested by Charles Morley. The cockpit vibrated and the distinctive smell of cordite filled the cabin.

'Fuse the bombs Charlie ... navigation lights off,' announced Carter. 'Right chaps, everybody alert, the Hun have been known to have an early crack at us over the Channel.'

Nobody answered, the reality of the operation now firmly in everyone's mind, the gunners gently traversed their turrets left and right, searching the sky.

Onward and upwards they droned though the dark, chill, space of night, checking this and that, searching the blackness outside for the slightest smudge which might be another aircraft on a collision course.

Carter made regular scans of the instruments and the darkness outside, punctuated at regular intervals by the crew check. Everybody was fully occupied with their own job and their own deep inner thoughts. Carter glanced across at Fullerton who sat perfectly still. He knew Fullerton would be feeling awkward, not wanting to say anything unless spoken to ... thinking about his own crew and their first operation ...

It was all perfectly calm as they approached the Assembly Point. Cocky Lobin gently bumped in the slipstream of the bombers ahead while the sound of the growling Merlin engines filled the mind. The reassuring fuselage vibration reverberated through the seats of all the crew as if Cocky Lobin was doing her bit to keep them awake and alert.

According to Armitage, they were about 2 minutes later than expected. There was no question of the bombers flying in formation in the darkness; they simply came together in a loose gaggle flying over the Assembly Point at their respective allotted time and height.

'Assembly Point Skipper! Maintain height 14,000ft speed one-seven-two,' called Armitage.

'Well done George, my heading is still one-three-four degrees?'

'Yes, maintain your heading.'

As Armitage watched his instruments the GEE signals stopped. The German jamming system had taken effect. He was now down to the H2S and dead reckoning. Armitage followed a set routine to establish the bomber's air position, once every 12 minutes. In the absence of GEE, this was either by DR, visual sighting or radio bearings. It took about 6 minutes to complete his calculations and do the plotting. This left him 6 minutes to warm his hands on the heater behind him, haul on his various layers of gloves, and then, after a pause, peel them off again in time for the next round of work. This was his procedure for the full 8 hours.

Armitage was happy in his work, and would not have swapped his job for anything. He felt for the gunners sitting in their lonely, isolated, frozen positions scanning the sky straining their eyes. He was thankful for the presence of Dave Muir whose wireless position was within a few feet.

Well below Cocky Lobin, there was some convection cloud[131] but above them only a very thin and broken layer of strato-cumulus, nothing like what had been promised.

'Visibility is really good,' said Carter to Fullerton.

'Yes, I can't believe how clear it is.'

'I've counted sixteen kites around us Skipper,' called Potts. 'It's like daylight up here. At least we know we're in the right place!'

There was no heating in the gunner's positions. In the case of the rear turret, it had an open hatch in front of the gunner's face as the Perspex misted up at altitude. His flight suit was electrically heated to ward off the bitter cold. Tommy Potts watched as an icicle formed on his oxygen mask.

Cocky Lobin violently lurched to the right, her starboard wing dipped.

Just ahead, another Lancaster appeared out of the gloom, right in front of them.

'Blasted slipstream,' called Carter, hauling back on the control column. Carter's hand flew to the throttles as he fought to control his bucking aircraft. The bomber in front seemed to be losing altitude, dropping away to starboard. Cocky Lobin responded instantly to the demand for more power and quickly settled as she climbed out of the turbulent slipstream.

'That probably won't be the first time tonight,' said Carter to Fullerton whose eyes showed the fright he had just received. 'Takes

131 'Convection clouds' grow by the process known as convection. Cumulus and Cumulo-nimbus are examples of this type of cloud. Convection in the atmosphere is the way air floats upwards on account of being warmer than the surrounding air.

a bit of getting used to … that other kite looks like it has a problem, probably turning back.'

'Engine temperature all good Eric?' asked Carter of his flight engineer, enquiring about the management of the fuel system.

'Yes Skipper, no problems here.'

'Dutch coast ahead, George,' called Morley from the bomb aimer's position. He was still shovelling window out through the small chute at the prescribed rate of one bundle per minute.

At his post, Armitage watched the H2S scope as the European coastline appeared as a distinct flickering green line.

'Skipper, Nav, ETA Dutch coast at 23:38. We are about five minutes too slow, looks like the tail wind has dropped off,' called Armitage as he again marked his position and began to recalculate based on his new estimate of wind strength.

'Roger, Dutch Coast at 23:38, I'm holding one-three-four, speed one seven zero.'

The Dutch Coast … the enemy coast … where angels fear to tread![132]

'Skipper, Nav, GEE's gone but we're bang on track.'

'Eric, engines look okay, how's the fuel consumption?'

'It looks okay so far Skip,' replied Biddle.

'Any windfinder information coming through Dave?[133]' asked Armitage of the radio operator.

'Nothing yet … wait a minute something's coming through now,' replied Dave Muir from his position. The morse code was ringing in his ears as he began to write down the information being sent from 5 Group HQ.

'Flak coming up Skipper,' called Charlie Morley. He could see the flickering rise of tracer followed by the flash of explosions. 'Search lights on the starboard side Skipper, must be Zeebrugge.'

A loud thud burst a mile ahead of Cocky Lobin. The German flak batteries along the coast were searching for the bombers overhead. Flak whipped past in red flashes.

'Skipper, Nav, standby in ten seconds for course change … Charleroi Leg … in five seconds … come left to bearing one-three-eight degrees, maintain speed one sixty two indicated,' called Armitage, clicking his stop watch for the beginning of the next leg … *so far so good …*

---

132 Quotation from the English poet Alexander Pope's *An essay on criticism*, 1709.
133 One of the tasks of the Pathfinders ahead of the Main Force was to measure the wind strength they encountered and compare it with the forecast. This information was then sent by morse code back to their 8 Group HQ. This information was then, in turn, transmitted to the other Group stations and then back out again to the bomber force.

'Twenty-one minutes and twenty three seconds to the next turn.'

'More light flak to starboard Skipper,' reported Morley.

'Skipper, some silly blighter still has his navigation lights on,' chipped in Frank Nellyer. 'I can see him sitting next to us, no more than a thousand yards on the port beam.'

Eyes looked out to the port side and sure enough, there was a Lancaster as bright as you please.

'Probably a sprog crew on their first operation … they won't be doing a second if they don't wake up soon,' said Nellyer, articulating what everyone was thinking. The situation wasn't lost on Ian Fullerton who made careful mental note.

'Is it one of ours, Frank?' asked Carter, hoping that it wasn't a 44 Squadron aircraft. The light was so good the recognition letters may be visible. There were strict rules for maintaining radio silence so Carter could not send out a radio warning.

'George, message from Group, wind two ninety degrees at fifty-five miles per hour[134],' called Dave Muir, writing down the message in his log and passing a piece of paper over to Armitage only an arm's length away.

'Skipper, do you want me to find out if its one of ours?' asked Dave Muir.

'Yes, have a quick go.'

'*maNyamazaan, upi lo lights ka lo n'Deke? Vuka! Kangela lo lights ka wena!*[135]'

Everybody that could get a look at the aircraft next to them did so, willing them to get the message.

'*maNyamazaan! Upi lo lights ka lo n'Deke? Vuka! Kangela lo lights ka wena!*' called Muir more urgently.

The word 'lights' must have triggered recognition. As they watched in hopeful anticipation, … the navigation lights blinked out.

There was a cheer from everyone.

'*Basopa lo Bandits!*' called Muir on the VHF. All around them, those Rhodesian pilots that could hear … nodded their heads in silent agreement.

'Hurrah! Well done Dave!'

'Whoever that is, get off the air!' screamed a voice over the R/T. There was no way of knowing who it was.

The crew settled down again, the constant loud drone from the engines lulling them back into quiet contemplation. Still the gunners

---

134 Wind from a direction on a bearing of 290 degrees, or roughly west-north-west.
135 Animals, who has his lights on? Wake up! Check our lights.

scanned the sky methodically left to right. The sense of having the enemy so close in the darkness was intimidating, Carter gently twisted Cocky Lobin left and right so as to help his gunners spot a nightfighter stalking from below.

Over occupied territory now and right over a whole nest of German nightfighter airfields, but so far all seems to be quiet ... time for another crew check ...

'All okay?'

The crew replied in turn.

Slowly, imperceptibly Carter become conscious of a beat developing in the steady drone of the engines as they become slightly unsynchronized. A quick check of the engine instruments showed that the starboard inner had dropped a few revs. Eric Biddle the Flight Engineer leaned forward between the pilots, he had spotted it too. He checked the boost and temperature gauges and gave Carter a thumbs-up sign and a shrug of the shoulders.

'Could be a little icing in the carb Skip.'

'Alright I'll adjust the throttles, but keep your eyes on it.'

With a slight adjustment of the pitch-levers the engines reverted to their steady drone.

'Skipper, fuel consumption is okay, just changing to number 2 tanks.'

'Okay Eric,' replied Carter. The sense of confidence that Eric Biddle gave, that he was on top of every situation, was an enormous comfort. It was something in his voice, the tone, it put the minds of all the crew at ease.

'So much for the layers of high cloud,' said Fullerton looking up through the top of the cockpit.

'Looks like Met have botched this a bit, there's no fog on the ground, no low or medium cloud, no bloody high cloud either,' replied Carter.

'I think that visibility must be at least fifty miles in every direction,' added Fullerton.

Nobody answered ... the implications were obvious.

'Chaps, this turning point we are approaching is over the battlefield of Ligny,' said Charlie Morley, ever educating his crew on historical events.

'When was that?' asked Potts, encouragingly. He secretly enjoyed listening to Morley's history lessons despite pulling his leg about it.

'The Battle of Ligny was on 16 June 1815 and was the last victory of the military career of Napoleon. Two days later he was defeated at Waterloo,' replied Morley in his school master voice.

'Let's hope this is not our bloody Waterloo!' chipped in Eric Biddle, expressing exactly what everyone else was thinking.

'Cannons to the left, cannons to the right,' quipped Tommy Potts from the rear gunner position.

'That was the Crimean War you little twerp,' laughed Morley. Listening to Charlie Morley's pearls of wisdom brought a smile to all their faces.

'Skipper, Nav, get ready for your next turn ... twenty seconds ... you will come left to eight-seven degrees,' called the ever-vigilant George Armitage.

'Skipper we are throwing beautiful vapour trails off all four engines[136],' called Frank Nellyer. From his position, he could see the puffy white tails flying off behind the aircraft, clearly reflecting in the moonlight.

It was as if someone had flicked a switch, all the aircraft at their height and below were suddenly throwing vapour trails.

'We won't have to worry too much about fighters finding us ... we are waving at them,' quipped Potts who had the best view of the vapour trails out the back of the aircraft.

'We shouldn't be throwing vapour trails at 16,000ft should we?' asked Fullerton to Carter.

'True ... normally only above 25,000ft, we don't normally fly that high,' replied Carter, now starting to feel the first pangs of real fear.

There was an uneasy silence amongst the crew of Cocky Lobin as they came to terms with the fact that their aircraft was revealing itself in the moonlight like a pretty woman at a dance. The difference being, this was a dance of death ...

*

Ju88G-1 (Schulte) *Luftbeobachterstaffel 3*, Luftwaffe 3 JD 1, 25,000ft above Halle Belgium.
30 March 1944, 11:42pm

Oberleutnant Gustav Lau, navigator/radar operator, affectionately called a *Funker*, stared at the two sets of radarscopes on the panel in

---

136 Vapour Trail or Contrail is formed when air condenses into tiny water droplets which freeze if the temperature is low enough. The time taken for the vapour to cool enough to condense accounts for the contrail forming some way behind the aircraft's engines. At high altitudes, supercooled water vapour requires a trigger to encourage deposition or condensation. The exhaust particles in the aircraft's exhaust act as this trigger, causing the trapped vapour to rapidly condense. Exhaust vapour trails usually occur above 8,000m (26,000ft), and only if the temperature there is below -40°C.

front of him. The Naxos system showed multiple H2S signals but too many to home into an individual aircraft. The radar information simply confirmed what could be seen in the moonlight, a large number of British bombers flying on a bearing of roughly 116°. From what he could determine, he was looking at the back end of the bomber stream.

The Ju88G-1 had been airborne for just under 2½ hours, shadowing the bomber stream. They had reported an estimate of aircraft numbers as well as confirming altitude and bearing. It was still unclear as to where the bombers were headed.

'Are you ready to make an attack Helmut?' asked Lau on the intercom.

'Yes, give me a target, Gustav,' replied the pilot *Hauptmann* Helmut Schulte. These men were both officers and called each other by their first names when they were on operations. They only respected the strict protocols and rank structure when they were about senior officers. As an NCO, the rear gunner *Oberfeltwebel* Hans Weitz was still bound by the obligation to refer to his other crewmembers as 'Sir'.

'We will make a standard attack *von unten hinten*, from underneath and behind, the stream is still too compact for me to use *Schräge Musik* from below,' instructed Schulte.

The SN-2 radar had three 2½ inch scopes, arranged alongside each other; a circular range scope, a scope with the pips on opposite sides of the vertical base-line, and an elevation scope with the pips on opposite sides of the horizontal baseline.

The radar could look down at a 45° angle and, there on the azimuth scope, was a green vertical line showing a contact dead ahead and below.

'Contact dead ahead, *Marie* 1,000m, 1,200m below.[137]'

Schulte put his aircraft into a steady dive rapidly increasing speed. His idea was to level out immediately below and behind his victim, kill him and then regain altitude. He was ever mindful of being issued fresh instructions from the 3 JD 1 HQ at Deelen. His job was not necessarily to shoot down the enemy but instead to direct other fighters onto the bomber stream.

As the hunter descended, the Ju88 began to buck gently as it hit the slipstream of the hundreds of bombers ahead of it. The sky was full of vapour trails making it difficult to pick up the exact aircraft ahead.

'Contact *Marie* 500m dead ahead.'

Schulte bled off speed to match the bomber.

There it was, a Halifax clearly silhouetted against the moon and

137 German R/T voice procedure used the code *Marie* for distance and *Lisa* for bearing.

stars, its four engines churning out the bright vapour trail. Schulte gently lifted the nose of his Ju88 to bring his cannons to bear.

The first tracer rounds flew past the front of Schulte's cockpit, disappearing into the night. More rounds hit the side of the aircraft. Schulte pushed down on his stick, thrusting the throttles forward, at the same time flicking the Ju88 into a tight diving turn.

More machine gun tracer chased the Ju88 as it pulled even tighter into the turn. Bombers appeared all around them, suddenly the real threat of a collision forced Schulte to level out. Hans Weitz was banging away with his rear-facing gun, his rounds returned tenfold as the surrounding gunners replied.

A bomber, caught in the crossfire, dropped away out of formation. It was not burning but a stream of smoke billowed from an engine.

'Stop firing Hans!' screamed Schulte. ' You are giving them a target!'

The vibration of the machinegun stopped.

Bathed in sweat, Schulte accelerated into the climb, his hands slippery inside his gloves.

'That was bloody close. What happened?' asked Schulte of his crew.

'We were spotted by a bomber to our left.'

'Is everyone all right?'

'We have taken a few rounds across the wing and the fuselage but there appears to be no serious damage,' replied Lau sitting behind his pilot. 'One round passed through in front of me. I can hear the wind whistling through the hole in the fuselage.'

*

Luftwaffe 3rd Jagddivision (Fighter) (3 JD 1) Division HQ, Deelen in Holland.
Thursday 30 March 1944, 11:58pm

'The front of the bomber force is passing Saint-Trond and Florennes, Herr Generalmajor,' reported the operations officer standing next to the plotting table.

'Yes,' replied Walter Grabmann softly, concentrating hard on the table as the 'chess' pieces were moved.

'Radar reports the bomber force has changed direction, now on bearing seven nine degrees, they are still headed towards the Ruhr,' said the operations officer.

The phones were constantly ringing as new reports flooded into the operations room. The telephone operators wrote down the information that was fed by clerks to the girls on the operations table where it was assimilated and plotted on the map.

The fighter control station NJRF 6, located two miles southeast of the town in St Trond in Belgium, took control of the battle. The Fighter Controller, surveying the Seeburg table below him, was sending the running commentary to the fighters as they flew towards their designated beacons. A nest of blue lights showed their progress.

Like a pride of lions the winged German hunters lay in wait for the bomber stream, preparing to spring their ambush and bring down their prey. There would be no choking dust, kicking legs, squeals of distress, guts ripped open by razor sharp claws, as the life is squeezed away … instead, the death rattle of machineguns, whipping tracer, flickers of flame igniting into consuming blaze, panic and screaming engines, to death dealt in exploding hell.

'Bombers reported over Aachen, Herr Generalmajor.'

'How many?'

'Reports say fifty.'

'Large force still reported approaching our border near Monschau, Herr Generalmajor.'

'Divert closest fighters to Aachen. Leave the others at beacons IDA and OTTO. They could still be aiming at the Ruhr. This could be another diversion,' clipped Grabmann.

'Fighters from III/NJG 1, report large number of bombers at the border near Monschau,' came another call from the operations desk. 'They are attacking.'

'This is the main force,' stated Grabmann decisively pointing to the black line marked on the operations map, stretching westwards from Charleroi.

'Turn up the fighter controller talking to III/NJG 1. Inform the pilot we want a commentary,' called Grabmann walking to the bank of radios against the wall.

The radio operator turned up the volume and the clear and precise words of the Fighter Controller at NJRF 6 at St Trond came over the speaker. Grabmann believed it was good for morale for the operations room staff to listen to an attack. NJRF 6 was only 18miles north of the planned track of the bomber stream. The southwesterly wind was pushing the bomber stream towards it.

Fighter Controller: Ypsilon 31[138] (Y31), this is *Spinne*, turn onto bearing zero-two-four degrees, target twenty-eight kilometres (18 miles), height 5,500m (18,000ft).

---

138 The German phonetic alphabet for 'Y' was Ypsilon.

The fighter controller at NJRF 6 used a call-sign, *Spinne* (Spider). He was not talking to the pilot but instead to the navigator/radar operator (*Funker*) sitting behind the pilot. Call-sign Y31 was a Bf110G-4b/R3 from III/NJG 1 based at Laon in France.

Radar Operator: *Spinne*, Y31, bearing zero-two-four degrees, height 5,500m. Standby …

The cockpit of the German nightfighter was a very busy place, not the least for the radar/radio-operator. He operated 2 radios (FuG10 and 16ZY), SN-2 radar, watching the FuG227 Flensburg for indications of Monica[139] emissions, or the FuG350 Naxos for H2S emissions, the radio compass in order to obtain fixes, plotting the fighter position and giving the pilot a course to steer when performing *Gebietsnachtjagd* (area night attack).

The Bf110 was equipped with both FuG202 and SN-2 radar. Window affected one of the radars, but not the other.

The pilot of the Bf110 accelerated onto the bearing given to him by the fighter controller.

In only five minutes, the attacking aircraft came back on the air.

Pilot (III/NJG 1):   *Spinne*, I can see them , they are above us, no more than 1,000 metres. There are hundreds …

The radio crackled from interference but the voices could be heard quite clearly.

Radar Operator: SN-2 is on, I have three targets, turn onto bearing six-two point five degrees.
Pilot: I can see the target, 600 metres.
Pilot: Target is a Lancaster, visibility is excellent, no cloud, half moon … we will get him!

The Bf110 crept up underneath the unsuspecting bomber. The pilot gently adjusted his speed to slowly edge underneath his target. This was to be a *Schräge Musik* attack.

---

139 British rear facing detection radar. The Germans had devised a way of tracking this radar that effectively brought the nighfighter directly to its target, better than any flashing light.

Pilot:	I am 50 metres below the target!

The pilot's voice cracked with excitement. He was looking up through the gun-sight on the canopy above him, his right finger on the trigger. He was aiming at the starboard wing between the two engines. The pilot was experienced, he knew that firing up into the bomb bay with 7,000lbs of high explosive inside would kill him as surely as it would kill the bomber.

The cannon fired, no more than five rounds.

Tracerless rounds arced up into the wing, it instantly caught fire as a shell burst into one of the fuel tanks.

Pilot:	It is hit! It is burning ...
Radar Operator:	It is a kill ... it is a kill! ...

A roaring cheer broke out in the 3 JD 1 operations room. Grabmann could not help but yelp in delight. This was the first kill of the night.

The Bf110 pulled away from the burning bomber above it to avoid being caught by debris if it exploded.

Radar Operator:	It is still burning, dropping out of the sky ... it is in a vertical dive ... the right wing is now fully in flames ... the crew are bailing out ... I can see two chutes ... now another. The aircraft is beginning to spin. There is another chute ...

The radar operator continued describing what he saw. His voice trailed off, he reported a massive explosion as the stricken bomber hit the ground, coloured cascades of Christmas Trees (marker flares) burnt on the ground marking the spot for all above to see. The bomber must have been a Pathfinder.

The radio was interrupted by more urgent messages, as the German fighter force literally collided with the bomber stream.

The fighter controllers at NJRF 6 no longer needed to direct their fighters, they were right in amongst them.

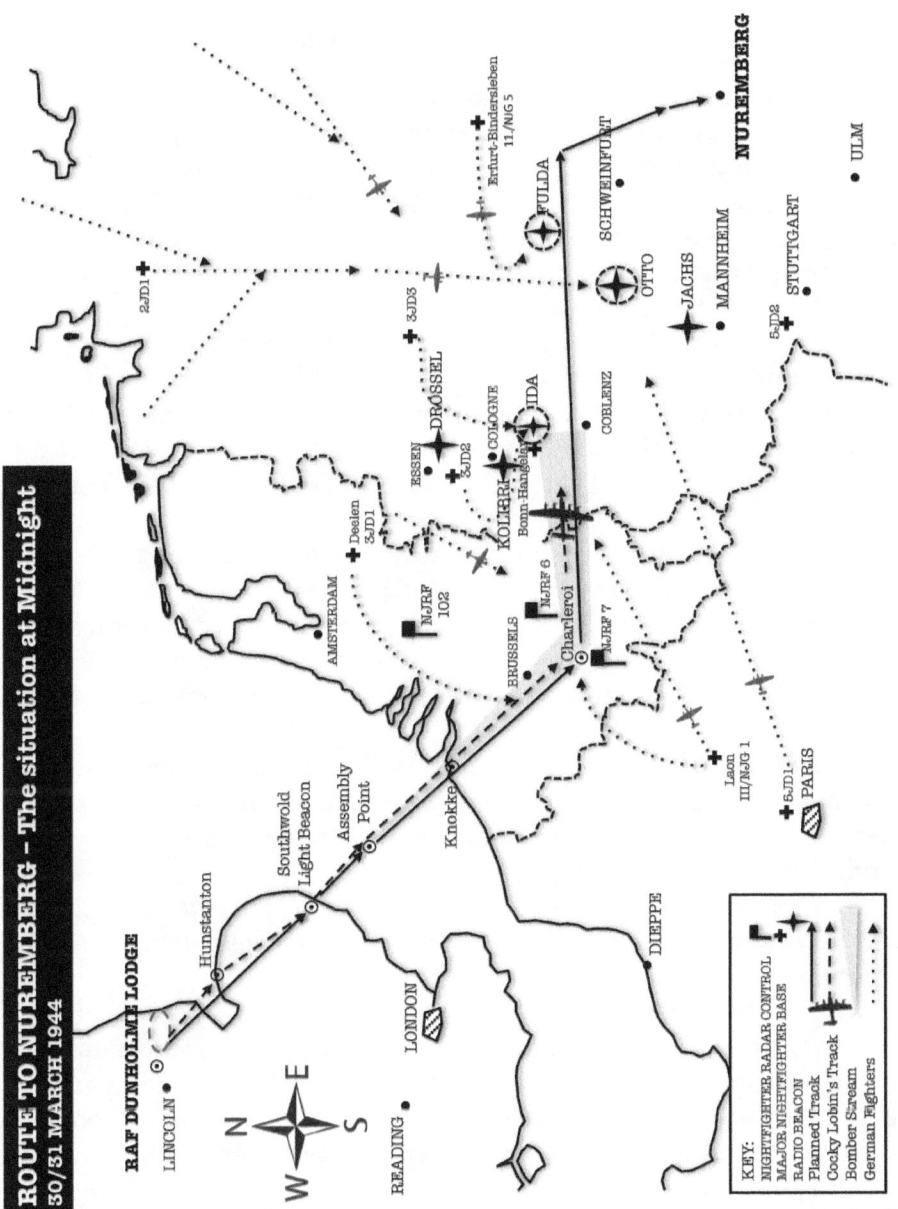

ROUTE TO NUREMBERG – The situation at Midnight
30/31 MARCH 1944

RAF DUNHOLME LODGE

LINCOLN

N
W E
S

Hunstanton

Southwold
Light Beacon

Assembly
Point

Knokke

LONDON

READING

DIEPPE

AMSTERDAM

Deelen
3/JD1

Brussels

N/RF 102

N/RF 6

Charleroi

N/RF 7

PARIS

Leon
III/NJG 1

5/JD1

ESSEN

3/JD2

DROSSEL

3/JD5

COLOGNE

KOLLER
Bonn-Hangelar

IDA

COBLENZ

2/JD1

FULDA

Erfurt-Bindersleben
11/NJG 5

SCHWEINFURT

OTTO

JACHS

MANNHEIM

STUTTGART

5/JD2

ULM

NUREMBERG

KEY:
NIGHTFIGHTER RADAR CONTROL
MAJOR NIGHTFIGHTER BASE
RADIO BEACON
Planned Track
Cocky Lobin's Track
Bomber Stream
German Fighters

257

*

RAF Dunholme Lodge, Lincolnshire
30 March 1944, Midnight

Section Officer Jill Evans woke suddenly with a start. She had been in a deep sleep, suffering from momentary disorientation. She shared a room with another Waaf officer, Ester Dumfries, a senior in Flying Control. Ester was on duty in the control tower. Jill looked at the alarm clock on her bedside table. The luminous dial said midnight. Looking into the darkness Jill breathed a soft sigh ... all was perfectly quiet.

They should be crossing the German border ...

She had been dreaming, something about deciding on where to eat in London ... worried about getting a table ... concerned that she looked her best for him ... for Arthur. *Where was Arthur ... why was he late ... it is so unlike him?* She had tried to get a picture of Arthur's face in her mind but all she could see was William Carter. He smiled at her ...

Turning on to her side Jill closed her eyes to go back to sleep but she knew that sleep was now going to be impossible.

In the past months Jill had steeled herself against sentimentality, there was no point in being any other way. The bomber crews came and went like passengers at a train station ... there one minute, gone the next.

Her brief but exciting encounter with William Carter in London had been as ill advised as it was unexpected. She had been angry with herself afterwards; she had sworn that there would be nobody else until this cursed war was over.

You are acting like a ruddy schoolgirl! What possible future could there be? He is a young man from the Colonies, we have nothing whatsoever in common.

The night's operation began to play over in her mind. She had drafted much of the intelligence briefing based on the information sent through from Group. She knew every aspect of the operation and had been party to many of the arguments around the route the bombers were to take. The weather ... it was risky, but then everything they did was risky ...

Jill had not gone down to the flarepath to see the boys off for many months, she found it too distressing, plus there had been no one special ...

She could not explain her actions, she had straightened her uniform, placed her cap neatly on her head and accompanied the other off-duty Waafs down to the runway. The younger ones were always excited, jabbering away eagerly naming men in the crews as each bomber took flight. It was exhilarating listening to the powerful engines racing away, their deep throaty roar beating in the chest, the ground shaking.

C-Charlie's wheels squealed as she turned onto the runway. Jill could see William's face clearly reflected in the runway lights ... *can he see me?* She waved at him sitting there in the cockpit concentrating on the beginning of the take-off run ... waiting for the green light from the signal hut.

Then in that brief captured moment, he had looked up and seen her. He waved his recognition, a smile clear on his young unblemished face ... it held an innocence ... yet a powerful inner strength. She had waved as hard as she could ... wishing him well ... yelling encouragement with the others above the thunder of the Merlins ... *give 'em hell chaps!*

They were off ... the Lancaster with the newly painted Cock Robin on the nose, edged forward, then all was lost in the howl of the engines and the whipping cavitation from the huge propellers. Jill could still smell the high-octane fuel and feel the blast from the propwash on her face, thrilling and terrifying at the same time.

When the last one had gone ... a strange silence fell over the Air Station ... a sudden feeling of emptiness ... the depressing feeling of being left behind ... the fear of never seeing friends again ... In the distance, the sound of the engines from Fiskerton carried on the breeze, 49 Squadron were taking their place in the line.

As Jill had turned to walk back to the mess, she noticed another Waaf close by was crying. Another girl Jill recognised from Met was comforting her. There were always a few tears when the boys left but this girl was in a terrible state.

'Can I help?' Jill had asked.

The tall girl had her arm around the obviously very young Waaf who was sobbing, sucking back her tears, clutching a handkerchief to her eyes.

'No Maam, it's just a broken heart. God knows we have all had a few,' replied the tall Waaf.

'You are Vera Johns aren't you, from Met?' said Jill.

'Yes Maam, and this is Maggie Smith. Poor girl has made the mistake of falling for an airman,' replied Vera smiling, still holding her friend tightly, giving her shoulders a squeeze.

'Come on Maggie, lets get a cup of tea ... they will all be fine, you'll see,' said Vera encouragingly turning her friend back towards the buildings.

'Who is it that she has fallen for? She's not …' asked Jill, suddenly very concerned. There were increasing numbers of young girls in the family way.

'Oh no Maam, no she isn't … given half a chance though …' smiled Vera. 'Hard lessons still to learn.'

'Thank goodness,' said Jill.

'It's Bill Carter … A-Flight, C- Charlie,' said Vera over her shoulder as she led her friend away.

A defensive … strangely jealous feeling struck Jill as she watched the women walking away.

'Maam!' came a call as Jill walked back to her office.

'Yes?' replied Jill, still deep in thought.

'I have a letter for you Maam,' said Mrs Ethel Greaves, out of breath, thrusting an envelope into her hand. On the front, a neatly written hand read simply, Section Officer Jill Evans.

The letter sat now on Jill's bedside table. It had invoked a stream of emotions that Jill had not felt for many years. She stretched out and turned on her reading light, then gently picked up the envelope as if it was a delicate flower. She began to read …

Dunholme Lodge
Thursday, 30 March 1944

Dear Jill,

I hope this note does not take you too much by surprise. I have been bursting to speak to you since our wonderful evening together in London. I don't have adequate words to describe how you made me feel. You must think that I am being silly – I hope not.

I know you have had a terrible time over the past year and this wicked war does not make things any easier, but I just wanted you to know that I feel very deeply for you.

I wrote this note so that you would know how I feel – just in case.

I hope we have the opportunity to see another film together, to talk … I really hope so.

Yours sincerely

William

The simplicity of the words, so heartfelt, brought tears to her eyes. The whole situation just seemed so ridiculous, *there is no future in this* ... yet Jill felt a stirring within her soul, a profound almost primal instinct that was beyond her control.

*

Jill Evans was not the only person struggling to sleep. Across the way in the Nissen Huts occupied by the non-commissioned Waafs, Maggie Smith had not been able to sleep at all. She lay in her bunk looking up into the darkness; all the other girls in her hut including Vera were sleeping soundly. She could hear them all breathing gently, including Tabitha Jackson, an LAC in Flying Control who had a tendency to snore.

It was absolutely no use at all. She had set her alarm for 5am so she could be up to see the boys back in.

It had been so disappointing. She had not been able to speak to him at all. Since the night in the Black Bull he had been distant, he didn't even tell her that he was going on leave.

Then she had been told, just before take-off, by one of the girls in the Orderly Room that he had a visit from a Canadian WD.

He must have met her while he was on leave.

She had tried so hard with the help of Vera to get close to him. They had painted the name on the plane ... *it took almost all night!*

It had been explained to her what bad form it had been to go out to the dispersal point. That had been a huge mistake that she regretted terribly. The final straw that had upset her the most, was that he had not seen her at the runway when they took off. She had waved and jumped up and down, so much so that Vera had to pull her back from the edge of the runway. He had waved but not at her, at the crowd, he had not seen her. Just the thought was too much.

Maggie Smith rolled over and buried her face in the pillow, trying not to allow her sobs to wake the others.

*

LAC Linda Potter, A Flight Clerk, did not sleep on nights when there was a 'maximum effort'. She sat at her desk drinking a cup of tea, a pile of unopened files for all the new crew that had arrived in the previous three days, sitting in a neat pile. It seemed a waste of time in a callous sort of way. She had lost count of the files that had come and gone across her desk – an endless stream of young men, bright excited faces, full of life and expectation – simply going out and

261

not coming back. There was an impersonal finality to it, no blood, no screaming anguish, just a quiet disappearance, fading away. All that was left behind was an empty bed, a few worthless belongings, a letter home, a final scribbled comment in the Log Book ... 'Failed to Return'.

Potter was the first to check the crews back in. If they did not return, she wiped the pilot's name and the aircraft number off the chalkboard. Perhaps because of her job, at the fateful intersection of life and death, or perhaps because she was a woman, reminding them of their mothers and sisters, they would give her things to look after for them before they went; a fountain pen, a folded photograph of a girl, keys, a favourite book, always promising to collect them when they got back. Potter had a cardboard box behind her desk where she kept these precious things. If they were unclaimed, she would wrap them up carefully with their other possessions to be sent home.

First, you wait for them to go ... and then you wait for them to get back ... the waiting was like something you could touch, like a pea-soup fog where everything is obscured, where terrible unseen things lay hidden.

Linda cared a great deal for her men. Her tears were shed in her bed at night, or stolen on long lonely walks around the station, sometimes in the pub after a few too many. She looked at the list of her boys on the blackboard, now out there in the treacherous darkness. She could picture their faces ... Pallister, Robinson, Charlesworth, Carter, Biggs, Smith, Meredith and Haworth.

Bloody Jack Haworth ... he was infuriating, demanding, petulant ... but exciting and dynamic with a smile that melted her heart ... every time. He only had to snap his fingers ...

Please come back Jack ...

16

Cocky Lobin, 20,000ft above the Rhine River
Friday 31 March 1944, 12:27am

'There goes another one, Skipper,' called Tommy Potts from the rear turret.

He was watching another bomber burst into flames and spiral into the ground. The explosion was a combination of reds and greens as the incendiary flares it was carrying burst on impact.

'That's the fourth one I've counted ...'

Nobody responded to Tommy's commentary, each trying to come to terms with what he was reporting.

'Stay alert chaps ...' was all Bill Carter could think to say.

Searchlights and bursts of flak filled the sky to the north of their track. The flashing northern horizon reminded Carter of a giant electrical storm rolling over the bushveld of Rhodesia.

'That's the Ruhr you are looking at,' said Carter to Fullerton who was staring out the cockpit. 'It must be the spoof raid going in.'

'Skipper, Nav, we are crossing the Rhine ... but we seem to be north of our track,' called George Armitage. '... And we are still behind schedule ... the winds must have changed dramatically in the last half hour.'

A massive explosion burst in front of and slightly above Cocky Lobin. The shock wave smashed into the aircraft, she bucked like a frightened horse.

'Jeesus ...'

The sky was a mass of churning orange flame, tinged with green. It lit up everything like a floodlight flashing on and off. The crew, for a split second, could see the reflection of the other bombers flying around them. Bits of debris spun across the sky dragging flames behind them, like a giant whirling Catherine Wheel.

'What was that ... was that a Lancaster?' shouted Charles Morley from the front turret. The burst had been so close that he had felt the heat flash across his face.

'It must be one of those Scarecrow things ... we've seen them before but that was really close,' replied Carter. Cocky Lobin was still shaking as she flew through the disturbed air, as if she shared the fright felt by her crew.

'CORKSCREW PORT SKIPPER! GO ... GO ... GO' screamed Tommy Potts.

Carter rolled full left aileron and smashed full left rudder, pushing the control column forward, at the same time his hand flew at the throttles. Cocky Lobin banked hard in a diving 45° turn to port.

The four Brownings of the rear turret were firing, spraying bright tracer across the sky. The g-forces threw anything loose around the inside of the cabin. Armitage lost his pens and pencils and his map flew up against the bulkhead. Dave Muir was tossed off his seat to land hard against the floor. Eric Biddle had been standing up behind the pilots in the astrodome as an extra pair of eyes. He was thrown off his feet, bashing his head in the same place as last time, easily reopening the still-healing wound from 6 nights before.

'Fook sakes!'

Cocky Lobin began to scream and shake, engines racing … *230mph … 250mph*. The altimeter was unwinding rapidly as the aircraft dived. Tracer rounds past above the cockpit disappearing out into the night in front of them.

After dropping 1,000ft in only six seconds, Carter pulled the aircraft out of the dive, keeping full left aileron on. He then reversed the turn, pulling back on the column and switching to full right aileron halfway through the climb. This caused the speed to fall sharply, praying the attacking nightfighter would overshoot.

'He's still there Skipper … I think its a Ju88,' called Potts.

'Where is he Tommy? … I can't see …' shouted Frank Nellyer swinging his turret desperately to bring his guns to bear.

'The bastards directly behind slightly above …'

'I can't see him Tommy!'

'The fooking Hun's shooting at us.'

Nellyer saw the source of the tracer and opened up with his guns. The cabin was instantly full of the smell of cordite … the loud TAK … TAKKA … TAK of Nellyer's guns.

With throttles wide open at full power, 3,000rpm, maximum combat boost +18, Cocky Lobin regained her original altitude. With speed down to 185mph and still in the starboard turn, Carter pushed the aircraft over into another dive. Picking up speed again, she descended through 500ft before he reversed the direction of the turn back to port. The crew held on for dear life, bracing themselves against the violent g-forces.

'Is he still there Tommy?' called Carter his voice laboured from the exertion, the muscles in his arms straining at the yoke.

'Can't see him Skipper … we may have shaken him off,' replied Potts, the adrenaline making his speech sound stilted … out of breath.

'I didn't even see the bastard … only a few tracer rounds,' called a frustrated Frank Nellyer,

Carter pulled back on the yoke again, still on full combat power to claw back to their required altitude. He was sweating profusely, perspiration dripping into his eyes making them water … the instrument panel became blurred as he tried to wipe it away. He was breathing hard from the strain, flying the Lancaster was like pushing hard in a scrumming machine.

The sky was still full of flak to the north and as they throttled back to their cruising speed, more flak opened up in the south. What seemed like hundreds of searchlights were swinging across the sky, feeling for the bombers.

The crew were silent, recovering from the two minutes of terror.

'Is everyone all right?' asked Carter.

One by one the crew acknowledged that they were unhurt, except for Eric Biddle, whose reopened head wound was bleeding all over his flight suit. It hurt like hell but Biddle didn't make a sound.

Charles Morley threw up silently in his bomb aimer position, his mind a jumble of fear and apprehension. He stuffed the sick bag down the chute he used for pushing out Window.

Glancing back at Biddle, Carter was shocked to see his face covered in blood.

'Bloody hell, Eric … you better get a bandage on that … can you help him?' said Carter to Fullerton, who was looking on equally shocked. He slipped off the jump seat and helped Eric back through the cabin to the bench just forward of the main spar. Dave Muir had the first aid kit out and between them, they cleaned the wound as best they could, wrapping a bandage around his head.

'Just as well you have such a hard noggin Eric,' commented Muir. 'Should end up with an impressive scar, something to explain to the ladies. Give you something more to talk about.'

'I do just fine with the ladies thank you very much … don't need a bloody scar … I am impressive enough as it is,' shot back Biddle, showing no signs of concussion.

Armitage had retrieved his map and notebook, a few instruments and a pencil.

'Skipper, Nav, I am going to have to take a shot at the stars … I have no idea where we are,' clipped Armitage. 'Before you threw us about … we crossed the Rhine … looking at the H2S it looked like the islands at *Bad Honnef*. That makes us about six or seven miles north of our track, about four minutes too slow. Make your bearing nine-four degrees, increase speed to one seven five, altitude 20,000ft.'

'Someone else just bought it, Skipper,' called Tommy Potts.

The crew of Cocky Lobin had no way of knowing, but they were only 9 miles south of the Luftwaffe beacon IDA, that at that moment, had over a hundred single-engined and twin-engined nightfighters orbiting it. They were shooting down bombers every few minutes. Explosions filled the sky to the north. Aircraft could be seen burning into the ground, bright plumes of exploding petrol.

The winds had dropped and changed direction to due west as they aligned with the old cold front. That part of the front over northeastern France had moved south faster than forecast. This had the effect of drawing what little cloud there was to the south, taking away all protection for the bombers.

The unexpected change in the winds, with the sudden and deadly nightfighter attacks had broken up the bomber stream. Bombers were now spread in a 40-mile arc stretching from Coblenz in the south to Cologne in the north. The flak defences of those two industrial cities were also shooting down bombers.

Most of the bombers were to the north of the correct track as was Cocky Lobin. Flying on such a broad track the bombers were literally ploughing through the nightfighter orbit around IDA and the Cologne flak defences. Vapour trails lit up in the bright moonlight pointing the way for the fighters. On the ground below the direction to the next turning point was marked by burning and exploding bombers as one by one they disintegrated into the German countryside.

'This is no bloody good at all. ... George I am taking her up as high as she will go ... height is our only hope,' said Carter to his navigator. He knew that staying at the planned height was suicide in these conditions. Carter pushed forward the throttles and applied increased boost.

*

Luftwaffe 1./*Nachtjagdgruppe 10* (Müller), 21,000ft above Beacon IDA, 3.8miles northeast of Bonn
Friday 31 March 1944, 12:40am

Hauptmann Friedrich-Karl Müller, the *Gruppenkommandeur* of 1./ *Nachtjagdgruppe 10* was flying in a gentle circle around the IDA visual flashing beacon, out at a distance of three miles. His navigation lights were on for safety reasons. As he looked around above and below him, the sky seemed to be full of lights. The Focke-Wulf Fw190 A-6/ R11 was throttled right back as he effortlessly maintained his height.

In his ear, Müller could hear the running commentary coming from the fighter controllers at 3rd Fighter Division at Deelen. From what he could gather, the main bomber force was heading straight for him and his waiting *Gruppe*.

The anticipation was extreme, almost unbelievable. The night was still bright and clear.

This was to be his first night battle using the new Neptune radar.

Without warning, a bomber appeared out of the dark on his starboard side flying directly towards him. He still had his navigation lights on and the bomber began shooting at him from the front turret. A collision seemed certain, his hands flew at the throttle and he pulled back hard on the stick.

The bomber pilot, seeing the danger, had dived below him.

Tracer from the mid-upper and tail gunners arched up towards him as the bomber banked away. On his port quarter, a bomber collided with one of Müller's single-engined fighters. The massive wing of the Lancaster cut the fighter in half, at the same time its starboard inner engine was ripped from its mountings throwing fuel across the wing in a fine spray. Müller watched in horror as the fighter's engine smashed into the bomber's cockpit, slashing it away like a giant cleaver, decapitating the pilot, then spinning off into the night. Both aircraft detonated into a fireball, the bomber's wing folding upwards from the root, tipping it onto its side as it began its flaming death-dive to earth.

Müller recovered his wits, shocked that the fighter controller had not given any warning at all. In moments the sky around him was full of bombers, some at his height but most below him, all throwing vapour trails. He flicked the Focke Wulf over onto a parallel course and had a contact on the Neptune radar immediately, 4,000m ahead and below. He switched off his navigation lights. Pushing the throttle forward, the fighter rapidly increased speed.

High above the bomber stream a *Behelfs Beleuchter* Ju88 released a string of illuminating flares. The effect of the bright light reflecting on the bomber's white vapour trails was electric, it was impossible to miss them as they trundled along in loose formation.

Not needing to use the radar, Müller dived on his first victim. His speed increased in the steep dive, the bomber appeared in the gunsight … *larger* … *larger* he aimed at the centre of the fuselage immediately behind the cockpit canopy.

The cannon shells thumped out, arching down … DUFF, DUFF, DUFF, … BANG!

It was as if a fuse had been lit … a split second elapsed before the bomber exploded. Pulling back on the stick, Müller took his fighter wide to the left. As he passed, he glimpsed a wing break off. The sky was a cascading mass of burning debris, an engine, the propeller still turning, whizzed past him as he pulled away.

There was no time to think about his first victim, as he pulled back into level flight another bomber appeared directly in front of him, no more than 1,000m.

Closing fast, before the rear gunner had any chance, he blasted the turret to pieces. As he watched, the bomber dived into the corkscrew manoeuvre. He followed it into its dive, easy to do as the tail was in flames.

Wait ... wait ... come on pull up.

The pilot of the bomber began to pull out of the dive, at the same time banking to the left, hoping that he had shaken off the fighter.

Müller watched as the bomber filled his gunsights.

DUFF, DUFF ... DUFF ... the recoil thudding into Müller's back.

Cannon shells exploded along the wing, walking into the fuselage. Engines on fire, the bomber entered its final spiralling plunge to earth. Counting three parachutes, Müller followed the bomber down making certain of its demise.

In less than three minutes, Friedrich-Karl Müller had killed two bombers. As he put his fighter back into the climb, the carnage was being repeated all across the sky as over two hundred fighters attacked the bomber stream.

Bright explosions lit up the landscape below as doomed bombers crashed into the countryside.

*

Luftwaffe 11./NJG 5 (Schreiber), 18,000ft, 9 miles East of Fulda, 98 miles northwest of Nuremberg
Friday 31 March 1944, 12:51am

Leutnant Wilhelm Schreiber of *IV Gruppe*, 11./NJG 5, in his Messerschmitt Bf110 G-4, had been aloft for 35 minutes on a track from Erfurt-Bindersleben of 236° directly towards the OTTO fighter beacon. The fighter controllers maintained the running commentary, instructing the approaching fighters to expect bomber contacts at any minute.

There was still some uncertainty amongst the High Command at 1JD as to the main target of the bomber stream. The Ruhr had been eliminated as well as targets north of the weather front that included Berlin. The options were still, Leipzig, Dresden, to the north, Frankfurt,

Stuttgart, Schweinfurt, Würzburg … and Nuremberg to the south. As the minutes ticked by and the bomber stream maintained its course to the east, so Frankfurt became less likely.

Schreiber's rear gunner, *Oberfeldwebel* Gunther Mahle was chatting to, *Leutnant* Frederich Dohle the *Funker*. The screens on the Lichtenstein SN-2 radar remained clear.

The perfect weather allowed the fighters to attack the bomber stream without radar assistance. Most continued shadowing the main force like a pride of lions in the Serengeti waiting for a weakened antelope to drop behind. More and more fighters linked up … the unrelenting slaughter of the bombers continued.

'Target, bearing 208 degrees, range 2,000 metres, height 5,400 metres,' called Dohle excitedly.

Schreiber flicked the Bf110 onto the new course. Ahead of him, at some distance, he saw a huge explosion in the sky … *that must be where the bomber stream is.*

'Accelerating to target,' called Schreiber, the sudden realisation that he was about to do battle struck him. He felt his body break into a nervous sweat despite the icy cold.

'Target 1,000 metres.'

The Bf110 raced across the sky towards its target that was on an angled converging course a few hundred metres above.

'Multiple targets dead ahead,' called Dohle as his screen flickered in front of him.

'Turn onto bearing 82 degrees, target 1,000 metres.'

Dohle turned his pilot to allow for an attack from below and behind.

'I can see him,' called Schreiber.

Ahead the bomber appeared out of the night, from below Schreiber could see the flames from the exhaust manifold. He continued to accelerate until the bomber was immediately above him, then carefully slowed to match its speed. Looking up, the outline of the bomber could be seen distinctly against the stars and moonlight.

The temptation to blast away was excruciating. The bomber filled the gunsight above his head. He had been warned about shooting at loaded bombers from below. Gently adjusting his position, Schreiber took aim at the port inboard engine and fired a long burst, desperate to ensure a kill.

The crew of the Bf110 watched in shocked amazement, flames licked out of the engine, in only a millisecond, engulfing the wing.

Diving and accelerating away to starboard, Schreiber attempted to get out of harm's way.

The bomber exploded in a bright, flashing, orange, haze. The shock wave from the explosion detonating so close smashed into the Bf110, standing it up on its tail. Debris was thrown out in a broad arch cascading down in streaks of churning flames. A chunk of red-hot metal struck the Bf110 cockpit canopy immediately behind Schreiber's head, smashing a hole through the perspex impacting the top of Dohle's radio and radar panel, landing in his lap.

Dohle screamed in shock as the blistering metal began to burn through his flying suit, he could feel the intense heat searing his thighs. He tried to lift himself up but the shoulder straps held him in place. He could smell his own flesh beginning to burn as he pushed at the metal chunk with his gloved hands. It was too big and jammed against his instrument panel between his legs, burning his knees. Screaming in pain and despair, the cockpit filled with the smell of burning leather and flesh.

There was nothing his crewmates could do to help him as he shrieked in agony, trying to lift his legs away from the metal. In tortured pain and desperation Dohle, smashed the release clip on his harness, flicked open the cockpit canopy above him and lifted himself up with all his might. As the gunner Gunther Mahle watched in distress, powerless to help, the radar operator pushed himself out of the canopy and dived into the night.

'Dohle has jumped Sir!' shouted Mahle. 'He has jumped, something was burning him.'

The metal chunk was now on the floor of the cabin burning through the aluminium. The Bf110 cockpit is so narrow and confined that Mahle could not stretch through to set off the fire extinguisher. The slipstream ripped off the canopy opened by Dohle above his seat.

Schreiber flicked the aircraft into a steep, banking, diving turn searching the sky below for a parachute.

English bombers continued to flash past through the stars like giant migrating whales focussed determinedly on their distant destination.

Cocky Lobin, 22,500ft above the village of Wahns
Friday 31 March 1944, 12:52am

Navigator George Armitage knew he was in the wrong place. He sat at his table, alone with his thoughts, always aware of his awesome responsibility. There had only been one wind report for over an hour, 290 degrees at 55 mph ... *rubbish!* The attack by the German fighter and the subsequent evasive action had added to the navigation error. What he did know was that his dead-reckoning turning point for Nuremberg was approaching in 3 minutes. He had recalculated his speed based on the aircraft flying 2,500ft higher than originally planned ... *but the wind ... what was the wind doing?*

'Dave, nothing from Group on the wind?' called Armitage in the forlorn hope that something new had come in since his last question 5 minutes before.

'Nothing on the wind George,' replied Dave Muir. 'Skipper, message from Group, Zero Hour is unchanged.'

'Thanks Dave.'

'Skipper, Nav, your turn coming up in two minutes. Are we sure we haven't got a Master of Ceremonies[140] on this show?' asked George in desperation. He was hoping that his errors in navigation would be rectified when the target was in sight as the TI (Target indicator flares) could be seen from a fair distance and the Master of Ceremonies would call them forward.

'No ... they didn't say anything at briefing. Strange ... you would have thought they would have had one on such a big raid,' replied Carter. The lack of a Master of Ceremonies had elicited some debate in the mess after the briefing but no explanation was given.

Carter's eyes were getting tired and he had to fight off the drowsiness that threatened to engulf him. The blackness outside was relieved only by the red glow of the exhaust from the port inner engine and the green glow of the instrument panel. They always seem to be uncomfortably bright in the dark night.

'Skipper, I can't see the markers at the turning point,' called Charles Morley from his position in the bomb aimer's blister.

Well now, we know for sure we are in the wrong place!

---

140 A senior pilot designated to direct the bomber stream onto the correct target. This was an extremely hazardous job as the Master of Ceremonies was required to orbit the target for a long period directing the bomber waves as they arrived over the target.

'Skipper, Nav, hold on zero-eight-seven for another minute ...' called Armitage. The nagging uncertainty of their position weighed on his mind ... it made him feel ill.

Why aren't their marker flares at the turning point?

Tommy Potts sat in his cramped turret unable to move more than a few inches in any direction, his hands were numb and his eyes hurt from the constant strain of watching the sky. The sickening sight of bomber after bomber hitting the ground below was relentless. He sat huddled up repeating Psalm 23 over and over again, *The Lord is my Shepherd, I shall not want* ... praying for himself and his crew ... praying especially for Bill Carter to get them home. He felt as if he was sitting on the edge of a cliff overlooking the end of the world.

Frank Nellyer was feeling the effects a few too many late nights while on leave with his mate Tommy Potts. They had a wonderful time on leave, going to the cinema, drinking beer and chasing the local Scottish girls. He and Tommy had more money than they had in their whole lives, a Sergeant's pay of 14s, 6d a day.

Slowly traversing his turret left and right, Frank followed a routine, like a game, watching a particular star in each quadrant. If it disappeared, it was being obscured by another bomber ... or a nightfighter! He hadn't actually seen a nightfighter yet, despite being on his 16th operation. Tommy had seen plenty, but Frank had only seen tracer aimed at their aircraft.

Frank wished he knew their proper names ... the names of the stars. He gave them names of his own, it helped to stay awake ... girl names, Jenny, Patricia ... mostly girls he had liked at school.

What is that! ...

'Skipper, Lancaster on the starboard beam about 300 feet above us,' called Frank Nellyer urgently.

'Good Frank, keep your eyes on him, we will probably converge on him with this new heading.'

'Okay Skip.'

For Nellyer staring into the black night sky to hold onto a fleeting black smudge was exhausting. Other black smudges could turn out to be a lot more sinister.

If we can spot them first, we stand a chance of living!

Putting his hand into his pocket, Frank pulled out a Benzedrine tablet, a wakey-wakey pill. They tasted awful. Still, he agreed with Tommy, they suppressed the need to pee.

*

At 12:45pm, the first PFF bombers had reached the end of the Long Leg and started to turn south to Nuremberg. German fighters and unreported wind changes had caused further dispersal of the bomber stream. The 220 miles from Liege to the turning point was by now clearly marked by the blazing remains of 41 Lancasters and 18 Halifaxes.

The turning point was a tricky one, above the forests of Thuringia with no recognizable feature or nearby town. Most of the aircraft turned well to the north of the right place and slightly short of it. This was the case with Cocky Lobin, who was above the tiny hamlet of Wahns about 6 miles north of the planned track and 15 miles short of the planned turning point. The target was now 88miles to the south; without the tail wind, this would be a 22-minute flight.

Cocky Lobin was just over 8 minutes behind the leading Pathfinders.

*

'Skipper, Nav, turn ... come round to one-six-four degrees for the target, speed one six two,' called Armitage. 'Charlie, we are going to need you to find the TIs[141], we could be as much as ten miles off track.'

'I am watching George. I can see a thick cloud layer well below us. Our boys are standing out like flies on a tablecloth. Still plenty of vapour trails about,' replied Morley.

'You Aussies know all about flies,' quipped Dave Muir.

'There're no flies on you Dave,' laughed George Armitage.

'Yes, but he's a fly in the ointment,' shot back Morley as the crew giggled over the intercom, the repartee fleetingly breaking the tension.

'Alright chaps, prepare for our attack run, eyes peeled for fighters,' called Bill Carter, trying to keep everyone focussed and alert. This was the most dangerous phase of the operation.

'An hour to go before the moon finally sets, not a moment too soon,' added Armitage. The tone in his voice indicated his frustration that this 'ropey show' was put on in the first place.

The gunners had stopped giving commentary on bombers shot down; they had lost count ages before. They just sat in their frozen turrets scanning the sky around them lit up with intermittent explosions and tracer fire as more bombers met their doom.

Dave Muir began to reel in his trailing aerial. Charles Morley switched on the gyros in the bombsight and the heaters on the camera housed in the bomb bay.

---

141 Target Indicator flares.

'Charlie, remember to increase your rate of windowing to two bundles a minute,' called Carter encouragingly, not wanting to sound like a nag, but with all the pressure approaching the target it was easy to forget the small things.

'Got it Skipper ... God I hate this job!' Morley's bomb aimer position was now covered in a thick layer of window that had blown out of the bundles as he shoved them down the chute.

Carter glanced at his watch; the first illuminator flares were expected in 3 minutes.

'Watch for those ground markers, any minute now,' instructed Carter to Fullerton sitting next to him.

'Where did that cloud bank come from?' asked Fullerton, pointing out ahead of them. As Carter looked out the side of the cockpit, he saw the well-defined edge of a sheet of cloud thousands of feet below. The cloud stretched in an uninterrupted mass to the far horizon ... the target was covered in cloud!

'Dave, have you got anything on this cloud base?'

'Nothing, Skipper.'

'How high do you think that cloud base is?' asked Carter to Fullerton.

'I'd say 11,000 feet or so.'

'Blast! Another bloody weather cock-up!' exclaimed Carter, his voice showing his concern. 'George, what have you got on the H2S?'

'Nothing I recognise, we should be crossing over Bamberg ... thirty-five miles to go.'

'Skipper, search lights and flak bursts to the east, plenty of it,' called Morley. 'That must be Nuremberg.'

Armitage rushed forward to the bomb aimer's position to look at the direction of the flak. He didn't hesitate.

'Skipper, turn onto one-three-five degrees, fly towards the flak belt. I knew the bloody winds had dropped. We are about eleven miles west of the correct track. My guess is that that flak is coming from Bamberg not Nuremberg.'

The thought of flying directly towards and through the flak belt was never appealing, but that was the case on every operation. Somebody was already getting a pasting up ahead.

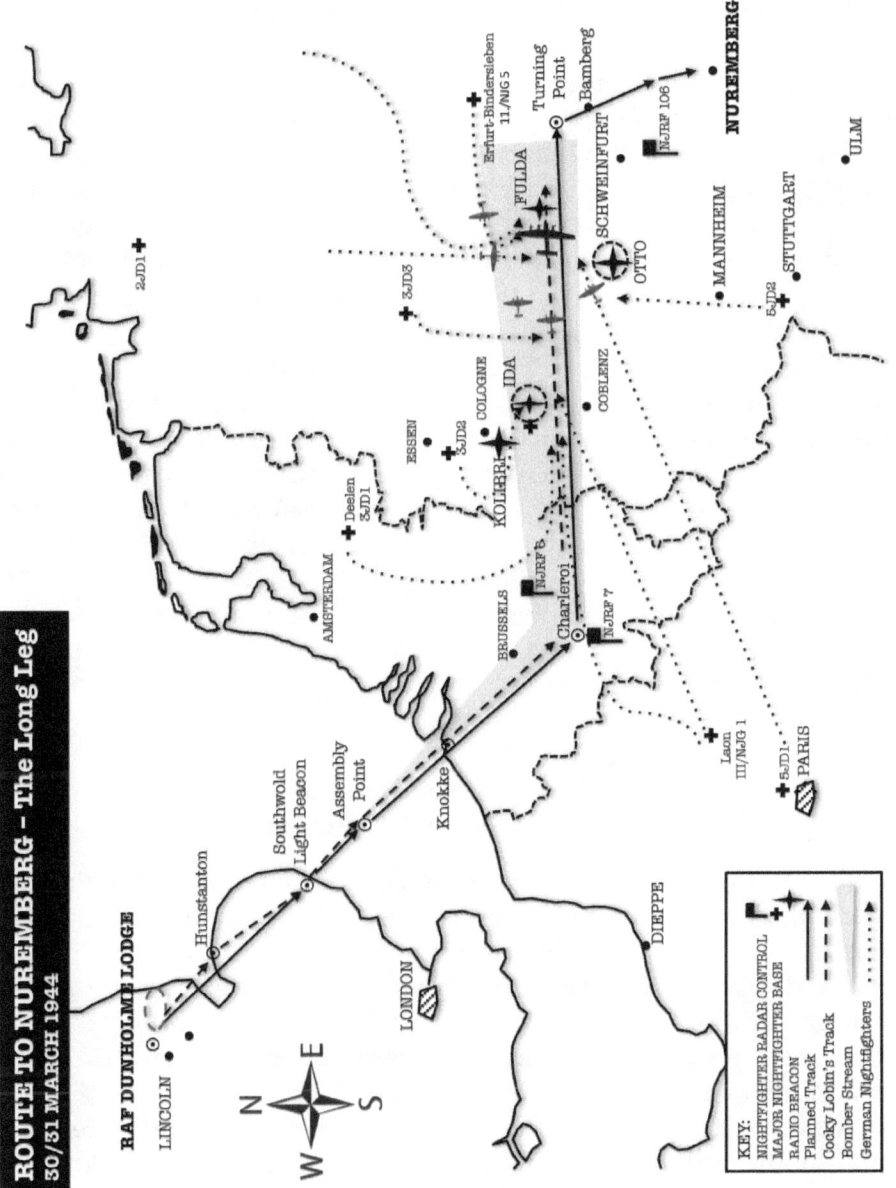

ROUTE TO NUREMBERG – The Long Leg
30/31 MARCH 1944

RAF DUNHOLME LODGE

LINCOLN

Hunstanton

Southwold
Light Beacon

Assembly
Point

Knokke

LONDON

DIEPPE

AMSTERDAM

BRUSSELS

Deelen
3/JD1

ESSEN

3/JD3

COLOGNE

KOBLENZ

Charleroi

Laon
III/NJG 1

PARIS
5/JD1

COBLENZ

IDA

NJRF 7

NJRF 6

FULDA

3/JD3

2/JD1

Erfurt-Bindersleben
11/NJG 5

Turning
Point

Bamberg

SCHWEINFURT

OTTO

NJRF 106

MANNHEIM

STUTTGART
5/JD2

ULM

NUREMBERG

KEY:
NIGHTFIGHTER RADAR CONTROL
MAJOR NIGHTFIGHTER BASE
RADIO BEACON
Planned Track
Cooky Lobin's Track
Bomber Stream
German Nightfighters

Unbeknown to the PFF Lancasters leading the force, the cold front had moved well away to the south. It was replaced by a V-shaped depression caused by warm air ahead of the front being compressed and pushed up over the front. This caused a thick layer of cloud from 1,600ft to 11,500ft. Not only was the V-Shaped depression covering Nuremberg, but the westerly winds had suddenly increased in velocity. The operation had been planned with Visual Markers (the Newhaven method) to be dropped on the Aiming Point, supported by Blind Marker-Illuminators dropped using H2S to flood the whole area with light. Further marking was to be done by supporters[142] coming up with the bomber stream.

What the leaders of the PFF force were now faced with was a cloud-covered target with only a limited number of release point flares or skymarkers (the Wanganui Method) that could be dropped at altitude to lead the bombers to the Aiming Point. They would cascade down with red and yellow stars providing a visual reference for the bombers following behind. The skymarker method was by definition hugely inaccurate, made worse by the strong wind.

The PFF leaders had 8 minutes to readjust, make an appreciation of the changed conditions, recalculate the wind and drop their skymarkers over the target.

*

Cocky Lobin 21,500ft above Bamberg
Friday 31 March 1944, 01:05am

Mosquitoes of 627 Squadron opened the activities of the Primary Marking Force at two minutes to 1 o'clock, offloading 500-pounders and 'window' at the rate of four bundles a minute to disrupt the 100-odd radar-predicted flak guns known to be defending the city of Nuremberg. Ten minutes later, 65 Pathfinders and Supporters had done their best, but the conditions were hopeless. Instead of a clear and vividly marked target for the Main Force bomb aimers, due to arrive at 01.10, there was one group of skymarkers over Nuremberg and another group ten miles to the north-east near Lauf. Both sets of skymarkers were being blown eastwards and falling towards the

---

142 The PFF did not only lead the attack, they were spread throughout the bomber stream referred to as 'supporters' or backers-up', their operation to re-mark the target with new flares as the first ones died out.

clouds.

*

'I can see a group of skymarkers in the distance on a bearing of one-six-four degrees,' called Charles Morley, now hunched over his bombsight. As the position of the aircraft was unclear, and the target obscured, he was not going to be able to use the automatic SABS bombsight.

'Skipper, Nav, turn onto bearing one-six-four degrees, maintain speed one six two miles an hour,' confirmed George Armitage. 'It will be all yours in five minutes Charlie.'

A searchlight broke through a gap in the cloud directly in front of Cocky Lobin. Below, on the northerly edge of the town of Bamberg, a battery of twelve 88mm flak guns using radar guidance, fired in one simultaneous barrage.

As the bomber passed through the searchlight cone a shattering explosion smashed into the nose. The perspex surrounding Charles Morley disintegrated into jagged pieces and blistering hot shrapnel ricocheted back and forth, filling the compartment with choking smoke. The bombsight was utterly destroyed, hanging by a single steel rod, the rest a twisted mess.

More bright explosions hit left and right, peppering the side of the fuselage, drilling holes through the thin skin. The smell of the exploding shells filled the nostrils, burning in the back of the throat. Cocky Lobin shivered from the onslaught. A large hole was punched through the tailplane making her buck wildly, a terrible vibration rattled the length of the fuselage.

Carter and Fullerton were unhurt but five or six panels in the cockpit canopy had cracks and holes in them.

Morley, with his oxygen mask torn away, lay unconscious on the floor, surrounded by pieces of window that now flew about like a blizzard in the freezing cold air.

'Charlie, are you okay?' called Carter, straining to keep the aircraft flying straight and level, she was pulling like a frightened horse, straining to dive.

'Charlie answer me!'

Carter felt the bite of terror in his gut.

'Charlie! ...' *Please answer ...*

Eric Biddle ducked down to check on Morley. Nothing could have prepared him for what he saw.

'CHARLIE! ...' screamed Biddle, the person he was looking at was

277

unrecognisable, Morley's face was a pulpy mass of blood, swollen from the force of the blast. Small slivers of perspex were sticking out of the skin, blood running down his cheeks, dripping off his chin onto the floor.

'Skipper, Charlie's been hit … there's blood everywhere, ' shouted Biddle.

Morley slowly came to his senses, rolling slowly onto his back; his oxygen mask hanging from a clip on his leather helmet. Window continued to flutter about like snow in winter. There was no feeling in his legs and his eyes were clouded over … *I can't see … I can't breath.* Blood flowed into his eyes, he could taste it in his mouth.

One arm seemed to have lost all feeling. It lay dead next to him, he willed it to move but it wouldn't. Charlie instinctively touched his face with his free hand feeling a sharp piece of perspex lodged there, his hand coming away a sticky, horrible mess. *My eyes! … I can't see.*

Forcing himself over onto his side, Morley pushed himself towards the main cabin, his chest heaved from the effects of oxygen depletion.

Morley raised his trembling hand, he could hear Biddle yelling at him but he could not see … *help … help me!*

Biddle bent down to take Morley's hand. Charlie gripped onto it … *please don't let me go Eric* … he could feel the cold blast of air on his face, the cold sucking his strength away.

'Get down there to give a hand,' instructed Carter to Fullerton, who immediately slipped off his seat, coming down behind where Biddle was crouched trying to pull Morley into the cabin. There was only enough room for one person to do it.

'We need to get him out quickly or he will pass out from lack of oxygen,' yelled Biddle, now pulling at both of Morley's arms, but his bulky flying suit was jammed against twisted metal. Fullerton went back into the cabin to get a portable oxygen bottle.

Out ahead of the aircraft more skymarkers began to drop, floating sharply to the east on the rapidly increasing wind.

'Skipper, Nav, turn onto one-seven-five degrees … this is the run to the target,' called Armitage. Stuck behind his desk he could not see the state Morley was in.

Dave Muir was receiving a coded morse message from Group … *di, di, di, … da, da, di, di, …*

It was all confusion, everything happening at once, noise and panic. Carter forced his mind to think, to concentrate, he wanted to see Charlie Morley to speak to him … *please be okay Charlie.*

'Skipper you are going to have to jettison the bombs yourself. The bombsight is US,' called Biddle, straining with all his might to pull Morley free.

The vibration in the aircraft intensified ... Carter was using all his strength to hold the control column back to stop the aircraft diving ... *I don't know how much longer I can hold it.*

'Frank can you see the engines? ... This increased vibration must be one of them,' called Carter, his voice showing the signs of the strain of holding the aircraft level.

'Skipper, I can see a bit of smoke from the starboard outer,' replied Frank Nellyer as he swung his turret about.

As he spoke the engine caught alight, flak had penetrated the crankcase, draining the oil, the engine was now grinding itself to pieces.

As Carter lent forward he managed to shut the fuel master cock to the starboard outer engine. Then he lent over to hit the engine fire extinguisher button which was to the extreme right of the instrument panel, just beneath the feathering buttons. The slight release of pressure on the control column was enough ... Cocky Lobin went into a dive.

Negative-g released Morley causing Biddle to fall forward, but still holding Morley's arms. Fullerton, struggling against the angle of the dive, leaned over Biddle to help pull Morley in.

Carter put his feet up onto the control panel, wedging his legs and then pulled back on the control column. He could not reach the fire extinguisher or the feathering buttons. The fire in the engine raged over the wing.

'Prepare to bail out everyone ... get your parachutes,' called Carter, his insides now gripped in the terror of what was now certain death.

Come on Cocky Lobin ... 16,000ft ...

The altimeter was now unwinding like a spinning top ... cloud base filled the forward view as Cocky Lobin steepened her dive.

Tommy Potts felt the aircraft tip forward, the force of the dive smashed his head against the roof of the turret, momentarily stunning him. Everything became blurred, he blinked hard to try and regain his senses. As he snatched a fleeting glance out the top of his turret, the sky was a mass of twinkling stars ... *is this it for me?*

Potts' parachute was on a hook just outside his turret, he slipped open the doors and pushed himself out backwards. Frank Nellyer dropped out of his sling seat and fell to the floor, pinned there as the g-forces intensified.

The engines were screaming, bits and pieces of loose equipment were flying around the cabin ... still a bone jarring vibration. There was a strong smell of burning oil.

Come on Cocky Lobin … please God help me … Carter swung the wheel controlling the elevator tabs to help him pull the aircraft up.

Dave Muir had his parachute clipped on and was crawling up over the main spar to get to the door in the rear. Tommy Potts was already at the door fighting to open it.

14,000ft … Come on …

Carter pulled back the throttles to try and slow the decent but the aircraft was in free fall, almost vertical now, beginning a spiral to port.

Almost imperceptibly at first, but then increasingly, Cocky Lobin responded, the propeller of the dead engine providing increased drag. Carter could see the clouds rushing up towards him … *12,000ft.*

'Someone get up here to help me,' pleaded Carter as the aircraft slowly pulled back to level flight just as they dropped into the cloud. He pushed the remaining engines back to cruising power just as Eric Biddle appeared next to him. The burning engine had been extinguished simply by the power of the dive.

'Feather starboard outer Eric, check fuel. You are going to have to help me with the control column, she's very, very, heavy.'

Nobody had jumped.

Without Carter calling them, they went straight back to their stations all saying their own personal prayers for salvation.

'Everyone okay?'

They all responded in turn, nobody else was hurt. Fullerton appeared behind Biddle.

'Bill, Charlie is in a bad way, he is losing a lot of blood, his face is a terrible mess,' said Fullerton.

'Do what you can for him, give him a shot of morphine from the first aid kit.'

'Should we jettison the bombs Skipper, and get the hell out of it?' asked Biddle.

'We are so close to the target, we should have a bash at dropping them in the right place.'

Cocky Lobin broke back out of the cloud at just under 12,000ft. Her sisters were lining up on the target 8,000ft above her.

*

Cocky Lobin 12,000ft above Erlangen
Friday 31 March 1944, 1:12am

What should have been a mass of exploding bombs and markers over the target was simply nothing. Just empty sky with the last of the moon reflecting off the endless cloudbank. Cocky Lobin should be about to release her bombs over the target, instead she was met with nothing but empty sky.

Fullerton remained in the back doing what he could for Morley who had passed out. At least the lower altitude dispensed with the need for oxygen.

'Have you got anything on the H2S George?'

'Sorry Skipper just a mass of ground clutter, I can't see the Pegnitz River which should be below us.'

'Look Skipper,' called Biddle, who was using a free hand to pull back the control column just below the yoke.

Out ahead of them there were two well-defined groups of skymarkers, 11 miles apart.

'Which ones are the target? George I need your help up here!'

*

Village of Schönberg, Middle Franconia District, Bavaria, 10 miles (16.7km) northeast of Nuremberg
Friday 31 March 1944, 1:13am

Frau Hanna Gregori heard the first rumble of bombers at just after 1 o'clock. At first, she thought the sound was thunder, but thunderstorms were rare in early spring. *Spring ... we have ten centimetres of snow on the ground outside!*

She lay in her bed looking up at the dark ceiling, straining her ears. She had not been able to sleep, tossing and turning, fearful for what had happened to Otto who had not returned home.

The rumbling sound increased, from a distant gentle drone to a loud, thumping, surging grumble. Schönberg had no strategic value so did not have air-raid sirens and anti-aircraft defence.

It is the Terrorfliegers. Where are they going? It must be Nürnberg.

Nuremberg had been attacked six times before; the last raid had been seven months before. Hanna had read all the details in the newspaper.

Hanna Gregori had heard many aircraft fly over but this was something different, this was the sound of many hundreds of aircraft. In the distance, the sound of exploding bombs carried on the strong westerly breeze.

She climbed out of bed and slipped into her heavy greatcoat. A cold shiver ran through her body despite the coat ... Something told her to put her boots on. Walking to the kitchen window, she pulled open the heavy curtain and in the distance to the north, a beautiful

281

cascading Christmas tree of lights was falling from the sky. The lights looked magnificent, shining and flickering, mesmerising.

Why would they be bombing Lauf, it is such a tiny town?

Then the first string of bombs fell. As Hanna watched in stunned shock, the sky to the north lit up ... CRUMP ... CRUMP ... CRUMP. The wooden floor beneath her feet began to shake and shiver like a frightened child. Crockery rattled on the sideboard, an old painting fell off the wall, splintering the heavy ornate frame.

She could not believe what she was seeing through the window; it was totally incredible ... *why would the British attack such a tiny village?*

Another string of bombs fell, this time much closer, they were falling in the *Spitalwald*, the flashes lighting up the low clouds overhead.

As Frau Hanna Gregori watched out her kitchen window, the true horror of war arrived at her doorstep.

*

M.A.N. Factory, Nuremberg
Friday 31 March 1944, 1:14am

The *Fliegeralarm* at the M.A.N. factory in Frankenstrabe, Nuremberg, had been blaring since 12:38pm. At first nothing happened. Men stopped briefly to look up at the roof of the factory as if they could see imaginary bombers flying high above. The shift supervisors and prison guards also hesitated, talking nervously amongst themselves.

Aurek Dabrowski looked across at his two companions Heniek and Iwan. They nodded knowingly at each other, there were no preparations for the prisoners to be taken to air raid shelters. In fact, nothing concerning air raids had ever been mentioned by the German factory workers. It would appear that the prisoners would take their chances in the open.

Earlier in the evening, an order had come down from the offices that the blackout must be strictly adhered to on this night. Normally the blackout was not enforced and the giant factory doors stayed open with bright light spilling out onto the surrounding streets. Work stopped as the doors and windows were closed and the thick curtains pulled across all the entrances. The lights remained on inside the factory so work could continue. At 12:15 pm the preliminary *Offentliche Luftwarnung* had been sounded. This was a precautionary measure as the bomber force was still many kilometres away.

One of the senior supervisors came rushing down the production line, calling for all staff to go to the shelters. After much confused screaming and shouting by the guards, the prisoners were herded into a storage shed and the outside doors chained and bolted. Now they knew ...

Outside, the citizens of Nuremberg were taking cover as they had been instructed to do. The older houses with basements had been adapted as air raid shelters with emergency access to the street if the house collapsed. The *Altstadt* had four huge towers on each corner with walls two metres thick providing shelter for those that lived in apartments. Out in the suburbs, communal shelters had been built. Firemen, reserve policemen and ambulance workers rushed to their posts.

All the public air raid shelters were connected by a communications network that kept them informed minute by minute as the bombers approached.

Aurek said a silent prayer to himself that the bombers would come and destroy this factory and this city with all its hate and oppression. He had no fear for his own life, he and his friends had long since come to terms with the fact that they were to die in this war. It was only a matter of time. They would prefer to die under the British bombs than by some Nazi SS stormtroopers.

The drone of approaching bombers steadily intensified. To Aurek the sound was strangely peaceful, reminiscent of the Gregorian Chants in the Church of the Assumption of the Holy Virgin Mary in Oborniki. The murmur was a soothing sound, promising forgiveness and redemption, but above all else ... hope. Aurek clamped his eyes shut and prayed.

A few early explosions could be heard some distance away. Steadily the bombing intensified, the windows of the storage shed, twenty feet above the floor, began to rattle. The prisoners sat huddled together on the floor, prayers were being said in Polish and Russian. Many of the men prayed for their own death, for a release from purgatory.

Bombs were now falling on the Altstadt and surrounding suburbs. A favourite dance hall, the *Norishalle,* was hit and flattened. In the sky above, the bombers milled above the clouds, looking for the correct place to bomb.

A string of bombs landed amongst houses across the road from the MAN factory where a fire was started. The explosions were so close that one of the storage shed windows above burst from the force of the impact.

Aurek pleaded ... *please bring the bombs closer.*

18

Cocky Lobin, 12,000ft above the village of Lauf, 11 miles north east of the planned Aiming Point
Friday 31 March 1944, 01:15am

George Armitage had made the decision … target the skymarkers to the east. There were more of them, and from the flashes below the clouds, it appeared to be where the most likely Aiming Point was.

Carter had altered course yet again to 115 degrees. Cocky Lobin was struggling to maintain height on three engines with +14 boost. The manual said clearly not to try and maintain height above 10,000ft on three engines. He just wanted to get his bombs to the target, *to get the bloody job done!*

Ian Fullerton had been sent down into the destroyed bomb aimer's compartment to give directions as best he could to the Aiming Point. The force of the wind through the broken perspex buffeted Fullerton so violently that he had to brace himself against the side of the fuselage, his goggles were misting up in the bitter cold. He looked down at the escape hatch he was sitting on … praying that they would not need to use it.

George Armitage was back at his position on the H2S set to try to identify the target through the clouds. As Armitage he switched the radar set back on, it lit up the Naxos detector on three German nightfighters prowling close by.

Carter's arms had started to shake from the exertion of holding the aircraft level. Eric Biddle had tied a piece of rope, cut from the inflatable life raft, around Carter's seat attached to the control column, to help take the pressure off his arms.

More skymarkers fell ahead of their track confirming in their minds that they were in the right place.

What the crew of Cocky Lobin could not see were the thousands of bombs falling from 8,000ft above them as the bulk of the main force arrived.

'Bomb doors open,' called Carter, pulling the lever to the left of his seat.

'Bomb doors are open Skipper,' called Dave Muir. It was necessary to check visually as the doors often jammed from flak damage.

Carter felt a change of trim as the two massive doors under the aircraft opened, fluttering into the slipstream, a tremble came up through the controls. Everything had to be very steady now, *keep the heading and airspeed correct. Airspeed steady at 160, heading 115 degrees, steady, steady.*

'Steady ... left a bit ... steady.' Fullerton was aiming at an imaginary spot below the brightest set of skymarkers.

'Ready Eric?'

'Yes Skipper.'

Biddle had his hand on the bomb jettison handle on the extreme right of the instrument panel. It was his job to twist the handle on Fullerton's command.

'Steady ... any second ... '

'CORKSCREW PORT ... GO ... GO ...GO,' screamed Tommy Potts from the rear turret.

Tracer seemed to fill the sky in front of the cockpit, whipping past like demented fireflies.

The rope helping to support the control column prevented Carter going into the dive; instead, he pulled it over turning Cocky Lobin onto her wing, dragging the huge aircraft into a turn, her bomb doors still hanging open.

Both gunners were firing into the night, chasing after the nightfighter as it dived away.

'It was a Me110 ... I saw it clearly ... it was so close,' called Potts. 'I am sure I hit it.'

Carter reversed the turn once again holding the aircraft on its wing searching the sky for the nightfighter. More skymarkers were falling, so close they lit up the inside of the cockpit.

'Ian, can you get us back to the target?' called Carter to Fullerton still in the shattered bomb aimer's compartment.

'I think we have overshot ... I can't see anything,' replied Fullerton.

The temptation for Carter to simply jettison the bombs was overwhelming; he could feel his crew willing him to do it ... to get them out of this.

There was silence over the intercom as they waited the few seconds for his decision.

'We will go around again chaps ... we are so close ...' stated Carter quietly, turning Cocky Lobin again as tightly as he could to port, pushing the throttles forward for more power. There was no comment from the crew ... just a collective intake of breath as they got ready for another run at the target.

Cocky Lobin turned through 180 degrees flying back towards the north. Out to the west of the track the flashes below the clouds continued now almost uninterrupted.

'Come round to two-four-two degrees, I think I can see the right spot,' called Fullerton.

'If you can see the target, I will fly directly towards it on this bearing,' replied Carter. *Then carry on for home!*

They were at such a low altitude that the chance of colliding with another aircraft on a converging course was remote. Being 'bombed' from above was a much higher probability.

'Steady ... only a few more seconds ... steady.'

Biddle had his hand back on the bomb jettison handle.

'Steady ... jettison!'

Donk ... Donk ... Donk ... went the bombs as they were released from their hooks. The aircraft reared up as its massive six-ton load dropped away. There was no waiting for the photo-flash from the camera ... there was no point.

'Bomb doors closed,' as Carter's left hand pulled up the lever and his right hand pushed the control column forward to build up speed. He could sense the massive release of tension in the crew as the engine's roar took on a higher note and the airspeed built up to get away from the target area as fast as possible.

'George, get us out of here!' called Carter.

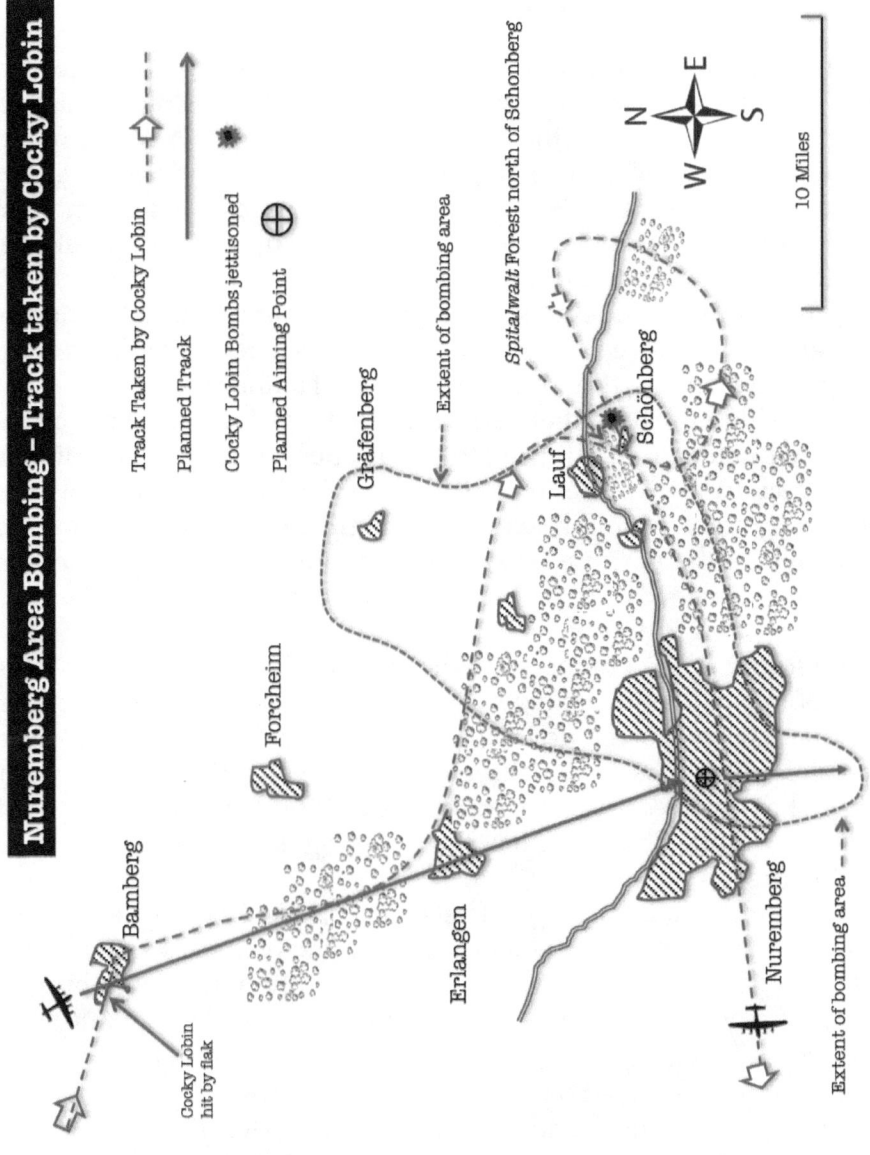

Nuremberg Area Bombing – Track taken by Cocky Lobin

Track Taken by Cocky Lobin
Planned Track
Cocky Lobin Bombs jettisoned
Planned Aiming Point

Bamberg

Cocky Lobin hit by flak

Forcheim

Gräfenberg

Extent of bombing area

Erlangen

Spitalwalt Forest north of Schonberg

Lauf

Schonberg

Nuremberg

Extent of bombing area

N
W   E
S

10 Miles

*

Village of Schönberg, Middle Franconia District, Bavaria, 10 miles (16.7km) northeast of Nuremberg
31 March 1944, 1:18am

Hanna Gregori stood outside the back door looking up at the sky. More brilliant, shining flares were falling through the clouds, making a spectacular sight. Then the bombs came in earnest. A string fell in the neighbouring fields, throwing up torrents of dirt and snow. As she looked to the east towards the village, giant explosions fell amongst the houses. In only a few moments, fires lit up the clouds above, bringing more bombs from the heavens.

An incendiary landed next to the Gregori barn. Inside the horses were squealing, as were the dairy cattle. More incendiary flares were falling in the fields setting haystacks alight. Hanna rushed across the muddy yard to the barn that had started to burn. She threw the doors open and ran inside. Hauling all the stalls open, she urged the animals out, her shouts lost in the roar of engines. The terrified animals ran out into the smoky exploding night, running hither and tither as more bombs fell in the surrounding fields. Opening the doors to the hen hock, Hanna shooed out the chickens that were flying against the wire mesh screeching in terror.

The sound of the bombers overhead, with the constant explosions of the bombs was a deafening roar. The horrific sound was so painful that Hanna was forced to hold her hands against her ears. Each explosion jarred the brain, the over-pressure sucking air from her lungs. Shock waves surged over her, knocking her about making it difficult to stand. She could feel the changing air pressure tugging at her clothing.

As Hanna chased out the last chicken, the flash of a massive explosion struck in a field across the way. The blast was so powerful that it threw Hanna off her feet, the noise was like a thousand thunder claps at once while the supersonic pressure wave blew muddy dirt and debris into Hanna's face, forcing her to bury her head in her hands[143]. The terrific force washed over her, carrying splinters of wood and tiny stones that cut into her hands as she held them over her head.

She lay stunned, ears ringing, covered in a thick layer of snow and mud. Trying to gather her senses, her mind was overwhelmed with the sheer horror of what was taking place around her. As she lifted

---

143 This was likely an 8,000-pounder.

her head, she saw across the fields that the bomb had literally swept a nearby farmhouse from the ground. There was nothing left standing, just charred wood and scattered brickwork.

Dead animals lay all about. A horse lay screaming, kicking out with its legs, throwing its head forward in a vain attempt to regain its feet, its stomach ripped open.

In the next-door field, Hanna saw her neighbour's barn on fire.

Rosemarie!

She scrambled to her feet, shaking off the thick layer of dirt. Suddenly the safety of Rosemarie her young neighbour was of paramount importance.

Rosemarie!

Hanna jumped over the wooden fence and struggled across the slushy field towards the Bongart homestead. Other neighbours in the surrounding farms were all outside their houses, shouting for buckets to put out the fires. To the east the tiny hamlet of Schönberg was burning. As Hanna looked back, the roof of her barn collapsed and the fire spread to the hay store next door.

Still more bombs fell in the fields and the surrounding forest, feeding the storm, adding more weight to its fury. The incendiaries set the undergrowth alight adding to the mayhem. Thick billowing smoke from the fires filled the air making it difficult to breath. All was noise, panic, sickening shock and destruction. Great towers of dirt flew into the sky marking the track of the bombs falling from above ... still the Earth shook ... CRUMP ... CRUMP ... CRUMP.

As Hanna reached her neighbour's gate, out of the smoky light charged a small herd of cattle bellowing in terror. She was unable to get out of the way as the lead animal hit her square in the chest knocking her to the ground. Winded from the blow, Hanna rolled to the side knowing that if she didn't she would be trampled to death. A hoof hit her in the small of the back, another the back of her thigh, each strike worse than the last, knocking her senseless. She lay in the mud next to the gate, gasping for breath, unable to move, her legs felt paralysed. Trying to call out, no sound would come, it was as if a great weight was pressing on her chest forcing the life out of her ... *please God! ... Rosemarie?*

Out towards the north a burning bomber broke through the cloud. Hanna twisted her head as the sound of the high-pitched engines carried to her. As if in slow motion, the bomber continued to drop from the sky, flying directly towards her. The engines on both wings were in flames screaming like a Valkyrie[144], choosing who shall live and who shall die. As the bomber came in over the trees of the forest, the propellers were still spinning. She thought for a split second that it was going to land ... but that was impossible.

The stricken bomber dropped further catching the top of the trees, then dived into the ground in the field next to the Gregori farm. It hit with a sickening thud, its wings and engines ploughing into the soft soil. Skidding across the icy snow, a wing tip hit a fence post, slewing the aircraft to the side.

On it came, kicking up snow and mud.

In stupefying shock, Hanna watched as the burning bomber burst over her farmhouse, demolishing it completely, its wing slicing through the remains of the burning barn, killing a cow trapped against the fence. Still it came on, dirt flying up in front of its nose as it slithered towards where she lay helplessly in the mud.

Hanna screamed in the dark, shutting her eyes against the impact that must come any second ...

As Hanna slowly opened her eyes, no more than thirty metres from where she lay were the remains of the bomber, its wings covered in muddy soil that had smothered the fires. She could feel the smouldering heat against her face, steam lifted from the hot engines. The dead bomber made unnerving wheezing sounds as the scorched metal cooled, like a hound panting after the chase.

She stared into the gaping maw of the bomb aimer's blister with the smashed cockpit above, looking in the ghostly light like the face of a terrifying monster from antiquity breathing fire and destruction.

Nothing moved inside the wreck ... the earth shook again as more bombs fell in the adjacent fields.

*

M.A.N. Factory, Nuremberg
Friday 31 March 1944, 1:18am

Aurek Dabrowski sat in the pitch dark with his back against the wall, his head tucked between his knees, holding as tightly as he could. Bombs were still falling in the city outside, the sound seemed to come from all directions at once, the thumping explosions with the constant surging moan of aero-engines.

Then it came ... the first impact ... very close ... then another even closer ... CRUMP ... CRUMP ... the force of the explosions beating

---

144 Norse mythology, from *valkyrya* 'chooser of the slain' is one of a host of female figures who decide which soldiers die in battle and which live.

inside the chest.

The outside wall of the storage shed burst inwards with the impact of a 1,000lb GP bomb only a few yards away. Those prisoners sitting against the sidewall were crushed under falling masonry. The explosion left a hole in the wall 10ft wide. Thick choking dust filled the room, covering all inside in a grimy film. Men coughed and spluttered, aimlessly milling around in the dark, unable to see inches in front of them.

Aurek did not move at first, his ears ringing from the blast. There was no sound anymore, just silence and choking dust. The air was stuffed with the stench of explosive, powdered masonry and humanity. He pulled his shirt over his nose and mouth to try to breath. As he watched, a star appeared from outside … it blinked yellow and then red.

A beacon …

'Heniek, Iwan … can you see the star?' called Aurek pointing upwards. He could not hear himself speak.

His two friends were by his side gazing at the star that still burned brightly, filling the room with a flickering light. Like him, they could not hear anything except the ringing in their ears.

'Come … we must follow the star,' urged Aurek scrambling to his feet, grabbing at the arms of his two companions, pushing through the surrounding men still shuffling about in disorientated shock.

A gust of fresh air entered the shed. Aurek felt the whisper of a breeze on his face. He shivered. In his tormented mind, it felt as if he had been touched by an angel.

They have sent a sign …

With increasing realisation, Aurek began to shout for the men to get out through the hole in the wall; he still could not hear his own voice …

The marker flare outside blinked out.

As Aurek looked left and right through the murk, the first muted sounds began to filter back into his ears.

Heniek and Iwan were by his side pushing towards the opening. Bodies lay sprawled on the floor, covered in dust, making it hard to walk without tripping. They stumbled towards the opening. More sound filtered through to Aurek as his hearing slowly returned. Those left unhurt slowly came to their senses, men poured through the hole into the street outside.

Once through the hole, the three friends bent over, coughing to get the muck out of their lungs, sucking in the fresh air. As they slowly recovered, the men looked furtively about, unsure of what to do next.

'We should escape to the forest,' said Iwan

'It is too far,' replied Heniek.

'I agree with Iwan. We have our best chance in the forest ... we can escape to the east. Come we have not a moment to lose,' urged Aurek, pointing towards Frankenstrabe. Each man took up a short length of pipe that lay in a pile near the hole in the wall. All about them, the other prisoners were aimlessly wandering about unsure what to do with their sudden, tenuous freedom.

The three men ran towards Frankenstrabe, turning right into the street leading to the east and the forests of the *Reichswald*. The bombs were still falling but way to the north, the flashes reflecting off the low cloud ...

*

Luftwaffe *Nachtjagdgruppe 10* (Müller), 14,000ft southern outskirts of Nuremberg
Friday 31 March 1944, 1:30am

Hauptmann Friedrich-Karl Müller in his Focke-Wulf Fw190 A-6/R11 had been in the air for close to 2½ hours, he knew he only had a few minutes of flying time left before he needed to land. He had followed the bomber stream since they had passed beacon IDA, all the way to the turn towards Nuremberg. Managing to get his radar on a target near Bamberg, he had got close enough to fire his cannon but could not confirm a victory as the enemy had spiralled away into the dark.

In his mind, he was going to try to reach Oberschleissheim (7 *Jagddivision*) north of Munich about thirteen minutes flying time away at his speed.

Müller was now following the tail end of the bomber stream passing over Nuremberg, turning for home. The moon would set in another 17 minutes, that would make further battle difficult.

As he made his decision to turn and begin a descent to Oberschleissheim, a target appeared on his scope a few hundred metres below at a range of 2,000m. With the classical instinct of a hunter, Müller accelerated towards his quarry. It took less than a minute to close the distance. The bomber was flying straight and level but one engine was stopped. Without any attempt at stalking his prey, he fired his cannon at the rear of the bomber. It instantly dived away into a corkscrew.

Müller cursed himself for not being patient. He followed the bomber into the evasive manoeuvre that lasted 5 minutes before the Lancaster settled back on its course almost due west.

Taking up station about a hundred metres off the port beam Müller watched the Lancaster as it trundled along. He was convinced that the gunners must be able to see him but they did nothing. Slowly he inched the Focke Wulf into a firing position, he was so close he could see the flames from the engine exhausts.

Moving his finger over the firing button, Müller took careful aim at a point close to the wing root. As he opened fire, the bomber again dived away, the shells passing harmlessly over the top.

Contemplating another crack at the bomber Müller decided against it. A brave adversary with nerves of steel they had certainly been watching him the whole time.

Hauptmann Friedrich-Karl Müller suddenly felt exhausted, he flicked his Focke Wulf onto a heading for Munich and dived away into the darkness of the early morning.

German nightfighters were landing at airfields throughout southern Germany and France to refuel and rearm.

The British bomber force could no longer be remotely described as a stream. Instead, bombers were spread in an arc from Schweinfurt to Ulm, a distance of over 100miles.

The headwind had increased in intensity and the bombers were still being pushed to the north.

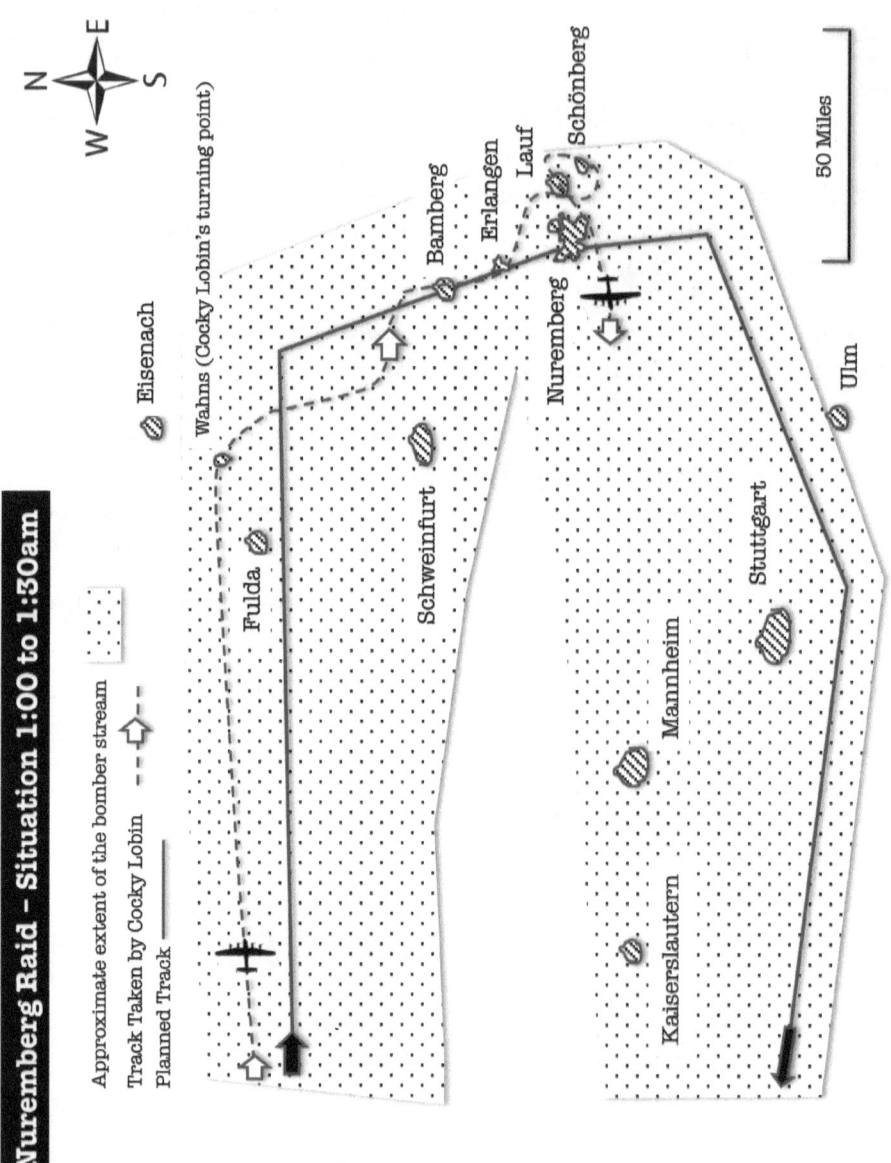

Nuremberg Raid – Situation 1:00 to 1:30am

Approximate extent of the bomber stream

Track Taken by Cocky Lobin

Planned Track

N W E S

Eisenach

Wahns (Cocky Lobin's turning point)

Bamberg

Erlangen

Lauf

Schönberg

Fulda

Schweinfurt

Nuremberg

Mannheim

Stuttgart

Kaiserslautern

Ulm

50 Miles

294

19

Village of Schönberg, Middle Franconia District, Bavaria, 10 miles (16.7km) east of Nuremberg
Friday 31 March 1944, 1:45am

'Frau Gregori! Are you all right?' called Rosemarie Bongart. 'We saw you fall.'

The sound of aero-engines had been replaced with the sounds of fire and destruction.

Hanna Gregori's ears were still ringing painfully, relieved to hear the child's faint voice. She blinked to try and focus in the dark.

Thank God ... Rosemarie is unhurt!

Hanna was still lying on her side against the gatepost, she could feel a tingling sensation in her legs as feeling slowly returned. She was covered in mud from head to foot, and her matted hair stuck to her face.

'Help me up Rosemarie,' called Hanna, lifting an arm towards the young girl.

The forbidding Lancaster still smouldered under its thick layer of mud. There had been no movement from inside.

It was a struggle to regain her feet, a sharp pain shot through her back making her yelp in agony. With Rosemarie supporting under her arm Hanna stood panting against the wooden fence, trying to regain her senses against the pain in her ears.

Both stared fixedly at the wreck of the bomber, as if it would leap up and attack them.

Towards the east, the village of Schönberg was burning, surrounding farmhouses and outbuildings had been burnt out. Incendiary fires still crackled in the nearby forest. Flames were pouring from houses on the outskirts of the village, leaping from one building to the next, engulfing them in seconds. Roof tiles snapped in the heat, the whole village was a sea of flames, lighting up the low hanging cloud above. Hanna shrank back from the terrifying sight ... *these are truly the fires of hell!*

The young Rosemarie began to cry as the horror of what she was witnessing sank in. She clung to Hanna, burying her face in the older woman's arms. Hanna turned towards her own house, there was nothing left standing, it was completely demolished while thick smoke still billowed from the hay store.

'Come child, we must help your father,' said Hanna softly, holding onto the girl tightly, taking a painful tentative step. The Bongart farmhouse was burning, Hanna could see Heinz silhouetted against the fire desperately trying to remove as much as he could from the house, throwing possessions in a pile in the middle of the muddy yard.

Looking towards the village, Hanna now feared for her husband Otto. It seemed impossible for anyone to survive the inferno. She prayed that he might be saved.

The Bongart farmstead was a horrifying sight, pigs lay burnt to death, the draft horses were screaming in panic. Heinz's small dairy herd had escaped into the fields and the road to the village.

As Hanna hobbled on, the strength slowly returned to her legs. The crack on her head had opened up a deep cut. As she touched her forehead, her hand came away with slick, greasy blood. As she looked down, she could see the front of her coat was covered in blood.

'Hanna! ... Hanna!'

She turned towards the sound, a man was running along the road from the village, she could see his outline ... *Otto?*

'Hanna ... it is me, Otto.'

The relief of seeing her husband overcame her, bursting into tears she lurched painfully towards him ... *Otto* ...

The couple embraced, tears running down their cheeks with the realisation that both had survived. They stood there amongst the flames and devastation, holding onto each other ... their most treasured possession had survived ... they were alive.

'Otto the house is finished ... that bomber landed on top of it ... there is nothing left,' said Hanna, tears in her eyes at the realisation that absolutely everything had been lost.

'We have each other Hanna...' replied Otto softly. 'We can build another house.'

Behind where they stood, a young man in flying kit tumbled out of the smashed cockpit of the Lancaster, falling to the ground painfully, giving out an agonising scream.

Hanna and Otto turned towards the sound ...

*

Nuremberg, *Reichsparteitagsgelände*
Friday 31 March 1944, 2:10am

Aurek Dabrowski and his two companions, Heniek and Iwan had passed safely by the entrance to the SS Barracks. The streets were still empty as the citizens of Nuremberg remained in the air raid shelters. They then passed the construction site of the Nazi *Innenhof Kongresshalle* in Bayernstrase with cranes towering above it.

The *Entwarnung,* all-clear sirens, had not yet been sounded.

There were no signs of bombing damage anywhere, but the sounds of fire engines could be heard in the distance. It was only a matter of a few minutes before the guards at the MAN factory would realise that the prisoners had escaped.

'We need to get out of these prison uniforms,' called Iwan as they hurried along, keeping to the shadows of the buildings. It was now pitch dark under the clouds and the moon had set.

There was no time to lose as the three fugitives made their escape, shuffling along in a slow laboured trot which was all their emaciated bodies could manage.

As they approached the intersection with Regensburgerstrase an Opel Blitz 3-tonne truck[145] with a canvas cover over the back, approached from the direction of the *KDF-Stadt,* the compound where the forced labourers were housed. The three men dived onto a clump of bushes just off the road and waited for the truck to pass. Instead of continuing on, it stopped at the intersection. It was the truck used by the prison guards for their own transport and sometimes as a means of moving the prisoners to a work site more quickly.

The driver remained behind the wheel while the passenger opened the door and climbed to the ground. He mumbled something to the driver that Aurek could not hear.

'It is *Unterfeldwebel* Horst,' whispered Iwan. He was one of the most feared of the prison guards, a man in his forties that had been passed over many times for promotion. His hate and frustration was vented on the prisoners.

'Come, we must sneak away,' hissed Heniek. 'We can't wait here.'

'Wait ... ' said Aurek, the flutter of an idea crossed his mind. 'I think there are only two of them.'

Unterfeldwebel Horst spoke again, raising his voice above the idle of the engine. His words were still lost but Aurek could now confirm that it was definitely him.

The German, wearing his steel helmet, began to walk across the road directly towards where the men were hiding. He was not carrying a machine pistol but had a Luger in a holster at his waist. This man would have no hesitation in killing them if he found them. They had seen him shoot numerous prisoners for things as trivial as dropping a tool on a factory floor.

Flattening themselves on the ground they waited, Aurek's mind racing with what he would do if they were discovered. Surrendering

145 Opel Blitz Type 3.6-6700A Cargo Truck, 6 cylinder petrol engine, range 255 miles.

was certain death.

On the man came with a slow deliberate stride … *he could not possibly have seen us!*

Horst stopped, unzipped his fly and began to pee.

Summoning all the energy he could, Aurek leapt up from behind the bushes and rushed forward, the metal pipe above his head. The German was standing only a few yards away, he heard the rustle in the bushes and turned his head to see an apparition appear out of the night running towards him. He gave out a yelp in surprise, his hands diving towards his pistol, backing away as he did so.

Aurek's first blow glanced off the shoulder, his arms so weak that he did not have enough power to slow the man down. Horst grunted from the impact, swinging up his forearm against the second blow aimed at his helmet. While Aurek's blow struck home, it simply ricocheted off the helmet giving off a loud metallic bang. Swinging with his free hand Horst's fist hit Aurek square in the face easily knocking him to the ground. Aurek went over backwards, sprawled in the muddy road.

'Who are you pig?' screamed Horst, lifting his pistol free of the holster, advancing towards the man on the ground. 'Ah, we have an escaped prisoner!'

Horst pulled the trigger, missing Aurek by inches as he summoned up his remaining strength to roll to the side.

Iwan and Heniek, seeing their friend thrown to the ground, rushed forward waving the steel pipes they were carrying. Horst did not see them coming, adjusting his aim at the man on the ground. Another shot cracked in the dark. The men were upon him, swinging the steel bars with all their might. A blow caught him on the knee, he cried out as the pain shot up his leg. Another hit him on the back of the helmet knocking it over his eyes.

The driver of the truck hearing the two shots ring out, jumped out of his seat and ran around the side of the truck his pistol in his hands. All he could see was the movement of bodies across the road, it was impossible to see what was going on.

'Stop!' he shouted.

Still the desperate fight continued. Aurek scrambled back to his feet, joining his friends raining down blows on the German. The man had fallen to his knees, his pistol smashed out of his hand.

'Stop or I will shoot,' called the driver, afraid to cross the road into the darkness.

With a loud grunt, Horst fell face first into the mud. Metal pipes flew in the night as three men vented four years of anger and desperation on the German, crushing his head to pulp.

The driver, realising that Horst was being attacked, spun around to get back to the truck.

Aurek saw him. He grabbed the pistol from where it had fallen and chased across the road. The driver shoved the truck into gear accelerating away. Aurek leapt onto the running board on the passenger side wrenching the door open. The driver who was only a young man himself, panicked when he saw the mud splattered ghoul spring into the cab, gun in his outstretched hand. He swung the steering wheel hard to throw the man off balance.

The bullet entered just above his temple, spraying blood and bone over the window. The driver slumped to the side, his foot wedged on the accelerator. The truck lurched off the road and ploughed into a tree. Aurek did not have time to brace himself as the impact threw him hard against the steel dashboard, knocking him senseless. The engine stalled.

*

Cocky Lobin, 10,000ft above the village of Heddesheim, 7 miles northeast of Mannheim
Friday 31 March 1944, 02:21am

'Dave have you had any more wind information?' asked George Armitage for the umpteenth time. His frustration was unbearable.

'No George, nothing in the last five minutes since last you asked,' replied Muir patiently.

Cocky Lobin could not maintain height above 10,000ft on three engines and had sunk into the cloud base that topped out at 11,500ft. George had them flying on a bearing of 268° roughly parallel to the planned return track but many miles to the north. The three engines made it necessary to fly as close to directly home as possible. Armitage suspected the wind into them had strengthened, slowing their speed. He was right, the headwind was at 65mph, it would take them another 4 hours to get home.

The clouds protected them against nightfighters, some small mercy, but it did not protect them from radar and flak. George figured that he was at a position roughly 11 miles south of where he actually was. His eyes flicked between his map and the H2S set anticipating the Rhine River that would give him an accurate fix despite the ground clutter.

Bill Carter was still straining against the control column helped by Eric Biddle who was holding the rope wrapped around his seat. The rope took some of the strain away and allowed Carter brief moments to rest his tired arms. The damage to the rudder and rear elevator also made the foot load heavy, with the result that his left leg was getting pins and needles from the pressure of holding the aircraft on the correct heading.

To the north, at 25 miles, was NJRF 103 the fighter control station that was tracking Cocky Lobin's position and relaying information to nightfighters circling the Beacon at JACHS. In fact, NJRF 103 had no less than sixty bombers on their scope, but as they were so spread out it was difficult to vector nightfighters accurately towards them. The cloud also hampered the nightfighters, made doubly difficult by the fact that the moon had set.

Less than 7 miles ahead of Cocky Lobin lay the major industrial complex of Mannheim straddling the River Rhine, with its massive flak defence.

The crew of Cocky Lobin were unaware of the danger.

On the ground the information from NJRF 103 had been relayed to the radar–predicted flak batteries scattered around the city. Bells were ringing loudly as the men of the gun batteries loaded the 88mm shells into the breach, slamming them shut with a loud metallic bang, barrels swinging towards the incoming track. The local Würzburg radar gave distance and height information to the German Kommando Gerät 40, which was a mechanical ballistic computer that calculated and transmitted the electronic firing solution directly to the heavy AA guns of the battery.

The searchlight crews had their lights off but aimed at the track indicated by the radar plot. Above them the cloud was as low as 2,000ft but beginning to break up. As the gun-crews studied the sky, increasing clear patches between the clouds revealed the stars beyond.

The first flak burst 1,000 yards on the port side of Cocky Lobin. It lit up the cloud in a bright flash. Then another ... and another.

The explosions were so close that they could be heard over the intercom and the engines. Carter could not believe the sudden onslaught of flak, George had not given any warning.

Where the fuck are we George?

Cocky Lobin began to buck wildly from the exploding over-pressure, making the ears pop. *It is so thick I could get out and walk on it*, thought Carter, fighting the controls. Biddle played out the rope to allow forward and backward movement, like an out-of-control *Laurel & Hardy* movie but with absolutely nothing funny about it. The smell and acrid taste of cordite in the back of the throat entered through the oxygen mask.

As if a stage curtain swung open, Cocky Lobin flew out of the cloud into clear sky.

Below searchlights flashed on, swinging across the sky in a macabre ballet, dancing that death may be delivered swiftly.

As Carter glanced to starboard, a searchlight picked up a nearby bomber, ridiculously close. Like a pride of lions sensing a kill, the others swung towards it, chasing after it like a lioness pursuing a gazelle, darting left and right. The tormented bomber twisted and turned trying to shake off the hunters, the flak came in a torrent of steel … the first claws went home.

The outcome was now shockingly predictable … first one hit, then another … the bomber lurched as if struck hard in the back. It staggered as more killing strikes went home. The mortally wounded Lancaster dropped a wing, an engine burst into flame. It began, slowly at first, with increasing speed, to give up the sky. She turned onto her back, more flames spreading across her wings, the hunters were all over her now, tearing her apart in screeching death. Almost mercifully, she blew up, spraying burning debris, like her very lifeblood, across the sky.

Where once there were seven brave men, with their lives still before them, there was nothing.

Still the searchlights swung, gleefully now, excited with their kill, seeking another.

It was Cocky Lobin's turn.

Carter saw it coming from the corner of his eye. It passed across their front, what seemed only a few yards, then reversed its course … it had them.

The giant eye held Cocky Lobin fixedly in its sight, unwavering, triumphantly.

Others streaked across the sky, Carter could see them coming … he had only a few seconds more.

He thrust forward on the column, yanking the rope from Biddle's grasp, rammed the throttles forward and let Cocky Lobin dive. Still the light held them in a blinding glare, Carter could see nothing except the light, his eyes forced shut from the pain.

With a rattle on the fuselage the flak came, punching holes in the thin defenceless skin, unstoppable.

Charlie Morley lay semiconscious on the floor just forward on the main spar, helpless and unprotected. A piece of flak the size of a tennis ball, entered through the bomb bay doors, up through the floor and into the small of Charlie's back. It tore through his spine, churning his insides, then up, burning hot, through the top of the fuselage out into the night. Charlie's body lurched upwards from the impact, then fell back, blood sprayed through the cabin over Dave Muir's crouching back, then over his radios.

Muir looked back. In the light of the searchlight he saw his friend's eyes flicker open looking pleadingly at him …

'Charlie!'

Muir pinned himself against the side of the fuselage, all he could do was hold out his hand towards his friend. Charlie's lips moved … *goodbye* … the bright light flickered away as Cocky Lobin pushed out of the searchlight cone.

Say a prayer for me …

Charlie Morley's life left him … his last glimmering image, the rolling granite hills of New South Wales.

5,000ft …

'Starboard inner's on fire Skipper,' shouted Eric Biddle.

'There's a bloody great flame going past the tailplane,' screamed Frank Nellyer.

'Ian, feather the starboard inner and push the fire extinguisher', called Carter, his eyes still straining to refocus from the powerful searchlight.

He glanced to his right to get some help. Fullerton lay slumped against the canopy, blood all over his face, pouring down the front of his flying suit.

Biddle leaned forward and hit the feather and extinguisher controls.

'Okay Skipper … Fire's still burning Skip … Shit!'

Thoughts rushed through Carter's mind as he continued to throw the aircraft about to keep away from the roaming searchlights.

We must be a choice target now, lit up in the night sky like a flaming comet and if we don't get this fire out we have HAD IT!

Carter pulled back on the control column … straining with every sinew … she would not respond.

'Abandon the aircraft! Everyone bale out … get out … get out now!' called Carter desperately, as the altimeter inexorably unwound.

4,000ft …

20

**Village of Schönberg, Middle Franconia District, Bavaria, 10 miles
(16.7km) northeast of Nuremberg
Friday 31 March 1944, 3:00am**

Hanna and Otto had heard the cry of pain from the bomber. At first, they could not believe their ears.

How was it possible for anyone to survive such a crash?

'What shall we do? These men are animals, they will kill us without thinking,' whispered Hanna, as if the wrecked bomber itself could hear her. She was still in great pain, her legs felt uncertain as she leant against her husband.

'We must go and investigate. Wait here, I will fetch a weapon from Bongart,' replied Otto, gently leading Hanna to a fence post.

'No ... these *Terrorfliegers* will kill us, they are monsters. The authorities have warned us never to go near them. We must call the army,' objected Hanna, playing over in her mind the newsreels she had seen at the cinema. Otto was already running towards where the Bongart's were standing staring at the ruins of their house.

To the east, Schönberg was still burning. The Bongart house was now burnt to the foundations. Poor Rosemarie stood clinging to her father as the last of the flames smouldered away. It began to snow very lightly, the gently floating flakes reflecting in the flames from the village.

Otto returned with Heinz Bongart who was holding a shotgun and a torch. Otto was armed with a pitchfork. Rosemarie ran to Hanna in absolute terror shaking from the shock of what she had witnessed.

Slowly the tiny party advanced towards the bomber.

'Hold the gun at the ready Heinz, don't hesitate to shoot,' instructed Otto. Heinz was also a veteran of the Great War and needed little instruction on weapons.

At first it was impossible to see anything just the silhouette of the bomber in the field. It was soft and muddy under foot, making it increasingly difficult for Hanna to keep her balance. Rosemarie was struggling to provide her support.

They approached the broken nose of the aircraft. Heinz flicked on the torch and there on the ground next to the aircraft was a man in a flying uniform with his leather helmet in place. His mask hung next to his face as he lay flat on his back. He did not move, as Heinz played the torch across his body they gasped in horror as they saw that the whole of his body below the waist was burnt. The trousers were burnt away in places revealing scorched skin, there was the smell of burnt oil and flesh in the air.

Stepping forward, Otto knelt down next to the man's face. Hanna hobbled forward behind him.

'He is just a child! ...' she exclaimed incredulously. 'How can this be?'

Heinz held the torch on the man's face, he looked like a young teenager, his fresh face untarnished by the rigours of age. His face looked peaceful.

The eyes opened. They recoiled as if the wounded man could leap up and devour them. Heinz instinctively lifted the shotgun.

'Please help me,' the man asked in the faintest of whispers.

'What did he say?' asked Hanna.

'I don't know, he is speaking English,' replied Otto.

'Where am I?' rasped the man, his eyes wide now blinking at the light shining in his face.

'We need to get him to a doctor,' said Otto. 'He is very badly injured.'

'I say we shoot the bastard,' blurted out Heinz, obviously in deep distress. 'Look what they have done ... they have taken everything from us ... we are left with nothing, how are we to survive?'

'We cannot shoot him Heinz, he is a prisoner of war,' retorted Otto, pushing the shotgun away with his hand.

'I say we kill him ... kill them all,' cried Heinz, his voice wracked with despair ... his fear for his future and the future of his daughter rushing into his mind with a flood of emotion ... as if shooting this monster would somehow relieve his pain.

'No ... come on Heinz, he is just a boy, look at him,' said Otto standing up, putting his hand on his neighbour's shoulder. 'Look at him Heinz, he could be your son Paulus.'

Heinz looked down at the young man ... *yes indeed he looks like my boy Paulus.*

Along the road from Lauf in the north, a small convoy of trucks drove towards Schönberg. Their hooded headlamps throwing tiny pools of light in front of them. The snow began to fall more heavily. When they saw the shape of the wrecked Lancaster they pulled off the road.

A group of men came struggling through the mud towards where the farmers stood.

'Stop!' shouted a voice. 'Put your hands up!'

A powerful torch lit up, shining into the faces of the farmers who stood looking back in surprise at the command.

A man obviously in charge stormed up.

'Why are you people standing next to this aircraft … you have been told never to approach a crashed plane,' demanded the man without any introduction.

Heinz returned the favour by shining his torch into the face of the officer. The SS insignia at his neck shone in the torchlight.

The man lifted his hand to shield his eyes.

'Turn off that torch you peasant! Can you not see that we are SS?'

'There is a wounded man here. He needs urgent medical attention. We need to get him to a hospital,' said Otto, totally unimpressed with the mention of 'SS'.

'Hospital! You have got to be joking … can you not see the destruction they have wrought? Your village is burning as are Lauf and Nürnberg.'

'He is a prisoner, it is our duty to give him assistance,' replied Otto, his contempt clear in his voice.

'No Otto!' Hanna interjected, realising her husband's temper was rising.

'Your duty! … What is your duty peasant?' spat the officer. 'Your duty is to feed the pigs … you even live like pigs!'

'Don't you speak to me like that …' demanded Otto raising his voice to the man who was half his age.

Ignoring Otto's objection the young officer pointed to the airman on the ground, 'Pick him up and throw him in the back of the truck … there are bound to be more tonight. Search the wreck in case there are any more left alive.'

'No …' shouted Otto stepping in front of the officer, who was a head shorter than him. 'I might be a farmer but I know what is right and wrong. I demand that we take this man to a doctor.'

'No Otto … please' pleaded Hanna pulling at his sleeve. She could see that Otto was about to make one of his principled stands. She knew how he hated the Nazis.

'He is right,' interrupted Heinz the shotgun still cradled in his arm. 'This man must be given medical attention!' Heinz also had no time for the SS and the Gestapo.

The young officer blinked in disbelief. He had never been confronted by a situation where two peasant farmers defied his instructions. Momentarily lost for words, the man weighed up the situation. His hand unclicked the holster and he lifted out his Luger pistol.

'If you say one more word I will shoot you. Do you hear me?' There was now something very sinister about this man. The four soldiers with him lifted their rifles.

Something snapped in Otto's brain.

The fight in the forest, being detained the day before on trumped up charges by the despicable Bürgermeister, and now this little SS turd throwing his weight about was just too much. *What are we fighting for? ... These disgusting animals ... calling us pigs!*

'You will leave this man alone. We will take him to the doctor,' demanded Otto defiantly. 'Now piss off back to the hole you came from!' he added pointing towards the trucks on the road.

The officer lifted his Luger pointing it directly at Otto's chest only a few feet away. With an automatic reflex, Otto swatted at the outstretched arm with the pitchfork. One of the tines dug into the man's forearm opening a deep cut. The man screamed in pain clutching his arm as the Luger fell to the ground. The other soldiers did not know how to react, clearly not prepared to fire on their fellow countrymen.

'Shoot them!' screamed the officer, spittle flying from his mouth.

'Take him away,' ordered Otto with the pitchfork now thrust into the officer's chest. He jabbed forward prodding the man painfully.

The young officer was lost for words, he looked around in disbelief as his soldiers looked on, lowering their rifles.

'Go ... leave us to deal with this ... you have more important work to do, your help is needed in the village,' said Otto, more conciliatory, pointing towards the flames on the hill.

'Come Sir,' said one of the soldiers. 'We will deal with these people later.'

He took his officer by the arm and led him back down towards the trucks.

'You have not heard the last of this Otto,' said Heinz, impressed with the fortitude shown by his friend.

'Those people are bullies hiding behind their uniform. Come let's make a stretcher and try to get some help for this man,' replied Otto, knowing in his heart that Heinz was right.

The bells of the *Kirche St. Jakobus* began to ring out into the night, as if to comfort the people of the village, to remind them of their faith.

*

Hirschau Germany, 60km east of Nuremberg
31 March 1944, 3:45am

The three prisoners, with their stolen truck, had made their escape on a rutted track deep within the *Reichswald* to the east of Nuremberg. From there, they had chosen a road travelling to the north until they struck a major road to the east. The road sign said 'Wernberg 65km'. Heniek was driving with Iwan in the passenger seat. Aurek lay in the back of the truck wrapped in a blanket. He was still semiconscious after the hard crack on the head that had opened a cut over his eye. Iwan could see Aurek lying in the back through the window in the back of the cab. Each jolt threw Aurek around painfully.

They had stripped the clothing off *Unterfeldwebel* Horst and the driver. Iwan was now wearing Horst's uniform that was at least two sizes too big in his shrunken state. Heniek's uniform fitted better. They each had a pistol at their waist and the Schmeisser machine pistol they had found in a trunk in the truck. Aurek was still wearing his prison uniform. All three men could speak German fluently but Iwan had the best command of the language. Their loose plan was to pretend that they were escorting an escaped prisoner back to a camp in Wernberg that they knew to be close to the Czech border, the region claimed by Germany called the Sudetenland.

Their goal was to get to a cabin that Heniek's uncle had in the Sudetes Mountains on the Polish – Czechoslovakian border, a trip of about 445km. The truck had a full tank of petrol but would likely not make it all the way.

The roads had been very quiet, they had seen only a few vehicles going the other way and had not had to negotiate any checkpoints.

If they tried to cross into Czechoslovakia there was certain to be a checkpoint. They had no papers, no identification, nothing of their own, but they carried the ID of the dead Horst and his driver. There was no resemblance whatsoever … the three Poles were walking skeletons. They were never going to bluff their way through a checkpoint, particularly since both uniforms were caked in blood.

As they passed a sign saying Hirschau 2km, the hooded headlights picked up a roadblock. There was a boom across the road, lit by a powerful security light. Next to the boom was a small guardhouse. Heniek braked hard with a loud squeaking noise from worn brakepads.

'What are we going to do?' called Heniek glancing across at his

307

friend, his nerves a jangled mess, made worse by the throb of hunger in his gut.

'Slow down, approach at walking pace, we may have to run the road block,' replied Iwan, his nerves in an equally raw state. The two men had already discussed the fact that if they were captured they would likely by shot out of hand … it made decision making easier … they had nothing to lose.

Aurek gave a groan from the back of the truck, his head was throbbing fit to burst.

The truck slowed down, Iwan double de-clutched expertly. A German soldier, his rifle slung over his shoulder, walked out into the road in front of the boom. He held up his arm indicating for the vehicle to stop. He appeared to be alone, but there were bound to be others close by.

'Steady friend,' said Iwan touching Heniek on the arm. 'Let me handle this. If the man is not convinced, ram the boom with all the power you can get out of this thing.'

Heniek brought the truck to a halt well short of the boom, he kept the revs up as he did so, his foot on the clutch, his hand on the gearstick.

The guard was clearly a little perplexed that the approaching vehicle had not driven right up to the boom.

Iwan lifted the Luger on his lap with his left hand and held its muzzle just below the wound-down window. Heniek had his pistol on the bench seat next to him, next to the Schmeisser. The soldier walked down the road towards them, approaching the passenger side window.

'*Guten Morgen,*' called Iwan before the man got to the window.

'*Heil Hitler! Papiere bitte,*' ordered the guard, in a mechanical fashion. Clearly, he was tired after pulling a night shift. He was simply going through the motions. He quickly noted that these men in the vehicle were not officers so he did not have to bow and scrape.

'*Unser Papiere sind im Regen ein bisschen nass geworden. Bitte entschuldigne Sie dies[146],*' replied Iwan, handing over the two ID tags.

The man took the documents and flicked on his torch, then swung it up into the faces of the two men in the truck. He held it there for a few seconds while he tried to reconcile the raw unshaven faces with the ID. The torch shot back to the tags in his hand.

Unconvinced the guard asked, '*wohin fahren Sie?[147]*' His demeanour changed to suspicion.

146 'I am sorry our orders got wet in the rain, here is our identification.'
147 'Where are you travelling to?'

Aurek gave a loud moan from the back of the truck. The man looked up in alarm, his mind was clearly racing.

'*Wir bringen zwei entkommene Gefangene auf die Wernburg*[148],' chipped in Iwan. It was the fluent German and neutral accent that had the man in two minds.

'Let me see the prisoner,' the man ordered. His footsteps could be heard on the gravel next to the road as he walked to the back of the truck.

Iwan opened the door to follow the guard. The truck was closed in with a canvas cover. Using both his hands, the guard undid the flap and threw the canvas open shining his torch inside. Aurek's gaunt face looked back, dried blood all over his forehead.

'Looks like you fucked him up,' smiled the guard.

'Yes, these Polish pigs have hard heads,' laughed Iwan.

It must have been the mention of 'Polish'. The guard's torch flashed back into Iwan's thin emaciated face.

Iwan smashed *Unterfeldwebel* Horst's SS dagger into the man's throat, stifling any sound. He twisted the hilt viciously and pulled it out. A terrible gurgling sound came from the man's throat as he tried to breath through his severed windpipe. Iwan grabbed his sagging body and held him up against the tailgate.

'Quick, help me,' hissed Iwan. Aurek leaned over and pulled on the man's shoulder straps while Iwan heaved him upwards into the back of the truck. Iwan then dashed forward towards the boom, lifting it up by leaning hard on the counterweight.

'*Hans, ist alles ganz recht?*' called a voice from the guardroom.

'*Ja*,' was all Iwan dared to say.

The truck came forward, Iwan leapt up into the seat and slammed the door shut. Heniek accelerated away. They knew that in a short time all the roadblocks would be alerted. They were not going to get a second chance.

The truck raced through the tiny towns on the way to Wernberg. Just short of the town, a large sign pointed to the east, Czechoslovakia 30km. Another sign said Prague 185km.

---

148 'We are carrying an escaped prisoner to Wernberg.'

*

RAF Bomber Command HQ, Code Name 'Southdown', Walters Ash, Buckinghamshire, 4 miles northwest of High Wycombe Friday 31 March 1944, 04:30am

... But I've a rendezvous with Death
At midnight in some flaming town,
When Spring trips north again this year,
And I to my pledged word am true,
I shall not fail that rendezvous.
Alan Seeger (1888 - 1916), Rendezvous, last stanza.

Wingco Felix Fawssett, Intelligence Officer – Targeting, was in his cramped office down 'The Hole', the Bomber Command Operations Room. He was the evening's designated duty officer, a role taken in turns by the senior staff at Southdown when the Command was on operations.

Fawssett yawned loudly, looking at his watch. He played over the operation profile in his mind as he had done all evening. The leading aircraft in the stream should be crossing the English Coast on the final return leg.

A disturbing phone call had been received from his good friend Sqn/Ldr Ronny Budge, the CO of RAF West Kingsdown, at just after 12:30am. RAF West Kingsdown[149] was the headquarters of the RAF 'Y' Service, responsible for a network of a dozen Y Listening Stations ranging from Montrose in Scotland to Strete in the Southwest. The intelligence that the Y network gathered was sent to RAF Sector Stations if the intercepted traffic was voice traffic, and to Station X at Bletchley Park in Bedfordshire for analysis if it was in morse code.

Ronny was a small, wiry man born in Devon with enormous energy and a great capacity to instil enthusiasm. He took his job desperately seriously and his team had made many successful discoveries of German tactics and radar equipment. Their job was doubly important

---

149 As RAF West Kingsdown was primarily a listening station the main equipment were radio receivers. American made Hallicrafter S-27, that covered frequency range of 28Mc/s to 143 Mc/s. For the high frequency range the RCA AR88 and National HRO sets were used. West Kingsdown had 68 of these listing sets. As West Kingsdown was also a direction finding (D/F) station there was either a R1481 that covered VHF low band 66Mc/s - 86Mc/s or R1132A that covered the higher frequency airband of 100Mc/s - 124Mc/s for direction finding. The whole of the Kingsdown network had a further 100 listening sets and 11 D/F sets.

on nights when major raids were undertaken[150].

Fawssett decided to give it a few more minutes before he phoned Ron again, as he had done every hour since 12:30. He got up to make himself another cup of tea; he had lost count on how many he had drunk through the night. There were three Waaf signallers on duty in the Operations Room, the sound of their typing and soft conversation was strangely comforting, providing a haven of normality on a night that was anything but.

The RAF West Kingsdown station was located at Hollywood Manor on School Lane in the North Kent village of West Kingsdown, on top of the North Downs[151]. A set of 90-foot masts stood high above the buildings. There was also a secondary station at Wrotham 3miles down the A20 with a 240-foot high mast.

Fawssett made his tea and walked back to his office. He picked up the phone and called Ron Budge. The phone rang only twice before it was picked up.

'Skylark,' the woman's voice said.

'Southdown here, can I speak to Squadron Leader Budge please?'

There were only a few seconds before Budge came on the line.

'Budge here.'

'Ron its Felix, any more news?'

'Well, we have collated about five hundred radio messages sent by the Germans in clear so far. I have to tell you it makes pretty horrific reading,' said Budge earnestly.

'What is the upshot of it all Ron?' asked Fawssett, dreading the answer.

'Taking into account, transcription error – you must understand the airwaves were literally alive between midnight and two am – we estimate we may have lost as many as sixty five aircraft shot down by fighters,' replied Budge, shocked by his own words. After

150 The radio operators also had to decode the Luftwaffe language that they heard. Like the RAF, the Luftwaffe used code words to give certain instructions or convey information. Once these code words were decoded, it made the job of the RAF pilots a lot easier. Important operational intelligence that was heard and could be acted on, was immediately passed onto RAF Group to be passed onto RAF Sector Stations and then onto aircrews as they were flying.

151 The RAF Y Stations, or Home Defence Units as they were known, concentrated on intercepting voice (R/T) traffic but also intercepting morse (W/T) traffic encoded by the famous German Enigma machine. Cheadle in the Midlands was the main W/T Intercept station for the RAF but Kingsdown also kept Station X fed with W/T intercepts. The name, Home Defence Units, was used to try and deceive the enemy about the true nature of these stations. German speaking operatiors wrote down all the R/T traffic in shorthand as it was heard and later transcribed into longhand and into a daily log that each operator kept.

a pause, Budge could sense the distress on the other end of the line. 'We did send out warnings to the Group stations Felix, as soon as the German fighter controllers began their running commentary. The 101 Squadron jamming was just not successful on this trip. Our own Corona[152] people couldn't keep up, we were just overwhelmed by the sheer weight of traffic. I've never seen anything like it.'

There was silence on the line as Fawssett tried to come to terms with the frightening information he had been given. The West Kingsdown people were good, very good. They were normally uncannily accurate.

'Are you still there, Felix?' asked Budge, through the prolonged silence.

'Are you sure Ron? ... It's ... it's unbelievable ... it's a catastrophe of monumental proportions,' whispered Fawssett, almost too afraid to say the words. Fawssett knew the answer.

'That's the situation so far ... the poor beggars are still up there. We are still getting radio traffic but much less concentrated. You can expect more losses ...'

Fawssett's stomach tightened into a knot, he suddenly felt ill.

'Thank you Ron ... please keep me updated,' said Fawssett distractedly, replacing the receiver as if it was a piece of Ming China.

Looking at his watch again, Fawssett considered whether he should call the Deputy AOC-in-C AVM Saundby.

What difference will it make, the men are already dead ... more are dying ... there is nothing anybody can do ...

West Kingsdown reported on nightfighters only ... there were still losses from flak, friendly fire, collisions and crashes when the poor blighters got home in damaged aircraft.

AVM Saundby will be in in less than an hour ...

Fawssett dropped his head into his hands ... *why did they let them go?*

---

152 Operation Corona was started from West Kingsdown. This involved German-speaking personnel countermanding the orders of German controllers and feeding false information using high-powered transmitters. To try and stop this the Germans switched from male controllers to female. the RAF swiftly copied this.

RAF Dunholme Lodge, Lincolnshire
Friday 31 March 1944, 5:00am

Section Officer Jill Evans had been up for three hours. Sleep had been impossible since midnight, her mind a jumble of emotions that she was struggling to come to terms with. In a way, she felt more vulnerable than at any time in her life. Carter's letter had awakened long-buried feelings that were now raw and exposed.

Eventually giving up on sleep altogether, she got up, put on her uniform and went down to the Waaf mess for tea and a sandwich. There were other Waafs on duty throughout the station. Some drifted in for a quick bite before rushing back to their posts.

Jill read the two-day old newspaper in the mess, unable to concentrate or take in anything she was reading. She decided to go over to the Intelligence Section offices next to the Operations Room.

She looked at the clock on the wall and asked the Waaf clerk if all the signals from Group were in the file. The girl confirmed they were, but that the file was with the Squadron Intelligence Officer, Sqn/Ldr Laurence Baxter.

Laurence Baxter never went to bed on a night when a large raid was on. It was his personal tribute to the aircrew. He had sent them on their way, the least he could do was to wait it out with them. He had his injured leg up on the desk; he said it was less painful when it was elevated.

Jill liked Laurence Baxter despite the fact that he was a bit taciturn. It was obvious that he had wounds much more serious than his leg … wounds of the mind. He was bitter at not being able to fly … stuck behind a desk … in constant pain. Jill could identify with his pain and the sense of loss, accepting his sometimes brusque, almost rude behaviour.

'Anything interesting from Group, Sir?' asked Jill standing in the door to Baxter's office.

'The southwesterly winds have strengthened considerably … our chaps are likely to be late getting back,' replied Baxter distractedly.

'Do we know how long?' asked Jill, a hint of concern in her voice.

'Maybe as much as half an hour, but that's not my principal concern, it's the blasted weather!'

'What is the situation with the weather?' asked Jill, now more concerned.

'Well, the reports are still a bit scanty but it seems good over France and the Low Countries and Southern England, but we have increasing northerly winds and snow, sleet and showers travelling south. While it is clear out now, we may have fog move in any minute,' said Baxter woodenly, as if he was reading the weather report on the BBC.

Jill felt a knot tighten in her stomach, the thought of the boys flying all the way home and not being able to land always worried her, but it happened more often than not.

'Have they activated the diversionary plan?' asked Jill, referring to the directive from HQ whenever bad weather closed in, to help the pilots find alternative airfields as quickly as possible.

'I suspect so, you had better ask Flying Control.'

'I will go up there and see. Can I bring you a cup of tea on the way back?' asked Jill with a smile. It was so sad to see this once active and virile man reduced to a sulking, moribund wreck.

Baxter didn't answer, merely flicking his hand dismissively.

Jill left Baxter's office to walk through the Ops Room to the adjoining covered passage to the control tower. There were four Waaf clerks on duty, the teleprinter was clattering away, a wireless was playing softly in the background.

As she walked past the large blackboard she hesitated to cast her eye once again down the crews on operations ... A-Able ... B-Baker ... C-Charlie ... Carter, Armitage, Morley, Biddle, Nellyer, Muir and Potts. Written below in tiny chalk writing, second-dicky Fullerton. An inexplicable shiver of foreboding washed over her ... the feeling people describe as 'someone walking over their grave'[153].

She was about to leave the Ops Room when the silky voice of Ann Shelton came on the radio. Jill paused ...

'Please turn it up?' asked Jill softly to one of the Waafs.

> *One of our planes was missing*
> *Two hours overdue*
> *One of our planes was missing*
> *With all its gallant crew*
> *The radio sets were humming*
> *We waited for a word*
> *Then a noise broke*
> *Through the humming and this is what we heard*

---

153   Its kind of just a moment out of time when the body convulses in an almost fear-like representation of something you didn't experience, something that bypassed your consciousness and went straight into your nervous system. The *heebie jeebies* is that kind of thing, but not quite.

We're coming in on a wing and a prayer
We're coming in on a wing and a prayer
Tho' there's one motor gone we will still carry on
We're coming in on a wing and a prayer

Jill closed her eyes and prayed.

What a show, what a fight
Yes we really hit our target for tonight
How we sing as we fly through the air
Look below there's a field over there
With a full crew abroad and our trust in the Lord
We're coming in on a wing and a prayer[154]

Feeling faint, Jill swayed on her feet. She leant on the doorframe, struggling to keep her composure.

With a full crew abroad and our trust in the Lord
We're coming in on a wing and a prayer.

Please bring them home... the words from William Carter's letter resonating in her head ... *I just wanted you to know that I feel very deeply for you.*

As the heady feeling passed, Jill regained her self-control and walked purposefully towards Flying Control.

The control tower was a two-storey building with a glassed-in observation deck on part of the roof of the second storey. On the ground floor were the offices of the Station Commander, the Met Officer and his staff. The first floor housed the radio room and the head of Flying Control plus all the duty controllers and radio operators. The second floor was windowed all the way around with a railed platform wrapped around the front facing the runways, this in turn, gave access to the observation deck on the roof. A few off-duty Waaf officers were already rugged up in their greatcoats on the observation deck waiting for the first arrivals. Duty observers stood with binoculars around their necks. The windsock on the roof was flapping loudly in the freezing cold north-easterly breeze.

154 The phrase 'Coming in on a wing and a prayer', from the 1942 film The Flying Tigers, was taken up by songwriters Harold Adamson and Jimmie McHugh in their WWII patriotic song *Coming in on a Wing and a Prayer*, 1943.

Jill skipped briskly up the stairs to the Flying Control room on the first floor. The room was buzzing with activity; the Station Commander Grp/Cpt Tony Fitzroy was at a window with his binoculars. Jill saw her roommate Ester Dumfries across the room. She made her way across to her through the rows of radios and the ops table showing the movement of aircraft on the ground and in the air. A blackboard was being wiped clean to mark the arrival of aircraft into the circuit.

Ester saw her coming across and smiled.

Before Jill could ask, Ester pre-empted her, 'HQ have activated the diversion plan ... it's still all a bit confused but the weather to the south is appalling'. Ester continued in her lilting Scottish accent, 'We are to take some of Waddington, Metheringham and Woodhall Spa's traffic as long as we remain clear. We may even get some 100 Group aircraft as their airfields are being snowed in with low cloud ... Should be a very busy morning.'

As Ester finished her sentence, a broken radio message crackled over the loudspeaker.

'Hello Darky... Hello Darky ... this is Splashboard S-Sugar[155],' called a distant voice through the static.

'Splashboard S-Sugar this is Bluestripe,' responded the controller calmly.

'Bluestripe, I need a heading to your Station, Over,' called the pilot through the static. The radio set up for 'Darky' calls showed a reciprocal bearing from the airfield to the aircraft with an approximate range. The operator checked the direction-finder on her receiver and responded.

'Splashboard S-Sugar, turn onto bearing three-zero-three degrees for six minutes.'

'Thank you Bluestripe, we are badly damaged ... I am on three engines ... I have no hydraulics ...' There was a fizz of static, the voice trailed off as the operator tried to retune. '... I have wounded on board ... I don't think I will be able to blow down the undercarriage[156].'

'Switch on the DREM lighting,' called Grp/Cpt Fitzroy. 'Make sure SBA is on ... prepare to receive aircraft. Controller, put him on runway three-four, that will bring him straight in. Leave runway zero-

---

155 DARKY was a system where a lost pilot could call for a bearing using the call-sign Darky. Most RAF Stations operated a permanent Darky Watch on a common frequency with a transmitter / receiver of limited range to avoid possible overlap with other stations. By taking bearings and comparing them by radio they could rapidly fix a lost aiarcraft's position.
156 The Lancaster had compressed air cylinders that could 'blow down' the undercarriage if the hydraulics were damaged.

four for our chaps … Notify the crash team and ground crews. We cannot have this aircraft block the runway under any circumstances.'

It was now frenetic activity as telephones were ringing with operators following the flow of instructions from the Station Commander and Flying Control.

'It's a Pathfinder from Thirty-Five squadron, that's why he is back so early,' whispered Ester to Jill. 'Their strip at Graveley is clouded in. Most of 8 Group and 3 Group strips have weather problems.'

'Splashboard S-Sugar, Bluestripe, can you hear me?' called the operator. There was no reply just hissing static. She repeated the call.

'Yes I have got you Bluestripe, my navigator is dead … '

'You are clear to land on runway three-four, your QDM[157] to our outer marker is three-zero-four degrees … QFE[158] nine-ninety … wind is fifteen miles an hour northeast … visibility is clear to 5,000ft. Call when you are downwind. Over' called the Operator in clear, precise, reassuring tones.

All eyes turned towards the beginning of runway 34, almost 800 yards south of the control tower.

We're coming in on a wing and a prayer.

Corporal Ron Boswell and his maintenance team on C-Charlie had just arrived at their hut next to the dispersal points for A Flight. Their aircraft was scheduled back at about 5:50am so they had plenty of time for a cup of tea and a natter with the other ground crews.

'Morning all …' announced Boswell loudly.

The telephone began to ring.

Chiefy Joe Kennedy picked it up. He listened to the instructions given in a clipped meticulous fashion by the Waaf in Flying Control.

'We've a damaged kite coming in on three-four … not one of ours. Sounds like it will be a belly-landing … poor sods. Ron, you and your crew get some tractors over there with steel cable, you may have to pull it off if it blocks the runway,' called Kennedy in his booming voice.

Ron had just poured himself a cup of tea and was looking at it longingly …

'Come on Ronny, get a wriggle on … they will be here any minute …'

'There it comes,' called a Waaf observer on the roof, talking into the

---

157 Magnetic heading to a station
158 QFE, the altimeter setting that will cause the altimeter to read the height above a specific aerodrome or ground level and therefore will read zero on landing.

speaking tube. Only the faintest of early morning light had cracked the eastern horizon, still too dark to see the aircraft, just its blinking nav lights. As they watched, it shot out a red flare to announce its arrival.

The sound of the engines carried to those at the control tower and on the ground.

'He's too high,' called Fitzroy holding the binoculars up to his eyes.

Everyone watched as the aircraft slowly approached, then it began to drop precipitously.

'Bluestripe … I cannot get the wheels down … I have no flaps.'

The beginning of runway 34 was only 250 yards from the A46 between Welton and Lincoln, with Heath Farm just across the road.

No one will ever know what happened next … The Lancaster seemed to rear up, her nose lifting … then she fell out of the sky … there was a terrible thump as she impacted short of the road, ploughing through a storage shed on Heath Farm. Then she skidded over the road, through the hedge, on through the security fence and approach lights, bursting into flames yards short of the runway. Her starboard wing ripped off, slewing the aircraft broad side on then she flipped over onto her back. A massive explosion sent bits of the plane high into the sky, spewing burning petrol over the grass …

The people in the control tower watched in total mesmerising shock … speechless …

The fire crews were at the crash immediately, spraying foam. The firemen in protective suits were trying to smash their way into the fuselage but the heat was too great, forcing them back. Someone inside the fuselage was screaming …

There was nothing anybody could do …

A young Waaf in the control tower burst into tears and ran from the room. The staff in Flying Control stood transfixed … nobody said a word … watching the crash teams desperately trying to save the aircrew.

Ron Boswell, only a few yards from the blazing wreck, sat on the seat of the tractor in sickened shock … He had seen a great many crashes but the sight and sounds of men burning to death was too much … slipping off the seat he fell to his knees and threw up. His body convulsing … the feeling of utter helplessness was overwhelming.

**Village of Schönberg, Middle Franconia District, Bavaria, 10 miles (16.7km) northeast of Nuremberg
Friday 31 March 1944, 5:15am**

Otto Gregori and his friend Heinz Bongart struggled under the weight of the stretcher carrying the injured airman. Hanna and Rosemarie followed on behind, Hanna hobbling painfully on the rutted surface of the road.

They had searched the broken hulk of the Lancaster finding it empty. It appeared that this very young wounded airman was the only man in the aircraft when it crashed. Otto had voiced the opinion that he must have been the pilot as how otherwise would the aircraft have been able to crash land in the way that it did?

'This is a very brave man,' Otto had said, looking down on the airman who was now unconscious again.

Heinz was flabbergasted at Otto's statement.

'How can you describe people who bomb innocent women and children and poor farmers 'brave'?' he had asked.

While Heinz was not prepared to hand over the prisoner to the SS, he was equally not prepared to treat him with any respect.

With Otto, this was now a matter of principle. He had taken responsibility for the airman and he would carry out his promise. The man was a soldier, Otto and Heinz had been soldiers, *they must treat the man with compassion as a fellow soldier*.

The fires in the town were still blazing but not as fiercely. The volunteer firemen were now at work, returning from their own burnt out houses.

The small party passed villagers sitting on the side of the road, surrounded by the few possessions they had saved from the fire. The church bells were ringing, providing a beacon of hope amongst the devastation. The authorities had set up an aid station for the injured in the Church and old Doctor Wiek, long since retired, was called back to service.

Otto led the way up the small rise to the Church grounds. The lights were on in the church bathing the walled Churchyard in a soft light, reflecting off the snow covering the ground. People were sitting about in the open, their faces revealing the sheer shock and disbelief of what had happened. Many of the women were crying, clinging to their young children.

Hanna saw her friend Magda Neumeyer sitting on the steps of the church holding her three young grandchildren. She limped up to her friend whose face was as white as a sheet, her vacant and unseeing eyes swollen from crying.

'Magda, thank God you are unhurt,' said Hanna, reaching down to take her friend's hand.

Magda looked up, her eyes empty. … 'Ange is dead … ' she rasped.

'My God!' shrieked Hanna her hands over her mouth. 'Magda, I cannot believe it …'

The memory of a young girl running in the fields, her skirts flying, screaming with the excitement of youth flashed through Hanna's mind. This young girl was dead, taken from her family and her children. *Why is this happening?*

'The house collapsed from a bomb … Ange had left the shelter as she had forgotten the milk for the children, I begged her not to go … Fredrik was searching for her in the rubble, they pulled her out … her body is inside.'

Magda began to cry again, the soft sucking whimper of a person who could not believe the tragedy that had befallen them. She had begged her daughter to bring the children to the country … now this …

Hanna sat down next to her friend, putting her arm around her shoulders. The woman was shivering uncontrollably. Hanna took the baby from Magda's arms, while the young Rosemarie sat holding the two children, too young to understand that their lives were now changed forever.

The injured airman began to moan as Otto staggered up the stairs of the Church with the stretcher. At the entrance was a line of bodies covered with blankets. Otto could see that some of the bodies were tiny children, others wore women's shoes. In the front, beneath the alter, Doctor Wiek was seeing to the wounded. Along the sidewall, a line of six British airmen stood under guard. On the floor, Otto could see two other injured airmen. As he got closer, he could see the exposed bone where the leg of one of the men had been all but severed at the knee. Volunteer nurses were stripping bed sheets to make bandages. Father Edmund, the parish priest, was helping them.

Otto and Heinz lowered the stretcher gently to the floor and Otto called Dr Wiek to look at the man. Wiek, who was in his late seventies, shuffled over and looked down at the man's burnt legs.

'It is very bad Otto, I can not do anything for him, I have no morphine left,' said the old man. 'His wounds need specialist treatment, the nearest burn hospital is in Nürnberg.'

As Otto looked down the young man moaned again, his eyes opened.

'Please help me … ' the man said holding up his burnt hand that looked like a scorched claw, with a half-burned glove hanging off it.

'What is he saying Herr Doctor?' asked Otto.

'He is asking for help Otto,' replied Wiek who had a good understanding of English.

'Please in my jacket is a letter for my mother … please take it,' groaned the man, clearly in the worst kind of agony.

Wiek translated and Otto knelt down next to the man opening the front of his flying jacket. Inside was his battle dress tunic. Otto felt inside and he gently lifted out an envelope.

'I did not have time to post it …' whispered the man. 'Please can you make sure my mother gets it?'

Otto looked at the letter, it had an address on the front of it that Otto could not read. He held it up to Wiek.

'The address reads Rotorua in New Zealand. Otto … this man is from New Zealand.'

'New Zealand! …' Otto could hardly believe it, that this man had come from the other side of the world to die here in Germany.

Otto nodded at the young man, *'Ich verspreche dir; ich werde alles tun dass deine Mutter diesen Brif erhaelten wird*[159],' he said patting the man softly on the chest. The airman smiled up at him, a reflection of relief as if some terrible burden had been lifted.

The man died then … his eyes so blue … his face so young … his life taken too early ...

The small group stood in silence, each trying to take in the enormity of what was going on around them. This church, this village, was their whole world … the town had been reduced to a smouldering ruin.

Otto made a decision.

'Come Heinz, help me bury this man in the churchyard,' said Otto.

A commotion broke out at the entrance to the church as the Bürgermeister burst in. He stormed up the aisle.

'What are you doing, Egg-thief?' he squeaked. 'You were locked up.'

'I was freed by these men from above, *Schweinchen*,' replied Otto sneeringly, pointing towards the sky. 'Your jail has been flattened.'

Otto indicated to Heinz to lift up the stretcher.

159 'I promise you, I will do everything I can to make sure your mother gets this letter.'

'Where are you going with this *Terrorflieger*?' demanded the Bürgermeister. 'They should all be taken out and shot,' he squealed, waving his arm towards the captured airmen along the wall.

Otto ignored the ugly little man. He and Heinz carried the stretcher towards the door, Heinz still had his shotgun across his shoulders.

'You cannot bury this animal in our churchyard, it will be desecrated,' screeched the Bürgermeister, following them out into the early morning light.

Otto stopped, set down the stretcher and turned on the small man.

'*Schweinchen*, if you come near me again this night, I will kill you … please do not mistake me,' he hissed, holding his mouth next to the man's ear so that no one else could hear.

The menacing tone of Otto's voice and the conviction in his stance, convinced the Bürgermeister that he meant every word.

They took the body to the far corner of the graveyard, Otto took shovels from the gravedigger's shed and he and Heinz began to dig.

Once the shallow grave was dug, they wrapped the body in a blanket and lowered it into the grave. Otto then fetched Father Edmund to say some words for the dead man.

The air hung with the stench of burning. Flames still flickered in the ruins of the village as Otto, Heinz and Father Edmund bent their heads.

Father Edmund begun to pray, '*Kraft der mir verliehenen Vollmacht gewähre ich dir vollkommenen Ablaß und Vergebung aller Sünden im Namen des Vaters und des Sohnes und des Heiligen Geistes. Auf daß der Weg dir leicht falle.*' The Priest continued the creed, '*ich glaube an Gott den Vater, den Schöpfer des Himmels und der Erde und an Jesus Christus, seinen eingeborenen Sohn …*'

Then we who are alive, who are left, will be caught up together with them in the clouds to meet the Lord in the air. Thus we shall always be with the Lord. Therefore, console one another with these words[160].

Otto looked towards the heavens. He contemplated meeting this young man one day in the clouds … *I would like to speak to him one day when we stand before the Lord in heaven … his mother will get his letter.*

The wind changed direction, taking away the clogging smoke, the air was suddenly fresh and clean, as the new day dawned.

---

160 A reading from the First Letter of St. Paul to the Thessalonians 4:13-18

*

Czech / German Border near Waidhaus
Friday 31 March 1944, 5:30am

Aurek, still groggy from his bang on the head, had donned the uniform of the guard they had attacked at Hirschau. It hung on him so loosely that he looked like a child dressed in adult clothing. In fact all three of them looked ridiculously incongruous, unconvincing to even the most dim-witted border guard.

'We are not going to be able to waltz up to the border like this in the truck,' said Heniek stating the obvious. 'It will be light soon … look at us, all three uniforms are covered in blood.'

'We are going to have to skirt the border-post on foot,' said Iwan. They had stopped the truck well short of the border, parked on a side road, then climbed a small hill overlooking the border. Below they could see a boom across the road with a number of buildings. As the light improved, they could count at least ten German guards. The boom looked sturdy enough to stop a truck even travelling at great speed. There was also a machinegun nest with guns facing in both directions.

'I agree, we need to move fast before the light improves,' said Aurek taking in the situation.

The three friends made their way down the hill with the weapons they had captured. For the first time in four years, Aurek believed that they may now survive this war. The first painful pangs of optimism filtered into his clouded brain. The despair and resignation that he had felt for so long were lifting, adding a new energy to his legs despite the hunger now burning in his stomach.

As is so often the case when so close to safety, the temptation to relax, increased the possibility of a mistake.

So it was.

The men were making too much noise moving through the forest undergrowth.

A German patrol along the border heard them coming. The light was still poor and the sky was heavily overcast. A light drizzle began to fall.

The three fugitives came to the path. At a distance of a 100 yards a German stepped out. He called to them to stop. He could see that each was wearing a steel helmet and dressed in uniform, but who were these men?

Aurek stopped.

'Go!' he hissed at his friends. 'Go into the valley ... I will catch up.'

The others did as he said. A dog barked from up the pathway.

'We are on a patrol,' shouted Aurek towards the man, the rifle loose in his arms.

'There are no other patrols! Come here!' ordered the German. It was clear that he was not convinced.

'We are from Waidhaus chasing an escaped prisoner,' called Aurek, buying time for his friends.

This seemed to work. The German grunted ... *it made sense.*

Aurek walked slowly towards where the man was standing.

The rifle he was carrying was a Mauser *Gewehr 43* with a 10-round magazine; he had another five magazines in the webbing. The rifle was cocked.

As Aurek got closer, the man seemed to relax. The light was still not good enough to see facial features.

'Have you got a cigarette?' asked Aurek conversationally.

Another three men came out from behind the bushes on the side of the path, their rifles were slung over their shoulders, these were old men, not crack German infantry. A dog barked again.

Only a few more seconds ...

Aurek stopped short of the man.

'I said come here!' the German called irritably. He was clearly tired from a night-patrol along the border.

Aurek did not move, holding the rifle with his finger on the trigger. The man had his rifle tucked into the waist, the muzzle pointing at the ground in front of Aurek.

'I need to get back to the chase. What do you want?' demanded Aurek with as much bravado as he could muster.

The man stepped forward.

Aurek lifted the rifle and fired directly into the man's chest. Correcting his aim, he took the next man in the head. The others dived into the undergrowth. Aurek rushed forward, rifle at the ready. One of the Germans was trying to scramble up the hill, Aurek hit him in the small of the back. Swinging the rifle back down the hill the other man was sliding down the steep bank. Aurek fired again but missed.

The dog up the road began to bark more excitedly, Aurek could hear it coming closer. More Germans appeared on the path, Aurek aimed carefully and hit the first one in the stomach. Now there was return fire ... he could hear bullets flying above him as the men up the path fired aimlessly into the dark.

The dog was closer.

Aurek slipped off the path and began to slide down the hill on his back using his legs as brakes.

The dog was now baying, it had his scent.

Aurek was paralysed with sickening gut-wrenching fear … the dog was so near he could hear it panting.

Turning to face it, Aurek fired, then fired again … the black shape was coming down the hill like a thing of the worst nightmares.

Aimed … fired … then the dog was on him. Its weight knocked him over onto his back, he held the rifle across his chest fending off the dog that was trying to bite at his face and neck.

It was a powerful animal, trained to kill. Against the first pale light in the trees above, all that Aurek could see was the giant dog's head, all snapping jaws. Saliva splattered his face as the dog's stale stinking breath entered his lungs.

Weakened as he was, Aurek fought on, holding the rifle across his face. The dog changed its angle of attack.

A bite went home … a stifled scream of anguish carried through the forest.

In the valley below Heniek and Iwan stopped, … looked back up the hill. They knew their friend was dead …

The glistening sun of the new day hit the tops of the tallest trees.

22

'All right chaps we've still got two good engines which should get us home if we are careful with the fuel. All the guns are out of action and it looks as though we have lost all our hydraulics,' called Bill Carter, doing his best to keep a positive tone in his voice.

'Rear Gunner to Skipper, my eyes are smarting and I'm soaked in bloody petrol.'

'Tommy, I think that some of the fuel we lost has been sucked into your turret, hang on as long as you can.'

Tommy Potts was stuck. His turret was out of action, he was covered in petrol, even the slightest spark would turn him into a flaming candle. He knew his best friend Frank Nellyer was badly wounded but he could not see him or do anything for him. It was not even possible to speak to him, to give him words of encouragement.

There was broken cloud on the approach to the English Coast. At 4,000ft, the wounded Lancaster was flying in the first sunlight of the day.

'Bluefrock, Bluefrock, this is March Tune C-Charlie, can you hear me, Over,' called Bill Carter.

'March Tune C-Charlie, we hear you clearly.'

'Bluefrock, I am on two engines, approximately ten miles to your southeast, I have severe structural damage ... request immediate clearance to land we have wounded on board.'

'I am sorry March Tune, our runways are blocked, we have crashed aircraft ... proceed to Watchtower (Woodbridge) ... fly on bearing three-five-six degrees for twenty-one minutes.'

Blast!

Cocky Lobin had flown across Germany and France on two engines. They were making at best a groundspeed of 100mph into the breeze. Both starboard engines were out which in turn had cut electrical power to some of the systems. The starboard inner engine generator drove one of the main services hydraulic pumps, the front turret hydraulic pump, the pneumatic system and no 2 vacuum pump. The starboard outer generator fed the mid-upper turret hydraulic pump and some radios. The upshot was that all gun turrets were out of action and the hydraulic system was compromised which meant they might not be able to get the flaps and undercarriage down. They only had VHF radio contact with the outside world.

The rear horizontal stabiliser was badly damaged, as was one of the rudders. Numerous holes from flak and cannon stretched across the wings and fuselage. The bomb aimer's blister in the front of the aircraft looked as if it had been in a collision, all mangled metal, open to the elements. The cockpit canopy had holes in it and the windscreen was badly cracked, making it impossible for Carter to see forward.

Charlie Morley and Ian Fullerton were dead, their bodies wrapped in blankets aft of the main spar. Dave Muir was wounded in the arm but still at his post. Frank Nellyer had a flak splinter in the eye that was bleeding fearfully. Eric Biddle was helping Carter fly the aircraft that was taking an enormous physical toll. George Armitage was at his post, none of his navigation systems, including the DF-loop, were working. He had been navigating on dead-reckoning, taking sextant sightings since Mannheim.

When Cocky Lobin had been coned by the searchlights, then put into the dive with the starboard inner engine on fire, Carter had ordered the crew to abandon the aircraft. Nobody heard him … a flak splinter had severed the wire to his intercom. He had recovered the aircraft at 1,000ft with the help of Eric Biddle and his rope. Carter could not believe his ears when he had discovered his crew were still with him. Biddle had since rigged a replacement intercom wire.

'Dave, call up Woodbridge and ask for an emergency landing, our ETA will be 05:59hrs.'

'Roger ETA 05:59hrs,' replied Dave Muir instantly, the pain in his arm so intense that it made his eyes water.

'What is our fuel position Eric?' asked Carter.

'Starboard number three tank took a hit and has drained, gauges indicate 393 gallons. I have transferred all the fuel from the starboard to the port tanks. We could almost get home Skipper,' replied Biddle.

'We have no room to stooge about looking for an airfield if we hit bad weather. No, we will put down at Woodbridge if they can take us,' said Carter, once again running mental arithmetic on fuel burn. 'How are Frank and Dave?'

'Frank's in a lot of pain Skipper, that eye is a mess. He lost a lot of blood. I have bandaged it as well as I can but we don't have any more morphine. Dave is also bandaged up but his arm is broken and still bleeding. There is a nasty chunk of metal sticking out of it.'

There was nothing else that could be said …

'Skipper, Woodbridge report poor weather but we are cleared to approach. They said we should call again when we get closer.'

'Thanks Dave.'

Carter's leg was aching from the enormous foot pressure caused by holding the bomber on a straight heading. Biddle had helped by wedging a fire extinguisher onto the pedal and still had the rope around the seat holding back the control column.

As Cocky Lobin crossed the sea on the outer edge of the Thames Estuary, a cloudbank was visible to the north stretching high above them.

The light improved with every mile.

As soon as Armitage indicated they were within range, Carter called Woodbridge.

'Hello Watchtower, this is March Tune C-Charlie, request QDM,' called Carter.

There was a crackle then a delay before a female voice came up on the radio.

'March Tune C-Charlie we are fogged in, visibility is down to 200ft. You must divert to Downham Market, all other fields in 3 and 8 Groups are out.'

Carter could hardly believe his ears.

'To hell with this ... Skipper turn onto heading three-one-seven, we can make it home ... ' called Armitage. 'We have to make it home ...'

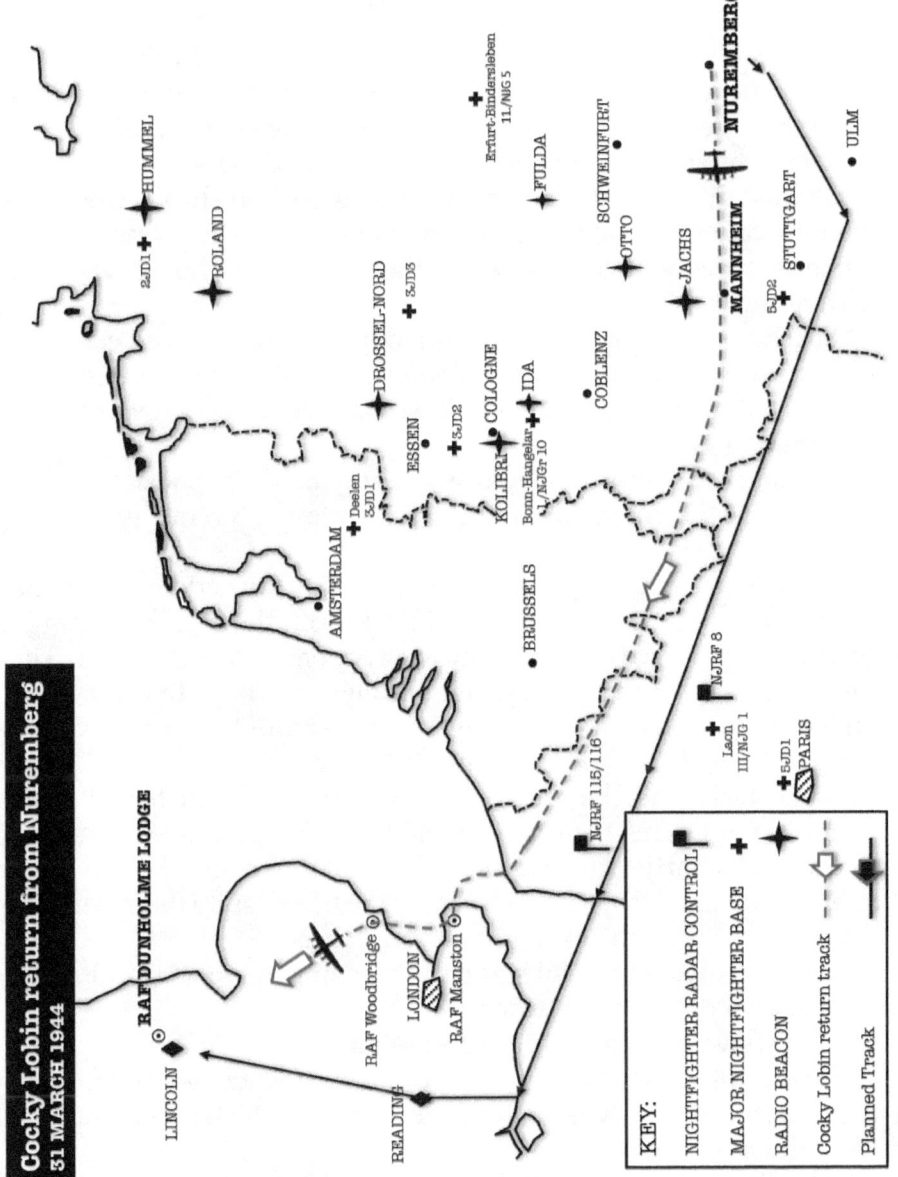

Cocky Lobin return from Nuremberg
31 MARCH 1944

NUREMBERG

ULM

STUTTGART

MANNHEIM

5./JD2

JACHS

OTTO

SCHWEINFURT

FULDA

Erfurt-Bindersleben
11./NJG 5

COBLENZ

IDA
Bonn-Hangelar
4./NJGr 10

KOLIBRI

COLOGNE

5./JD2

ESSEN

DROSSEL-NORD

5./JD3

ROLAND

HUMMEL

2./JD1

Deelen
3./JD1

AMSTERDAM

BRUSSELS

NJRF 8

Leon
III/NJG 1

5./JD1

PARIS

NJRF 115/116

RAF Woodbridge

LONDON

RAF Manston

RAF DUNHOLME LODGE

LINCOLN

READING

KEY:

NIGHTFIGHTER RADAR CONTROL

MAJOR NIGHTFIGHTER BASE

RADIO BEACON

Cocky Lobin return track

Planned Track

RAF Dunholme Lodge, Lincolnshire
Friday 31 March 1944, 6:20am

The first 44 Squadron Lancaster, K-King had crossed the threshold to runway 04 at 5:59am. The sound of the others filing into the circuit beat in the skies above. It was overcast with the cloudbase at 2,000ft. The wind was still from the northeast at about 15mph.

Halfway up the active runway, the usual off-duty crowd had gathered waving excitedly at the returning crews. In Flying Control, clipped instructions were issued to the orbiting aircraft giving them each a number to land.

At 6:02am Sqn/Ldr Haworth landed in A-Able followed closely by Pallister, Robinson and Wingco Thompson. All was throbbing noise as the huge bombers taxied back down past the control tower to their dispersal points.

Ground crews stood patiently waiting at their pads, tools and equipment at the ready, dreading what state the aircraft were going to be in.

The crashed Lancaster from 35 Squadron lay burned out. There had been no survivors. The crash teams had put out the fire, then dragged the wreck a 100 yards away from the approach to runway 34. They then returned to runway 04 to wait for their own boys to come in.

By 6:20 only three aircraft were not accounted for, C-Charlie (Carter), D-Dog (Charlesworth) and R-Roger (Frost).

Winnie Daly had the crew bus next to Gavin Pallister's B-Bravo dispersal point. The Lancaster turned off the perimeter track and spun around smartly. The engines were shut down and the crew came tumbling out, almost sprinting towards the bus despite their tiredness. They were all jabbering excitedly, *we are alive ...*

'You are truly a beautiful sight this morning Winnie,' said Pallister as he did every time he returned.

'Good show last night, Sir?' asked Winnie.

'It was a total cods-up, we are still not sure where we bombed but I don't think it was Nuremberg!' exclaimed Pallister, the sound of frustration in his voice.

In the de-briefing room, Jill Evans waited at her usual table with the other intelligence personnel. Her boss Sqn/Ldr Laurence Baxter was hovering.

Pallister was next through the door, the crew of U-Uncle were already at a neighbouring table, smoking and eating sandwiches.

Jill was unprepared for the response to her first question.

'It was a bloody shambles,' announced Pallister loudly. 'I don't think we got more than two wind reports on the way to the target. The weather report was hopelessly wrong ... the target was covered in cloud to 12,000ft. I don't think we got anywhere near the aiming point. There were skymarkers everywhere ... some ten miles apart.'

'What sort of fighter activity was there?' asked Jill in her usual gentle way.

'We were slaughtered up there!' stated Pallister emphatically, his crew nodding their agreement.

'I saw the first one go down near the German border,' said the rear gunner. 'I stopped counting when I got to twenty-five.'

'I got to fifteen!' chipped in the rear gunner from the crew on the neighbouring table.

Baxter had been listening to Pallister's comments and stepped forward.

'So how many of our aircraft did you see go down?' asked Baxter pointedly.

'Approximately thirty!' snapped Pallister, his frustration now really bubbling over.

'Now steady on ... nobody has reported anything like that number. Just write down ten Jill,' instructed Baxter.

'Bloody hell Sir, we were there, ask any of my crew ... we were lambs to the slaughter,' blurted out Pallister, now visibly upset that he was not being taken seriously. 'Anyway you don't have to believe me, just you wait and see!'

Haworth and Thompson were now both in the debriefing room and it seemed that they too had seen a great many battles.

'There were also those blasted scarecrow things again,' said Pallister to Jill as they wound up their debriefing.

The last of the waiting crews finished their debriefing and went off for breakfast and a sleep.

Jill glanced at the clock in the room ... it read 06:30.

Pallister and Robinson came back into the room.

'Is Bill Carter back, did we miss him?' asked Robinson.

'No he isn't. Let me call Flying Control,' said Jill trying to hide the concern in her voice.

Pallister looked at his watch, *he's more than half an hour late.*

Nobody dared say what they were all thinking.

Jill put down the receiver.

'Flying Control say they have not heard from him or Frost and Charlesworth. They may have diverted to another airfield or put down at the emergency strips at Manston or Woodbridge,' said Jill trying to keep her emotions in check. She was feeling sick to the stomach.

'I can't eat until he's back, or we know where he diverted,' said Pallister.

'Me too,' agreed Robinson. 'We will go and wait at Flying Control. If he is not back in the next twenty minutes, he would probably have put down somewhere else. Hopefully the blighter phones us straight away and doesn't go off for a pint!'

*

6:30am

The main gate to Dunholme Lodge was still closed to outside visitors. A car carrying four Canadian WDs pulled up outside the gate, one jumped out of the passenger seat and ran up to the guard house, it was now drizzling hard, she held her cap to her head as she ran.

'I need to know whether William Carter is back,' she blurted out to the guard.

'We don't have that information and even if we did I couldn't give it to you,' said the Sergeant in a broad Yorkshire accent.

'Please can you find out … we … we are engaged,' she pleaded, looking into the man's eyes.

'No …'

'Please … I just need to know … just a simple answer yes or no … his aircraft is C-Charlie. Please …'

The Sergeant knew Bill Carter, an officer who always smiled and said hello.

'Let me see what I can do … no promises mind,' relented the Sergeant, picking up the field telephone to the Orderly Room. 'Come on, get out of the rain … you will catch your death out there,' he added making room for her.

Ann watched his every move as he wound the handle on the phone. Someone picked up on the other side, she heard him ask about Bill Carter.

'Yes … I see …'

He put down the receiver, the expression on his face showing the news.

'I phoned the Flight Office … C-Charlie is overdue,' said the Sergeant. 'They are over an hour overdue … they could have landed elsewhere but they don't know yet. I … am sorry.'

332

'I don't believe it ...' cried Ann Woodcroft.

'I am sorry ...' said the Sergeant again, seeing the distress on the girl's face, tears in her eyes. 'Why don't you go off into the village and get a cup of tea ... come back later, there may be news then.'

'Yes ... ', said Ann weakly, trying her best to fight back the tears. She turned towards the door, spits of rain were now running down the windowpanes. She pushed open the door, then turned towards the Sergeant, 'I'll come back a bit later.'

'Yes lass, you come back a bit later,' whispered the Sergeant as he watched the girl run towards the car, hunched over against the rain and cold. He shook his head ... *be prepared for the worst ...*

*

6:32am

In front of the control tower, the group of Waafs had dwindled in number. Maggie Smith and Vera Johns were still waiting.

'They are overdue, aren't they?' said Maggie, knowing the answer.

'Yes, they are, but anything could have happened, they may have landed somewhere else,' replied Vera encouragingly.

'I can't imagine not being able to speak to him again ... He needs to know how I feel about him ... please bring him home,' pleaded Maggie softly, looking into the heavens, praying with all her might.

'You may have to accept Maggie, that he is not coming back. You need to be strong,' said Vera, trying her best to bring her young friend around to the reality. A reality she had lived through herself too many times.

'How long ... before we lose hope?' whispered Maggie, her eyes filling with tears.

Vera looked at her watch as she had done countless times already.

'Flying Control say ... no later than seven o'clock ... but that is stretching it,' replied Vera, taking her friend's hand and squeezing it.

As Vera looked out across the runway, the weather was noticeably deteriorating. Low clouds were scudding across from the north, she could feel a few spits of rain on her face. She knew that unless the boys got back in the next few minutes Dunholme Lodge would be clouded in.

Jill Evans had left the debriefing room to follow the two Rhodesian pilots across to Flying Control. On the top observation deck, the Waaf crew still had binoculars up to their eyes scanning the horizon in all directions. Jack Haworth was standing on the 1st floor deck talking to Chalky White. Linda Potter, carrying her clipboard, was on the deck

333

next to him, the B-Flight clerk stood next to her. The survivors of Ian Fullerton's crew stood waiting for their Skipper to return from his first 'dicky' flight. All were studying the horizon towards the south ... willing for the sound of engines.

Wingco Stuffy Thompson climbed the steps onto the deck and spoke to Haworth, his voice carried easily to those standing on the ground below.

'Looks like we will have to call it a day on those three overdue aircraft,' said Thompson to Haworth.

'It does not look good Sir, but their aircraft may be damaged, the headwind on the return flight was enough to add an hour to the flight,' replied Haworth with none of his usual flippancy. He tried to sound optimistic but that was not how he was feeling. The set of his jaw and the way he gripped the rail on the balcony said it all.

'Our squadron has been stood down from operations to sit out the moon period,' stated Thompson in his usual formal way. 'You should send as many of your men on leave as possible.'

'Bit bloody late isn't it!' spat Haworth uncharacteristically, turning towards his commander. 'You saw what it was like last night ... they should never have sent us ... God knows how many good men have been lost.'

Thompson did not react to the outburst, his job to maintain the 'stiff upper lip'.

'Just send your men on leave ... you had best go yourself ... it's been a rough two months,' replied Thompson, understanding the pain his flight commander was feeling. 'Who will run the Flight while you are away? ... Maybe you should give young Carter a crack at it ... '

Thompson stopped himself, realising what he had just said ... It was an easy mistake to make ... he had so much on his mind. All those on the balcony and on the ground below were looking at him.

He coughed to clear his throat, 'Well ... you know what I mean ... horrible business ... I had best get back to my office,' added Thompson, clearing his throat again, turning on his heel, he took the steps two at a time, acknowledging the salutes as he went.

Haworth watched him go, his own words to his men haunting him.

... God willing we will all come through this thing together.

*

Jill Evans stood on the path in front of the control tower. She had heard the words exchanged by Haworth and Thompson. The reference to William sent a shiver down her spine ... *they were writing them off already.* She saw the two Waafs she had spoken to the night before, she could see the younger one had tears in her eyes.

The taller girl looked over.

'He's overdue Ma'am,' said Vera.

'Yes ...' was all Jill could say, the three woman stood in silence looking across the windswept airfield, the drizzle increasing.

Maggie cracked.

'I can't take it any more,' she wept into her friend's shoulder. Embarrassed by her tears in front of the senior officer, she held her handkerchief to her face and ran off towards her billet. The two older women watched her go.

'Terrible thing, a broken heart Ma'am,' said Vera smiling weakly at Jill.

'Indeed Vera ... a truly terrible thing,' agreed Jill, her face turned to the wind ... her mind a churning turmoil ... *too many things unsaid ...* She looked at her watch, *ten to seven.*

*

At the dispersal point for C-Charlie Ron Boswell stood forlornly with his crew. Even the dog Paddy had stopped playing, sitting instead next to Ron's leg, looking out towards runway 04.

Ron could not bear to speak ... to say what everyone was thinking. The other A-Flight Lancasters all stood proudly in their pads, their ground crews already clambering over them.

Chiefy Kennedy came walking over from the crew hut, his hands thrust deep into his greatcoat.

'I phoned Flying Control, they have not heard anything. Your boys are way overdue, I think we have to face it ... Come on, let's get out of this weather and have a cup of tea.'

Ron could not believe it. Bill Carter and his crew! He had felt close to these men, fifteen operations they had done together ... their indomitable spirit, their laughter. There was nothing to say ... just a sick hollow feeling in the pit of the stomach. He took one more hopeful

335

glance towards the approach to runway 04, then in silence trudged off after the rest of his ground crew as they made their way across the wet grass towards the hut.

Paddy barked …

'No, we are not throwing the ball,' said Ron smiling thinly at the dog.

The dog barked again, his head was fixed ahead as if he had picked up the scent of a pheasant.

'What is it Paddy?' asked Ron, straining his eyes in the direction Paddy was looking. 'Have you spotted a rabbit lad?'

Paddy barked again, more loudly, he jumped up and ran a few steps forward.

Ron thought he was imagining it at first … it could be a truck passing on the road to Lincoln. Then the sound was unmistakable.

'It's a kite!' shouted Ron back at his crew. They all stopped to listen. 'Its another bloody kite!

The phone began to ring in the maintenance hut …

*

7:00am

There was a crackle on the VHF radio at Flying Control. The operator of the radio adjusted the tuning. The other staff in Flying Control stopped what they were doing.

'Bluestripe, this is March Tune C-Charlie, we need clearance to land, I have wounded on board, request QDM.'

It was the distinctive voice of Bill Carter.

'March Tune C-Charlie you are clear to land runway 04. Wind is north-north east at fifteen miles an hour. Cloud base is down to 1,000ft, turn onto bearing two-eight degrees,' replied the Controller.

Someone stuck their head out the window to those below and shouted, 'Its C-Charlie.'

Jill Evans put her face in her hands, fighting back the tears, *C-Charlie* …

'Bluestripe, I am on two engines, I have no hydraulics, we will attempt to blow down the undercarriage, we have no fuel left to go around again,' called Carter, the strain in his voice unmistakable.

'C-Charlie, call finals, you are number one in the circuit,' confirmed Flying Control.

'Wilco,' replied Carter.

Carter could hear the tone of the SBA radio beam in his ears.

'All right, Eric this is it, there are no second chances,' said Carter

336

to Biddle in the seat next to him. Now he had the familiar dots and dashes in his ear from the SBA system. 'Everyone brace yourselves for an emergency landing.'

We're coming in on a wing and a prayer.

Biddle was watching the instruments while Carter was fighting the control column. The aircraft continued to vibrate alarmingly.

We must be losing bits and pieces.

Rain appeared on the shattered windscreen reducing forward visibility to nil.

'Speed one-thirty, height 1,500ft,' called Biddle.

The SBA buzzed in Carter's ear.

'We are over the approach beacon. Turn on the stopwatch Eric.'

Slowly Cocky Lobin dropped altitude, feeling her way through the cloud. The seconds ticked away, measured to the runway threshold.

'We will only try to blow down the wheels at the last moment.'

'1,000ft, speed one-thirty mph.'

'Blast, we should be out of the cloud.'

I can't see a bloody thing!

Biddle held the stopwatch tightly in front of his face.

We are running out of time.

'There it is! Ruddy beautiful!' called Biddle triumphantly as they dropped out below the cloud. They could see the blinking DREM lighting of the funnel in the dull overcast light, the recognition signal for Dunholme Lodge blinking in the gloomy light.

'We are too high ... blow down the wheels Eric.' The knob was just forward of the flight engineer's panel. Eric lowered the undercarriage lever into the down position, then hit the compressed air. There was a loud hissing sound as the air drove the wheels down. Both sat transfixed, watching the lights on the instrument panel as if they would leap out and bite them.

'Undercarriage down, Skip ... we've only got one green light Skipper!'

'The port looks fine, look out of your window and see if the starboard leg is down.'

Biddle twisted his head to look at the starboard main wheel. 'It appears to be down but we can't be sure it's locked.'

'Bluestripe this is C-Charlie, we are on finals, we only have one green, starboard leg is down but we don't know if it's locked, Over.'

'Roger C-Charlie can you do a circuit and be number two for landing, we have another aircraft in distress,' replied Flying Control, they had just been contacted by a crew from 4 Group also in a badly damaged aircraft.

'Bluestripe, no … we have no fuel … we must come in now,' pleaded Carter.

Things were happening fast now.

'Flaps to 25 degrees.'

Once again, the compressed air system went to work to lower the flaps.

'There's the outer marker.'

700ft …

The damaged rudder could barely keep the aircraft straight, the two port engine throttles were being used by Biddle to help steer the aircraft. Carter's leg was shaking as he held the rudder in place, the pressure was excruciating.

'Eric you will have to direct me, I can't see a thing through the windscreen.'

'Inner marker, 200ft … left a bit … left … we are on the centreline.'

Eric's hands were on the throttles, ready to pull off the power.

'Crew BRACE … BRACE!'

Cocky Lobin floated in over the threshold at 150ft, she drifted over the runway, her tail hanging out to port.

The crowd at Flying Control held their breath as the aircraft continued to drift off line.

She dropped out of the sky as the power was cut, hit the concrete hard, bounced up, then down again. Suddenly well off line, one main wheel on the grass, throwing up a spray behind it. Carter was powerless to stop the aircraft's drift against the crosswind.

The bomber swerved, travelling over the soft grass next to the runway at 100mph. She veered more violently, now directly towards the control tower. The tail dropped onto the grass, bouncing viciously knocking poor Tommy Potts' head against his guns.

A leak in the air pressure system released the undercarriage locks and the wheels collapsed. She crumpled onto her belly, tearing up great chunks of turf, sending it flying high into the air like the wake behind a boat. The broken and contorted bomb aimer's compartment made the aircraft look like it had an ugly sneer.

On she came. The people in the control tower stood riveted to the spot as the aircraft continued its skidding approach. A woman screamed.

Sliding and twisting like a frightened whale the stricken aircraft approached, all grinding, screeching metal. The Waafs on the path below the Control Tower scattered in all directions.

Cocky Lobin slid to a grating, squeaking halt no more than 40-yards short of the control tower ... black smoke and steam lifted off the mud-splattered fuselage. An acrid smell of burnt rubber filled the air.

In the distance, the fire trucks and crash tenders were speeding across the airfield, their bells ringing madly. Ron Boswell was bouncing along on top of the airfield tractor, Paddy the Irish Setter, a streak of red fur as he raced over the sodden turf.

Bill Carter and Eric Biddle sat in their positions, shaken to the core, unable to move from exhaustion and the sheer terror of the violent impact of the crash. Carter's head was bleeding from a hard thump against the side of the cockpit and his left arm was in a numbed spasm. It had been wrapped around the control column for so long that it had locked in position. He sat trapped in his seat powerless to move, both legs shaking from the sudden release of pressure.

With a deep sigh, utterly drained, Carter allowed his head to slip forward to rest on the control column, his body shaking violently from nervous reaction.

Unable to speak, all Eric Biddle could do was stretch over and place a hand on the shoulder of his trembling Skipper ... saying a silent prayer for their deliverance Psalm 143 ... *In Your righteousness bring my soul out of trouble. And in Your loving kindness, silence my enemies , destroy all those who afflict my soul.*

At first, nobody in the Control Tower moved, just staring fixedly into the crushed face of the bomber.

Jill, standing next to Vera in front of the tower, was the first to move. Clutching her cap in her hand, she ran towards the bomber ... all her reserve was gone, she needed to see him ... to hold him ... to be with him.

Jack Haworth, still on the balcony of the control tower, turned to Linda Potter standing next to him.

'Potter ... remind me to talk to Carter about the correct use of the undercarriage ... and the runway,' smiled Haworth, the look on his face unabashed delight.

'Yes Sir,' replied Potter, '... the undercarriage and the runway!'

> *We're coming in on a wing and a prayer*
> *We're coming in on a wing and a prayer*
> *Tho' there's one motor gone we will still carry on*
> *We're coming in on a wing and a prayer.*

Postscript

On the night of 30/31 March 1944, the night of the Nuremberg Raid, 44 (Rhodesia) Squadron lost two crews, 13 men killed, 1 taken prisoner. None of those killed were from Rhodesia, all were from England. By the most extraordinary coincidence, both aircraft were shot down by the same pilot, Lt Wilhelm Seuss of 11./NJG 5 flying a Bf 110 G-4.

The 53rd aircraft shot down on the night was flown by P/O C. A. Frost from Birkenhead, Cheshire. All the crew died and are buried at the Hannover War Cemetery. The aircraft was KM-R (Roger) Lancaster ME629. They were on their 6th operation.

KM-R (Roger) Lancaster ME629

RANK	NAME	POSITION	DESTINY	BURIAL PLACE
PO	Charles Albert Frost	Pilot	KIA	Hannover War Cemetery 4.J.1-3
Sgt	Fred Stanton	Flight Engineer	KIA	Hannover War Cemetery 4.J.1-3
Flt/ Sgt	Tom Ashton	Navigator	KIA	Hannover War Cemetery 4.J.1-3
FO	Harold Alan Devon	Bomb Aimer	KIA	Hannover War Cemetery 4.J.1-3
Sgt	Arthur James Johnson	Wireless Operator	KIA	Hannover War Cemetery 4.J.1-3
Sgt	James Henry Carr	Gunner	KIA	Hannover War Cemetery 4.J.4
Sgt	John Hamlin	Gunner	KIA	Hannover War Cemetery 4.J.5

The aircraft crashed while on the Long Leg, in an open field 600m north of the tiny village of Lautenhausen, 7.9 miles east of Bad Herzfeld. The crash site is 23miles north of the planned track, illustrating the effect of the poor wind forecasts that were lighter than expected and pushing them north of track. The crash site is only 47miles from the Erfurt-Bindersleben airfield where 11./NJG 5 was based. Lt. Seuss must have literally flown into KM-R shortly after taking off, his gun camera registered the kill at 12:52am at a height of 5,800m (19,028ft). On page 252 of Martin Middlebrook's book, *The Nuremberg Raid*, he quotes Lt Seuss. It was his second kill, his first with *Schrage Musik*. It was, he said, so simple. He was flying a borrowed aircraft – his own machine had not yet been fitted with the upward-firing cannon – and all he had to do was to slide beneath his victim and aim between the two port engines.

The second 44 Squadron aircraft lost was the 67th victim of the night. KM-C (Charlie) Lancaster ND795 was flown by P/O T. G. W. Charlesworth from Shareshill, Staffordshire. Six of the crew died and are buried at the Durnbach War Cemetery. They were on their 7th operation.

The aircraft crashed into a house in the village of Untereßfeld, 3.3miles southeast of Bad Königshofen, 7.8miles west of the planned track. It is unclear if anyone on the ground were killed. Charlesworth must have turned short of the correct turning point off the Long Leg. They were flying south on the final leg towards Nuremberg. I have not been able to verify the time of the crash, but based on the known time of the loss of R-Roger and the planned speed for the approach to the target, it must have been at +-1:07am.

341

KM-C (Charlie) Lancaster ND795

RANK	NAME	POSITION	DESTINY	BURIAL PLACE
PO	Trevor George W. Charlesworth	Pilot	KIA	DURNBACH WAR CEMETERY, Coll. grave 5. A. 1-6.
Sgt	K. A. Jeffrey	Flight Engineer	KIA	DURNBACH WAR CEMETERY, Coll. grave 5. A. 1-6.
Flt/ Sgt	R. P. G. Hill	Navigator	KIA	DURNBACH WAR CEMETERY, Coll. grave 5. A. 1-6.
FO	E. M. Dunn	Bomb Aimer	Prisoner of war	
Sgt	Samuel Percival	Wireless Operator	KIA	DURNBACH WAR CEMETERY, Coll. grave 5. A. 1-6.
Sgt	George Walter Scott	Mid Upper Gunner	KIA	DURNBACH WAR CEMETERY, Coll. grave 5. A. 1-6.
Sgt	L. J. Evans	Rear Gunner	KIA	DURNBACH WAR CEMETERY, Coll. grave 5. A. 1-6.

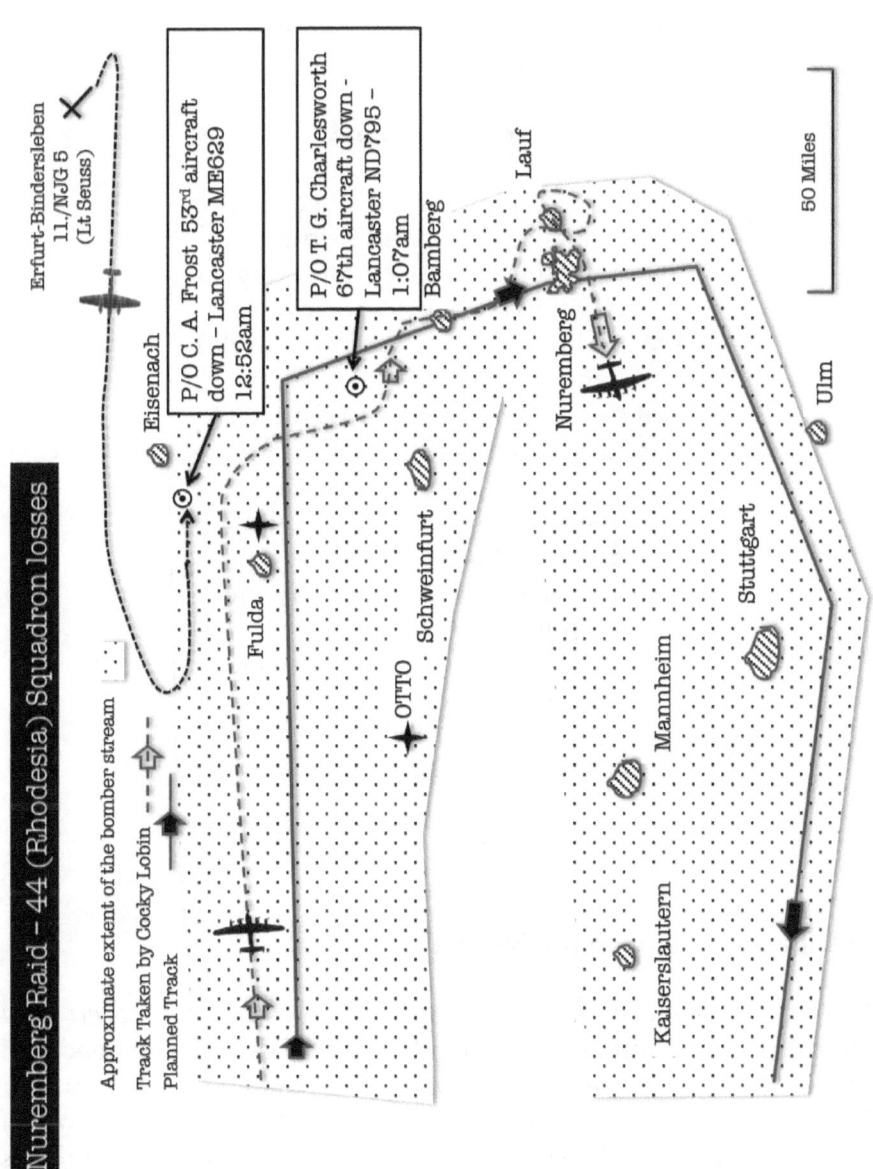

Nuremberg Raid – 44 (Rhodesia) Squadron losses

Approximate extent of the bomber stream
Track Taken by Cocky Lobin
Planned Track

Erfurt-Bindersleben
11./NJG 5
(Lt Seuss)

Eisenach

P/O C. A. Frost 53rd aircraft
down – Lancaster ME629
12:52am

P/O T. G. Charlesworth
67th aircraft down -
Lancaster ND795 –
1:07am

Bamberg

Lauf

Fulda

OTTO

Schweinfurt

Nuremberg

Mannheim

Kaiserslautern

Stuttgart

Ulm

50 Miles

The two 44 Squadron aircraft were shot down only 50 miles apart, 15 minutes flying time. What is staggering is that during that same short period, 14 other aircraft were shot down. This illustrates the carnage that took place on that fateful night. It is unimaginable for us living today to appreciate what it must have been like.

Bomber Command

A long cold night, a star filled sky,
A blacked out world below.
The grim faced crew on faith rely
They'll live to see tomorrow.
The searchlights sweep, the hell sent flak,
A thousand shards of steel.
But on they press their bold attack
And hide the fear they feel

For near six years, night after night
Squadron after Squadron
Shattered the dream of Nazi might,
Its power a sham illusion
They shared a duty, fate and fear
That forged uncommon pride
And paid a price in lives so dear,
More than fifty thousand died.

By John M Milne (57 Squadron RAF)

What went wrong on the Nuremberg Raid?

The hours between midnight and 07:25 on the 31st March 1944 became known as Bomber Command's 'Black Friday.' The dead and wounded aircrew for the night's operations totalled 745. A further 159 aircrew were taken prisoner, some of them badly injured. Loss of aircraft amounted to 108, 94 were shot down by nightfighters and flak over enemy territory.

At 15:25 on the afternoon of the 30th, a weather Mosquito confirmed to Bomber Command that the outward flight in the moonlight had little chance of cloud cover, and, if the cloud seen over Nuremberg persisted, it would rob the Pathfinders of the ability to mark visually by moonlight. A further forecast was handed to the AVM Sir Robert Saundby at 16:40. It read: 'Nuremberg: Large amount of strato-cumulus with tops to about 8000ft and risk of some thin patchy cloud at about 15 to 16 000ft.'[161]

Many years after the war, Sir Robert recalled: 'I can say that, in view of the met report and other conditions, everyone, including myself, expected the C-in-C to cancel the raid. We were most surprised when he did not. I thought perhaps there was some top-secret political reason for the raid, something too top-secret for even me to know'.

The conditions reported by the Mosquito were not passed down to the stations. Every effort was made to keep from crews the unpleasant fact that they were to fly a constant course through a well-defended part of Germany for 265 miles in bright moonlight with little chance of cloud cover. At a dozen air stations, met officers forecast that there would be cloud cover at operational height. No one, not even the Pathfinder squadrons, was told of the 'large amounts of strato-cumulus' now forecast for Nuremberg.

From the original force of 782 heavy bombers that had taken off for Nuremberg, 725 crossed the Belgian coast. The others had aborted for various reasons: engine failure, oxygen supply problems, unserviceable radar sets and so on.

As the bombers flew due east from the Charleroi turning point, they began to drift north of the correct track and to fall behind time. The wind had veered due west and had decreased, and the Windfinder system had already broken down. The leading Pathfinders were detailed to transmit the 'found' winds back to their Group HQ who would in turn broadcast these to all the bombers on the half-hour. That night, the few reports that did get through were so conflicting that it was impossible to send out common forecasts. In addition, too many aircraft transmitting wind forecasts on the same frequency cancelled each other out.

Just after midnight, the first bomber was shot down by flak over Liege; at the same time, over 200 nightfighters were on their way to the IDA and OTTO beacons, straddling the course of the Long Leg. The diversionary feints had failed to fool the Luftwaffe generals.

The 45-mile section of the route between the German frontier and the Rhine cost the RAF ten Lancasters and two Halifaxes and two more bombers had been damaged.

The Germans circling at the IDA beacon were listening to the running commentary from the Deelen (3 JD 1) underground ops room,

161   The weather over Nuremberg was confirmed in a later report by the Germans, cloud nimbo-stratus moving northwards, base 1,640ft, extending to 11,500ft.

and were justifiably amazed to be told that the main bomber-stream was heading straight for them in the clearest weather conditions possible, under a brilliant half-moon.

The bomber crews were deeply shocked to meet nightfighters in such strength so early in their flight, waiting dead on track in every semblance of an ambush laid with advance information. And, as if this wasn't enough, a completely unforeseeable weather phenomenon occurred at this point. Vapour or condensation trails, rarely found below 25,000ft, started to appear behind each bomber flying at 19 to 20,000ft. The dead-straight streams of pure white cloud in the bright moonlight were welcomed enthusiastically by the waiting Germans.

This situation was no different, and no less avoidable, than the tragic day on 25 October 1854 when the Light Brigade threw itself against the Russian guns at Balaclava. The comparison is stark.

> *Cannon to right of them,*
> *Cannon to left of them,*
> *Cannon in front of them*
> *Volley'd and thunder'd;*
> *Storm'd at with shot and shell,*
> *Boldly they rode and well,*
> *Into the jaws of Death,*
> *Into the mouth of hell*
> *Rode the six hundred*[162]

Unbeknown to Bomber Command, many of the German nightfighters were equipped with a newly-developed and deadly form of armament the Luftwaffe had named *Schrage Musik*; literally translated, it means 'slanting music', more colloquially, 'jazz'. The pilot would approach the bomber from below, unseen by both gunners, and line up an aiming point on either side of an inner engine; both wings at this point carried the fuel tanks. Because they attacked from the very close range of 70 to 80 metres, it was considered too risky to aim at the unprotected belly of the bomber and possibly to detonate the bomb-load.

At a quarter to one, the leading bombers reached the end of the Long Leg and started to turn south to Nuremberg. German fighters and unreported wind changes had caused further dispersal. The 220 miles from Liege to the turning point was by now clearly marked by the blazing remains of 41 Lancasters and 18 Halifaxes. It is unlikely

162 *The Charge of the Light Brigade*, Alfred Lord Tennyson written in 1854, third and last stanzas.

that a single hour, before or since, has seen a greater rate of aerial carnage.

The target was now 75miles to the south; without the tail wind, this would be a 20-minute flight. The turning point was a tricky one, above the forests of Thuringia with no recognisable feature or nearby town. Most of the aircraft turned well to the north of the right place and slightly short of it.

The Luftwaffe fighters kept attacking. The first half of that short leg to Nuremberg claimed ten more bombers; and as the leading Pathfinders flew past the searchlights of Bamberg, only 30miles from the target, they suffered yet another critical setback in the shape of a thick blanket of cloud, less than 2,000ft at base and extending up to 11,500ft. Not only was Nuremberg covered by cloud, but also the winds from the west had suddenly increased in velocity and were blowing the big bombers sideways to the east. So, instead of flying over Erlangen and on to Nuremberg, some of the Pathfinders had crossed another small town, Forchheim, and then approached Lauf, much smaller than the real target but with similar characteristics on the H2S radar screens, being situated on the Pegnitz River and surrounded by woods.

Thirty-nine bombers were shot down on the final approach and over the target area. The force had by now lost 79 aircraft, exceeding the Leipzig total of six weeks earlier. Of all the aircraft shot down on the outward flight, there was only one from which the entire crew survived; from one crew in every three there were no survivors at all.

Mosquitoes of 627 Sqn opened the activities of the Primary Marking Force at two minutes to one, offloading 500-pounders and 'window' at the rate of four bundles a minute to disrupt the 100-odd radar-predicted flak guns known to be defending the city. Ten minutes later, 65 Pathfinders and Supporters had done their best, but the conditions were hopeless. Instead of a clear and vividly marked target for the Main Force bomb-aimers due to arrive at 01.10, there was one group of skymarkers over Nuremberg and another group ten miles to the north-east near Lauf, both being blown eastwards and falling towards the clouds.

It was Zero Hour by now and 559 Main Force bombers should have started to arrive. During the first five minutes, only 33 aircraft bombed. The majority of the force had turned from the Long Leg well north of the right track and were, therefore, some minutes flying time further from the target than planned.

Seeing two groups of markers, the Main Force crews were

understandably confused; so were the Backers-up among them whose duty it was to renew the skymarkers. They managed to re-mark the group over Lauf which now gave off the most light and attracted by far the greater number of bombs. Some of the later Pathfinders placed their markers accurately over Nuremberg, but the damage had been done, and soon there was a ragged line of skymarkers more than ten miles wide. The wrecks of nine aircraft shot down on their bombing runs formed a long straight line from Bamberg to Lauf. The creep-back started early and soon measured 15 miles.

Altogether, 512 aircraft bombed in the Nuremberg area; what had happened to the other 119 bombers that should have done so?

A chapter of accidents misled at least a hundred of them. Both radar sets in a marker Mosquito had failed and the dead-reckoning navigation had been adversely affected by the changing winds. Just before Zero Hour, the crew found a well-defended industrial area they presumed was Nuremberg, especially as they had been briefed to expect clear weather there. The bombs and markers were released and within a few minutes, the indicator flare had attracted seven Lancaster Supporters and their bomb loads. Another Lancaster in the area was shot down and the blazing wreckage was the final signal for many bomb-aimers to assume they'd arrived on target, and 48 crews took back clear bombing photographs ... of Schweinfurt! In the most supreme irony, damage was done to all three of the ball-bearing plants ... Harris' hated panacea targets.

Thirteen other bombers released their loads when they realized they were lost; these fell on unspecified targets, including Bamberg, 30 miles north of Nuremberg, and a small town 60 miles north.

When the bombers flew away from Nuremberg and Schweinfurt they were pursued for a short way by the German fighters and several more combats took place; it would be wrong at this stage to talk of a 'stream' for the bombers were spread over a huge frontage. The tail wind which had helped them along from the Belgian coast to the target in just over 100 minutes was now a heavy head wind, and the flight back would be for most a long, boring drag of three hours or more. The force lost three more aircraft before leaving Germany, all near Stuttgart.

Just over an hour after leaving Nuremberg, those aircraft that were following the planned route flew over the Rhine north of Strasbourg and on into France. Night-fighters were responsible for the destruction of five or six bombers between the German border and the Channel coast. Two more were shot down by flak, and there was a tragic collision north of Metz. Both aircraft were at least 40 miles off course.

It was almost 06:00 before the last stragglers reached the coast and flew out over the English Channel.

Six hundred men of the Light Brigade … 745 dead and dying bomber crew … brave beyond measure.

> *When can their glory fade?*
> *O the wild charge they made!*
> *All the world wonder'd.*
> *Honor the charge they made!*
> *Honor the Light Brigade,*
> *Noble six hundred!*

Sixty-eight years and three months after the Nuremberg Raid, the Bomber Command Memorial opened in Green Park on the banks of the Thames.

On the wall of the Churchyard in the village of Ste Marguerite des Loges in Normandy, 27 miles east of Caen, is a tiny granite plaque. The plaque, made from Rhodesian Black Granite, is easy to miss, mounted on the wall next to the gate to the cemetery in Le Bourg Street. Above the plaque is a sign in white with a green background that reads in French, *Commonwealth War Graves*. Below the sign the plaque reads …

EN SOUVENIR DES AVIATEURS
RHODESIENS MORTI
AU CHAMPS D'HONNEUR DURAND
LA SECONDE GUERRE
MONDIALE
---- IN MEMORIAM ----
IN MEMORY OF THE RHODESIAN
AIRMEN KILLED IN ACTION
IN FRANCE DURING WORLD WAR II
---- LEST WE FORGET ---

A tiny tribute to a few good men, from a tiny country in Africa. We must remember them.

Analysis

German assessment of damage at Nuremberg: '133 killed (75 in city itself), 412 injured; 198 homes destroyed, 3,804 damaged, 11,000 homeless. Fires started: 120 large, 485 medium / small. Industrial damage: railway lines cut, and major damage to three large factories; 96 industrial buildings destroyed or seriously damaged. Bombs dropped (target area). 30 'mines', 145 HE (11 duds), 60,000 incendiaries. Bombs dropped (decoy sites): 6 'mines', 110 HE and numerous incendiaries.'

Although this provided confirmation of the determination of many crews to press home the attack, Nuremberg citizens had good reason to be grateful to their nightfighters whose activities spared them the full force of a saturation attack such as those suffered by Berlin, Cologne, Dresden and Essen and several other centres pounded to rubble by area bombing.

Scarecrow

There was no such thing as a special exploding shell used to terrify bomber crews. The RAF High Command had no idea of what was causing the explosions and attempted, as far as possible, to dissemble on the subject. On one occasion the Air Ministry put out a press statement insisting, under headlines, 'The Scarecrow flare is a German bluff', that crews had nothing to worry about. These mysterious explosions were simply bombers blowing up in mid-air from the upward-firing *Schrage Musik* cannons.

Conclusion

In the summer of 1971, in interviews with Alastair Revie, author of the book *The Lost Command*, Arthur Harris said: 'Churchill spoke to me with pride and admiration of the thousand battles of Bomber Command. But he knew, as I did, that when you're fighting 1,000 offensive battles in the course of the longest continuous battle of the war, it is difficult to find changes of tactics every time that will fox the enemy; and one of the changes you have to include occasionally is to do what the enemy thinks you would not dare to do: avoid extensive diversionary operations for once and take a fairly direct route to the target, as with Nuremberg.

'I do not make excuses … there is no need. To guess wrong a few times out of a thousand, as at Nuremberg, is deeply regrettable, especially in view of the slaughter that could be involved on such occasions in the terrible circumstances of air warfare.

'The scale of losses at Nuremberg was due to the weather, as well as to the main trouble we were suffering from at that time; the fact that .303 machine guns in a night bomber are not much use against cannon-firing nightfighters.'

'I am asked if there was a security leak on that occasion. I just do not know even at this distance in time, but it may be that a security leak coincided with a straightforward operation and was helped by the wrong bombing weather. As it happened, not for the first time, conditions in the night sky on 30th March 1944 turned out to be much more in favour of German fighters than of British bombers.'

'There are those who say we should have known that the moon would be bright, that the clouds would vanish, or that a wind would blow up later.'

'I say we are not gods to know such things to perfection. But I also have to say that I am full of admiration for our met people. Meteorology is more of an art than a science even today, even with the benefits of computers and other technological aids. In the war, we knew nothing of jet streams, and there was all too little information available about fronts building up in the Atlantic and that sort of thing.'

'Also, my met officers in the Groups would give an opinion, as at Nuremberg, if the prospects were reasonable. At the morning conference, the weather conditions were rated either "possible" or "impossible", and nobody was obliged to stick his neck out. Where doubts arose, all the Group met officers had to do was to assure me that they considered prospects unfavourable, and that was that.

'Do you honestly think that I would have risked aircrew unnecessarily when I valued them as much as I did?'

'My feelings towards the boys who flew in Bomber Command are beyond expression. They knew the odds were constantly against them to the point that they were playing never-ending games of Russian roulette. I do not know why or how they went on as they did. I am lost in admiration for them.'

The Rhodesian Air Training Scheme[163]

Whenever the Rhodesian Air Training Scheme is mentioned, a large number of people appear to think that it refers to RAF wartime training, and that Rhodesia played a small part in what was, essentially, a Canadian and Australian venture. The Rhodesian Air Training Scheme was an important part of the Commonwealth Air Training Organisation and continued for many years after the end of World War II.

From the 1 May 1940 until the 31 March 1954, the Royal Air Force had a presence in Rhodesia in the form of the Rhodesian Air Training Group. RATG trained a large number of aircrew for the RAF, from all over the Commonwealth, as part of the Empire Air Training Scheme.

During the years of World War II, and after, the Royal Air Force was the sole military force to fly in Rhodesian skies. After the end of World War II, in common with all other units, RATG was run down and continued its training task at a much-reduced rate. On 28 November 1947, The Southern Rhodesian Air Force was re-established as a permanent unit and from that date until the RATG closed, both the RAF and the SRAF took to the skies above Rhodesia.

RATG was organised as a headquarters with training units and supporting units reporting to it and operated from 14 May 1940 to 1 January 1946. RATG Headquarters was located in the Salisbury suburb of Belvedere. Supporting the Headquarters and tasked by it, was a Communications Flight provided by Southern Rhodesia Air Services that was located at the nearby Belvedere Airport.

The organisation of the RATG consisted of four Elementary Flying Training Schools that undertook basic flying training of the pilot cadets. Four Service Flying Training Schools brought the pilot cadets up to 'wings' standard. A Combined Air Observers School trained Navigation/Air Observer and Air Gunner cadets. The provision of instructors for these units was undertaken by a Flying Instructors School and service and maintenance of the group's aircraft was in the hands of two Aircraft Repair Depots.

---

163 Dave Newman, *RATG An Overview*, www.rhodesiaandtheraf.blogspot.com. au. Article *RAF Training in Southern Rhodesia 1940-1954* by Ray Sturtivant (Aviation News - 18 December 1980)

The Elementary Flying Training Schools comprised:

No. 25 EFTS
Located at Belvedere, Salisbury, until it closed on the 16 November 1945, with a relief landing ground at Parkridge from May 1943. The unit flew DH Tiger Moths, Fairchild Cornells and NA Harvards.

No. 26 EFTS
Operated from RAF Guinea Fowl, near Gwelo, from 8 August 1940 till the 14 August 1945, with a relief landing ground at Senali. It flew DH Tiger Moths and Fairchild Cornells.

No. 27 EFTS
Sited at RAF Induna near Bulawayo from 28 January 1940 (prior to the official opening of the Group), until the 21-Sep-1945. DH Tiger Moths and Fairchild Cornells were used by the unit.

No. 28 EFTS
RAF Mount Hampden near Salisbury was the site of this unit from 1 April 1941 and it absorbed No. 20 SFTS on the 7 September 1945. It closed on the 30 October 1945. Its relief landing grounds were Oldbury from Mar 1943 and Rainham from Apr 1943 and it flew DH Tiger Moths, Fairchild Cornells and NA Harvards.

The Service Flying Training Schools comprised:

No. 20 SFTS
Flew from RAF Cranborne near Salisbury from 10 July 1940 to the 7 September 1945. From September 1943, it had a satellite at New Martinsthorpe and relief landing grounds at Sebastopol by April 1943, Hienzani from 7 September 1943 and Inkomo from September 1945. It flew NA Harvards, and was absorbed into No. 28 EFTS.

No. 21 SFTS
Operated from RAF Kumalo near Bulawayo, from 8 October 1940 to the 18 May 1945 and out of its satellite Wollendale by February 1943. It had a relief landing ground at Marrony by August 1943 and flew Airspeed Oxfords.

No. 22 SFTS

Based at RAF Thornhill near Gwelo, from 25 March 1941 to the 30 September 1945. It used relief landing grounds at Sendi from April 1943 and RAF Moffat. It flew NA Harvards.

No. 23 SFTS

From 8 July 1941 to the 30 September 1945 it flew from RAF Heany near Bulawayo with relief landing grounds at White's Run still March 1945 and Sauerdale till April 1945. It flew Airspeed Oxfords.

Navigation/Air Observer and Air Gunner training was conducted by No. 24 Combined Air Observation School at RAF Moffat from 3August 1941 using Airspeed Oxfords, Avro Ansons and NA Harvards. On the 12 May 1943, the school was re-designated No. 24 Bombing Gunnery and Navigation School. Two new units, No. 29 Elementary Navigation School and an Aircrew Pool were formed and these three units continued the training task, with the same aircraft, until 13 April 1945.

To provide flying instructors for the groups schools, the Rhodesian Central Flying School was established at Belvedere on 3 September 1941 flying DH Tiger Moths. On 20 May 1942 the unit was re-designated No. 33 Flying Instructors School and it remained at Belvedere. The aircraft inventory was increased to include DH Tiger Moths, Fairchild Cornells, NA Harvards and Airspeed Oxfords. On 2 November 1942, the unit re-located to RAF Norton south of Salisbury. Another change of designation occurred on 9 May 1944 when the unit became the Central Flying School (Southern Rhodesia). It remained at Norton using the same aircraft types until 9 October 1945.

Supporting the flying effort and providing aircraft servicing and repair were No. 31 Aircraft Repair Depot at RAF Cranborne and No. 32 Aircraft Repair Depot at RAF Heany. Both were establish on 1 August 1941 and each had a NA Harvard on strength for communications work.

Kubani ena Bulalile Cocky Lobin?

Who Killed Cock Robin?

Zonke nyoni lapa moyo ena kala, ena kala
Ena izwile ena ifile lo nyoni Cocky Lobin
Ena izwile, ena ifile,
ena izwile ena ifile Cocky Lobin …

All the birds in the sky cried and cried,
When they heard of the death of the bird Cock Robin,
When they heard of the death of poor Cock Robin.

Kubani ena bulalile Cocky Lobin?
Meena kuluma lo Sparrow
Na lo picannin 303 Browning kamina
Meena bulalile Cocky Lobin!

Who was it that killed Cock Robin?
It was I said the Sparrow,
With my tiny .303 Browning,
It was I who killed Cock Robin.

Zonke nyoni lapa moyo ena kala, ena kala
Ena izwile ena ifile lo nyoni Cocky Lobin
Ena izwile, ena ifile, ena izwile ena ifile
Cocky Lobin …

All the birds in the sky cried and cried,
When they heard of the death of the bird Cock Robin,
When they heard of the death of poor Cock Robin.

Kubani ena bona ene ifile?
Meena kuluma lo Mosweeto
Na lo cleva bomb sight kamina
Meena bona ene ifile …

Who saw him die?
It was I said the Mosquito,
Through my clever bomb-sight,
It was I who saw him die.

Zonke nyoni lapa moyo ena kala, ena kala
Ena izwile ena ifile lo nyoni Cocky Lobin
Ena izwile, ena ifile, ena izwile ena ifile
Cocky Lobin.

All the birds in the sky cried and cried,
When they heard of the death of the bird Cock Robin,
When they heard of the death of poor Cock Robin.

Kubani ena digga lo grave?
Meena kuluma lo Jackal,
Na lo mukulu foshol kamina,
Meena digga lo grave.

Who will dig his grave?
I said the Jackal
With my big shovel,
I will dig his grave.

Zonke nyoni lapa moyo ena kala, ena kala
Ena izwile ena ifile lo nyoni Cocky Lobin
Ena izwile, ena ifile, ena izwile ena ifile
Cocky Lobin.

All the birds in the sky cried and
cried,
When they heard of the death of
the bird Cock Robin,
When they heard of the death of
Cock Robin.

Kubani ena kuluma lo prayers?
Meena kuluma lo Owl,
Ndaba meena kona maningi fundisili,
Meena kuluma lo prayers.

Who will say the prayers?
I said the Owl
Because I am so well educated
I will say the prayers.

Zonke nyoni lapa moyo ena kala, ena kala
Ena izwile ena ifile lo nyoni Cocky Lobin
Ena izwile, ena ifile, ena izwile ena ifile
Cocky Lobin.

All the birds in the sky cried and
cried,
When they heard of the death of
the bird Cock Robin,
When they heard of the death of
poor Cock Robin.

Kubani ena bora lo booku?
Meena kuluma lo Vulture.
Ndaba mena kona maningi culture,
Meena bora lo booku.

Who will write in the book?
I said the Vulture,
Because I have so much culture
I will write in the book.

Zonke nyoni lapa moyo ena kala, ena kala
Ena izwile ena ifile lo nyoni Cocky Lobin
Ena izwile, ena ifile, ena izwile ena ifile
Cocky Lobin.

All the birds in the sky cried and
cried,
When they heard of the death of
the bird Cock Robin,
When they heard of the death of
poor Cock Robin.

Based on account by William Dives DFC, *A Bundu Boy in Bomber Command.*

A RUTHLESS ESCALATION TO A COLONIAL WAR

Set in the country Rhodesia, now called Zimbabwe, in the late 1970s, the counter-insurgency war reaches a whole new level with Soviet and Cuban involvement. Internal settlement negotiations threaten vested interests. British Rapier missiles and Soviet SAM-7s add to a dangerous mix with horrific consequences. The northern neighbour, Zambia, provides logistical and technical support for the build up of Cuban and freedom fighter forces for an invasion of Rhodesia. MIG-19s and MIG-21s are game changers for old Rhodesian Hawker Hunters.

This story follows the bravery and commitment of a celebrated US war correspondent who has been sucked into a war she was sent to cover. Her path crosses that of a Rhodesian Selous Scout infiltrated into Zambia to try and turn the tide. Cold War rivalry, political intrigue and paralysis, are the backdrop to this fast paced, brutal, violent story where nothing is as it seems … one unspeakably ruthless act changes the World's view on the difference between freedom fighters and terrorists … forever.

Due for release in 2014

Winner of the Bronze Award in the Military/Wartime Fiction category in the 2012 Independent Publisher (IPPY) Book Awards in the United States.

A DESPERATE COLONIAL STRUGGLE ON A CONTINENT TORN BY WAR

Set in an almost forgotten guerrilla war in what is now called Zimbabwe during the 1970s, this is a journey into the world of young men fighting and dying at the behest of their political masters. The strain of having to survive close-quarter skirmishes preoccupy the combatants, who helplessly find themselves caught up in a conflict spinning out of control.

Mike Smith, an insecure nineteen-year old national serviceman, is immersed in a bloody insurgency witnessing horrors that seem too much for a young man to have to bear.

Tongerai Chabanga, a commander of the liberation movement, must withstand political pressure from his leaders outside the country to prosecute the war in a manner he disagrees with. At the same time, he is faced with the atrocities perpetrated of a depraved Soviet Spetznaz military advisor who threatens to undo the work he has done.

A COLONIAL WAR IN SOUTHERN AFRICA SPINNING OUT OF CONTROL

Set in the country now called Zimbabwe in the late 1970s, the Bush War has escalated into a desperate fight for survival. In a bid to stem the tide of freedom fighters flooding into the country, the war has spilt over into neighbouring Mozambique. External raids by special forces, the Selous Scouts and the Rhodesian Light Infantry, are required to hunt down the leaders of the liberation movement. They are hopelessly outnumbered, jumping from ancient Dakotas and rugged Alouette III helicopters. Chinese trained freedom fighters mount sabotage raids on key installations from bases in Mozambique, aided by spies in high places.

This story follows the harrowing, day-in-day-out combat and relentless pressure put on the combatants. Cold War rivalry, political paralysis and undercover agents put the men on the ground, on both sides of the conflict, in mortal danger. They not only have to defeat the enemy on the battlefield, they also have to endure the mistakes, bigotry and self-interest of their leaders. On the Freedom Fighter side, the fighting men and women are subjected to unspeakable hardship and brutality. Death stalks them from bomb, bullet, disease, hunger and their own leadership.

This is the story of the 'Steely-eyed killers' …

www.ingramcontent.com/pod-product-compliance
Lightning Source LLC
Chambersburg PA
CBHW020528020726
47494CB00006B/1673

ISBN 978-1-936556-57-1

Right Place, Right Time Copyright 2015 Leslie McKelvey

Published 2015
Printed by Black Velvet Seductions Publishing
A division of Savage Publications

Visit us at:
www.blackvelvetseductions.com

www.blackvelvetseductions.com

Dedication

Men are often the inspiration for romance novels, and this story is no different. There have been quite a few men who have influenced my life, but in this instance I can narrow it down to two.

To Bill: you were my first real love and my first Marine. You are the physical embodiment of Bear; the build, the walk, the attitude, the laser-pointed look, and the military bearing. When I picture Bear in my head you are the man I see. I could not have created this character without you, and I am so glad that you were a part of my life.

To my husband, Scott: you are Bear's heart and soul, which makes you my heart and soul. You are a man of quiet confidence, excellence of spirit, and dedication to integrity. Your skill, knowledge, and command presence make you, like Bear, a man to be reckoned with and never taken lightly. God has blessed you not only with boundless patience (and being married to me, I know you need it), but also with the understanding and supportive nature that has allowed me to write my books and live my dream. You are my soul mate, the man I can't live without, the man I will always love. You are my Bear.

Chapter One

As Beth Drummond flew down the narrow, wooded trail, her lungs burned and her heart raced. With one hand tightly gripping her camera's telephoto lens, she tried to shield it from the branches and brambles that ripped at her clothes and left red, angry scratches on her bare arms. Blood roared in her ears and drowned out even the sounds of her footfalls. She didn't think the people who had been shooting at her had just given up and gone home, so she kept running, praying her legs would carry her to the ranger station. If not, she'd run until she couldn't or until they caught her.

The trail veered sharply to her left, and she skidded to a stop, pressing close to a Rocky Mountain Maple. She tried to breathe deeply and evenly, struggling to hear anything over the internal *whush-whush* of her loud, galloping pulse. Moving slowly, she peered around the trunk back up the trail. Nothing. But that didn't mean they weren't coming. She was about to start running again when a pair of muscular arms snaked around her from behind and a large hand clamped itself over her mouth. She inhaled sharply and thrashed about, trying to twist away from him, but his grip only tightened, effectively immobilizing her. She tried to kick, but he'd pinned her legs between his. A turtle on its back should be so helpless.

"*Don't* move." The words were a harsh whisper in her ear. "And *don't* scream."

She went stock still. The hand was so big it covered nearly her entire face, and the body at her back was male, tall, broad, and hard. The top of her head just reached his shoulder, and she felt the bunched muscles in his arms and chest as he held her close and tight. Her throat closed up, and her heart beat so hard and fast she thought it would burst, but she did as the stranger commanded. Without a sound, he pulled her away from the tree and backward into a stand of brush. The thick branches closed around them like a cloak.

Her heart literally stopped when, not fifteen seconds later, the men who had been chasing her for the last several miles ran by. Her only advantage had been her knowledge of the area and the terrain, but apparently even that had not been enough. She'd had no idea they had gained so much ground on her. How had she not heard them? They made no attempt to move quietly. She closed her eyes and listened as they crashed through the brush. When the sounds of their headlong run faded, her limbs gave out and she sagged against the stranger.

The stranger. Although he had saved her from the men chasing her, that still didn't ensure he was a good guy. And she was a woman, alone. Fear revived her frozen heart, sending her pulse into a full gallop, and she stiffened. Now that her pursuers had gone, and quiet once again ruled the forest, the only sound she could hear was the roaring of blood in her ears and the stranger's calm, even breaths. *Come on, Beth*, she thought, *you've been in worse situations. Remember Afghanistan?*

His heartbeat was steady and strong against her back, and she sent a silent prayer heavenward. *Please, please, please let him be a good guy or, at least, not another bad guy.* When she tried to move, he tightened his hold on her waist, his lips near her ear.

"Not yet. They may double back."

Beth jumped when a shout cut through the woods like an axe.

"Do you see her?"

"No!"

The voices were close, too close, and she hunched back against him. Fear filled her in a cold, dark surge, but his presence was strangely comforting. Even when the three men joined up mere feet away, he remained silent and motionless, seemingly unaffected by their proximity and their weapons. She fought the urge to turn and bury her face against the man's chest, as if doing so would infuse her with his apparent calm. Her pulse neared heart attack range. She stared at the gun-wielding thugs and tried to regulate her breathing.

The tallest of the trio was Hispanic and thin with dark hair, dark eyes, and swarthy skin. His associates were of similar lineage and coloring, one with his long hair pulled back into a ponytail and the other with a short, shaved haircut. The tall one was obviously the leader as the others watched and waited for him to speak.

After a brief silence, the tall man looked at the man with a ponytail and said, "Head back toward the meadow. She can't have gone far." The man nodded and ran back the way they'd come.

Shaved head spoke. "I'll head toward the ranger station. That's probably where she's going."

The tall man nodded and glared. "Don't come back until you find her. And bring her alive. I want to know what she saw."

Beth watched as the three men split up, each heading in a different direction. Even though she knew she was far from safe, her legs sagged as relief washed over her. Had it not been for the stranger's steely arm around her waist, she would have dropped to her knees. Once the men disappeared from view, he let his hand fall from her face.

She jerked away from him and spun round. Her gaze was inexorably drawn upward. He was one of the tallest men she'd ever seen, well over six feet and probably closer to seven, his blonde hair cut in a high and tight. Broad shoulders filled out the shirt of woodland camouflage, the long sleeves rolled up to reveal muscular forearms. Sharp blue eyes cut straight through her, like a pinpoint laser. His features were chiseled, his jaw sharply squared and shadowed with blonde stubble. He looked her up and down once, though there was nothing sexual in his perusal. He glanced at the camera hanging around her neck, and when their eyes met again, the intensity of his gaze pierced her like an arrow.

She lifted her chin. "Who are you?"

"I'm the guy who can get you out of here if you can keep up."

She backed up a step. "And why should I trust you?"

He rested his hand on his hip, and her heart fluttered wildly when she saw the pistol.

"If I'd wanted to hurt you, we wouldn't be having this conversation." His gaze turned frosty. "Do you want to get out of here or not?"

She was good at no-brainers and nodded.

"Then we need to move." He grabbed her hand and pushed through the shrubs, moving with unexpected stealth for a man of such stature. His eyes swept one way down the trail, then the other, and he skewered her with a look. "Stay close, and keep quiet." Without another word, he crossed the trail and melded into the trees on the other side, drawing her with him.

He was fast, sure-footed, and silent, his feet seeming to barely touch the ground. Beth felt like a clumsy oaf as she tried to step where he stepped and move how he moved, and several times she failed. Dead branches snapped beneath her feet, and anger burned hotly in her chest, anger at herself. Her lack of grace was the equivalent of sending up a flare, alerting the gunmen to her location. *Get it together, Beth. Get your blasted feet on straight.*

She had learned from Chief Dancing Eagle, a local Native American man, how to traverse through wilderness areas because wildlife didn't usually stand still to be photographed. Normally she had no trouble moving like a resident of the forest, and she had an impressive portfolio to prove it. She'd been fleet and surefooted before her rescuer had shown up, managing to avoid the horror movie faux pas of falling and giving the killers the chance to catch her. But, as she trailed behind him now, it was as if she had two left feet. He leapt over a fallen tree with the grace and ease of a gazelle, and when she tried to imitate him, her boot caught on an errant branch. Her hand was jerked out of his, and her camera went flying as she landed face first in the dirt.

She lay there for a moment, dazed, but when she tried to get up, he planted a hand between her shoulder blades and pressed her back into the ground. Before she could protest, he sprawled out beside her and pushed her against the trunk of the prostrate conifer.

"Stay down."

Suddenly she heard the sound of running feet and sucked in a breath, her eyes flying to his face. Her lungs spasmed, unable to expand as a band of near panic tightened around her chest. His expression darkened; he shook his head once and pressed one finger to her lips. Somewhere on the other side of the fallen tree, the person paused for several tense, silent moments, and then the footsteps retreated until she could no longer hear them.

Beth blinked and exhaled slowly, blood pulsing through her veins at warp speed. The stranger slowly lifted his head and peered over the top of the log, moving with a grace and fluidity that was mesmerizing. Even though they were the ones being hunted, he did *not* look like prey. Those steely eyes surveyed the area with all the cunning and confidence of a highly skilled predator. If he hadn't just saved her life, his expression would have terrified her. He waited another couple of minutes and then carefully rose. When no one burst from the brush with guns blazing, he grabbed her camera, tossed it to her, and held out a hand.

"Let's move."

Beth quickly checked her camera, and then looped the strap over her neck and slipped her fingers into his. He hauled her to her feet. Without another word, he spun and those long legs ate up the distance as he went from zero-to-sixty in half a dozen heartbeats. She lengthened her stride and managed to keep up, barely. Her lungs started to burn again, and her muscles protested vehemently, but she choked down her discomfort and focused on him. Even at a run he appeared serene and unruffled, and she tried to absorb his calm. Oddly enough, his composure helped her regain hers. She tightened her grip on his hand.

The sun was well into its downward descent into the west, shadows lengthening across what was barely more than a deer path. They were moving south/southeast. She pushed thoughts of the armed men aside and focused on moving as quickly and quietly as possible as the trail narrowed and the terrain roughened. Several times the trail forked off, but he didn't hesitate or even glance at the branching paths. Apparently, he knew exactly where he was going. After about twenty minutes at a near dead-run, she heard the sound of rushing water and prayed they would stop soon. Her mouth was dry, and her lungs were begging for more oxygen. Trees started to thin and less than a minute later, she and the stranger stood on the banks of a rushing stream.

Without even pausing, he released her hand and crossed the tributary, hopping from rock to rock as if the path was marked and only he could see it. Beth stopped, took several deep breaths and then followed, making certain to plant her feet where he had planted his. Her camera had survived its flight into the brush, but she doubted it would recover from a swim.

He reached the opposite bank and turned toward her. She was aware of his gaze and tried to move faster while keeping her balance and staying out of the torrent. Once she put foot on the bank, he spun away without a word and started running downstream. Beth squared her shoulders and followed. She was actually starting to enjoy his unspoken challenge. He'd said he'd save her if she could keep up. Well, she was *going* to keep up or die trying. She focused on his broad back and set her stride to match his.

After about a mile they reached an eddy in the stream. The water lapped at the shore. Rock-studded sand edged with trees created a small clearing that would be a perfect campsite. He ran to the far side of the glade, reached into the bushes, and pulled out a pack. He shrugged into it, reached back into the brush, and retrieved a rifle. Beth stared, and a shaft of apprehension pierced her.

"Let's go," he said brusquely. "We need to put some more distance between us and them before we make camp."

"Camp?" He *couldn't* be serious. She gaped at him and wondered if perhaps he'd spent too much time in the wilderness. "We need to get to a ranger station, try to get out of here."

His brows drew together. "You heard them. That's where they're going."

"There's more than one station," she argued.

He gave her a tolerant look, the same look one would bestow on an argumentative toddler. "And there's more than one of *them*. You want to chance that?" He shouldered the rifle. "My car is east of here parked at Drake's trailhead."

"That trailhead is more than ten miles," Beth said. "It'll be dark soon."

He lifted one blonde brow. "That's why we keep moving until we make *camp*." He glanced at the sky. "We've got about an hour of daylight left. We can cover three, maybe four miles in that time."

"And if they're heading in the same direction?"

"We'll stay off the main trails. None of them had packs, so they weren't equipped to be out here for more than a few hours, unless you know something I don't."

She thought back and shook her head. "I didn't see any packs."

"Then we keep moving."

Indignance filled her, but before she could even form a retort, he started jogging, his long legs covering far more ground than hers. Beth planted her hands on her hips and stared after him, but then realized he wasn't waiting for her. In fact, he didn't even look back to see if she was following. Obviously, he thought her smart enough to realize she had little choice. As he disappeared into the trees, she huffed and sprinted after him. *Challenge accepted.*

They moved quickly and quietly and stayed well off the established, marked trails. She wondered if he was listening as hard as she was. Thankfully, the only sound was the chirp of birds, the soft rustle of their feet over the ground, and the occasional cry from an unseen wild animal.

She had to admit that, as much as she preferred having an unobstructed view when she went on her photo safaris, there was a distinct advantage to her current position. Watching him made their run infinitely more bearable. He ran through the trees seeming more animal than human. His muscles moved with fluid grace and easy, unrepressed strength as he smoothly and soundlessly traversed the narrow path. Fascinating. And then there was his backside. Tight and ultimately grab-able, it warranted a warning label, which would just give her even more reason to look at it. A pulse of attraction vibrated inside her, and she gulped. There were a million questions she wanted to ask him, but she thought it wise to imitate him and keep her mouth shut for the time being. From his actions and the brief, terse conversations, she discerned he was the sort of man accustomed to leading and being in control. Being in control required knowledge of the facts which required questions; questions he hadn't asked, *yet*. She imagined once they made camp and were relatively safe, he would start the interrogation, and for some reason she doubted she'd be able to get a word in edgewise.

The sun had just dipped below the mountains to the west. Darkness swallowed up the land like a carnivore gorging on its prey. They'd been moving for close to half an hour, and just as she was about to ask him to stop for a moment, he paused. Beth bent over and rested her hands on her thighs, taking deep breaths. Although she kept in top shape because hiking the trails of America's wilderness lands demanded she do so, she was not accustomed to prolonged runs over the rough and tumble terrain. Not to mention she'd been running for several miles *before* her enormous rescuer had saved her. A water bottle appeared in her periphery, and she glanced at it and lifted her gaze to his. To her annoyance, he wasn't even breathing hard. He said nothing, those blue eyes boring into hers, his face expressionless. Apprehension skittered up her spine. Straightening, Beth took the bottle.

"Thanks," she said softly.

"You're welcome." He shrugged out of his pack, dropped it on the ground, and then crouched and started searching through it. "Think you can make it another couple of miles? I've got an idea where we can make camp, but if you're worn out, we'll stop now."

Beth took a long drink of the water, careful not to drink it all. "I'm fine." She handed the bottle back to him. "I may be sucking wind, but I will go as far as you need me to."

He rose, finished the water, and handed her an energy bar.

"Okay then." He pulled another bottle from his pack, tossed it to her, and finished off his energy bar in two bites. "The spot I'm thinking of is a little tough to get to, but we'll be able to see anyone coming. And, if anyone *does* manage to track us that far, it'll give us an opportunity to get away."

"Sounds perfect." Beth opened the bar and took a healthy bite. "Lead on."

After she finished her energy bar and took a few more drinks of water, he did just that. He moved like a Marine sniper, quick and lithe, as if the pack and the rifle slung across his back weighed nothing. As they ran, dusk expanded its hold on the Rockies, the sky to the east draped in navy blue with faint pinpricks of light. Every so often he glanced over his shoulder at her, and she had a feeling he was pacing himself so as not to wear her out. The very idea irritated her. She was accustomed to others trying to keep up with *her*, not the other way around.

"Stop checking on me," she said when he looked at her again. "If I break a leg and can't go on, believe me, you'll be the first to know." She frowned. "I *will* keep up, and you can take that to the bank."

The briefest smile curved his mouth, and she was momentarily stunned by the change in his appearance. In that split-second, he'd gone from handsome to drop-dead gorgeous. *Wow, bet you have to beat them off with a stick when you flash those pearly whites.* She had no doubt women would drop their panties when he turned on that smile, but then it was gone, and the blank mask was back. *Bummer, but now I can look at his butt again.*

As the final rays of sunlight vanished, he stopped in a small clearing several dozen paces from the foot of a sheer vertical rock wall. Beth leaned against a tree and tried to catch her breath. She hurt in places she hadn't even known had muscles, and she knew she would really feel it in the morning. The sound of his pack hitting the ground made her look up, relief flooding her at the thought of finally making camp. When he pulled a coil of heavy-duty nylon rope from inside the pack, she slowly straightened. She glanced at the wall, looked at the rope, and hoped like hell her math was wrong. Nervous tingles traveled from her head to her toes and back.

"Um, what's the rope for?" *Please tell me you're going to use it to make a tent, string a hammock, tie me up, anything but what I'm thinking.*

He glanced at her, glanced at the wall, and then gave her a small, grim smile. "I told you camp would be a little tough to get to."

Her stomach dropped. "You're kidding." She looked up and fear churned in her gut. She'd witnessed the brutality of war up close. She spent her days chasing wild animals that could easily kill her, and now, she was being chased by people who would *definitely* kill her. However, heights were *not* her thing. Her heart did a double back-flip. "Oh, crap."

He rose and started tying knots in the rope. "Don't worry. I'll go up first. Then you can climb up. I'll anchor you."

Beth just stared at the rock face and tried to wrestle the near-panic back to simple fear.

He approached her. "Remember to use your legs, not your arms." Her arms automatically went up when he reached around her waist. Heat crawled up her neck. "Find a handhold, and then a foothold, then use your legs to push yourself up until you find another handhold." After he had tied the rope between her legs and around her midsection, he stepped back. Her cheeks burned but, thankfully, he seemed unaware as he added, "It's easier than it looks."

Beth laughed shortly, her eyes still on the rocks. "I'll bet."

"You'll do fine. And if I have to, I can pull you up."

She glanced at him. "And what happens if *you* fall?"

He lifted one blonde brow. "I won't fall."

"Right." Beth looked at the wall again. "Of course not."

He looped the rest of the rope over his shoulder then shrugged into the pack. "Relax. It'll be over before you know it."

Her pulse notched up. An image of flailing limbs and the ground rushing up, and the sensation of air *whooshing* by, flashed in her brain. "Well, you're right about that," she said under her breath as she leaned her head back. "One way or another it *will* be over."

"Here, carry this."

The rifle appeared in front of her, and Beth stared at it. She fought not to remember the last time she'd held a rifle, but the memories were harder to box up this time. She squeezed her eyes shut briefly and forced the words out. "I don't . . . I don't like guns."

He frowned. "You don't have to like it. You just have to sling it across your back." When she hesitated, he huffed and slid the sling over her shoulder. "I can't carry it all *and* climb."

Heat crawled up her neck. She adjusted the sling and forced herself to think logically. The rifle was an inanimate object after all and not something to worry about. Getting away— *that* was *far* more important. Now was *not* the time to let her past get the better of her. Picturing her pursuers helped her focus, and she gave him an apologetic look. "Right. Sorry."

"Don't be." His expression softened just a bit, or so it seemed in the deepening night. "We've made it this far." He spoke with confidence, and the deep, rough timbre of his voice soothed her. "The finish line for this evening is about sixty feet up. Think you can handle that?"

She wasn't at all sure she could. "I don't know," she replied, "but I will give it my all."

He clapped her on the shoulder. "That's all I ask. Let's get this party started." He turned away, but then turned back. "You may want to move your camera. It'll be tough to climb with that telephoto between you and the rocks. You don't want to break the lens."

Without another word, he put his pack on and moved toward

the rocks.

Shooting a glare at him, she slung her camera across her back like the rifle. "I knew that," she said under her breath.

She followed behind him, her heartbeat jumping a point for every step they took. However, when she got close to the cliffs, she realized that what had at first looked sheer and nearly vertical was not quite so intimidating. Beth sent a silent thank you heavenward and took a deep breath.

"All right," he said, "here we go. When I get to the top, I'll jerk on the rope twice. Then you start up, okay? And keep it quiet. We don't want to help them find us."

Beth nodded and watched as he began carefully picking his way up the cliff face. She made mental notes of where he put his hands and feet, hoping to imitate him when her turn finally came. Then she rolled her eyes. He was nearly a foot taller than her. For this leg of the trip, she would have to blaze her own trail.

All too soon he disappeared from sight as night deepened. She suddenly felt very alone and very vulnerable. Her stomach knotted, and she looked around. By the time it got this dark, she was usually sitting near a cheery fire or safe inside a hunting blind. Her mind started to play tricks on her. Trees loomed. Her pursuers danced in every shadow. Beth closed her eyes and kept a hand on the rope. When she felt the tug, a sigh of relief escaped her. Sending another silent prayer into the cosmos, she started up.

Her progress was painstakingly slow as she felt her way, darkness almost vocal in its claim of the mountains. She couldn't see the handholds, so she had to feel for them, which made it harder going. She half expected her rescuer to start pulling her up, but he didn't. However, the rope remained taut, so she knew he was aware of her progress. Pausing, she looked down before she realized what she was doing, and a wave of dizziness spun her. She squeezed her eyes shut. It looked like she had a bottomless pit beneath her, the ground swallowed in shadow. A cold surge of panic burst upward from the pit of her stomach. Beth sucked in a breath and pressed herself against the rocks, her heart beating so hard she was sure the pounding would push her backwards off her perch.

"You okay?"

He spoke in what was little more than a whisper, but she heard him readily enough. Again, the husky resonance of his voice calmed her. Beth took a steadying breath and whispered back, "yes, just trying to find another handhold."

"You're doing great. Take your time."

She had no idea how far she'd gone before a strange yet oddly familiar mechanical sound reached her. The deep, reverberating *whump-whump* was distant but growing closer, and she turned her head in its direction. The glare of a spotlight sliced through the fabric of darkness better than the sharpest blade. The calm she had borrowed from him evaporated. She gasped softly as her pulse launched into a full sprint. "Oh, crap."

Suddenly the rope went taut, and she felt herself move up, but not under her own power. Apparently he, too, had noticed the blazing light. Beth briefly thought about helping, but realized she would probably do more to hinder. Branches and leaves grabbed at her hair, face, and clothes, and she realized she was being pulled *through* a wall of brush, *fast.* She closed her eyes and shielded her face as best she could. Then she was out of the foliage and lying on the hard ground. Beth took several deep, ragged breaths and tried to gather her wits. When she finally did, she realized it wasn't hard ground she had collapsed on, unless the ground normally moved up and down like it was breathing.

As if sensing her intentions, his arms immediately locked around her. "*Don't* move."

Beth looked down into his face, and the sound of the helicopter washed over them. It was close, *very* close, and her throat closed up. A few seconds later light penetrated the bushes. It moved slowly back and forth and illuminated the rocks with disco-ball dots and strange, moving, leaf-shaped shadows. Beth blinked as she realized they were in a small cave. She froze and held her breath, as did he, his chest hard and unmoving beneath her. The light paused, and her heart stopped. Certain they had been spotted, she closed her eyes and waited for the ensuing gunfire. An explosive breath escaped her when, after several long, tense moments, the aircraft moved on. Without having to be told, she remained motionless and tried once more to absorb his calmness. She felt his heartbeat, slow and steady, and started counting. By the time she reached ten, her pulse had eased down several points. When the rapid *thump-thump* of helicopter blades finally vanished, she was almost back to normal. She was surprised at the effect he had on her. His unruffled demeanor soothed her fears and imparted a serenity she knew wasn't her own. It suddenly hit her that if he hadn't intervened earlier she'd most likely be dead. Beth's heart flipped once, and she gulped.

Several minutes had passed before he gave her a small nod. She took a deep breath, moved away from him, and sat cross-legged on the ground.

She was wrong; they weren't in a cave. Beth ran a hand over the wall, vertical and horizontal striations telling her this "cave" had been carved, not naturally formed. His pack leaned against the back wall, and large bushes obscured the opening from view. The sage sprouted from the very rock itself. Thank goodness. If not for that cover, they would have been like ducks in a shooting gallery.

Glancing at her savior, she took her camera from her neck, then removed the rifle and held it out to him. He watched her closely, but he took the gun without a word, putting it aside.

"Who are they?"

The direct, sharp tone of his question startled her, and she blinked at him. "I don't know."

His tone didn't change, but his posture certainly did, his shoulders squared and tense. "Why are they chasing you?"

She saw the drawing down of his brow, his hands clenched into fists the size of footballs. Not only did Beth see the scowl, she also *felt* it and cringed, both physically and emotionally. She looked down at her camera and wound her fingers around the telephoto lens, memories surging to the surface despite her efforts to the contrary. Her annoyance had morphed into shock and disbelief. The cold wave of despair and helplessness that followed chilled her. She shuddered and squeezed her eyes shut, but that only gave her mind a better screen on which to play. Fear rose like bile, hot and thick in the back of her throat. She choked it down. After several deep, steadying breaths and a brief silence, she forced herself to meet his gaze. "Because I saw them kill four people, and I have the pictures to prove it."

Chapter Two

Ted "Bear" Bristol kept his face neutral as he digested what the pretty photographer had just said. When he didn't reply, she stared at him, and he saw the indignant flash in her eyes. He realized she thought he didn't believe her. If the situation hadn't been so serious, he would have smiled at her expression.

She grabbed her camera and started fumbling with buttons. "I'm *not* making it up. I can show you right now."

He leaned forward and plucked the device from her hands before she had a chance to turn on the digital display screen. "No," he said in a harsh whisper. He checked to make sure it was set to "off" and held it out to her. "*Any* light will stand out like a beacon, so keep it off." Her eyes widened, and she bit her lip as she took the camera from his outstretched hand.

"Sorry," she said in a low voice. "I wasn't thinking."

"No worries. I can think enough for both of us."

The glare was back as her gaze flew to his face and her brows drew together in a frown. He wondered if she thought he was mocking her. Deciding to test her mettle, he let her believe that falsehood for the moment and returned her stare in kind. He had recognized one of her pursuers, and dangerous didn't even *begin* to describe the man. Bear had to get this situation figured out, and *fast*. First and foremost, he had to know if she was involved in any way, or if she was just in the wrong place at the wrong time. And, if she was the latter, what sort of woman was she? That determination could very well decide whether or not they survived this ordeal.

She battled with him visually, her eyes glittering with annoyance, her lips pressed into a thin line. He studied her closely, looking for the clues that would tell him what he needed to know – a flicker of guilt, a hint of nervousness, the telltale signs of deception he had learned to recognize over the years – but he saw none of that. Finally, she blinked several times, and he watched as the irritation slowly faded. Her expression shifted to one of self-reproach. He'd bet his life she was just unlucky, but he kept his guard up and continued to assess her.

She put the camera aside and wrapped her arms around her knees. "I guess that's a good thing – that you can think – because it's obvious *one* of us is incapable of logical thought."

"A temporary lapse, I'm sure." He chuckled, trying to lighten the mood. He knew she would reveal more about herself and what she knew, if anything, if she felt comfortable with him. "Don't take this the wrong way, but it doesn't bother me at all when a pretty girl loses her head."

She blinked at him.

"*I* prefer to be the cause of a woman's temporary insanity, but since we've just met," he paused and shrugged, "I suppose guys with guns will have to suffice."

Her mouth dropped open. She stared at him, and after about ten silent seconds, he saw realization dawn. She laughed shortly, shook her head, and rolled her eyes. A smile blossomed. "Thank you."

He wiggled his eyebrows at her and tried not to stare at the lush curves of her mouth. Lips came in at number two on his list of favorite traits in a woman, and she had a pair that definitely met with his approval. He forced the inappropriate thought aside. "Don't mention it."

"I suppose now you want me to tell you what happened."

"Do you *want* to tell me?" He saw the shadow that flitted over her face and recognized it instantly: sorrow mixed with disbelief tinged with regret. He'd seen it more often than not over the past several months, in the mirror.

"Not really," she said softly, "but I guess since you saved my ass, I kind of owe you."

"You don't *owe* me anything other than the necessary information to get us out of here alive."

"So you risk your life to help a complete stranger and expect *nothing* but information in return?"

"Damn straight."

She lifted her chin. "Really? Why?"

Her questioning his motives and the wariness in her gaze irritated him for some reason. He guessed a man was behind her suspicious inquiry, and given what she was currently going through, he knew she was wise to be cautious. However, *he'd* done nothing to earn her distrust. Hell, he'd saved her life.

A flicker of irritation sparked in his chest. If she was putting on an act, it was a damn good one. Needing space, Bear rose and took a step back, bumping his head on the ceiling. He looked at the overhanging rock in annoyance and reined in his temper. His fingers moved to the rope around his waist and started to work the knots loose. Then he put on his neutral mask and turned his eyes on her. "Because I'm one of the good guys, that's why."

She lifted one patrician brow and pursed her lips, giving him a look that said she was less than fully convinced of his noble intentions. That flicker of irritation burned a little brighter, and he frowned.

"I really don't care if you believe me or not, but if you want to get out of here without seeing your *friends* again, you may want to start *answering* questions instead of *asking* them because *this* is getting us nowhere." Even in the darkness, he saw the flush that stained her cheeks, and she looked away. He immediately gave himself a mental slap for feeding her uncertainty when he should be reassuring her. *Way to go, asshole. So* not *helping.*

"Can I ask . . . one more question?" Her voice was low, subdued, the dulcet tones penetrating his introspective fog and wrapping around him with surprising warmth.

Bear watched her for another moment and wanted to high-five himself. In the face. With a chair. He'd blasted her for asking questions, when in reality she'd asked very few. After he was free of the rope, he walked over to her and crouched down. "I'm sorry. That was uncalled for. Ask whatever you want."

She leaned her head back and met his gaze directly. "What's your name?"

He smiled, realizing that of the few questions she'd asked, his name hadn't been one of them. Given their situation, the query seemed trivial, even ridiculous, yet there it was. And, it gave him the opportunity to ask the same of her. After a second or two of silent perusal, he held out a hand. "Ted Bristol, but my friends call me Bear."

"Ted. Bear. Teddy bear?" One finely arched brow rose as she grasped his fingers. Her grip was firm, her skin soft and warm. "Seriously?" She laughed shortly. "So, if that's what your *friends* call you . . . what should *I* call you?"

He wanted to point out that saving her life kind of penciled him into the *friend* category, but instead he smiled and said, "Sweetheart works for me, but I *totally* understand if you're uncomfortable with that."

He was rewarded when she laughed softly and blushed. She stared at him, and he found himself transfixed by her eyes. They were a vivid golden brown, almost amber colored, and lined with thick, dark lashes. The outer corners tipped up like a cat's, giving her a distinct feline appearance. As inappropriate as it was, he was unable to look away. He didn't want to look away. Several long, silent seconds passed before her flush deepened, and she dropped her gaze.

"Well, I was out here to find a bear, and I guess I did." She shrugged. "I was thinking more of the mama and her two cubs I was tracking, but I suppose some higher power knew black and furry wasn't the sort of bear I needed to find."

He was impressed that she was able to joke, given the situation, and smiled. "Guess so."

"You realize I could make about a hundred jokes right now, *Bear*," she said.

He nodded.

He kept the blank mask firmly in place, watching her as she studied him. She certainly *seemed* like nothing more than an innocent bystander, but he couldn't be too careful. A chuckle fought for freedom, but he managed to keep the laughter in and continued his perusal.

She was pretty, although a little worse for wear. From the riot of dark mahogany strands escaping her braid and the state of her clothing, he judged she had been out here for a couple of days at least. She was tall, probably 5'9" or 5'10" and nicely built, slender and athletic like a swimmer, but far from skinny. He preferred women with curves, and she had them in all the right places. The khakis fit her closely, the wrinkled fabric doing nothing to detract from the shapely arc of her hips and derriere. Her button-up shirt wasn't fully buttoned, revealing a grubby white tank top and an enticing hint of cleavage. His gaze moved up, back to the lips he found so inviting. He gave himself an inward shake and forced his eyes elsewhere. Her skin was tanned the color of coffee with too much cream. A grimy smear marred the delicate line of her jaw, another swipe of dirt streaked the side of her pert nose, and yet another darkened an elegant cheekbone. Clean her up, and she'd be a stunner.

Not only was she an attractive woman, she also had grit. She'd kept up with his breakneck pace without a word of complaint and had climbed the rock face with surprising speed and agility for someone who was obviously frightened and doing it in the pitch dark. He'd seen the anxiety in her eyes, but she'd done it anyway, making it two-thirds of the way on her own before the helicopter's appearance. Those things, more than anything, impressed him, and he was not a man who impressed easily.

Their gazes locked, and she seemed to search his eyes, looking for what he didn't know. Apparently, she didn't see what she wanted to, and a glimmer of disappointment flashed before she looked away. Pursing her lips, she leaned against the rock wall and tried to untie the rope that was wound around her waist and between her legs. He reached out to help, but she pushed his hand away. *Ah, so she has a stubborn streak. Let's see how long that lasts.* After several unsuccessful attempts, she huffed, blew a strand of hair out of her eyes and frowned.

"I'm sorry." She tossed him a rueful look. "Would you help me, please?"

Bear fought a smile and knelt at her side. "Stand up." She did so, which brought him eye-level with her slender waist. He began to work the knots loose, taking his time, testing her again. She remained still, but when his hands followed the rope between her legs, he heard her indrawn breath and felt the tensing of her muscles. To her credit she said nothing and didn't waver, but when he was done, she moved away from him and sat down, her back against the wall.

"I've been out here for three days, tracking a mother bear and her cubs," she said, her eyes downcast. "I finally caught sight of them yesterday, late, a few miles below Drake's Meadow." She paused and glanced at him. "I assume you know where that is."

Bear nodded and began to coil the heavy-duty cord. *Tracking wildlife, eh?* The part of him that was tense and on-guard relaxed a hair. She continued.

"I slept in a hunting blind I use a lot when I'm out here, and planned to pick up their trail this morning." She chuckled and ran a hand over her brow. "If I had gotten up when I was *supposed* to, none of this would have happened."

Bear eased down onto his backside. "What *did* happen?"

"I overslept." She shook her head and rolled her eyes. "I slept right through my watch alarm." He saw the expression of self-reproach as her gaze turned toward the brush that covered the mouth of the cave. "As much as I love being out here, getting away from people and life and politics, being alone at night can sometimes be sort of . . . ." Her voice trailed off, and she glanced at him. "Let's just say when I come out here alone, I don't sleep very well most of the time."

His senses told him she was what she seemed to be, and not involved with the tall man who had been so determined to chase her down. There was a possibility she was playing him, but he'd learned to listen to his gut, and it was seldom wrong. That mystery mostly solved, he wondered why she would venture into the woods by herself. Not only was it unwise to start with, it obviously put her on edge. Perhaps *that* was why she did it, the adrenaline. He could relate.

"Which begs the question, why do you come out here alone?" he asked dryly.

"I don't have anyone to come with me," she replied matter-of-factly. A small smile lifted the corners of her mouth. "And . . . I must admit part of me kind of likes the risk factor." She shrugged. "That's why I take pictures of dangerous predators for a living instead of working at Sears Portrait Studio. Sears would be steadier pay, but it wouldn't be *nearly* as much fun as being stalked by a cougar."

He chuckled. "Can't imagine why your friends don't want to join you for *that*."

She gave him a wry grin. "I know, right?" She sighed. "But, my friends would rather get a mani-pedi than trek through the wilderness, so I'm on my own."

He gave her a sidelong glance and a half-smile. "Maybe you need new friends."

She looked at him directly. "Maybe I just found one."

"Maybe you have," he said in a low, suggestive voice with a wink and a wicked grin.

Something electric zipped up his spine. She squared her

shoulders and returned his unrelenting gaze, although he sensed it was a fight for her to do so. She pulled the water bottle from a pocket on her khakis, fiddled with the lid, took a long drink, and then recapped it. Liquid sloshed softly as she rolled the bottle back and forth between her hands. After about ten long, pregnant seconds, she dropped her chin and started to pick at the label. She was nervous, and he had a feeling *he* was the cause of her anxiety, not the fact she was being hunted. He didn't understand it. *He* wasn't chasing her with a gun, but then again, he intimidated most people, and that could be the cause of her tension.

"Go on," he said softly. "Tell me what happened next."

She seemed relieved and a little surprised by his gentle tone. "Well, by the time I caught up to the bears, it was almost two o'clock. They were at the stream that cuts through the meadow, and I was at the western edge in the trees. I'd just gotten my camera set, when all of a sudden this helicopter pops up over the eastern ridge, dive bombs into the meadow, and buzzes over mama and her cubs. Scared the crap out of them, poor things."

"Helicopter. So, it *was* your friends that just passed us by."

She frowned but nodded. "More than likely."

"What did you do?"

"At first, nothing. I was startled, and then pissed off. The only aircraft allowed to fly up here are Bureau of Land Management or Forestry Service, and neither one of those agencies would purposely harass the wildlife." She tucked several stray strands of hair behind her ear and glared at the floor. "I was going to wait until they landed, then get their names, give them a piece of my mind, and report them to the rangers."

"Wait." He pinched the bridge of his nose for a moment then met her gaze. "Being in the woods alone at night makes you a little jumpy, but you didn't think twice about confronting an unknown number of people doing only God knows what, possibly armed six ways from Sunday, in a remote mountain wilderness . . . *alone?*" He paused and rubbed his chin. "You've got a set of stones on you, I'll give you that."

Her eyes narrowed and the angry sparkle was back. "I was *thinking* about it, but I didn't *do* it, obviously. I guess I was still capable of logical thought at that particular moment."

He chuckled. "Thank goodness." When she opened her mouth to speak, he held up a hand. "Relax, I'm teasing. Please . . . go on."

Her brows rose as if she was surprised he would tease her. "Okay."

She paused and licked her lips. That small, unwittingly sensual mannerism sent another zing of current through him, catching him off guard. He gave himself another inward shake, harder this time, and focused on what she was saying as she continued.

"The helicopter landed on the eastern side of the meadow and four men got out."

"Four?"

She nodded. "The three you saw chasing me and one more. He was obviously the leader, and he wasn't dressed for hiking."

"What do you mean?"

"He wore a suit," she replied, "a *nice* one, and I could see the flashy jewelry from where I was across the meadow. They stood there, talking for a while, and then I heard the sound of ATVs."

Bear couldn't resist. "Guess it's a good thing you decided not to give them what for. I can see you taking on *four* of 'em, but more?" He let his voice trail off and waited, anticipating her reaction.

Her head snapped up, and a fierce scowl darkened her brow. "Do you enjoy provoking *every* person you meet, or am I just special?"

He pretended to think about it and grinned at her. "Yes."

She glared at him. He thought briefly about telling her she was cute when she was angry, but decided he'd better keep that observation to himself. She pursed her lips and lifted one patrician brow.

Bear let the chuckle out. "Okay, I'll stop." She didn't look convinced, her arms crossed over her chest. He held his hands up, as if in surrender. "I promise. Go on. Tell me what happened then."

She watched him silently, her expression wary, but he merely smiled at her and waited for her to continue. Finally, she let out a frustrated humph and continued.

"Well, the four men waited, and three ATVs drove out of the woods and across the meadow to meet them. Suit guy took a few steps forward to shake hands with the three newcomers, and they started talking."

His brain was kicking into gear. "What did they look like?"

She closed her eyes for a moment then shrugged. "Like the other three, dark hair, dark skin."

"How long did the conversation last?"

"About five . . . maybe ten minutes."

"Could you hear what they were saying?"

She shook her head. "I was too far away. The only reason I could see them at all was because of my zoom." She glanced down at the massive lens. "Like I said . . . if I had woken up when I was supposed to . . . ."

Bear rolled his eyes. "*If.* I really *hate* that fucking word." She looked at him strangely, and he waved a hand at her. "Never mind. Go on."

She uncapped her water bottle and took another sip. "When they were done talking the two main guys shook hands again and then . . . then . . . ."

She paused and her expression shifted. He saw the fear in her face and realized now was where the story turned deadly. He knew exactly what she was going through. Reaching out, he took her hand and gently laced his fingers through hers. She looked at their twined hands for a few seconds and then took a deep breath and continued in a hushed voice.

"And then things went crazy. The guy with a shaved head grabbed the suit guy, and they started fighting. At the same time, the tall guy and the one with the ponytail pulled out guns and pointed them at the three ATV guys." She turned haunted eyes to him. "Tall guy and ponytail shot the ATV guys point blank in the chest with no reason, no provocation that I saw. Just . . . blew them away." She blanched, and her grip on his hand tightened. "Then the tall one walked over and . . . and shot each of them in the . . . the head, like they were . . . *animals* that needed to be put down."

She closed her eyes. Bear scowled when he saw the lone tear that trailed slowly over her dirty cheek, and wished he could take the memory from her. Living with the image in your head of someone being murdered wasn't something he'd wish on anyone. He sighed and sandwiched her hand between his. Her fingers were long and elegant with short manicured nails, and he absently rubbed a thumb over her smooth skin.

"It's okay," he said. "You don't have to say anymore. I get the picture."

"That wasn't the worst part."

Shit, it gets worse? He looked at her in silent question and waited for her to continue. Her cheeks were pale, her brows drawn together as if she was trying to make sense of something she couldn't wrap her head around. Her expression, more than anything, convinced him she was indeed a victim and not a conspirator. He wasn't sure how else to comfort her, so he continued to hold her hand. It took her a few seconds to find her voice, and when she did, she spoke in little more than a whisper.

"Um, shaved head and ponytail had suit guy by the arms. The tall guy said something to him, something that made suit *really* mad, and then tall guy laughed. Suit guy struggled to get away from the other two as tall guy bent over and picked up one of the dead men's weapons. He waited a moment, then shot suit guy three times in the chest." She blinked slowly. "After the other two dropped suit guy's body, tall guy did something really weird."

Bear leaned toward her slightly. "What?"

"He took a handkerchief from his pocket, wiped down the gun, and then put it back in the dead man's hand and fired into the air."

Dread pooled in Bear's stomach, and he started to rethink his position on the word "if." Now that he was certain she was just an innocent bystander all the scenarios playing out in his head ended badly, and he ground his teeth together.

"Why would he do that?" she asked, more of herself than him.

"Why would he put the gun back in a dead man's hand and pull the trigger?"

Bear sighed heavily. "Don't you watch *any* TV?"

"Not really."

Bear released her hand and pressed his fingers against his temples, rubbing in small, tight circles. *She wasn't kidding when she said that wasn't the worst of it.* "Because of what the tall guy did, any forensic evidence will show that suit guy was killed by the dead ATV guy. I'm guessing that's what tall guy was going for."

"Why?"

"So he doesn't get blamed for it." He rubbed the back of his neck and looked at the ceiling. His brain was spinning various scenarios, none of which he cared to think about because they all ended in bloodshed, *lots* of bloodshed. "How did they see you?"

She shook her head. "I'm not sure. I just know that after tall guy shot into the air, it got *really* quiet. The auto advance was firing, but I was too far away for them to have heard *that*." Her eyes went vague. "I hadn't even realized I was taking pictures until then. I lowered the camera to check the last few frames and next thing I know," she paused and focused on him, "they're shooting at me. I just ran."

Bear stood slowly and walked toward the brush covering the mouth of the man-made cave. He looked through the leaves and over the dark forest spread out before him and listened intently, but the helicopter was either shut down or long gone. His gut told him that was temporary. He knew the men trying to kill her would be back, most likely in greater numbers.

"Bear?"

He glanced over his shoulder at her. "Yeah?"

"What should we do now?" Her voice was low, apprehensive.

Bear rubbed his chin and walked to where his pack was propped against the back wall. The fact she'd asked him that question said she was ceding control, at least temporarily, to him. With control came responsibility, a responsibility he was all too familiar with. Could he do this now? Given what had happened over the last several months, he wasn't at all sure. The last time he'd held someone's life in his hands, he'd failed. One look at her face, however, and he knew he had no other choice. *This is what you signed up for, bud, so suck it up and do your job.*

"Now . . . we have something to eat, drink some water, and get some rest. We need to be up and out of here as soon as it's light." After opening the rig, he pulled out a jacket and tossed it at her, then continued to root through his belongings. "Sorry, but since we can't have a fire, all I have to offer you for an entrée this evening is another energy bar or trail mix."

"With M&Ms or chocolate chips?"

The hopeful lilt in her voice made him pause, and he looked at her. Her expectant but cautious expression made him chuckle, and he wrapped his fingers around the Ziploc bag full of homemade trail mix. "M&Ms."

Her eagerness waned a bit. "Plain . . . or peanut?"

He laughed softly and handed the bag to her. "Plain, although there are peanuts in there, but I'm sure you can pick those out."

She grabbed the bag and practically ripped it open. "Outstanding. I've been *dying* for something sweet, and something *without* peanuts."

Without another word, she dove into the blend of dried fruit, nuts, oat clusters, and chocolate. Bear watched her for a few moments, warmed and heartened by her childlike enthusiasm over something as seemingly trivial as trail mix, especially under the current circumstances. He shook his head and unpacked his sleeping bag and two more water bottles.

He unzipped and unfurled the sleeping bag over the rough, rocky ground, then sat down on it and watched her eat. She glanced at him and paused in mid-chew, swallowed, and held the bag out to him. He waved a hand at her and offered her another water bottle. She took it from him, pausing when their fingers touched.

"Thanks."

He smiled. "Don't mention it."

Using his pack as a makeshift pillow, Bear stretched out on the sleeping bag, alternating bites of an energy bar with sips of water. He watched her covertly from beneath half-closed lids. She was concentrating on the M&Ms, and her soft pleasure noises made him smile. When she'd had her fill, she closed the bag and finished off the first water bottle he'd given her. After shrugging into the jacket, she looked at him and seemed surprised he was watching her. Bear patted the sleeping bag next to him.

"We need to share body heat," he said when she didn't move.

She chewed her lip, and he imagined she was silently debating the wisdom of sleeping with a virtual stranger. It was nearly a minute before she nodded and rose, and when she did, he almost laughed. The jacket swum on her, but it was made for a 6'8", 280 pound man and not a 5'10", 160 pound woman. Shuffling over to him, she lay down at his side, careful not to touch him, and propped her head in her hand.

"Don't you have another blanket or something?" she asked after a brief silence.

She sounded nervous, but whether it was about the chill of the deepening night or sleeping with him, he wasn't sure.

Bear shook his head. "Don't need one. I'm hot-blooded." He wiggled his eyebrows at her, but that didn't seem to assuage her misgivings.

"Shouldn't we get *under* the sleeping bag?"

He lifted one brow. "We could, and then the rocks will leach our body heat right out. It's wiser to put some sort of insulation between us and the ground."

"Right." She gestured toward the sage bushes at the mouth of the cave. "Those would be great insulation."

"And get rid of our only cover?" He could almost hear the mental slap she gave herself.

She sighed. "The temp will probably drop into the mid to upper 30s by morning."

He looked at her out of the corner of his eye. "I'm aware. You keep the jacket; I'll be fine." *You're fresh out of delaying tactics. So, what now?*

There was a mutinous set to her chin as she stared at him, and the inner debate was almost audible. After about twenty seconds she sat up, removed the jacket, and spread it over his torso.

He half rose. "You're going to need this more than I will."

She planted a hand on his chest and pushed him back down. "Relax, big guy. You said we need to share body heat." Her movements were sure and quick, but he saw the uncertainty in her eyes that told him she was anything but confident. "So, let's share body heat." Minutes dragged out as she fussed and arranged and rearranged the jacket, as if she was gathering her courage. Finally, she took his hand, lifted his arm, and lay down at his side. There was an inch or so of space between them, and she gingerly put her head on his shoulder. Then, she tugged the edge of the jacket over herself. "There. Now we'll both be warm."

Something in his gut pulled taut. *You aren't kidding.*

"And *don't* get any funny ideas," she added with a sharp look in his direction. "Just because you're bigger than me doesn't mean I won't hurt you."

Bear rolled his eyes, but the opportunity to tease her again was too good to pass up. "Don't worry. I'll save any funny ideas for *after* you've had a shower, which certainly won't be *tonight*." He smiled as she gasped softly and tensed, but he settled his arm around her shoulders before she could move. "Now *you* need to relax. I'm kidding . . . sort of."

She huffed, and his smile widened. Her body was stiff at his side, but he pretended not to notice as he made adjustments to the jacket to ensure she was covered. Her hand fluttered over her hair briefly, then she slid it between their bodies, and then she laid it against her thigh, as if she wasn't sure where to put it. Bear grasped her wrist lightly and flattened her fingers on his stomach, covering them with his own. It did nothing to help *him* relax, but after about a minute, she relaxed and snuggled against him.

"Get some sleep," he said softly. "I have a feeling we're both going to need it."

She nodded against his shoulder but said nothing more, the trill of crickets serenading them. She yawned and tucked in beneath his jaw. Oddly enough, he started to drift off before her softly spoken words roused him.

"By the way, my name is Beth, Beth Drummond."

Beth. He liked it and smiled. "Pleased to meet you."

There was a long pause, and then she whispered, "Thank you for saving my life."

It wasn't the first time he'd heard those words, but he couldn't remember the last time that phrase of gratitude had warmed him as it did now. "You're welcome. Now go to sleep. Dawn will be here before you know it."

She yawned again. "Good night, Bear."

His throat tightened. The sleepiness in her voice was an unconscious signal that said she trusted him enough to sleep in such close proximity. Given what she was facing, he wondered if she would come to regret that. He would do everything in his power to protect her, but there were some things even *he* couldn't accomplish. If they made it out of this alive, her future was almost assured to veer sharply off whatever course she thought it was on. Identifying the bad guys, a trial, Witness Protection . . . . Sometimes he really hated his job. He choked his misgivings down and closed his eyes.

"Good night, Beth."

Chapter Three

The roar of an explosion rolled over them, the shockwave vibrating through the Humvees and setting her teeth on edge. Beth watched in horror as the lead Hummer was thrust more than ten feet into the air. When it fell back to earth, fire and black smoke erupted from the shattered windows in curling, billowing clouds.

"RPG!" Coop shouted.

Before Beth could move, he reached behind him and opened her door, then shoved her out. The rest of the Marines launched themselves from the vehicle. Coop pushed her into a drainage ditch on the side of the road the exact second the Humvee they'd just exited exploded in a blast of piercing noise and roiling heat.

Beth came awake with a start, feeling the flames and tasting the smoke just as she had that fateful day.

"It's okay, Beth," Bear whispered. "It's just a dream."

She gasped and scuttled away from him, memories washing over her in a painful wave of serrated images that cut like glass. Tears clogged her throat and stung behind her eyes as the mental pictures played. She didn't want to be here, not again. Her breathing was sharp and ragged, and she pressed the heels of her hands against her forehead in a vain attempt to stop her brain's projector. It wasn't helping. She felt the anxiety attack coming on, and there was no ER close by that could drug away her demons this night.

"Beth, look at me."

The deep resonance of Bear's voice sliced through the soundtrack roaring in her ears. She blinked and met his gaze.

"It's just a dream," he said, those blue eyes boring into hers with pointed intensity. "Put it back in its box, close the lid, and walk away."

She tried, but couldn't. Technicolor images splashed the screen inside her mind's eye, snapshots from earlier that day mixing in with the older ones. Panic clawed its way up her throat, and she shook her head as it started to spread to the rest of her in sharp, painful tingles. She was on the verge of hyperventilating. Bear put a hand on her shoulder, squeezing gently.

"Beth." He nudged her chin up with his knuckles. "Beth, close your eyes."

"No, no, no, no!" She tried to twist away from him, her vision blurred with tears. "I can't . . . I don't want to . . . oh, God!"

He cupped her head in his hands. "Beth!"

She froze and stared at him. He hadn't raised his voice much, but the increase in volume was enough to startle her to full attention.

"It's a memory," he said from between clenched teeth, his gaze relentless and unblinking. "*You* control *it*, not the other way around. Now, close your eyes."

As if they had a will of their own, her eyelids squeezed together.

"Put it away," he said softly, his voice tinged with steel.

She felt the tears trickling down her cheeks, the tracks freezing in the cold, early morning air. "I can't," she choked out, "I can't!"

"Yes, you can." His fingers started a slow massage of her scalp. The contact was warm, comforting, distracting her from the terror that threatened to overwhelm her. "It's *your* memory; *you* own it, now *put it away.*"

She tried to shake her head, but he was holding her too tightly.

"Do it."

Her breath came in short, explosive gasps, but she pictured herself shoving the film reel into a large, wooden box.

"Shut the lid."

She imagined the heavy lid falling into place with a resounding *thunk.* Her lungs stopped their spasms and began to work in a more even rhythm.

"Now turn around and walk away from it."

In her mind, she was inside a projection room. She looked at the box for a long, silent moment, then walked away and left through the only door. The doorknob was cool in her hand, the hinges squeaked slightly. The panel closed behind her with a soft click, and the panic receded slowly, almost grudgingly as she felt her self-control return. Several more seconds passed, and she was finally able to draw a deep, cleansing breath. When her pulse was back to normal, she opened her eyes and stared at him.

"Wh-where did you learn that?" She asked in a whisper.

A small smile danced about his mouth. "Let's just say I've seen a couple of therapists in my day."

"Well . . . thank you," she said, unable to hold his penetrating gaze.

"Any time." he paused. "Want to talk about it?"

"No." A chill of dread made her shudder, and she moved away from him, needing the space. She sat cross-legged, elbows on her knees, and shook her head slowly. "It's been more than two years since I've had that dream."

"Sometimes fresh trauma can aggravate old wounds," he said. He touched the inside of her forearm gently. "Was that dream connected to this scar?"

She jerked away from him and clapped a hand over the mark, as if by covering it up she could make it, and everything connected with it, disappear. His eyes narrowed.

A sudden tightness in her chest constricted her airways as she looked at the thin, red line that ran from her elbow to her wrist. Was he always so observant?

The scar was a remnant, ever raw and achingly fresh, no matter that the wound had physically healed long ago. It was always there, a constant reminder of how life could turn on a dime and shatter a person's soul. A flash of anger warmed her. She had thought – hoped – she was past the nightmares, past the overwhelming terror and the soul-crushing loss and the utter helplessness that boiled inside her, red-hot and seething, always ending in tears. Suddenly, she wanted to yell at him, as if by doing so she could release her pent up anger and the demons that lurked in the dark corners of her mind. What had happened today certainly wasn't his fault any more than what had happened years ago. Still she fought the urge to scream about the unfairness of it all, to vent all of her fear, rage, and sorrow on him.

"I'm sorry. It's none of my business." He patted her knee once and backed away. "I'm here if you change your mind. I know how it feels to have images in your head you want to get rid of . . . and can't."

The low, even tone of his voice defused her fury. She didn't want to yell at him anymore; she wanted something else from him: the comfort of another human being who understood. Her ex had never understood what she'd been through, and her best friend thought talking about it over and over would somehow make it go away. She dared a glance at him, and the concern she saw etched on his handsome face made her throat tighten. Tears stung as she tasted again the sharp bitterness of loss and took a deep, hitching breath.

He studied her carefully, his lips slightly pursed, his eyes narrowed as if the secrets of her heart were painted on her face and he was trying to decode them.

"Come here," he said in a whisper.

She looked at him, uncertainty winding through her until he held out a hand. His fingers were long and surprisingly elegant for a man of his size and build. She stared at the digits for a moment before slipping her hand into his. He stretched out on the ground and pulled her against his side. Beth pressed her face into the crook of his neck as he wrapped his arms around her.

His embrace enfolded her, and so did his strength and composure. It was like bathing in serenity, and in spite of everything that was happening she relaxed against him.

"Thank you," she said after a brief silence.

He rested his chin atop her head. "You're welcome. Now get some sleep. It'll be light soon."

****

Beth yawned and her eyes fluttered open. She was lying on her side, and she stiffened when she felt the weight of an arm draped over her waist, and a large body curled around hers. Memories came flooding back, and she gasped softly.

"You okay?"

Bear's voice cut through her fear, and she rolled toward him. She met his eyes briefly before resting her head on his shoulder. The warmth of his body soaked through her, and she relaxed against him. The pre-dawn air had a definite chill, and her breath turned into frothy, wispy puffs.

"Yeah. Forgot where I was for a moment."

A chuckle rumbled in his chest. "The way you coiled up, I half-expected you to turn around and start hitting me." He paused. "You weren't dreaming again, were you?"

For a moment, she couldn't find her voice. She swallowed hard and shook her head. "No, no dreams, and if you were a man named Michael Ellison I *would* have hit you."

He laughed softly. "I'm glad I'm not him."

Beth smiled and closed her eyes. "Me, too."

"He an ex?"

She wrinkled her nose and choked down the self-reproach that always came with the mention of Michael's name. "I think the word *ex* is too good for him." She counted Bear's heartbeats as his pulse pattered against her cheek. "Try biggest mistake of my life, at least in the relationship department." Beth paused in her counting and thought about it for a moment. Disjointed images glared to life: Michael partying all night and sleeping until dawn, his disdain for people who actually had jobs, catching him in the act of infidelity. "Actually, I think he's the biggest mistake I made *ever*, in any department."

"Bigger mistake than taking pictures of gun-wielding murderers?"

"Well, maybe not *that* big, but he comes in a close second."

He whistled softly. "Wow. That's a pretty big title for one mortal man to hold."

It was sad really, but what she remembered most about their time as live-in-lovers, aside from walking in on him with his pants down, was their apartment's filthy bathroom. Not only did Michael refuse to work *outside* the home, he couldn't be bothered to work *inside* the home either. She shuddered as she recalled the scent of urine that she could never quite scrub out of the tile floor. "If you'd lived with him, you'd understand."

"I'll take your word for it." He pulled the jacket closer around her shoulders, and Beth was happy to let the subject go. Another minute or so passed before Bear said, "We need to get up and moving. It'll be dawn soon."

Beth made a disappointed sound and, instead of getting up, snuggled closer. "Five more minutes, Dad?" He chuckled again, and she had the strangest urge to kiss his neck. The stubble on his jaw abraded her nose and sent strange shivers over her skin as she inhaled his scent. He was warm and smelled like soap, despite their marathon of the previous evening.

"Okay, as long as you don't ever call me dad again."

She closed her eyes and smiled. "Deal."

Like a human stopwatch, five minutes later he eased away from her and sat up, running his hands over his short hair. He reached into his pack, grabbed two water bottles, and handed one to her. Beth reluctantly sat up and bit back a groan as a deep, steady ache stiffened her muscles. It didn't matter how carefully she moved, the pain was right there. He took a mouthful of water, swished it around, and then spat it out. He glanced at her, and an I'll-bet-you're-hurting smile curved his mouth.

"Sore?" he asked.

Beth rolled her eyes. "No, not at all," she said, her voice dripping sarcasm. "You?"

He chuckled. "Nope. I do this sort of stuff a lot."

"Really?" She huffed. "You spend a lot of time running away from killers?"

He thought about it for a moment. "Actually, I spend more time chasing them than running away from them."

"You're some kind of cop? Yeah, right." She glanced at him, and the blankness of his expression made her pause. "*Are* you a cop?"

He grabbed the bag of trail mix and dipped a hand into the nutty concoction. "Not exactly."

What the hell does that mean? Beth stood and stretched, but kept her eyes on him. "So, what are you, exactly? Sorry, but you don't look like Forestry Service or Bureau of Land Management, so what are you?"

He took another handful of trail mix then sealed the bag and tossed it to her. "I'm just a guy who was going to camp in the woods for a few days."

A spark of irritation flared inside her. "Of course you are." She tossed the trail mix back, crossed her arms over her chest and narrowed her eyes on him. "Because campers *always* go around chasing killers." Saying the word *killers* brought memories back to the forefront of her mind, and a heated flash of annoyance burned the inside of her chest cavity. "I hear it's actually surpassed roasting marshmallows and making smores in popularity among the 'like to rough it' set." His chuckle sent her from irritated to just shy of angry. She stomped to his side and looked down her nose at him. "*Are* you a cop?"

"It's not important."

Indignance filled her. "The hell it's not."

He stood, grabbed the corner of the sleeping bag, and started to roll it up. "Get something to eat. If we get started in the next few minutes, we should reach my SUV and be out of here before noon."

Beth gaped at him, fury simmering. He turned his back and walked along the front edge of the cave toward another stand of sage. Apparently, they were done talking. He pushed through the foliage and disappeared. She stared at the spot, trying to wrap her head around the conversation. Then she realized she was alone, and she didn't want to be alone. Her anger morphed into apprehension. Approaching the wall of brush, she peered through the maze of branches. There was another cave on the other side of the natural barrier.

"What is this place?" she asked, her voice echoing oddly off the curved rock walls.

Bear's face popped up over the bush in front of her, and Beth jumped back, startled.

"Native American cliff dwellings," he replied. "Now, if you don't mind, I'd like a little privacy."

Beth blinked, and then realized what he was doing. Chastised, she moved back and sat down on a rock, picked up her water bottle and the trail mix, and began to eat. As she munched on some oat clusters, she gazed around the cave. Her eyes widened when she saw the cave paintings on the ceiling above her. Last night in the dark, they had been invisible, but now, as the sun began to bathe the earth in pale, golden light, the crude, primitive drawings seemed to jump off the walls. Fascinated, she grabbed her camera. Just before she took a picture, Bear's voice stopped her.

"Hey. Flare, remember? Your auto flash will go off in this light and if anyone's watching . . . ."

Beth groaned and ran a hand over her face. "Right. Sorry, I wasn't—"

"Thinking," he finished for her. He shook his head, gave her a lopsided grin, and tapped his index finger lightly against her brow. "Better start, Beth, or we may not reach my SUV."

For the thousandth time since meeting him, she choked down her growing sense of inadequacy. She felt small, incompetent, but he was right. Beth looped the camera strap around her neck, unable to meet his piercing gaze. "Why don't *you* just do all the thinking and I'll follow you? Ever since we met, I have had two left feet and no brains." She glanced at him. "I'm not normally so clumsy or scatterbrained."

A chuckle rumbled in his chest. "I have no doubts about that."

"I'm usually quite agile," she continued, "I impressed Chief Dancing Eagle anyway, and I'm pretty smart . . . most of the time."

Bear grinned and finished packing the gear. "It happens when a person gets rattled."

"*You* didn't have any trouble leaping tall logs in a single bound," she pointed out.

"*I* wasn't rattled." He gave her a quick smile as he propped the pack against the wall and took a drink of his water. "Now, why don't you let me take a look at those pictures while you utilize the little girl's room? And those are the last of our water bottles, so conserve until we can refill them."

"Okay." She handed the camera to him. "So where is the little girl's room?"

"There are half a dozen cliff dwellings on this rock face," he replied, turning the display on and shielding it with his hands. "Pick one. Nobody lives here anymore. Just be as respectful as possible."

She looked at him, but he was scrolling through the shots she'd taken yesterday. With a sigh, she pushed through the sage and walked several caves down until she found a spot where she could relieve herself in relative privacy. When she was done, she walked back the way she'd come and bumped into Bear's formidable form. She stutter-stepped and her feet got tangled together, nearly sending her through the concealing wall of bushes covering the cave mouths.

"Whoa," he said, grabbing her arms to keep her from falling. "Careful. There's only a bunch of sage brush between you and a sixty foot drop."

Her heart thudded in her chest, and she looked up into that sharply planed face and nodded slowly. His eyes searched hers, and her heart started to pound for an entirely different reason. His features were harsh, forbidding, softened only by the fullness of his mouth. That mouth was the sort that could tempt even the most virginal to partake in the sin it promised. Warmth pooled in her belly. He really was something to look at. Then she remembered what *she* must look like, and heat climbed up her neck. She'd left her toothbrush and hair brush in the blind with her sleeping bag and pack, and she hadn't bathed in three days.

"Thanks," she finally managed to get out. "I'll be more careful."

He released her and held out her camera. "Here you go. If I were you, I'd take the memory card out of your camera and put it somewhere safe. That way, if something happens to the camera you still have the pictures."

Something in his face, the careful blankness, the too-calm expression, set her nerves jangling. "Why? What did you see?"

"You haven't looked at them?"

She shook her head slowly. "Didn't have time. Running, remember?"

He rubbed his chin, his expression completely neutral. "Well, the bad news is what you have on that memory card can definitely get you killed. The good news . . . ."

His voice trailed off, and Beth took a step toward him. "What good news?" When he didn't answer, she fisted her hands in the front of his shirt. "*What* good news?"

He sighed heavily. "Those pictures can also save your ass, provided we get them to the right people."

"Who?" Beth didn't let go, even when he covered her hands with his. She was angry, at herself, at him, at the entire situation, and his lack of elaboration wasn't helping. She jerked on his shirt. "*Who* are the right people, and how do we get those pictures to them?"

"I'm still working on that, Beth." He gently pried her hands loose and held them in his much larger ones. "First and foremost, we have to get out of here." He released her, stepped around her, and started walking. "After we reach my car, we'll head to the closest ranger or sheriff station and take things from there."

Beth didn't know Bear well, but she knew from the set of his jaw and the squaring of his shoulders they were done talking. He strode past the cave she had used as a restroom and two more. Confusion and irritation bounced around her insides like annoyed bees as she stared at his retreating back. He just kept walking. As he'd done yesterday, he trusted her to realize she didn't have much choice but to follow. She had the insane, childish urge to pick up a rock and throw it at his broad back, but that would just piss him off. The last thing she wanted to do was anger the one person who stood between her and almost certain death. Her angry sails deflated. As he disappeared around a curve in the rocks, she shook her head, huffed in frustration, and followed.

The sun had just cleared the eastern horizon when they reached the top of the ridge. Bear's gaze scanned first left and then right. After a moment, he walked toward a tumble of boulders and crouched down next to it. Beth trailed behind him, sat down on the ground at the base of the rocks, and took a long swallow of water as he divested himself of his pack. He pulled a topographical map from inside one of the outside pockets and flattened it on the ground.

"We're here," he said, pointing to a spot on the map. He pulled a compass from his pocket and checked his bearings. He narrowed his eyes on a distant point for a moment before turning his eyes back to the map. "It's roughly six miles from here to the trailhead, which will take at least three hours given the terrain between here and there." He looked at her. "How you holding up?"

"It's a little early in the day to start asking me that, isn't it?" She took another drink. "I'm fine, thank you for asking. And how are you this lovely morning?"

One corner of his mouth rose, and a twinkle entered his eye. "Quite well, thank you."

"Glad to hear it." She saluted him with her water bottle and gave him a smile. "Lead on, mon Capitan. I'll either follow you to the end or die trying."

His expression darkened a bit, and he looked away from her.

"Don't say that. Flippant remarks have a strange way of becoming self-fulfilling prophecies."

The sarcastic retort on her tongue stuck there, her vocal chords refusing to voice it. The shadow that had passed behind his eyes was fleeting, but obvious enough that she wondered at its cause. It was the first time she'd seen an expression other than mild annoyance, concern, or amusement on his face, and she didn't like it, not even a little bit. It made her feel uneasy, and she glanced around. Realizing how little cover they had caused apprehension to coil around her esophagus and squeeze. The image of a helicopter popping up in front of them flashed in her mind's eye. As if reading her thoughts, he rose and extended a hand to her.

"Let's get off this ridge." He scanned the horizon. "I don't like being this exposed."

Her pulse leapt, and she let him pull her to her feet. "I'm with you on that."

He quickly made his way off the ridge and started down the other side, Beth on his heels. Here on the rocky slope of the mountain there was nothing to shield them from prying, searching eyes, no place to hide. The tree line seemed so distant. She thought she heard the *thump-thump* of rotor blades. Her heart gave a painful jerk, and she froze, listening carefully. Realizing her imagination was playing tricks on her, she scurried after Bear, stretching out her stride to catch up. It wasn't until they were completely shielded by trees and foliage that her heart stopped somersaulting.

As familiar with the Rocky Mountains as she was, this was a section of the park she had never ventured into before. Bear seemed completely at home here, however. It was more than an hour before he stopped on the banks of a large stream. Despite the cool morning, Beth was working up a sweat, and it took everything she had not to disrobe and dive into the water. Instead, she dropped to her knees and splashed her face and neck. Then, she took a small handful of wet sand and started scrubbing. Bear had pulled out his map again, but he was watching her. She could feel it. When she'd scrubbed the majority of grime from her face, arms, and neck, she rinsed the sand off, sat back on her heels, and looked at him over her shoulder.

"What?"

He smiled, shook his head, and went back to his map and compass.

"Not going to ask how I'm holding up?"

"You seem to be doing just fine." He glanced at her then rechecked his headings. "I'm sure if you twist an ankle, you'll let me know." He gestured toward his pack. "Grab something to eat if you're hungry. My food is your food."

She hesitated, not entirely comfortable with rummaging through his pack. Thankfully, she only had to search two pockets before she found an energy bar. "Thanks," she said, waving the bar at him. He nodded, and she ripped open the wrapper. "What I wouldn't give for some chicken fried steak right now." She took a bite of the bar and tried to imagine it was something other than what it was. "Or some biscuits and gravy. Yum."

Bear chuckled and reached for the trail mix. "Tell you what. I'll buy you a big breakfast when we get out of here. There's a little diner on the outskirts of Boulder that has the best chicken fried steak in the western hemisphere."

"Oh, *that* would be outstanding," she said with a small groan. "But, what I'd like even more than food is a bath. Or at least a really long, hot shower." She gave him an apologetic look. "My apologies if I offend."

The smile on his face said she didn't need to worry, and he shook his head. "No apology needed. Despite what I said last night, I never turn down an opportunity to sleep with a beautiful woman, no matter how long she's been running around in the woods."

Beth opened her mouth to speak, but nothing came out as heat crept into her cheeks. She snapped her jaw shut and tucked unruly strands of hair behind her ear. After clearing her throat, she finally found her voice, but she couldn't look at him. "Well, then . . . thank you. I think."

He laughed. "You're welcome. Now, finish that bar, and let's see if we can't hone in on some chicken fried steak for lunch."

"I'm all for that. How much farther?"

Bear glanced at the map again. "Just over four miles."

Beth chuckled. "Well, if I didn't need a shower already, I certainly will once we get to your car." She gave him a sidelong glance. "Any chance I can get a bath and a change of clothes *before* we hit the diner?"

"I think that can be arranged." He stuffed the map into a pocket of his pants. "I could stand to be hosed down as well."

She looked at him and the image of what he'd look like naked popped into her mind. He was magnificent in woodland camouflage. Without the shirt and pants? "I'd be more than happy to volunteer for that job." The words jumped out of her mouth as if rocket-propelled, and her face flamed.

"You just want to get me out of my clothes," he said, a teasing note in his voice.

Heat flooded her face, her breasts tingled, and she gulped. She glanced at him, but thankfully he was looking at the map. Beth stuffed the last of her energy bar in her mouth and chewed, hoping her flush would fade before he noticed it.

"By the way, do you always sleep with men you've just met?"

The question brought her head up sharply, and she nearly choked on the last of the energy bar. When she saw the mischievous twinkle in his eyes, her indignation sputtered out and died. Another challenge. She watched him through narrowed eyes as she finished chewing, swallowed her mouthful, and gave him a saucy smile. "Well, I must admit that when a man saves my life, I do like to show my . . . *gratitude* . . . ."

Bear stared at her for a moment and then burst out laughing. "Good to know." He shook his head and chuckled as he tossed the empty water bottles at her. "Let's refill the water bottles." He knelt by the pack and started rummaging through it again. "I have some water purification tabs in here somewhere."

Beth knelt at the edge of the stream and refilled the bottles, smiling when she heard his, "Aha!" He joined her and dropped the small, white tablets into the bottles as she handed them to him.

"Y'know, it's sad," he said as he capped the last bottle and gave it a shake. "There was a time when one didn't need water purification tablets. One could drink right out of that stream and not have to worry." He walked back over to his pack and put the extra bottles away. "I guess those days are long gone."

"Yeah, but just think. Now we have cell phones and iPads and the Internet to make up for all that." She watched the tablet dissolve. "Who needs clean water and air when we have Google and electric cars? After all, *everyone* knows electricity comes from *magic*."

He gave her a lopsided grin and shrugged into his pack. "I detect a note of sarcasm there."

"Really?" She gave him a wide-eyed, innocent look. "And here I thought I was hiding it so well."

"I guess I'm just more observant than most."

Something warm blossomed deep inside of her. That he could be so calm and infuse humor into even this situation sparked something that had been long dormant, and she chuckled. "Apparently. Sorry, if that offends you, but my politics revolve around common sense and not common opinion."

"A girl after my own heart." His smile widened, and she was again surprised by the change in his appearance. A mischievous light entered his eyes and gave him a boyish look, young and impish. The granite features softened, making him *far* more approachable.

The shift transformed him from intimidating to heartbreakingly handsome. Her stomach clenched, and her insides turned to mush.

"You ready?" he asked.

Beth shook herself and forced a smile. "Yeah. Let's go."

They stayed on a narrow trail for the next several miles, keeping a good pace, but things slowed when they started up a particularly steep grade. The ground was covered in shale, pine needles, and dead leaves, making ascending the hill difficult at best. Bear was having better luck than she, probably because he was heavier and didn't slip as easily. She lost her footing and came down hard onto her right knee, cursing fluently under her breath as pain shot through the joint and up her leg.

"You okay?" Bear asked.

Beth gritted her teeth, frustrated to the point that tears stung behind her eyes. "Yeah." She gained her feet, looking up in surprise when Bear grabbed her hand and held tight.

"Come on," he said. "Try to put your feet where I put mine. It'll be easier."

After that, he started stomping up the trail, leaving indents in the ground for her to use like stairs. She had to lengthen her stride considerably, but at least she stopped slipping. Her knee throbbed, but she was damned if she was going to start bitching now when they only had about a mile left. Ignoring the pain, she put one foot in front of the other, following in his tracks until they neared the top of the ridge.

"So," she began, concentrating on placing her feet, "how did you find me yesterday? How did you even know someone was in trouble?"

"I heard the gunshots."

Beth glanced at his broad back. "This *is* Colorado and gunshots aren't *that* uncommon, even in a National Park."

He looked over his shoulder at her and gave her an indulgent smile. "Hunters don't usually use pistols."

She stared at him. "You can tell the difference?"

Bear nodded and continued to trudge uphill. "Was about to make camp when I heard the shots, so I grabbed my binocs and started scanning the woods in that direction. I saw you dashing headlong down the trail, and then saw those guys chasing you." He paused as he neared the top of the ridge and helped her up. "I stashed my pack, decided on an intercept point, and prayed I was fast enough to reach you before they did."

Before she could thank him for being fast enough, he turned around and pushed her. *What the hell?* Beth cried out as she lost her footing. She would have somersaulted backwards down the slope if not for his iron grip on her hand. He shoved her behind a large maple tree and forced her down on her backside. He positioned himself between her and the trail. A moment later a helicopter burst over the ridge. Beth clapped her hands over her ears at the sudden, violent assault of noise. The chopper rose into the sky, seemed to hang there for a moment, and then spun around and swooped back toward them. Her heart launched into her throat as she imagined the bad guys shooting at them from the helicopter and braced for the gunfire. He immediately covered her body with his and she realized the woodland camouflage he wore would help hide them from searching eyes. She curled into a ball and tried to make herself as small as possible. The aircraft passed over them and turned, following the ridge north.

It wasn't until the sound of the helicopter's engines faded that he moved. His eyes scanning the forest with laser-like intensity, he slowly stood, his large frame pressed close to the maple. Beth remained still, more than content to follow his lead. When he finally looked down at her and extended a hand, she sucked in a breath and closed her eyes as relief washed over her.

He pulled her to her feet. Her heart beat a frenetic staccato against her sternum, her breathing shallow and ragged as unadulterated fear threatened to drown her. A sharp-clawed, icy hand raked up her spine, and she started to shake, full realization hitting her like a two-by-four to the temple. She was the only witness to four murders. What happened had been choreographed to the last detail, which spoke of something organized and far more dangerous. Although she didn't watch much TV, she *did* read. Whether it was the Mob, drug dealers, or some other form of organized criminal network, she was well aware of what could, and *had* happened to the people, and their families, who testified against such illegal enterprises. She pressed her face against Bear's chest as a wave of nausea hit her, and his arms closed around her.

She thought of her parents at their house in Florida. Their distance gave her some measure of comfort, but what about Andrew and the rest of her friends? The thought they could already be in someone's crosshairs sent apprehension rising in her like a poisonous tidal flow. She pictured Andrew, his deep green eyes, his genteel charm, his winning smile. Not only was he her mentor, he was her closest friend. The idea of never seeing him again made her lungs clamp down and spasm painfully.

"It's okay," he said in a low, soothing voice. "They're gone."

It took her several moments to draw breath. "But they . . . they won't stay gone, will they?"

His hands moved in slow circles over her back. "No."

Her eyes stung, and she squeezed them shut, refusing to cry. When she finally stopped trembling she pulled back and looked up at him. "My . . . my life as I know it is over, isn't it?"

"No." His expression hardened, and his eyes turned steely.

"My friends . . . my family . . . ." Emotion clogged her throat, and she covered her face with her hands. "Their lives could be over, too."

His scowl deepened. "I am going to do whatever it takes to make sure that doesn't happen."

"How? How can you do that?"

He studied her face for a moment and sighed softly. "I'm a Federal Agent, Beth. I work for the FBI."

"FBI?" She stared at him, incredulous. "What the hell are you doing out *here*?"

That shadow passed behind his eyes again, and he turned his gaze back up the trail. He gently loosened her arms from around his waist. "I took a leave of absence," he replied, stepping out from behind the maple. "It's been a tough couple of years, and I needed some time off." The corners of his mouth rose, but that was as far as the smile went. "Lucky for you I decided *not* to go to Cabo."

"Well . . . ." she paused, contemplating what kind of shape she'd be in if he *had* gone to Mexico. She took a breath and said, ". . . I'm glad."

"Me, too."

"Really? *You're* glad?"

Bear chuckled and started back up the trail, still holding tight to her hand as his eyes swept back and forth. "Yeah. This has been the most interesting camping trip I've been on . . . *ever*."

She tugged on his hand, and he stopped to look at her over one shoulder. "How did we not hear them?"

A muscle twitched in his cheek, and he clenched his jaw. "They were flying NOE."

"What?"

"Nap of the earth," he explained.

She remembered Coop had taught her that, back *then*. She quickly pushed the thought aside. "That means they were flying at low altitude and following the lay of the land, right?"

He nodded. "The ridge itself served as a sound barrier until the chopper flew over it."

"Isn't that dangerous?"

"In this terrain?" He nodded. "Very."

Her mind was working much better than yesterday. "That means whoever was flying that helicopter is probably very familiar with this area." Even from behind him she saw the tightening of his jaw.

"Most likely."

Her voice came out in a choked whisper, that icy hand clawing at her windpipe. "And *that* might mean . . . ." She couldn't say the words, but Bear seemed to understand.

"It's a distinct possibility."

Her heart somersaulted. "So, now we have to worry about the good guys, too?"

"*No*." Bear turned to her, his expression fierce. "If they're working with the bad guys, they're *not* good guys anymore." He continued walking.

"And how do we figure out which is which?"

Bear paused and faced her. There was a cold fire burning in his eyes, lines of anger harsh about his mouth. If he hadn't saved her life, she would have found him terrifying.

"I'll find out who they are. *Trust* me."

Chapter Four

The end was in sight, the parking lot and his SUV just another short climb away. He glanced back, but she was concentrating on foot placement and not looking at him. He saw the wince every time she put weight on her bruised knee, but she uttered not a single complaint. Roughly five minutes later they reached the top of the trail. To be on the safe side, he took Beth's hand and pulled her behind him as he walked into the brush rather than following the footpath into the lot. Better safe than sorry.

Bear crouched behind a tree and indicated for Beth to do the same. To her credit, she did so without question, but he heard her sharp inhale. She moved gingerly, and he knew that her knee was bothering her, but she'd said nothing.

He divested himself of his pack and the rifle. He then turned his eyes to the gravel-covered clearing that served as a parking lot for hikers. The clearing was roughly one hundred fifty feet in diameter, outlined by tall trees and thick brush. Those intending to hike the trail would get a permit at the ranger station on the way in, then park here and walk from this point. On any given spring or summer weekend, this lot would have at least a dozen vehicles in it, but because it was mid-week in early spring there were only three cars in the lot: his Escalade, an old, battered, muddy, red pickup truck, and a heavy-duty pickup painted Forestry Service green with the FS logo on the side. He could make out the silhouette of a person inside the cab, but from this distance it was impossible to get a good look. His senses started tingling.

Beth half rose. "A ranger," she whispered.

Bear put a hand on her shoulder and kept her from standing. "Don't you think it's funny he's just sitting there?" He kept his voice low and when she spoke, thankfully, so did she.

She frowned. "It's part of his job to check the trailhead lots."

"Yeah, emphasis on the word *check*." He looked at the FS truck. "They're *supposed* to check the lot, make sure any cars have the proper permits, and then move on to the next trailhead." He gave her a sidelong glance. "If he's doing his job, he shouldn't be sitting *in* the truck. He should be *outside* of it looking at permits, which, with only two cars in the lot, should take . . . what? Five minutes?"

"Right, I see your point." He heard a sharp intake of breath and glanced at her. "Oh, crap." Her eyelids fluttered, and she moved closer to him. "Did you happen to notice the tires on your SUV are flat?"

He hadn't. He turned toward the Escalade and carefully pushed the branches of a bush aside. When he saw she was right, he swore under his breath. From this angle, he could only see two tires, but two were enough. They wouldn't be driving his Escalade anywhere. His eyes narrowed. "The tires on that old beater are intact."

"So?" She looked askance at him. "What are you going to do? Hotwire it?"

"Wouldn't be the first time." When he looked at her, her incredulous expression almost made him laugh. "What? I *did* have a life before joining the Bureau, you know."

She blushed and dropped her gaze. "I realize that. I just didn't know they let car thieves into the FBI."

"It was a juvenile offense, and I learned my lesson the first time."

"Was it *that* bad?" Beth glanced at him. "I would think someone like you would rule the roost . . . *anywhere.*"

A long forgotten memory flashed briefly. Bear pushed it aside. He laughed softly and focused on the FS truck. "You'd think so, but the established predators, the inmates who run things on the inside . . . . When a big guy like me shows up, the first thing they do is take him out, make an example." He looked at her, and she watched him with wide eyes. "That way everyone knows *they* rule the roost, and even a giant can't stop them. My second night in juvie was spent in the infirmary. I had three broken ribs, a broken arm, broken nose, and a concussion. I was sixteen."

"That's awful," she whispered. "I'm so sorry."

He shrugged and returned to watching the lot. "It was a long time ago, and it made me turn my life around, so it was actually good it happened." He gave her a quick smile. "I call it providence." When something crackled, Beth jumped and reached for his arm. His gaze slid to the FS truck, and then he closed his eyes and listened intently. The sound of a muted conversation was barely audible, and he realized the crackling had come from a two-way radio. His gut was telling him to tread carefully, that the ranger could be foe instead of friend. He had to find out for sure. Bear put a hand on Beth's shoulder and gave it a reassuring squeeze. "Stay here. I'll be back in a minute."

She nodded, and he melted into the forest. He quickly skirted the lot, moving closer to the FS truck. When he caught sight of the truck through the bushes, he paused, crouched and slowly crept forward. About ten feet from the passenger side door, he froze.

". . . headed back now. Any sign of her?"

The ranger pushed the button on the radio. "No. I'm telling you she probably headed west."

"She hasn't shown up at the west station. A BOLO went out saying she's armed and dangerous, but my contact at the sheriff's department says there's been no sign of her. She has to be somewhere between the meadow and you."

The ranger frowned. "You're talking hundreds of square miles of rough, rugged terrain with dozens of crisscrossing trails. Plus there are the other trailheads and the river. She could be ten miles downstream if she decided to get wet." He shook his head. "You sure this woman is going to be a problem?"

"Stop asking questions and do what you're paid to do. We need to find her. Just stay where you are and radio me if you make contact. If you can, detain her, but don't do anything stupid. We'll be there soon."

The ranger scowled. "Roger that."

Bear ground his teeth together. So much for going straight to the local authorities. Both the ranger and someone in the sheriff's department were involved.

She'd never make it into Federal custody. It didn't matter whether the *contact* in the sheriff's department worked for her pursuers or was just a loose-lipped employee, he couldn't take that chance. His mind worked furiously, but he was coming up dry. With a low, frustrated growl, he slowly and silently moved backwards, brush closing around him like a shield. When he couldn't see the truck anymore, he half-rose and quickly made his way back to where Beth was waiting.

"What happened?" she asked in a whisper as he crouched behind the tree.

Bear ran a hand over his face. "Well, we won't be going to the local authorities."

"Why not?"

What did he tell her? His throat tightened uncomfortably. She thought there were just a small handful of men after her, not rogue law enforcement officers who worked for an international criminal organization. He decided to give her the truth, but only part of it. Best to ease into it and see how she reacted.

He sighed. "Because the guys chasing you have someone in the sheriff's department and the local Forestry Service on their payroll. A BOLO has gone out, saying you're armed and dangerous." He focused on the FS truck, frustration burning hotly in his chest. "Now *they* don't have to look for you because law enforcement will do it for them."

She blinked at him and paled.

"Gun crimes in a National Park come under FBI jurisdiction," he continued. "That means if local law enforcement finds you, they'll arrest you and take you to the closest sheriff's station. They'll hold you there until they can transfer you into federal custody."

"Maybe we should let them find me." She squared her shoulders and glanced at the green truck then looked at him. "I mean, they can't *all* be bad guys, can they? Maybe I'd be safer in a jail cell, and then you could sort all this out, and it would be over."

Yes, it would *definitely* be over, but not how she thought. Bear's gut knotted. "No."

"Why not?"

He clenched his jaw. He didn't want to panic her, but he didn't want to lie to her either. She deserved to know what she was up against. "You'd never make it into federal custody."

Her eyes went wide. "What do you mean?"

His frown deepened. "Because the guys you took pictures of would have no trouble getting to you in a jail cell, especially since they have inside help." He looked away from her, wishing he could remove the stark fear from her eyes, and wishing he didn't feel just a bit of it himself. "You have *no* idea who you're dealing with." He waited for the hysterics or demands for more information, but they didn't come. He looked at her, surprised by the grim determination he saw in her eyes.

Her voice was clear and low. "Mexican mafia, drug cartel, Nortenos, MS-13 . . . let me know if I'm getting warm."

His brows rose. Admiration tinged his voice. "You're not so scatterbrained today."

"Nope, brain seems to be functioning normally now." She sat down, rested her elbows on her knees, and covered her face with her hands. "Kind of wish it wasn't."

Bear knew exactly how she felt and waited for her to look at him. She was breathing deeply and evenly, her posture stiff and tensed. He understood she needed a minute to process the gravity of the situation. After taking several more breaths, she peeked between her fingers.

"So, what now?"

He was impressed, again. He'd expected tears, not stoic resignation. "Now . . . ." He looked toward the truck. "We get out of here. Once I get you someplace safe, we can work on the rest of it."

She nodded slowly. "Okay. I'm assuming you have a plan?"

"I wouldn't call it a *plan*." He turned to her and put a hand on her shoulder. "But it will require your participation. How is your knee?"

Her brows rose. "Um . . . okay. Why?"

"I need you to get the ranger out of his truck." When her brows rose higher, he gave her a smile. "Relax. You won't need to say anything. All you have to do is run."

Her eyes turned into saucers. "Run *where*, exactly?"

When he glanced at the ranger and then back at her, her chin nearly hit the ground. She blinked at him several times, and he saw her throat move as she swallowed hard.

"Just get him to chase you and I'll take care of the rest." He squeezed her shoulder slightly. "Trust me. I *won't* let him hurt you."

She looked at the ranger for several long seconds as she started more deep breaths. Finally, she set her jaw and turned her eyes back to him. "Well," she began, "I think you know I can run."

"Yes, you can. Now, here's what I want you to do."

Chapter Five

Beth stared at the Forest Service truck, her heart pattering against her sternum, her knee throbbing with every beat. She hoped it would hold out for the upcoming sprint.

The truck sat at the edge of the lot near the only road in or out, roughly sixty-five feet from where she was crouched. Bear had said to give him five minutes. She glanced at her watch as it counted down. When the allotted time had passed, she rose, took several deep breaths, and started running.

She burst from the bushes. Bear had said to run straight across the clearing and head down the road, which would bring her within about thirty feet of the green truck. Hopefully, the ranger would be slower than she was so Bear could eliminate him from their current equation. If it worked, they would have one less bad guy to deal with.

The door to the pickup popped open, and the ranger stepped out, staring at her as she got closer. Beth's heart started to race. *Focus on the road,* she told herself. *Focus on reaching the road.*

"Ma'am! Ma'am, I need to talk to you." The ranger started running, and she could tell he was moving to intercept her. "Stop!"

Adrenaline surged through her. She ignored him and kept her mouth shut, running as if the killers were hot on her heels.

"Ma'am! Stop!"

He ran towards her, but she paid him no heed.

"I said *stop!*"

The ranger closed the gap and grabbed for her. Her heart surged into her throat, but she side-stepped and spun away from him in a move that would have made a professional running-back proud. She heard him grunt and stumble, but didn't bother to look. Digging deep, she put on a burst of speed.

Trees arched over the single lane road that led from the trailhead lot to the closest highway. The gravel-covered lane went straight for about a hundred yards, and then curved sharply to the left and descended, disappearing from sight as the trees thickened. As she continued her breakneck pace, she became aware of heavy footfalls behind her and realized the ranger was catching up. Beth lengthened her stride and kept her eyes on the narrow path.

She rounded the curve in the road and kept going, focusing on the apex of the trees as the path descended. *Run until you hear the signal, just run.* She heard a strange whistling sound followed by a loud *thwack* and a pained grunt, and then all went quiet. She hadn't taken more than three more strides before a shrill whistle split the air. That was the signal. Beth skidded to a halt and looked back over her shoulder, her lungs laboring for air, her breathing deep and heavy. Her eyes widened at the sight of the ranger sprawled out in the middle of the road, unconscious. A large branch that hadn't been there a few seconds ago hung out over the road, moving gently back and forth. A moment later Bear stepped out of the thick brush.

"Man should watch where he's going." He grinned at her. "See what happens when you run into tree branches?" He approached the fallen ranger. "Nice job, by the way. I particularly liked that little spin move you did."

Beth stood for a moment, hands on hips, breathing in huge gulps of air. Her knee throbbed, but she ignored it. Bear bent over and rolled the ranger onto his stomach. He then waved her forward.

"Get his cuffs."

Beth blinked, but took the ranger's handcuffs from his utility belt. Bear gave her a look that said she should know what to do next, so she cuffed the unconscious man. "Why did you have me do that?"

Bear looked at the ranger speculatively, rubbing his chin. "We have two advantages. One, they don't know who you are, and two . . . they think you're on your own. I want them to keep thinking that." He glanced at her. "Wait here."

Beth watched as he jogged back to the bushes where they had crouched earlier. After a few moments, he reappeared with a length of rope in his hands. He ran back to where she stood. After he securely tied the ranger's ankles, he rose, dusted off his hands, and looked at her.

She narrowed her eyes at him and fought a smile. "You *really* enjoy your job, don't you?" she asked, still breathing heavily.

He shrugged, and one corner of his mouth lifted. "One does what one is born for." As carefully as he could, Bear rolled the still unconscious ranger into a large bed of ferns at the side of the road.

"So, now what?"

He gave her that killer grin and wiggled his brows at her. "Want to learn how to hotwire a truck?"

Beth thought about it for a second then shrugged. "Sure."

"Let's go then."

Beth looked toward the cluster of ferns for a moment and started after Bear. She took one step and a sudden jolt of pain shot through her knee. She cried out as it buckled. She was aware of falling, butterflies swooping wildly in her stomach as the ground rushed up to meet her. Steely arms caught her and lifted her against a hard chest. She looked at Bear in surprise.

"How do you *do* that?" she asked.

"What?"

"Move like that?"

He shrugged and started walking back toward his SUV, gravel that covered the narrow road crunching beneath his boots. His arms were hard and his chest even harder, yet he held her as gently as if she was something delicate and breakable. "If I didn't move like a wraith, I'd have been dead a long time ago."

Beth gulped. "Well, then I'm glad you move like a wraith." Heat crept up her neck, and she dropped her gaze. "Thank you, again, for saving me."

He chuckled and walked back toward the lot. "Happy to be of assistance."

She closed her eyes and thought of laying her head on his shoulder the way she had last night. Despite the fact he was a virtual stranger, sleeping next to him had felt right, natural, and being held in his arms now felt delicious. A flutter of heat ran through her and pooled in her midsection. She started to lean her head toward him, but caught herself and straightened. She glanced up at him and felt her flush intensify when she saw a small smile on his mouth. Had he been reading her mind?

After what seemed like mere seconds they reached the black Escalade. Even while holding her, he had the dexterity to reach into his pocket and retrieve his keys. Beth heard a small *beep*, the SUV clicked, and then the rear hatch of the Escalade started to rise. Bear strode to the rear driver's side door, opened it, and gently put her down on the plush seat.

"Your throne, my lady," he said, his tone formal but his lips twitching with a barely restrained smile. "Once I take care of a few things, I will transfer you to your new chariot." He walked around the vehicle looking at the tires with a frown, and then moved to the rear hatch.

Annoyance flared inside her. "I *can* help, you know." She stood up, took a step, and found herself holding onto the door frame as she bit back a cry of pain. Bear stopped what he was doing to put her back in her seat and then stood there with his fists on his hips. Beth flushed and dared a glance at him, surprised to see him smiling. She had expected irritation or the blank slate, but he actually seemed amused by her temerity.

"Relax, I can handle a first aid kit," he said before moving to the rear of the Escalade. He looked through the interior of the vehicle at her and chuckled. "Besides, I kind of enjoyed carrying you, and you didn't seem to mind it either."

Beth huffed. "I didn't have much choice."

Bear was focused on something in the cargo area, but the smile widened just slightly. "You could've stayed with the ranger."

"You didn't give me a chance to make that decision." She shot him a glare and ran a hand over her disheveled hair. "You just picked me up like a sack of potatoes and started walking."

"Should I have let you fall?" He glanced at her. "Letting a lady do a face plant when I was in a position to stop it seems rather rude."

Beth crossed her arms over her chest. "So is gloating because you *think* I enjoyed being held by you. Pointing it out doesn't help your case either."

"Touché."

Her heart did a hard *ka-thump* when a shotgun appeared in his hand, and he dropped one round into the open chamber. He then racked that round and slid several more shells into the weapon. He put it back where he'd taken it from. She watched as he checked several other firearms before he seemed satisfied. Apparently the cargo area of his Escalade contained a gun safe. Once he was done with that, he walked off into the brush in the direction of the spot they'd stashed their stuff. When he reappeared, he had her camera and, oddly, nothing else.

"Where's your pack, the rifle?"

He put the camera in the cargo area and grabbed something else, but she couldn't see what it was. "I'll get those in a few." He locked that laser-like gaze on her, his eyes twinkling impishly. His expression started Beth's heart on a steady climb up her throat. He slowly walked around to where she sat.

"I've scoped out the area, and there are no signs of any pursuit," he said, holding a large first-aid kit in his hands. "Let's take a look at that knee, but let's do it quickly."

Beth frowned. "I'm fine." He crouched in front of her and started to roll up her pant leg. Shivers shot up her calf into her thigh and higher.

"Of course you are. You always walk like the Hunchback of Notre Dame, right?" She gulped as he gave her that killer smile and added, "Silly me for thinking something was wrong."

More shivers pulsed up her leg as his fingers brushed her skin. She was immensely thankful she'd shaved before heading out into the wilderness. Usually she didn't, reserving that chore for the hour long bath she took upon returning home from one of her photo safaris. Beth ground her teeth together, and her heart started to thud as his hands seemed to inch from her ankle, over her calf, and finally brushed the sensitive backside of her knee. She closed her eyes, willing away images of his hands moving past her knee, up her thigh, to a spot between her legs that even now ached to be touched. It was ridiculous to even think about getting intimate with him given the situation they were in, but for some reason she couldn't stop thinking about what it would be like.

His voice intruded on her thoughts, but the warm, rough depth of his voice was a welcome intrusion.

"What?" he asked. "No snappy comeback?"

"No," she said from between clenched teeth. "Just get on with it." His chuckle made her frown, and she opened her eyes expecting to lock gazes with him, but he was examining her knee. He cupped the back of her knee in one large hand, his thumb brushing gently over the swelling.

"Well, it's going to bruise real pretty, but I think you'll live. Let's get this wrapped so we can get the hell out of here."

He put the kit on the ground and opened it. He moved quickly and fluidly, his eyes moving between her knee and their surroundings, ever alert. She watched as he pulled an instant icepack from inside the blue and white box and crushed the inner capsule that would activate the cooling crystals. He paused and peered around, seeming to listen intently. Apparently satisfied they were still alone and undetected, he took an ace bandage, wrapped it once around the pack, and pressed the pack to her knee as he wrapped the rest of the bandage around her leg. After securing the elastic cloth with several small metal clips, he grabbed a bottle of pain reliever, opened it, and deposited two pills into his hand.

"It's just ibuprofen," he said as he handed the white capsules to her. "It'll help with the pain and swelling until we can get a real medical professional to look at it."

Beth put the pills in her mouth, retrieved her water bottle from her pocket, and took a long swig. "I told you, I'm fine."

Bear closed the kit and stood. His sharp gaze again scanned the woods. "Good. That means you can drive then, right?"

Her heart did an unexpected vault, and she almost choked. "What?"

"You're going to have to drive out of here."

Cold fear stopped her heart mid-cartwheel, and she gaped at him. "I thought we were going together."

"Not right now." She continued to stare, and after a few tense, silent moments he sighed and ran a hand over his eyes. "I need you to trust me, Beth." He glanced at the FS truck. "They have my info. I gave it to them to get a parking permit, so they know I'm out here somewhere." He met her gaze. "If we both vanish, they'll figure out I'm helping you, and there goes any advantage we may have had."

She thought about that for a second. "So, you're just going to . . . send me off?"

The panty-dropping smile was back, and he wiggled his eyebrows at her.

"Temporarily. Yes."

"You have a plan?"

"I'm making this up as I go."

An uncomfortable ball curled in the pit of her stomach, and she took another drink of water. It didn't help. "Okay." She took a deep breath, held it for a moment, and let it out as she met his eyes. "What do you want me to do?"

"That's my girl. I want you to drive back to the main highway and head south. About four miles down the road you'll see a gravel lane on the left. It leads to an abandoned lumber mill."

Beth nodded. "The old Chatham Mill. I know the place."

"Good." His expression sobered. "I want you to park inside one of the buildings at the mill and hide, somewhere away from the truck in case they come looking for it."

"Wait." Her stomach curled up, as if it wanted to hide from the cold fear pooling in her midsection. "You think that truck is theirs?"

"Yeah," he said with a glance at the pickup, "or it would have four slashed tires, too."

"Of course." She swallowed the lump forming in her throat. "So, *after* I steal the murderer's truck and hide at the mill, what do I do?"

"Wait for me."

"For how long?"

"If all goes well, I should be there by dark."

"And if all *doesn't* go well?"

"Then get someplace where you feel safe," he replied as he reached into his pocket and pulled out his wallet. He took a business card from within the stitched leather and held it out to her. "And call this guy."

Beth took the card and read the name. "Special Agent Jack Vaughn, FBI." She looked at him. "Who's he?"

"He's the only guy I trust one hundred percent."

Something cold and hard clogged her throat and for a moment she couldn't breathe. Bear only had *one* guy he trusted to back them up? Panic started to swirl, and she fought it, taking more deep breaths. *Bear knows what he's doing, Beth. He's got this. You can't wimp out now.* When the dread receded to a manageable level, she exhaled slowly and met his gaze. "Okay." She licked her lips and nodded slowly as she slid the card into the front pocket of her shirt. "Say everything *does* go well. What's *your* part of the plan? I assume you're going to do . . . *something.*"

He grinned and lifted one blonde brow. "Of course I'm going to do something."

He paused as if gauging her reaction, and Beth sighed softly. "So enlighten me, genius. While I'm hiding in some rat-infested, spider-webbed, bug-filled hole somewhere, what are *you* going to do . . . sunbathe?"

"I'm going to make new friends."

"Make new friends?" She wished she had a clue in hell what he was talking about. Beth looked around. "There's no one else here. How are you going to make new friends?"

The curve of his mouth expanded and lit up his face. "I'm going to save the ranger."

Suddenly, his head snapped around and then Beth heard what had drawn his attention: voices, male voices conversing in Spanish. Bear grabbed her hand and pulled her out of the Escalade.

"Hide." He pushed her toward the edge of the clearing.

Beth gaped at him. "What about you?"

He glared at her. "Just go. Don't worry about me."

She thought about defying him, but one look at his face made her think better of it. "Be careful," she said. He nodded at her, grim lines bracketing his mouth, and waved her on. Beth limped into the brush. She listened intently as she moved to where they'd stashed their stuff, trying to keep Bear in sight through the trees and foliage while making as little noise as possible. She'd expected him to grab one or more of the guns from the SUV, but he didn't. Fear stiffened her lungs, and she fought for air as she moved toward the cluster of bushes that hid the pack and rifle. If nothing else, Bear's .308 might come in handy.

When she disappeared from sight, Bear quickly shut the passenger door and then moved to the back of the Escalade. His senses went on high alert. He wasn't nervous, just hyper-aware of every sound, every movement, and the normally muted hum of nature was suddenly much too loud. He jerked the car cover over the guns, not wanting to start a firefight unless he had to. He wished he had his rifle, and prayed he'd hidden it well enough to keep it concealed from the approaching strangers. How they'd managed not to run into these men before now made him realize how fortunate they'd been thus far. Either his luck was holding, or it was about to run out.

His pulse went up a point as he listened to the voices and pretended to unpack something. Seconds later two men meandered out of the woods. He glanced at them covertly. One was tall, probably 6'3" and the other was a head shorter. They both had black hair, swarthy skin, and dark eyes, the shorter one's pecs and biceps bulged beneath the fitted white t-shirt he wore. Their gazes jerked to him, and they paused for a second before walking toward him.

"Hey, gringo," the taller one said. "What are you doing here?"

Bear put on a surprised face and turned toward them. "Hey. Where'd you guys come from?"

"Hiking," the shorter one said, scowling darkly.

"Ah." Bear turned back to his imaginary packing. "I was doing some camping. Planned to go home today, but . . . ." His voice trailed off, and he glared at the wheels. "Not going anywhere with four slashed tires." He faced them, and they backed up a step, obviously nervous. The shorter one reached behind him. Bear pretended not to notice. "Say, is that pickup yours?" He gestured to the red truck, and the tall one nodded. "Could you give me a ride back to the ranger station so I can call a tow truck?"

The tall one's eyes narrowed, and he jerked his head toward the FS truck. "Get the ranger to call one for you."

"Ranger's not here," Bear replied smoothly.

"Where is he?"

Bear shrugged. "Don't know. He wasn't here when I got here. His truck's here, but he must've gone down one of the other trails or something." He planted his fists on his hips. "So, can you give me a ride?"

The shorter one smiled and pulled a pistol from behind him. Bear pretended to be surprised and groaned inwardly. This wasn't how he wanted to play it, but he would if he had to.

"I don't think so, gringo." The taller one pulled a pistol as well, and Bear put his hands up. The shorter one took another step forward. "See, I like Escalades, so I'm going to have to commandeer your vehicle."

Bear frowned. "Why? I mean, unless you've got three Escalade tires in the back of that pickup, you're not driving my car *anywhere*."

Short guy grinned. "Once I kill you it won't matter. I'll just come back later and get it."

Like hell you will. Bear affected a worried expression, but remained mute.

The tall one's eyes narrowed. "Come on, Mateo. We don't have time for this."

"Relax, Alvarez," Mateo said, scratching his chin with the barrel of the 9mm. "We have plenty of time for this. After all . . . ." he paused and leveled the pistol at Bear's chest. "It takes less than a second to shoot someone. And I've always wanted a black Escalade."

You better hope you're as fast as you and everyone else thinks you are, because this is about to get ugly. Bear eased his hands down and imagined grasping the pistol on his hip when a shot rang out. The man named Mateo jerked, spun away from him, and landed face-first on the ground. From the direction the guy had spun, Bear knew where the shot had come from, and he knew the sound of his own rifle. The report of the .308 and his gut told him his golden-eyed photographer had just saved his life. And here she claimed not to like guns. If the situation hadn't been potentially lethal, he would've smiled.

The taller guy reacted quickly, but Bear was faster. He didn't recall pulling the trigger, but in the next second, another body joined the first. He paused, took a breath, and waited. Nobody else moved. *Thank you, Beth.* With a sigh, he holstered his weapon and crouched and checked both men. Neither had a pulse. He looked at the two corpses for a few seconds, then straightened and started walking.

Beth rose out of the bushes when he got within several paces, his rifle in her hands. Her expression was inscrutable. She cycled the bolt with the speed of someone who knew how to handle a gun, and his brows rose. He stopped in front of her. She handed the weapon to him, and they stared at each other for several long, silent seconds. He studied her face, noting the clenching of her jaw, the slight tremble in her chin, and the rapidly blinking eyelids. This must be a first for her, at least he hoped it was.

"I thought you didn't like guns," he said at last as he shouldered the rifle. He saw the convulsive swallow, and she glanced briefly at the two dead men.

"That doesn't mean I don't know how to use them," she said flatly.

Without another word, she limped past him and sat down on the open tailgate. Bear watched her for another second or so and then retrieved his pack. He approached the back of the Escalade and put his burdens in the cargo area. Beth was staring into the woods, her expression distant, and a cold flash of regret scored through him. He leaned against the SUV's frame and watched her face.

"You gonna tell me who taught you to shoot like that?"

She shook her head and dropped her chin. "Not today. Let's get out of here first."

He wanted to prod, get her to open up a little, but now was probably not the right time. There could be more of them closing in, so he let it go. "Of course." He crossed his arms over his chest. "We have a much better chance, thanks to you." He took a deep breath. "Thanks for saving my life. I guess this means we're even."

She laughed shortly and stared at her lap. "Yeah, not even close. You've saved my butt three . . . no, four times since we met, so I still owe you."

"You don't owe me anything."

She sniffed and dashed a hand over her eyes. "Because you're one of the good guys?"

He put two fingers under her chin and turned her face to him. "Yeah, because I'm one of the good guys." He smiled. "And because sleeping with me was payment enough. I'd be greedy to ask for more."

She blinked rapidly and chuckled again. "So, I'll probably have to sleep with you again before we get out of this, won't I?"

That's it, joke with me, and reach out instead of turning in. It was a good sign. Bear pursed his lips and rubbed his chin. "It's a distinct possibility." He sat down next to her and covered her hands with one of his. "And I'll behave the same way I did last night."

She wound her fingers through his, and his insides tightened when he saw a single tear trail down her cheek, even as she smiled. The sight of that solitary, silver droplet made his abdominals tighten in protest.

"Always a gentleman."

"I try." He wiped the tear away. "Now, come on. If we're going to get out of here, I have to show you how to hotwire." He gestured at the truck. "Welcome to my classroom."

Chapter Six

The engine of the red pickup roared to life, and Beth laughed excitedly.

"I did it!"

Bear chuckled. "Yes, you did. Now, if the whole photography thing doesn't work out, you have something to fall back on."

Her expression sobered. "I guess it *is* sort of wrong to be so excited about hotwiring a truck."

"That was my reaction the first time I did it." He smiled. "Just don't get *too* comfortable with it. This old jalopy is easy, but newer cars? They are *much* harder to steal, most of them anyway."

One winged brow shot skyward. "I would ask how you know that, but I don't think I want to know."

He laughed softly. "Good. I'd hate to have to fill you in on my sordid past. Just remember, stealing cars is *bad*. Criminals steal cars." When he saw her expression darken, he wanted to kick himself.

She glanced toward the bodies which were still where they had fallen. "Guess this is my day for criminal activity."

The remorse and guilt in her expression started a wave of angry heat inside him. "Hey, there was *nothing* criminal about what you did."

"Really? What about thou shalt not kill?"

He put a hand to her cheek and turned her face to his. "The correct translation is thou shalt not *murder*, actually, and what you did is the opposite of that. You *saved* a life. Yes, you had to take a life to do it, but taking someone's life in defense of another is *not* murder. What you did was *heroic*, not criminal."

"And stealing this car?"

"In situations like this sometimes you have to . . . *bend* the rules a little. Just *don't* make a habit of it."

"Well, thanks for the tip, but I don't think that's going to be a problem." She slid behind the wheel. "I'm putting my evil ways behind me. This is the first and *only* car I ever plan to steal."

He chuckled. "We didn't *plan* to steal this one."

She paused and nodded. "Right. Point taken."

Bear closed the door and leaned on the open window frame. "Now, you remember what you're supposed to do?" He saw a flash of fear in her eyes, but it was quickly replaced by what looked like determination.

"Yes." She hesitated a moment then reached for her camera, which sat on the seat beside her. "And here." She took the memory card from inside the device, looked at it for a moment, and handed it to him, her expression solemn. "You said put it somewhere safe." She met his gaze. "I can't think of any safer place than with you."

Bear knew, for her, handing that memory card to him was the equivalent of her handing over her life to him. It wasn't something *he'd* ever do willingly or lightly unless he had no choice, but she hadn't hesitated a bit. He palmed the one-inch-square piece of plastic. "Are you sure?"

Her smile answered an emphatic *no*. "As sure as I am about anything right now." She shrugged. "Besides, if anything happens to me, you know who to take it to. I don't."

His jaw clenched. "*Nothing* is going to happen to you." When she lifted her eyes to his, something inside him shifted, and the wave of protectiveness that crested in his chest was much stronger than what he normally felt when protecting a witness. This wasn't work. *This* was personal, and he didn't like it one bit. He took a deep breath and held it, but it took a moment to regain his composure. "You're going to be fine, I promise."

She tipped her head to the side and laid a hand over his. "You can't promise that, Bear, but I appreciate the thought, and I will do my best not to disappoint." She smiled. "After all, you still owe me some chicken fried steak."

He returned her smile. "*When* we get out of this, I'll buy you chicken fried steak every day for a month if you want."

Beth studied his face for a few seconds, and then leaned toward him and kissed his cheek. His stomach flipped. He had the sudden, insane desire to turn his face and capture her mouth, and it took every ounce of willpower he had not to. She pulled back, and color surged into her face.

"I *do* want." Her lashes fluttered down, hiding her eyes from him. "I *love* chicken fried steak, and I think I'd enjoy the company that comes with it just as much." Without looking at him, she put the truck into gear. "I better get going. I'll see you soon."

He didn't move. "Yes, you will. Be careful."

She gave him a quick grin. "You, too."

He backed away from the truck. "Always."

Bear watched until Beth disappeared from sight in the dirty pickup. Cold, barbed fingers of worry invaded him. He liked to be in control, but once she left his line of vision, Beth and anything that happened to her was out of his control. It was one thing to plan an op and then turn trained, skilled agents loose to do their jobs. It was quite another to plan on the fly with an unarmed, untrained civilian, especially if that civilian was Beth. That last thought jolted him. In the brief time they'd spent together, she'd impressed him with her grit and her willingness to follow him even if it scared her. Those golden eyes were quickly casting a spell he knew he couldn't fall under. He had to be close to her to keep her safe, but getting too close could be just as dangerous.

"Get over it, Bear," he told himself. "She's a witness, nothing more."

It didn't matter that he'd said it aloud. It just didn't ring true. Beth wasn't some frail, fainting female. The stop-spin she'd done to stay out of the ranger's grasp was a move worthy of Emmitt Smith, legendary running back for the Dallas Cowboys. And then there was the fact she'd shot someone to save him. Finally, a ray of light broke through his concern. The woman was nothing if not capable, even if she wasn't a Federal agent.

He sat down on the open tailgate of the Escalade and waited. About five minutes passed before the familiar *whump-whump* of helicopter blades severed the quiet. He stood, looked into the sky, and his pulse started a slow but steady climb. The aircraft either belonged to the Federal government or the men chasing Beth. Either way, it was bad news. Good news was Beth wasn't here anymore. He glanced at his watch and estimated she was probably just hitting the main highway. Thankfully, the thick brush and trees lining the roads would provide her some measure of protection. The sound grew closer, the helo obviously approaching his location. After closing and locking the Escalade, he retreated quickly into the forest, his rifle in hand, brush and saplings closing like curtains in his wake. He found a concealed spot close enough to the trailhead lot to have a clear line of sight, and hunkered down.

Less than a minute after he took cover, the aircraft cleared the trees and hovered over the clearing. Bear pressed close to a gnarled trunk and readied his rifle, using the scope to get a closer view. A Hispanic male looked down into the lot from the cab of the helo and yelled at the pilot, also Hispanic. So, it was the bad guys and not the Feds. He wasn't sure if that was better or not.

About ten seconds later, the chopper began to descend. Once on the ground, the man sprinted to the bodies and checked for pulses. Bear tensed and flexed his fingers around the barrel of the rifle. The man from the helicopter looked over his shoulder at the pilot and shook his head. He waved an arm for someone to help him, and a second man sprinted from the cab of the aircraft. The two men loaded the bodies, and then one of the men returned with a gallon jug of water. He splashed the blood pools until there was little left to tell of what had happened here. Once he finished his task, he ran back to the helicopter.

Well, that's good. At least now I won't have to explain the bodies to the ranger or anyone else.

The helicopter's engines spun up, the chopper rose, and then disappeared behind the tree tops. He glanced at his watch again. Beth had been gone less than fifteen minutes, but she should be almost to the mill. Knowing she'd soon be out of the line of sight gave him some measure of comfort. Bear didn't move until he couldn't hear the rotors, and then he waited another five minutes before leaving his hiding place.

As soon as the engine noise had died down, he'd heard murmuring and then shouting from the bushes where he'd left the ranger. He was surprised the ranger hadn't woken sooner with all the shooting, shouting, and noise from the helicopter.

Bear walked back to the Escalade and opened the rear hatch, reaching for a bottle of water. He unscrewed the cap, drained the bottle, then capped it and tossed it inside the vehicle. The shouting grew louder, and he glanced at his watch. The ranger continued to call out. Bear ignored him and sat down on the tailgate. After another fifteen minutes had passed, he shouldered his pack and rifle and started jogging toward the sound.

"Hello!" he called when the ranger's voice died. "Hey, is someone there?"

"Help!"

Bear made a pretense of searching the bushes close to the ranger before he finally pushed back the large ferns to reveal the now conscious man. "Shit, what happened to you?"

"It doesn't matter." The ranger winced and rolled onto his side. "Get my cuff keys, please. They're on the key ring attached to my belt."

Bear grabbed the keys, dropped them, and gave the ranger an apologetic look before picking them up again. The ranger rolled over to expose his hands, and Bear fumbled with the keys for a few seconds before unlocking the cuffs.

"There," Bear said, holding out the keys as the ranger moved to a sitting position. The ranger put the keys away as Bear took a knife from his belt and cut through the binding on the man's ankles. Then he stepped back. "You okay? That's a nice bump you've got on your forehead."

"I'll be fine." The ranger touched the growing lump on his brow. "Can you help me up? My feet are asleep."

Bear extended a hand. "Sure. Not going anywhere anyway. Someone slashed my tires."

"I guess you're driving the Escalade?" the ranger ground out as Bear helped him to his feet.

"I *was*," Bear replied with a rueful chuckle.

The ranger took a step and swayed, and Bear grabbed his arm.

The ranger shot him a grateful look. "Thanks, man. Guess I'm not as steady as I thought."

"Guess not. What'd you do . . . run into a tree?"

"Something like that." When they reached the FS truck, the man eased down on the seat and held out a hand. "Thanks, again. Name's Miller, Brent Miller."

"Ted Bristol," Bear responded, shaking the man's hand firmly.

Miller reached across the seat and picked up a clipboard. After glancing through the sheaf of papers, he looked at Bear quizzically. "Permit says you got here yesterday and planned to stay for a week." He put the clipboard aside. "Leaving early?"

"Well, I came out here for some peace and quiet." Bear leaned against the open door. "With all the gunshots and helicopters flying around I figured something was going on, and peace and quiet were out of the question."

"What's wrong with a few gunshots? You don't like hunters?"

Bear lifted one brow. "Not when those hunters are close enough to shoot *me*."

Miller gestured to the rifle over Bear's shoulder. "I'd say that evens the odds."

Bear was starting to get irritated, but he kept his face impassive and smiled that smile most people took as genuine even when it wasn't. "When I came out here, I really hadn't planned on getting into a firefight. Figured I'd play it safe, quit the woods, and take my buddy's advice instead."

"And what was your buddy's advice?"

"Go to Cabo and spend my time and money on senoritas and tequila."

"Ah." Miller sighed. "Well, I can help with that. Why don't you wait in your vehicle? I'll call a tow truck for you. Shouldn't have to wait more than an hour or so. Then, if you want to go to Cabo you can."

"Sounds good." Bear started to walk away, paused, and turned back. "You sure you're okay? Maybe you should call an ambulance instead of a tow truck."

"I've had worse bumps on the head, trust me." Miller waved him off. "I'm fine, and thanks again. I appreciate you getting those cuffs off me. I would've been here for hours before anyone else came looking."

"No problem. Thanks for your help."

Miller nodded. "Anytime."

Bear walked to the Escalade and put his pack and rifle in the back on top of the locked, hidden gun case built into the floor of the cargo area. After closing the lift-gate, he walked to the driver's seat and slid behind the wheel. He unlocked the glove compartment and grabbed his cell phone, but there was no service. Not that he'd expected any. He hadn't been lying when he'd told the ranger he'd come to the woods for peace and quiet.

He closed his eyes and leaned his head back, and immediately Beth's image filled his mind. He hated to admit it, but he liked her. She had a wry wit and a sarcastic bent he enjoyed, and sleeping beside her had been surprisingly easy. Not to mention she'd saved his life. *That* certainly increased her stock price and piqued his curiosity. For someone who professed not to like guns, she knew how to use them.

In the end, it didn't matter. He couldn't let things between them progress any further. He was a Federal agent, and she was a witness to a Federal crime. That's as far as it could go.

There was a tap on his window, and Bear opened one eye. Miller stood there, and Bear rolled down the window.

"Yeah?"

"You're in luck." Miller smiled. "Tow truck will be here in half an hour. Guess it's a slow day for them."

Bear nodded. "Must be. Now, hopefully, they'll have my tires in stock so I don't have to wait for parts to be delivered."

"Shouldn't have to." Miller leaned on the window. "Truck stop is pretty big and has a full garage. And Escalades aren't uncommon."

"Great. I'll wait here."

Miller gave him a lopsided grin. "Not like you can go anywhere anyway."

"Right." Bear looked at the man out of the corner of his eye and glanced at the green truck. "Your tires aren't flat. Shouldn't you be moving on to the next trailhead lot?"

Miller nodded and pushed his sunglasses up on his head. "I will after I talk to the sheriff. The tree that hit me also stole a vehicle from this lot, so this is officially a crime scene." Miller shrugged. "You could file a report with them about the tires, for your insurance company."

Bear laughed. "I *could*, if I want to pay more for a deductible than I will have to pay for brand new tires." He shook his head. "I'll pass, but I hope you catch the tree that did that to you. Is that what all the helicopters are for . . . finding the *tree?*" A shadow of uncertainty passed behind the ranger's eyes, but it was quickly gone. Nevertheless, Bear knew what he'd seen.

"You guessed it," Miller replied with a short, uneasy laugh. "Easy job, finding a tree in a forest."

Good, Bear thought. *Keep looking in the forest.* "I don't envy you, man." Bear extended his hand. "Thanks for calling the tow truck, and I hope everything works out."

Miller shook his hand. "I'm sure it will. Hope you find that peace and quiet you're looking for."

"Me, too. Thanks again."

Miller nodded and walked back to his truck. Bear ground his teeth together and looked at the ceiling of the Escalade. Great, the lawmen were on the way. If the ranger hadn't already done it, the local cops would run his plates and know very quickly he was a fellow law enforcement officer, and then the interrogation would start. He glanced at his watch and growled in frustration. Hopefully, Beth was safely hidden away at the mill, and the tow truck would arrive before the lawmen. That would give him the head start he needed.

* * *

Beth shut off the truck's engine and peered through the windshield. The abandoned mill was surprisingly intact for a business that had gone under nearly a decade past. She opened the window and stuck her head out. Much of the equipment remained in place. The machines looked like metal ghosts waiting to be awakened so they could gobble up acres of forestland once again. Sunlight found entrance through a myriad of holes in the soaring roof, but the interior space was still dominated by darkness and shadows that seemed to shift and dance every time she turned her head. She jumped when a bird took wing, exiting the corrugated metal structure through one of the many broken windows. Once the jay's flapping died away, an eerie quiet descended over the place, and a shudder ran the length of her spine once, and then again. This was a place where nightmares came to life, in broad daylight.

"Oh, I hope I'm not here after dark." Her whispered words were like a shout in the cavernous interior of the main mill. She gripped the steering wheel tightly. A chill that wasn't in the air settled over her, and she wrapped her arms around herself. "I wish Bear was here." She closed her eyes, pictured him, and tried to absorb the calm that always seemed to emanate from him. It wasn't as effective as being physically close, but it helped.

Hide, preferably away from the truck in case they come looking for it.

Her eyes snapped open as she recalled his voice, and she could picture the scowl that would furrow his brow if he saw her still sitting in the truck. Even so, Beth spent another minute or so hoping Bear would show up, but he didn't. She was alone, or at least she *thought* she was. She looked around, half expecting the thugs from the previous day to pop up from behind the rusted generator, the frayed conveyor belt, or another piece of the aging, decaying equipment. When all remained still and quiet, she sighed softly and got out of the vehicle.

She reached into the bed of the truck and shouldered the canvas bag Bear had put there during her attempt at hotwiring. He'd told her he'd put some supplies in the tote, and although she had no idea what, she didn't think now was the time for an inspection. Once she was hidden, she could rummage through the bag. Testing her knee, she removed the ice pack and looked around for a place to hide.

Finding nothing in the main mill that appealed to her, Beth approached the rear of the facility. Large, corrugated metal doors were held together by a thick chain mottled with rust. She pushed her head through that gap and peered around. There were half a dozen buildings scattered around the several-acre clearing, all in various stages of decay. She decided on a smaller, two-story building near a fence at the back of the property. The structure was roughly sixty feet long and half as wide. It was close to the woods, so if worse came to worst, she could always flee into the forest and hide there.

There was enough play in the chain holding the metal doors together to allow her to squeeze between them. As soon as she left the main mill, she would be totally exposed and easily viewable from almost anywhere on the property. Beth took a deep breath and started walking. With each step, her pulse ratcheted up, and adrenaline pumped, the pain in her knee waning as the chemical washed through her. Her heart started to thump uncomfortably as she moved out of the shadow of the mill and crossed the broad, flat expanse of gravel-covered earth toward her selected hiding place. Not wanting to be caught out in the open, Beth quickened her pace.

She half ran, half limped around the side of the building and collapsed against the structure's rear wall, her breath coming in short, shallow gasps. Closing her eyes, she forced herself to breathe more deeply and listened for anything unusual. All was quiet. Looking to her left, she spied an air-conditioning unit and sat up a little straighter. The unit seemed oversized for the building it was connected to, taller than Bear and twice as wide. Beth slowly got to her feet. Large, insulated ducting ran from one end of the unit into the back of the building. *Hmm, that might work.* She could just go in the front door of the structure and hide inside, but that seemed too obvious, and the bad guys would expect it. She wanted to be as sure as possible no one would find her unless she wanted them to. She walked up to the unit, unfastened the latches holding the front panel in place, and let the four-by-four-foot piece of sheet metal slide to the ground. Beth stuck her head inside.

There was little inside the shell of the air conditioner aside from clusters of cut wires, tubing, rusting bolt mounts, and metal rails. She wondered if the remaining machines on the property were similarly hollow. Apparently, the mill wasn't as intact as she had first assumed. Beth tossed the canvas bag into the unit, climbed in after it, then lifted the front panel into place and tried to secure it as best she could from the inside.

A grate with a filter covered the mouth of the ducting, and it was secured by four large, rusted screws. She pulled her Swiss Army knife from her pocket and went to work. The tiny blade snapped and sliced her finger. Pain, hot and sharp, triggered a curse that left her mouth on a gasp before she could think to stop it. She went completely still and silent for a moment. All remained quiet, and she took a slow, relieved breath. Her gaze swiveled back to the metal grille.

"Great. Now what?"

She stared at the grate in frustration then looked around the unit. Her eyes fell on the bag. Perhaps there was something inside she could use. After all, Bear seemed prepared for *everything*. Seeing no other options, she opened the tote.

The first thing she saw was the pistol, the dark, brushed metal gleaming softly in the shadowy interior of the unit. There was a yellow sticky note threaded through the trigger guard, and she chuckled. Apparently, Bear not only kept first aid kits, guns, and ammunition in his Escalade, he also kept office supplies. Careful of her now bleeding finger, she removed the note and unrolled it.

The safety is the lever on the left side of the barrel. Flick it down to expose the red dot before you shoot. Red means dead. Don't forget that.

Beth already knew that, Coop had taught her to shoot during the down-time in Afghanistan, but she turned the gun over in her hand and pushed down on the specified lever. As Bear had said, the red dot was revealed, and the gun was ready to fire. All she'd have to do would be point and squeeze the trigger. Something cold and thick started to burrow its way up her throat, and a snapshot of what she'd seen through the scope of Bear's rifle flashed. She flicked the safety back on and quickly dropped the gun into the bag as if it burned her to touch it. The movie version of what had happened earlier started to play, but she did as Bear had taught her. She closed her eyes and clenched her hands, her nails digging into her palms. The reel of film was heavy as she mentally put it in the box, closed the lid, and walked away. Oddly, the door to the projection room seemed very far away and appeared to be moving farther. Her heart jumped. Beth fought the fear and forced herself to breathe as she continued toward that imaginary panel. Without the soothing timbre of Bear's voice coaxing her, it took a little longer to get there, but eventually she closed in and her pulse eased down.

When the door clicked shut, she opened her eyes and took a deep, cleansing breath. Her brow was damp with perspiration. She wiped her forehead and then sifted through the contents of the tote, which included Bear's heavy jacket, the bag of trail mix, several water bottles, and the first aid kit. The kit contained a small pair of scissors, and she slipped them in a pocket, hope burgeoning inside her. They weren't much, but they were better than nothing.

Beth quickly bandaged her finger and kept rummaging. Finally, her hand wrapped around something cold, metal, and heavy, longer than her hand and oddly familiar. She slowly pulled the item from the dark interior of the bag, and when her treasure was revealed, she smiled and sighed.

"Bear, I think I love you."

The Leatherman tool was even handier than her Swiss Army knife, and she almost laughed as she unfolded one of the many utensils it included. It was larger than any Leatherman she'd seen or owned previously, and she guessed it was probably special issue for law enforcement and military personnel. After finding the screwdriver blade, she went to work on the screws and in a matter of minutes the grate was down. Beth pocketed the hardware. Gazing into the dark interior of the three-by-three-foot metal duct, she took a deep breath and exhaled slowly. Cobwebs fluttered like ragged strands of ancient lace.

Y'know, going in the front door seems like a much better idea now.

She stared into the maw of the duct for another moment or two, and then picked up the tote and shoved it inside. She hoped pushing the bag ahead of her would dislodge the cobwebs, spiders, or other creatures lurking in the darkness. She shuddered, climbed into the duct, and popped the grate back into place.

The metal pinged and creaked as she inched along. Crawling on her battered knee made it painful going, but she gritted her teeth and continued. Her eyes soon adjusted to the gloom as thin veins of light found cracks and gaps in the flexible tubing. To her relief, there was nary a spider to be seen. Beth sent a silent prayer heavenward and kept moving.

She stopped a few feet from the outlet vent and rolled onto her back, listening intently. All she could hear was her own breathing and the ticking of her watch. Thoughts started to swirl. Had the men chasing her figured out who she was?

Andrew wasn't expecting her home until tomorrow, but when she didn't show up at the appointed time, he would go looking for her. His first stop would be her apartment. Her heart twisted as she imagined some bloodthirsty killer waiting behind her front door and slitting Andrew's throat as he entered. The pain that ravaged her felt as real as if it had actually happened, but when her pulse started to skyrocket, she reminded herself it was all in her head.

Beth blinked back tears and drew on what Chief Dancing Eagle had taught her, how to be like the animals, how to be quiet and still and become part of the surroundings, how to breathe to bring the heart rate down. It took longer than expected, but finally she managed to rein in her racing thoughts. It helped to think of Bear – the sexy grin, the blue eyes that could pierce or caress depending on his mood – so she pictured him and took deep, even breaths.

"All right, Bear. I'm hidden away from the truck. I just hope you get here before dark."

****

Bear smiled at the cashier and put his credit card back in his wallet. "Thanks, again." He turned to leave the truck stop's garage and nearly bumped into a shorter, uniformed man.

"Ted Bristol?" the man asked.

Bear groaned inwardly when he saw the sheriff's badge and the nameplate that read "Carter" on the man's chest, but he kept his expression neutral. He'd already spoken to a deputy, but thankfully the interview had been short and cursory. This man was close to six feet tall and burly with a barrel chest and broad shoulders, and his expression said he was anything but in a hurry. He wore the stereotypical cowboy hat, had a handlebar moustache, and aviator sunglasses, the mirrored lenses hiding his eyes.

Bear fought the annoyed growl that wanted to break free as he slid his wallet back into his pocket. "Who wants to know?"

"I'm Sheriff Ben Carter. Are you Ted Bristol?"

Bear pasted a bland smile on his face. "Guilty."

"*Special Agent* Ted Bristol?"

The lackluster smile stayed firmly in place. "That's me."

Carter hooked his thumbs in his gun belt, the leather creaked softly. "I was just at the trailhead lot talking with the ranger and my deputy, and I have a few questions to ask you."

I'll bet you do. Bear fought another growl and made sure to keep his expression neutral.

Carter glanced at the cashier who was watching the exchange with unabashed interest, and then he removed his sunglasses and jerked his head toward the exit. "Would you come with me, please?"

Bear nodded. "Sure thing." They walked outside to the police cruiser, and Bear crossed his arms over his chest as he faced the sheriff. "What can I help you with, Sheriff Carter?"

Carter leaned against his car and slid his sunglasses into his breast pocket. "I wanted to talk to you about your little trip into the woods yesterday, ask you what you saw."

"What I saw?" Bear lifted one brow. "Well, I saw trees and I saw the river . . . saw a twelve point buck I'm sure many a hunter would love to get a clean shot at. Saw several helicopters or one helicopter several times. You want to be a little more specific?"

"There was an incident in the park yesterday," Carter replied, his brows drawing down. "Couple of tourists reported being shot at. Did you hear anything or see anything?"

"Oh, I *heard* something, but I didn't *see* anything, and I didn't go looking."

A look of surprise crossed Carter's face. "You're a Federal agent, you heard gunshots, and you didn't make any attempt to find out what was going on?"

Bear hid his irritation. "I've been a Federal agent for almost seventeen years, and I wouldn't have lived this long if I did stupid things like that."

Now Carter looked offended. "Stupid things like *what?*"

"Like looking for trouble and confronting an unknown number of armed individuals without backup." Bear gave Carter a bored look. "I heard several shots from several types of handguns – at least one .40 cal and a .44 magnum if I don't miss my mark. I was alone and armed with a .308 rifle, a .45 caliber pistol, and a Bowie knife. I've been shot several times in the line of duty, Sheriff. I'd prefer *not* to do it while I'm on vacation if I can avoid it."

That seemed to sober the sheriff somewhat, but the set of his posture and the determined gleam in his eye said he wasn't about to relent just yet. "Crime on Federal land falls under the FBI's jurisdiction."

Bear pressed his thumb and forefinger into his eyes for a moment. "Thanks for the heads up. After almost two decades, I think I know my jurisdiction." He sighed. "Look, I hiked into the park, heard the shots, turned around, and made camp just after nightfall. I was back hiking shortly after sunrise and made it to the lot around noon today. What else can I tell you?"

"Why didn't you tell Ranger Miller you were FBI?"

"Because I don't normally go around telling every person I meet what I do for a living."

Carter gave him a long, assessing look and took a piece of gum from his pocket. After unwrapping it, he popped it into his mouth and started to chew. "You afraid he might ask you to do your job?"

An angry wave crashed through him, heating his chest and barreling upward. His fist itched to make contact with the portly sheriff's jaw, and he jerked on his inner reins, but he didn't bother to hide his annoyance any longer. "Of course not, but it wouldn't matter if he did. I took a leave of absence from the Bureau so whatever Fed is assigned this case won't be me. I'm not on the roster." He glared at the man. "I would tell you to call the Denver field office, but I have a feeling you've already done that."

Carter's smile said he had. "Your superiors have nothing but nice things to say about you."

"So why the third degree?"

"Just doing my job."

"Seriously?" Bear frowned. "Your job involves interrogating fellow law enforcement officers? That's new."

"Well, I just find your behavior curious."

"How so?"

"Assault with a deadly weapon on Federal land," Carter drawled, "and you don't seem to care."

Bear growled. "We've been *over* this."

"No need to get defensive."

"I'm going to get *offensive* shortly. If you have an accusation to make, make it."

"No accusation." Carter looked him up and down. "But you seem a mite touchy, if you ask me."

The anger that had surged upward from his midsection started to radiate outward. Heat was usually relaxing, but this warmth made his muscles tighten, and his teeth grind together. "I *didn't* ask you." Bear fixed the sheriff with a fierce stare. "And I'm not *touchy*, I'm *pissed*. Maybe my superiors didn't tell you, but I watched a fellow agent and a close friend get gunned down three weeks ago, and I helped bury him the day before yesterday." He paused and the rising temperature of his blood dropped several degrees, and then began another steady climb as he continued. "I came out here to get away from that shit. I drove four hours, hiked more than five miles, only to be right back in the middle of the same BS. So I hike back, the tires on my SUV are slashed, I find a ranger handcuffed in a ditch, and now *you're* in my face because you find my behavior *curious*." He clenched his fists at his sides and let the growl free. "You think I'm touchy *now* . . . ? Keep pushing, I *dare* you."

"I'm sorry." Carter's expression was solemn. "They didn't tell me about your friend."

"Yeah, well at the FBI we don't usually answer questions without being asked first." He sighed and dropped his chin. "I'm not trying to be evasive, Sheriff Carter, but I don't know how I can help you. I told you what I heard – shots – I told you what I saw, which was *nothing*. I didn't tell Ranger Miller I was FBI because it wouldn't have mattered. Had I volunteered to help, the Bureau would still have sent someone to replace me."

Carter watched him carefully for a moment then pushed away from his car. "Would you mind coming down to the station to make a formal statement?"

"Not at all," Bear lied. "When they finish with my tires, I'll drive on over."

The sheriff extended his hand, and Bear shook it firmly.

"Sorry for being hard on you, Agent Bristol," Carter said with the barest hint of a smile. "I guess I just don't like it when big-city crime spills out into my jurisdiction."

Bear narrowed his eyes on the man. "What makes you think this is big-city crime?"

He crossed his arms as the sheriff hesitated. Carter hooked his thumbs in his gun belt, the toe of one boot tapping rhythmically against the cruiser's tire. Bear tipped his head and waited.

Finally, Carter sighed and pushed his hat back. "Found spent casings in the meadow, .40 and .44 caliber, and 9mm." He looked at Bear out of the corner of his eye and gave him a rueful smile. "You really know your firearms."

"Been doing this a long time."

"Yeah, well, pistols aren't the types of weapons we normally have inside the park. Rifles, yeah, shotguns, sure, but handguns? And taking potshots at people, no less." He gave Bear a wry look. "That's more your style . . . *city* style."

Bear ran a hand over his face. "Unfortunately, they *all* seem to be my style recently. And there are *plenty* of pistols outside the city limits."

Carter nodded. "True, but most of those are owned by law-abiding citizens, not criminals shooting at tourists."

Tourists, Bear thought. *Tourists in leather jackets, dress pants, and*

$400 loafers. Riiiight. "Did the complainants give you a description of the shooter?"

"Female, dark hair, tall, slender." Carter shrugged. "They saw her as she was running away, so they didn't get a good look. The person who attacked Ranger Miller matched the description." The sheriff adjusted his hat again. "He's with a sketch artist now."

"Hmm." Bear lifted one brow. "If *she* had the guns, why was *she* running away? Shouldn't it be the other way around?"

Carter rubbed his chin. "There were three of them, so the report indicated. Maybe she realized she bit off more than she could chew."

"At least three high-powered pistols with more than twenty rounds combined against three guys? I'd take those odds any day." He gave the sheriff a pointed look. "Doesn't make sense, Sheriff. Maybe you should take another look at the complainants."

"Maybe I should." He met Bear's gaze. "In the meantime, I'll stay here until your car is done and escort you to the station. It's a little hard to find if you're unfamiliar with the area."

Bear could tell by the look in the older man's eyes there would be no getting out of this. Frustration burned through him. He didn't want to be here. He wanted to find Beth and get her someplace safe. But, unless he wanted to draw unwanted attention, he'd just have to fill out a statement and do it fast. Bear forced a smile and clapped a hand on Carter's shoulder. "Well, I grew up around here, but thanks for the company. Can I buy you a cup of coffee while we wait?"

Chapter Seven

Beth yawned and rolled onto her side, moving carefully so as not to make any noise. Night was quickly approaching, the light filtering through the cracks growing dimmer as time passed. Her watch read 4:47 p.m., and as the sun seemed to fade, cold uneasiness expanded through her. The darker it became, the harder her heart beat, and she prayed Bear would arrive soon. The last place she wanted to be when the sun disappeared was alone in this deserted facility. It was creepy enough in broad daylight.

Just as she was about to doze off, she heard the familiar sound of a car's engine. She froze, straining to hear, but the sound was muted. Then again, she was at the far edge of the property and noise wouldn't travel that distance clearly. Something both warm and cold blossomed in her chest as the possibilities danced through her brain. The thought of seeing Bear made her want to faint with relief, but she knew it might not be Bear. A substance closely resembling panic climbed into her throat, and for a moment she felt like she was choking. Beth focused on her FBI agent and fought to rein in her galloping pulse.

"The truck is here! Check the buildings!"

It definitely wasn't Bear, and her muscles first spasmed and then froze with fear. Beth closed her eyes and tried to breathe as deeply and evenly as possible. There could be two men, or there could be a hundred, she had no way to know for sure. The best bet was to remain silent, hidden, and still and see what, if anything, she could discern by listening. Her stomach knotted when the thought that Bear might show up now jumped into her head. *Oh, no, no, no.* Her heart raced, pounding against her sternum until it ached. She reached into the bag for the pistol. When her fingers found the cool metal, she took hold of the grip and held the gun to her chest. Strangely enough, the weapon's presence was a comfort.

She heard the bad guys going from building to building, slamming doors, shattering windows, and toppling furniture. Every *crash* made her pulse go faster, and each *bang* made her cringe. The men were shouting at each other in Spanish, and as they drew closer, their anger seemed to escalate. She didn't know how much time had passed before they entered her building, but her heart nearly stopped when she heard them rummaging around inside the two-story structure. Fear ballooned inside her. Tears stung as she carefully flicked the safety off the pistol and tightened her grip. She tried to breathe normally, but her heart was fighting to break through her breastbone and climb out of her chest.

"Any sign of her?"

"No. The engine on the truck was cold, so she's probably long gone. Do you really think she'd hang out when she knows we're looking for her?"

"She killed Mateo and Alvarez! We have to find the bitch!"

"She's not *here!*"

Something smashed loudly against the back wall of the building. The duct vibrated from the force of the impact, and a gasp was forcefully expelled from her lungs. She blinked and felt the tears slide down the side of her face as one of the men let out a long, forceful stream of Spanish. She had studied the language in college, but he was speaking so fast she only caught a few words: *violar, desentrenar, desollar* . . . rape, disembowel, skin. That was enough to make her insides curl up and freeze. When he finished his terrifying tirade, silence fell. Beth held her breath.

"Let's get out of here. Perez is waiting for us."

"*Sonofabitch!*"

A gun went off, and Beth clapped a hand over her mouth, unable to swallow the whimpers of terror caught in her throat. She curled into a ball, trying to make herself as small as possible as more shots, close to a dozen she guessed, ripped through the air like short, abbreviated claps of thunder. When they stopped shooting, they finished taking out their frustration on the hapless building. The walls vibrated as furniture impacted them, the tinkling of glass adding an almost musical note. The violence of their rampage shook everything, even the duct. Beth braced herself against the inside of the tubing and squeezed her eyes shut. Panic burgeoned in a burst of sharp, cold twinges that impaled her insides like invisible shrapnel. Their angry eruption was almost worse than what she'd been through in Afghanistan. At least there she had been surrounded by dozens of Marines, not alone and virtually defenseless.

It seemed like forever before they finished venting their rage on the ill-fated building and left. A preternatural quiet descended, but still she remained silent and immobile. She feared it was just the eye of the hurricane passing, and more violence would be forthcoming. She counted to one hundred, slowly, the silence deafening. Only when her lungs started to burn did she realize she still held her breath. She exhaled in a sharp gasp.

Several minutes passed. Then she heard two engines start, breaking the quiet. Apparently, the shooters were reclaiming their truck. She listened as the vehicles drove away, and the sound of the motors faded. With shaking hands, she reengaged the safety and held the pistol to her chest. Her heart hammered beneath the weapon, the gun visibly moving with each beat. Gradually, silence reclaimed the mill, and her fear deepened. Now if Bear showed up, he might think she'd gotten tired of waiting and left, and *he* might leave. Then she'd really be in trouble. Regardless, she couldn't move. She trembled with fear, her limbs frozen and numb.

Beth remained immobile and silent even as the light faded completely, and darkness claimed the mill. She had stopped caring about the spookiness factor. The duct had proved an effective hiding place, and it was unlikely the thugs would return, which eased her fear just a bit. She'd wait inside her cozy little metal cocoon until morning and then hike out herself if she had to. She shivered and reached into the bag for Bear's jacket. Immediately his scent surrounded her, and she pressed her nose to the fabric. A glance at her watch told her it was after five p.m., and she felt a flutter of worry. She hoped Bear was okay.

Time continued its relentless march, and with each passing minute, her concern for Bear multiplied. Worry no longer fluttered in her chest; now it beat against her heart and lungs with strong, eagle-like wings in a rhythm that had her pulse in a slow but steady climb. When the worry started moving up her throat, she fought to keep it down, her airways constricting. Just as she thought she might choke, the sound of a familiar voice reached her ears.

"Beth! Beth, where are you?"

The words were little more than a hoarse whisper, but she recognized the voice as if it were her own. She gasped, bolted upright, and hit her head on the top of the duct. Pain radiated across her forehead, but she ignored it and quickly scuttled toward the grate, making a lot of noise, but not giving a damn. As she kicked the grate out of the way, the front panel of the air-conditioning unit came off. Bear stuck his head inside, and she launched herself at him, a hushed sob escaping her. She wound her arms around his neck, and he held her tightly, pulling her from inside the unit as if she weighed nothing. Her feet dangled above the ground as tears squeezed out from beneath tightly closed lids.

"It's okay, Beth. I'm here, and you're okay."

"Th-they were h-here." Beth pressed her face into his neck and tightened her hold.

"I know and I'm sorry. I got here shortly after they did. I've been waiting in the woods for them to leave, and I wanted to make sure they were gone." He sighed and cupped the back of her head with one hand. "I wouldn't have let them hurt you, I swear. I'd have killed them first." He chuckled. "Nice hiding place, by the way."

"Were they the same ones?"

"The only one I recognized was shaved head. Looks like your friends called in reinforcements."

She jerked back and glared at him through her tears. "*Stop* calling them my friends."

Bear gave her a look filled with regret and gently pressed her head to his shoulder. "I'm sorry."

Beth nodded against his neck. The steady, even beat of his heart and his whispered reassurances calmed her. Her fear receded like water swirling down a drain as his pulse thrummed against her cheek in a slow, steady rhythm. She took a hitching breath and pulled back to look at him.

"Are *you* okay?" she asked softly. "I was so worried you'd show up when they were here and—"

"I'm *fine*," he interrupted. "And I *did* show up while they were here. I was just cool headed enough not to go barging through the front door and confront them, even though I *really* wanted to."

Beth bit her lip. "Is that supposed to be a jab?"

He chuckled. "No, it was supposed to be a comment on how worried *I* was about *you*."

Beth thought about that for a few moments. "I was . . . I was afraid you'd leave if you got here and the truck was gone."

Bear gently put her back on her feet, but his hands remained clasped behind her back. "Not a chance." A fierce scowl darkened his features. "Not a chance in hell."

"What . . . ?" Her voice died, and she gulped. "What did you do with the bodies?"

A faint smile curved his mouth. "I didn't have to do anything. Your friends—" She frowned, and he chuckled. "I mean the guys in the helicopter came looking and were kind enough to remove their departed compatriots for us."

"Why?"

He pursed his lips and seemed to ponder that for a few moments. "Could be any number of reasons, first and foremost not giving law enforcement a reason to get involved, but it doesn't really matter." His smile widened, and he wiggled his brows. "That's just less explaining on my part. If the bodies were still there, you'd probably have wound up spending the entire night here." His expression sobered. "*Are* you okay?"

Beth searched his eyes and was warmed by the concern she saw there. She nodded. "What took you so long?"

"After I made friends with the ranger, he repaid me by sending the local sheriff my way."

"What?" She blinked at him. "I thought you didn't want to involve the local authorities."

He frowned. "I didn't, but I didn't have much of a choice."

"What did you say to him?"

"I told him I heard the shots but didn't see anything, and he asked me to write out a formal statement. That's why it took me so long to get here. Believe me, if there had been bodies, I'd probably still be at the *lot*. The cops up here still write reports by hand, if you can believe *that* shit."

Beth rested her hands on his chest. "Did he buy it?" He looked away from her, and she saw the tensing of his jaw.

"I don't know, maybe. But I sort of lost my temper with him."

"Why?"

He fixed that blue, pinpoint gaze on her and ran his fingers over her jaw. "Because I was worried about you." He searched her eyes for a moment. "Are you really okay?"

Beth nodded. "I am now."

She slid her arms around his waist and laid her cheek against his chest. He rested his chin on top of her head, his hands moving slowly up and down her back. They stood together for several minutes, silent and unmoving. Beth reveled in the feel of his arms around her. His heartbeat was strong and steady, his embrace like flesh-covered steel that would protect her from anything and everything. She knew with startling clarity that at that moment she was the safest she'd ever been.

"You ready to get out of here?"

His voice was low and velvety, and she almost said no. She would have been content to stand there forever. It took her a moment to gather her wits and finally she nodded. "Absolutely."

He pulled back and locked eyes with her. "It's about a mile back to the SUV. How's your knee holding up?"

Beth smiled. "I'm fine."

He pursed his lips. "Would you tell me if you weren't?"

"No."

He chuckled, shook his head, and released her. "I didn't think so."

The temperature had dropped several degrees, and it took everything she had not to pull him back, to soak up more of his warmth. She *wanted* to be close to him, and that realization shook her. She had always been fiercely independent, but with each smile he drew her closer. He was more than just physically appealing. His blatant masculinity, his strength, his toughness, called to the feminine side of her. It suddenly occurred to her that she was one of those women who would drop their panties for a smile from him.

"I'll go as far as you need me to, Bear," she said, his courage bolstering hers.

"And if you can't, I'll carry you."

She met his gaze, and those piercing eyes froze her like a deer in headlights, her heart fluttering wildly. His expression was thoughtful, assessing, and he tipped his head to the side. As he studied her face, she found breathing difficult and absently wondered how many other women had felt exactly the same way when he turned those eyes on them. Had they met under different circumstances, out of all the women he could no doubt pick from would he have even looked twice at her? Her mind balked at responding, and she knew it was because she was afraid the answer would be *no*.

"You'll tell me if it gets to be too much?" he asked.

Beth's attention snapped back to him, and she nodded. "Yes, I will. Let me get your bag, and we'll head out."

"Yeah." He smiled. "I need that gun back." Bear glanced at the air conditioner. "I'd get it, but I don't think I'd fit."

Beth chuckled and climbed inside the unit. "You *wouldn't* fit."

Less than two minutes later, she was back outside with the bag. Bear shouldered the black canvas duffel and then held out a hand. She slipped her fingers into his and gave him a small smile.

"Onward, fearless leader," Beth said. "I need a shower."

****

Bear scanned the parking lot of the motel as Beth quickly slipped into the room, using his body as cover. His senses were on alert, but he was otherwise relaxed. All seemed quiet. He had specifically requested lodging on the far end of a small roadside inn, well away from the office and prying eyes. The Escalade was backed into the spot directly in front of the door in case they needed a quick getaway. He waited for another moment, eyes alert, but the only sound was the vibrating hum of tires on the nearby highway and the musical trill of crickets. When he was certain they hadn't been followed and weren't being watched, he grabbed his pack and the duffel from the back of the Escalade and entered the room.

The room itself was unremarkable, but at least it was clean and had an ideal location. It was close enough to any services he might need, but isolated enough to ensure relative privacy. He stayed here often and knew the owner, an older woman named Emily Harper. She was a widow in her mid-to-late fifties, with a penchant for younger men, who flirted with him outrageously every time he stopped in. He knew better than to flirt back, or no doubt he'd find himself with an unwanted guest in the dead of night. She'd flat out told him as much. Tonight especially that would *not* be a good thing.

Bear immediately pulled the heavy drapes closed and then dropped the pack and bag on the dresser. Beth eased down into one of the two chairs flanking a small, round table near the front window with a soft groan. She leaned her head back and closed her eyes. Bear knelt in front of her, grabbed her foot, and removed her shoe.

"You don't have to take my shoes off for me," she said with a wry twist of her lips, "but I appreciate the assistance. Thank you."

Bear tossed her a smile and rolled up her pant leg. "You're

welcome." Her knee was turning a lovely shade of purple, and it was quite swollen. Concerned, he frowned and gently probed, but nothing *felt* broken. "Does that hurt?"

She sucked in a breath. "No, not at all."

He looked up at her. "Stop being so stoic."

Her eyes glittered with annoyance, and she leaned back in her chair. "Fine. It hurts."

"You shouldn't have been walking on it." He frowned. "You should've let me carry you."

"Why?" She lifted one arched brow and crossed her arms over her chest. "So you could tell me again how much I enjoy it?" A scowl darkened her features. "*Not* going to happen."

Ah, the independent female and her ruffled feathers. Bear fought a smile, amused by her indignation. "So, it's okay that you enjoy being held by me, it's just not okay for me to point it out?"

She gave him a bored look then tugged her pant leg down and stood. "I'm going to take a shower."

Bear also rose. "No, you're not."

She blinked and gaped at him. "Excuse me?"

"You're not going to shower just yet."

Her hands dropped onto her hips. "Look, you asked me not to call you 'dad' again, but you're acting just like him."

He usually preferred self-reliant women, but at this moment her stubbornness was starting to irritate him. Bear tamped down a spurt of annoyance and ran a hand over his face. "In case you hadn't noticed, this isn't the Ritz-Carlton. No complimentary toiletries and all I have is a bar of soap."

Her expression turned indignant. "I can deal with bar soap. Seriously?"

"Seriously?" he repeated. "And how are you going to comb your hair before you suds it with bar soap? For obvious reasons, I neither need, nor do I carry a brush."

"So I'll use my fingers."

He rubbed his eyes and sighed. "Yeah, *that* will take all night. We *do* need some sleep."

Her cheeks flushed. "Then what would you suggest, Mr. Know-It-All?"

Her expression almost made him chuckle. She obviously didn't like being told what to do, a personality trait he identified with. Bear put his hands on her shoulders and gently pushed her back into the chair despite her attempts to resist. He sat on the edge of the bed facing her, and she glared at him.

He almost told her she was cute when she was flustered, but decided against it. There was no point in advertising the fact that he found her attractive. He understood her frustration. She wanted to be back in control after being so out of control, able only to react to the situation at hand instead of being able to influence or mold it. The image of a day not so long past flashed in his head, a day where he had been twisted up by something he couldn't control. He knew *exactly* how she felt.

"I'd suggest you sit down, put your feet up, and ice that knee. There's a large truck stop down the road a few miles." He rested his elbows on his knees. "I'll grab some supplies, toiletries, and some dinner, and be back here in half an hour, an hour tops." He gave her a small smile. "Does that work for you?"

"Do I have a choice?" she asked. Her expression was a mix of sad resignation and childish petulance, and he swallowed the chuckle that almost escaped.

He decided to give her back some of the control she felt she'd lost. "Yes."

She seemed taken aback by that simple statement. She fixed those golden eyes on him, her mouth opening and closing several times as if she was searching for something to say. After a few moments, she snapped her jaw shut, rolled her eyes, and sighed.

"Works for me."

He'd already anticipated a positive response, but hearing her agree made him smile. "Good." He stood. "Now, I'll go get some ice. *You* stay put and out of sight."

"And where exactly would I go?"

Bear chuckled and pulled his trail mix out of his pack. After emptying it into the plastic liner for the ice bucket, he took the Ziploc bag and walked toward the door. With his hand on the knob, he turned and paused. Beth had taken off her other shoe, and was now resting her feet on the edge of the bed, her gaze shuttered, her brow furrowed. She looked sad, pensive, and he felt an almost overwhelming desire to reassure her. He wanted her to smile again.

"I'll be right back," he said. "Don't go anywhere without me."

She looked at him out of the corner of her eye and pursed her lips.

Bear fought a grin and decided that teasing her was quickly becoming his favorite pastime. However, first and foremost, he had to keep her safe. He glanced at her hiking boots. "Put your shoes and socks under the bed."

Her brows drew together. "Why?"

"So no one sees them. They're definitely not *my* size."

Her eyes widened. "Who would see them but us?"

He shrugged. "You never know."

Beth blinked at him and slowly shook her head. "You *really* need a life *outside* the FBI."

Bear laughed and left the room.

He kept telling himself he didn't like the resilient Miss Drummond, but he knew he was lying. She had trekked through the woods to his Escalade without a word, even though she'd started to flag the last quarter mile or so. He knew she had been tired, frightened, and in pain, but she'd just kept trudging on. When he'd asked her to lie down in the Escalade's back seat, she had done so immediately and without question. But, she wasn't a doormat. He liked the fact that she had enough common sense to quietly obey when necessary, but enough spine to question him when she needed to. She was a participant, not just a follower, and that made her infinitely more appealing. *Damn it.*

The icemaker sat against the outer wall of the separate building that housed the office and Ms. Harper's living quarters. As he approached the noisy, aging machine, he saw Ms. Harper waving at him from behind the front desk. Hoping acknowledgement of her wave would be enough, Bear lifted one hand in return salute and smiled. He groaned inwardly when she left her post and walked to the office door. She stepped outside, leaned against the door jamb, and cocked one rounded hip, her chest thrust forward proudly.

"You settling in okay, Ted? Need anything?"

"No, thank you, ma'am." He opened the icemaker. "Just getting some ice."

"There are buckets in the rooms."

He paused. "I'm making an icepack. Sore shoulder."

Her smile said I'll-be-happy-to-rub-you, w*herever.* He guessed she was trying to look coy, but she just looked desperate, and he almost felt sorry for her. It wasn't that she was unattractive. Bear imagined that in her day she had been a real head-turner. She was still a handsome woman, but she just wasn't his type. *And,* she was almost old enough to be his mother.

"Y'know, before I took over this place, I was a massage therapist," she said, her expression saying much her mouth did not. "Maybe you should let me take a look at it."

Bear forced a smile. "I appreciate that, and thank you, but no. A little cold therapy is all I need, ma'am."

"Why won't you call me Emily?" She tried to appear hurt, but the flirtatious sparkle in her eyes gave her away.

"Because my mama would kill me," Bear replied.

Emily Harper sighed. "And I suppose I'm almost old enough to be your mama."

Inwardly, he winced. "Almost, ma'am, though you do not look it."

She looked at him for a long moment. Bear kept his face expressionless and hoped his apparent lack of interest would send her back inside as he reached for the ice scoop. A few more seconds had passed before she made a disappointed sound.

"You are *such* a handsome devil." She jerked open the screen door, and then paused and looked at him again. "You'll let me know if you need anything, won't you?"

He was quickly tiring of her practiced flirtations, but he ground his teeth together and forced another smile. Being raised by a genuine Southern belle had instilled him with a sense of chivalry he just couldn't fight, at least not unless pushed to the extreme. "I will, ma'am. Thank you. You have a good evening." He gave her a small smile as she devoured him with her eyes one last time before returning to her post behind the desk. Bear chuckled, shook his head slightly, and started scooping ice.

After filling the Ziploc bag, he sealed it and started walking toward the room. His pace was relaxed and unhurried, but his eyes surveyed the area, alert and watching for any movement. Thick woods encroached on the back of the motel and gravel covered the seventy or so feet of "defensible space" regulated by state law. In the darkness, it would be easy to hide amongst the thick pines, maples, and other indigenous trees, but he sensed nothing out of the ordinary for now. After taking a final, lingering look around the modest property, he unlocked the door and entered the room.

Beth was dozing in the chair, her head propped in one hand, her lashes a dark sweep above her cheekbones, and there was no sign of her shoes or socks. Bear smiled and walked over to the vanity to get a hand towel. After wrapping the ice, he moved back to the bed and sat down on the edge next to her feet. Her toenails were painted a pale blue with silver glitter, which told him her friends weren't the only ones getting pedicures. She had a delicate gold ring on her right middle toe. The nail color and the jewelry suited her, and he found he liked them. They showed that not only was she tough, she was also feminine, and something warm invaded his chest cavity. He could easily imagine her running around barefoot in a gauzy skirt and a peasant blouse with a wreath of flowers on her head and blue toenails. It was a nice picture. Hopefully, if he did his job well, he would get the opportunity to see it in real life.

Bear forced himself to focus and gently touched her leg. "Beth."

Her eyelids fluttered open, and she gave him a beautiful, sleepy smile. "Hi. Back so soon?"

He chuckled and gently laid the icepack on her knee. "Haven't left yet. Just got an icepack, remember?"

She rubbed her eyes. "Right."

"So, you'll be okay until I get back, right? I'm the only registered guest, so don't answer the phone or the door, don't make any calls, and stay out of sight." He paused and wondered if he should tell her about Emily Harper. He had a feeling if he didn't, he would regret it, so he went with his gut. "By the way, the motel's owner is a fiery redhead who sort of has a crush on me, and she would *not* be happy if she saw you in my room. Got it?" He felt a little silly for listing the rules for her, but it had become a habit over the last seventeen years. Some people really *did* need to have their hands held, although he was thankful Beth wasn't one of them.

"Yes, *dear*." She smiled and shook her head. "I'm not one of those witnesses like you see in movies. I'm not going to leave the room or call my ex-boyfriend or do anything else to unwittingly expose myself. I promise to stay in this chair with icepack in place until you return."

"Well, you don't have to do *that*." He stood. "But the rest of it sounds good. Any special requests?"

"Chicken fried steak."

Bear laughed. "Okay, but I meant for the shopping list." He rose and watched her as she thought about it.

"Disposable razor," she replied, "and some body lotion, don't care what kind."

"You got it. I'll be back as soon as I can."

He turned toward the door and stopped when she grabbed his hand. Bear looked down at her, but she was studying his fingers intently, as if they were the most fascinating things she'd ever seen. Her expression was solemn, and as the silence stretched out, color brightened her cheeks. He wondered what was going on in her head, but decided to let it play out instead of asking. If she wanted to tell him, she would. If not, he didn't want to put her on the spot.

"Thank you," she finally said in a whisper, "for everything."

"Hey, *you're* the one who saved *my* ass today, remember?" She said nothing. Because she still had hold of him, Bear used his other hand, curled a finger under her chin, and tipped her face up so he could look her in the eyes. "You don't have to thank me, but you're welcome."

A memory of the many times he'd seen his father do this with his mother popped into his head. Every morning before his father went to work, he'd get up from the breakfast table, tip his mother's face to his, and lean in for a kiss. For some reason, Bear felt as if it would be the most natural thing in the world to lean over and kiss Beth. He had a feeling she wouldn't mind. But, as nice as that idea was, he couldn't act on it. He was the professional, after all. He gave her a small smile and let his hand fall.

Her eyelids fluttered slightly, and her color deepened as if she was reading his thoughts. He saw the convulsive swallow before she dropped her gaze to her lap and released his fingers. He felt a wisp of sadness as the moment passed, but part of him was relieved. He wasn't about to go down this road and get involved with a witness. Not again.

"I'll be back ASAP," he said softly.

Beth nodded but kept her eyes downcast. "I'll be right here."

He wished she would look at him, but she didn't, and he finally opened the door and stepped outside. Before closing the thin, pressboard panel, he glanced at her again. Her gaze was still fixed on her lap. That wisp of sadness grew into a sliver as he closed the door behind him.

Beth took a deep, shaky breath when she heard the Escalade roar to life and pull away. She had been almost certain he was going to kiss her, and her heart had leapt with excitement and anticipation. But, as quickly as the feelings had appeared they had vanished, leaving her shaken and disappointed.

"Stop it, Beth," she said to the empty room. "Get a grip."

She leaned her head back and closed her eyes, but Bear's image immediately filled her mind's eye. Her lids snapped open, and she glared at the ceiling.

"I *said* stop. You feel this way because he saved your life. If you got to know him, *outside* of this mess, you probably wouldn't even *like* him."

The words sounded hollow. As she thought about her situation and Bear's part in it, emptiness swirled inside her, and for some reason it made her angry. She sat up a little straighter in her chair and frowned.

"Elizabeth Anne Drummond, knock it off. He's an FBI agent. You're a witness to a crime. That's all it is and all it will ever be. He's just doing his job; he doesn't care about you beyond that." Her anger receded, and a veil of sadness draped itself around her shoulders, dark, heavy, and damp. Deflated, she stared morosely at the icepack. "Besides, he's too tall. You'd break your neck just trying to kiss him."

Frustrated, she put the icepack on the table, rose, and limped to the bathroom. After relieving herself, she washed her hands, splashed her face with cold water, rinsed her mouth, and then stared at her reflection. Bear was right. Her hair was a mess. Most of it had come loose from her braid and lay tangled about her head and shoulders.

"Is he *ever* wrong?"

Beth grabbed a towel and dried her face as she walked back to the window. Careful not to move the curtain she peered through the inch-wide space between the drape and the wall. It was dark so she couldn't see much aside from the motel sign and the building marked "Office."

She was just about to return to her seat when movement in her periphery froze her. A lone figure was walking across the parking lot toward their room, but in the dim light she couldn't tell if it was a man or a woman. A finger of worry trailed slowly up her spine. If they were the motel's only guests, where had this person come from? As he or she got closer, Beth realized it had to be a woman, and she felt a faint, warm surge of relief. Her relief lasted all of two seconds. The woman passed beneath an overhead light, and her flaming red hair glowed. Bear had joked that the motel's owner had a crush on him, and again he hadn't been wrong. Fear started to balloon as she realized the redhead was headed to their room. And she no doubt had a master key.

"Oh, crap."

Beth retreated to the bathroom as quickly as her knee would allow. No sooner had she closed the lavatory door than she heard a key in the lock. She pressed herself against the door and held her breath. Apparently the woman's crush went a little deeper than even Bear knew, and a shiver of dread chilled her. Beth looked at the ceiling, her pulse at a near gallop.

And just when I thought things couldn't get any worse....

Chapter Eight

Beth's heart raced as she listened to the woman rummage through Bear's things. She gasped when she realized the pistol was still in the bag. *Damn it.*

She moved away from the door and opened it just a hair. Pressing her eye to the narrow crack, she watched as the woman went through Bear's pack. In one of the outside pockets she found what looked like a wallet, only thinner. The redhead opened it and gasped softly.

Beth saw the flash of light on metal and realized it was probably Bear's badge. The woman ran a finger slowly over the emblem.

"FBI? Why, Ted, you sly dog. I *knew* there was a reason I liked you."

The motel owner held the badge to her chest for a moment and closed her eyes with a sigh. After about a minute of silent reflection, she put the badge back in its pocket and opened the main compartment. Less than ten seconds passed before she pulled out a folded flannel shirt. She held it between her hands for a moment and then pressed her nose to the fabric. She inhaled deeply before she unfurled the garment and held it up against herself. The woman ran her hands over the material in slow, loving strokes, and the look of rapture on her face made Beth shudder. After a few more moments of what Beth considered highly inappropriate touching of a shirt, the woman refolded the garment and laid it on the bed. Then she unzipped the black tote bag. Beth's stomach lurched when the woman's eyes widened.

"Well, well, what have we here?" the redhead asked.

The woman lifted the pistol out of the bag with both hands, as if it was a sacrifice to be offered to the weapons gods. She turned the gun over, wrapped her fingers around the grip, and pointed it at the mirror hanging over the dresser. A laugh escaped her as she pretended to shoot her reflection. After a few minutes of playing "Charlie's Angels," she caressed the barrel of the .45 before putting it on the dresser next to the tote. Beth bit her lip and tried to regulate her breathing.

Red seemed disappointed with the rest of the bag's contents, frowning as she straightened and picked up the pistol once more. Her expression turned pensive as she stared at the black metal and then, with great reverence, she returned the .45 to its former place and zipped the bag. She turned to survey the room.

"Now, what else do you have in here?"

Beth's pulse skyrocketed when the redhead's eyes turned toward the bathroom. Thankfully, Beth wasn't as left-footed as the previous day and was able to retreat to the shower without a sound. Images of the motel owner entering the bathroom and sweeping back the shower curtain made her gut clench, so Beth backed into the far corner and pulled the shower curtain back slowly until it was almost completely open. If the woman just glanced in the lavatory, Beth would remain unseen. If Red chose to closely inspect the tiny room, it would be another story.

Beth held her breath and tried to remain absolutely still as the light flicked on, and the door softly creaked open. About five or so nerve-racking seconds passed, then the light flicked off, and darkness engulfed her as the woman pulled the door shut. Beth counted to thirty before she exhaled.

Thank you, thank you, thank you. Hurry back, Bear. Please hurry back.

****

Bear had two large, plastic bags in each hand. The aroma of chicken-fried steak and biscuits wafted up to him. He put the bags on the hood of the Escalade, retrieved his keys and opened the door. The sound of a car pulling into the vacant spot next to him made him glance over his shoulder. The patrol car parked and the engine died. He frowned. Bear closed the driver's door and leaned against it.

"Evening, sheriff," he said as the man got out and put on his hat. "I would ask you what brings you out this way, but I think I know the answer to that question."

Carter chuckled and hooked his thumbs in his belt as he walked around his car. He glanced at the plastic bags and lifted one bushy brow. "Shopping, Special Agent Bristol?"

Bear gave him a bored look.

"Mind if I take a look?"

Bear crossed his arms over his chest. "Be my guest." A flicker of uneasiness went through him. Most of the items he'd purchased were purposely asexual. The perfumed bath set he could explain easily enough, however, the hair-styling tools he'd rolled up in a pair of sweat pants would definitely rouse Carter's suspicions if the sheriff found them. Bear's synapses started firing as he anticipated the questions he knew would be forthcoming should that happen.

"Thank you." The sheriff picked up each bag in turn and glanced at the contents, putting it back when he was satisfied. When he looked inside the next to the last bag, he paused and his brows rose. Reaching into the white plastic, he pulled out a rectangular box with metallic flowers and leaves embossed on it. "Grandma Rose's Organic Bath and Body Collection . . . with jojoba, rose oil, and essence of lemongrass." He looked at Bear from beneath bushy eyebrows. "Funny, but I pictured you as more of an 'Old Spice' kind of man."

Bear pinched the bridge of his nose. "Actually, soap and deodorant are as fancy as I get."

"So you're buying girly bath products for—?"

"A friend," Bear replied, maintaining a tight hold on his temper. "It's a gift."

"A gift for who?"

Bear frowned. "A gift for *whom,* and *that* is none of your business." He returned the older man's pointed look in kind, more than willing to meet the sheriff's unspoken challenge. "You stop by for a cup of coffee, Sheriff Carter, or are you following me?"

The sheriff put the bag back. "No, no, not following you, Special Agent Bristol. I was just driving by and saw you leaving. Thought I'd stop and give you this." He reached into a pocket and pulled out a folded piece of paper. "Sketch artist finished up about an hour ago."

Bear took the paper, unfolded it, and looked at the drawing, making sure to keep his expression impassive. It was a relatively good likeness of Beth, but the eyes weren't quite right. And she was much prettier than the artist's rendering. He glanced at the sheriff. "Mind if I keep this?"

"Not at all."

Bear watched the man's face carefully as he folded the paper and put it into his pocket. "Is this the *only* reason you stopped?"

A you-should've-seen-this-coming smile curved the older man's mouth. "Well, I thought since I was here, I'd ask if perhaps you'd remembered something else."

Bear rolled his eyes and choked back a growl of irritation. "And here we go."

"Now I'm sorry, but I just think it's strange."

Bear leaned a shoulder against the SUV and faced the sheriff. "What's strange?"

"I think it's strange you didn't run into my suspect." Carter pushed his hat back on his head and looked up at him. "The ranger says you showed up roughly half an hour after she attacked him. How is it two people using the same trails leading to the same trailhead didn't at least *glimpse* one another?"

Bear smiled, barely able to keep the condescension out of it. "I don't know, sheriff. How is it dozens of search-and-rescue volunteers with bloodhounds, helicopters, and infrared can't find one missing hiker?" When he saw the sheriff's frown, his smile widened. "I've been on SAR missions in these mountains before, so I don't find it at all odd that two lone individuals with dozens of trails to choose from, in thousands of acres of heavily wooded forest didn't see each other. What *I* find odd is that *you* do." Bear narrowed his eyes on the man. "So what's really going on? What is it you're not telling me?"

The sheriff stared at him belligerently for a moment, and then sighed and dropped his chin to his chest. "Well, I shouldn't say anything about an ongoing investigation, but no doubt you'll get the info from your fellow agent as soon as he gets here."

"Who are they sending?"

"Special Agent Fellowes. Know him?"

Bear nodded. "Yeah. He's good, and he has a great team behind him. His top techs, Vargas and Paulson, are first rate." He waited a moment. "What is it I'm going to eventually find out from Fellowes?"

"We found more than casings in the meadow."

"Drake's Meadow?"

"Yep."

Bear knew the sheriff expected him to be curious, even if it was only a professional interest, so he put on the appropriate expression. "Okay. What else?"

"Blood." The sheriff took his hat off and ran a hand over his thinning hair. "Several pools actually. It's too much blood for anyone to have gotten up and walked away, and then there's the brain matter."

Bear pretended to be surprised, but inside he was dying to hit something. This was getting more and more complicated. Damn it. He had hoped to have a little extra time to get a handle on the situation before more officers and agencies got pulled in, but apparently life had other ideas. "So," he began, "what started out as assault with a deadly weapon has turned into a probable homicide investigation?" Carter nodded, and Bear rubbed his chin. "Find any bodies?"

Carter shook his head. "Not yet. Crews have been searching the meadow and the surrounding woods. They'll pick up the search again at first light."

Bear quirked one brow. "Using your logic at least one of them should have *glimpsed* a corpse by now."

Carter gave him a sour look and tossed his hat onto the roof of his car. "Can we call a truce, Special Agent Bristol? We *are* supposed to be on the same side."

"I know that. I was beginning to wonder if *you* did."

"I don't want to fight with you."

Bear's brows drew together. "This is a fight *you* picked, sheriff. *I* was minding my business."

"I know." The sheriff looked at the ground for a moment, then met Bear's gaze. "I know and I'm sorry. I guess I get a little touchy with outsiders sometimes."

"Really?" Bear pressed his lips into a thin line. "I couldn't tell."

Carter ignored the remark. "Your superiors say you're one of their best agents." He paused, his expression uncertain. "I'm asking for your help."

"I'm not assigned to this case."

Carter glared at him. "Then give me your *opinion*."

Bear studied the shorter man for a few moments. "All right. Was the blood fresh or dry?"

"Mostly dry. Given the temperature and humidity, my investigator estimates the blood was on the ground roughly eighteen hours, but he'll know more once he finishes his tests."

"When did you find it?"

"Just before 9 a.m."

"Well, eighteen hours would be around 3 p.m. yesterday." Bear rubbed his chin. "What time did your complainants report being shot at?"

The sheriff pulled a notebook out of his breast pocket and flipped through the pages. "Between 2:30 and 3:00 p.m, in Drake's Meadow."

"You still like the woman for this?"

"Until someone convinces me otherwise. Witnesses put at least one gun in her hand."

Bear stared over the top of the man's head at the neon on the truck stop. "Okay, try this on for size. They say she shot at them in Drake's Meadow between 2:30 and 3:00 p.m. Your investigator says the blood is eighteen or so hours old. If your man is right, that would put the victims in the meadow around the same time our female shooter killed someone."

"That's right."

"So," Bear continued, "did they report hearing any shots *before* she started firing at them?"

Carter stood up a little straighter and went through his notes. "No."

"And after she shot at them, between 2:30 and 3:00, she ran away. The *armed* woman who possibly killed someone just turned and ran."

Carter's expression hardened just a bit. "That's what they claim."

"Then where are the bodies?" Bear gave the man a pointed look. "If this woman *did* shoot someone, and the timeline matches up, she wouldn't have had time to hide them." Bear stuffed his hands in his pockets and rocked back on his heels, studying the older man's face. He didn't have to wait long for the realization to register. When it did, he wanted to gloat, but he kept his expression neutral. "I think you need to talk to your alleged victims again."

Carter rubbed his brow. "That was my inclination, too."

The hairs on the back of his neck prickled and Bear pounced. "But?"

"I asked my deputy to contact them and arrange a meeting so I could ask them a few more questions."

"And?"

Carter grabbed his hat from the roof of the car and put it back on. "I just got a call back about ten minutes ago. The names and contact information they gave us were false."

"Big surprise."

Carter pinched the bridge of his nose and made an exasperated sound. "Look, Special Agent Bristol, this isn't the sort of stuff we're accustomed to dealing with up here." He sighed and jerked his hat off again. "We handle drunk drivers, barroom brawls, shoplifting, some minor drug possession, domestic violence, and speeders. This crap? This is a little out of our league."

Bear wanted to tell the sheriff it was actually *waaaay* out of his league, but instead he just nodded. "Then let us handle it. This crap is right up our alley."

Carter appeared not to have heard him. "This kind of thing just doesn't happen up here."

"Didn't used to." Bear sighed. He sympathized with the man's dilemma. Times were definitely changing. "But I know DEA and local LEOs were up here last summer raiding illegal pot grows, and they're gearing up for next summer's raids. The cartels are pushing hard up here, especially now that marijuana is legal. In addition to the illegal grows on Federal land, now the cartels can steal from the dispensaries, too. Like it or not, big city crime is here."

"It's a shame." The sheriff looked at him speculatively for a moment and nodded. "I'm almost sorry you won't be working with us on this, Special Agent Bristol." A small smile curved his mouth. "I think I'm starting to like you."

"That'll pass." Bear gave him a wry grin. "Fellowes is much more personable."

"Well, personable is good, but sharp is better." Carter narrowed his eyes. "*You* are sharp."

"Thank you, but Fellowes is sharp, too, or he wouldn't be where he is. I think he's after my job, actually. And, he's not as *touchy* as I am."

Carter chuckled. "Good to know." He extended his hand, and they shook. "I appreciate your insights and your patience."

Bear smiled. "I was about to say 'anytime' but I think I'll refrain."

A grin lit the man's face. "Alright, Special Agent Bristol. I'll let you alone then." He walked around to the driver's side of the patrol car. "Still like to find that woman, though. If she's not the shooter, she could be a witness."

Bear pretended to think about it for a second. "That seems more likely."

"Yes, it does. I'll run it by Special Agent Fellows when I meet with him in the morning, see if he agrees with you."

"Oh, when you talk to Fellowes . . . why don't you leave me out of it? This *is* his investigation."

Carter gave him a knowing look. "Don't want to step on anyone's toes, eh?"

"Serves me better not to. The man has been looking for a reason to get me in trouble, and I'd rather not help in his quest."

Carter nodded. "No problem. You have a good rest of your night."

Bear lifted one hand. "You, too, sheriff. Good luck."

The sheriff nodded, got in his cruiser, and drove away. Bear watched the taillights until they disappeared, picked up the bags from the hood, loaded them into the car, and slipped into the driver's seat. He sat there for a moment, staring in the direction the sheriff had gone. He replayed the conversation with the Sheriff and was pretty sure he'd convinced the man Beth wasn't a killer or a crazy woman with a gun, but only time would tell. With a rueful shake of his head, Bear started the Escalade and drove back to the motel.

As before, he backed into the spot in front of the room, shut off the engine and got out of the vehicle. To his surprise, he found himself looking forward to the rest of the evening, though he had little planned other than food, a shower, and sleep. As he grabbed the bags from the back seat, he wondered absently if Beth was still sitting in the chair with the icepack on her knee. He opened the door to the room and stepped inside.

He immediately noticed Beth was *not* in the chair. The icepack lay on the table mostly melted. A sliver of apprehension wormed its way up his spine as he dropped the bags onto the bed.

"Beth?" The bathroom door opened a crack, and he walked toward it.

Beth left the bathroom and met him halfway, her golden eyes dark with worry and her posture tense. A sense of foreboding tickled up his spine.

"I think we may have a problem."

His abdominals tightened, and he lightly grasped her arms. "What happened?"

"Well," she began, in a low voice, "you were right when you said the redhead has a crush on you."

He frowned at her, a flash of uneasiness chilling him. "What do you mean?"

"She came into the room while you were gone and went through your things." Beth looked up at him, and her brows drew together. "And she knows you're an FBI agent."

"Damn it, my badge." Bear closed his eyes briefly and choked down the growl of frustration. "Did she see you?"

Beth shook her head. "I hid in the bathroom. She turned on the light and stuck her head in the door for a few seconds, and that was it." She gave him a pointed look. "I have a feeling if she had found a *woman* in your room, you and I would *not* be having this conversation."

He stood and ran a hand over his face. This was all he needed. Aggravation simmered and bubbled, heating his chest cavity in red, angry waves. "Maybe I should've flirted with her. Playing cool obviously isn't working."

"I wouldn't do *that*." She almost sounded amused, and he watched her as she went back to the chair, sat down, and put the mostly melted icepack on her knee. She had looked at him for several seconds before a wry smile curved her mouth. "I'd think you'd be used to this by now."

He frowned. "Used to what?"

Her brows rose. "Women falling all over themselves to get to you."

His frustration shifted from Emily Harper to Beth. *Oh, yeah, and a badge bunny is just the sort you take home to mom.* "And why would I be used to *that?*"

Her eyes widened. "Are you serious, or are you fishing for a compliment?"

She'd lost him, and he didn't try to hide his incredulity. "Are *you* serious?"

"C'mon, Bear." She looked at him as if he'd sprouted a third arm. "Women must *throw* themselves at you. I mean . . . *look* at you." She moved her arm up and down, gesturing to all of him.

He crossed his arms over his chest. He realized she was paying him a compliment, sort of, but nevertheless a spark of irritation warmed him. It was true he received more than his share of female attention, but the shallow interest in his physical appearance and the "glamour" of his job had long ago worn thin. He often wondered if he'd ever find a woman who had the spine to stick it out when things weren't unicorns and rainbows. His job required him to stay fit, and he enjoyed working out, but it had been years since attracting a woman had figured into his efforts. He wanted someone to like him for who he was and not what he did or looked like. *Wow, I must be getting old.*

"Do you really picture me as the type who spends a lot of time in front of a mirror? I have more important things to do." He walked over to where she sat and looked down at her. "Most people don't approach me at *all*. I tend to intimidate them, and that doesn't usually lead to *anyone* throwing themselves at me."

She craned her neck to look up at him, her eyes huge in her face. Her fingers tugged at the snap on one of the pockets on her cargo pants, and she licked her lips. "I guess I can understand that," she said after a brief, taut silence. She focused on the worn carpeting, shifting in her seat as if uncomfortable. "I suppose if I hadn't met you the way I did, you'd intimidate me, too."

Bear looked at her bowed head for a moment, mildly perplexed, and then eased down onto the edge of the mattress facing her. "I wouldn't think much intimidates you." When she glanced at him, he decided to let her off the hook and smiled. "There aren't many women I know who spend days alone in the woods chasing and photographing animals that can eat them."

She gave him an *aw-shucks* smile and shrugged. "Yeah, well animals don't have ulterior motives. *Them* I understand. People? Now *that's* another matter."

He leaned forward and covered her hand with his. "I don't have ulterior motives where you're concerned."

Beth looked at him. He saw the disappointment in her eyes, even if it was fleeting, and his heart did an uncharacteristic spin. Her expression turned pensive, and she wound her fingers through his.

"I know, Bear. I know you don't." It was his turn for disappointment, but he made sure to keep it hidden. Now was *not* the time or place. She stared at him for another couple of seconds and then looked toward the plastic bags. "Do I smell food?"

Thankful for the reprieve, he smiled and grabbed the bag with the take-out containers inside. "You do. One chicken-fried steak with biscuits, mashed potatoes, green beans, and peach cobbler." He handed her one of the Styrofoam boxes and took the other.

Beth opened the box, held it beneath her nose, closed her eyes, and inhaled deeply. "Bear Bristol, I think I love you."

Bear almost dropped his dinner, but somehow he managed not to. Thankfully, she hadn't seen his bobble. When she was done inhaling the fragrance of the food, she put the box on the table and looked at him.

"Cutlery?"

"Oh, yeah." He reached into the bag and retrieved the plastic dinnerware the waitress had included. "Here you go."

"Thank you, sir. You are a god among men."

The compliment caught him momentarily off-guard. Bear looked askance at her as she attacked her food, and he chuckled when she closed her eyes and said, "Mmm, mmmm!"

"I take it you approve?"

She looked at him out of the corner of her eye. "Can we have this for breakfast tomorrow? After all, I do believe you promised me chicken-fried steak every day for a month."

He unwrapped his utensils and opened his take-out box. "I said *after* we get out of this situation. We're not out of it yet."

Beth scooped a large mouthful of steak into her mouth. "Right now I don't care. At this moment, all I care about is this amazing meal." She gave him a sidelong glance. "Next time I'm buying."

"And how exactly would you do that?" he asked, teasing. "If I remember correctly you left all your stuff in a hunting blind."

Her fork froze in mid-air. She blinked a couple of times then turned her head to look at him. "Oh, crap," she whispered. The color drained from her face.

Bear sat straight up, concerned. "What?"

"If they find that hunting blind . . . my ID . . . my name and address . . . ." Her eyes widened, and he saw the fear reflected so clearly in those golden depths. He wanted to kick himself for opening his mouth, but there was little he could do about it now. Her eyelids fluttered. "They'll know who I am . . . where I live."

He'd already considered that possibility. Bear put his food aside, took her food and put it aside, and then took her hands in his. "It doesn't matter. It just means you can't go home right away, that's *all.*" He squeezed her fingers and wiggled his eyebrows at her. "I wasn't planning to take you home just yet anyway."

She closed her eyes. He saw the convulsive swallow and wondered if all that had happened was finally catching up to her. *Don't panic on me now. I need you to keep it together.*

A rush of protectiveness roared through him, and he was helpless to stop it. This wasn't the first time he'd had to babysit a witness or keep someone safe, but what he felt was morphing into something he couldn't allow. Despite his best efforts to the contrary, the situation was becoming personal.

"Beth, look at me, please." Her eyes remained closed, and he put a hand behind her neck. He clenched his teeth and turned the request into a demand. "*Look* at me."

Beth inhaled sharply and did as he commanded.

"I *will not* let them hurt you, do you understand me?" His thumb stroked the line of her jaw. "As long as I am breathing, *nothing* will hurt you."

She blinked rapidly, and her chin trembled. "Don't talk like that," she whispered. Her gaze wandered over his face, and she pressed a hand to his cheek. "I don't know what I'd do if anything happened to you."

Eyes boring into hers, he leaned toward her until their foreheads nearly touched. "We are going to get out of this," he said in a low, vehement voice. "*Both* of us."

"Do you really believe that?"

"Absolutely."

She didn't appear convinced. His gaze drifted to her mouth, and the desire to comfort her almost had him tipping his head to seal his mouth to hers. But, no matter how much he wanted to, no matter how right it felt, Bear wasn't about to cross that line. Their eyes met, and he read the desire in those golden pools. He felt himself waver slightly when she licked her lips. Taking a deep breath, he steeled himself, forcing his libido back into its cage. Needing the distance, he released her, stood, and gave her a slight smile.

"Finish eating, Beth. I'll go grab us a couple of Cokes from the machine."

Chapter Nine

Beth stared at the closed door for nearly a minute, her heart pinging around the inside of her chest. For the second time in as many hours, she had been almost certain he would kiss her, but again it hadn't happened. A flash of heated frustration warmed her midsection at the same time a sobering chill of disappointment swirled in her belly. The contradictory sensations were separate and distinct at first, and then they expanded and blended. Her stomach cramped. She sucked in a breath and held it for a moment before she exhaled slowly and leaned back in her chair.

"What is wrong with you?" she asked aloud.

"Talking to yourself?"

Beth jumped and turned toward the sound of his voice. When she saw Bear standing in the doorway with two soda cans held easily in one hand, heat surged into her cheeks. "I'm going to put a bell around your neck," she said in a breathless rush. She grabbed her food and picked up her fork. "And yeah, I talk to myself sometimes." One shoulder lifted in a shrug, and she focused on her food.

Bear put one can down on the table then sat down on the bed facing her. "As long as you don't start answering yourself, you'll be okay."

"Then I'm sunk." She stabbed a piece of chicken fried steak and glanced at him. "I already do that."

A chuckle escaped him. "Then we're both sunk because I do it, too."

That killer grin flashed, and she frowned inwardly at the inappropriate surge of attraction. *Not the time or place, Beth. Keep it together.* "At least I'm not the only crazy one."

He looked at her, smiled, and gave her a wink. "*That's* for sure."

And just like that, the tension that hung heavy around her neck vanished. They finished their meal in silence. When she was filled to the gills, she tossed her fork and napkin into the Styrofoam container.

"Okay, now I'm ready for a bath and some sleep." She glanced at the clock and her eyes widened. "Holy cow, it's after nine o'clock."

Bear gathered the trash and put it in the can by the dresser. Then he grabbed two of the plastic bags from the bed, briefly examined the contents, and handed them to her. "There you go. Mind if I hop in first? It'll only take me about five minutes, and then I can do some laundry while you soak."

Beth gaped at him. "You do laundry?"

"Yeah," he replied with a chuckle and a wiggle of his eyebrows, "unless you want to get all nice and clean and put back on the same clothes you've been wearing for three days."

She grimaced. "Right. Good idea." She looked into the bag and pulled out a rectangular box. After reading the embossed label, a tiny sliver of uncertainty wormed up her back. "Um, Bear?"

He was rooting around in his pack. "Yeah, what?"

"Are you married?"

He continued to search. "No."

Beth heaved an inward sigh of relief. "Girlfriend, fiancé?"

He stopped what he was doing and looked over his shoulder at her. "No and no. Why?"

She stared at the box for a moment then asked, "Are you gay?"

He faced her and crossed his arms over his chest, looking at her as if she'd just asked to have his baby.

She blushed and dropped her gaze. "You're better at picking out toiletries than my girlfriends." She glanced into the bags again. "Grandma Rose's bath collection, razor, shaving cream, facial cleanser, facial moisturizer with SPF 30, toothbrush, toothpaste, floss, unscented antiperspirant." She paused and looked at him. "Did you forget anything?"

He lifted one blonde brow. "You tell me."

She held up the box. "This is pretty high end stuff."

Bear shrugged and turned back to his bag. "My best friend's wife uses it. I saw it and made an impulse buy."

Beth opened the box and removed a bottle of shampoo. She opened it and inhaled the delicate floral and citrus scent. "Excellent impulse. This stuff smells good enough to eat."

"You didn't get enough dinner?" he asked. He pulled a Ziploc bag containing sunscreen, insect repellant, a bar of soap, toothpaste and a toothbrush, and deodorant out of his pack. "I can go get you some more if you're still hungry."

"No, that won't be necessary." She put her items on the table. "I am full. And thank you for all this." She started rummaging through the bags again. "Did you forget the hairbrush?"

"Ah." Bear reached for the last remaining bag and turned it upside down. A pair of rolled up men's sweatpants, a plain white t-shirt, and a pair of flip-flops dropped onto the bed. He unrolled the sweatpants and a brush, a pick, and a wide-tooth comb fell out.

A self-satisfied smile curved his mouth. "No, I did not." He picked them up and held them out to her. "The sandals are yours, too. Didn't think you'd want to go walking around barefoot, no matter how clean the carpet looks."

Beth took the styling tools. "Dare I ask why you rolled them up in the sweatpants?"

He tossed the sandals to her and shrugged as he grabbed the sweats and t-shirt and walked toward the bathroom. "Didn't want anyone else to see them. Toiletries I can explain." He paused in the bathroom doorway and looked at her as he ran a hand over his high-and-tight. "A brush and a comb? Not so much."

Beth put the brush and combs in one of the bags and slipped into the flip-flops. They were far too large, probably Bear's size, but they'd suffice. "Who else but the clerk would see them?"

"The sheriff."

Her head snapped up, and she stared at him, her heart vaulting into her throat. "What?"

Bear sighed and put his items on the counter by the sink. He turned slowly toward her and leaned against the vanity, crossing his arms. "I ran into Sheriff Carter at the truck stop."

"What did *he* want?"

He straightened and walked toward her, reaching into his pocket as he eased down on the edge of the bed. "Said he saw me leaving and wanted to ask me a few more questions." He held out a folded piece of paper. "I was going to show you this later, but this is as good a time as any."

Beth looked at him for a moment, her stomach knotting, took the paper from him and unfolded it. When she looked at the image, she sucked in a breath and the room dipped slightly. The eyes weren't quite right, at least *she* didn't think so, but it looked enough like her to get the job done. "Oh, crap."

"Now that they know what you look like, it's only a matter of time before they find out who you are, if they haven't found the hunting blind already." He rested his elbows on his knees. "Depending on how widely law enforcement disseminated this, they might already know."

A hollow ache bloomed inside her. If the good guys knew who she was, and one of the good guys was a bad guy, then the bad guys knew who she was, too. Her life and her friends' lives flashed before her eyes. Beth refolded the paper and handed it back to him, fighting to swallow the amphibian lodged in her throat. When the frog finally went down, she met his laser-like gaze and tried to hide her feelings. "There's nothing we can do about it, is there?"

His expression was neutral, his eyes narrowed just slightly, his voice low and calm. "No."

Needing a distraction, she picked up the can of Coke, opened it, and took a swig. "Then I just stay out of sight until we get this all figured out, right?"

He nodded. "Right."

She took another drink and looked at him. Inside she was falling apart, but she didn't want him to see that. She felt like shattered safety glass: brittle, fragile, and cracked, held together by only the thinnest protective film. That film was quickly reaching its limit, and she could almost hear the snapping as pieces slipped and fell away. Thus far, she'd held her own, but she didn't know how much longer she could keep it up. Her mind whirled with fearful possibilities. If they knew who she was, they would very quickly know who and where her friends and family were. Guilt choked her as she thought of the position she had put everyone she loved in, and all for the sake of a few photographs. Suddenly, she needed to be alone. "Well, go on. Get your shower, because once I get in there you may not see me again until midnight."

He studied her face and she did her best to keep her expression neutral, even as the world seemed up to open up beneath her feet. She doubted she'd fooled him. He seemed to have the ability to read her like a book, but the last thing she wanted was his sympathy. A flash of regret darkened his gaze for a split-second, and then his voice broke into her thoughts.

"Do *not* stress about this," he said softly. "They may have your likeness, they may even have your name and address, but they don't have *you*. They don't know where you are, and they're *not* going to find out." He laced his fingers through hers. "Trust me, Beth."

She studied the sharp planes and angles of his face and had a sudden desire to photograph him. He would be especially stunning in black and white. She could picture it: dark background, angled lighting, water beaded on his skin . . . *yum*. Beth squeezed his hands and was amazed that his slightest touch calmed her. Only a moment ago, she had been close to drowning in fear, and now she wanted to take his picture. Unbidden, she smiled. "I *do* trust you, Bear, with my life."

His expression was pensive, and he reached out to tuck a strand of hair behind her ear. "I promise you that trust is not misplaced." He lifted her hands and pressed a brief kiss to her fingers, and electricity pulsed up her arm. "You're safe with me." He dragged his knuckles over her cheek, his touch like gossamer, and then he rose and walked toward the vanity. He picked up his toiletries and clothes, and gave her a smile before entering the bathroom and closing the door.

When the water came on, she allowed herself to imagine her hands running over his skin where water now sluiced. She hadn't seen him without clothing, but she had a *very* good imagination, and she'd felt the hardness of his chest and abdomen when he'd held her. It hadn't felt as if he had an ounce of fat on him. She could picture the rounded pectorals and bit her lip. Would he have a six-pack, or an eight-pack? Her money was on the latter, and she gulped. His back was broad, and she wanted to run her fingers over that vast expanse, drag her nails over his skin. And then there was his ass, that tight, round ass she'd had the pleasure of staring at the night before, and earlier today. Beth groaned as heat roiled low in her belly.

"For goodness sake, Beth! Get a *grip!*"

A couple minutes later, the water shut off. Beth took the now completely melted icepack and walked to the vanity where she put the Ziploc bag in the sink. Her knee actually felt better, even though the bruise continued to darken. A moment later he opened the door. His brows rose when he saw her standing there.

"A little anxious are we?"

She shook her head, gulped, and tried not to stare. The t-shirt stretched over his chest, drawing her eyes to the hard, chiseled planes. *Wow, an eight-pack it is.* Biceps bulged, pulling her gaze upward to shoulders that were broad and densely muscled. The fit of the shirt made him look even bigger than he had before, and her breathing hitched. Beth forced her eyes away, walked back to the table, and grabbed her bags.

"Just getting rid of the icepack." She glanced at him, careful to look only at his face. "My turn?"

He finished toweling his head. "Absolutely. Just leave your clothes on the floor. I'll get them once you're behind the curtain." He wiggled his eyebrows at her and gave her a boyish grin. "Not as much fun as *before* you're behind the curtain, but it'll have to do."

Heat surged into her cheeks. She toyed with the idea of turning the water on and standing naked outside the shower until he came in to retrieve her clothes. Would he be so hard to read then? She thought about it for a second and realized the answer was . . . probably. A chuckle escaped her, and she shook her head.

"What's so funny?" he asked.

She bit back a sigh. "Nothing." She approached him. "Out of the way. And *don't* come looking for me before dawn. I may just sleep in there."

Bear laughed and hung his towel up on a nearby bar. "I shall remain outside unless I hear splashing and cries for help." He faced her, and his expression sobered somewhat. "You don't mind if I wash our clothes together, do you?"

She walked into the bathroom and glanced over her shoulder. "Not as long as you don't have a problem washing women's panties." She gave him a sinful, maybe-I'll-let-you-wash-something-else smile.

His brows rose, and the twinkle in his eyes said he was up for her insinuated challenge. "Not at all," he replied in a silky voice, one corner of his mouth quirking up just slightly. "I'll even *hand* wash them, if you ask me *very* nicely."

Heat flooded her face as the image of *his* soapy hands caressing *her* flashed in her mind. Oh, what they could do to each other in the shower! She closed her eyes and took a deep breath as she realized she had just engaged him in a game he had probably mastered *decades* ago, one she was ill-equipped to play. "Um, no, machine wash is fine."

He'd won, and they both knew it. Bear's lips twitched and then he nodded. Without another word, he sat down on the bed and picked up the remote control. When he saw her still watching him, he waved a hand at her. "Go on. I'm looking forward to washing your *delicates.*"

Beth wrinkled her nose at him and closed the bathroom door with a little more force than was necessary. Just before she turned on the water, she heard him laugh softly and smiled.

After she'd shampooed, conditioned, and scrubbed herself clean, she plugged the tub drain and turned the hot water up until steam billowed like roiling translucent clouds. A peek out the shower curtain showed her that her dirty clothes were still there. Mildly perplexed, she poured some of Grandma Rose's bath and body foam under the torrent, and a tangy floral scent quickly filled the tiny room. She breathed deeply of the delicious aroma. Then she sank down into the bubbles with a sigh.

She listened as she soaked, not quite sure what she'd do if she *did* hear him come into the room. She shaved, and after she finished and put the razor aside, she slid back the shower curtain and glanced at the floor. Her clothing was gone. Obviously Bear had used his usual stealth when retrieving her garments, because she hadn't even heard the door open. With a chuckle she closed her eyes, let the curtain fall back into place, and sank down into the water.

It wasn't until the water had lost most of its heat that Beth finally unstopped the drain, turned on the shower to rinse off, and grabbed a towel from the wall-mounted rack. It was then she noticed the large flannel shirt hanging from the hook on the back of the bathroom door. It was Bear's shirt, but it was a different color from the one the motel owner had been fondling earlier. She imagined he was washing that one.

After a liberal application of Grandma Rose's Organic Body Quench and a swipe of antiperspirant, Beth slipped into the shirt. It smelled like Downy fabric softener. However, beneath that was another scent, *his* scent, a mix of sandalwood and skin. Beth inhaled it and smiled.

The flannel was soft against her skin and fell to her knees. She rolled the sleeves up and fastened the top button, but she was still exposing a good amount of cleavage. She looked in the mirror and pursed her lips. Oh, well. There wasn't anything she could do about it. Once she was clothed, she gathered up her toiletries and left the bathroom.

Bear wasn't in the room, but she hadn't expected him to be. The room felt much larger without him in it, and she realized she missed him. He was probably still doing laundry. He couldn't leave their clothes unattended with Ms. Harper snooping around. It wasn't as if Bear could sheepishly admit to being a cross-dresser. There was no way he'd fit in her panties. Beth chuckled at that image and grabbed the tiny hair dryer from the wall.

After drying her hair and brushing her teeth, Beth looked at the bed. She was exhausted, but beneath her weariness was newly awakened fear. She didn't want to dream again. Her thoughts drifted to the previous night when terror had jerked her out of sleep into a waking nightmare, and the way Bear had calmed her. She closed her eyes and imagined herself back in that projection room. She opened the box, looked at that old, familiar reel, but let it sit where she had previously put it. Then, she mentally sorted through the images of the afternoon and put those snapshots alongside the reel. With a deep, slow breath she lifted the lid and let it fall into place. It made the same, familiar *thunk*. A warm blanket of calm enveloped her. The knowledge that Bear would soon be there further deepened her confidence. With a sigh, she pulled back the covers and slipped into bed.

The sheets were crisp and white and had a fresh, outdoorsy scent. She snuggled into the pillow and yawned, weariness stealing the strength from her limbs. Another deep, eye-watering yawn escaped her, and her eyelids started to droop. She flicked on the TV in an attempt to stay awake until Bear returned, but it was no use. She was warm, she was clean, and she was, for the time being, safe, with Bear. Her vision started to blur, and she closed her eyes.

Bear entered the room with an armload of laundry. He smiled when he saw Beth was fast asleep in spite of the news anchor's droning voice. He tossed the pile of freshly dried clothes on the bed, stifled a yawn, and glanced at the clock, 10:13 p.m. He stretched, then engaged the chain and wedged a chair beneath the doorknob for good measure. The last thing he wanted was to have Ms. Harper come into the room in the dead of night. The fact she'd been pawing through his things was disturbing enough.

He turned and stood at the end of the bed, his heart thumping a little harder as he watched Beth sleep. Her lips were slightly parted, her hair like skeins of dark silk against the white sheets. He'd been right. She was a looker when she got cleaned up. To distract himself, he folded the clothing and put the garments on the dresser.

Bear took a deep breath and remembered how it had felt to have her pressed against him the previous night. Although a part of him wanted to experience that again, his common sense won out. Clamping down mercilessly on his attraction and his libido, he walked to the vanity and brushed his teeth.

After rinsing his mouth, Bear straightened the room, put all the toiletries into the tote bag, and then bagged the trash and put it in the tote as well. When he was satisfied they could make a quick getaway if needed, he turned off the lights, plunging the room into darkness. Faint skeins of illumination found entrance around the edges of the curtains, and as his eyes adjusted, he moved to one of the chairs near the window. He eased down into it. His size often proved problematic when dealing with standard types of mass-produced furniture, like the chair he was now wedged into. But, he didn't have much choice. He put his feet on the edge of the bed and froze when Beth stirred. Her eyes slowly opened, and she blinked several times, then leaned up on one elbow and looked at him as if she wasn't quite sure what she was seeing.

"What are you doing?"

Bear adjusted his feet. "I'm going to try and get some sleep."

"In that chair?" Her dark brows rose. "Really?" When he didn't reply, she gestured to the mattress. "You didn't notice the king-sized bed?"

The fact he *wanted* to get into bed with her irritated him for some reason, and he frowned. His shirt had slipped off her shoulder, baring the graceful curve of her neck, and the delicately chiseled collarbone. The thought of pressing his lips to that smooth arc of skin made his insides clench. Bear ground his teeth together and fought the desire to do just that.

"Unlike the men you may be accustomed to dealing with, I would never assume I could just hop into bed with you." He gave her a pointed look. "Before I get in bed with a woman, I like to *know* that's where she wants me."

Her eyes widened slightly, and she looked at him for a moment, her expression uncertain. Bear silently cursed himself, but at least he wasn't thinking about kissing her neck anymore. Finally, she blinked and pulled back the covers to expose the other side of the bed. She patted the mattress a couple of times and waited.

He searched her eyes, but for what he wasn't sure. "Why?" he asked at last.

A frown flitted across her brow. "You'll never get any sleep jammed into that chair. You don't fit." She stared hard at him, and he returned her stare in kind. It wasn't long before she dropped her gaze. Even in the darkness he saw the flush in her cheeks, the color deepening as she continued. "And . . . because I feel safer when you're close."

Those last words had been hardly more than a whisper, but he'd heard them clearly enough. He fought a smile. "I'm five feet away, Beth."

She lifted her eyes to his, and an angry sparkle glittered in those amber pools. "Fine. Sleep in your chair." She shot him a glare and turned away from him, flouncing dramatically down on her side. After punching her pillow several times, she jerked the sheet up over her shoulders, ignoring him.

Bear looked at her stiff back for a moment, debating the wisdom of getting closer to her. He knew she was naked except for his flannel shirt, and the thought of what lay beneath that shirt made his pulse beat a little faster. His chest went taut as he imagined his hands moving where the flannel now lay, brushing the curves and hollows of her body. He growled softly and shook himself.

Even if he wasn't fighting the itch to caress her skin, the chance of him actually sleeping while stuffed into a chair meant for regular-sized people was almost zero. His feet would hang off the end of the king-sized mattress, but it would still be vastly more comfortable than the chair. At least there was a *chance* he'd get some rest, which he would need if he was going to resolve the dilemma they were in. Finally, he rose and sat down on the edge of the mattress. He stripped off his shirt, tossed it on the nearby chair, and turned toward her with a sigh. "I'm sorry, Beth, and thank you." He slipped beneath the covers, but kept to his side.

She glanced over her shoulder at him, her expression wary, and then settled back onto her side facing away from him. "Don't mention it."

He looked at the back of her head. "Feel safer now?"

She was silent for several long, still seconds. Then she sat up, reached across his body, and grabbed his hand. She lay back down and pulled on his arm until he rolled onto his side toward her. His body automatically spooned around hers, and she moved closer to him. She tucked his hand in the hollow between her ribs and hip.

"Yes," she said softly. "I feel safer now."

I sure don't, Bear thought, *but at least* one *of us will sleep.*

Her head was nestled beneath his chin, and he closed his eyes as the scent of her hair drifted to him. He fought the urge to bury his face in the dark tresses and started counting backwards from one hundred. To his surprise, after a few minutes his body relaxed despite their proximity, which was unusual. Being in bed with a woman didn't normally involve sleep for him. It involved sex. No, sleep was something he usually did alone. Having another body close when he was accustomed to sleeping by himself was usually enough to keep him awake until well after dawn. But, this felt different. He hated to admit it, but it felt like she belonged there.

"Good night, Beth," he whispered.

"Good night, Bear."

****

Emily Harper stood on the bed of the empty room that adjoined Bear's, her hands clenched into fists. She tried to rein in her temper as she quietly replaced the picture that covered the peephole. She stared at the wall angrily for a few moments then climbed down, carefully smoothed the bedspread, and left the room, her insides vibrating.

"I thought you said you were alone, Ted," she said in a heated whisper. "You shouldn't have lied to me. You really shouldn't have."

With brisk strides, she crossed the gravel-covered parking lot to the office and sat down on the rolling stool behind the desk, impotent rage burning hotly in her chest. She had hoped to glimpse the large man half-dressed or, better yet, naked, as she had on several of his previous visits. However, seeing him in bed with a woman was *not* what she had anticipated. *She* had planned to slip into bed with him and show him what he was missing, but that was shot to hell.

She drummed her painted fingernails on the counter. "What to do, what to do?" Many of the single men who stayed at the Rocky Mountain Inn, even the younger ones, were more than happy to have her share their bed, but not Ted Bristol. Oh, no! Apparently *he* was too good for the likes of her. As she stoked her own angst, she heard the phone ring in the background, but paid it little heed. Only when she heard the *beeeeep* indicating a fax was incoming did she stop her petulant reverie. She rarely got faxes. Her anger forgotten for the moment, she hopped off the stool and rushed to the fax machine.

As the sketch of the dark-haired woman was revealed a ray of sunlight broke through her inner storm. She held the fax up to get a better view. Although she couldn't be sure, it certainly *looked* like the woman sharing Ted Bristol's bed.

She's wanted, eh? What are you doing hiding a fugitive from the law? Emily Harper laughed softly. *Well, that certainly explains why you didn't tell me about her, Special Agent Bristol. You were obviously worried I'd turn her and you in.* She giggled and stared at the drawing. *I should call Duffy. The girls at the salon would be so impressed if my nephew, Deputy Duffy Harper, was the one to find her.* She glanced at the clock. *But, it's too late now. Duffy won't answer my call at this hour.* Her mind worked furiously. *He gets up at 5:00 for work, so I'll call him then. Yes, it certainly will look good for the Harpers to capture a fugitive from justice.* She laid the paper on the desk next to the fax machine and sighed happily. *And if it's not her, at least everyone around here will know the Harpers take their civic duties to heart.*

Emily took the next half an hour getting ready for bed and set her alarm for 5:00 a.m. When Duffy arrived and took the fugitive and her accomplice, Ted Bristol, into custody, she planned to look her very best. She wanted Ted Bristol to have a really good look at what he *could* have had.

****

Beth knew before she came fully awake that it wasn't her ex Michael's shoulder her head rested on, it was Bear's. And it was Bear's leg hers was thrown over. She couldn't remember a time she'd ever slept better and, thankfully, she hadn't dreamed. He was shirtless, his skin warm and smooth beneath her fingertips. His stomach was hard and flat beneath her hand, moving gently as he breathed, and she couldn't help but smile. She let herself imagine waking up like this every morning, rolling over and seeing his sharply chiseled face softened in sleep, snuggling up against him. An arrow of sadness pierced her. With a soft sigh, she tried to roll away from him.

His embrace tightened. "Five more minutes, Mom?" he asked in a hushed voice.

Surprised, and thrilled, Beth settled back against him and pressed her face into the crook of his neck. "Make it fifteen and you have a deal." She slid her hand up his chest until it rested on his shoulder. "And *don't* call me mom."

He yawned. "You got it."

Unlike the previous morning, he didn't pop up when the allotted time had passed. Instead, he glanced at the clock and stayed where he was, much to Beth's secret delight. The pulse in his neck beat slowly and steadily against her cheek, and the hard planes of his body fit with hers as if they were two adjoining pieces of a jigsaw puzzle. Warmth skittered over her skin and was followed by chills. She knew she shouldn't feel what she felt, or think what she thought, but with Bear so close, her mind refused to focus on anything else. There was an ache inside her, and the fact she was wearing only his shirt just made it worse. A few buttons were all that stood between being clothed and being naked in his arms.

He must have sensed the tension in her because he eased his arm out from under her head, leaned up on his elbow, and looked down at her. His brows drew together, concern clear in his bright blue eyes.

"What is it?" he asked.

Beth returned his gaze for a few moments, and then closed her eyes and pressed a hand to his chest. Her insides tightened at the feel of his skin, smooth and warm beneath her palm with just the slightest spattering of soft, curling, blonde hair. She swallowed hard and shook her head. "Nothing."

"C'mon, Beth. Talk to me."

But she didn't want to talk. He was so close and warm, and she wanted to get closer. Taking a deep breath, she opened her eyes. She let her gaze wander over his face for a moment, memorizing each harshly carved feature. His breath fanned warmly over her cheek, and she focused on his mouth. The thought of kissing him sent heat to her scalp. She dropped her chin and focused on his chest. "Nothing, Bear."

"Beth . . . ."

Aw hell, just do it. You might not get another chance. Beth met his gaze briefly and then leaned up and kissed him. He stiffened, but it didn't matter. She was committed. Fireworks crackled inside her, and she pressed closer to him, her arms sneaking around his waist. It took several seconds, but then the tension in him eased, and his mouth softened against hers. She wanted to shout for joy.

Beth moaned when his arms enfolded her, and he pulled her tightly to his chest. She may have started this particular venture, but Bear wasted no time taking control. He cupped her head with one large hand as his mouth moved expertly over hers. Beth sighed and surrendered. He deepened the kiss; his tongue melded seamlessly with hers. Her nipples pebbled and ached. She clung to him as heat built low in her belly. Shivers of pleasure spiraled out from her core to her fingers and toes, and her skin went hot. She dug her fingers into his back, trying to press him closer.

Suddenly he stiffened and jerked away. He turned his head slightly toward the window, his expression fierce.

Beth made a frustrated sound. "Bear, what—"

"Sh." He pressed a finger to her lips. "I thought I heard something."

She froze, and her heart started to pound for an entirely different reason. With the grace of a panther, he uncoiled himself from the bed and moved to the window. He pushed the curtain aside a hair and peered through the narrow opening. She saw his jaw tighten, and a cold splash of fear doused the passion that had started to burn.

"Get dressed," he said in a whisper. "Your clothes are next to the tote bag."

Beth didn't hesitate. "What is it?"

"Sheriff's car just pulled up in front of the office."

In less than a minute, she had finished lacing her boots and pulling her hair into a loose ponytail. She glanced at the clock. "What is he doing here at 5:50 a.m.?"

"Yeah." He looked at her, his expression grave. "That kind of bugs me, too." He glanced outside again. "It's not Sheriff Carter. Must be one of his deputies."

Beth moved to his side. "Get dressed. I'll keep watch." He relinquished his post, and she put her eye to the opening. "He's talking to your crush. It looks like they know each other." Before she knew it, he was dressed and standing behind her, peering over her head out the window.

"Any idea what they're talking about?"

She moved away from him, her stomach in knots. "No, but she just pointed this direction, so it's a safe bet it has something to do with you."

Bear scowled. "Dammit." He straightened and looked around the room. His eyes narrowed as he looked toward the back wall. "Think you can fit through that?"

She looked over her shoulder at the narrow window next to the mirror. "Maybe?"

"Well, you're going to have to try because he's coming this way." He practically leapt across the room to the sink area. He opened the window, popped the screen out, and sat it in the sink. "Up you go."

She turned sideways and stuck her head and shoulders through the narrow opening. He hooked his arms around her thighs and gently pushed. Getting past her chest proved a little difficult, and a little painful, but after that, it was relatively smooth sailing. Bear had to give her an extra shove on the butt to get her backside through, and she fell to the ground with a pained gasp.

"Now," he began, glancing over his shoulder, "get inside the tree line and head south. You'll run right into the truck stop, but stay out of sight. When you see me pull in, meet me in the southeast corner of the lot."

"Got it." She turned.

"Beth."

She turned back and looked at him questioningly, and her heart leapt when she met that pointed stare. He was concerned. A faint flower of hope bloomed inside her, fragile and tenuous. His gaze wandered over her face for a moment then he said, "Be careful."

She nodded. "You, too. See you soon." She half-ran, half-walked to the tree line, her knee protesting with each step. Before she disappeared, she turned and gave him a short wave.

Bear watched her until she disappeared into the forest. He then snapped the screen back into place and closed the window. He glanced around to make sure there was nothing that would give away her presence. He grabbed his flannel shirt from the bed where she'd tossed it and the flip-flops from the floor and stuffed them inside the tote. He waited.

Chapter Ten

Bear put toothpaste on his toothbrush and started to brush his teeth. Only seconds later there was a knock at the door. He kept brushing, walked over to the door, and opened it. He feigned surprise when he saw a uniformed man standing there with a nameplate that read "Harper" and a cowboy hat in hand. *Ah*, Bear thought. *So that's why Beth thinks you two know each other.*

"Morning, offisher," he said through his mouthful of foam. "Hold on jushta shecond." He jogged back to the sink, spit the froth out, and rinsed his mouth. Then he wiped his chin with a hand-towel and walked back to the door.

"Sorry about that," he said with a smile. "Wasn't expecting company. What can I do for you this morning um . . . Deputy Harper? Say, is your mom the one who runs this place? She sure keeps things spick and span."

Harper was young, mid to late twenties Bear guessed, with brown eyes and sandy blonde hair cut in a high-and-tight. His features were soft but not completely devoid of masculinity. He was just over six feet tall with wide shoulders and a slight paunch. Harper looked him up and down, and Bear doubted the young man's gaze missed much. He had an air of intelligence about him that bespoke of higher education, but there was also an arrogance that didn't sit well on his 'public servant' shoulders. Bear felt an immediate surge of dislike, but he kept his face expressionless.

"Actually, Emily Harper is my aunt," Harper replied, "and yes, she does run a tight ship. Always has." He tried to peer around Bear's bulk. "Um, my aunt was under the impression you had company last night even though you registered as a solo guest."

He met Bear's gaze directly, but Bear could tell he was hiding something. Bear laughed. "What would lead her to that conclusion?"

The deputy shrugged. "She says she saw a brunette in your room last night."

Bear feigned puzzlement and rubbed his chin. "How would she

see *anyone* in my room? I've kept the windows and curtains closed since I arrived." He glanced around. "Does she have hidden cameras in here or something?"

Deputy Harper shuffled his feet, and an annoyed look briefly shadowed his features. "Of course not, but she says she saw a brunette woman in your room, a woman who looked an awful lot like this." He held up the sketch.

Bear's eyes flicked over the drawing. "Ah, I have one of those. And I *wish* I could say that person spent the night, if you know what I mean." He paused and gave Deputy Harper a grin, "but I was, and am, alone." He stepped back and made a sweeping gesture with his arm. "You're welcome to come in and look around if you like."

Deputy Harper cast a wary eye at him and rested one hand on his pistol as he entered the room. After checking under the bed, in the armoire, and in the bathroom, he opened the window by the mirror and peered outside. He turned and surveyed the room once again before he walked to the door.

"My aunt says you're an FBI agent," Harper commented, leaning against the jamb.

Bear gave him a knowing look and a small smile. "Now how does she know that? I didn't use my official ID to register."

Harper straightened, his expression guarded. "You must have mentioned it."

Bear lifted one brow. "No. I don't go around telling people who I work for, especially when I'm on vacation."

"Maybe she just guessed."

"Maybe. Especially since the only other explanation is that your dear, sweet aunt came into my room when I wasn't here and went through my things." He paused and a faint flush crept up Harper's neck. "Not that it really matters." Bear crossed his arms over his chest. "Is there anything else I can help you with, deputy?"

Harper shook his head. "No, thank you. My aunt has your contact information if I need to speak with you."

Bear reached into his pocket, pulled out his wallet, and took a business card from inside. "Here." He held the card out to the younger man. "Now *you* have all my contact info."

Harper took the card, glanced at it, and put it in his left breast pocket. "Thank you, Special Agent Bristol. Sorry to bother you so early in the morning, but when my aunt saw the sketch, she was sure she'd seen a woman matching that description in your room." He glanced over his shoulder at his aunt who was waiting outside the office, arms wrapped around herself, her expression anxious. Then he leaned forward a bit and smiled. "Personally, I think she spends too much time up here alone. Too much solitude can make a person . . . imagine things."

"I wouldn't know." He held out a hand, and the deputy grasped his fingers. "If you'll excuse me, I need to load up and head out."

"Leaving so soon?"

Bear nodded. "Yes. Think I'll go south of the border for a few since camping didn't work out." He walked to the door and crowded Deputy Harper outside. "Tell Sheriff Carter I said hello."

Harper put on his hat, touched the brim and walked toward the office where his aunt waited. They spoke for a few moments before Harper took his aunt's arm and steered her into the office. Bear double-checked the pistol on his hip, opened the hatch on the Cadillac, and loaded his bags. Once his things were safely stowed, he went into the room and shut the door.

Common sense said for him to get in the Escalade and go get Beth, but his agent senses were tingling so intensely it was like a buzz-saw was traversing his spine. Instead, he waited by the window and watched. Less than two minutes later, a dark blue Ford Bronco pulled into the motel lot behind the deputy's patrol car, and three men got out of the SUV. The hackles on the back of his neck jumped to attention when he recognized one. Shaved Head. The other two weren't familiar, but it wasn't much of a leap to assume they all worked for the same people. The three men looked around the modest property for a minute, before they turned and entered the motel office.

When the door shut behind them and the blinds closed, Bear left the room and ran the thirty yards across the parking lot, keeping as low as possible. Once he reached the SUV, he slipped the knife from his belt and jammed it into the driver's side rear tire and then the front one. Air hissed from the gashed rubber, and he scuttled to the deputy's car where he punctured the rear tire. Then he pressed himself against the rear quarter-panel of the vehicle and listened. It was quiet, too quiet. Bear carefully peered over the trunk of the black-and-white, but with the blinds drawn, he couldn't see anything. Slowly, in a crouched position, he moved backwards toward his vehicle. A short, sharp cry that sounded like a woman's voice was cut off mid-scream. He paused and his pulse jumped when he heard two soft pops. Light briefly illuminated the edges of the window, glaring in the early morning light like a photographer's flash. There were two more pops and flashes, and his pulse jumped another notch.

"Shit."

He ran toward the Escalade and had just opened the driver's door when he heard a gunshot and the rear passenger window exploded. Bear jumped into the driver's seat and closed the door, using the metal panel as cover. His gun was already out, and he carefully lifted his head to take aim. The side view mirror shattered, peppering his face with shards of glass and molded plastic. Bear growled and squeezed off two rounds. The closest shooter went down, two dark spots dead center in the chest.

Out of the corner of his eye he saw another thug running. *Shit.* They were going to try to flank him. He fired two more shots, one hitting the dirt directly in front of the sprinter, and the other impacting his thigh. The man screamed and went down.

The only one left was Shaved Head, and Bear's abdominals clenched when the man popped out from behind the Bronco with what looked like an Uzi. A lightning bolt of adrenaline seared through his bloodstream. Bear rolled out of the vehicle and hugged the Escalade as he maneuvered himself around behind the SUV. Shaved Head shouted and started blasting away.

Bear was pissed. Not only was he bleeding, but this guy was going to destroy his Cadillac. He flattened out on the ground and took aim at Shaved Head's lower leg. He squeezed off two shots, firing underneath the vehicle. Shaved Head howled in pain and went down as his shin bone shattered. Shaved Head rolled onto his side and returned fire. Bear sighted down the barrel and smiled grimly as he squeezed the trigger. He knew what would happen, picturing it a split second before Shaved Head's head snapped back. Blood and gray matter splattered the ground and the Bronco's tires, and the Uzi fell from the man's dead fingers.

Another gunshot split the air. Pain sliced through his left shoulder and Bear realized with no small amount of annoyance that he'd been hit. Thankfully, he was right-handed, and he rolled onto his right side, brought the .45 to bear on the only soldier still breathing and emptied the magazine. He reloaded and went still.

The quiet that fell after the final gunshot was eerie, almost preternatural. Bear's heart was pumping, his breathing heavy as he waited for something else to happen. After about a minute, when no more truckloads of murderous thugs pulled into the lot, he got to his feet. He glanced at his shoulder, which was bleeding profusely, but didn't appear serious. It looked like the bullet had only grazed him.

Bear made his way across the parking lot, checking pulses as he did so and finding none. He briefly searched Shaved Head's pockets for ID using the cuff of his shirt to avoid leaving prints, but all he found was a wad of cash, a throwaway cell phone, some keys, and lip balm. It was a safe bet neither of the other two had ID either. Shaking his head, he walked to the office. The door stood wide open and behind the counter were Emily Harper and her nephew, Deputy Harper. They'd each been shot once in the chest and once in the head. Bear sighed heavily. Deputy Harper's pistol was still snapped into its holster; it didn't appear he'd even attempted to draw his weapon. The look of surprise on both faces said volumes.

After a fruitless pulse check, Bear carefully went through the deputy's pockets until he found the man's cell phone. Hoping he was wrong, he hit the redial button with his cuff-covered finger. About five seconds later, a phone started ringing. Bear followed the sound until he found himself standing over Shaved Head. Unfortunately, he hadn't been wrong.

"Son of a bitch," Bear said under his breath. Now he knew who at least one 'contact' in the sheriff's office was. His heart heavy, he walked back into the office and returned the phone to the dead deputy's pocket. He glanced at Emily Harper, her bright blue eyes lifeless and forever fixed on the ceiling. He thought about closing her eyelids, but he didn't want to leave any more forensic evidence behind. Analysts would have enough to process already.

Bear rose, bowed his head, and said a silent prayer over the two corpses. Then he left the office and walked quickly to his Escalade. Thankfully, most of the damage was cosmetic. The hood, windshield, and window would need to be replaced, but the engine roared to life on the first turn of the key. He took a final look around the lot and at the bodies that littered it, before he hopped into the SUV and left the motel.

****

Beth hid just inside the tree line on the eastern side of the truck stop, watching every car and truck that entered or exited the facility. A couple of Escalades pulled in, but they weren't Bear's. She'd been waiting about half an hour when an eighteen-wheeler parked directly in front of her, blocking her view, and she huffed angrily. She moved north, searching for a clear vantage point, and that's when she recognized Bear's SUV pulling into the lot. Her brain spasmed, and her lungs froze when she saw the shattered headlights, the bullet-riddled hood and windshield, and the blown-out windows. She hoped she was imagining things, but a blink and a shake of her head only sent cold fear pulsing through her when the damage remained. The possibilities made her soul recoil.

"Oh, my God."

Heedless of her sore knee, Beth sprinted through the trees to the southeast corner of the lot and waited. The Escalade approached and turned, presenting her with the passenger side of the vehicle. She saw him lean over the seat and open the rear passenger door.

"Get in and get down, and watch out for the glass."

A million questions were poised on her tongue, but when she saw the blood on his face, they died in her throat. He had a myriad of cuts and scrapes on his cheeks, chin, and brow, but he didn't look seriously hurt. He looked angry. Beth immediately climbed in and sat on the floor behind the front seats, closing the door behind her.

"Are you okay?" she asked.

"Fine." He glanced at her and then put the car in drive. "Have any trouble?"

"Not as much as you apparently."

"Just doing my job, sweetheart."

Without another word, he pressed on the accelerator.

Beth looked at his profile from her hiding place. The thin lines of blood running down his cheek and the clenched jaw had reality hitting her upside the head again, with more force this time. How close had she just come to losing him? Her stomach curled in on itself, and she squeezed her eyes shut as the movie reel threatened to turn itself on. She had no idea what had happened after she'd left the motel, but it had obviously been bad. She'd heard shots, but this *was* Colorado. With the mountainous terrain, she hadn't been able to identify what direction the shots had come from, but now she knew.

Bear's expression was cold and as hard as granite, his brows drawn together ominously. Something hard, dark, and rough lodged in her throat, and the familiar heat of panic began to pulse through her. Suddenly, she needed to touch him, to reassure herself he was indeed okay. She reached between the seats and put a hand on his arm, her fingers tightening around his bicep. He glanced at her, and when she met his gaze, his expression softened.

"Are you *really* okay?" she choked out.

He turned his eyes back to the road and covered her hand with one of his. "I'm fine, Beth."

She closed her eyes and pressed a shaking hand to her mouth while her other hand remained firmly affixed to his arm. Her mind was spinning in a million different directions, and she had to keep pressure on the box in her mind to prevent it from popping open and flooding her brain with images that would leave her a sobbing, shuddering mess. She tried to take deep even breaths, she tried to remember what Chief Dancing Eagle had taught her, what Bear had taught her, but she was torn between those calming practices and keeping the box closed. *Get a grip, Beth. The last thing Bear needs is for you to lose it now.* Tears gathered behind her eyes, and she squeezed her lids shut tighter, knowing if even one escaped, it would start a landslide of emotions she might not be able to control.

His fingers rubbed hers, and she pulled strength from that simple contact. Gradually, her panic receded, but she didn't relinquish her hold until he pulled the Escalade over and killed the engine nearly half an hour later. He turned around in his seat. Beth gulped and opened her eyes.

"Think you can bandage me up?" he asked with a small smile.

Afraid her voice would break, Beth nodded. She took several deep breaths and fought to remain dry-eyed and tremor free as she opened the door and stepped outside. Bear had pulled off the main highway and down a narrow, overgrown dirt lane until the trees and brush obscured the main road from view. She could still hear the drone of tires on the highway, but all she could see was forest. Steeling herself for what she knew was coming, she approached the back of the Escalade.

Bear was already sitting on the rear hatch, first aid kit open and ready. She watched as he soaked several large gauze pads with alcohol. It was then she saw his bloody shoulder. She'd never been much for the sight of blood, and she'd already seen enough of it to last a lifetime. The fact it was Bear's blood made it worse. Her stomach rolled dangerously.

"Oh, my God, your arm."

He scowled, stuck two fingers through the tear in the fabric, and ripped the sleeve clean off. Beth jumped, and her stomach dropped when she saw the gash. It was about four inches long and creased the outside of his shoulder above the left bicep. He grabbed one of the alcohol soaked pads and pressed it against the bleeding wound. She flinched, but he didn't, his expression stoic.

He gave her a pointed look. "I need you to wrap it."

"Bear, you need stitches."

"I know." He nodded toward the first aid kit. "There are some latex gloves in there. You can bandage me up until we get someplace I can get stitches."

Beth swallowed hard. Her stomach was pinging around her middle like a drunken sailor, which made her distinctly nauseous, but she inhaled deeply as she took a pair of latex gloves and put them on. Trying to breathe slowly and evenly, she took the gauze from his shoulder and inspected the gash. Thankfully, it wasn't deep, but it continued to bleed. Beth picked up the bottle of alcohol and gave him a pointed look.

"This may hurt."

He gave her a don't-I-know-it smile. "No 'may' about it. Go ahead, Doctor Drummond. Do your worst."

Beth grabbed several large pads and held them below his injured shoulder. Then she slowly poured alcohol over the wound. His breathing didn't even hitch. He continued to watch her face, that same half-smile firmly in place.

"Before you wrap it, pack some gauze in the wound," he said gently. "It'll help stem the bleeding."

Beth only nodded as she put the alcohol and soaked pads aside and dried his skin. Her stomach rolled again, an action dangerously close to a full 360, but she clenched her teeth and focused on the task at hand. After putting a couple of smaller gauze pads against the gash, she took a long bandage and began to wrap it around his muscular arm. Once the bandage was secure, she turned her attention to his face. She moved to stand between his legs and examined the numerous lacerations, shards of glass protruding from many of the wounds. Now her stomach *did* do a complete 360, but she forced herself to focus on him and not the gymnastics going on in her middle.

"Are you going to tell me what happened back there?" She searched the kit briefly and found a pair of tweezers. "It looks like a mirror exploded in your face."

"Pretty close."

Beth pulled a long shard of silver glass from his forehead and her insides twisted as more blood oozed from the wound. She gulped.

"So tell me, please. It'll give me something to concentrate on *other* than this."

"You *are* a bit pale."

"Yeah, well I already told you I don't like guns." She glanced at him and blanched. "I don't like blood either."

He chuckled and related the tale. His tone was bland, matter-of-fact, as if he was relating the events of an ordinary day at the office. Beth listened as she picked pieces of fiberglass and mirror from his face. The depth and timbre of his voice helped to calm her roiling stomach. When she finished, she put the tweezers aside and ran an alcohol pad over his entire face. It hurt her to do it, but it was as if he felt nothing. Several of the cuts started to bleed afresh, and she gently pressed clean gauze to them. It was then she realized how close they were, and her heart did a back-flip as those sharp blue eyes met hers. Scant inches separated them, and she was suddenly very aware of the heat and proximity of his body. Beth gulped and dropped her chin.

Needing to do something, *anything*, she searched through the kit with one hand until she found some butterfly bandages. After checking to see if the blood flow had slowed, she dressed the larger cuts on his face. Then she stepped back and almost heaved a sigh of relief. It was done.

"There." she said. She removed the gloves and tossed them on the small pile of trash with the used gauze pads and bandage wrappers. A glance at him made her heart thud and the box in her head started to quake again. As much as being close to him calmed her, right now his bandaged face and the bullet-ridden Cadillac were anything but calming. She could almost hear the soft, maniacal laugh of panic as it wound through her and started a slow, viper's climb up her throat. She took a couple of steps back and tried to sound nonchalant. "You should survive until you can see an actual doctor."

"Thank you, Miss Nightingale." He flexed his arm. After testing his shoulder, he gave her a nod of approval. "Nicely done. As soon as I change my shirt, we can be off."

Beth nodded, and she realized she was losing the emotional battle as the box burst open and splattered her mind's eye with vivid, Technicolor snapshots. She swallowed hard and said in a hushed voice, "Okay. I'll be right back."

She felt his gaze on her as she walked into the forest, fighting to keep the tears at bay. When she'd gone about twenty paces or so and the greenery closed around her, she leaned against a tree and covered her mouth with her hands. A cold wave of despair rushed through her chest cavity. Its touch was soft, almost comforting at first, but then the chill turned sharp and cutting. Taking a deep, hitching breath, she slid down the trunk until her knees were in her chest and choked back her cries. Eleven people dead in two days, and Bear had almost made it an even dozen. She and Bear were on the run for their lives, and everyone she knew and loved could be a potential target as well. And for what – money, drugs, power? The thought of what could have happened to him brought on a fresh cascade of tears, and it was all she could do not to burst into great, heaving sobs. She felt like she was drowning, the weight of hopelessness crushing the air from her lungs, sucking her into a vortex she fought to escape, but couldn't. Beth rested her brow on her knees and wrapped her arms around her legs as she tried desperately to get hold of herself.

She didn't know how much time had passed before she felt him near. Beth lifted her head slightly, saw him crouched in front of her, and the dam gave way. The concern in his blue eyes, the starkness of the bandages against his skin brought it all into razor sharp focus, and she quit fighting. She pressed her forehead against her knees and sobbed as his arms wound around her shoulders. He laid his cheek atop her bowed head.

"It's okay, Beth," he whispered, his hands rubbing her back, "I'm fine, really."

Beth couldn't have spoken if she'd been able to form any coherent words in the first place. Her heart ached, her lungs ached, her throat ached, her soul ached. He spoke soothingly in hushed tones, but she was so overwhelmed she couldn't understand what he said. Even his nearness and the sound of his voice couldn't stem the tide. Too much had happened too fast, and despite the fact she hated crying, she realized on an instinctual level that right now it was necessary. As all the twisted, jumbled emotions drained out her eyes and down her cheeks, it seemed to free up space inside her. The torrent and the tension began to wane. Also, her hearing improved. She realized he was telling her how proud of her he was, how brave she'd been, how what they were going through was nothing compared to chasing down dangerous wildlife all on her own, how he liked her blue nail polish. It was several minutes before the tears were completely spent, but neither his arms nor his voice wavered in the slightest. He kept her wrapped in that fortress-like embrace and spoke softly until she regained control of herself.

Finally, she sniffled, wiped her eyes, and took a shaky breath. With her brow still on her knees, she said, "I – I'm. . . I'm s-sorry."

Bear's voice was low and gentle. "You have *nothing* to apologize for, Beth."

She lifted her eyes to his, and the tenderness in his expression was almost her undoing. She blinked rapidly as tears somehow managed to replicate. "You . . . ." A shaft of pain skewered her, and she turned away. "You could've been *killed.*"

"But I wasn't." He ran a finger along her jaw and gently turned her face to his. He studied her features, his expression pensive. "I'm more pissed off than hurt, and if anyone had to get injured, I'm glad it was me and not you."

Her chin trembled. "Don't say that."

He brushed a lock of hair from her cheek. "Don't cry," he whispered.

A tear escaped, and she ran a fist over it and frowned at him. "Don't tell me what to do."

"Don't cry . . . please?"

She memorized his face, and more tears welled. "Promise me you won't do anything like that again."

A wistful smile curved his mouth. "You know I can't promise that."

She looked at him, beseeching him with her eyes. "Promise me you'll *try*."

For an answer, he cupped her head and pressed his lips to her brow in a lingering kiss. Beth's lashes fluttered down, and she curled her fingers around his muscular forearms, absorbing the strength that always seemed to emanate from him. She wanted his arms around her again; she wanted to feel safe and protected again. She wanted to drown in him and never resurface. As if sensing what she needed, he gently pulled her into his arms. Something warm and soothing replaced the cold fear and anguish that had previously owned her. She felt freer, lighter, as if fetters she'd unknowingly worn for years simply fell away.

After several moments, he pulled back slightly and rested his forehead against hers.

"I promise I'll try."

Beth took a shaky breath. "Thank you."

****

Laine Vaughn had just made herself a cup of tea and picked up the newspaper when her cell phone rang. She glanced at the caller ID and smiled.

"Hey, Bear," she said jovially after pushing the button and putting the phone to her ear. "You must have great cell service if you're calling me from the middle of Rocky Mountain National Park."

"I do, I'm not, and I need a favor."

Laine sobered immediately, the tone of his voice setting off alarm bells in her head. "Anything, Bear, you know that."

"Are you at home or the hospital?"

"Home. Technically I'm still on my honeymoon." She sat up a little straighter in her chair as a dark flutter of apprehension danced through her. "Why? What's going on? What do you need?"

"I need you to move the Suburban out of the garage and leave the door open. I'll be at your place in five and the fewer people who see my Escalade the better."

She blinked. *What the hell?*

There was a brief pause. "Is Jack there?"

Laine frowned and her chest tightened. Something was wrong here, terribly wrong. His clipped voice and lack of animation were enough to tell her that. And, he hadn't flirted once. "No," she replied. "He got called into the office for something, but he said he'd be back in a couple of hours, why?" She walked to the hall closet and retrieved her medical kit. For some reason, she had a feeling she'd need it.

"Because he can't be involved just yet," Bear replied, "and I'm going to ask you to do something you won't want to do."

Dread expanded through her in a strange cold, tingling wave that made her breath catch. She put the kit on the kitchen island and leaned into the granite counter. "What's that?"

"I'm going to ask you to lie to your husband."

Chapter Eleven

Bear sat on a barstool in Laine's kitchen. Beth stood at the end of the island, as she nibbled on one thumbnail. He wanted to comfort her, tell her this was the one place they were safe with people who fully understood what they were going through, but Laine was in full doctor mode as she removed the bandage. Beth stayed where she was, watching, until Laine started probing the bullet wound. He kept his face expressionless in spite of the throbbing in his shoulder, but Beth blanched and went pale, as if she could feel the pain herself. She turned away, walked across the kitchen, and pushed through the screen door onto the enclosed back porch without a word. Maverick, Laine's wolf-dog hybrid, followed, pushing past the mesh covered panel with ease. The animal gave Beth a doggy smile and trotted over to her, plumed tail wagging with enthusiasm. Bear's eyes narrowed when Beth smiled slightly, crouched down in front of Maverick, and started rubbing the thick, gray and white fur.

Laine paused in what she was doing and followed the direction of his gaze.

"Maverick likes her," Laine observed as she disinfected the wound. "That means she's a good person."

Something warm and long dormant fought to break free in his chest, but he wrestled it back. Now was *not* the time. "Yes, she is." Bear continued to watch Beth, but he felt Laine's eyes on him.

"I'm not even going to ask if she shot you."

And so it begins. Bear scowled at her.

Laine smiled. "I didn't ask."

I think you've been spending too much time around Jack. "Really?"

"So, who *did* shoot you?"

"Bad guys."

Laine pulled a syringe and a vial from her kit. "You know, as a doctor I'm supposed to report all gunshot wounds to the local authorities." She extracted several CCs of fluid from the small bottle and tapped the syringe.

Bear pursed his lips. "Thank you for doing your civic duty, Doctor Vaughn. I will look into the matter right away." He watched as she swabbed his shoulder and injected him. "There. You've notified the local authorities."

Laine laughed softly and shook her head as she prepared to stitch the wound. "Smart ass."

"Better than being a dumb-ass," he shot back. "But enough about me." His eyes swept over her. Her chestnut hair was pulled back into a sensible ponytail, her face devoid of makeup. There was a faint smattering of freckles across her aristocratic nose, and those intelligent, green-gold eyes returned his gaze with a sparkle of mild amusement. She looked beautiful, like always, and Bear smiled. "Looking good, Dr. Mrs. Vaughn. Or is it Mrs. Dr. Vaughn? Or are you still going by Wheeler?"

Laine rolled her eyes, grinned, and started sewing.

"Regardless," Bear continued, "marriage seems to agree with you."

"It does." She gave him a pointed look. "It would agree with you, too, if you'd date a girl more than twice."

"Hey, I'm open. It's not *my* fault they all decide they 'just want to be friends' at that point."

"Maybe not," she agreed, focusing on his shoulder, "but you don't do anything to try to change their minds."

Bear looked at her in mock reproach. "If they don't recognize what a catch I am, then to heck with them," he shot back.

Laine laughed and shook her head. "I love you, Bear, but sometimes I'd like to smack the crap out of you."

"You don't because you know I'd enjoy it."

"That I do," she said with a wry twist of her lips. "You're lucky, you know. A couple of inches to the right and the bullet would've hit the joint." She paused in her stitching and met his gaze. "If that was the case, you'd be in a lot worse shape and there wouldn't be anything I could do for you in my kitchen."

Bear had no reply for that, so he nodded and looked again at Beth. She was sitting on the edge of a chaise longue, Maverick's head in her lap, and for the moment, she seemed relaxed. That warmth in his chest lifted its head again, and it was a little harder to rein in this time.

Laine's voice broke into his reverie. "Tell me you hurt them worse than they hurt you."

He felt her gaze and glanced at her. "If dead is hurt worse, then yeah, I did."

Her expression sobered and she blinked at him. Taking a deep breath, she continued to stitch his shoulder. "And what about her? Did they hurt her, or did you?"

He scowled. "How can you even ask that?"

She glanced toward the patio. "It's obvious she's been crying.

And Maverick's got his head in her lap. That's his 'I know you're hurting and I'm here for you' position." She looked at him out of the corner of her eye as she finished stitching the wound.

"Well, she *is* hurting, but it's not because of me."

Laine pressed a fresh bandage over the neatly stitched laceration and taped it firmly in place. "Are you certain about that?"

Bear frowned and looked at Beth. Was he partly to blame for her pain? His insides recoiled at the mere thought, and then the memory of their brief kiss flared to life. Maverick watched her adoringly as she scratched behind his ears, and then he licked her cheek. Beth buried her face in the dog's fur, and he suddenly envied the canine.

"Or, is she hurt because they hurt *you?*" Laine studied him closely, and a small smile curved her generous mouth. "That's it, isn't it?"

Bear lifted one brow and gave her a bored look. As usual, she'd nailed it, but he wasn't about to give her the satisfaction of knowing she was right. Not yet.

"Don't try to fool me, Bear Bristol." She stood in front of him and examined the lacerations on his face. "The fact I can't read you says you're hiding something."

"She's frightened, and she has good reason to be." He tried to look at Laine, but found his gaze drawn back to Beth. "I'm just a lifeline for her right now, nothing more."

"Keep telling yourself that if it makes you sleep better at night."

A disgruntled huff escaped him. "I've slept better the past two nights than I have in a while."

As soon as the words were out of his mouth he wanted to take them back. Laine's smile practically screamed I-knew-it and she glanced over her shoulder at Beth.

"Hmm . . . I wonder why that is."

"Don't read anything into it, Laine."

"Too late."

"I've slept better because I've been exhausted." He knew it wasn't true, not completely, but again, he wasn't going to give Laine the win.

"Okay." She snapped off the gloves and leaned against the counter. Her expression was smug, self-satisfied, and he could almost hear her saying, "You can't fool me, dude." Instead, she said, "She clean you up?" When Bear nodded, she crossed her arms over her chest. "Did pretty well for someone with, I'm assuming, no medical training."

Nice try, Laine. She was still fishing, but he wasn't going to indulge her. He shook his head and shrugged into a fresh shirt. "She's a photographer."

Laine's eyes widened and her mouth dropped open. "Oh, my gosh. I *knew* I'd seen her somewhere before." She grabbed the newspaper from the counter and started shuffling through the pages.

When she found what she was looking for, she folded the paper in half and handed it to him.

The black and white image of Beth stared back at him from the upper half of page five, and she looked *nothing* like the police sketch. The contrast was stunning. In the photo she was made-up, coiffed, and dressed in a sharp, fitted pantsuit. She leaned against a wall next to a five-by-seven-foot print of a bear. The animal's lips were curled in a savage growl to reveal razor-sharp teeth and its claws were extended as it leapt through the air for a fish. The detail was exquisite. Individual droplets of water were frozen in midair. He could see each hair of the bear's coat. The bear's nose was flared, the individual pores clearly visible. Even the hapless fish looked so real Bear could imagine it leaping from the page. It was an awesome shot, and his respect and admiration for her grew. The article's headline read, 'First Gallery Showing for Local Photographer Receives International Attention.'

Bear started reading. "Local photographer, Beth Drummond, will have her first showing at the Mile High Gallery in Denver, Colorado, on Friday, blah, blah, blah . . . . 'Invitations have been sent to art collectors, critics, and enthusiasts from as far away as Japan, New York, and London,' said gallery owner, Andrew Shaw, 'and the responses are beyond enthusiastic. This showing will truly draw an international crowd' . . . ." Bear's voice trailed off as he read the date. "Shit."

Laine looked at the paper. "What?"

"The showing . . . it's a week from tomorrow."

"And?"

Bear pinched the bridge of his nose. Just as her career was going to take off, life had stepped in to throw her a cruel curveball. He tasted the remorse and regret like bile. "Unless I can channel Superman, she may not be there."

Laine's brows rose. "It's that serious?"

"It's even more serious than that serious."

It was quiet for a moment, and when Laine spoke next her voice was hushed. "Is this where you ask me to lie to Jack?"

"I don't want to, Laine, I don't want *you* to." He rubbed his temples. "But ever since JC's death . . . ." He stared across the family room and out the window. "Jack is the *only* guy at the office I trust completely, and I don't want to drag him or you into this unless I absolutely have to."

"We can help—"

The very idea of putting more bodies in the crosshairs made his abdominals tighten. "No." Bear stood in one fluid motion and looked down at her, brows drawn together. "Absolutely not. It's too dangerous."

She gaped at him. "And what about the Escalade, Bear? Jack's going to notice that, so what do I tell him when he starts quizzing me about the broken windows and the bullet holes?"

"The car cover for the Escalade is in the cargo area. I'll cover it before I go so he won't see them." He ran a hand over his eyes and returned to the barstool he had been sitting on. "If he asks, tell him you're keeping an eye on it for me while I go to Cabo. He knows how much I love that car, so unless you give something away, he has no reason to look." Even as he said the words, he knew they weren't true, but he didn't know what else to say. Jack had been called into the office, which probably meant he was now involved in this mess. Once he found out the Escalade was in the garage, it would be the first thing Jack would check out. Bear knew he'd need Jack's help, but not just yet. He had to get the rest of his plan worked out first, or it could very well blow up in all their faces.

"I take it you want the Suburban?" Laine asked.

"If you don't mind?"

"Not at all, but I'll need to explain that, too."

Bear sighed and rubbed his neck. "Tell him I drove it to the airport. Jack knows it'd be a cold day in hell before I'd leave my Caddy in the airport parking lot."

"And why didn't I just take you?"

He gave her a sour look. "I didn't want to inconvenience you." Both her brows rose and he pinched the bridge of his nose. "I know. I wouldn't believe it either." He sighed. "I don't know what to tell you, Laine, but right now Jack is the least of my worries."

He planted his elbows on the counter and scowled at the sink. He was trying to imagine every probable scenario, everything that could go wrong, and mentally prepare himself for the worst possible outcomes. If the cartel didn't already know who Beth was, they soon would, and now he was also on their radar, which widened the circle of danger to include everyone and everything both he and Beth knew and loved. He pulled in a breath. *Focus. Beth is your primary concern right now. The cartel won't go after a Fed unless it's a last resort, and Jack won't leave Laine alone until this wraps. The farther away Beth and I are, the safer everyone else will be.*

"Bear," Laine began, resting a hand on his arm, "you're scaring me."

He sighed heavily then met her gaze. "Now you know how *she* feels."

"Does *she* know what's going on, I mean *really* know?"

"No." He shook his head once. "Not all of it."

Laine seemed to ponder that for a moment, glancing at the dark-haired woman and the dog. "What else can I do?"

"I need some cash, some supplies, and a place to hole up for a while." He rubbed his chin. "It has to be someplace that can't be traced back to me . . . or *you.*"

His mind worked furiously, but he was coming up empty. As

soon as Sheriff Carter had arrived at the motel and put together the pieces that included him, an APB would have been put out for him and the Escalade. This meant his place and all of his friends' places were now off-limits, not to mention their time in Jack and Laine's home was rapidly expiring. He glanced at Laine, whose brow was furrowed in thought as she absently chewed on her thumbnail. After a few minutes her eyes widened and she straightened, and he saw the proverbial light bulb go on.

"The cabin," she said, snapping her fingers. "The cabin at Dunbar Lake, you can stay there."

"You guys buy a cabin since I last saw you . . . three days ago?"

Laine frowned and shook her head. "No, silly. Jack's sister, Hillary, and her husband, Mason, have a cabin right on the water. You met them at the wedding. It was all they could talk about. Built it on the twenty-acre parcel Hillary inherited from her and Jack's grandfather."

"Doesn't Jack have twenty acres up there as well?"

Laine nodded. "It adjoins Hillary's." She sat down on the stool next to him. "She and Mason invited us up last weekend. Mason spent most of those two days trying to convince Jack to build on his parcel, or sell."

Bear frowned. "Those two didn't strike me as the 'cabin' sort."

"They're not," Laine said with a roll of her eyes. "That *cabin* is worth close to a million dollars, has three bedrooms, three baths, a hot tub, gourmet kitchen, even satellite television and internet service." She rested her elbow on the counter and propped her chin in her hand. "Hillary's idea of 'roughing it' is not being able to wash her hair for twenty-four hours after a perm."

Bear thought about it for a moment, and a sprig of hope started to take root. "And what would they think about you sending guests to their expensive little hideaway?"

Laine stood and walked around the island to a key-shaped rack mounted on the wall by the back door. She lifted a ring from one of the pegs and walked back over to him and returned to her seat. Her smile was calculating, conspiratorial, and she dangled the ring in front of him.

"What they don't know won't hurt them." Laine pressed the keys into his palm. "Hillary gave me a set and insisted that Jack and I use the cabin while they're gone. I think she's hoping something will change Jack's mind about building or selling, and I'm guessing their preference would be the latter."

Bear looked at the keys. "Where are they?"

"Switzerland, for the next two weeks." Laine snorted derisively. "Apparently the skiing in *Colorado* isn't good enough for them."

"But it can trace back to you and Jack."

She shrugged. "Everything is in Mason's name." She smiled and patted his arm. "It'll take anyone a while to connect the dots if they even manage to line up those particular dots in the first place." Laine met his gaze and framed his face with her hands. "Now, I know you, Bear Bristol, and I have no doubt you'll have this situation resolved *well* before then."

Bear looked into the eyes of his best friend's wife, a woman he'd have happily romanced if circumstances had been different. But, they hadn't, and now he was happy to have her as one of his truest, closest friends. "I love you, you know that, right?"

Her cheeks dimpled as she gave him a what's-not-to-love smile, and then she leaned forward and kissed his cheek. "I love you, too, big guy. Now, come on. We have some work to do." She released him and walked over to a bookcase in the family room. She moved a set of classic Dickens novels aside to reveal a wall safe and started pressing buttons. "I've got $2000 in here, and that should be enough, but if you need more," she paused while inputting the code for the combination lock and then looked at him over her shoulder, "you let me know."

Bear chuckled. "Jack said you kept a wad of cash at the house. I thought he meant a couple hundred bucks in a cookie jar or something."

The twelve-by-twelve-inch metal door swung outward and Laine grabbed the neatly stacked, wrapped bills. "Nope. My dad hated banks and always kept a couple grand hidden in the house. I just followed his example." She tossed the money to him and shut the safe. "Now, you won't need many supplies because Hillary and Mason keep the cabin fully stocked."

"What about servants?" Bear asked as he absently counted the stacks of twenties. "I seriously doubt those two keep their cabin all stocked and shiny by themselves."

Laine chuckled. "When they're not at the cabin, the only guy you will see is Malcolm, the caretaker." She approached him, a sly smile on her face. "Hillary specifically told me," she paused and continued in a voice with a genteel Southern drawl, "'Now, you and Jack shouldn't go running about naked on Wednesdays between nine a.m. and one p.m., or you'll scare the life out of poor old Malcolm.'" Laine rolled her eyes and sat on the barstool next to him. "Apparently it's *fine* to cavort without clothing the rest of the time, just not those four hours on Wednesday. I wonder if she knows this from personal experience . . . ?"

Bear shook his head, stood, and stuffed the money into his pockets. "I'd rather not know, thanks." He looked around the kitchen and met Laine's gaze. "I guess that does it then."

"Not yet," Laine said with a shake of her head. She glanced at Beth, who was stretched out on the chaise longue with Maverick, his head on her chest. "I'm sure you have some weaponry you need to transfer from the Escalade to the Suburban, so why don't you take care of that while I get Miss Beth some clothes? We're about the same size." She gave him a knowing smile.

Bear smiled back. "Fine, but don't be filling her head with any wild stories about me. I don't want her thinking I'm anything other than bulletproof and immortal. Oh, and take a look at her knee, will you? She banged it up pretty good."

"Of course."

Bear watched as Laine crossed the room and opened the door leading to the screened in porch. She stuck her head through and said, "Hey, there. My, you two look comfy."

If there was one person on this earth he would entrust Beth to, aside from Jack, it was Laine. In addition to her doctoral skills, she had been *exactly* where Beth now was. With a soft sigh of relief, he left the house through the side door and made his way to the garage.

Beth looked up at the sound of Laine's voice, and a spark of jealousy burned hot in her chest. She'd seen the way Bear had looked at Laine, heard him tell her he loved her, and envied what that must feel like. Ever since they'd entered the house, she'd felt almost invisible, as if Laine's presence made her smaller, less significant. But Laine was newly married to Bear's best friend, and if the photos that decorated the walls of their home were any indication, the two of them were madly, hopelessly in love. Beth stomped on the green-eyed monster and sat up. Maverick woofed softly and laid his head in her lap.

"He likes you," Laine said as she sat on the edge of a chair facing her. Maverick licked Beth's arm and then padded over to Laine, nudging her hand with his nose. Laine rubbed the dog's ears and met Beth's gaze. "I've learned over the years that Maverick is an excellent judge of character. And so is Bear, so if they like you, then I like you." Her smile sobered just a bit. "I wish we were meeting under different circumstances."

"Me, too." Beth dropped her gaze. "This must be a huge inconvenience for you."

Laine chuckled. "Not at all. Helping friends is never an inconvenience, and when you have friends like Bear, it can be downright exciting."

Beth didn't want to like the chestnut-haired woman, but it was hard not to. She gave Laine a small smile and shrugged. "I suppose." Not knowing what else to say, she looked toward the kitchen and half rose out of her chaise. "Where *is* Bear?"

"Vehicle exchange," Laine replied, standing and backing up a step. "He's transferring his weaponry from the Escalade to my Suburban since the two of you can't go driving around in that shot up jalopy." She turned hazel eyes on Beth and smiled. "I thought, while he was doing that, you and I could put together a few outfits for you."

Beth looked up at the pretty doctor and stood. She was about an inch taller than Laine, but she still felt small beside the woman. Laine carried herself well, with confidence and pride, but there was nothing at all arrogant about her. She was friendly and kind, and Beth had no trouble imagining what Bear, and the woman's husband saw in her.

Jealousy hissed softly and Beth clenched her teeth. *Go away, you green-eyed monster. I don't like you or how you make me feel. Laine and Bear are just friends.* Swallowing her self-consciousness, she smiled.

"That would be nice," Beth said. "I am rather tired of khaki."

"All right then." Laine grinned and linked arms with her. "This is going to be fun." She started walking and Beth had no choice but to go along. Laine cast an assessing eye her way as they walked through the kitchen and upstairs to the bedrooms. "Now, you're a little bustier than I am, but as long as we stay away from any fitted, button-up shirts, we should be fine. I have a sweater I *know* will look divine on you."

Twenty minutes later Beth found herself outfitted for a week long getaway, and to her own surprise, it *had* been fun. The king-sized bed looked like a tornado of women's clothing had landed and fizzled out in the middle of it, shirts, pants, and other items tossed haphazardly about. At the foot of the bed on top of a cedar chest was a small red Brighton suitcase. Inside that bag were enough clothes to easily go from casual to formal, plus almost anything else one would need for a short vacation, or a few days on the run from a murderous drug cartel.

"And *this*," Laine began, reaching into the closet, "is the only evening wear you will need."

Beth sat on the edge of the bed, already overwhelmed, but when she saw the beautiful, floor-length nightgown her jaw dropped. The fabric was a sheer, shimmering gold color with delicate, braided spaghetti straps and it was trimmed in lace with a lace-edged slit that would reach her left hip. The plunging décolleté and back would reveal vast expanses of skin, and Beth felt the heat rise in her cheeks when Laine tossed it to her.

"It has a matching satin robe and slippers," Laine said, pulling out the additional items. "And with your coloring . . . it will look *fabulous* on you. The color *almost* matches your eyes." She folded the robe and laid it in the open suitcase, slid the feather-topped slippers into a plastic bag and dropped them in as well.

Beth rose and approached the full-length mirror, the glowing gown held against her. "Laine, I can't take this," she whispered. "It's too beautiful. Besides, who would I wear it for?"

She looked at Laine in the mirror and the woman lifted one winged brow. The flush in Beth's cheeks intensified and she dropped her gaze. She draped the gown over her arm and looked at the floor.

"It's not like that with Bear and me."

Laine walked up to her and stood at her back. "Of course it's not." She smiled. "I've seen the way you look at him, *and* the way he looks at you."

Beth's heart twisted painfully. "He doesn't look at me in any way."

"*Exactly*, which means he's hiding something."

Beth's brows drew together, and she looked at the woman in

silent question. Laine sighed, sat down and patted the mattress next to her. Beth eased down on the edge of the bed and laid the gown across her lap.

"I've been exactly where you are, Beth," Laine said. "When Jack and I first met . . . well, he was *all* business, and I was the one who initiated the first kiss." She laughed shortly. "*And* the second. Both times he shut me down. He was Special Agent Jack Vaughn then, and I didn't *want* to be with *Agent* Vaughn. I wanted to be with *Jack*. But, he was determined to be *professional*."

Beth's eyes went wide. "What did you do?"

Laine looked at her lap and a hint of pink bathed her cheeks. "Well, I figured I was stuck with *Agent Vaughn*, so I swore to myself I wouldn't give in to my own weakness. I was so attracted to him I couldn't stand it, but it seemed he could've cared less." She fingered the lace on the gown's hem. "But, I was wrong. When *he* kissed *me*, every promise I'd made to stay strong, every vow I'd taken that he wouldn't melt me again just . . . ." She paused and looked out the window. "They just flew away. He *did* care, and once *Jack* kissed me . . . I couldn't have said no if I had wanted to."

Laine laid a hand over Beth's and chuckled. "I won't lie to you. Bear's a tougher nut to crack, but he's also well worth the effort." She sighed. "Bear is so 'by the book' that sometimes I think he wrote the damn thing, sleeps with it, and rememorizes it every morning over coffee."

"He's hurting," Beth said absently. When Laine tipped her head to the side and looked at her in silent question Beth sighed. "It's nothing he's said or done, but a couple of times I've seen the briefest shadow in his eyes, and it only lasts a second or so." She shrugged. "Maybe I imagined it."

There was a brief silence before Laine said softly, "No, you didn't."

Beth glanced at her and was surprised by the shimmer of tears in Laine's eyes.

"We buried a good friend and a fellow agent a few days ago." She blinked and a single tear fell. "His name was JC, Juan Carlos Acosta. He was killed in the line of duty and . . . Bear saw it happen. He watched as it unfolded, but he couldn't get there in time to stop it."

Beth closed her eyes as she imagined Bear watching a good friend get gunned down, unable to stop it, and that ache inside her grew. "Oh, God."

"I think he blames himself," Laine continued. "As soon as the funeral was over, he took a leave of absence, said he would be unreachable until he decided otherwise, and left."

"It *couldn't* have been his fault." Beth scowled. "Bear's too good. If there was *any* way he could have saved that man's life he would have, even if it meant sacrificing his own."

Laine squeezed her fingers and her expression was pensive. "For someone who's only known him a few days, you seem to have a pretty good read on him."

Beth blinked and opened her mouth to speak, but no words came out.

"Hey," Laine said, "let me take a look at that knee. Bear said you did a number on it."

"Oh, that's not necessary," Beth said with a shake of her head. "I'm fine."

"Why don't you let me be the judge of that?" Beth stared at her for a moment, then relented and rolled up her pant leg. Laine examined the bruised, swollen knee. After a few minutes of poking and prodding, she sighed. "Well, it's going to hurt, but I don't think anything's broken. Ice it as much as you can and try to stay off it."

Beth nodded. "I will. Thanks."

Laine smiled. "No problem. Now, I'm going downstairs to make something to eat," she said, patting Beth's hand and standing. "You haven't eaten yet, have you?" When Beth shook her head Laine smiled. "Good. Now, if you want to take that nightgown, please do, and consider it a gift. It's never been worn." She smiled. "And if you don't want to, that's okay, too. Just . . . come on down to the kitchen when you finish packing."

Beth stared out the open bedroom door for several minutes after Laine had disappeared from sight. She clutched the buttery-soft, filmy material to her chest, warring with herself. When the smell of eggs and coffee reached her, and she heard the sound of Bear's voice, the war came to an abrupt end. He sounded normal, but she knew what she'd seen in his eyes, and now she knew why it was there. Carefully, reverently, she folded the delicate garment and put it inside the suitcase, determined to help him with his demons as he had helped her.

"It wasn't your fault, Bear," she whispered as she zipped the bag closed. "It *wasn't* your fault."

Beth changed into the jeans and flannel shirt Laine had put aside for her, grabbed the suitcase and picked it up. She made her way down the stairs and toward the kitchen, listening to the easy chatter between Laine and Bear. Jealousy tried to lift its head again, ghosts of her past whispering in her ear, but Beth stomped on it once more and with extra force this time. She had no reason to be jealous of Laine, and it bothered her that she was even capable of such a petty emotion. Bear and Laine were good friends, lucky to have each other, just like she and Andrew were.

When she reached the archway leading into the kitchen/family room, she put the suitcase on the floor. Laine was handing Bear a sheaf of papers. Neither of them had noticed her yet, so she leaned against the wall and just listened.

"Here are directions to the cabin," Laine said. She went back to the stove, picked up a large frying pan, gave it a shake, and then flipped the omelet. "It'll take you four or five hours to get there, and the code to the gate is written on the bottom of the directions." She slid the omelet onto a plate and put it in front of Bear and then poured more egg mixture into the pan. "I want you to call me as soon as you arrive."

"No." Bear picked up a fork. "When they check phone records, they'll see I called you."

"Right," Laine agreed, "to ask me about storing the Escalade and borrowing the Suburban, which is exactly what I'll tell them if—"

"When," Bear corrected.

Laine huffed. "Fine, *when* they ask me why you called." She lifted the edge of the omelet with a spatula and adjusted the heat on the stove. "The second call was to tell me you landed . . . wherever."

Bear laughed and shook his head. "They'll be able to triangulate the call using cell towers, Laine. That information will definitely *not* put me in Mexico. And remember to clear your browser history, hard delete."

Laine frowned at him. "If you don't call, how will I know you made it safely?"

He gave her a bored look. "This is me we're talking about, Laine. You'll know if I *don't* make it."

"That's *not* funny."

He lifted one blonde brow and cut into his omelet. "It's not supposed to be."

Beth stepped into the room. "Is there a gas station or a truck stop close to the cabin?" she asked as she moved to sit beside Bear.

Laine flipped the omelet and glanced over her shoulder. "There's a gas station with a mini market about twenty. . . twenty-five miles from the cabin, why?"

Beth leaned her elbows on the granite counter. "Do you have a favorite restaurant or coffee shop here in town you frequent?"

Bear and Laine's eyes met. Something passed between the two of them and the green-eyed monster whimpered. Beth mentally ground it under her heel and waited, trying not to feel as if she was fading into the background again as Bear and Laine looked at each other.

After a brief silence he turned to her, watching her face closely. "Bridges' Café," he said. "What are you thinking?"

Beth met that laser-like gaze. "Think of a name."

He frowned. "A name?"

"Yeah," Beth said. "Just . . . make one up."

"Dick York," Laine said. When Bear arched a brow at her, she shrugged. "It's one of the guys who played Samantha's husband on 'Bewitched'." He smiled and Laine frowned. "What? I like classic sitcoms."

Beth chuckled. "Fine, Dick York it is." She paused as Laine slid an omelet onto a plate and put it in front of her. "Thank you."

"You're welcome." Laine poured more egg mixture into the pan and smiled at her. "Hope you like ham and cheddar."

Beth nodded. "I do."

"Great, we're all happy with the food." Bear looked from Beth to Laine and back. "Now, Dick York?"

Beth glanced at the clock. It was nearly 11 a.m. "Well, Laine, you said it'll take a few hours to get to the cabin, right?" When Laine nodded, Beth continued. "You and your husband should go to Bridges' for an early dinner, say, four o'clock-ish, and wait for someone to call looking for Dick York. That way, you'll know we at least made it to the gas station." She took a bite of omelet and sighed as the perfectly cooked egg melted on her tongue. "Oh, my goodness. This is amazing."

When the silence stretched out Beth glanced up from her plate. Laine had an I-knew-I-liked-you look on her face and Bear was watching her with a barely concealed smile.

Beth swallowed her mouthful. "What?"

Laine chuckled and went back to cooking. "I think you may have found your match, Bear." She gave him a sidelong glance. "You might want to think about getting past a second date with this one."

Heat seared Beth's cheeks and she turned her attention back to her eggs. She felt Bear's gaze on her and suddenly swallowing was more than difficult, it was almost impossible.

"We have to go on a first date before we can go on a second, but we'll see, Laine. We shall see."

Chapter Twelve

Laine had just finished loading the dishwasher when she heard the front door open.

"Doc? Laine, where are you?"

She closed the dishwasher, surprised that Jack was home, and relieved. Bear and Beth had left less than an hour ago. "Kitchen," she called back.

About ten seconds later her husband appeared and her heart did the now familiar jump when those grey eyes met hers. He walked over to her, wrapped his arms around her waist, and leaned in.

"Hi, honey," he said in a low, velvety voice. "I'm home."

Laine smiled. "Mmm. Yes, you are."

His mouth covered hers and Laine melted against him. The thought of making love to him on the kitchen counter warmed her, until she realized he wasn't alone. When she heard someone clear their throat, her eyes snapped open. She looked at Jack in surprise, and then over his shoulder. On the other side of the island stood a man she vaguely remembered from her wedding reception. He was around six feet tall and on the thin side with dark hair, green eyes, and sharp, pointed features. He wore wire rimmed glasses and a black overcoat, and he couldn't have looked more like an 'agent' if he'd had FBI tattooed on his forehead. He smiled at her, which made him considerably easier to look at, and his cheeks flushed slightly.

"Afternoon, Mrs. Vaughn," he said.

Her brows rose and she looked at Jack. Her husband gave her a sheepish smile.

"Babe, this is Special Agent Fellowes. You remember him from the wedding, right?"

"Mm hmm." She unhooked Jack's hands from the small of her back and stepped away from him, hitting her leg on the trash can. Realization dawned. *Shit.* She smiled at their visitor, hoping it didn't look as forced as it felt. "Nice to see you again, Special Agent Fellowes."

Fellowes strode around the island with his hand extended.

"Sorry to intrude, ma'am."

"Oh, don't apologize." She shook the man's hand. "I'm sure if Jack could've told me you were coming," she paused and gave her husband a pointed look, "he would have." She turned another smile on the agent. "Would you like a cup of coffee?"

"No, thank you, ma'am." Fellowes adjusted his glasses. "I just have a few questions to ask you and then I'll be on my way."

Laine gave him a blank look, then shrugged and gestured toward the family room, thankful they were moving away from the proverbial scene of the crime. "All right, have a seat, Special Agent Fellowes."

The agent preceded them into the family room and Laine sent a quick glare Jack's way. Her husband shrugged, mouthed "Sorry," and followed his coworker. When they were seated comfortably, Special Agent Fellowes took a computer tablet from the bag over his shoulder. Laine sat next to Jack, but not close enough for him to touch her.

"Okay, Mrs. Vaughn . . . ."

Jack scooted closer and put his hand on her leg. She laced her fingers through his and squeezed, just a little harder than necessary. "Please, call me Laine."

Fellowes blushed slightly. "As you wish, Laine." He tapped the tablet's screen. "Okay, then, let's get to it." He glanced at her and then refocused on the computer. "Have you seen or spoken to Special Agent Bristol recently?"

"Yes." Laine nodded. "I spoke to him earlier today."

"And when was that?"

Laine glanced at Jack, but he said nothing and his face was oddly blank. "Ten . . . ish, I guess. Why?"

Fellowes ignored her question. "What did you talk about?"

Laine thought that was rude, but let it pass. "He asked if he could borrow my Suburban and leave his Escalade here."

Fellowes glanced at her. "You didn't think that odd?"

Laine shrugged. "A little. I mean, he's supposed to be in the middle of Rocky Mountain National Park, but aside from that, no. He loves that Cadillac, and we let him park it here whenever he's going to be out of town for more than a few days." Fellowes glanced at Jack who nodded in agreement. That sparked Laine's temper and she sharpened her tone. "Are you going to check with my husband each time I answer one of your questions, *Special Agent* Fellowes? Maybe you should just ask *him* and leave me out of it."

Color surged into the agent's face. "I'm sorry, Laine." He glanced at Jack again. "I'm going to need the information on that Suburban, Jack."

"Sure thing, Bill."

Laine scowled. "Why are you so interested in what Bear's driving?"

Again, Fellowes ignored her question and asked another of his own. "Did he actually come by and change vehicles?"

"Yes."

"Tell me exactly what happened."

Laine gaped at him, but he was looking at his tablet. She took a breath. "Well, he showed up about ten minutes after he called. I'd already backed the Suburban out of the garage, and I left the door open so he could drive in. He parked, covered the Escalade, shut the garage door and came inside."

Fellowes looked up. "He came inside?"

"Yes. How else do you suppose he got the keys?"

"You could've left the keys in the ignition."

Laine pursed her lips. "Sorry, Special Agent Fellowes, but I went to school at Harvard and did my internship and residency in Chicago. I don't *leave* keys in the ignition . . . *ever.*"

Fellowes nodded. "Understandable. When he came inside, how did he look?"

Laine didn't bother to hide her exasperation. "He looked like Bear. How was he supposed to look? *What* is this about?"

"I'm sorry, Laine," Fellowes said, "but I can't discuss an ongoing investigation."

"Investigation?" She turned to Jack and then looked at Fellowes again. "Should I be worried about him?"

"Just answer his questions, babe," Jack said softly. "How was Bear when he showed up here?"

"He seemed *fine.*"

"He wasn't injured in any way?" Fellowes asked.

Laine half came out of her seat. "Injured? No, why would you ask that?"

"So, he seemed normal?"

Laine turned to Jack, and he squeezed her knee reassuringly. She looked into Jack's silver eyes for a moment and then turned back to their visitor. "Yes, Special Agent Fellowes. Perhaps a little more subdued than usual, but he's been like that since Agent Acosta's death."

Fellowes looked at her and his expression sobered.

"I don't understand why you're asking *me* about Bear," Laine said. "Ask *him.*"

The man sighed. "I'd like to, Laine, but I can't find him."

"So . . . track his cell phone or something."

"Either his cell is malfunctioning or he's turned off the GPS capability."

Laine crossed her arms over her chest. "He *did* say when he took his leave of absence that he was going to be incommunicado until he decided otherwise, Special Agent Fellowes. Maybe you and the FBI should respect that and give him his space."

"I'd like to, ma'am, but things have changed." He tapped the screen a few more times. "What did he say while he was here? Did he mention where he was going?"

"Sort of." She gave Jack a pointed look. "He said he was going to take *your* advice, whatever *that* means."

Fellowes looked at Jack.

"I told him to go to Cabo, Bill. Said he should spend his time with tequila and senoritas."

Fellowes made a note of that. "Can I take a look at his car?"

"Sure." Jack rose. "Come on, I'll show you." He leaned over and brushed his lips over her cheek, before meeting her gaze. "I'll be right back."

Laine nodded and waited until the side door closed behind them. Then she ran into the kitchen, retrieved the bloody cotton, bandages, and other used medical supplies from the trash and ran back into the family room. She had planned to dispose of the evidence once the dishes were done, but again life had shown up with its twisted and often annoying sense of humor. With the press of a button, she turned on the gas fireplace and tossed the incriminating trash onto the flames. She turned up the fire and glanced over her shoulder toward the garage. All she could see from her vantage point was the door going up. She looked at the flames as they began to devour the blood-stained evidence, the alcohol soaked pads flaring and then blackening.

"Come on, come *on*."

The flames readily chewed through the gauze, paper, and cotton, and less than a minute later all that remained was a faint trace of ash. Laine turned the gas down, sat down on the edge of the hearth and held her hands toward the flames. After a few moments she heard the side door open and schooled her face into an impassive mask.

"Cold, babe?"

She looked up at her husband as he moved to her side. "A little chilly." She glanced at Special Agent Fellowes. "And scared, actually. Is everything okay out there?"

The two men looked at each other as Jack eased down beside her. "I'll tell you later. Anything else, Bill?"

"I'm going to send out a forensics team to check the garage and tow the Escalade, but that can wait until tomorrow." He looked between the two of them. "Is that all right or do you want me to get a warrant?"

"It's fine." Jack looked at Laine. "Isn't it, babe?"

Laine's insides clenched, but she nodded. "Of course." She looked at Special Agent Fellowes. "Is there anything I can do to help?"

"You already have." Fellowes tapped his tablet a few more times, put it in the bag and slipped the strap over his shoulder. "Well, that's it for now. If you remember anything else, Laine, have Jack give me a call." He gave her a sad smile. "Sorry to intrude. You two have a nice day."

Jack rose. "I'll see you out."

Laine watched the two men until they disappeared from sight. She heard them converse briefly in hushed tones before the door closed. Resting her elbows on her knees, she waited for her husband to reappear and prepared herself for the barrage of questions she knew was coming.

Jack's hawk-like gaze met hers the moment he entered the room, and he slowly walked toward her. His eyes were narrowed, assessing. Her heart began to thud, but she kept her face blank as he crouched in front of her. He ran a finger over her cheek and tipped his head to the side.

"You okay?"

She looked into those silvery eyes she loved more than life and nodded. "I'm fine. Is *Bear* okay?"

He narrowed his gaze on her face. "You're *very* good. But then, you always were. I think that's part of the reason I fell in love with you."

Laine's brows drew together. "What are you talking about?"

"You know exactly what I'm talking about." His expression hardened just slightly and Laine instantly recognized *Special Agent* Vaughn. He laced his fingers through hers. "And now you're going to tell me *everything* you *didn't* tell him."

She met his gaze for a moment, then leaned forward and kissed him. Jack cupped her head with one hand and met her tongue with his. When the familiar heat started to coil inside her she ended the kiss and rose. "No." She looked down at him and shook her head. "No, I'm not."

*****

Beth approached the payphone, her hair hidden under a baseball hat, a pair of dark glasses covering her eyes, her hands stuffed into thin, soft gloves. After popping the necessary quarters into the machine, she dialed the number Laine had pulled from the Yellow Pages. On the second ring a perky, female voice answered.

"Bridges' Café. How can I help you?"

"Um, hi, I'm supposed to meet someone there, but I'm running late. Could you check and see if a Dick York has arrived?"

"Why, sure. You just hold on a second."

The phone made a muffled sound as if it was being held to someone's chest, and then Beth heard the waitress shout the name several times. When the waitress came back on the line, she actually sounded disappointed.

"Sorry, hon, but I guess he's running late, too. Blind date?"

Beth sighed and a shaky laugh escaped her. "Um, yeah. He's supposed to be a great guy and I didn't want to screw it up. Thanks."

"No problem. And if he asks, I'll tell him you called and are having car trouble."

"Appreciate it. Thanks, again."

"You're welcome." The young woman giggled. "Have a nice day."

Beth hung up the phone, turned and walked back to the Suburban.

"All clear?" Bear asked as she got into the passenger seat.

"We're good. I just hope Laine was there to get the message."

Bear started the engine. "Oh, she was there. So was Jack."

"I did suggest that she and her husband have an early dinner." Beth snapped her seatbelt on. "That would mean he would be there."

Bear gave her a sidelong glance. "He wasn't there because she asked him to take her to dinner. He's looking for me."

Beth's head snapped around and a chill of uncertainty slithered up her spine. "Why would you say that?"

"I checked my phone just as we entered the Denver city limits, shortly before I called Laine." He put the Suburban in gear and carefully pulled back onto the road. "There were half a dozen missed calls from the office, and a half-dozen more from Jack's cell. That means they've been to the motel and want to talk to me."

She inhaled sharply, apprehension bubbling like cold, liquid tar in her belly. "Can they track your cell?"

He shook his head. "I disabled the GPS and left it in the Escalade. But it does mean they've probably checked phone records and have questioned Laine. And, they know what we're driving." A grim smile curved his mouth. "Once we get to the cabin, we won't be leaving . . . unless we steal a different car."

Beth closed her eyes and leaned her head back. *What I wouldn't give for a glass of wine, some Adele, and a steaming hot bubble bath right now.* "I was kind of hoping we wouldn't have to leave until this was resolved."

"It's my goal to wrap this up and have you back in Denver before your showing."

Her eyes opened and she slowly turned her head to look at him, that thick, viscous liquid in her middle expanding outward. "How did you . . . ?"

"Laine recognized you." He gripped the steering wheel, his gaze moving back and forth between the road in front of him and the rearview mirror. "There was a story in today's paper about you complete with your picture." His expression was neutral. "Why didn't you tell me?"

Beth sighed in resignation. "Given what was happening, I didn't think it was important."

He glanced at her. "That showing could be the biggest break of your career. It could *make* you."

Her heart twisted and her brain fired off a snarky line about Murphy's Law, but she bit it back. "It could, but only if I'm *alive* to be there." She looked out the window and her synapses crackled again. Her vocal chords activated before she even really thought about it. "Then again, if I'm dead, my pictures will probably be worth more money."

"*Don't* talk like that."

His expression was a dark warning, and she knew it would frighten anyone but the people who knew him best. The thought that she knew him enough to not be scared buoyed her a bit. "I'm kidding, Bear." She shrugged. "Sort of."

"Beth—"

The tone of his voice told her he was getting annoyed, so she tried to lighten the mood. "Okay, okay." She sighed and rested a hand on his arm. "I wouldn't want all your hard work at keeping me alive to be for nothing." He glared at her and a sad chuckle escaped her. "There's no use crying over spilled milk, Bear, and let's face it, we're both swimming in a big puddle of spilled milk. When we get past the 'make it out alive' part, *then* I'll worry about the showing." When he didn't respond, she gave him a small smile. "Come on, lighten up. If you're *this* serious for the foreseeable future, you're going to be a real drag to be around. After all, you're the little ray of sunshine in this duo, not me. You're the only thing holding me together."

He scowled and turned his gaze back to the road.

Beth tried another tack, hoping she could distract him and satisfy her own curiosity. "So . . . tell me about Laine."

"What about her?"

"Where'd you meet?"

His expression said "Really?" but his mouth said, "She didn't go over that while you two were trying on clothes together?"

"No." Beth chuckled. She sobered as she remembered the burning pang of jealousy she'd felt, thankful that sour emotion was no longer clotted in her chest. She tried again with him. "So, where'd you meet?"

Bear shook his head. "Well, I met her about three years ago, a day or so after she dug a bullet out of Jack's shoulder, about twenty minutes before she was taken hostage by a domestic terror group, and about thirty minutes before Jack was shot and almost killed." A small smile curved his mouth. "I could give you the official FBI version, but it sounds much more exciting coming from Laine and Jack themselves."

Holy mother of real-life action movies. Beth turned her eyes back to the road. "Wow." Not only did the doctor have better style, a better education, and a better career, she had a better story, too, and Bear loved her. That pang of jealousy was back and harder to ignore. "Probably sounds like a Tom Clancy audio book when *she* tells it." She winced inwardly at the petulance she heard in her own voice.

"Just like yours will when all is said and done," Bear commented. He lifted one brow and looked at her out of the corner of his eye. "Do I detect a note of jealousy?"

Beth scowled and crossed her arms over her chest as heat

surged into her cheeks. She was busted, and rightly so. "Yes," she said after a brief pause. When Bear chuckled, she ran a hand over her face and sighed. "I know. It's ridiculous. You don't have to tell me."

"Glad I don't have to point it out."

"She just seems so . . . *perfect*." Beth tried not to sound childish, but it didn't work very well. "She's beautiful, intelligent, confident . . . ."

"Gee," Bear mused wryly, rubbing his chin, "those are all words I'd use to describe *you*."

Beth looked at him, and her heart thumped uncomfortably in her chest. Next to Laine she'd felt invisible, as if Bear didn't see her anymore. "You . . . ." Heat flooded her face and she turned her gaze to her lap. "You think I'm . . . ?"

"Yes, yes, and I guess I have to rethink the confident part," he replied. He wiggled his brows. "I do believe I already mentioned the fact you're beautiful."

Her heart leapt again and her chest tightened. "I . . . I thought . . . ." She closed her eyes and cleared her throat. "I thought you were just being nice."

"I was, but it doesn't mean what I said was untrue."

She could feel him watching her and wished she could crawl into the nearest hole. She hadn't been fishing for a compliment but it sounded as if she had, and her face felt as if it would burst into flame. "Thank you."

"You're welcome."

They drove in silence from that point, although she saw him glance at her occasionally in her periphery. Each time he did, she wanted to squirm in her seat. She wondered what he was thinking, if her abysmal performance since they'd left the mini-market had altered his opinion of her. She hoped not.

After about ten minutes they left the main highway and started to ascend a narrow, gravel-covered lane that cut through the trees and up the side of the mountain. It was slow going. After they crested the peak and started down the other side, Beth caught glimpses of a lake as they wound through the crags and ridges. It looked like a dark blue jewel set midst the pines and maples, small but deep, if the color was any indication. Late afternoon sun glinted off the surface in pale gold and yellow flashes, and then it disappeared from view. It would be a perfect backdrop for wildlife shots, and she wondered briefly if the wildlife was the only danger lurking in the woods.

More than half an hour passed before the road dead-ended at a tall, metal gate. Elaborate wrought iron fencing extended in either direction into the woods, the foliage eventually swallowing the metal spires in a sea of green. Set in one of the brick columns flanking the gate was what looked like an old-fashioned gas lamp and a keypad.

"I guess this is it," Bear commented as he put the Suburban in park and rolled his window down. "Where's the gate code?"

Beth reached into the glove box and retrieved the printout Laine had given them. She unfolded the papers and read off the numbers. Bear punched the appropriate buttons and the gate moved gracefully to the side.

"That was easy," she commented.

Bear glanced at the trees overhead and then along the fence line. "That's how I like it."

Once they were through the gate, it rolled shut and Beth felt a flutter of uneasiness. The sun was almost gone, hidden behind the peaks to the west, the air heavy and damp. She leaned her head out the window and inhaled deeply of the forest's earthy scent, the smell of grass, dirt, leaves, and other various smells combined into a perfume she reveled in. The driveway continued on for what seemed forever until they came around a small hill. The house appeared to their left, and faced west toward the lake. Bear gently pulled to a stop and whistled softly.

"You sure this is a cabin and not a ski lodge?" Beth asked as her gaze wandered over the immense A-frame. "Funny, but when she said 'cabin' this is *not* what I pictured."

Bear rested one hand on top of the steering wheel. "Well, Laine told me this place was worth almost a mill, but to be honest, it's not what I pictured either." He shook his head. "This isn't a cabin, it's a damn mansion in the woods."

In addition to the central part of the house, there were two wings off either side of the "A" and the several acres surrounding the main building had been covered with bright green, meticulously manicured lawn, which looked oddly out of place.

If one turned left from where they were, the gravel lane descended a gentle slope to a broad expanse of smooth concrete and a subterranean, four-car garage that ran along the north side of the house. If one drove straight, the driveway circled around in front of the house and back on itself in an elegant oval.

"I knew there was a reason I disliked that guy," Bear said under his breath. "If anything defines the word 'pretentious' it would be this place. Guess that means it suits him."

"Wonder if he's adopting?" Beth asked absently as Bear drove around the oval and parked in front of the enormous structure. She got out of the Suburban and closed the door. When Bear moved to her side, she looked up at him, but he was staring at the house.

She faced the "A" frame. "Y'know," she said, "when I realized I was going to be on the run, this is not the sort of place I imagined I'd be hiding out in."

Bear planted his fists on his hips. "Me either."

"It's weird, but I kind of prefer the Rocky Mountain Inn." The image of the kiss they'd shared flashed briefly in her mind, flooding her with heat. Then she remembered what had happened later and cold flashed over her skin and permeated to her very soul. She gulped and dropped her chin. "Then again, maybe not." She squeezed her eyes shut, trying to will away the picture of a bleeding Bear. "Definitely not."

He chuckled and draped an arm over her shoulders, pulling her against his side. "For what it's worth, I'd rather be in a place like the Inn than this million-dollar clip joint, too."

She looked up at him as his gaze wandered over the façade of the house. The last vestige of sunlight glimmered briefly on the uppermost part of the two-story front windows, and then the glass went dark. Only moments later, lights began flickering on, first outside, and then inside, until the entire building and the surrounding area was bathed in a golden glow. Her stomach clenched, and she moved closer to Bear.

His eyes narrowed. "Must have the lights on a timer."

Beth leaned into his side. "Or it's not vacant."

He looked down at her and met her gaze, and his expression darkened slightly. He stepped away from her, removed his pistol from its holster, and gripped the weapon with the confidence and ease of someone who was intimately acquainted with firearms.

"Let's go see if anybody's home."

Chapter Thirteen

Bear thought briefly about telling Beth to stay with the Suburban, but he decided not to. She had been pretty compliant until now, but if he had a choice of staying behind in a car or going with someone, he knew which one he'd pick. He didn't really want to leave her alone outside anyway. He walked slowly toward the house, her fingers hooked through one of his belt loops as she stayed a step behind.

He walked up the stairs to the expansive front porch that wrapped around the entire building. It was decorated with large potted plants, banks of ferns, and sofas done in dark wood with bright, jewel-toned pillows. His brows drew down. Pretentious didn't begin to describe the owner of this place. Moving slowly, eyes darting back and forth, he crossed to the massive front doors.

The double-portal entry was made with heavy, ornately carved wood inset with beveled glass that sparkled like finely cut jewels. Bear paused, lifted his hand, and knocked soundly. Beth moved closer and tightened her grip on his belt loop. He glanced at her over his shoulder and gave her a reassuring smile. He knocked again, waited a while longer, then pulled the keys from his pocket and unlocked the door.

They stepped into the entry and he heard her gasp softly. Before them was a double staircase reminiscent of something out of *Gone With the Wind*, the space soaring upwards more than two stories. A chandelier made from deer antlers hung some fifteen feet above their heads, the golden light it cast glinting off the highly polished wood floors. In between the stairs was an archway made from large logs carved into what looked like real trees, the branches and leaves and even birds outlined in vivid detail as the boughs gently curved upward from either side and met in the middle. Bear slipped the keys back into his pocket, and closed and locked the door behind them.

"I don't think anyone's home," he said in a low voice.

"Boy, they must really like their space." She released his belt loop but stayed close. "This place is enormous."

"Let's check out the rest of it." He brought the gun up. "Stay with me."

"Don't have to tell me twice."

Bear walked forward through the arch and found himself in what could only be called a great room. It was a sunken living room lined with oversized, plush furniture. More deer-antler chandeliers dangled above. A fully stocked bar lined the south wall to his right. Barstools covered with cow hide sat empty and waiting. The room itself was about sixty feet square, the hardwood floors almost completely covered with thick, expensive rugs. Directly across from them was a floor-to-ceiling, double-sided fireplace that was at least fifteen feet wide made from what looked like river rock. On either side of the edifice were soaring, two-storey archways similar to the one they'd just walked through.

"I stand corrected," Beth said. "This is nicer than any ski lodge I've ever been to."

Bear looked around and shook his head. "Probably cost more, too."

He quickly crossed the room, the rugs deadening the sound of his footsteps. He opened the only door in the room and discovered it was a full bath, complete with a ball-and-claw tub and antique fixtures. He closed the door and proceeded through the archway.

On the other side of that enormous fireplace was the kitchen/family/dining room, which was even larger than the great room. The back wall was entirely made up of windows and looked out onto a wide deck with chaise longues, a large, brick barbecue, an outdoor kitchen, and a sunken hot tub.

"This guy must entertain a lot," Beth commented as she walked past him.

He smiled when she checked the lock on the sliding glass door and then looked at him. He walked to a door set between a fireplace and the wall-mounted TV and opened it. A set of stairs led down, probably to the garage. Bear closed the door and turned around.

The other two-thirds of the space was dominated by a professionally appointed kitchen. Separating the family room from the kitchen was a split-level, granite-topped island bigger than the Escalade. Bear crossed to a closed door in the southeast corner of the room, flipped the light switch on the wall, and discovered an enormous walk-in pantry with enough canned food and dry goods to feed an entire Third World nation.

He backed out of the pantry, closed the door, and turned to Beth. She eased up onto one of the barstools lining the island and watched him, her expression guarded.

"What now?" she asked.

"Now," he said, "we check upstairs, unless you want to wait for me here."

Beth shook her head and slipped off the chair. Bear looked around again and noticed the stairs in the northeast corner of the room. He nodded toward them.

"God forbid they should have to walk back to the foyer to go upstairs," he mused as he crossed the room and took the stairs two at a time. From the sound of it, Beth was close on his heels.

The stairs opened up into a walkway that ran from the back of the house to the front and overlooked both the kitchen and the great room. It ended at an open catwalk that crossed over the great room and led to the southern wing of the house and another hallway that ran exactly parallel to the one they were in.

Bear opened one of the two doors in this hall and slowly stepped into the room, his pistol at the ready. He looked around what could only be the master bedroom and whistled again. A massive, custom-made bed at least eight feet square dominated the sparsely furnished space and sat beneath an enormous picture window. On the wall closest to the bed were another fireplace and a door. He flexed his fingers on the grip of the .45.

A walk-in closet that was bigger than his bedroom made him shake his head in amazement. He checked the space for anyone who might have been hiding, then reentered the bedroom and walked to the opposite side. Beth watched from the outer hallway as he opened the only other door and found himself in the master bath, which also opened to the hall.

"More money than sense," he said under his breath as he closed the door on the second enclosed toilet. "I'm surprised they don't have separate tubs, too."

He walked back into the bedroom and smiled when he saw Beth lying on her stomach in the middle of the colossal bed. Her hands were running slowly over the plush, faux fur comforter. At least, he *thought* it was faux fur.

"You're definitely sleeping in this room," she said, flipping onto her back.

He moved to the edge of the bed and sat down. "Why is that?"

She leaned her head back into the mattress, looked at him upside-down, and smiled. "You'll actually *fit* in this bed. You can stretch out, be comfortable for a change."

He couldn't stop the smile. "What, you don't want to share with me anymore?" he teased. He was rewarded by the color that brightened her cheeks and the widened eyes. Yep, it was official. Teasing her was now his favorite pastime. A chuckle escaped him at her expression, and he decided to have mercy on her. "We still have more rooms to check, unless you want to stay here."

"Right." She sat up. "Sorry."

He extended a hand to her. "Don't be." Bear pulled her to her feet. She took a step, got her legs tangled in the draped corner of the comforter, and stumbled. He caught her neatly and hauled her up against his chest. The same electrical shock that had seared through him when she'd kissed him that morning crackled to life again. Bear let his gaze wander over her face for a split-second, imagining another kiss, *wanting*, oddly enough, another kiss. Keeping his expression neutral, he gave her a tight smile and set her back on her feet. "Careful."

Her flush deepened and she nodded mutely. Stuffing her hands into her pockets, she bit her lip and waited for him to move. That sliver of sadness he'd felt at the Rocky Mountain Inn grew into a shard and he turned away from her before it registered on his face. Strangely, it was becoming harder and harder to remain aloof with her. She had a way about her that put him at ease, something that made him feel like *Bear* instead of *Special Agent* Bristol. And, he couldn't deny he was attracted to her. *You can't be attracted to her, so get your head screwed on straight and DO YOUR JOB.* Scowling, he left the master bedroom and stepped into the hall.

He looked down into the great room as they crossed the walkway above the space to the other hallway. There were four doors set in this wall, and he opened them one by one. The first door led to a bedroom about a third the size of the master suite. The second door was for a large Jack-and-Jill bathroom, and the third led to another bedroom. The fourth door opened into a study/office.

He leaned against the jamb as Beth stood opposite him and peered into the room. "Guess nobody's home," he said.

"Which means the lights *were* on a timer," she observed. She looked at him out of the corner of her eye and smiled. "My bad."

Bear chuckled. "Let's go unload the Suburban, and then see if you can open the garage door. I'd rather *not* leave the car parked in front of the house." He holstered his pistol. "Don't want to announce to the neighbors that we're home."

She lifted one winged brow. "And have them descending like vultures? We *can't* have that now, can we? I don't think we have enough wine for all of them." She laughed softly and turned to walk back the way they'd come. "Somehow, I doubt we have to worry about any unannounced callers, and if anyone *does* come knocking, we just won't answer."

There it was, that sense of humor and sarcasm that pulled at him like a magnet. "I'd rather be safe than sorry," he replied with a smirk.

Bear watched the gentle sway of her hips and parried the bolt of lust that wanted to impale him. She was *working* those jeans. Something in his gut contracted as he thought about the night, and possibly nights, to come, here, alone, with her. The softness of her hair, those golden eyes, the dusky skin that he *so* wanted to touch; it was going to be incredibly hard to stay focused with only her to distract him. He ground his teeth together and forced himself to think about the task at hand. The cartel had an insider at the sheriff's office, which meant whatever information law enforcement had the cartel probably had as well. Then there was the matter of *his* office. He and Jack had already dealt with one traitor, but that had been nearly three years ago. It seemed a new one had sprung up in the former rat's place. The image of JC's murder flashed in his mind and the pain of it ripped through him like a chainsaw, teeth and claws bared and churning. He paused and squeezed his eyes shut as his internal organs were shredded and splattered against the inside of his chest. Sorrow blossomed in a tornado of cold regret and for several seconds he couldn't breathe.

"Bear?" The voice was Beth's but it sounded as if it came from far away. "Bear, what's wrong?"

He heard the concern in her voice, but the whirlwind inside him had him in full lockdown. He couldn't move, couldn't take a breath, and he couldn't pull himself out of the internal storm to reassure her. He felt her hand on his arm and suddenly the winds calmed to a dull roar. Finally, he opened his eyes and looked into those golden-brown pools lined with the impossibly thick lashes. She blinked and her brows drew together, and she pressed her fingers to his cheek. That small but intimate contact gave him the strength to break free of the poisonous memories and solidified his resolve. Keeping her alive was his number one priority. He covered her hand with his, turned his face, and kissed her palm, and an enormous sense of gratitude replaced the previous internal carnage. *She* had saved *him* this time, and it was several seconds before he found his voice.

"I'm fine." He smiled. "Let's get unpacked. I don't know about you, but I'm starving."

He stepped around her and Beth watched him go, a mixture of uncertainty and frustration spinning inside her. That shadow had passed behind his eyes again, but it had been darker this time, far more pronounced. She had a feeling he was anything but fine, but as he descended the grand staircase and crossed the foyer, she sighed and followed him.

After they unloaded their bags and several firearms, Beth walked through the house to the door that led to the garage. She flipped the light switch on the wall and jumped when overhead fluorescent lights crackled and buzzed to life. Then she descended the stairs into the garage. The vast space was empty except for a Mercedes Benz G550 SUV. Once the Suburban was inside, she hit the button again and the door whispered shut.

She watched as Bear got out of the vehicle and walked toward her. His expression was neutral, and he gave her a smile as he gestured toward the stairs.

"After you, my lady."

Beth looked up into that sharply planed face for a moment, then gave him a curtsy and mounted the stairs. Once she reached the main floor, she crossed to the island and sat on one of the barstools. Bear followed close behind, and even in the large room, she felt his presence. It was a comfort to have him near, but it also made her nervous. She searched for something to break the quiet.

"I know I already asked this," she said as he walked toward her, "but what now?"

He walked to one of the refrigerators and opened the door. "Hungry?"

She looked at his broad back. "I could eat. You?"

He gave her a wry look over his shoulder and returned to perusing the icebox's contents. "I thought Laine said they kept this place stocked."

"No point in having fresh food if you're going to be out of the country for a couple weeks," Beth observed, putting her elbow on the counter and propping her chin in her hand. "Just because they're rich doesn't mean they're blatantly wasteful."

Bear rubbed his chin. "Not much in here except for condiments and eggs. Maybe we'll have better luck with the freezer." He leaned over, opened the freezer, and smiled. "That's more like it." He held up two individually wrapped, thick-cut steaks. "Pop these in some water, maybe a couple minutes in the microwave on defrost and they should be ready to grill."

Beth slid off the stool. "You cook, and I'm going to take a shower."

His brows drew together. "You're really big on this 'clean' thing, aren't you?"

She looked askance at him. "Yeah. I get OCD about hygiene for a few days after a photo safari."

Bear tossed the steaks into the stainless steel sink. "Okay. How would you like your steak, madam?"

"Medium," she said over her shoulder as she walked toward the foyer. "And if you can rustle up a baked potato or something that would be *divine*."

He chuckled and turned on the tap. "Will do."

Beth walked to the entry, grabbed her suitcase, and walked up one side of the double staircase. She paused on the landing and looked to her left, toward the master suite, silently debating with herself. Did she want to sleep with him? *Oh, hell yeah.* But, did he feel the same? Bear wouldn't kick her out if she put her things in the master bedroom that much she knew. As the gentleman he was, however, he might choose another bedroom if she did. Last night they hadn't had a choice. Tonight, there were three beds to choose from. She decided to avoid the potential hurt feelings and err on the side of caution. After chewing her lip for a moment and swallowing her disappointment, she turned right and went to the first spare bedroom.

There was a padded bench at the end of the king-sized bed and she hefted the suitcase onto it. She opened the bag, took out the toiletry case, and crossed to the door that opened into the Jack-and-Jill bathroom. Less than a minute later she was naked and standing beneath a steaming shower. As the water beat into her shoulders, she thought back to the look on Bear's face when he'd paused in the hallway. Self-reproach and self-recrimination she had recognized immediately, and then the flash of pain had darkened his eyes. It almost appeared to have knocked the wind out of him. She closed her eyes as she imagined the event that had rocked someone as strong and solid as Bear. She had witnessed four murders, but to see someone she knew and cared for gunned down? Close enough to watch but not intervene? Her heart thumped painfully in her chest and a tremor ran through her as everything inside her recoiled from the very idea. She braced herself against the tiled wall, but even the hot water couldn't dispel the chill growing in her chest. Here she was asking him to help *her* keep it together, but who helped *him*? He'd been as steady as the Rock of Gibraltar, but she knew his pain ran deep. She'd felt it in that few seconds as if it was her own. *It's time to start pulling your weight, Beth.* She pushed away from the wall, took a deep breath, and finished bathing.

After dressing, Beth dried her hair and left her room. The smell of grilling meat immediately assaulted her and her mouth watered. Beth crossed the connecting hallway and walked past the master bedroom, taking the back stairs into the kitchen.

She choked back a laugh when she saw Bear at the grill, a pair of tongs in one hand and an apron around his waist. The garment was obviously a woman's, pink in color and edged with lace, and it looked pitifully small on his massive frame. He frowned and glanced over his shoulder as he stirred something in a small pot on the stove.

"What?" He looked down at himself. "What's so funny?"

Beth walked across the room and sat on a barstool. She waved an arm, gesturing at him. "It's a nice look, but I'm sure you could've found something *without* ruffles. And pink? Really? I would think blue is more your color."

He grinned and turned back to the meat. "It's about functionality, not fashion," he said. "Besides, I didn't feel like searching every drawer in the place. You'd think people with this much money would be organized enough to put all the aprons in one location."

Beth chuckled. "You'd think."

He gestured to his right. On the end of the island were an open bottle of red wine and two glasses. "Like some?"

Beth sighed softly. "Oh, you are a god among men."

A wry smile curved his mouth. "You've already told me that."

"And it's as true now as it was then." She grinned and got off her seat. After walking around the island, she poured two glasses and then walked toward him. "Your Merlot, my good man."

He took the glass she offered and met her gaze. He held the

goblet toward her. "To you. This is the most fun I've ever had while being chased by ruthless killers."

His tone was jaunty, but his words stopped her cold. The memory of the man she'd killed followed by the murders she had witnessed assaulted her without warning, the lid on the box popping open as if it was spring-loaded. Her stomach clenched and her pulse jumped. Synapses fired, her brain having more than a little trouble reconciling her current reality with the belief most people held that stuff like this only happens to "other people." She felt slightly lightheaded and grabbed for the edge of the counter. Bear's expression immediately changed and he dropped his chin.

"I'm sorry," he said in a voice tinged with regret. "That came out wrong."

She saw the concern in his eyes, realized that once again he was swallowing his own pain to assuage hers. A flash of self-reproach warmed her and she straightened her spine. "No." She shook her head, forced the memories back into the box, and took a deep, steadying breath. "No, that's okay. It's better if I remember why I'm here. We're not on vacation, after all."

He sighed. "Beth—"

"Really," she interrupted, "it's okay." She tapped his glass with hers and took a slow sip. She thought about it for a moment as she swallowed, and then lifted her eyes to his. "I don't have a basis for comparison, but I don't imagine I'd like being in this situation anymore . . . if I was . . . with anyone . . . else . . . if that makes . . . *any* sense."

She felt his gaze on her as she walked back around the island and returned to her seat, grabbing the bottle on the way. *Ah, nothing like a little liquid courage, eh Beth?* She didn't usually drink much, but right now it seemed like the thing to do and she needed every bit of help she could get. After emptying her glass, she poured another, the tart liquid settling warmly in her belly.

"For what it's worth," he said, "I think we're relatively safe for the next twelve to sixteen hours."

Beth mulled that over. The last twelve hours had seemed like quite a stretch of time. Now, she realized with painstaking clarity that it was hardly more than a heartbeat in the grand scheme of things. A cloak of depression hung over her, threatening, looming, and she didn't know if she had the strength to fight it.

"C'mon, Beth," he said, swirling the wine in his glass. "If you're *this* serious for the foreseeable future, you're going to be a real drag to be around."

A stab of indignation cut through her, but when she met his gaze she saw a spark of amusement in his eyes. He was baiting her, provoking her to fight. Again, it was as if he knew exactly what she needed, and right now she *needed* to fight. The cloak of depression seemed to lighten and lift a few feet. She looked at him over the rim of her goblet and arched one brow. "Using my own words against me?"

He shrugged and took a sip. "They're as true now as they were then."

"What are you? A human tape recorder?"

Bear waggled his brows at her. "I have been accused of having . . . an above average memory." He turned, checked the steaks, and stirred whatever was in the pot again. "Wouldn't be very good at my job if I didn't."

"Could you be a little less efficient, please?" She rolled her eyes and took a drink. "You're making the rest of us look bad."

He chuckled, grabbed one steak with the tongs, and placed it on a plate. "Now that's the Beth I know and love."

Beth blinked and almost choked on her mouthful of wine. After clearing her throat, she put the glass aside. "Is that the bitchy and complaining Beth?"

"No, the feisty and smart-assed Beth," he corrected with a low laugh. He put the second steak on another plate, moved to the microwave and opened it. Inside the appliance were two large potatoes in plastic wrap and her stomach growled in anxious anticipation of the coming meal. Bear glanced at her. "I like a girl who can use sarcasm even when her life is in danger."

She rolled her eyes again. "I thought you said we were safe for the next twelve to sixteen hours."

He gave her a pointed look and unwrapped the potatoes. After placing them on the plates, he scooped green beans out of the pot and plopped them next to the potatoes. Once he'd arranged the food to his liking, he picked one plate up and reached across the island to sit it in front of her. "I *said* relatively safe, and I *could* be wrong."

Beth stared at him as he took a glass butter dish and a plastic tub of sour cream from the refrigerator and put them on the counter. He then retrieved salt and pepper, cutlery, and a set of linen napkins, placing them next to the condiments. She watched him for another few seconds. "Well, hell."

Bear looked at her strangely and moved to sit beside her, his plate in hand.

She shook her head and picked up her fork. "I guess I should just forget about the guys killed in the meadow and the guy *I* killed and enjoy this while I can, right?"

Bear seemed to ponder that before he shrugged and flipped his napkin open. "Might as well. A good attitude is better than a bad one any day."

"That's a good way to look at it."

"That's the *only* way to look at it." He cut into his steak. "The bad guys don't care what kind of mood I'm in and whether I spend these moments pissed off or not." He skewered a piece of meat with his fork and looked at her out of the corner of his eye. "Therefore, I choose to take it as it comes, enjoy the times when I'm not in danger, and deal with the danger as it happens."

Beth took a bite and chewed thoughtfully. "Isn't it better to be prepared?"

"I'm *always* prepared," he replied, "but that doesn't mean I have to wallow in it waiting for the other shoe to drop." He took a sip of wine. "If I did that, I'd *really* be a bear." Unbidden, she smiled, and so did he. "Now that's a beautiful smile. I hope to see it often."

Heat flooded her cheeks and she turned her eyes to her plate. He chuckled and continued eating. They finished their meal in comfortable silence. When Bear stood and picked up his plate, she put a hand on his arm.

"Uh uh," she said. She took the plate from him and placed it on top of her own. "You cooked. I'll clean up."

"Beth—"

He was gearing up to argue with her, so she cut him off. "Nope." She stood, grabbed the dishes, and turned away from him with a flourish and a grin. "Go . . . take a shower . . . sit on the porch and finish your wine . . . whatever." She put the dishes in the sink, faced him and planted her hands on the edge of the counter. "I'll do the dishes and join you shortly."

He glared at her and her smile widened.

"You can scowl at me all you want." She shrugged. "It's not going to change anything, so move it." His frown deepened, but she sensed her imminent victory. A soft laugh escaped her. Tipping her head to the side, she gave him a small wave. "Buh-bye."

Bear stared at her for another moment, grabbed his wine glass and stalked out of the kitchen. His expression was that of a petulant child being sent to his room. Beth giggled again and started filling the sink with hot water.

Twenty minutes later the kitchen was spotless, the dishes washed, dried, and put away, and even the grill had been given a good scrubbing. Satisfied with her handiwork, Beth refilled her goblet and meandered toward the front of the house. A thrum of anticipation and apprehension shivered over her skin. He wasn't in the great room. She surmised he was on the porch, but when that, too, proved empty she looked around, uneasiness scratching her spine. It was then she noticed lights through the trees near the lake, and she sucked in a breath. Had they been found? She focused on them and as her eyes adjusted to the glow from the three-quarter moon, she realized there was a long, narrow dock and boathouse at the edge of the water. The pier was outlined by low wattage light fixtures, their glimmer more like flashes of sunlight on water than incandescent illumination. At the end of that pier was a large silhouette, which told her that her favorite FBI agent had taken a walk. Wrapping her arms around herself, she strode briskly across the broad lawn.

His glass of wine stood empty on one of the pilings, and he had his hands stuffed in his pockets, his head tipped back. Beth looked skyward for a second and then moved to his side. She tried to discern his mood, but it, like his expression, was unreadable to her.

"It's gorgeous out here," she said in a low voice.

"Yes, it is."

She sat her glass on another piling and waited for a few moments. "Makes me wonder if the guys who are after us ever pause to appreciate the beauty of the night sky, or anything else for that matter." His jaw tensed and the mood polarized.

"All they appreciate is money, power . . . and death."

She couldn't see his face well in the dim light from the outdoor bulbs lining the dock, but she felt his sorrow as it radiated out from him. It cut her, as if it was her own. Taking a breath, she faced him and put a hand on his arm.

"It *wasn't* your fault, Bear."

He looked at her. The blank mask was back, but Laine had told her that meant he was hiding something.

She said again, "It *wasn't* your fault."

"What are you talking about?"

His voice had taken on a sharp edge, but it was too late to stop now. Beth forced herself to meet that pinpoint gaze and took another breath.

"Laine told me about Special Agent Acosta."

The expression that dropped over his face was dark and forbidding and had a sound like that of a vault door being slammed shut. She cringed inwardly as it echoed through her. Before her courage deserted her, she touched his jaw and plunged ahead.

"It *wasn't* your fault . . . just like that man's death in the meadow wasn't *my* fault." She ran her fingers over the stubble on his cheek. His eyes narrowed just slightly and the muscles in his jaw worked. His sorrow had shifted to anger and she now had a pretty good idea how it felt to slam headfirst into a brick wall, but she couldn't let it go. Her throat nearly closed up, but she forced the words out. "Just because you were close enough to see it happen doesn't make you responsible."

"It was *my* operation," he said from between clenched teeth. "He was *my* agent. That *makes* me responsible."

His anger ignited hers and her tone sharpened. "Did you know he would die when you sent him in?"

He blinked. "No, but there is always that possibility."

Beth rested her hands on his chest and stared hard at him. "And he knew that, too, just like I know that every time I go into the forest I could wind up the entrée du jour for some bear or wildcat." She stepped closer and framed his face with her hands. "But the possibility of dying didn't stop him from doing his job, did it?"

He fixed her with a glare, lines of anger harsh about his mouth.

A shiver coursed through her. After a brief, pregnant silence, he shook his head once. Beth dropped her hands and stepped back, her heart breaking at the frost in his expression.

The box in her mind popped open and the memory unfurled. Unlike most of them, this wasn't terrifying, just painful. Beth saw the red-rimmed eyes of a dead Marine's widow, a woman who had, despite her own loss, offered words of wisdom and comfort during one of the darkest times of Beth's life.

"Mourn his loss," she said softly, tears stinging, "but *do not* take responsibility for it." She straightened her spine. "That lies with the person who pulled the trigger, and by shouldering the blame that isn't yours, you dishonor your friend's memory." His posture tensed and his eyes blazed with cold fury.

"What do *you* know about death, aside from what you've seen the past couple days?"

His caustic tone stung and she backed up another step as her heart faltered. That he would make a snap judgment about her life when he knew virtually nothing about her did more than sting. White hot pain blazed through the center of her chest, as if a lightning bolt had found its home in her. *Oh, if only you knew.* More memories threatened to spill forth, but she squeezed her eyes shut, refusing to let them out. Not here, not now. Her chin trembled and she clenched her teeth to stop it. Dropping her gaze, she closed her eyes and took a deep, hitching, breath as the force of his anger punched through her. "I know more about it than you think," she whispered.

Without another word she turned and walked slowly toward the house.

Chapter Fourteen

Bear stared after her retreating form. Pain ripped through his midsection, cutting and sharp, and he felt strangely hollow, as if his internal organs had splattered onto the wooden planks beneath his feet. Her words, although caring and sweet, had forced him to examine things he didn't want to look at. He felt gutted, empty, and it didn't matter that logically she was absolutely correct.

Even from where he was, he heard the front door slam, and the sound jarred him. His anger evaporated and another deeper, more painful emotion pulled him under. It was like drowning in broken glass, all sharp edges and stabbing shards as fragmented memories surfaced.

A macabre slide show played, flashes of the day JC had died intermingled with snapshots of the time since he'd first set eyes on Beth. First he felt the blast of fear as he saw JC go down and saw Beth being chased. Next was the heart-pumping surge of adrenaline as he raced to get to his dying friend and to Beth. After that the autopilot that had taken over, and blocked out his emotions, kicked in. Lastly, the frigid dread and rush of sorrow that even his autopilot couldn't block out enveloped him. He tasted them as bitterly now as he had on both of those days.

Instinctually, his training kicked in and Special Agent Bristol took the helm. Bear took a deep breath and focused on what was most important right *now*: Beth. That searing pain scored through him again. The look on her face, the pain in her golden gaze, the expression of resolute determination and absolute belief that he had done no wrong . . . . Bear hung his head and closed his eyes. He'd let his control slip a fraction, directed his rage and anguished frustration at her, and she had reacted as if he'd hit her. Guilt rose like bile as he remembered his harsh question. He *had* hit her, not with his fists, but sometimes words inflicted more pain than physical violence.

"You're an *asshole*," he said to himself. "And what the *hell* do you know about her life?" He thought of her parting line, but inwardly he recoiled at examining it more deeply. Death was something he knew too much about, and he didn't want to imagine that Beth did too. Deciding that was a conversation for another time, he ran his hands over his face and stared into the heavens. After several long seconds passed, he looked over his shoulder at the lights from the house, then sighed, turned, and started walking. At the very least he owed her an apology. He just hoped she'd forgive him.

He didn't find her in the great room or the kitchen. As he mounted the back stairs, he found himself not wanting to face her, which surprised him. He'd never been one to shirk his duties or avoid confrontation. He had the scars, emotional and physical, to prove it.

"Move it, Bristol," he scolded himself. "You *don't* get to sit this one out."

Bear paused in the doorway of the master bedroom, but it was empty. His brows drew together and his gaze swung around across the open expanse over the great room to the doors on the other side of the house. Only one was closed. He stared at that carved wooden barrier for a moment, and then crossed the walkway with long, sure strides, determined to set things right. Their position was too precarious not to.

He tapped gently on the door and slowly opened it. To his right was an enormous picture window with a long, padded bench seat beneath it. In front of him was the bed, and to his left was a door that probably led to the bathroom. The room was empty. *What the hell?*

Just as he turned to continue his search, the bathroom doorknob turned and the door opened. Beth was just tying the sash of a golden satin robe, her gaze downcast as she stepped into the room. She looked amazing, almost angelic as the golden fabric shimmered in the dim light. Bear gulped and his abdominals tightened. As if sensing his presence, she looked up and froze.

The silence stretched between them and she remained motionless. Finally, after nearly half a minute, she spoke.

"What are you doing here?"

He wasn't sure how to respond to that because he didn't really know the answer. When he didn't reply, her chin went up a notch.

"I'm not going to apologize for what I said," she told him flatly.

Her stubborn declaration warmed him. "I didn't ask you to."

"So, if that's what you want—"

"I'm not asking for an apology."

He saw her convulsive swallow and felt her defiance fade, a chill of sadness cooled the air between them. She seemed to ponder his remark before she nodded shortly and walked to the window seat bench. She sat sideways on the cushion, pulled her legs to her chest, and wrapped her arms around her shins. Without a word she rested her cheek on her knees, her gaze turned toward the lake. Moonlight glinted darkly off her hair and cast a ghostly reflection of her on the glass. She blinked and he saw a tear as it left a silver track over the bridge of her nose and down her face. Slowly he walked over to where she was, sat down a few feet away, and leaned his back against the window.

"I owe *you* an apology, Beth," he said softly, lacing his fingers together and resting them in his lap. "I had no right to talk to you like that. I don't know anything of your life." He sighed. "I guess I just don't want to believe a pretty girl like you is closely acquainted with death, but I should know by now it touches all of us at some point."

She said nothing, but he saw another tear slowly trail its predecessor. Regret pulled at him. Maybe if she knew a little more about his life, she would understand.

Bear focused on the door leading to the bathroom. "I know I didn't pull the trigger when JC died, at least . . . I didn't pull it fast enough. That's the problem." In his periphery he saw her head turn toward him, but he couldn't look at her. "I knew what was going to happen a split second before it did . . . I *knew.* I was watching the whole thing through the scope of a Remington 700 rifle from the roof of a building across the street, and that sixth sense I was born with started tingling." He shook his head and leaned forward, resting his elbows on his knees. "Had I pulled the trigger at that moment, my friend might very well be alive today."

Remorse almost choked him and he closed his eyes, but telling half the story would accomplish very little. If he was going to be honest, he needed to be *completely* honest.

"And it gets worse."

"Bear—"

"Tall guy, from the meadow?" He paused and looked at her out of the corner of his eye. "He's the one who killed JC." Her eyes widened and she sat up a little straighter, but thankfully all he saw was shock in her expression and not reproach. He wasn't sure he could have taken that. "Had I pulled the trigger at that moment, you probably would *not* be in this position." He turned his gaze back to the bathroom door. "It's my fault you're here."

His muscles clenched as the realization pummeled his insides. It felt as if all his internal organs expanded and contracted at once, fighting each other for space in his chest. Bear took a deep breath and pressed his thumb and forefinger into his eyes.

"It's. *Not.* Your fault."

Her words flowed over him like a soothing balm, but he couldn't look at her. He felt her move. A moment later she knelt beside him. The faint perfume of her hair drifted to him and he inhaled it. Her fingers brushed his cheek as she took his head in her hands. She turned his face to hers, and he felt her gaze wandering over his features.

"Look at me," she whispered.

He didn't want to. In spite of her comforting reassurance, part of him was afraid of what he might see in her eyes. And, yet, he *did* want to look at her. He hated to admit it, but every time she smiled at him his heart beat a little harder. And when she had giggled . . . he had been tempted to tickle her just to hear her laugh like that again. Mentally bracing himself for whatever he might see, he opened his eyes.

Her fingers lightly grazed his jaw. "Had you shot that man at that moment, I would never have met you." Her eyes narrowed slightly. "When this all started, I just thought I was in the wrong place at the wrong time, call it happenstance, chance, bad luck, whatever. I've had quite a bit of that over the past few years actually." She traced the outline of his mouth. "Then I realized I was actually in the *right* place at the *right* time, the place and time I had to be to meet *you*."

He gaped at her. "If I had killed that son of a bitch when I had the chance, you wouldn't have *needed* to meet me. You'd be on your way home with a memory card full of pictures of mama and her cubs." He clenched his jaw as that boxer in his chest stepped up his attack, his ribs aching from the internal pressure. "If I had done what I knew I should do . . . none of this would be happening and *you* . . . you would be safe."

"If." Beth pressed a finger to his lips. "Didn't you say something once about *hating* that word?"

He frowned, but inside a faint ray of hope pierced the guilt and regret threatening to suck him under. "What are you, a human tape recorder?" he asked, only half-joking.

Her expression was solemn. "I'm just human, and I was beginning to think you weren't."

He lifted one brow. "Just beginning? I must not be working hard enough."

A faint smile hovered on her lips. "I have evidence you're not bulletproof . . . or immortal. Immortals don't bleed, at least . . . they're not *supposed* to."

He focused briefly on her mouth, the gentle, full curves, and warning bells started to ring softly. "Where is this evidence of yours?"

"You're wearing it." She touched his shoulder gently. "Here." She looked at his forehead, leaned up, and pressed her lips to the bandage-covered laceration on his brow. "And here." A gentle kiss on his cheek. "And here . . . ."

She pressed her mouth to his and every muscle in his body went taut. The warning bells rang louder, and while part of him knew this was wrong, that it couldn't happen, another part of him relished the contact and craved more of it.

A millisecond of panic shot through him, and it automatically kicked him into *agent mode*. Putting his hands on Beth's upper arms, he carefully pushed her back and rose. He ran a hand over his face and moved away several paces, needing the distance so he could grab hold of the reins again. After a few seconds he took a deep breath. When he finally forced himself to face her, the look in her eyes almost undid him.

"This," he said from between clenched teeth, gesturing between the two of them, "*can't* happen, Beth. It *can't*."

"It *can*." She dropped her chin. "You just won't *let* it."

He felt the pull of desire and the simmer of frustration as he fought for control. "I *can't* let it."

"Why not?" She stared at him for a moment, and then he saw the convulsive swallow. She stared at him for another second or so and then turned and walked back to the window, her posture ramrod straight. When she spoke next, her voice was little more than a whisper, but he heard the tremor of uncertainty in it. "If you're not attracted to me, just say so."

Frustration closed in on a boil and Bear ground his teeth together. "That's *not* it, and you know it."

"Then *what?*" She spun to face him, hands on hips. "What is it, Bear? Tell me."

His body's instant response to the silent challenge in her eyes and the shimmer of her skin went against everything he thought he knew about himself, every ounce of training he'd had. Anger roiled inside him, anger at himself and his sudden lack of control. He decided he much preferred it to the blatant longing and uncertainty of only moments ago. Anger he knew how to deal with, anger he knew how to channel.

"I'm a Federal agent and you're a Federal witness." He stood toe to toe with her and scowled. "You are under my protection, and no matter what happens I *will not* take advantage of that position. I *will not* take advantage of you."

She stared at him with wide, incredulous eyes. "Take *advantage* of me?" She exhaled sharply. "*I'm* the one who's been kissing *you*. How could that possibly be you taking advantage of me?"

Bear remembered the heat of her kiss, the pressure of her mouth, the feel of her body against his. Clenching his hands, he fought between keeping her at arm's length and jerking her to his chest. He wasn't accustomed to being questioned in this sort of situation, or any situation for that matter. Then again, he'd never really been in *this* sort of situation before. Beth wasn't the typical witness and because he was operating outside the jurisdiction of the FBI, technically he wasn't acting as an agent. The normal protocols and procedures didn't really apply here, but they were all he had to go on. Unfortunately, they weren't working. Why did she refuse to understand the position she was putting him in, and why couldn't he just walk away?

"I'm the agent, and you're the civilian." His knuckles cracked as his fists tightened. "I'm in the position of power, and no matter how much I want you, I will *not* abuse that authority."

"Even if I *want* you to?"

God, he wanted to. He *really* wanted to, and it frightened him. Maintaining distance and objectivity weren't things he usually had trouble doing, but whenever their eyes met, his protocols and procedures wanted to fly right out the window. More accurately, he wanted to *toss* them out the window and forget about everything but her. The last time he had done that, it had ended in disaster and regret. Picturing the woman who had destroyed his heart when he was still a rookie, another witness he'd protected, helped him gain his proverbial feet. He backed up several paces, pulled in a deep breath, and then slowly let it out. "You're scared, and you're vulnerable. You're not thinking clearly."

"You're right." Her cheeks brightened and her gaze was smoldering. "Because as crazy and stupid as it sounds . . . all I can think about . . . is getting you in bed."

The look of blatant longing she gave him sent something other than hot fury expanding through his core, and it was an emotion he didn't want to identify. He recognized the sting of rejection in her vivid eyes, the shadow of insecurity, and yet she still gazed upon him with desire. *Damnation.* Unbidden, his feet moved, taking him closer to her, closer to something he knew he shouldn't want but did, with everything inside him. For the first time in over a decade he was more than a little tempted to ignore his instincts, his training, and his experience. But he *couldn't.* As much as he wanted her, the *last* thing he wanted was to give in and have her regret what happened between them. He *never* wanted to feel that sort of pain again. He glanced at the pulse fluttering beneath the skin of her throat, steeled himself and looked at her directly.

He kept his face expressionless. "*Stop* it."

"Why?" An angry spark glittered to life in her eyes. "Afraid you might feel something *other* than power?"

His brain effortlessly manufactured a harsh retort, and when it almost escaped his mouth, he realized his control was slipping. He took a deep breath. No one had ever gotten under his skin like this. It was obvious to him she wasn't *trying* to get under his skin. She was just being herself, but that was it. There was no guile about her, no agenda, other than seducing him. But even that he knew he could take at face value. She wasn't using her feminine wiles because she had ulterior motives. He wasn't sure she realized she *had* feminine wiles. Suddenly that emotion he didn't want to identify expanded again, and he didn't need to examine it to know what it was. He not only wanted her, he also cared for her, far more than he should. The realization only made him angrier. It was insane.

He gritted his teeth. "Beth, *stop.*"

"No." She tilted her chin in defiance. "Not until you tell me why you won't take what I'm offering. Why are you so different from almost every other man I know?"

"I'm not," he ground out, "except I carry a badge and a gun." He leaned toward her slightly. "Aside from that, I'm pretty much *exactly* like every other guy you know."

She flattened her hands on his chest and that small, but intimate, contact sent sparks shooting along every nerve. Bear closed his eyes briefly and tried to mentally reinforce the wall that was so quickly crumbling.

"Then *why* do you keep pushing me away?"

Her softly spoken query was the final straw and before he could censor himself, the words exploded outward.

"Because *I* don't want to be something you *regret!*"

He didn't realize he'd shouted at her until his roar reverberated off the windows and bounced back, vibrating through him. Fixing his gaze on the ceiling, he tried to pull in his frustration with little success. He was frustrated with her for pushing, with himself for caring, and the entire situation in general. *Yeah, asshole, and THIS is helping.*

He had expected her to recoil from him, as most people did when he raised his voice to that level, but she didn't move. Taking several deep breaths, he squeezed his eyes shut as remorse grated through him. He dropped his chin and forced himself to look at her.

What he saw in her face dissolved his defenses. Instead of the fear or shock he had expected, she looked at him with quiet understanding, as if the final piece of a puzzle had been conveniently dropped into place. Her eyes searched his, and she pressed a hand to his cheek.

"Regret?" She framed his face and stood on tiptoe. "The only thing I would regret about being with you . . . is not having done it sooner." She wound her arms around his neck and pressed the length of her body to his.

He tensed, but against his will his arms slid around her waist, his fingers splaying over her back. That glimmer of panic brightened. He looked down into her face and desperately fought to maintain his distance and his professional demeanor. "Beth . . . ."

"I'm not expecting a declaration of love or a marriage proposal, Bear. I'm only asking for one night." She lifted her head and brushed his lips with hers. "Just give me one night. Can you do that?"

He tried to remain stiff and unyielding, but then something inside him shifted and his body betrayed him. He pressed a hand to her cheek and rubbed his thumb over the silky-smooth skin. "I *can't* . . . ."

A sad, wistful smile curved her mouth, and he found his gaze drawn there. He was acutely aware of her breasts against his chest, her softness melding perfectly with the planes and angles of his body. He couldn't remember when having a woman pressed against him had felt so natural and so right. That whisper in his head got stronger, encouraging him to give in.

"Yes, you can." Her smile widened slightly. "Tell Special Agent Bristol to take the night off. He can come back tomorrow, but tonight I don't want to be with *him*. I want to be with *you*."

Bear realized he was fighting a losing battle, but he refused to throw in the towel. It went against his nature. His heart thumped uncomfortably inside his chest, and for a second he had trouble drawing a breath. "Beth, please."

She pressed a finger to his lips. "Put your rule book aside. Tonight you're not a Federal agent; tonight you're just a man."

She kissed him again, and he nearly lost it. Special Agent Bristol hovered nearby, Bear felt him, but what *Beth* made him feel effectively silenced any of his alter-ego's protestations. He burned like he'd never burned before, not even with . . . . That was odd. At the moment he couldn't even remember his past love's name. When he sensed his defeat was imminent, he rallied what resolve he had left and pulled away. "Beth . . . ."

"And I'm not a Federal witness," she said as if he hadn't spoken. When she pressed her lips to his this time, he *did* lose it. He went on the offensive, taking what she offered the way a starving man would trounce on a steak. They explored each other's mouths and the firestorm ignited. Hot, heavy, pulsing need filled him until he could barely breathe. Her arms wound tighter around his neck, and he instinctively pressed her closer. She pulled back just slightly and it took all of his will not to jerk her back. Her lashes fluttered up. She looked at him with those golden eyes that seemed to see straight through his heart to his darkest fears. "Tonight I'm just a woman who desperately needs you and even more desperately wants you."

Oh, dude, you are SO done.

She kissed him once more. It was a deep, sensual kiss, one that sent heat blistering through him. Her lips were soft and warm and tasted of tears, tears *he* had caused. *Never again.* He marveled that in spite of how he'd hurt her, she was fearless, unwavering in her desire, and something inside him gave way. The warning bells were quickly drowned out by that voice in his head, the voice of Bear and not Special Agent Bristol. His breathing quickened and his groin tightened and desire roared through him. It was like a tidal wave crashing onto shore, drowning out the voice and the warning bells and destroying everything in its path, including any willpower he had left. She finally pulled back just enough to end the kiss, her lips barely a hair's breadth from his.

"One night, Bear. Give me one night."

He gave it one last try, but even before he spoke the words, he knew they would matter very little. "One night may be all you get."

She pressed closer to him. "Then I'll take it."

His gaze raked over her face and he felt the scowl, but it didn't seem to frighten her in the least. *This* battle she had won and they both knew it.

"Damn you," he whispered. "I *told* you I was just like every other guy you know."

"No, you're not." She met his gaze. "I don't want any of *them*."

He gave her a solemn look. "It would probably be better for both of us if you did."

Beth ran her fingers over the closely shorn hair on the back of his head, her expression thoughtful. "A couple of hours ago you said we had a half a day, maybe a little more, of relative safety."

"I did."

She tipped her head to the side. "Then make love to me, Bear. You've got ten to fourteen hours to remind me why I'm fighting so hard to stay alive."

It sounded more like a command than a request, and his mind flew back to that morning when she had walked away from him to weep in secret. She had wept for *him*. "Don't tell me what to do," he said softly, replaying their earlier conversation. A smile blossomed on her lips, and his heart did the now familiar thud.

"Make love to me . . . please?"

He knew he shouldn't cross this particular boundary. He'd done it only once before, a long time ago, with catastrophic results. He kept that painful remnant alive inside him as a constant reminder, like a tattered flag on display, and it had always been enough to keep him on the straight and narrow. Until now. As he made that final, conscious decision to disregard what his head and training told him and follow his heart, he experienced a moment of complete panic. He briefly sorted through his memory and tried to recall a time when he'd felt something similar and couldn't. The emotions he'd experienced when JC had died were just as deep, but different. His mother often complained he'd been born without a fear gene, citing incidents from his youth and adulthood that had, on several occasions, almost claimed his life. Physical pain and external danger he had no trouble staring down. Guys with guns and ruthless criminals were just a part of his average day. Returning fire and taking the life of someone trying to take his was a cakewalk. Turning off Special Agent Bristol, acknowledging what he really wanted, and taking a long, hard look in the mirror, however, was not so easy. Special Agent Bristol was perfectly happy with his life, his job, casual dating, and occasional casual sex. Bear's throat constricted as he realized *he* wasn't happy with that, and there was *nothing* casual about what he felt for the woman in his arms.

Bear released her and took a step back, his eyes locked with hers. When he saw the flash of anxiety in those golden pools, he realized she wasn't as fearless as he'd thought. He was hit with a primal, nearly overwhelming urge to reassure her, to alleviate all her fears regardless of his own. He slowly slid his fingers into her hair and lowered his head. His mouth covered hers, and he felt the tremor that went through her because it passed through him as well. He deepened the kiss and her fingers curled around his forearms, her lips warm and firm beneath his, her body trembling. His heart started to pound in a strong, steady rhythm against his sternum, but this pressure didn't make his ribs ache. It made *every* part of him ache. Bear ended the kiss and rested his brow against hers, knowing what was going to happen and, oddly enough, completely at peace with it. In spite of everything, it felt right.

"The things I do to keep witnesses happy," he whispered. In one swift motion he bent down and tossed her over his shoulder, and she cried out in surprise. "Fine, but if we're going to do this we're going to do it in the master bedroom."

"Why?" she asked in a breathless voice.

"Because I'll actually *fit* in that bed." He strode across the room, out the door, and across the hall. "And . . . it'll give me room to work."

Chapter Fifteen

Beth was nearly giddy with anticipation as he walked into the master suite and kicked the door shut behind them. Moonlight cast an ethereal glow over the room as it poured in through the enormous picture window. She closed her eyes as her heart started to thunder against her breastbone. He strode to the side of the bed and, without a word, tossed her into the middle of the enormous mattress. She gasped and pushed the hair out of her face.

Before she could move or say a word, he came over her on all fours. A hand was planted firmly on the bed on either side of her shoulders and his legs straddled her hips. His gaze raked over her face, and she couldn't tell from his expression if he was aroused, angry, or perhaps a little of both. She was betting on the latter. She had pushed hard for some reason, something quite out of the norm for her. She let men pursue her, not the other way around. With Bear, however, *everything* was different. Every time she thought about just letting it go, of not being with him, a sense of apprehension bordering on panic engulfed her. It made no sense.

His eyes narrowed. "If you have *any* doubts about this," he said in a low, harsh voice, "tell me now."

She traced his brows, the line of his nose, his jaw. "Do you?"

"Only about a million," he replied. "However, at this precise moment I can't remember a single one of them."

Beth had no doubt she wanted him, her body ached to have him touch her. She also had no doubt how she felt about him and that making love with him would only solidify those emotions. She didn't just *want* him, she *needed* him. What she didn't know was how *he* felt. Sadness bloomed inside her like a flower. She had asked him for one night, and he had said that might be all she could have. A band of sorrow constricted around her heart as she realized she wanted more, much more.

"And I hope you never remember them." She searched his eyes. "Because I don't want to be something you regret either."

"I have the feeling," he paused and dropped down onto his elbows, "that the only thing I will regret about being with you . . . is not being able to be with you again."

An image of the day they would eventually part ways tried to manifest. That band tightened around her heart, making each beat an arduous chore. But this was what she had asked for. Forcing the mental picture away, she memorized his features, committing each to memory, and reached for the buttons on his shirt. "Then let's make the most of the time we have."

He framed her face, his thumbs stroking over her cheekbones. His expression was inscrutable, but as he lowered his head, she saw the blaze of desire in his eyes. His lips moved over hers and her body came alive, warmth fanning over her skin like a lover's breath. His tongue met hers, his touch exceedingly delicate and in direct contradiction to the violence of the passion rising in her. His exploration was cautious, deliberate, and the heat inside her expanded exponentially, leaving her breathless. Her limbs liquefied as he delved deeper, but he didn't intrude. He was searching, seeking, and dizziness spun her.

As devastatingly erotic as his kiss was, her fingers literally itched to touch him. Beth tugged the shirt from his trousers and worked the rest of the buttons loose. She sighed and caressed his chest. The ache in her belly sharpened. His skin was warm and smooth and taut over the dense musculature beneath it. The spattering of hair on his chest was delightfully soft and springy, her skin tingling as she moved her palms over it in slow circles. She let her hands roam, mapping his shoulders, his back, the chiseled planes of his abdomen. When he ended the kiss and pulled back, she moaned softly in protest, her lips aching for more.

Bear rose up onto his knees, shrugged out of the flannel, and tossed it to the floor, his eyes never leaving her face. Her breath caught. Never in her life had she seen a finer model of masculine beauty. Her gaze traveled over him, from the line of his sharply squared jaw, over the impressive breadth of his shoulders, to the massive chest that was so hard planed and yet was the softest place she'd ever laid her head. She reached out and traced the distinct line that ran from his sternum to his navel. He was as still as stone but warm to the touch, like granite warmed by the sun, and she fanned her fingers over his abdomen. Her heart fluttered as she closed her eyes and felt the gentle movement of his muscles as he breathed.

She took hold of his belt and looked at him in silent question when he gently grasped her wrists. He shook his head and released her. With nimble fingers he untied the sash of the robe and pulled it open. She flattened her hands on the bed and sucked in a breath. Now all that stood between them was a filmy layer of golden silk. Beth's heart did a somersault, her eyes locked with his.

"Stand up," he whispered.

Beth blinked at him and then rose, resting one hand on his

muscled shoulder as the mattress shifted beneath her feet. From their relative positions on the bed, him kneeling and her standing over him, she should have felt more in control. She didn't. Her heart began to pound. He placed his hands at her waist and looked up at her, but there was no sign of surrender in his steely eyes. He was leading, and all she could do was yield. Her breathing quickened when he reached up, slipped his fingers inside the collar of the robe, and slid it off her shoulders. After the garment lay in a heap of golden satin on the faux fur comforter, he pulled the gown up and over her thighs, his hands grazing her skin, his fingers exploring and causing her breath to catch in her throat. His gaze never left her face.

He moved off the mattress and stood, taking a step back as he let his gaze wander slowly over her, not just once, but several times. Cold and heat flashed over her skin as his eyes devoured her.

He whistled softly. "*You* . . . are *beautiful*," he said softly.

Beth chewed on her lip as he continued his perusal, and when his eyes finally met hers, her heart leapt.

"Take it off."

With slow, tentative movements she slipped first one strap and then the other off her shoulders. She dragged the gown downward, a flush heating her skin as the flame in his eyes burned brighter. She pushed the negligee over her breasts, hips, and down her legs. The way he watched her made her incredibly aware of her femininity. Michael had never looked at her like that.

When the garment lay about her ankles, she straightened. His brows rose and his gaze met hers.

"Your turn," she said softly.

The panty-dropping smile lifted the corners of his mouth and his eyes twinkled. "All right, although my performance won't be nearly as graceful as yours."

"I doubt that, but that's okay." Beth fought a smile. "I'm not looking for graceful."

His smile widened and he started to undress. She was mesmerized by the fluid movements of his body. He removed his shoes, socks, and pants, and her heart started to ping against the inside of her chest. As she allowed herself to drink in the picture he presented, a pang of self-consciousness and uncertainty stabbed through her. He was just too handsome. She was accustomed to dating attractive men, at least men *she* thought were attractive, but as far as she was concerned Bear took *attractive* to a whole other level. If she were to glimpse him in a social setting, she would admire from afar but never have the nerve to approach him. She would sit at the bar or table and watch as her friends drooled and plotted, and eventually one of them would go on the offensive. Then she would sit at the bar or table and watch as that friend flirted, seduced, and eventually took him home. It had happened before, more than once, and it had never really bothered her. But, she'd never had feelings for the men on her friends' radar. She'd never begrudged her best friend Melody's ability to go after and get what she wanted, until Melody went after someone Beth wanted.

She felt that hurt now as sharply as if her former best friend had just entered the room, fixed a smoky gaze on Bear, and lured him away. It wouldn't have been the first time Melody seduced one of Beth's boyfriends. The image of Michael and Melody together flashed in her head, shattering her confidence with one vivid snapshot. Her stomach curled in on itself and she took a deep, slow breath.

Those laser-like eyes missed nothing. His brows drew together. "What?"

He stood there naked as the day he was born, and her lungs contracted. A Greek god could not have been more exquisite. Beth squeezed her eyes shut. "You are *so* out of my league," she finally whispered.

"What the hell are you talking about?"

It took every ounce of strength she had to meet and maintain his gaze. He was so beautiful, and it was more than just his physical appeal. His strength, his compassion, his sense of humor, everything about him, from the way his brow scrunched when he scowled to the depth and timbre of his voice, called to her on a level she'd never before experienced. He was smart, skilled, dedicated, everything she could ask for wrapped in a package to make a woman sigh. She closed her eyes briefly and took a deep, steadying breath. "I wonder how many women's hearts you've broken without ever even knowing it."

He took a step forward and frowned. "I'm not like that."

"Yes, you are, but not because you try to be." A lump formed in her throat and butterflies took off. "You're beautiful. Bear. But, you'd know that if you ever really *looked* at yourself, and I'm not just talking about in a mirror."

His brows drew together. "I'd rather look at *you*."

He climbed back onto the mattress and knelt in front of her. Beth's heart jumped into her throat as his hands slid around her thighs with a barely-there touch, but one that she felt to the core of her being. He dropped his chin, pressing his lips to her belly. His tongue slowly circled her navel and a gasp escaped her when her stomach muscles contracted. She ran her fingers over the crisp hair on top of his head and fought to stay upright. Her knees trembled. His calloused fingers rasped lightly over her backside and up, and the flame burned hotter even as goose bumps peppered her skin. Then his hands moved back down her legs with the same gossamer touch and she bit back a moan. When he reached her ankles, he jerked her feet out from under her and she landed on her back on the mattress. Beth bounced once and gasped.

Bear stared at her for a few moments, and the blank mask was back. He finally broke eye contact, his gaze moving slowly over her, but she couldn't tell from his expression what he was thinking. A pang of worry pierced her. Did he find her as appealing as she found him? His eyes finally returned to hers and she gulped. The heat in those azure pools first sent chills through her, and then fire.

He crawled up the bed until he loomed over her on all fours, the muscles in his chest and shoulders moving with sinuous grace. "I thought you were beautiful after two days in the woods covered in dirt with your hair all tangled." His knuckles rubbed against her throat and he dropped down onto his elbows again. "*Now*," he began in an awed, hushed voice, "now, you're stunning."

Her skin tingled where he touched it and as he continued his caress, the zings of electrified current spread through the rest of her. "I wouldn't think much stuns *you*."

His eyes darkened. "If I wasn't *stunned* . . . I wouldn't be *here* right now. *Trust* me."

Her stomach flipped and she took a shaky breath. "Well, then . . ." Beth cupped his neck. "I should take advantage of the situation."

"You should."

She stared at him for a moment. What she did next would have consequences. That much she knew. Beth closed her eyes, lifted her head, and kissed him.

Their lips melded together and the shadows vanished. Beth felt hot and cold in alternating flashes, and a tremor coursed through her as he explored her mouth, deeply and lazily. His tongue wound around hers in a slow, sensual dance, and her insides turned molten. He stretched out beside her and the contact of their bodies sent a buzz of awareness through her that pushed her senses into overdrive. Her breathing hitched. Bear slid an arm around her and pulled her closer. Her breasts tightened as their softness pressed into the steel of his chest. The curling hair there brushed her nipples and they pebbled, sending a violent surge of need to her core.

Beth had never experienced anything so all-consuming. The fire burning through her devoured everything in its path except her awareness of him. Nothing and no one else existed at this moment. She felt the outline of each finger as his hand wound around her waist and splayed over her back, his ridged abdomen as it pressed to hers, each beat of his heart and her own. His skin was warm and smooth beneath her fingertips, and she couldn't touch him enough. Her pulse skyrocketed. A wave of dizziness washed over her, but instead of fighting it, she gave in to it. She moaned softly and clung to him.

His hand twined in her hair. He gently pulled her head back, his lips trailing down her throat, searing her skin. She gasped.

"I'm going to say this one last time," he whispered against her skin. "If you're having second thoughts, tell me now."

Beth dragged her head up and looked into the eyes of the man who was rapidly working his way into her heart. He met her gaze and she gulped at the passion she saw there. "I've been having second thoughts about *this* ever since I kissed you this morning."

His response was immediate. His mouth captured hers, and he jerked her to him with such force she gasped. Lips that were soft, yet hard, demanded entrance. She automatically surrendered. A shock of pleasure rocked her as her breasts were crushed to his chest and his tongue stroked hers. The taste of him, the friction of his skin against hers, his hardness against her softness sent goose bumps skittering over her skin and started a slow, steady, growing tension between her legs. She needed to be closer. Beth wrapped her arms around his neck and tried to disappear into him. Her leg wound over his as his mouth moved expertly over hers. Her lips felt bruised, abraded, but there was no way she wanted him to stop. She'd never been kissed like this before, never felt this searing hunger as it built in her belly and spiraled outward. His erection was hard against her pelvis, and a jolt of pure, unadulterated lust sizzled through her. Her core throbbed and contracted as she imagined what he would feel like inside her.

The only thing I will regret about being with you . . . is not being able to be with you again.

A tug of sadness pulled at her briefly, not enough to dampen her desire, but enough to let her know it was there. Beth embraced it. The knowledge that this could be her one and only time with him made her want to savor the experience and seemed to heighten her sensitivity. His fingers trailed lightly down her back, and a chill followed in their wake. A shiver coursed through her. His mouth against hers was gentle, yet insistent. Heat built in the pit of her stomach and worked its way outward as he kissed her deeply. She felt feverish and cold at the same time, the desire to be one with him building to a level she'd never felt before.

Bear's lips left hers and trailed leisurely over her cheek and jaw as light as butterfly's wings. Slowly, he moved down. He kissed the pulse in her throat, his tongue flicking lightly against her skin, and Beth inhaled sharply. His mouth followed the line of her collarbone to her shoulder, his hands gently gripping her waist. He feathered kisses over her décolleté as his fingers slithered upward. She sensed where he was going and what he was going to do, but nothing prepared her for the way her body reacted. When he cupped her breast and lifted it to his mouth, scorching heat shot through her and she gasped.

His tongue swirled around her taut nipple, warm and wet, and her hips jerked as pleasure rippled out from low in her belly. For such a large, formidable man his touch was exceedingly gentle, like the practiced hands of a sculptor moving carefully over pliable clay. He was in no hurry and Beth bit her lip, her hands cupping his head as he suckled her. The pleasure seemed to radiate from her breasts to her vulva and back, each volley increasing in speed and intensity, like a pinball caught in the machine.

Suddenly his head snapped up, and the pinball stopped bouncing.

Beth moaned in frustration. Her body protested the abrupt interruption, until she opened her eyes and saw his face. She remembered that look, from when they'd hidden behind the fallen tree only minutes after she'd first met him. His eyes were sharp, razor-focused, and staring out the window. Beth sat up and turned.

All thoughts of sex vanished and her heart vaulted upwards as the unfamiliar pickup truck rambled slowly past the garage and toward the front of the house. Bear jumped to his feet, slipped into his boxers, and retrieved his pistol from the holster on his pants.

"So much for not tipping off the neighbors." He gave her a sharp look. "Stay there."

Beth nodded.

The gun held down along his leg, he walked toward the windows overlooking the oval driveway. Beth scrambled to the edge of the massive bed, grabbed his flannel shirt, and slipped it on. She buttoned it quickly, her eyes fixed on Bear's tense form. Outside she heard the truck door open and then slam shut.

"Who is it?" she asked.

Bear shook his head, his expression darkening. He turned and grabbed his pants, pulling them on quickly. "Don't know, but it looks like he's coming inside." He crossed the room to the door and opened it a crack. "Come here," he said without looking at her. When she touched his back, he turned to her and cupped her chin. "I want you to go down the back stairs into the garage and hide. No matter what you hear, stay hidden until I come to get you. Can you do that for me?"

Beth nodded. His eyes narrowed on her face, and he kissed her hard and fast. When he pulled back, he opened the door, stepped into the hall, and looked at her. Beth slipped past him and froze when the front door crashed open. She glanced at him and he nodded grimly. Her heart beating a brisk staccato against her ribs, she ran down the hall and quickly descended the stairs.

Bear watched her go and then focused on the intruder. The upper hallways were cast in shadow, and he stepped to the railing, leaning a shoulder into one of the many heavy beams that ran from the main level to the roof. The sixteen-by-sixteen-inch timber wasn't large enough to completely hide him. However, he knew it would take someone with sharp eyes to pick his form from out of the darkness so long as he didn't move. He flicked the safety off the pistol and looked down into the great room.

The front door closed just as loudly as it had opened and the person started to sing, loudly and quite off-key. It was a man and he tightened his grip on the gun. The intruder's words were thick and slurred, and Bear's tension level dropped a notch. A moment later a short, stocky, older gentleman with salt and pepper hair stumbled into the great room. He was built like a bulldog with a thick neck, chest, and arms. A curse escaped him when he stumbled down the three steps that descended into the sunken living area, and then tripped over a coffee table. More profanity ensued as he struggled to his feet. When he was finally upright, he seemed to muster his dignity before walking to the bar. Bear half-smiled when the man grabbed an expensive, half-full bottle of bourbon and started to guzzle it.

His insides unclenched as he watched the stranger drain the bottle. He had expected tall guy and ponytail to be in the truck. The fact that it was just an aging drunk made him decidedly less nervous. This had to be Malcolm, the caretaker. That he'd opened the gate and had keys to the house were evidence of that. Bear pursed his lips and waited for the inevitable. It wasn't a long wait. Less than five minutes had passed before Malcolm slid off the barstool and onto the floor, the now-empty bottle falling onto a thick rug with a barely audible thump. Bear waited another minute or so and smiled when the man started snoring softly.

Bear descended the great stairs and carefully approached the unconscious man. He prodded the drunk with one foot. The man's snoring stopped for a second, then continued at a louder volume. Bear sighed.

He made his way to the garage and flicked on the light. "Beth." He heard a sound behind him and spun around. There was a small doorway that allowed access to the space under the stairs, and he backed up a step as it swung inward. A moment later, Beth peeked around the door jamb, and when she saw him, relief swept her features. He held out a hand and she slipped her fingers into his. Bear pulled her upright, and wasn't at all surprised when she wrapped her arms around his waist, her face pressed against his chest. His heart gave a thud and warmth filled him as his arms enfolded her. He rested his chin on top of her head and closed his eyes. She was shaking, and the familiar protectiveness swelled inside him yet again.

"It's okay, sweetheart." His hands rubbed over her back. "Our intruder is more a danger to himself than us." He paused as the scent of her hair drifted to him. Resisting the urge to bury his face in the mahogany tresses, he inhaled deeply and released her. "Come on. I'm going to need your help."

She preceded him up the stairs, and he found his gaze drawn to her long, tanned legs. They were sleekly muscled and shapely and he had the sudden urge to run his hands up them. Beth looked better in his shirt than he did, and his desire rekindled as he imagined those legs wrapped around him. Bear clamped down mercilessly on his libido. They had things to do.

When they stood over the fallen drunk, Beth put her hands on her hips and frowned. "Is this the caretaker?"

Bear crouched and started searching the man's pockets. "Since he had the gate code and keys I'd have to say yes." He finally found a wallet, flipped it open, and removed the Colorado driver's license.

"Malcolm Guthrie, 68. Guess Wednesday morning isn't the only time he shows up at the Lockhart's place." He glanced up at her.

"What are we going to do with him?" she asked, a puzzled frown creasing her brow.

She seemed perplexed rather than alarmed, and he was impressed, again. He gave her a reassuring smile. "I have an idea." He rose. "Go get dressed."

Twenty minutes later Bear was behind the wheel of Malcolm Guthrie's pickup, the older man snoring softly in the passenger seat as they drove toward the gas station. Beth followed in the Mercedes. When they were about a quarter mile from the station, Bear stopped on the shoulder of the tree-lined highway and waved her forward. She pulled alongside and lowered the passenger window.

"What now?" she asked.

"Spin around and wait for me." He glanced at Guthrie as the man snorted and stirred. "I'll be back shortly."

Beth nodded, waited for a lone car to pass, and then flipped a U-turn and pulled onto the opposite shoulder. Bear put the pickup in drive and accelerated. It took him less than thirty seconds to drive the final quarter mile to his destination.

He stopped the Dodge about a hundred yards away from the gas station on the opposite side of the road and put it in park. After wiping down the steering wheel and anywhere else he had touched, he carefully moved Malcolm Guthrie behind the wheel. He belted the man in, closed the door, and leaned through the open window.

"Sorry, Malcolm. Hopefully this will be your first DUI, although somehow I doubt it."

Bear wrapped Guthrie's hands around the wheel, put the truck in neutral, and carefully adjusted the steering wheel. His eyes moved back and forth between the wheels of the truck and the gas station, and when he thought he had the angle right, he braced his legs and put the vehicle in drive. Thankfully, at this time of night the mountainous, two-lane highway was virtually deserted. Making a last adjustment, Bear stepped back and let the truck go. Once it crossed the empty road, he moved back into the trees and watched.

The downhill slope helped the truck pick up speed, and by the time it crashed into the northeast corner of the gas station's main building it was moving at about fifteen to twenty mph. He waited until the clerk came out the front doors and ran toward the truck. As the clerk checked on Malcolm Guthrie, Bear turned and sprinted back up the road to where Beth waited.

She jumped when he tapped on the driver's window. He opened the door and she slid across to the passenger seat, anxiety clear in those wide, amber eyes.

"Is everything okay?" she asked as she fastened her seat belt.

Bear buckled up, started the engine, and put the Mercedes

into drive. "Everything is fine, sweetheart." He checked his mirrors and pulled onto the road. "Malcolm will wake up in county jail with a headache, his truck will probably be impounded, his insurance rates are *definitely* going up, and he may lose his job, but everything else is A-okay."

"Okay? You just crashed him into the mini-market."

"Should we have put him in the spare room to sleep it off?" he asked with a sideways glance at her. When she scowled and pursed her lips he chuckled. "Relax. He wasn't going fast enough to get hurt or cause any substantial damage to the store. And, this way, he'll get some medical attention, have time to sober up, and he won't be endangering anyone else, at least not *tonight.*"

She leaned her head back and sighed. "So, now we go back to the house, pack up and leave, right?"

He shook his head. "I don't see any reason to." He saw her head turn toward him in his periphery and smiled. "I doubt there's a connection between the caretaker and the guys chasing you, and I doubt the man will even remember being at the cabin. Right now we're relatively safe, hidden, and off the radar. Until I know otherwise, the safest thing to do is stay put."

He glanced at her and she met his gaze. By the look in her eyes he could tell she wasn't sure if she liked that or not. Her face was carefully neutral, but she couldn't mask what was in her eyes. He recognized the spark of desire, which was quickly extinguished by a shadow of sadness. Beth nodded and turned her face toward the window.

His mind started to turn over what was going to happen once they got back to the cabin. Heat curled inside him as he remembered her passionate response to his lightest touch, the satin of her skin beneath his fingers, the way her nipples had hardened against his tongue. He gripped the steering wheel a little tighter and pulled sharply on his inner reins, fighting the urge to pull over and take her on the side of the road. They rode the rest of the way in silence.

After they reached the gate, he entered the code and waited for it to roll out of the way. He looked at her and realized she was still wearing his flannel shirt. It hung to mid-thigh and the memory of long, sleek legs made him smile. Even in black yoga pants the curves were evident and he pictured those supple limbs wrapped around him. She really had no idea how attractive she was, which only made her more attractive to him. He much preferred down-to-earth women, and Beth Drummond was nothing if not down-to-earth.

They parked in the garage a few minutes later and Bear watched her covertly. She didn't say anything as she opened the car door and got out, but he sensed her uncertainty and she was visibly tense. It was as if she didn't *want* to go back upstairs and pick up where they left off. Or, more accurately, he had a feeling she was worried *he* wouldn't want to resume their prior activities. She was anticipating rejection.

His smile had widened a bit before he wiped it off. If only she knew he was reading her mind she would be mortified, especially if she could also see what was in his. He left the Mercedes and followed as she made her way silently up the stairs.

Once in the family room Beth moved to the fireplace, away from the stairs, and turned on the gas. Moments later blue flames sprang to life. He watched her closely. She kicked off her shoes and curled herself into a nearby chair, wrapping her arms around her legs. She turned her gaze to the flames, and he knew she was deliberately avoiding eye contact. Her expression was resolute, but he noticed the convulsive swallow as he continued to stare. Apparently she had expended all of her bravado earlier, and if he still wanted her, he was going to have to take the lead. That was fine with him. He'd made the decision to cross the line with her, and he wouldn't change it unless he knew she no longer wanted to go there. He watched her for a few more seconds and moved to the refrigerator. After retrieving a bottle of water, he snapped off the cap and took a long drink.

"I'm going to take a quick shower," he said. He wished she'd look at him, but she merely nodded and stared at the fire. Bear took another drink, capped the bottle, and put it on the end of the counter. "Don't go anywhere." She shook her head once and rested her chin on her knees. A sliver of concern cut into him. Had she decided she no longer wanted to be with him? Perhaps Malcolm Guthrie's interruption had brought her to her senses. Now that he'd admitted to himself how much he wanted her, he wasn't about to just let it go. Quitting wasn't in his nature. *Time to go on the offensive, bud.* He smiled, turned, and quickly walked up the stairs to the master bedroom.

He bathed quickly and then slipped into his sweatpants and a muscle shirt. Barefoot, he padded down the hallway and the stairs into the kitchen/family room. Beth stood at the windows overlooking the deck, a tumbler of something in her hand. He watched as she took a slow sip. They made eye contact in the reflection on the glass for a couple of seconds before she focused on something else, her expression sad but determined. He wondered what she was thinking and hoped it wasn't what he thought it was. His abdominals tightened. Bear grabbed his water bottle and sat down on a barstool.

"All right, Beth," he said. He emptied the water bottle and put it aside. "Talk to me."

She took another drink, took a deep breath, and turned to face him. He recognized not only the melancholy in her eyes but the resolve as well. She stared at him for a moment.

"I'm," she paused, dropped her chin, and sighed. "I'm sorry, Bear."

He was mildly puzzled at her response and frowned. "Exactly what are you sorry for?"

She walked up to the end of the island and put the tumbler on the smooth, granite surface close to the sink. She stared at the counter. "People want to kill me, you're doing everything you can to keep me and yourself alive, and all I'm doing is providing a . . . a *distraction*. I'm – I'm sorry."

So that's it. It was obvious to him she felt guilty, as if she had coerced him into something he didn't want. She couldn't have been more wrong. She wasn't the only one who had fantasized about more after their first kiss. "Beth—"

"No, it's okay. I get it." She squeezed her eyes shut and flattened her hands on the island. "You don't have to say anything."

Maybe not, but he was certainly going to *do* something. "Good." Bear rose, towered over her, and when she finally looked up at him he scowled. "I didn't feel like talking anyway."

He recognized the uncertainty in her golden gaze, but the desire was still there, and she blinked at him. Grasping her waist, he picked her up and settled her on the end of the breakfast bar. This brought them almost eye-to-eye. Her eyes went wide and she gasped as he put one hand on either side of her, effectively penning her in. Beth leaned back slightly and pressed a hand to his chest. He smiled. Using one knee, he nudged her legs apart and stood between her thighs.

"What are you doing?" she asked in a breathless voice, her eyes wide and incredulous.

He closed in on her until their lips nearly touched, and smiled. "Finishing what you started."

Chapter Sixteen

Bear kissed her and the flames rekindled so quickly it took his breath away. Fire spread from low in his belly until even his scalp was tingling. She seemed shocked for a moment, unresponsive. Bear nipped at her bottom lip and she gasped softly. Then the hand that had been holding him at bay clutched the fabric of his shirt and pulled. His tongue entered her mouth, gently probing, exploring. *Ah, so it's cognac in that tumbler.* She touched her tongue to his and sighed. Her surrender started an explosive chain reaction inside him and he was instantly hard.

Beth wound her arms around his neck and suddenly he needed to get his hands on her bare skin. With slow, deft movements he unbuttoned the flannel shirt. When the last button gave way, he slipped his hands inside the garment and around her waist. His groin throbbed when he realized she was not wearing a bra. He spread his fingers over her back and pressed her closer, and he grew even harder as her bare breasts brushed his chest. A low moan escaped her, and she wrapped her legs around his waist.

Her invitation was clear, and although he was ready and willing to take her up on it, he wanted more. He didn't want there to be a trace of uncertainty or guilt when they made love, and he didn't want her to regret *anything*. To him, that meant her pleasure was first and foremost, and he intended to pleasure her well.

Bear trailed his lips over her jaw to her throat. Her pulse thrummed there, and he pressed his mouth to the visibly pulsating spot. She inhaled sharply. He grazed his fingers over her skin, amazed at the smooth texture, and then cupped her breasts. His thumbs stroked softly over her taut nipples and she moaned again, arching her back. Bear looked at her, and the picture of brazen sensuality she presented sent lust through him like a shockwave. It started at his core and radiated outward as if a bomb had gone off. Her eyes were closed, her lips moist and parted, her head thrown back, her skin flushed and glowing. He continued to stroke her breasts, enjoying their weight and warmth in his hands. She bit her lip and moaned softly, and his groin twitched in reaction. Her chest was heaving, her breathing rapid, and when he lowered his head to take one nipple into his mouth, she tensed and cried out. He smiled. *That's it, sweetheart. Let everything else go.*

Slowly, he eased her onto her back, but she seemed unaware. Her teeth worried her lower lip, small, urgent whimpers coming from her mouth, her hands gripping his shoulders. Bear continued to lave his tongue over her nipples and she trembled. Taking the other dusky peak into his mouth, he suckled her lightly as he slid her pants down over her hips and pulled them off. Her breath caught. His penis throbbed when he realized that not only wasn't she wearing a bra, she wasn't wearing panties either. Even better.

He dragged his tongue away from her breasts and over her stomach to her belly button. Her abdominals clenched. She gripped the edge of the granite counter when he made slow, wet circles around her navel.

"Bear . . . ."

He ignored her and pressed his lips to the inside of her thigh. She jumped and sucked in a breath. He kissed her other thigh as he pushed gently against her knees, opening her to him. His erection swelled as he looked at her for a moment, and then covered her with his mouth.

She shuddered and moaned, and the sound only fueled his need for her. Her clitoris was engorged, and he swirled his tongue around the tiny bundle of nerve-endings in slow, deliberate circles. He kept the pressure light but constant and after a minute or so her legs began to shake. Her abdominals were fluttering, alternately contracting and relaxing in visible waves. Her reaction told him he was doing something very right.

"Bear . . . !"

He slid his hands beneath her backside and lifted her slightly, his mouth still on her. God he loved the taste of her, the way her clit hardened beneath his tongue. He felt the tensing of her muscles and a sense of satisfaction washed through him. It wouldn't be long now.

"Bear . . . stop . . . ."

Her plea was breathless and thick with passion, and he knew it wasn't a serious request. His senses were sharp, and all he sensed in her was desire, raw, hungry, and pushing toward the summit. He ignored her and lapped at the swollen nub, like an animal would lap at water. Her entire body was trembling now, ragged gasps escaping her.

"Bear . . . please, stop!"

The note of desperation in her voice gave him pause and lifted his gaze to hers. "Why?"

Beth covered her face with her hands, then slid her fingers into her hair and stared at the ceiling. Pink surged into her cheeks, her breasts heaving with every labored breath.

"Because," she paused and he saw the convulsive swallow, "when I come . . . ." She lifted her head and met his gaze, and the fire he saw there made his pulse quicken. "When I come, I want you inside me."

"Okay." He smiled and tightened his grip on her hips. "We'll schedule that . . . for when you come *again* . . . ."

Her eyes widened and her flush deepened. "Oh, God . . . ."

He dropped his chin and sucked lightly on her clit. She lay back and stifled a moan. His smile widened. *You wanted me, you got me, baby. Now let me take you all the way.* He flattened his tongue against her and started moving in firm, leisurely circles. She tensed and a shudder coursed through her. When the tremors increased, he fixed his mouth over her clit and suckled harder. She gasped. Her abdominals fluttered, tensing and relaxing, the speed and strength of the contractions growing as he continued his tender assault. *That's it, sweetheart. Let it all go.* Suddenly a cry of pleasure was wrenched from her lips and her back arched. She went silent and froze there for a few seconds, and then she started to shake, wails of release echoing off the vaulted ceiling as she climaxed. It was a beautiful thing to see. Bear didn't stop, and neither did she. This was what he had wanted from the moment he'd given in to her. Even if nothing else happened between them, he was, at this moment, a very happy man.

He took his cues from her, reducing the pressure as her orgasm softened from shuddering spasms to undulating ripples. When at last she took a huge gulp of air and went limp, he pulled back. Placing his hands on the edge of the counter on either side of her hips, he straightened and then leaned over her. He watched her for a moment, enjoying the rapid rise and fall of her breasts and the soft gasps. Her eyes were closed, her lashes a dark fringe above her cheeks. She looked magnificent.

Now that he had pleasured her, his body reacted ferociously, lust roaring through him. All he had to do was drop his pants and he could take her, the breakfast bar putting her at the perfect height. Oddly enough, despite what he'd just done, the idea of making love to her on the kitchen counter didn't appeal to him. There wasn't *nearly* enough room on this granite slab for everything he wanted to do to and with her. He slid his arms around her, pressed his face into her neck, and nuzzled her ear. She wrapped her arms and legs around him, hooking her ankles in the small of his back with a sigh. His groin pulsed and he straightened, taking her with him. He crossed the room and ascended the stairs.

Beth rested her brow on his shoulder, unable to hold her head upright. Her heart still fluttered wildly, and she knew it was due to more than the explosive climax he'd given her. This was what she had wanted, what she had pushed so hard for, and it was beyond anything she had imagined. She wound her arms more tightly around his neck and closed her eyes as he walked into the master bedroom and kicked the door shut behind them. Her body was still humming, as if her orgasm hadn't completely stopped. She felt him, hard and throbbing beneath her and settled herself more intimately against him. He paused, looked at her, and then strode to the bed.

Instead of throwing her onto the mattress as before, he jerked the faux fur comforter off and sat down on the edge of the bed with her still wrapped around him. He cupped her backside and looked at her. This time there was no mistaking the flame in those sharp blue eyes. His expression turned wistful as he brushed a finger over her cheek.

"You are so beautiful," he whispered.

Her heart throbbed and she wondered absently how many women would kill to hear those words from his lips. "And *you* are an Adonis."

His eyes narrowed slightly. "Does that make you Aphrodite, or Persephone?"

"Aphrodite, I hope." She looked at his mouth. "He spent more time with *her.*"

"Beth—"

She kissed him quickly, not wanting to hear again that their time was limited. Fire erupted in her and that wonderful tension sprang to life between her legs as he grew even harder beneath her. Suddenly the shirt was in the way. She wanted to see him, touch him, taste his skin. Beth pulled back long enough to jerk his tank top off of him and shrug out of his flannel shirt. She stared at him as his hands moved slowly up her back and pressed her closer. When her nipples brushed his chest and hardened, she took a shaky breath, delicious shivers fanning out from her breasts through the rest of her. She bit her lip. His gaze searched hers and then focused on her mouth.

He brushed her lips with his and pulled back, as if gauging her reaction. His eyes narrowed slightly, and he kissed her again. Beth closed her eyes. His hand cupped her head and he turned to lay her gently on the bed. His tongue made cautious entrance into her mouth as he came over her. The weight of his body was a welcome pressure, and she felt his erection, hard and pulsing. A low moan escaped her and the ache in her belly sharpened.

He kissed her slowly, deeply, with a mixture of strength and gentleness that sent her heart racing. She wound her arms around him, her fingers digging into the muscled expanse of his back. When he ended the kiss and pulled away, she moaned in frustration.

Opening her eyes, she looked at him and gulped as he pulled off his sweatpants. In that split second, she wished she had her camera. He really did look like some Grecian statue of male perfection, if she discounted the enormous erection. But she knew even if she asked, he'd never pose for her. That just wasn't *him.* She leaned up on her elbows and just looked at him.

"Oh my."

His gaze moved slowly over her, and met hers with that direct sharpness that she'd come to know. "You can say *that* again."

His expression was solemn as he came over her on all fours, and she gulped at the unconcealed hunger in his eyes. There was fire in those blue orbs, but there was something else she couldn't put her finger on. Was it sadness, regret, disappointment? She didn't know and she refused to care.

His head came down and he captured her lips. Beth sighed softly and gave over to the passion unfurling inside her. She ached to be one with him and pressed her hips toward him. Bear growled softly and continued to explore her mouth, sending liquid heat along every nerve. She felt him hard against her stomach. When she moved her hips again, he pulled back. Beth whimpered.

"Bear . . . !"

"Hush," he whispered against her lips.

She moaned softly as he deepened the kiss. He stretched out next to her, leaning on one elbow so he half-covered her body with his. She tensed when his fingers drifted over her belly and downward. They slid past the crisp hair at the juncture of her thighs and between her legs. Beth sucked in a breath. He gently parted her and very quickly found what he was searching for. A groan was pulled from deep within her as he began a slow and steady stroking of her clit. The ache in her belly tightened and wound in on itself, shivers of pleasurable anticipation fanning over her skin.

He slipped one finger inside her as his thumb massaged her clitoris. She trembled and he growled. The sound rumbled deep in his chest and through her. An inferno followed, hotter than the surface of the sun. Her hips began to move against his hand, almost of their own volition. Her skin was aflame, her insides pulled tight, her breath coming in short, ragged gasps. The tingles started to swirl beneath his fingers and expanded with each stroke of her flesh until her head spun.

His mouth left hers to trail down her throat. Beth moaned when he ducked his head, took one nipple in his mouth, and gently nibbled. The coil between her legs cracked. She tried to pull him on top of her but to no avail. He outweighed her by more than one hundred pounds of rock hard muscle and bone, and she knew she wouldn't move him if he didn't want to be moved.

Suddenly he did move, rolling onto his back and taking her with him. She looked down at him in surprise as she straddled his hips, her fingers braced against his chest. His hand was flat on her belly, his thumb still massaging that tender nub of flesh. He cupped his other hand behind her neck and pulled her toward him until their lips nearly touched. The coil fractured again and started to spin apart.

"This is what you wanted, Beth," he whispered. His eyes searched hers. "So take it."

Beth's heart did a back flip, bouncing uncomfortably between her lungs and sternum. He was right, but not completely. She wanted much more than to make love with him, but if this was all she could have, she would content herself with this. Gazes locked, she moved her hips and took him inside her. He was so large it almost hurt. A gasp was forced from her lungs and for a moment, she couldn't breathe.

Ecstasy shot through her and she froze as he inhaled sharply. His eyes were smoky and she saw the tensing of his jaw as she began to move her hips in a slow, sensual rhythm. The sensation overwhelmed her. It was as if her entire body had been dipped in Icy-Hot, heat and cold washing over her in intermittent waves. She closed her eyes and kissed him.

There was nothing gentle about his response this time. His mouth ravaged hers and for a moment, she felt as if she was drowning. The pressure between her legs strengthened and ripples of pure pleasure spun through her in widening circles. She reared up, leaned back, and planted her hands on his muscular thighs. Her hips moved just a little faster, and his fingers grasped her waist. She reveled in the feel of him deep inside her. He pressed against the entrance to her womb and a shudder ran the length of her body. Somehow that coil held together, but it grew with each measured thrust of his pelvis until she had the sensation of being turned inside out. She looked at him, and what she saw in those usually guarded eyes made her heart quiver: desire, sadness, determination, and passion. Her lashes fluttered down and she moaned, breathless, as their bodies moved as one.

Beth arched her back when he rose to a sitting position and swirled his tongue around one rigid nipple. Her hips jerked as white hot heat seared through her from her breasts to her vulva and back. She wrapped her arms around his head as his mouth moved from one peak to the other, licking, nibbling, caressing. Pressing herself more firmly against his mouth and his pelvis, the wave started to crest. Part of her wanted to move faster, but she knew if she did it would be over far too soon. She didn't want it to be over . . . ever. She bit her lip and moaned.

She maintained the easy, languid tempo, and every stroke sent pulses dancing through her with increasing speed and intensity. Bear groaned deep in his throat with each swivel of her hips, and the sound of his pleasure only added to hers. Just when she thought her body had reached its limit, the wave dipped almost imperceptibly and then surged higher. Rapture pierced her, wrapped around her, enveloped her, and she trembled. Ragged cries erupted from the core of her being. She knew a moment of intense fear as not only her body but also her heart became one with him. At that moment the coil shattered. She rocked her hips once as agonizing pleasure swelled through her, and then again as a scream clogged her throat. Her orgasm detonated, and violent shockwaves wracked her body. Beth pressed her face against his shoulder, and every muscle in her body tensed. He gripped her waist tightly and jerked her against him, seating himself to the hilt. Her hips moved on their own now, fast and hard, and pleasure spiraled outward from low in her belly like a supernova. Her gasping cries filled the cavernous room, but she barely heard them over the roar of blood in her ears. Tears stung and she closed her eyes as the physical and emotional riptide pulled her apart and under.

Bear watched her closely, reveling in the sight, sound, and feel of her climax. The expression of rapture on her face took his breath away and threatened to send him over the edge. She was hot and wet and tight around him, her muscles clenching and unclenching, constricting and pulling him deeper. Her skin glowed pink and when she threw her head back and cried out in release, he felt the familiar tingling at the base of his penis. He fought it. The longing in her golden-brown gaze had touched something deep inside him, something in a place he'd kept under lock and key. She had asked him for one night, and he planned to make good use of that time.

He felt her orgasm starting to ebb, the contractions easing. Bear flipped her onto her back and surged forward powerfully, heat swelling through him when she gasped and looked at him in surprise. Leaning up on his elbows, he framed her face and memorized every detail: the sweeping brows, the thick lashes, the narrow nose, the sculpted cheekbones, the full, generous mouth, and the golden eyes with flecks of paler amber and darker chocolate brown. Something tightened in his chest and his groin as he started to move. He slowly left her body and pushed forward, and she let out a soft mewl of pleasure. That soft, telling sound lit the fuse. He took a deep breath as sizzling pulses traveled from his penis through the rest of him.

The pace she'd set before her climax had been unhurried and languorous, and he wanted more of that. The rhythm of his hips was strong and deliberate, soft yet relentless. Beth pulled her knees up and locked her ankles behind his back. Bear groaned softly as shocks of pleasure built inside him to such a level that his pulse raced and electricity shivered over his skin. The feel of her as his body rhythmically melded with hers was like nothing he'd experienced before. This was more than just sex. Connections were being made here, deep but fragile bonds. Fear seized his heart with an iron fist as he thought of those bonds being inevitably severed. He paused and looked down at her.

Her eyes were closed, and he blinked when he saw the tracks of her tears. Her legs were still tightly wrapped around him, her hands clutching at his back, her breasts moving with each gasping breath. He blinked again, thinking he was imagining them, but when he ran his thumbs over her cheeks, the cool wetness proved he was not seeing things. His throat tightened.

"Beth." Her eyelids fluttered up and his heart lurched at the shimmer in her eyes. "Am I hurting you?"

She took a short, shallow breath and shook her head. "No." More tears gathered and a pensive smile curved her mouth. "No."

Her answer didn't reassure him, but before he could say or do anything, she kissed him. A vortex of sensation completely sucked him under. Every coherent thought, every word, every idea was completely and utterly overwhelmed by how and what she made him feel: appreciated, wanted, *needed*. In the time since his last relationship he'd guarded his heart with fierce determination, but he felt himself giving it to her without reservation as their tongues entwined. Oddly, the realization didn't frighten him. It freed him.

He deepened the kiss, the movements of his tongue matching the movements of his hips. He took her frantic murmurs into his mouth, and they traveled through him to where their bodies were joined with such seamless ease and urgency. The tingling increased and strengthened, urging him to move more quickly. Rather than giving in to the desire, he forced himself to slow. He focused on kissing her, on each hushed sigh and whimper, on the tightening of her muscles around him. The frequency and pitch of her moans increased, and she tried to move her hips faster. He groaned as the pulsing in his groin expanded exponentially, threatening to overpower him. Burying his face in her neck, he fought it, determined to pleasure her again before he allowed himself release.

He searched for her hands and wound his fingers between hers, their palms pressed together. His hips pushed forward, deeper, harder, and he felt the rush of heat and moisture as her body responded. He bit her neck lightly and she moaned. She trembled beneath him, and with each measured thrust, she gasped. Her ragged breaths frayed his control, and Bear felt himself swell and harden as the ache in his groin grew. His body wanted to lose itself in her, to give in to the animal urge to rut, but *he* didn't want that. He wanted to prolong their connection as long as he could. Waves of pleasure pulsed through him as he forced himself to slow even more. Every square inch of him was burning, and he wished it would never stop.

Beth's hips matched the movements of his, and he felt her climax building. The contractions started softly at first, but grew stronger. A groan was ripped from his throat as she tightened around him, released, and tightened again. Her frantic whimpers only pushed him further. Her nipples were hard against his chest, brushing his skin with each undulation of his pelvis. Their hands entwined, her breath hot on his skin, he felt the pull as the earth opened beneath him. She coiled like a spring and a shock of pleasure washed over him as the spring gave way. A startled cry burst from her mouth and her muscles clamped down on him, her body quaking. The dam inside him exploded and he groaned. He buried himself in her, his hips rocking back and forth as excruciating, tingling waves of pleasure erupted from deep within him. Her vaginal walls clenched and unclenched around him with incredible force. Ragged gasps escaped him with each frenzied spasm. His head spun and, after what seemed like both a fleeting moment and an eternity, the tremors eased. Releasing her hands, he cupped her bottom and gave one final, powerful thrust.

Beth tried to catch her breath and couldn't, blood thundered through her veins. Throbbing waves of pleasure continued to crackle through her, gradually fading like fireworks against the night sky. Finally she took a huge, shuddering gulp of air. As the last shivers left her, she felt her heart break. It was over. Her eyes were closed, but the tears still found a way out.

She'd never before experienced such profound, intense emotion for a man, not ever. Not even Michael, whom she had briefly thought of marrying, had touched her as deeply as Bear. It was as if he had demanded a piece of her soul, and she had given it to him. And she'd do it again, without reservation, even knowing how fleeting their time together would be.

I love you, she thought.

Her eyes snapped opened and fear pierced her like an arrow. Had she spoken the words? She wasn't sure if what was in her heart had escaped her mouth. Bear leaned up on his elbows, and she squeezed her eyes shut, knowing she would see the answer in his face. His fingers gently stroked her brow, her cheekbones, the line of her jaw, and a ball of uncertainty roiled in the pit of her stomach.

"Beth."

"Hmm?" It was all she could manage.

"Look at me."

The uncertainty blossomed into full-blown apprehension. Beth shook her head as another tear slid down the side of her face. She felt him take a deep breath, hold it for a second, and then let it out. He traced her lips with one finger.

"Please."

The ache in her chest intensified. Her chin trembled and she ground her teeth together. *Might as well get it over with. There's no getting away from this one.* After a brief, pregnant pause, she forced herself to meet his gaze. His expression was tender, wistful, and his brows drew together slightly as he continued to trace her face with his hands. His eyes searched hers and she saw the affection, and the sorrow reflected in those pools of blue. Her breath caught. It was the first time he'd ever looked at her without erecting any sort of shield or barrier between them. This man was *not* Special Agent Bristol. This man was *Bear.*

"Whatever feelings you think you have for me . . . ." His voice trailed off and his eyes narrowed. "When this is all over . . . they'll go away."

The last phrase had been a whisper, but he might as well have shouted at her so deeply did it cut. She stared at him. "Why . . . why would you say that?"

Another shadow flitted over his face. He clenched his jaw as he left her body, moved away from her, and sat up. He turned his gaze out the window for a few seconds, sighed and glanced at her over his shoulder. "Because once you're safe . . . you won't need me anymore."

His tone was soft but matter-of-fact, and it was like a fist to her midsection. Beth blinked and exhaled sharply. She stared at his broad back, and her stomach knotted as the pain of his words knifed through her. He'd spoken flatly and without inflection, but she felt his wound as if it was her own. "Is that . . . ?" She paused and swallowed the lump lodged in her throat. "Is that what you *want*?"

He moved to the edge of the bed and sat there, hands braced at his sides. "No, actually, it's not." He shook his head. "For the first time in more than fifteen years it's not, but it will still happen." He rose and walked toward the bathroom. "It always does."

****

Bear stared at his reflection, hating himself more with each passing minute. He had crossed that line, knowingly and willingly, and what bothered him most was that he'd cross it again. Even if he could relive these last few days over and over in an attempt to correct all his mistakes, being with Beth was the one thing he would not change. He turned on the water in the sink and thrust his hands beneath the flow. After looking at himself for another moment, he leaned over and liberally splashed his face, the cold water like a slap. Bracing his hands on the edge of the counter, he watched the water drip off his chin. He took a fluffy white hand towel from a nearby stack and dried himself, then tossed it aside and reached for the doorknob. Time to face the music.

To his surprise Beth was not in the bedroom. A chill of concern made his abdominals tighten. He grabbed his sweatpants from the floor and slipped them on, then crossed the room and exited the suite.

The house was dark, moonlight spilling through the enormous windows and puddling on the floor in silver rectangles. He was puzzled for a moment, wondering why Beth had bothered to turn off all the lights, until he remembered the lights had turned on by themselves. That mystery solved, he glanced across the house to the spare bedroom. He hadn't bothered to close the door with Beth dangling over his shoulder, but it was closed now. With a small sigh, he walked toward it.

It pushed open with nary a sound. She stood at the end of the bed, dressed in the golden negligee, tucking things into the suitcase Laine had let her borrow. He wondered why for a second, before his brain caught up, and he realized this was what she thought he wanted. It wasn't, not even close. His breath caught, and his heart did an uncharacteristic leap as he allowed himself a few seconds to drink in the sight of her. The gown skimmed her body and looked more like a dusting of sunlit glitter than actual fabric. For a moment he forgot why he was there, completely captivated by the graceful movements of her body. He wanted to touch her again. He wanted to pleasure her again and again, until she begged him to stop. They would eventually be forced to part ways, but he refused to think about that now. Reality could wait. For the next eight to ten hours, they could pretend lives didn't hang in the balance and concentrate on each other. After that, he'd play it by ear and hope they had more time together. He shook himself and leaned against the jamb.

"What are you doing?"

She jumped, gasped, and spun to face him, eyes wide. "Oh, crap." She pressed a hand to her heart and closed her eyes for a moment. "I really *am* going to put a bell around your neck."

He wondered if she knew how little that gown concealed, and he felt desire stir. He asked again, "What are you doing?"

Beth glanced at the suitcase and shrugged. "Making ready in case we have to run." She sat down on the padded bench. "Didn't think I should leave my . . . I mean Laine's stuff scattered everywhere."

"Okay." A pang of guilt wormed its way through his middle. In light of their last conversation, she was making the logical assumption that they were done. He'd given her what she'd asked for, and it was back to business. *Not yet, sweetheart. Not quite yet.* "Now what are you *really* doing?"

She looked down at her lap. "I . . . I thought I'd give you your space." She flipped the lid of the suitcase closed and avoided looking at him. "You should sleep in the master suite. I mean, you'd probably like the chance to stretch out for a change instead of having to share."

His feet padded across the thick carpet until he towered over her, arms crossed over his chest. It bothered him that after all the effort she had put into seducing him, she now seemed resigned to just let it go. A flash of indignation warmed his chest, but he immediately chided himself. This was his fault. She glanced up at him, and he saw the plea in her eyes. That golden gaze was asking him to tell her she was wrong, to reassure her and pull her back. She moved before he had a chance.

Without a word, she rose and moved to the picture window, presenting him with her back. The moonlight illuminated the outline of her body through the sheer material, and his gaze was drawn to the long, sleek legs. He took in the elegant curves, the graceful lines, and the shimmer of moonlight on her skin. Bear walked up behind her. He was close enough to touch her, but he fisted his hands at his sides.

"And, if that's *not* what I'd like?" he asked.

She met his gaze in their reflection on the glass

"Well . . . ." Her voice died and she cleared her throat softly. "Unlike the women you may be accustomed to dealing with, I would never assume I can just hop into bed with you." She lifted her chin. "Before I get in bed with a man, I like to *know* that's where he wants me."

"That's where I want you."

"Is it?" she whispered.

He said nothing. After visually battling with her reflection, he turned her to face him. She took a deep breath and looked at the floor.

"I don't know what you've been through, Bear." She paused, clenched her jaw, and then lifted her eyes to his. "But I'm not *her.*"

"I know." He rubbed his knuckles against her cheek and sighed softly. "I never wanted her as much as I want *you.*" Her eyelids fluttered and her mouth opened in surprise. Before she could say anything, he grabbed her hand and walked out of the room, pulling her behind him.

"Bear . . . !"

"You asked me for one night." He gave her a sidelong glance and smiled. "Night's not over yet."

Chapter Seventeen

Light tugged Beth from the soundest sleep she'd had in months. She reached for Bear, but her eyes came open when all she found were cool sheets. He was not in bed. Beth rolled over and looked around, but the room was empty. Dawn was just breaking, pinkish gold light bathing the outside world in a warm glow that flowed gently in through the windows. That was when she saw her camera.

It sat on the sill of the huge windowpane on top of a folded piece of yellow paper. She reached for the paper and unfolded it.

Found a clean memory card in the Lockharts' study and transferred all non-incriminating shots. Thought you might want your other pictures back.

Her brows drew together, and she picked up the camera. She turned the device on and scrolled through the photographs. Sure enough, the pictures of the murder were not there.

Beth put the camera down on the bed and got to her feet. After slipping into Bear's flannel shirt, she walked toward the windows overlooking the lake. She yawned and stretched, sucking in a breath at the sharp ache between her legs. Heat suffused her cheeks. The last time she'd looked at the clock had been shortly after midnight, and she'd been on her way to orgasm number five. She gulped as a pang of desire twinged inside her yet again.

Movement near the water caught her eye and she froze. Unable to see what it was, she walked back to the bed, grabbed her camera, returned to the window, and put her eye to the viewfinder. She smiled when she saw Bear standing on the end of the dock wearing what looked like swim trunks. He stretched for a few minutes and then dove cleanly into the water.

A chill went through her. It was early spring and they were well above 8,000 feet, sporadic patches of snow stubbornly clung to the shaded areas where little sun penetrated. At this altitude and time of morning, the air would be cold, and the water was no doubt colder. She shivered again. "No, thank you."

She watched him until the trees obscured her view. A pang of disappointment made her chest ache. Beth looped the camera around her neck, grabbed her sweatpants and went in search of her slippers.

A few minutes later she wore Bear's enormous jacket and leaned against a tree at the shore. Bear swam back toward the dock. His arms moved in strong, sure strokes, and he sliced through the water like a shark. When he got within about fifteen feet of the pier, Beth lifted the camera to her eye and focused on him. She knew he'd never pose for her, but she could always take his picture when he wasn't paying attention.

He tapped a large piling, flipped, and swam away again. Beth just stood there, content to watch as she snuggled deeper into his coat. It smelled like him, and she inhaled deeply of his scent. A cold, hard lump formed in her throat as she imagined him never returning. She swallowed hard and focused on him.

He swam to the opposite shore, turned around, and swam back. He did this several more times before he planted his hands on the end of the dock and lifted himself out of the water. The auto advance fired, taking pictures continuously as he swung one foot up onto the rough, wooden boards and stood. Her breath caught. Water glistened on his skin in droplets turned a pale orange color by the rising sun, the early morning light accentuating the sharply defined muscles. She continued to take pictures. He reached for a towel lying on the dock and his head snapped up. That sharp gaze found her immediately and a frown creased his brow. Beth smiled, lowered the camera, and walked toward him.

Bear toweled himself dry, his eyes locked on her. His skin was flushed with the cold and covered in goose bumps.

"Looks a mite chilly," she said.

"A little." He tipped his head to the side and shook it, drying his ear. "I just figured out how they saw you."

Her brows rose. "How?"

"Sunlight off the lens casing. I saw the flash a split second before I heard the auto-advance." His brows drew together. "What are you doing?"

Apparently, Special Agent Bristol was back. Sadness pricked her heart, but Beth forced a smile. "Taking your picture."

He frowned again. "Why?"

"Because I wanted to." She looked at the camera and capped the lens. "And because I knew if I asked you, you'd have said no."

He frowned and tipped his head the opposite direction to dry his other ear. "I don't like having my picture taken."

"You could make a lot of money having your picture taken, trust me." When his brows shot up, she smiled and dropped her chin. "But I know that's not your style. You like the job you have." She crossed her arms over her chest. "What is it with you military and law enforcement types not liking your picture taken?"

"We have dangerous jobs," Bear replied, rubbing his head with the towel. "The more anonymous we are, the better, which precludes having our pictures taken. Firefighters can get away with that shit because people are always happy to see *them*. Cops and military . . . not so much." She saw the shift in expression as he latched onto what she'd just said. "You spend a lot of time with cops and military types?"

The film reel threatened to jump out of the box, but she slammed the lid shut and held a mental hand there. "I used to." She thought about leaving it at that, but after the night they'd spent together, it seemed somehow wrong to keep that part of her a secret. "I was a . . . a war correspondent for the Associated Press . . . an *eon* ago. I spent some time in Afghanistan with a Marine unit."

He didn't seem surprised. "See any action?"

She swallowed hard. "A little." A smiling face flashed in her mind's eye, but she forced it back into the darkness. "That's where I learned to shoot."

His gaze was speculative. "That explains a lot, including the scar." He hung the towel around his neck and watched her for a few more seconds, his expression assessing. She could almost hear the wheels in his head spin. "I need to show you something."

Her stomach flipped. "Something good, or something bad?"

Those laser-like eyes focused on her. He stared hard for a moment then sighed. "I just think it's time you know what you're up against, I mean *really* know." His eyes narrowed a fraction. "You up for that?"

She hesitated, then returned his gaze and nodded. "Yeah." Beth glanced at her camera. "But first you should take a shower and get dressed. It's cold out here." She started to unzip the jacket but he stopped her.

"You need it more than I will." He laced his fingers through hers. "Hot-blooded, remember?"

The look he gave her was completely neutral, but she felt the flush to her scalp. "Um . . . yeah . . . I remember."

He chuckled and started walking. "Come on, Aphrodite. I don't know about you, but I could use some coffee, and some breakfast. I find myself oddly famished this morning."

****

Bear emerged from the shower to the smell of bacon and his mouth watered. He dressed quickly and made his way to the kitchen. He appeared just as Beth lifted a large skillet filled with scrambled eggs from the stove. He watched as she shoveled three-fourths of the eggs onto one plate and the rest onto another. After placing a half-dozen or so slices of bacon on the first plate, she turned. When she saw him standing there, she jumped and dropped the dish. Bear caught it neatly. She stared at him for a moment and then scowled.

"Really?" She braced her hands on the edge of the granite. "Would you *please* stop sneaking up on me?"

"I wasn't sneaking." He shrugged. "That's just how I walk."

She glared at him. "Well walk . . . *louder*."

He chuckled. "I take it this is mine?"

She said nothing, rolled her eyes, and turned back to the stove. Bear sat down at the dining table. A steaming cup of coffee already waited for him, and he put the plate next to it. Beth sat at his elbow. He watched her covertly for a moment before he started to eat, and when the first bite of egg hit his tongue, he looked at her in surprise.

"These are great." He took another forkful. "What do you put in them?"

"A little cream, salt and pepper, cayenne, and feta cheese," she replied. She stabbed a piece of egg with her fork. "They didn't have any milk, but I found a carton of half-and-half on the bottom shelf in the back. It was still good, so food poisoning isn't a concern."

"Well, this is delicious." He took a sip of coffee. "Thank you."

"You're welcome."

They ate the remainder of the meal in silence, but Bear glanced at her often. His brain was trying to say something, but he ignored it. He didn't need it to tell him what his heart already knew. He'd broken his own unwritten rule by falling for her, a witness, and it was going to cost him, big time. He just hoped it didn't cost her as dearly.

Beth finished her last piece of bacon and rose, taking her plate in one hand. Bear took it from her and stood.

"You cooked." He stacked their dishes and carried them to the sink. "I'll clean."

"Bear."

He waved a hand at her and started running water. "Go . . . take a shower . . . sit on the porch and have another cup of coffee . . . whatever." He squirted some dish soap into the water, put the dishes in the sink, and planted his hands on the edge of the counter. "I'll do the dishes, and then we'll talk."

She stared at him mutinously. "You wash, I'll dry."

He admired her stubbornness, but this time it triggered something devilish in him, and he deliberately changed gears. "How's your knee?" She blinked and he fought a smile. "I've been meaning to ask."

Her expression turned wary. "A little sore but otherwise, fine. How's your shoulder?"

"Fine." Bear turned off the water. "But I didn't spend any time on my shoulder last night." He picked up a sponge, swirled it over a plate, and fought a grin as color surged into her cheeks. "*You*, on the other hand . . . ."

She gaped at him, and he saw her gulp. A flash of hunger shone in her eyes and her blush deepened. He wiggled his eyebrows at her. *You won the last round, sweetheart. My turn.* After nearly half a minute of staring at each other, she exhaled sharply, turned and walked toward the stairs. "Fine. I'm going to take a shower."

He chuckled. "I'll meet you in the study when you're done."

Twenty minutes later she entered the study dressed in jeans, a pale blue sweater, and her hiking boots. He sat at a desk, scrolling through the pictures from her memory card. As soon as their eyes met, he felt the familiar spark, and it was much harder to smother or disregard than it had been before they'd made love. Bear clamped down ruthlessly on his attraction for her and focused on the computer monitor. He gestured for her to come near. He saw the apprehension in those golden-brown eyes, but she nodded once and walked over to him. *That's my girl.* The decision to tell her had not been an easy one, but he was going to need her cooperation. He knew she would be more agreeable if she knew everything. She sat down on the arm of the large executive chair he sat in. Bear tapped a key and she tensed.

"Meet one Hector Perez," he said. In the photograph, Tall Guy was just exiting the helicopter, the blades a blur overhead. "He's the head enforcer for the Cárdenas Cartel out of Mexico City. They're one of the largest drug-smuggling organizations in the western hemisphere. They've established themselves in Texas, Arizona, New Mexico, and California, and they're looking to expand north. The DEA has been dealing with these guys a lot over the past couple of years, and some of it has fallen in my court."

She exhaled slowly. "So, I was right about it possibly being cartel related."

"Yep." He pulled up the next picture. "And *this* is Ramon Cárdenas."

"Suit guy," she whispered. "Is he *the* Cárdenas . . . ?"

Bear shook his head. "No." He opened up the Internet browser and typed quickly.

"Wow. You can Google drug lords now?"

"Technology is great, isn't it?" He hit the return button. "*That* Cárdenas is . . . ." He paused as a number of links appeared on the screen. He clicked on one and it opened up a newspaper article containing a photograph of an older, distinguished gentleman with salt and pepper hair, dark skin, and even darker eyes. The resemblance between Ramon and the older man was unmistakable. ". . . Diego Cárdenas, also known as The Don. Ramon is his only son and heir apparent."

He glanced at her, gauging her reaction. Under normal circumstances this wasn't information he'd share with a witness, but this wasn't a normal situation. And, Beth was far more to him than just a witness. She had a right to know the dangerous potential here, but he was worried. Most civilians he'd dealt with would've shut down *long* before now, but not her, not *yet.* Her expression was somber, her gaze focused on the monitor. She took a breath, glanced at him. When he saw the resolve in her eyes, he wanted to kiss her. Instead, he reopened the media viewer and moved to the next image.

"So, who are Shaved Head and Ponytail?" she asked in a low voice.

"Don't know. Probably just enforcers, but I'm sure I could find rap sheets on both of them if I looked. They're not important." He split the screen so Hector Perez, Ramon Cárdenas, and Diego Cárdenas were visible. "These guys are the main players."

"What are they playing?"

"I'm not sure. Perez is the Don's right hand man, but Ramon has never done anything in the organization except enjoy the fruits of his father's labor." He leaned back in the chair. "He's been enrolled at and expelled from some of the most expensive Ivy League universities in the nation, he's known as a playboy, and he has more speeding tickets than the Don has cocaine." He rubbed his chin. "Ramon and Hector used to be inseparable." He looked at her out of the corner of his eye. "Hector is Ramon's cousin. The story says the Don took Hector in when he was just a boy after his mother, the Don's sister, was caught in the crossfire of a gang shootout. Hector was always there to get Ramon out of trouble, clean up his messes, and keep him safe. They grew up together, and they were more like brothers than cousins."

Beth turned wide, disbelieving eyes to him. "But Hector . . . *killed* Ramon."

"Ever hear of Cain and Abel?"

She exhaled sharply and blinked at him, her jaw hanging slack. Several seconds had passed before she looked at the monitor again. After another brief silence she said, "So, what about the ATV guys? What part do they play?"

Bear's mind was spinning at warp speed. "I'm not sure."

She leaned over to look him in the face. "But you have a theory." When he nodded her brows drew together. "What is it?"

Bear looked at her for a second before he opened a photograph of the men on the ATVs. "I don't recognize any of them, but I do recognize this." He isolated a spot on the lead man's neck and enlarged it. An elaborate "G" done in flowing script superimposed over an undulating Mexican flag was visible just below the man's ear. The tattoo was only a few inches square, but the bright colors were unmistakable. "*That* is the mark of the Giraldo family." He paused and rubbed his chin, thoughts ricocheting through his brain.

"Who are they?"

"They're a competing cartel with their roots in Oaxaca. They're smaller, not as well equipped or financed, but scrappy. They fight for and defend every inch of territory they have with a ruthlessness that makes the Don look like Santa Claus."

Beth frowned. "So, the son of a drug kingpin who has never been involved in the cartel's business is suddenly meeting with soldiers of a rival cartel." She looked at him. "Why?"

Bear knew there could be a hundred different reasons, but only one kept running through his brain to return front and center. "I think Ramon was trying to impress Daddy."

"What do you mean?"

He pursed his lips and reopened the three split-screen photos. "Rumor has it the Don wants to retire, but he hasn't because he's not sure Ramon can handle the organization." He sighed. "I think Ramon wanted to show Daddy he was wrong."

Beth gaped at him. "You think he was negotiating some sort of . . . *trade agreement* with their rivals?"

"Or maybe a cease-fire." He met her gaze. "It's always more profitable to work *with* your competitors than expend the time, money, and bodies to fight them." He gave her a pointed look. "Hector is second only to the Don in the organization. If Ramon had succeeded and been crowned the new king, where would that have left Hector?"

Her brows rose. "Still second."

"Exactly." Something in her expression changed, and he almost heard the shift of gears.

"So . . . Ramon arranges a meet with his family's rivals in the hopes of brokering some sort of . . . *truce* to prove to his father that he *can* run the cartel. Hector kills the rivals, kills Ramon, but makes it *look* like the Giraldo soldiers killed Ramon." She paused and took a breath. "Hector goes back to the Don, tells him the *Giraldo* men killed Ramon. The Don promotes Hector, and Hector now gets to be in charge and lead the cartel in the war he just started, which takes the focus off Ramon's death and makes him look like the most loyal of subordinates." She ran a hand over her eyes. "Brilliant."

"That's pretty much what I was thinking." Bear rested a hand on her leg. "For someone who doesn't watch a lot of TV, you seem to have a knack for this kind of thing."

"Yeah, well, I read a lot." She squeezed her eyes shut. "Although I think from now on I'm going to switch genres. Romance, yeah, romance. This sort of shit doesn't happen in romance novels, does it?"

Unbidden, he smiled. "I don't know."

"If it does, I'll just try another genre." She rose and moved to the window. "Maybe autobiographies or self-help. This shit *can't* happen in self-help or it wouldn't be self-*help*." She froze, then spun and stared at him. "Wait. Why are you telling me this now?" Her eyes narrowed. "You said you recognized Perez from the first, so why *now*?"

Bear was impressed. She was quite sharp, but that only increased his uncertainty level. He'd been mapping out his plan ever since he'd woken up with Beth in his arms, but he was unsure what her reaction would be. Up until now she'd been completely sensible, ceding control to him, but his next words could bring her levelheadedness to an abrupt end. He hoped her intellect would override her gut reaction and plunged ahead. "I need to leave."

Her mouth dropped open. "Leave?"

He took a step toward her. "I need to go to Denver and end this. I said those pictures could save you if given to the right person, so I need to get them there. If I don't, you'll spend the rest of your life running and looking over your shoulder, or you'll have to start your life over, as someone else."

She took a step toward him, her expression one of shocked disbelief. "Take me with you."

He shook his head. "It's too dangerous. You'll be safer here."

Her expression turned incredulous. "Will *you* be safe?"

Her concern warmed him. "I'm always safe."

She shook her head and backed away from him. "Bear . . . ."

He cupped her head, his brows drawing together. "Trust me, Beth."

"It's not *you* I don't trust." She jerked away from him. "It's *them*." Her fear was a palpable thing, filling the space between them.

"I'll be fine." He knew he couldn't guarantee that, but he saw no other recourse. And, once he was committed, he was *committed*. He wouldn't take any unnecessary risks, his plan was solid but, as he'd recently experienced, a plan could very easily fall apart.

She blinked several times and he braced in anticipation of tears. Instead, an angry flush crept into her cheeks. "Is that what Special Agent Acosta said right before he went in?" she asked in a whisper. There was the faintest shimmer in her eyes. "I'll be *fine*?" Her voice was hushed, filled with fear, but there was also an edge of sarcasm that he felt to his core.

He was amazed that a one hundred sixty pound woman could wield a verbal knife with such cutting precision and brute strength against a man more than a hundred pounds heavier. Bear looked over her head for a moment and took a steadying breath as he tried to gather his insides from off the floor, again. He knew her reaction was instinctual and not deliberate. He'd been on the receiving end of the latter more than once, so he recognized the difference. She didn't mean to mock him, but that didn't lessen the sting. Carefully and deliberately, he put the pain from her words inside a compartment in his head, and closed and locked the door. He kept his face impassive and his voice level.

"Stay in the house and keep the doors and windows locked." He met her anguished eyes and clenched his jaw. He wanted to reassure her, but right now he couldn't. Any promises he made would be disingenuous and he knew she'd know that. "I'll leave the shotgun and a pistol and some extra ammunition, but if anything happens, *anything*, you dial 911 and hide. And keep the guns with you. It'll take the sheriff a while to get here. If you *have* to run, the keys to the Suburban are on the visor."

Beth stared after him as he turned on his heel and left the study. Her heart turned to ice. When he disappeared from view, searing pain cut through her, as if her chest had been sliced open from the inside. The frozen internal organ fell to the floor and shattered. Her knees wobbled and she sank down in the chair he had vacated. Fear blossomed in her belly in a dark, cold, tar-like pool, and it expanded until it felt like it was being forced out her pores. She understood he was just doing what he needed to protect her, but it didn't matter how confident she was in his abilities. No matter how much he wanted her to believe otherwise, she knew he wasn't Superman.

She heard the door to the garage close and shot to her feet. *He's really leaving.* Panic scraped beneath her sternum in sharp spasms. She raced up the hall, across, and down the opposite hall to the back stairs. She jerked open the door to the garage and leapt down the steps, entering the cavernous subterranean room just as the door whispered shut. Beth pounded on the button and the door slowly rolled up.

Once there was enough space for her to fit beneath it, she skittered under the heavy panels and ran up the driveway. As she did, what she'd said to him replayed in her mind, and now guilt joined the cold sense of loss in her belly. *No, no, no. I can't let you leave like this.* Alarm surged through her and she stretched her legs out as the Mercedes headed away. Beth crested the top of the driveway and put on a burst of speed. Just as she was about to yell his name the brake lights went on and the vehicle stopped. Tears were cold on her cheeks. Her heart pounded vigorously against her ribs, and relief washed over her when he opened the door and stepped out. Without even slowing, she threw herself against him. It was like throwing feathers against a brick wall. His arms closed around her and her feet came off the ground as he lifted her against his chest.

"I'm sorry!" she gasped. Her arms wound around his neck. "Oh, God, I'm sorry. I shouldn't have said that to you."

"It's okay, sweetheart," he said softly. He cupped her head with one large hand and pressed a kiss to her temple. "Everything's okay."

His voice was a deep rumble that vibrated through her, but she heard a note of humor. She pulled back to look at him. "Would you *stop* being so damn understanding?" Her eyes searched his. "Get mad at me, yell, do *something*."

He shook his head slightly. "I'm not angry with you, and I yelled at you last night, something I do not plan to do again."

Beth closed her eyes and dropped her chin. "I . . . *was* . . . pushing."

He chuckled and kissed her brow. "Perhaps, but I prefer to save my anger and my vocal chords for situations that warrant them." He put her feet on the ground. His eyes narrowed slightly as he watched her closely. "This isn't one of those times." Bear curled a finger under her chin and tipped her face up. "I've been doing this a long time, Beth. I get it. You're scared, and you should be, but I'm not going to do anything stupid. Believe it or not, I'm really good at my job."

She focused on the cleft in his chin. "You already promised me you'd try not to get hurt again."

"And I will do everything I can to keep that promise." A pensive smile lifted the corners of his mouth just slightly. "Y'know, I don't like getting hurt any more than the next guy. I just handle it better than most."

Beth flattened her hands on his chest, his heart beating a slow, steady cadence against her palm. She thought of never seeing him again, and a shaft of pain stabbed through her with such power she thought she heard the rending of flesh and bone.

"The last man who saved my life . . . I watched him die." She had to force the words out her painfully tight throat. Tears stung and her chin trembled. "I held him as he bled to death." The box started to shake, but she mentally planted both hands on the lid and put her full weight behind it. She couldn't imagine something like that happening to Bear. She *wouldn't.* Her chest was already so taut her lungs could barely inflate, as if her torso was clamped into a vise. She knew if she even entertained the thought of him being seriously hurt or killed, she'd completely shut down. Pausing, she tried to clear her mind and took a hitching breath. "He died protecting *me.*" Something cold and sharp lodged in her esophagus. Squeezing her eyes shut, she swallowed it down and whispered, "I don't want that to happen to you." *And I can't go through that again.*

"It won't."

The tone of his voice was low, reassuring, and firm. It did little to alleviate her fear, but there was little she could do. He had to do what he had to do, and she was in no position to stop him. Nor did she have a better idea. *Okay, Beth. It's time to suck it up. He doesn't need to be worrying about YOU.* "Promise me you'll be careful."

"I promise."

She opened her eyes and looked at him. "And that you'll come back to me."

He pressed a hand to her cheek. "Can't think of any place I'd rather be, sweetheart."

Part of her knew he was just saying that to appease her, but the rest of her didn't care. Fear, dread, sorrow, longing, panic, and despair curled in her belly, winding through her insides and squeezing like soul-sucking tentacles. Beth took a shaky breath, nodded, and stepped back.

"Then go and do what you need to." She tried to hide what she was feeling, but she knew he saw right through her. Wiping her cheeks, she forced a smile. "I'm not going anywhere."

She stuffed her hands into her pockets and waited for him to get back in the Mercedes, but he didn't. His gaze was focused on her face, and it felt like that laser-pointed look was boring straight into her soul. Although his expression betrayed nothing, she wondered if he was as conflicted as she was. Somehow, she doubted it. He looked calm, cool, and composed, like he always did.

He took one step toward her, lowered his head, and covered

her mouth with his. A ray of hope broke through the dark emotions congealing in her chest, and a wonderful sense of rightness settled over her. Heat spread through her like sunlight breaking the horizon. He cupped her head in his hands, and she wrapped her fingers around his forearms, her knees wobbling. His tongue melded with hers and started desire curling in her belly. She moaned softly. His kiss was ruthless, demanding. When he ended it, a disappointed whimper stuck in her throat.

"I'll be back this evening," he whispered, his lips nearly touching hers. "I promise." A zing of excited anticipation shot up her spine. "Will you be okay?"

All she could do was nod once. Bear brushed his lips over her brow and released her. Beth just stood there, muscles frozen, eyes closed, unable to breathe as she listened to him get back in the Mercedes. The engine revved, and she heard gravel crunching underneath the tires as it drove away. By the time she had the strength to open her eyes, Bear was gone.

****

"This is ridiculous."

Laine looked at her husband, filled his coffee cup, and put it in front of him. "I agree."

Jack scowled. "Why won't you just tell me where he is?"

Frustration bubbled hotly in her belly, and she crossed her arms over her chest. "He asked me not to."

"Laine—"

She scowled. "Just stop, Jack." She turned her back on him, poured coffee into another mug, and started the third pot that morning. Jack had been pushing since they'd gotten up, and she was getting tired of battling him. "At least *you* know he's alive, which is considerably more information than *I* had when the two of you used me as bait to catch Ripley." There was a brief silence.

"Wow." He exhaled slowly. "*That* was a little below the belt."

A shiver of guilt brought her frustration level down. From his bed by the screen door to the porch, Maverick barked softly, as if agreeing with Jack. Laine tossed the animal a glare and then faced her husband. "Does that make it any less true?"

The two of them went silent as another forensics technician walked in. There were at least half a dozen people wandering in and out, including Fellowes. The Escalade even now sat on a flatbed tow truck in the driveway, and Laine noticed several neighbors peeking out their windows as the commotion continued. The technician smiled and murmured a "thank you" as he took the cup from Laine's outstretched hand. She gave him a thin smile and nodded.

It had been like this all morning. Fellowes had shown up promptly at eight o'clock with a truck full of crime scene technicians and additional agents in tow. Now, nearly three hours later, they had dusted the garage, the Escalade, and even the kitchen for fingerprints, taken photographs, and bagged only God knew what other evidence. Thankfully, they had started in the kitchen and cleaned up after themselves, which had surprised her. Jack could have saved them the trouble by telling them she had scrubbed the house from top to bottom the previous evening, but he had seen fit to keep his mouth shut for some reason. Laine leaned against the sink and waited until the technician walked back outside. As soon as the door closed, Jack spoke.

"Doc, I need to find him."

God, she hated this. She tried to clue him in without betraying Bear's confidence. "He's not *missing*. He doesn't *want* to be found. There's a distinct difference." She met her husband's gaze. "When he *wants* to be found, he will be found."

His grey eyes studied her, and she saw the anger glowing in the silvery depths. He rose from the barstool and walked around the island to stand toe to toe with her. She gulped.

"Is our first fight really going to be about Bear?" he asked in a low voice.

"I don't know." Laine lifted her chin. "Is it?" He didn't say anything, but his brows drew together ominously. Inside she was shaking, but she stood her ground. "It takes two to fight, Jack, and I'm not fighting. *You're* pushing."

He sighed and planted a hand on either side of her, pinning her against the counter. "Laine—"

He was relentless, and she was reaching her breaking point. She and Jack didn't keep secrets from each other. Her insides were tied in knots and tears stung as she took a shaky breath. "Please . . . please stop."

His expression softened. "Talk to me, Doc."

"I *can't*." When he opened his mouth to speak, she pressed a hand to his lips. "He's protecting you, and so am I."

His scowl was back. "How are the two of you protecting *me*?"

Laine frowned. "Because if I tell you where he's gone, you are obligated to tell the Bureau or risk your career. You could go to *jail*." She gave him a pleading look. "You know Bear would never put you in that kind of position, so don't ask *me* to."

Jack looked at her for a moment, his face tight with frustration. Laine rested a hand over his heart and dropped her chin.

"Please, Jack, just let it go for now. When he needs you, he'll call."

He sighed heavily and pressed his forehead to hers. "Laine . . . you have *no* idea what he's wrapped up in, how dangerous it is."

"Yes, I do."

Jack looked surprised. He straightened and met her gaze. "He told you?"

She shook her head once. "He didn't have to." Laine closed her eyes for a moment and then glanced at Maverick. "He was worried, Jack, *really* worried, even though he tried to hide it." When she met her husband's eyes this time, she didn't bother to hide her anxiety. "If it worries *Bear*...?" Her voice trailed off and she pulled in a deep breath. "If it worries *Bear*, it's a safe bet it would *terrify* the rest of us."

Jack studied her. "Okay," he said at last, "I'll stop asking where he is if you answer one question for me."

She ran a hand over her eyes. "Jack."

"Was he really okay when he stopped in here?"

She looked at her husband in surprise, and for a few seconds she couldn't speak. He was clearly worried about his friend, and she wondered what was going on that had two of the strongest, most capable men she knew concerned. Finally, she nodded. "He was fine, shot in the shoulder, but otherwise fine."

Jack gaped at her.

"It wasn't serious," she continued before he could say anything else. "It was hardly more than a scratch, for Bear anyway." She saw the relief flood Jack's face and almost spilled what she knew, which was not much. Instead she said, "For someone as big as Bear, all bullets *ever* seem to do is graze him. I sewed him up and he was as good as new."

There was a long pause before Jack closed his eyes and whispered, "Thank God."

He pushed away from the counter and hooked his thumbs through his belt loops. Laine looked at him briefly and wrapped her arms around his waist, needing his strength. She was thankful he didn't pull away. He embraced her, sighed, and rested his chin on top of her head.

"Okay, babe, we'll do it Bear's way... *this* time." He pulled back and looked down at her, and she saw the hurt in his eyes, hurt *she* had put there. He traced the line of her jaw and his expression hardened. "But never again. No more secrets between us... *ever*."

Tears welled and she nodded. "Agreed." She tucked in beneath his chin. "I'm sorry."

He sighed again as his hands moved over her back. "I know."

Laine tightened her hold on him. Her emotions rose into her throat and threatened to choke her. "I love you," she whispered.

Jack pressed a lingering kiss to the top of her head and rested his cheek there. "I love you more."

Chapter Eighteen

Bear parked the Mercedes in front of a small Hispanic market, locked the vehicle, and started walking. The mouth-watering aroma of authentic Mexican food wafted through the air, but it was impossible to tell which taqueria was responsible for the glorious scent. There were three of the eateries on this block alone. A dark-haired woman with three small boys was walking toward him, and when he nodded and said, "Buenos dias," she didn't reply. She said something in hushed Spanish to her children, ducked her head, and hurried them on their way.

After several blocks he stopped in front of a nondescript storefront, and his pulse ticked up a notch. The windows were heavily tinted and the rather plain sign over the door read *Los Cigars del Mundo*, Cigars of the World. Although the place looked unremarkable, he knew it was anything but, and so did the rest of the law enforcement community. A glance down the street showed him several plain, unmarked panel vans, and he knew any one of those vehicles might conceal a surveillance team. He could almost picture the agents scrambling to find out who he was and why he would be visiting a known cartel front. Then again, those plain, unmarked vans might very well be just what they appeared. There was no way to know unless he approached one, and he had more important things to do first. Taking a deep breath, he grasped the door handle, pulled, and stepped inside.

Four large men stood side-by-side, legs braced, arms crossed, forming a human barricade of considerable size and obvious strength. Unable to move further inside the store, he clasped his hands and waited. Thankfully, he didn't recognize any of them. They stood about three feet inside the door. Bear noticed the bulge beneath the expensive, tailored blazers that spoke of weapons not so well concealed. This actually made him decidedly less nervous. If Hector had been on the property, as soon as the door had closed behind him, he'd have been executed. Score one for the good guys, at least *this* round. He fixed the tallest one with a bored look.

"This is a private club," the man said in a heavily accented voice. "Get out."

"I would like a minute of your boss's time," Bear said in a low voice, "if he's available."

"He's not." The man took a step toward him. "Leave."

Bear pursed his lips and rubbed his chin. The men visibly tensed, almost as if he'd gone for a weapon. After a taut moment Bear said, "Tell him it's about Ramon's murder."

The tall one's eyebrows rose. A few seconds passed and he said something in hushed Spanish to one of the other columns of the wall. The second man turned on his heel and disappeared through a thick, red velvet curtain that separated the front of the store from the back. The heavy material sighed softly as it fell back into place.

Bear glanced around at the floor-to-ceiling humidors lining the walls on either side of him, his eyes flicking over the attractive, dark-haired woman sitting behind a counter to his left. Her expression was cold, distrustful, and he had no doubt that her hands hidden behind the counter contained at least one gun, maybe two. The smell of tobacco smoke and leather permeated the air. Bear clasped his hands in front of him and waited.

About a minute later, the messenger returned and whispered something in the tall one's ear. The tall one's gaze flicked over him, and then he stepped forward. Bear knew the drill. He lifted his arms and the man patted him down, grunting when he found Bear's pistol. He grunted again when he found Bear's badge. The man took his gun and badge and prodded Bear in the shoulder, pushing him toward the back of the room. The wall of men parted down the middle. The tall one gestured for Bear to walk ahead of him and followed a pace behind.

The back of the store was definitely a man's world with dark, heavy, leather-covered furniture, posters of beautiful women from cigar labels adorning the walls, and thick, dark carpet cushioning the floor. The soothing lilt of Spanish guitar exited wall-mounted speakers, the tone of the music in sharp contrast to the mood of the people in the room. The only light came from about half a dozen elaborate bronze table lamps. Heavy lampshades muted the incandescent glow. On a large, thickly cushioned couch sat Diego Cárdenas, arms resting on the back of the sofa, one ankle on the other knee, a cigar held easily in his right hand. A hot burst of anger burned in Bear's chest as he gazed upon the man who was, ultimately, responsible for JC's death, but he kept it hidden. It would do him no good to lose his temper here.

The Don's cold, dark eyes moved over him slowly, one brow shooting skyward when the tall man put Bear's pistol and badge on the massive, elaborately-carved coffee table in front of the kingpin. Cárdenas leaned forward and picked up the badge.

"Special Agent Ted Bristol." The man's voice was low, melodic, with the perfect measure of Spanish accent to give his words a graceful, alluring quality. The Don flipped the badge shut and put it back on the table. He took a puff of his cigar. "Do you have a warrant?"

"Do I need one?" Bear crossed his arms over his chest. "I'm just here to talk, Don Cárdenas."

The Don studied him. "My condolences on the passing of your co-worker, Special Agent Bristol. The world is a very dangerous place for law enforcement these days."

That anger roiled and expanded outward from his gut, but Bear ignored it. "And for children as well, apparently." He saw the tensing of the Don's jaw, but, other than that small tell, the man looked completely unflappable. "My condolences on the death of your son, Don Cárdenas. I'm truly sorry for your loss. A parent should never have to bury a child." Oddly enough, he meant the last part.

The Don stared at him for a long, silent moment before taking another puff of his cigar. "Thank you, Special Agent Bristol, although I do not think you came to see me about my son."

"Actually, that's *exactly* why I'm here."

The Don gave him a tolerant smile. "You cannot stop what is going to happen. The men who took my son from me must pay, Special Agent Bristol. Surely you understand that."

"Where's your right-hand man?" Bear asked. "Shouldn't he be at your side during this time of . . . mourning?"

The smile vanished. "Hector?" Those dark eyes flicked over him again. "You know I'm not going to tell you that."

Bear frowned slightly. "I don't care where he is, as long as he's not *here*."

The man watched him carefully and took several puffs of his cigar. Finally he said, "Hector is taking a few days off. He is trying to come to grips with Ramon's death." The Don leaned forward and tapped the cigar against the edge of an exquisite silver ashtray probably worth three months of Bear's salary. Cárdenas relaxed against the couch. "He just lost his brother, after all."

"And you lost a son."

Dark brows drew together. "Yes, I did."

"More than enough provocation to start a war."

The Don narrowed his eyes. "Wars have been started for less."

Bear reached into the waistband of his jeans, knowing what would happen as he did. The muzzle of a gun was immediately pressed into his back between his shoulder blades. His abdominals clenched and he hoped whoever was holding the weapon didn't have an itchy trigger finger. Slowly, he lifted his hands, a flash drive between his right thumb and forefinger. "You and I need to talk, in private. I have something here you need to see."

The bodyguard snatched the flash drive from Bear's hand and put it on the table next to the gun and badge. The Don picked it up, turned it over a few times, and then lifted his eyes to Bear's. He twitched two fingers of his left hand and one of the bodyguards took the flash drive, walked to a door in the back of the room, and disappeared through the thick panel. The man reappeared minutes later with a laptop, the flash drive plugged in and humming.

"It's clean, Don Cárdenas," the man said. He handed the computer to the Don and returned to his post at Bear's back.

The Don nodded. "Thank you, Manuel. Now all of you can go." Cárdenas spoke softly, but the words were edged with steel that was unmistakable.

"Sir?" the tall one asked.

The Don's brows rose and he looked at his guard. "What do you think he's going to do, Carlos . . . commit suicide by trying to kill me?" He waved a hand at them. "Get out, all of you." Once they were alone, Cárdenas gestured for Bear to sit on the couch next to him and handed him the laptop.

Bear started typing. "You said Hector is taking time off?"

The Don nodded. "I did."

Bear pulled up a photo of Hector, Shaved Head, and Ponytail. The three were standing next to the helicopter. "These guys taking time off, too?" He turned the screen so Cárdenas could see it.

A shadow of surprise danced over the man's aristocratic features. He pointed to Shaved Head. "That is Beto Gonzalez. The other man is Arturo Montoya." Cárdenas fixed Bear with a sharp gaze. "Beto is dead, as are four more of my men, but you already knew that, did you not?"

"I did." Bear nodded. "My apologies, Don Cárdenas, but they *did* shoot at me first. Even cops are allowed to *return* fire."

Cárdenas ran a hand over his brow and took another puff of his cigar. "I can see target practice is something I should insist on."

Bear chuckled darkly. "*I* would." He opened a picture of Montoya. "Do you have any idea where Montoya is right now?"

The Don was starting to look annoyed. "No."

"Do you know this guy?" Bear opened a photograph of one of the ATV guys and spun the laptop.

The Don focused on the screen, and even in the dimly lit room, Bear saw the color that slowly climbed into the man's face. His dark eyes took on an unnatural sparkle, and he sat up straighter.

The Don spoke through clenched teeth. "I do not know his name, but I imagine that is one of the men who killed my son."

Bear turned the screen away from Cárdenas and pulled up another picture. "Actually," he said, "*this* is the man who killed your son."

He put the laptop on the coffee table, and the picture Beth had taken of Hector shooting Ramon filled the screen. She'd captured the precise moment Hector had fired, the flash from the muzzle like a frozen sparkler in the center of the image. All four men were easily identifiable, the details crisp and clear.

The Don stared at the screen with wide eyes, his mouth open in shock. Bear had a feeling this was the first time in a *very* long time Cárdenas had been surprised by anything or anyone. The fact the man was showing those emotions told Bear the pain the Don felt ran deep. Bear recognized the flash of anguish, then disbelief, then rage that danced over Cárdenas's face.

"Hector?" He blinked and fixed Bear with an accusing glare. "Where did you get this?"

"From someone who just happened to be in the wrong place at the wrong time." Bear frowned. "Hector is trying to kill her." The Don looked askance at him and Bear ground his teeth together. "He's tying up his loose ends, Don Cárdenas, and even *you* could be on that list."

"You're lying." The Don put his cigar down and rose. "You . . . *manufactured* that . . . Photoshop or some such program . . . ."

Ah, denial. He had been expecting that. Bear sighed. "If you want to show that image to your computer tech, he can verify it hasn't been tampered with." He rested his elbows on his knees. "Why would I do that?"

"To stop a war," Cárdenas shot back. He walked around behind the couch and started to pace. "You want to keep me from going after the Giraldo organization."

"You and the Giraldo family have been sparring for decades. An all-out war between your two organizations just means more dead gang-bangers and job security for everyone from the Director to the Coroner." Bear stood. "Law enforcement won't step in unless innocent civilians start getting caught in the crossfire, and that's not usually your style because that's how your sister was killed. Besides . . . ." He leaned over, tapped a few more keys, and pulled up the picture of Ramon shaking hands with the head ATV guy. "Stopping a war was actually your *son's* idea."

The Don stopped pacing and inhaled sharply. He braced his hands on the back of the couch and stared at the image. With a growl he strode to a sideboard decorated with nearly a dozen crystal liquor decanters and swept an arm over the surface of the cabinet. The decanters crashed against the wall, to the floor, and against a fifty-six-inch plasma television. The TV shattered and toppled from its perch. The smell of brandy, whiskey, and several other varieties of alcohol filled the room with fumes.

"*Madre de Dios!*"

The Don's bodyguards tore through the curtain, guns drawn and Bear lifted his hands. The tallest one poked an Uzi in his chest and backed him up against the nearest wall, eyes glittering angrily. He tensed as he felt the release of adrenaline and an image of Beth flashed in his mind. What happened next could very well determine their fate.

"Poner sus armas hacia abajo. Ahora!" *Put your guns down. Now.*

The guards looked at Cárdenas uncertainly. The Don glared at each man in turn, his teeth bared in a snarl, savage fury blazing in his eyes.

"*Ahora!*"

The men holstered their weapons and stood there, obviously unsure what to do next.

"*Salte!*" *Get out.* When he spoke next he used English. "Do *not* make me tell you a second time."

The curtain trembled as it fell behind the last departing bodyguard. Bear looked at the softly moving velvet for a moment, and took a breath and turned his eyes to the Don. His pulse was at a gallop, but as Cárdenas returned to his seat on the couch and picked up his cigar, it gradually came down. Bear walked slowly to a large, overstuffed chair across from the man and eased down onto the plush seat.

"What do you want from me, Special Agent Bristol?"

"I need to stop him before he kills anyone else." Bear rested his elbows on his knees. "And I'm going to need backup."

One dark brow rose. "The FBI is not with you on this?"

Bear thought about it for a moment. "Technically . . . ? No."

A wry smile curved the Don's mouth. "So, an alleged drug lord and the FBI's finest join forces to bring down Hector Perez."

Bear nodded. "That's the idea. We work together we both get what we want."

"I doubt that. *I* want him dead. What is it *you* want?"

The memory of JC's murder flooded his brain but he forced it out. "I want him to pay." He gave the Don a small smile. "But we'll discuss details later. Maybe there's a way we can *both* win."

Cárdenas narrowed his eyes on Bear's face. He put his cigar down again, reached into an interior pocket on his suit jacket, and pulled out a small, gold case. The Don removed a business card from within and held it out to him.

"These are my private numbers, Special Agent Bristol." He put the case back in his pocket. "When you are ready . . . call me."

Bear slipped the card into his wallet and rose. He picked up his gun and holstered it, then grabbed his ID and slid it into his back pocket. "I need you to give me your word you won't go after him yourself."

The Don's eyes narrowed. "If it gets out that I am hunting someone from my own organization, it makes me look weak, as if I do not know what is going on under my own roof." Cárdenas tapped his cigar against the silver ashtray. "Besides . . . it is bad for morale."

"Sir—"

"You are probably the most polite FBI agent I've ever met," the Don observed. He puffed slowly on the cigar. "You have my word I will not go after him . . . *yet*." The man smiled, but north of his mouth the frost remained firmly in place. "You will find him faster anyway. After *that . . .* I make no promises."

Bear understood with absolute clarity he was treading on dangerous ground, but he had to take the Don at his word. He knew in his gut that the Bureau was compromised. JC's death was proof enough for him that Hector had an inside man, a man that could get him and Beth killed. Until he could find out who the mole was, Bear couldn't get the FBI involved, and if Cárdenas's soldiers got in the way . . . ? They'd all just be more meat for the grinder.

"There's a reason they say 'revenge is a dish best served cold'," Bear said softly. "When it's served hot, it usually winds up burning the server instead of the recipient."

The coldness in the Don's eyes thawed just a bit, and the man laughed softly. "You are an old soul, Special Agent Bristol." His gaze turned assessing. "You and I have a lot in common." Bear frowned and the Don laughed again. "I know . . . I know. You are *nothing* like me."

"True, but that's *not* what I was going to say."

"My apologies." Cárdenas inclined his head. "What then?"

"I was going to say that apparently traitors aren't unique to the dark side." A picture of the faceless man who had given up JC flashed in his head, followed by the image of Deputy Harper and his aunt. "Hector wasn't alone when he killed your son. Whether your men were tricked, manipulated, or helped him knowingly, he may have more allies in your house you don't know about."

"Is this when you tell me to be careful and watch my back?" The Don seemed amused.

Bear's brows drew together. "I shouldn't have to tell you that."

Cárdenas nodded and his gaze turned to the laptop where the picture of his son was displayed. Bear saw the flash of raw emotion before it was carefully masked.

"I will find out who betrayed me on this end," Cárdenas said softly. He looked at Bear. "For now . . . Hector . . . I leave to you. But—"

"I know," Bear interrupted. "Once I find him that will change."

The Don nodded slowly and closed the laptop. Bear looked at him for a moment, turned and took a step.

"Do you not want your pictures back?" Cárdenas asked.

Bear glanced over his shoulder. "I have another set."

"Of course you do."

Bear paused and faced the man. "If it's any consolation, Don Cárdenas, remember that your son was trying to make you proud." He didn't know why he offered the comforting words to one of the most ruthless, notorious drug-lords he knew. What he did know was he needed Don Cárdenas to hold up his end of the bargain, and grief often made men do strange and terrible things.

A sad smile curved the Don's mouth. "I suppose . . . there is a first time for everything."

The two men stared at each other for a long, silent moment

then Bear nodded. "Thank you for your time."

"Thank *you*, Special Agent Bristol." Another puff on the cigar. "I will be waiting for your call."

Bear turned and pushed through the curtain, walked past the bodyguards and the suspicious clerk, and out into the early afternoon sunshine. Closing his eyes for a few seconds, he took a deep breath of fresh air. "Somehow," he mused, "I doubt that."

As he walked back towards the Mercedes, his thoughts focused on Beth again. Although he should feel more optimistic that this part of the mission had gone according to plan, he knew they weren't even close to being out of the proverbial woods. The fun was just beginning.

****

Laine cut the sandwich from corner to corner, arranged it on a plate, and dumped a healthy portion of Fritos next to the ham and cheese. It was a couple of hours past lunchtime, but while the FBI had been in the house, her stomach had been in knots. Even the thought of food had made her nauseous. Now that she had her house back she was hungry. She pulled a pickle from a jar and bit into it.

Moments later the door opened and Jack walked in, Maverick on his heels. As Jack disconnected the leash, she retrieved a can of soda from the fridge and sat it on the island.

"Made you a sandwich," she said. She finished her pickle and watched Maverick plod over to his bed. "Ham and cheddar."

Her husband hung the leash up near the back door and walked over to her. There was a mischievous light in his eyes, and he wiggled his brows at her. Laine caught her breath when he looped an arm around her waist and ducked in for a kiss, his lips moving expertly over hers. She sighed softly and laced her fingers behind his neck. He ended the kiss slowly and pressed his lips to her brow.

"My favorite," he said in that soft, gravelly voice that turned her insides to mush. "Thank you."

Familiar heat swirled in her middle. "You're welcome," she said, breathless. It took her a moment to gather her wits, and then she leaned her hands on the edge of the counter and watched him as he slid onto a barstool opposite her. "Are they gone?"

The Coke can hissed when he popped the top. "Yes." Jack took a drink. "Fellowes and all his people are gone." He picked up one half of the hefty sandwich and gave her a wry look. "He said he'd call me if they found anything noteworthy, although I doubt *that* will happen. You keep a tidy home, Mrs. Vaughn."

Her cheeks warmed. "Yes, well he said they were going to take the Escalade and check the garage. He never said *anything* about them searching the *house*."

Suddenly his expression shifted and he sat up straight in his chair, his eyes focusing on the key-shaped rack by the door. She blinked and kept her face impassive, but she had the strangest sinking sensation in her stomach. He seemed to be taking a mental inventory, and she groaned inwardly when he turned and rested that steely, razor-sharp gaze on her.

"You sent him to the cabin."

She said nothing. She picked up a chip, popped it in her mouth, and chewed.

"Laine."

She sighed and stole his Coke. "Well, at least Bear can't accuse me of *telling* you."

"Why?" He stared at her, incredulous. "You know eventually they're going to look there, right?"

A spot of anger flared beneath her sternum and she gaped at him. "Oh, now you're worried about them *finding* him? I thought that's what you wanted."

His brows drew together. "Babe."

Laine frowned, pulled a stack of ham out of the bag, and started to make another sandwich. Maverick appeared at her side and she tossed him a slice. After downing that in one gulp, he moved to her other side, doggy-grin flashing. Just as she was going to give him another piece of ham, the dog winced. She frowned. Maverick shook his head and whined softly, ears flat against his skull. He pawed at his ears, lifted his head and barked. She immediately went into "diagnosis" mode and started cycling through possibilities for this display of pain.

She dropped the ham and wiped her hands on a dish towel. "Maverick? What is it, boy?"

Jack put his sandwich down. "What's wrong with him?"

"I don't know. My first thought is a bad tooth or a sore mouth, but I checked him over a couple days ago and he was fine."

Maverick barked again, the sort of bark that told her he was hurting. She knelt and took his head in her hands, but he wiggled away and started to sniff the underside of the counter. His nails clicked softly on the wood floor as he walked around the end of the island, whining. Moments later, he growled and started clawing at the top of the cabinet, where the wood of the cabinet face met the overhang of the counter.

Jack slid off his bar stool and moved out of the way as the dog pushed past him. "*What* is he doing?"

A cold chill slithered around her spine. "I don't know." There was something terribly wrong here. Maverick never behaved like this. She crouched next to the dog and tried to examine him, but the dog jerked away from her and growled again. His claws left long scratches in the wood. He barked once more and then bit at the underside of the breakfast bar. Then it clicked. Laine craned her neck around, examining the underside of the counter, and froze, fear coiling around her heart.

"What is it?" Jack asked.

She looked at him and pressed a finger to her lips. "He's just hungry. Maverick, I'll get you some dinner in a bit. Just hold on, boy." She gestured for Jack to come near. "My, you are impatient this afternoon. You'd think I never feed you."

When Jack was crouched beside her, she pointed to the small, circular device affixed to the underside of the breakfast bar. Fear coiled and undulated inside her like a python, squeezing her internal organs until she couldn't breathe. Jack's eyes widened and then narrowed as a fierce scowl darkened his features. He met her gaze, pointed at Maverick, and pointed to the back door. She nodded.

As she put Maverick outside, Jack ran upstairs. She could hear him rooting around in the closet, and moments later, he reappeared with a small, electronic device in his hands. It was silver, slightly larger than a deck of cards, and had a collapsible antenna. A set of LED lights ran vertically up the front of the device. He pointed at the stereo and made the motion of turning a dial. Laine turned the stereo on and up and faced her husband.

He activated the device and the lights on the front blinked green. With sweeping motions, he swung the machine back and forth. When the device got within a foot of the kitchen island, the lights on the front started dancing and flashed red. He clenched his jaw. She followed him as he moved slowly through the downstairs. By the time he found the third bug, his face was a storm cloud. A muscle in his cheek was twitching, and she could feel the anger radiating outward from him. Leaving the listening devices in place, he stalked back into the family room and tossed the device on the sofa.

Laine exhaled sharply and sank down on the couch. Fear and dread raced through her, and when Jack crouched in front of her, the emotions grabbed her heart and twisted.

"What's going on, Jack?" she whispered.

He looked at her silently for a few seconds, then sighed and took her hands in his. When he spoke, his voice was hushed. "Ever since JC's death, Bear has been convinced we have another mole at the Bureau. The higher-ups think he's being paranoid but," his brows drew together, "it looks like he might be right."

Tears stung and she squeezed her eyes shut.

Jack laced his fingers through hers. "The only good thing about this is we just narrowed the list of suspects considerably."

She blinked at him. "And the bad news?"

He cupped her face. "Now they know where to find him."

Her eyelids fluttered. "Oh, God."

Jack jumped on that like a hawk on a ground squirrel. "What? What is it?"

"He wasn't alone."

He blinked and his brows shot skyward. "*What?*"

She rose and retrieved the newspaper from the stack near the fireplace. When she found Beth's picture, she handed the paper to him.

"*She* was with him. He's protecting her, I don't know why or from what, but all this centers around her."

A sense of foreboding dropped over her shoulders like a cloak. He shook his head and exhaled. "Jesus." He wadded up the paper, tossed it aside, and clenched his fists.

"Who is she, aside from a photographer I mean?"

Jack stood and ran his hands over his hair. He paced several times, but then sat down beside her and rested his elbows on his thighs. His expression sent her pulse thrumming against her windpipe in violent staccato.

"We think she's a witness to what we suspect is a cartel hit. Local LEOs discovered five bodies at an inn north of Boulder yesterday morning, including a local sheriff's deputy and three known cartel soldiers. Bear was the only guest at the motel."

Laine sucked in a breath as the floor fell out from under her. Jack dropped his chin and pinched the bridge of his nose.

"Fellowes told me they fished six more bodies out of the river this morning, three bearing tattoos for a rival cartel. Five of the ten were shot execution style."

The fear chilling her blood was rapidly morphing into something much more potent, fingers of panic winding around her lungs with insidious intent. "The others . . . ?" she asked in a choked whisper.

Jack sighed heavily. "We think Bear shot the rest of them in self-defense." A string of angry curse words left his mouth, and then he thrust his hands into his hair, his expression pained. "Damn it, Bear. Can't you *ever* do anything simple?"

Dread rose like bile in her throat and she closed her eyes, trying to choke it down. Bear wasn't the sort of agent other agents worried about, but Jack was clearly worried, his eyes dark and shadowed. His concern, more than anything else, communicated the seriousness of the situation. When Jack rose and started to pace, she grabbed his hand, needing the physical contact. He stopped and looked down at her, and Laine tugged gently on his fingers. His expression softened. He crouched in front of her again and ran a finger over her cheek.

Her throat was painfully tight, her vocal chords frozen. The thought of something happening to Bear nearly undid her, so she forced the unwelcome thought aside and tried to channel her husband's best friend. No matter how bleak the situation looked, Bear always seemed to find a way out. And when he and *Jack* joined forces, they made Superman look like a lazy, incompetent fool. Laine swallowed hard and met her husband's concerned gaze. "So what do we do now?" she asked.

"This is serious shit, babe." He tucked a fall of hair behind her ear. "These guys make Ripley look like an upstanding, law-abiding citizen, and there are *dozens* of them."

Laine stroked the stubble that darkened his jaw and searched his eyes. "So . . . *what do we do now?*"

"I don't suppose I can convince you to visit my mother or head to the bungalow in Oceanside for the next week or so?"

A soft, sad chuckle escaped her. "Really?" She ran her fingers over his cheek. "In this situation, *no*. Besides, given your propensity to get hurt, you may need a doctor, you and Bear both."

He was silent, his gaze wandering slowly over her face. "I knew there was a reason I fell in love with you." He watched her for a bit longer. Finally, he rose and took her with him. "Pack a bag." Grim determination glittered in his silver eyes. "We're going to the cabin."

Chapter Nineteen

Beth walked into the house, closed and locked the door behind her. After Bear had left, she'd spent the better part of the morning meandering aimlessly through the large dwelling, looking for something, anything, to occupy herself with. She'd put the sheets from the bed in the wash and after a failed attempt to read a Tom Clancy novel, she had picked up her camera and headed outside despite Bear's request that she stay in the house. The call of the outdoors was just too much. Her mini-safari took her around the entire lake, and she had encountered an elk, several pronghorns, and about a dozen different bird species. Even a gray wolf had taken a peek at her before disappearing into the forest.

She went to the kitchen and put her camera and the pistol on the end of the breakfast bar. The clock on the stove read 5:12 p.m. and her stomach growled loudly, reminding her she hadn't eaten since breakfast. She smiled as she remembered Bear catching the plate of eggs. With a melancholy sigh, she opened the fridge and started searching for something to eat.

She found a can of Chef Boyardee ravioli in the pantry and spooned the contents into a bowl. As the pasta took a turn in the microwave, she poured herself a glass of wine, sat down on a barstool, and looked out the back windows. Darkness fell quickly in the mountains, and tonight was no exception. Already it was impossible to see past the square of light cast onto the deck through the wall of windows. A pang of loneliness wormed through her, and she realized the feeling was all too familiar. It was a sensation she felt often, even in the midst of a group, as if she was physically present but didn't belong somehow. In fact, the sadness always seemed to be there. It hovered, visible and palpable, but just out of reach. She took a deep breath as her heart whispered the one exception to this cycle of isolation and unintentional emotional solitude. Bear.

Her diaphragm spasmed, as if she'd just had the wind knocked out of her. Even with Michael she'd been an outsider, having little in common with his circle of friends and the world he lived in. Now that she thought about it, she and her *ex* had little in common. Had they met *before* her trip to Afghanistan they might have meshed a little better and had a slightly better chance of lasting, but they hadn't met before Afghanistan.

Michael had won her over with his puppy-dog eyes and boyish grin, but she'd never understood his "struggling artist" mentality. Her parents had been true, tie-dyed-in-the-wool hippies, but her father had always taught her to work and pay her own way. Michael thought it was better to live in squalor, or his girlfriend's apartment, and "sacrifice for his craft" rather than clog his creative outlets with such a menial thing as earning a living. The two men couldn't be more different, and Bear was better at . . . well, *everything*. Heat surged into her cheeks and she took a deep breath.

The timer went off and Beth jumped, coming back to reality with a start. The ding resounded through the room and off the vaulted ceiling with an eerie echo. As she pulled the bowl from the microwave, she wondered absently if Bear liked canned ravioli. Somehow, she doubted he would turn down a meal, *any* meal. The thought of him was bittersweet. It made her both happy and sad, but she couldn't stop the smile. With his image hovering in her mind's eye, she sat down and started to eat.

Half an hour later she was relaxing in front of a fire, the dishes had been washed, dried and put away, and a second glass of wine was settled warmly in her belly. Beth swirled the last swallow briefly before emptying the goblet. She sighed softly as she rose, walked to the sink to wash the glass, and put it away. Once that was done, she took the memory card out of her camera and walked slowly up the back stairs.

She entered the study and sat down in front of the computer Bear had used earlier. As soon as she moved the mouse, the monitor glared to life and she was transfixed for a moment. The three men who had turned her life upside down stared back at her from that flat screen, and a shiver ran down her spine. Beth shook off the chill and closed the image.

After inserting the memory card into the port on the computer, she scrolled through the shots she'd taken that afternoon. The pictures of the pronghorns were especially nice, but for some reason she just couldn't get excited about them. That same coldness fanned over her skin again and she rubbed her arms.

A soft click from behind her sent her pulse to the moon and she jumped out of the chair, spinning toward the sound. There was no one there. Her lungs froze, her eyes darting about the study, but she was quite alone. Pressing a hand to her heart, she exhaled sharply and then sucked in a breath.

Her gaze was drawn to the cordless phone sitting on top of a low, squat cabinet along the wall behind the desk. On the device a red light was flashing and the counter read twelve. Beth blinked and saw her hand reach for the replay button, almost as if she was watching from outside herself. In her head she told herself not to push that button, but she did it anyway.

"Two . . . thirty-three . . . p.m."

There was a brief silence.

"Bear, it's Jack. Listen very carefully. You need to take Miss Drummond and get out of the cabin, *now.*" He sighed softly. "It seems you were right about us having another turncoat at the Bureau, and the bad news is I think they know where you are. Get out of there and meet me at our favorite rest area."

Beth couldn't draw a breath. She sagged against the edge of the desk and stared at the phone.

"Two . . . fifty . . . p.m."

"Bear, it's me again. I don't know who else to call. I hope you got my message, and I hope I see you and your new friend soon. Be careful."

The messages from Jack continued, one roughly every thirty minutes or so, until the last message. Beth immediately recognized Laine's voice.

"Bear, please, call us. I'm really worried about you, and Beth. Please . . . let us know you're okay."

Beth blinked. Fear flooded her and adrenaline started pumping, urging her into action. If the men chasing her knew her location, she needed to leave, *now.* Bear's voice echoed in her head. *If you have to run, the keys to the Suburban are on the visor.* She ran out of the study and up the corridor.

As she crossed the adjoining hall, she heard a strange rattling and froze on the landing. A glance over the railing between the sweeping double-staircase told her someone was at the front door, a large shadow darkened the beveled glass. Her heart started to ping between her spine and her sternum so quickly she knew if she could see it she would see nothing but a red blur. The shadow shifted and pounded violently on the carved oak. That was enough to get her moving again.

She dashed down the back stairs and jerked open the door to the garage. Halfway down the steps she cursed softly. The firearms were still upstairs. She briefly entertained the idea of returning for them, and then the front door crashed open in an explosion of cracking wood and shattering glass. Beth jumped down the last several steps and pushed past the door into the garage. She made straight for the Suburban.

She climbed in and pulled the keys from the visor as she shut the door. The engine roared to life on the first turn and she jerked the lever into reverse. Just as the interior garage door flew open she stomped on the gas and barreled backwards, the exterior door no match for the SUV. Metal crumpled and shrieked as the vehicle shot through the barrier and up the sloping drive. At the top of the hill Beth braked and jerked on the wheel.

The Suburban shuddered and skidded as the front end swung around to face the direction of the gate. She heard several loud pops and the passenger window shattered. She screamed and ducked. Shards of glass peppered the right side of her face. Jerking on the gear shift, she put the Suburban in drive and pounded her foot on the accelerator.

She hadn't driven more than fifty yards when the headlights illuminated the tall, thin form of Hector Perez. He stood in the middle of the road with what looked like a submachine gun in his hands. She'd already had the gas pedal floored, so she tightened her grip on the wheel. Suddenly she wished she'd had the foresight to fasten her seatbelt.

Flashes glared in the darkness and the front windshield rippled as bullets punched through the safety glass. Her left cheek stung and she threw herself across the passenger seat, inadvertently jerking on the wheel. She felt the tires leave the gravel covered road and churn into the grass. Before she could right herself there was an enormous burst of sound and the SUV vibrated violently as it came to a bone-jarring stop. Beth was forcefully catapulted into the dashboard and fireworks exploded inside her head. There was a brief, intense surge of pain and then . . . nothing.

****

The first thing Bear saw when he rounded the blind curve toward the cabin was the Suburban, the front end wrapped around the trunk of a Rocky Mountain Maple. The front windshield was riddled with bullet holes, one headlight flickered dimly, and the driver's door was wide open. The Mercedes skidded to a halt as he stomped on the brake and threw it in park.

For a moment he couldn't move, fear and dread pushing past the blood in his veins. He remembered the sensation. Seconds before JC had been gunned down he'd felt the exact same emotions, and they filled him as completely now as they had then. His eyes scanned the scene, looking for any sign of Beth or Perez, but there wasn't any.

"Shit."

He jumped out of the Mercedes and ran to the Suburban. Beth wasn't there. He had known she wouldn't be, but finding the vehicle empty hit him like a fist between the eyes, cold, hard, and enough to rock him back a step. Especially when he saw the blood on the dashboard. He checked the engine, and the lack of residual heat told him it had been at least an hour since the crash. Shoulders stooped, he looked toward the house and an invisible hand thrust its talons into his abdomen. Light spilled from the garage onto the cement pad, twisted, mangled metal littering the driveway. *Maybe she's hiding inside.* Even as he thought it he didn't believe it, but he still had to know for certain. Bear ran down the driveway, through the garage, and up the stairs into the house.

"Beth!"

Those claws scored the inside of his chest, causing sharp pangs to radiate outward from beneath his breastbone. The house was deathly quiet. He ran through the great room toward the foyer. When he saw the ruined front door, something cold and jagged punched clean through him. He raced up the stairs to the master suite, kicking open the doors. Nothing. He crossed to the south side of the house and did the same thing. When he finally entered the study and found it empty, he felt like the air had been sucked from his lungs. He leaned on the door jamb for a moment and tried to breathe.

His mind was spinning, but Special Agent Bristol's voice was loud in his head. If Perez had wanted Beth dead, he'd have simply killed her and left her body for him to find. No, Perez had *taken* her, which meant Hector wanted something else. All he had to do now was figure out what that was.

Bear moved behind the desk and sat down. The monitor lit up, the image of a leaping pronghorn filling the screen. It looked as if the animal was literally clicking its heels together. A ball of fear, regret, and apprehension coiled in his throat. She really was talented, and he prayed he would get the chance to tell her so.

He stared at the photograph for a moment before he rose and walked toward the door. A soft click made his head snap around. He zeroed in on the telephone immediately. Apparently the ringer was turned off, but every time the answering machine activated the device clicked. He should know. He had the exact same model at home.

The red light on the face of the telephone was blinking, and the counter read 16. Just as he was about to punch the replay button he heard the sound of a vehicle. Bear unholstered his pistol and walked quickly toward the front of the house.

His feet made no sound as he descended the stairs. The glare of headlights slashed through the two-story windows briefly and he moved to the side of the decimated front door. Back against the wall, he regulated his breathing and waited. A car door opened then closed, and hurried footsteps raced toward the porch.

"Bear."

He recognized Jack's voice, but he instinctively brought the gun around. Jack was just coming through the archway from the great room, and he held up his hands. He must have come in through the garage. Bear blinked and lowered the pistol. Seconds later Laine rushed in. When she saw him, her eyes welled with tears and she ran toward him. Bear exhaled sharply, caught her, and held her with one arm while he holstered his pistol. He met Jack's gaze.

"Sorry, brother."

Jack shook his head. "No need to be."

"I mean about asking Laine to lie to you."

Jack thought about that for a minute and shrugged. "Apology

accepted." He frowned. "*Don't* do that again."

"I won't." Bear frowned back. "That being said, why the hell did you bring her here?"

"I'm sorry. Have you *met* my wife?" Jack crossed his arms over his chest. "And by the way, she didn't tell me, I guessed."

"Realized the cabin keys were missing?"

"Something like that." Jack glanced at his wife, and there was no mistaking the love in his gaze. "I didn't want to bring her . . . but you know how she is."

"I do." Bear closed his eyes and held Laine tightly. "You still should've tied her up in a hotel room or something." She was shaking and her tears were hot on his neck. "It's okay, Laine. I'm fine."

"I was so scared," she whispered. She pulled back and looked up at him. "What happened?"

He sighed. "I don't know. I drove into Denver to see someone and I just got back. All I know is they have Beth." He released her and leaned against the wall. Saying the words made his heart drop to the floor. Was she still alive? Had they hurt her? Imagining what Perez could do to her nearly buckled his knees, but he steeled himself and forced the macabre pictures away. "Any idea how they found out?"

Jack's expression darkened. "Looks like you were right about us having another traitor in house." He leaned against the elaborately carved banister. "The only up-side is the list of suspects just got a whole lot shorter."

His agent senses immediately tingled. "What happened?" Bear asked.

"Fellowes and a forensic team were at my place this morning." Jack scowled fiercely. "A couple hours after they left, I found three bugs in the downstairs." He reached for Laine's hand and pulled her to him. "When I realized the keys to the cabin were gone, all I said was, 'You sent him to the cabin.' I didn't say which cabin or where."

Bear rubbed his forehead. "That means whoever was listening had to have the expertise and access to cross-check your personnel file with real estate data bases to find a match. That's not a simple search because the cabin is in Mason's name and *not* your sister's . . . ." He sighed and tipped his head back, focusing on the antler chandelier. "I *hate* it when I'm right."

"Vargas has the skill for that," Jack observed quietly. "So does Paulson, and he and Fellowes are pretty tight. Everyone knows Fellowes wants your job."

"Right now he can have it," Bear shot back. "Even so, I don't think it's him. He's too straitlaced for that, but he'd be a perfect patsy. And I've already looked into Vargas. It's not him."

"Do you . . . ." Laine's voice trailed off and she tucked in under Jack's chin. "Do you think Beth is still alive?"

He had been pushing that thought aside ever since finding the

SUV, but hearing Laine say it gathered dread in his belly like a black, gelatinous, carnivorous pool. The pool looked calm, but there were teeth just below the surface, sharp teeth that would devour him if he even touched that water. Bear clenched his jaw. "If they had wanted her dead, they would have just executed her." He shook his head. "No, they want something else."

"What?" Jack and Laine asked in unison.

Bear chewed the inside of his cheek, his synapses firing at the speed of light.

Jack's expression darkened. "Who did you see in Denver, Bear? Who was so important that you risked leaving her here alone?"

Laine had extricated herself from her husband's embrace and eased down on the stairs, her eyes wide and moving slowly between the two of them. Oddly, she remained mute.

Bear scowled and pushed away from the wall. Frustration and uncertainty weighed heavily on his shoulders, but second-guessing himself at this point was futile. "You know who."

"Why, Bear?" Jack's eyes glittered angrily. "After everything we've been through because of that man? You *cannot* get in bed with him."

Bear stood toe to toe with him. That pool in his middle was no longer dark and gelatinous. It was hot, red, and swirling with self-reproach and wrath. "I will get in bed with whomever I have to if it means putting an end to this and getting her back alive."

Jack gaped at him. "He *can't* be trusted."

The sharp blade of betrayal cut through him, and it only increased the temperature of his rage. "Neither can anyone else, apparently." He returned Jack's stare for a few tense seconds before he spoke. "I'm going to check the house again. Maybe they left something that'll tell us where they're headed."

A shrill ringing made him tense and his head swung around. He glanced at Jack and walked slowly through the archway into the great room, apprehension growing with each step.

"Your phone?" Jack asked, falling into step behind him.

"I left it in the Escalade."

There was another ring and Bear followed the sound into the kitchen. The cell phone on the kitchen counter was unremarkable, and next to it sat Beth's camera and the pistol he'd left. Picking it up, he glanced at the caller ID. Unknown.

"I take it that's not yours?" Laine asked softly.

Bear scowled. "No." He pushed the answer button and put the phone to his ear. "What?"

"Bear?"

Her voice was low and tear-filled, and his lungs seized up as air was forcibly expelled from them. "Beth." He leaned against the granite, overwhelming relief and pure fear spinning inside him.

"Bear, don't do any—!"

He growled when she was cut off. When he heard a muffled cry of pain, he almost choked on the fury that erupted upward from his gut. "Beth!"

"Evening, Special Agent Bristol."

Bear took a deep, silent breath, held it for a moment. Then he exhaled slowly and reined in his emotions. "Evening, Hector. It is Hector, right? I'd hate to think I was talking to a lackey."

There was a soft laugh. "No, when it comes to FBI agents, I like to deal with them personally."

Anger exploded inside him, hot and potent, his vision edged in shades of red and orange. "So, I've seen." He tightened his grip on the phone. "Am I to assume this isn't a social call?"

"If you ever want to see your pretty photographer again, be at the Chatham Mill by sunrise. And, if I even *think* you've called in your coworkers . . . . I'll make certain she lives *just* long enough to die in your arms."

The line went dead. Bear held it to his ear for several more seconds, his heart pounding like a drum in his chest. Finally, he put the phone down.

"Bear?" Laine slid onto a barstool, her eyes fixed on his face.

Bear stared out the back windows. "He wants a meet."

"No," Jack said, "he wants to kill you, *both* of you."

"I know."

Jack stood behind Laine, his hands on her shoulders. "What do you want me to do?"

"Nothing, Jack. It's only my ass in the fire right now and I plan to keep it that way."

Jack snorted. "As soon as I figured out where you were, I should've called Fellowes and clued him in." He lifted one brow. "Looks like both of our asses are on fire."

Bear wanted to kick himself. Not only had he endangered Beth by leaving her alone, now Jack and Laine were in the line of fire as well, but he had to focus on Beth. He walked toward the back windows and his pulse was running faster than it had been at the cigar shop. He had a lot to do and a very limited amount of time in which to do it, but Beth's life hung in the balance. He squeezed his eyes shut as his brain started to assemble a plan. The pieces snapped together, and with each item he ticked off his mental list, the sense of impending doom receded. He concentrated on Beth, on getting her back alive, and his sense of confidence and control returned. Thankfully, he was good at this sort of thing and he worked better under pressure. He couldn't think of a time when those two skills would be more beneficial. The good guys had to win in this scenario. They *had* to.

"Bear?"

Bear focused on Jack's reflection in the glass. "Are you still buddies with that pilot out of Boulder, the retired Marine?"

"Dan Guilder?" Jack nodded. "Had lunch with him last week. Why?"

"Think he'd be willing to do some . . . *off the books* work for the Bureau?"

Jack's brows drew together. "I think I'd be able to talk him into it."

Bear did a one-eighty. "Give him a call. If he's in, we'll meet at his hangar at one a.m." His doubts vanished as he put Special Agent Bristol firmly behind the wheel. This is what he did, it was what he was good at, and he didn't plan to fail now. A growing sense of buoyancy lightened the weight pressing on his heart, and he planted his fists on his hips. "Tell him to bring some Red Bull. It's going to be a long night."

"What's the plan?"

Bear approached the island and leaned his elbows on the breakfast bar. "Still putting it together." He gave Laine a pointed look. "I suppose if I tied you up and left you here, you'd never speak to me again."

Laine scowled at him and crossed her arms over her chest. "You got that right."

"She did point out we might need a doctor," Jack said. His expression sobered. "There *is* blood in the Suburban."

Bear pinched the bridge of his nose. "Sorry about that, by the way."

Laine looked at him in disbelief. "I don't care about the car, Bear." She got off the barstool and walked up to him. "What matters is getting Beth back in one piece and breathing." She put a hand on his arm. "You and Jack are the best I know. If anyone can save her, it's you two."

Instead of lightening the load, her pep-talk added to the weight. Bear straightened. "No pressure."

Jack moved to his wife's side. "This is what you *do*, Bear."

Uncertainty grated through him. "Yeah, and look what happened last time."

"That was *not* your fault," Jack said from between clenched teeth. "When we find the person who gave JC up and bugged my house . . . they're going to answer for *everything* they've done."

Bear remembered how Beth had defended him, told him JC's death wasn't his fault. He could picture those golden eyes and the expression of absolute trust on her face. She believed in him, even when his own confidence faltered. He stared at the counter, his spine straight in spite of the immense pressure on his back and shoulders. Now was not the time to cave. He couldn't let her down. He *wouldn't*. More pieces of the plan dropped into place.

"Okay then. Laine, get Beth's things . . . actually, *your* things.

They're in the spare bedroom."

Laine arched a brow. "The *spare* bedroom?" She stared at him for a moment. "Okay."

Bear ignored her implication, unwilling to answer her unspoken question. "Jack."

"Yeah, bud?"

Bear looked at Jack for a few seconds. He needed to make sure Jack didn't overhear anything that might come back to bite him later. Bear was more than willing to take the hit if he had to, but he wasn't about to let Jack get in any deeper than he already was. "Make your call and promise him whatever you have to. I don't care what it is. I'll even give up my season tickets to the Broncos if he wants them. Then transfer the guns from the Suburban to your car." He met Jack's gaze. "I'm hoping you have the quad-cab?"

Jack nodded. "I do."

"Good." He walked to the other end of the counter, stuck the pistol in the waistband of his jeans at his back, and grabbed the camera and the phone. "I'm going to make a few calls of my own."

"Who are you calling?" Jack asked, his brows drawing together.

He had known Jack would ask, but he didn't have time for this, especially when he knew Jack knew the answer. Bear met his gaze. "Don't worry about it."

"Bear—"

A flash of annoyance warmed him. "Jack, you said this is what I do, so let me do it." He gave them a grim smile. "Once we get to the main road, we'll call 911 and report a break-in. As soon as they find the Suburban, it'll ping the Bureau and Fellowes will be all over it." He turned to walk away, but paused. "Write down the names of everyone who was at your house today. I already had our mole narrowed down to four individuals, but hopefully, I can knock a couple more names off that list." Without waiting for a reply, he crossed the room and mounted the stairs.

****

Laine leaned against the side of the quad-cab, Jack beside her. Everything Bear had asked them to do was done, Jack's pilot friend had agreed to help, and now they were waiting on Bear to finish his calls. She was anxious, and more than a little fearful. Bear was still inside the cabin, and she moved closer to Jack as a chill of apprehension went through her.

"I think this situation is a whole lot more complicated than we realize," Jack said softly.

Laine glanced at him but he was looking at the house. "Why do you say that?"

"Bear has feelings for our missing photographer."

"You're right, he does."

Jack looked at her. "How do you know? He hasn't done or said anything to indicate that."

She gave him a small smile. "So how do *you* know?"

He dropped an arm around her shoulders. "Call it a hunch."

"Well, I *know* he has feelings for her and it's more than just a hunch." When he looked at her in silent question, she turned her gaze to the master bedroom window. "Her things were in the spare bedroom," she paused and met Jack's eyes, "but the only unmade bed was in the master suite."

Jack groaned and grabbed his forehead with one hand. "Damn it, Bear. And you yell at *me* for poking hornet's nests."

"Plus I found one of Bear's flannel shirts in her suitcase . . . I mean *my* suitcase." She crossed her arms over her chest. "She's *way* more than a witness to him, but I knew that before I sent them up here."

"Shit." Jack leaned his head against hers. When he spoke again, his voice was somber. "Does he realize he's setting himself up for a remake of what you and I went through?"

Laine was silent for a moment. "Of course he does." Her heart ached for her friend and she took a deep breath. "But, sometimes love smacks you upside the head when you least expect it and don't even *want* it to, and *rarely* is it convenient."

"You can say that again."

Laine poked him in the ribs. "Hey!"

"I'm just saying." He chuckled and kissed her temple. "I didn't want or expect to fall in love with *you*, but I did, and it sure as hell wasn't *convenient*."

Laine had no reply for that because Jack was right. After a brief silence she whispered, "Will she have to go into WITSEC?"

Jack sighed. "Given what she's in the middle of, probably."

She remembered what that had felt like; being separated from everyone she loved, including Jack, using a new name, a fictitious history, the constant lying and deception. Her eyes stung. "God, I don't want to imagine what that would do to him, or her." A heaviness settled on her heart. "You know even if he's dying inside he'll never show it, right?"

"I know," Jack whispered, his voice laden with sadness.

"We have to fix this, Jack." She faced her husband. "We *have* to. I don't want him to go through what we did."

Jack cupped her face, his expression tender. "It may be out of our hands, babe, but even if we can't stop it, we are going to give it one *hell* of a try." His thumbs rubbed over her cheekbones. "And, no matter what, we'll be there for him. You're not the only one who loves him."

She closed her eyes as Jack kissed her. Her arms wrapped around his waist.

"Hey, would you two stop making out? We have things to do."

Laine pulled away and smiled when Jack tossed an annoyed glance at Bear's back.

"On second thought . . . ."

She looked at him with mock reproach. "Jack."

He chuckled. "Relax, babe, I'm kidding. Bear's like a brother to me, and we're going to do everything we can."

"Thank you."

He smiled at her and her heart flipped.

"Anything for you, Doc, and for him."

Chapter Twenty

Bear pulled off the highway and drove slowly toward the mill. The eastern sky turned lighter with each passing minute, and although he usually enjoyed the sunrise, this particular dawn only made him more aware of what was at stake. The trees rustled slightly as a faint breeze caressed the leaves, birds started to chirp, and all of these "normal" things only hammered home how *not* normal this morning was. Shaking off his apprehension, he parked the Mercedes behind the main building and climbed out, tucking the tablet beneath his arm. The computer was a prop, but a very important prop that could mean the difference between Beth living and dying.

The chain that had held the large doors closed had been cut and lay in a puddle of rusted metal on the ground. At the doors he paused, took a breath, and then pushed through the corrugated barrier.

The interior of the mill was darker than outside, but his eyes adjusted quickly. He walked toward the center of the space, his pulse picking up just a hair as the first act of this proverbial play began. When Hector Perez appeared from out of the gloom with Beth in front of him, Bear's heart thumped once against his ribs and then continued beating at a slightly more elevated rate. Perez had one hand on Beth's neck, the other gripping a pistol that was shoved into her ribs. A flash of anger heated his blood, but he kept his face impassive.

"Nice to see you again, Special Agent Bristol," Perez said.

Bear felt the kick of adrenaline. He met Beth's gaze briefly and fury bloomed beneath his heart like a molten flower. Her left cheek was sliced open, her lip bloodied and swollen, and the right side of her face was peppered with small cuts and lacerations. She had a lump on her left brow and she held her left arm carefully across her body as if it hurt to move it. The front of her sweater was blood-spattered, but despite the tears shimmering in her eyes, she looked angry, not afraid. His chest swelled with pride. *That's my girl.*

"You okay?" he asked.

She gave him a curt nod and winced when Perez tightened his grip on her neck.

"She's fine."

Bear lifted one brow. "I wasn't asking you."

Perez's lip curled. "You should be more polite."

"And *you* should let her go."

"Maybe I should kill her."

Bear kept a tight rein on his anger, pulled out the tablet, and started tapping the screen. "You could . . . but I think you have bigger things to worry about." His gaze flicked toward Perez, gauging his reaction. Although the cartel soldier had an infamous temper, the fact he'd managed to pull off the murder of his boss's son told Bear he was also a planner, and knew when to exercise restraint. Bear prayed he was reading the man correctly, or Beth would pay for it.

"Such as?" Hector sneered.

"Such as getting out of here alive."

Beth's eyes widened and she whispered, "Bear." But, it was too late.

He felt the muzzle of a gun pressed into the center of his back. Obviously Ponytail was still hanging out. Frustration simmered hotly, but Bear reined himself in and slowly lifted his hands.

"I plan to get out of here alive." Perez sneered. "It is you and the pretty lady who will not be leaving."

Bear gave him a bored look. "Before you start shooting, you may want to take a look at this." He turned the tablet toward him.

"I'm not interested in your gadgets."

"You *should* be." Bear kept his hands up as he tapped the screen and then faced it toward Perez. "See this? This is a map of the local area. That green dot in the middle is us. This blue line here?" He glanced at the tablet and pointed. "That's the highway, and those four moving red arrows . . . those represent the Don and his men." He looked at the screen again. "From here it looks like they're about . . . four minutes out give or take." Bear lifted one brow. "You said not to call *my* coworkers. You said *nothing* about not calling *yours*."

Perez laughed and tightened his grip on Beth's neck. "You're lying."

Bear saw her wince, but she remained silent, her eyes fixed on him. He fought the surge of anger welling in him and kept his face expressionless. *Hold it together, sweetheart. Hold it together.*

"You have a decision to make, Hector." Bear showed him the tablet. "I can arrest you and take you into custody, or you can try to kill both of us and then face your boss. How far do you think you'll get with the Don right behind you?"

"You forget I know you. You'd never work with the likes of Don Cárdenas."

"Didn't have to." Bear gave him a grim smile. "You want to know the *one* good thing that happens when you kill a Fed, Hector? The wheels of justice start to spin a little bit faster. Even judges who think you're just a member of a downtrodden ethnicity being taken advantage of by *the man* tend to frown on the murder of an FBI agent."

Perez pulled Beth in close. "What are you babbling about?"

Bear's smile widened slightly. "After you killed Special Agent Acosta it took me *two* seconds to get warrants and install GPS trackers on every one of the Don's vehicles. A few hours ago I made a call to *Los Cigars del Mundo* and told the Don where he could find you." He shrugged. "You want to wait here to find out if I'm telling the truth that's on you." Bear paused. "You've got about three and a half minutes."

"Hector." It was Ponytail, and he sounded nervous.

Bear fought the smile. *Good, you should be nervous.*

Perez scowled. "Quiet, Arturo! He's playing us."

"And if he's not?"

"Then we will deal with the Don when he gets here."

The gun in Bear's back suddenly went away and he heard the sound of running feet. He turned and glanced over his shoulder as Ponytail high-tailed it for the door. Hector cursed and pointed the gun at his accomplice's retreating figure, but it was too late. Ponytail had already slipped between the large metal doors and disappeared from sight.

Bear looked at Hector and sat the tablet on a nearby conveyer belt. "I guess he'd rather *not* deal with the Don." He kept his tone light, well aware that overt sarcasm might very well push Perez over the edge. Distracting the man long enough for his plan to work was crucial, but with each minute that ticked off the clock, Bear knew the margin of victory grew slimmer.

"It doesn't matter." Perez glared at him. "Now I have nothing to lose. Say goodbye." He pressed the muzzle of the pistol against Beth's neck.

His insides seized up in protest and he took a step toward the armed man. "You *really* want to die here today?" Bear asked. He heaved an inward sigh of relief when the 9mm swung toward him. "It doesn't have to end this way, Hector. Let her go."

"Why?" Perez's eyes took on a fanatical glint. "Like you said, how far will I get with the Don right behind me?" He flexed his fingers on the grip. "It would've worked, you know. If not for this meddling bitch—"

The thump of helicopter blades broke the relative quiet of the morning and beat against the crumbling walls and roof of the mill. Birds took to wing and shards of broken windows tinkled to the cement floor, shaken out of the panes by the wind and vibration. Perez tensed and glanced at the ceiling, the gun back at the base of Beth's neck.

"What the hell?" Perez looked at him with wide, angry eyes. "What *is* that?"

"That's your ride out of here." Bear lifted his hands and took another step toward Perez. "Let her go and you'll be halfway back to Denver before the Don arrives." He glanced at the tablet. "You've got about three minutes."

Perez stared at him for a long moment, and Bear wondered if the man had lost it. He had the look of a cornered animal, eyes bright and wild, skin flushed, his breathing rapid and shallow, and he didn't seem to care that the clock was ticking down.

Perez bared his teeth. "I wanted to look in your eyes when I killed Acosta, show you I had won, but you denied me that. So, I brought you here. I want to see your face when I kill her, see the pain and defeat, and I will not be denied again."

Rage surged upward and nearly choked him, but venting his temper would only start a chain reaction. He wrestled his emotions back and started counting down in his head as he lifted one brow. "My expression wouldn't be any different than it is right now, so you've gone to a lot of trouble for nothing." *Five, four, three . . . .*

The man laughed. "Should we test that theory?"

"That's not an option," Jack said, pressing the muzzle of the shotgun to the base of Perez's skull. "The *only* way you take another breath is if you let her go . . . *right* fucking now."

Bear's insides coiled like a spring as Perez hesitated. When the man finally dropped the gun and let go of Beth's neck, the wave of relief that hit him nearly buckled his knees. Beth let out a hushed sob and ran toward him. Bear kept his gaze on Perez and his face blank as his arms closed around her. She tucked in beneath his chin, her left arm held tight to her side, her body trembling.

"Wise move, Hector." He glanced at the tablet then met Jack's gaze. "Get him out of here. We'll be right behind you."

Jack nodded. "You got it, brother." He prodded Perez with the shotgun. "Move."

Once Jack and Perez left the mill, Bear pulled back and cupped Beth's chin. "Are you okay?"

She smiled and a tear rolled down her cheek. "I am now," she whispered.

He gently touched her left shoulder and she winced. "I take it you weren't wearing a seatbelt." She shook her head and he sighed. "Let's get you in the chopper and to a hospital."

Bear cupped her good elbow and walked her quickly out of the mill and across the lot to where the helicopter sat, blades whirring. Jack had handcuffed Perez to a metal bar inside the cabin of the aircraft, and the man glared at Bear as he helped Beth on board. Once she was safely strapped in, Bear looked at Jack.

"Get her to the hospital and then get him to the Federal Building," he shouted over the roar of the engines. "I have something I have to do."

Jack's eyes narrowed. "What are you talking about? Get in and let's get out of here."

Bear shook his head and backed up. "I need to deal with Cárdenas."

"Bear, you can't." Jack stared at him. "He'll kill you."

Bear had already considered that, and although death by cartel wasn't on his bucket list, neither was being killed at a later date by a car bomb or a sniper. He didn't plan to put every person he knew and loved in the crosshairs either. "I don't have a choice." He tapped the pilot on the shoulder. "Thanks again, Dan. Now get them out of here."

"Bear!"

It was Beth calling to him. The terror in her voice kicked his protective instincts into full gear, and nearly kicked *Special Agent Bristol* to the curb. He turned, looked into her eyes, and almost changed his mind. He had known she wouldn't go along with this particular element of his plan. He *hadn't* known his reaction to her would nearly paralyze him. The fear and sorrow he saw in those golden pools pierced him like arrows. The sensation was almost like being shot, but the pain went deeper than nerve endings and soft tissue. Regardless, he had one more loose end he had to tie up; otherwise, Beth would forever be looking over her shoulder. He let his gaze wander over her face for a moment and steeled his resolve.

"I'll see *you* later, sweetheart, I promise." He looked at Jack. "I'm counting on you, Jack. Take care of her."

Jack's brows drew together and he looked at Bear in dismay. Finally, he nodded. Beth glanced between the two of them and started fumbling with her harness.

"Go!" Bear shouted. He backed away and the helicopter spun up. He shielded his eyes with one hand as Jack easily restrained Beth.

"Bear, no!" she cried, tears streaming down her face. Dust roiled, obscuring his vision, but he could still hear her, the panic in her voice, and the fear for him. "Let me go! Bear!"

He watched until the helicopter disappeared over the trees. When he could no longer hear the aircraft, he walked back into the mill and waited. Less than a minute passed before multiple vehicles pulled up outside the main building. The engines idled for about thirty seconds before shutting off, and a preternatural quiet descended over the property. Bear sat on the conveyor belt next to the tablet and took a deep breath. Between the weight pressing down on his shoulders and the tightness in his abdomen, it was difficult. The heaviness was too familiar, the wound too fresh. *Well, here comes the final act. Hope I don't see you today, JC, but if I do, we'll have a cold one together.*

The first men through the door were the four from the cigar shop. Bear nodded to the tallest one, Carlos, and rose. Three more men entered, briefly searched the mill, and when they gave the all-clear the Don walked in. He was impeccably dressed, as if he was attending a business luncheon instead of a clandestine meeting in the hills of Colorado. In all the man had twelve bodyguards with him, which made Bear wonder vaguely why they had needed four vehicles. He clasped his hands in front of him as Cárdenas approached.

The Don got right to the point. "So, where is Hector?"

"On his way to the Federal Building," Bear replied.

"What?" The Don's brows rose and he blinked slowly. "You . . . *betrayed* me?" He took a step forward. "You *told* me I would find Hector here."

"I said you *could* find Hector here," Bear corrected him. "And, if you'd arrived five minutes ago you would have."

"You are playing *word games* with me?" Rage glittered in his dark, flat eyes. "I have killed men for less."

Bear pursed his lips. "That is *not* the sort of thing you should say to a Federal agent."

"You should know better than to cross me, Special Agent Bristol." The man was fairly shaking with anger. "Perez killed my son."

"And he killed one of my best friends."

"Forgive me if I do not think the two are comparable."

"Maybe they're not." Bear shrugged. "But, if you'd set aside your anger and look at this through the eyes of the man who built a multi-million dollar business and has managed, somehow, to stay out of prison . . . you'd see I'm doing you a favor."

"Really?" The Don bristled. "I cannot *wait* to hear this."

Bear glanced at Carlos. "See, I have no doubt that no matter where I put Hector – prison, solitary confinement, witness protection – you can get to him. If something happens to him while he's in custody . . . makes it harder to pin it on you." He picked up the tablet. "If they find you standing over Hector's body? That's a little tougher for you to explain."

Cárdenas put his hands in his pockets. "And exactly how would they find me?"

Bear tapped the screen and then turned it toward the drug-lord. "Because they're going to be here in about twenty minutes."

The man's expression turned black with fury. "Now I *will* kill you."

"You could." Bear thought about it for a moment. "But you won't."

"Why not?" A deadly smile curved the man's mouth. "Do you know what I could do to you in twenty minutes?"

"A lot. After all, your ancestors invented the Inquisition." Bear lifted one brow. "But I think . . . *deep down* . . . you're starting to like me."

The Don clenched his jaw and took a deep breath, his eyes narrowed dangerously.

"Besides," Bear continued, "I thought this meeting should be about your son . . . not the man who murdered him."

He tapped the screen and put the tablet down. Moments later the sound of a vehicle sent the Don's bodyguards reaching for their weapons. The men closed around the kingpin and the tall guy pressed the muzzle of his Uzi into Bear's side. The tension was palpable, filling the interior of the mill like an invisible fog. Bear's pulse jumped a notch.

The next minute stretched out, each second elongated and pronounced. A car door opened and closed, and finally a tall man walked through the main doors, sunlight from behind casting him in silhouette. He was lean and well-dressed, dark-haired, dark-eyed, and athletically built. He had a moustache, goatee, and sharp features. Two more men trailed behind him a few paces.

Cárdenas's men lifted their guns as the newcomer slowly walked toward them, his hands raised. The two men at his back were armed, but their weapons were pointed at the ground. Bear knew the slightest untoward movement or unexpected whisper could set this powder keg off and result in a bloodbath, so he broke the quiet and introduced the two men.

"Don Cárdenas," Bear said in a low, even voice, "meet Julio Giraldo. Your families have been fighting for a generation, but I do believe this is the first time you two have actually *met*, is it not?"

The level of hostility skyrocketed and Bear saw fingers move to triggers. Cárdenas stared at his nemesis, eyes glittering dangerously, posture ramrod straight. Giraldo moved with the confident grace of a dancer, and the fact that nearly a dozen guns were pointed at him didn't even seem to register. He stopped when he was a few feet from the wall of men separating him and Cárdenas, his hands still lifted in a gesture of submission. The rest of the Don's men closed in behind him.

"My condolences on the death of your son, Don Cárdenas," Giraldo said. His voice was soft but authoritative and sincere. "I am truly sorry for your loss."

"What is *he* doing here?" Cárdenas asked in a hiss, looking over his shoulder at Bear.

Bear frowned. "I thought perhaps you would want to finish what your son started."

"Ramon contacted *me*, Don Cárdenas," Giraldo said. "He had hoped to negotiate a cease-fire between our two organizations. He thought if we joined forces, or at least stopped killing each other . . . ." Giraldo glanced at Bear and smiled, ". . . both of us could benefit."

"So," Bear said, "you can either concentrate on Hector Perez and getting vengeance, or you can focus on what your son was trying to do." He crossed his arms over his chest. "I know which one *I'd* choose, but that's just me."

"Perez betrayed us both," Giraldo said. "I will not hold what he did against you if you will at least entertain the idea of a truce."

Cárdenas looked from Giraldo to Bear and back. Then he faced

Bear and gave him a forbidding smile. "So, now the FBI is mediating treaties between alleged drug cartels?"

"Nope." Bear leaned against the conveyor belt. "Just me. My employers have nothing to do with this. However, if what happens here keeps bodies from stacking up like cordwood, I think the FBI will be happy to ignore the fact that I didn't exactly have their blessing."

The Don chuckled. "You walk a very fine line, Special Agent Bristol." Cárdenas motioned for his men to lower their weapons. "How you stay on that tightrope and keep your badge is indeed a mystery."

"I've been told that." Bear shrugged. "A number of times, actually."

Bear and the Don stared at each other, and his pulse eased down when he saw what looked like respect in the kingpin's eyes. He neither wanted nor needed the drug lord's esteem, but it did increase the chances that he would be breathing when this little drama finally wrapped up.

"What happens now?" Giraldo asked. "Your fellow agents will be here in minutes. That is not enough time."

Bear nodded. "You're right." He picked up the tablet and started tapping the screen. "That's why you and Don Cárdenas will each choose *one* man, and the four of you will get into Mr. Giraldo's vehicle and drive away. Wherever you decide to continue this little discussion is on you, and I'd rather *not* be privy."

Cárdenas lifted one dark brow. "And how do we get past the FBI?"

Bear motioned the men forward and pointed to the map displayed on the computer. "Here, in the southeast corner of the mill property is an old logging road. It's overgrown and rough and you'll probably scratch your SUV, Senor Giraldo, but it should be clear."

"Should be?" Cárdenas and Giraldo said in unison.

"That road has been out of use for more than ten years, and it was never an 'official' road in the first place." He turned back to the map. He didn't want to tell them the FBI wouldn't be on the logging road because they would be monitoring and following the tracking signals from Cárdenas's SUVs. "Trust me, the road will be clear, and it'll take you back to the main highway just south of Boulder."

"What about the rest of my men?" Cárdenas asked.

Bear rubbed his chin. "That's easy, but you're not going to like it. Neither are they." When Cárdenas and Giraldo looked at him expectantly he sighed. "They need to leave all their weapons here, and I mean *all* – firearms, knives, whatever – including any in the vehicles, and go back the way they came. The FBI will stop them, but as long as they don't find any guns only those with outstanding and active warrants will be detained. The rest will be sent on their merry way, and if anyone *is* taken into custody . . . ? I'm sure your lawyers will have them released before *you* even make it back to Denver." He met each man's eyes. Don Cárdenas expression was speculative, his brows drawn together, and Bear frowned. "What?"

"How did you arrange all this?" Cárdenas looked around. "And what do *you* get out of it?"

"Well, I knew it would be easy to get *you* here." He glanced at Giraldo. "Senor Giraldo?" He pursed his lips. "I e-mailed him a few . . . *interesting* photographs and suggested that if he was still interested in a truce you might be persuaded to go along with it, providing he didn't show up with an army and display any aggression."

"Special Agent Bristol was most convincing," Giraldo said, a small smile hovering on his mouth. "And the photographs didn't hurt." Giraldo glanced at Bear. "But I, too, am curious. Why would you facilitate a union between two of your enemies? Is that not counterproductive to the goals of the FBI?"

"Perhaps." Bear chose his next words very carefully. "But, merging two companies, regardless of what kind of companies they are, takes time and resources. If the two of you are busy laying a framework for the organization, agreeing on ground rules, consolidating assets, etc., you'll be too busy to do . . . *other* things." He smiled. "Also, statistically speaking, the chances of a successful union between your two . . . *organizations* aren't good. The bad blood between the Cárdenas and Giraldo families runs deep. Chances are actually better that you'll destroy each other, which means *we* won't have to do it."

Cárdenas' eyes narrowed and Giraldo's brows rose. After a few tense, silent moments, Cárdenas burst into laughter. His men looked at him and then at each other, obviously unsure what their boss found so amusing.

"You are right, Special Agent Bristol." Cárdenas nodded. "I am starting to like you."

"That still doesn't tell us what *you* get out of this," Giraldo pointed out.

Bear shrugged. "I'd like to think you won't kill me." His expression sobered and he faced Don Cárdenas. "And I'd like your word that you won't go after Beth Drummond."

Cárdenas looked surprised. "The photographer? I have no reason to hurt her. I have her to thank for finding my son's true killer."

"Your *word*."

"Why?" Cárdenas narrowed his eyes and tipped his head. "To you I am nothing more than a drug dealer and a murderer. My word means nothing to you."

"Under normal circumstances that would be true." Bear met the Don's dark eyes. "But these are not normal circumstances, so in this case your word will have to do. If you give it . . . I will take it as such."

Cárdenas studied him for a few moments. "This woman is important to you."

Bear kept his face impassive. Giving this man any information other than what he wanted Cárdenas to have could be extremely dangerous, not only for him but also for Beth. "No more than any other witness. She's an innocent civilian who was in the wrong place at the wrong time. She doesn't deserve to have her entire life uprooted, nor does she deserve to live the rest of her life in fear. After all, she *did* prevent a war between you two gentlemen, and war is never good for business. If for no other reason, she deserves some sort of consideration for *that*."

Cárdenas thought about it, then pursed his lips and nodded shortly. "You have my word no one in my organization will harm Miss Drummond. In fact, consider her under my . . . *protection* from now on."

"We have no quarrel with her," Giraldo added.

"I appreciate that." Bear's brows drew together. "Just know that if anything happens to her that is *remotely* suspicious . . . yours will be the first doorstep I darken." He glanced at the tablet. "Now, you and Senor Giraldo need to decide what you're going to do. You have less than ten minutes before my coworkers show up."

Cárdenas and Giraldo looked at each other.

"I would like to pursue a cease-fire, Don Cárdenas," Giraldo said, "but it is your decision. If you do not wish to proceed, my men and I will leave, and it will be business as usual. No hard feelings."

Bear planted his fists on his hips. "What's it going to be, Don Cárdenas?"

The Don looked at him for a few seconds, his expression guarded. He started to pace, glancing between Giraldo and Bear as he did so. Finally, he focused on his head bodyguard. "Carlos, come with me. The rest of you . . . wipe down your weapons, *all* of them, then leave them and go." As his employees started piling all their firearms and other assorted weapons in a pile, Cárdenas turned to Giraldo. "We will talk, Senor Giraldo, and that is all I can promise you at this point." He gestured toward the exit. "After you." Giraldo nodded, smiled, and walked toward the double doors. Cárdenas moved to follow him, but stopped and faced Bear. He looked him over from head to toe as if assessing his worth. "Well played, Special Agent Bristol. But do not think that what happened here today will gain you any special consideration if we meet in the future."

Bear lifted one brow. "Wasn't sure it would get me any special consideration *today*."

"And I *will* take care of Perez."

"Again . . . *not* something you should say to a Federal agent."

A wry smile curved the Don's mouth. "I meant from a legal standpoint."

"Of course you did."

Cárdenas laughed. "Good day to you, Special Agent Bristol. I wish you luck with your superiors. If you need me to vouch for you . . ?"

Bear gave the man a small smile. "Yeah, *don't* think that will help."

"Probably not." Cárdenas turned and walked away. "And please tell Miss Drummond she has no need to look over her shoulder. She is safe . . . as are you for the time being."

"Until we meet again," Bear said under his breath. He watched until the last man filed out of the mill, before he leaned against the conveyer belt and scrubbed his face with his hands. "And now, the *real* fun begins."

Chapter Twenty-One

Bear had just finished sorting the nearly three dozen firearms left by Cárdenas' men into piles by type and caliber when he heard the SUVs pull up outside the main mill. He counted to ten and looked up when Fellowes and several more agents in TAC gear rushed into the mill. Hearing noise behind him, he turned and glanced over his shoulder. Apparently Fellowes had surrounded the mill before giving the order to enter. Nice. At least the kid had remembered something from his time at the Academy.

"Clear!"

The shout resounded through the cavernous interior of the building and the same cry was repeated several times. Fellowes holstered his weapon and walked up to him.

"What the hell happened, Bristol?"

Bear frowned. "Nothing happened. As you can see I'm unhurt, thanks for asking. There are no bodies, no smoking guns, and no blood spatter." He picked up a knife one of the Don's men had left, flicked out the blade, and tested the sharpness with his thumb. "I'm assuming you stopped the SUVs somewhere between here and the highway."

Fellowes looked at him sharply. "We did." He grabbed the arm of a passing agent and gestured to the piles of weapons. "Bag these and get them to forensics. Tell them I want a rush on any fingerprints."

Bear gave Fellowes a sidelong glance. "They've been wiped down, so you won't find anything on the *guns*." He closed the blade and tossed it onto the 'miscellaneous' pile. "But I doubt they wore gloves when loading the magazines, so print them and the *bullets*. And check ballistics. I'm sure you'll find at least a couple of matches there."

The agent nodded and walked off. Bear looked at Fellowes and smiled when he saw the man's glower.

"What's wrong, Fellowes? Case not going the way you expected?"

"You realize you have a *lot* of explaining to do, don't you?"

Bear nodded absently and picked up the tablet. "Yep, but my

debriefing will have to wait for a bit."

"Why?" Fellowes asked flatly. "You have something to do that's more important?"

"I do. Have a hot date with a patient at Memorial Hospital, or aren't you at all concerned about Miss Drummond's health?"

"I heard she's fine."

Bear gave him a bored look. "So you *do* care. How sweet."

"You could lose your job for this, Bristol." Fellowes shook his head. "This is *way* off the reservation, even for *you*."

Bear almost laughed and crossed his arms over his chest. "So fire me. Oh, wait, you can't because I outrank you." He scowled. "Make your suggestions to the Director, Fellowes, and we'll take it from there. Maybe Hume will even give you my job. Right now, I don't give a shit." Bear turned and strode toward the door.

"Bristol, we're *not* finished."

"*Yes*, we *are*." He glanced at Fellowes over his shoulder. "And I'm not the only one who has some explaining to do, but we'll save that for the Director."

Bear walked outside and closed his eyes, turning his face to the sun for a moment. Taking a deep breath, he let the morning roll off him as he exhaled slowly. He pictured all the people he cared about – his family, Jack, Laine, Beth – and allowed himself to feel the lightness of relief for just a moment. It enveloped him like a warm cloud, buoyant and optimistic. While he wished he could indulge in the emotion fully, he knew it wasn't over yet, not even close. In fact, the hardest part was still just a burgeoning shadow on the horizon. Bear set his jaw, opened his eyes, and walked toward the Mercedes.

He reached for the door handle and the sound of speeding tires on gravel made him look up. His hand fell to his side when he saw the patrol car. Sheriff Carter skidded to a halt mere feet away and popped open the door. Bear walked around to the front of the Mercedes and leaned against the hood.

Carter approached him slowly, his movements tightly controlled, but Bear felt the anger coming off him in waves.

"Morning, Sheriff," he said in a bland voice. "Glad you could join us."

Carter stopped a few feet away, legs spread, arms crossed over his barrel chest. "You lied to me, Special Agent Bristol."

"I did what I had to do to protect my witness." Bear straightened. "Tell me you wouldn't have done the same."

"I could have helped you." Carter took his sunglasses off and stuck them in his front right pocket. "We're on the same side."

Bear gaped at him. "Would *you* have taken that risk? Would you have risked someone *else's* life on that?" He took a step toward the sheriff. "Perez and his men didn't fly themselves up here, and Deputy Harper didn't get a bullet in the brain because he was helping *me*." That brought Carter up short. Bear saw the flash of pain and regret in the man's eyes and lowered his voice. "You have some housecleaning to do, Sheriff. Save your anger for someone who really deserves it."

"As if the FBI is so lily white," Carter growled.

"Not even close." Bear frowned. "That's what I'm going to do next . . . get rid of the rats in my own house."

Carter blinked, sighed and pushed his hat back on his head. The man's shoulders hunched forward and he pinched the bridge of his nose. "Do you . . . do you have any idea who I should be looking for?"

Bear shook his head. "No, but you might." He took the tablet and tapped the screen a few times. "Miss Drummond didn't get a shot of the pilot's face, but she did get a picture of his left forearm." When he found the photo he was looking for he handed the device to the sheriff. Carter's eyes widened and color crept slowly up his neck, and Bear sighed. "I take it you recognize the tattoo?"

Carter couldn't have looked more deflated if he was a balloon that had been popped. He handed the tablet back and leaned against the Mercedes. "Son of a bitch." He looked into the sky for a few moments and ran a hand over his face. "I'm going to need a copy of that photograph."

"Already e-mailed you one . . . and you need to check out Ranger Miller while you're at it." Bear watched the sheriff for a few seconds then put a hand on the man's shoulder. "I'm sorry, Sheriff. I know how it feels to have to pull the knife from between your own shoulder blades." His hand dropped back to his side. "Just . . . don't do anything foolish."

Carter looked at him out of the corner of his eye. "Like what?"

"Like try to take him down yourself." Bear glanced at the mill and met Fellowes eyes as he exited the building. "He's part of a Federal investigation now, so let the FBI do the heavy lifting. Make Fellowes earn his paycheck."

"Is that what *you're* going to do?" Carter asked. "Make Fellowes earn his paycheck?"

Bear eyed the other agent for a moment before meeting the sheriff's direct gaze. "No, but in my case it's personal."

"Pretty personal here, too." Carter looked at Fellowes through narrowed eyes. "I've known Duffy Harper since he was six years old."

"I killed the man who killed Harper." Bear put the tablet on the hood and crossed his arms over his chest. "The pilot didn't have anything to do with that."

Carter shook his head. "Duffy may have been *book* smart, but he wasn't *street* smart. He would never have gotten into this mess on his own. I doubt he knew who Hector Perez was."

"One thing I've learned during my time at the Bureau is to *never* be surprised by anything anyone does. *You* may not think he had the stones to run with Perez, but you could be wrong." He gave the sheriff a pointed look. "Don't jump to conclusions because you're grieving. I know you want to believe the best of Deputy Harper, but . . . people change. There may be no best to believe in."

"What are you saying?"

Bear faced the sheriff. "I'm saying don't act unless you're *sure.*" His brows drew together. "And, if you need any help, you have my number." Bear picked up the tablet and walked around to the driver's door. "Maybe Harper was a gullible shill, maybe he was a full-fledged accomplice. Until you know for sure . . . don't do anything you can't *undo.*"

****

Beth heard the door open and feigned sleep. The last thing she wanted was to tell another nurse she was fine and hear them tell her to get some rest. She didn't want to rest. She wanted Bear.

Her eyes stung as she remembered the look of stoic resignation in his azure eyes as he'd watched the helicopter lift off. She had realized in that split second he knew he could be killed in the coming minutes, but he had accepted his fate, whatever it might be. Her heart ached and her stomach knotted. Taking a ragged breath, she turned her face toward the window.

The edge of the bed dipped beneath someone's considerable weight. Beth's eyes snapped open, and her heart rocketed into her throat. She stared at the mesh reinforced window for a few seconds before slowly turning her head. When she met that familiar laser-like gaze, the air was forcefully expelled from her lungs as her diaphragm contracted violently. Tears welled and when he smiled at her, her heart nearly exploded.

"Bear."

"Hey, sweetheart."

Relief washed over her like water, warm, soft, and soothing. Beth closed her eyes, sat up, and reached blindly for him. Pain shot through her shoulder and she sucked in a breath.

"Hey," Bear said with a chuckle, pulling back to look at her, "take it easy. Laine said you have a broken collarbone, bruised ribs, and a concussion, so let's not add to the list of injuries." He tucked her hair behind one ear, his finger trailing slowly down her neck. "I'm so sorry."

Tears obscured her vision. "For what?"

"For not being there." His brows drew together and she recognized the self-reproach in his expression. "I should never have left you alone."

Beth touched his cheek. "If you had been there, he would have killed us both." She let her gaze wander over his sharply-hewn features. Then she leaned forward and tucked in beneath his chin. "It happened the way it was supposed to. I'm just happy you're safe. I was so afraid I wouldn't see you again."

He chuckled and pressed a kiss to her brow. "You can't get rid of me that easily." His hands moved slowly over her back. "You *do* know I'm bulletproof and immortal, right? Do *not* believe anyone who tells you anything different, including Laine."

Beth's throat closed up and more tears gathered. She wanted to ask him what had happened at the mill, but part of her was afraid of the answer. As his pulse thrummed against her cheek, she decided it wasn't important. All that mattered was that he was back and alive and in her arms again. She clung to him and let the minutes tick by, perfectly content in the fortress of his embrace.

He laid his cheek against her hair. "You're not falling asleep on me, are you?"

She took a shaky breath. "Not a chance."

"Do you want to talk about what happened?"

"There's not much to talk about."

He ran his fingers through her hair. "They didn't . . . hurt you?"

The pause had been brief, barely discernible, but she heard it. Beth shook her head and relaxed against him, warmth rushing through her at the concern in his voice. "No. After I crashed the Suburban I was in and out for a while . . . ." She thought about it, trying to remember. "The next thing I remember clearly was being at the mill. Perez and his friend handcuffed me to a chair, told me to be quiet, and left me alone."

Bear took a breath. "Good."

Something popped into her head and she sat up. Bear moved to look her in the face, his brows drawn together in concern.

"What is it?" he asked.

"They were talking about someone." She squeezed her eyes shut for a moment, then met Bear's sharp gaze. "While I was in and out, Perez asked Ponytail if he'd heard from Alejandro."

"Alejandro?" Bear cupped her head, his expression fierce. "Are you *sure*?"

She nodded. "They were speaking Spanish, but I studied Spanish in college. Still can't speak it well, but I understand most of it." He rose and started to pace, and Beth watched his face. She knew his brain was working at light speed. The crackling of synapses was almost audible. "Even if I didn't understand the language, I know I heard them say Alejandro. Ponytail said . . . ." Her voice trailed off as she tried to reconstruct the memory. "He said Alejandro had booked their flight and would meet them at the terminal with their new passports."

Bear stopped pacing, his gaze focused on the window, and the look in his eyes sent a chill through her. She scooted to the edge of the bed and reached for his hand, uncertainty winding around her chest.

"Bear, what is it?" She laced her fingers through his and was relieved when he squeezed her hand lightly. "What did I just do?"

He was silent for a moment, and when he spoke again his voice was low and deadly. "You just confirmed the identity of our traitor."

"Are you sure?" she asked in a whisper.

He nodded and sat down next to her. "I had it narrowed down to two." He sighed heavily. "I was hoping I was wrong, but you just circled one of those last two names." Bear looked down at their intertwined fingers for a few silent moments then turned to her. "I may need you to do something for me."

Her reply was automatic and instant. "Anything."

"That was easy."

"So am I, apparently." Heat flooded her cheeks, and she looked down at her lap. "That *is* how you like it, isn't it?"

"*Don't* talk like that." He curled a finger under her chin and tipped her face up. "*You* are amazing." His gaze wandered over her features. She saw a flicker of something in his eyes that sent apprehension fluttering to wing inside her. His brows drew together. "You should rest. I need to get to the Federal Building and see how Mr. Perez is faring."

"Will I see you later?" That blank wall dropped into place and her heart hit the floor.

He rose. "We . . . we won't be seeing much of each other from here on out."

The wings of apprehension brushed against her lungs, freezing them. "Why?"

His expression was carefully neutral. "It's not my case. I'm a witness, not an agent, and the State's Attorney frowns on the fraternization of witnesses." He took a breath, held it for a moment, and exhaled slowly. "In a situation like this, they want to make certain our testimony isn't tainted. We would be separated anyway, just like they separate suspects. My being here now is going to make my superiors *and* the State's Attorney *distinctly* unhappy."

Beth tried to swallow the lump in her throat, but it was firmly lodged, rough edges pressing painfully into her esophagus. She nodded silently and laid back down, a cold, hard ball solidifying in her belly. After tugging the blanket back over her legs, she focused on her toes. Her eyes stung, but she clenched her teeth and fought the tears that wanted to form.

"Then you should go," she said when she finally dislodged the lump from her throat. "I don't want you to get in trouble because of me."

Bear scowled at her. "If I was worried about getting in trouble, I wouldn't be here in the first place."

He dropped his chin and crossed his arms over his chest, and there was a long pause. He seemed to be searching for something to say, which was odd. Bear wasn't a huge talker, but she had never seen him at a loss for words. When he finally spoke, his voice was low and even and completely devoid of any hint as to what he was really feeling, like his face. Even the boyish grin seemed genuine, though the warmth stopped short of his eyes. Nevertheless, he put on a convincing show.

"Good news is you'll make your showing."

Beth forced a smile. "Yeah, that is good news." Her traitorous eyes started to leak, and she dashed a hand over them. "Andy will be happy, but I'm going to look like hell."

He took a step toward her and cupped her chin. She lifted her eyes to his. The thought she might never look into those azure pools again sent a sharp, metallic shaft of pain through the center of her chest.

"You . . . will be beautiful," he whispered.

He studied her for a few seconds before he lowered his head and covered her mouth with his. Beth fisted one hand in the front of his shirt as he kissed her softly, deeply, and everything inside her started to sing. The song was cut short when he ended the kiss, pressed his lips to her brow, and turned on his heel. He paused at the door, one hand on the knob, eyes focused on the glass.

"By the way, Cárdenas gave me his word that the cartel won't come after you. It *is* the word of a drug kingpin, but for what it's worth," he paused, "I believe he was sincere."

She wanted him to look at her, but his gaze remained firmly fixed on the window. "What about Perez?" she asked softly.

He slowly turned his head and there was a cold fire burning in his eyes. "I'll take care of Perez, don't you worry. Soon . . . soon you won't have to look over your shoulder anymore. You'll be safe."

Bear flexed his fingers on the knob and opened the door halfway. Beth sat up a little straighter when he hesitated, closed his eyes briefly, and let the door close again.

"It's probably better this way, Beth," he said in a low, flat voice. She saw the tensing of his jaw. "The sooner I get out of your life, the sooner you can start living it again."

"And if I'd like you *in* my life when I start living it again?"

He rubbed his eyes. "Look, I understand you think you have feelings for me, but we were in the middle of a highly stressful, dangerous situation, and that can do strange things to a person's emotions." His hand fell to his side, and he looked at a spot on the wall over her head. "I know. I've been there."

The flash of pain in his eyes was unmistakable and he faced her, hands stuffed into his pockets. Her heart flip-flopped.

"You have to understand," he began, his voice carefully modulated, "witnesses often develop . . . *attachments* to the agents protecting them. We learn about it at the Academy and are trained to deal with it. Nine times out of ten, when the danger has passed and the person's life returns to normal they realize, with no small amount of embarrassment, that what they thought was love just isn't there anymore. It never really was." A small smile curved his mouth and he stared at the floor. "They're mortified and apologize profusely, but we just take it in stride. It's one of the hazards of the job."

Beth studied his face. "You said nine times out of ten." She paused and took a breath. "What about the other *one*?"

His jaw tensed. "Oh, the same thing happened to her." He looked up. "It just took her longer to realize it."

Her stomach dropped. "How much longer?"

He sighed and there was a brief pause. "Just over a year. We didn't start dating until after her case was closed, and about a week after our year anniversary, she just broke down over dinner, said she couldn't do it anymore." His brows drew together. "She said she wasn't in love with me, and that she hadn't been for a while, but she hadn't said anything because she thought it was just a phase." He laughed. It was a short, sharp sound that made her wince. "And because she didn't want to hurt my feelings."

Beth closed her eyes. "Oh, Bear."

"Thankfully she broke the news *before* I proposed, and the jeweler was kind enough to take the ring back."

Her heart broke for him and she blinked back tears when the mask fell into place.

"Whatever you think there is between us, it isn't real." He opened the door. "Just give it some time."

He left without looking back. Beth held her breath as the door whispered shut, tears trickling slowly down her cheeks.

When the door closed, Bear felt something inside him close as well. He stood there for a moment and took a deep, slow breath. He felt a presence at his elbow and looked down into Laine's hazel eyes.

"What did you do?" she asked in a whisper.

"What I had to do." He ran a hand over his brow. "You understand transference just as well as I do, probably better."

"I do, but I don't think Beth's feelings for you are that superficial."

"It wouldn't be the first time a witness has *fallen in love* with me, and it probably won't be the last." An ache throbbed to life inside his chest, a dull and persistent pang of longing. "Once her life returns to normal, so will her feelings."

She put a hand on his arm. "Bear, I think you're wrong." She searched his eyes. "Beth doesn't exhibit the classic symptoms of transference, the over-the-moon, school-girl like behavior, the childish, almost fairy-tale-idea that when the situation is resolved, they'll live 'happily-ever-after'."

He wanted to believe that, but he couldn't. "People are different, Laine. Not everyone will display the 'classic' characteristics."

Laine's expression was thoughtful. "True, but what Beth exhibits is almost completely opposite."

Bear felt the frown even as a spark of hope flared. He snuffed it out without mercy. Before he could respond, two men dressed in suits approached. He recognized them immediately and turned to face them. "Special Agents Devereaux and Jones. I take it you're here to guard Miss Drummond?"

Devereaux nodded. "Can think of about a hundred things I'd rather be doing on my Saturday, but such is life."

Bear pinched the bridge of his nose. "Really?" he muttered. "Did you think the FBI was a Monday through Friday, nine-to-five?" He fixed the agent with a pointed look. "If so, you're in the wrong line of work, brother."

Laine bristled. "Agent . . . Devereaux, is it?" She lifted one brow. "I imagine Miss Drummond would rather have done something other than be kidnapped and held hostage by ruthless drug dealers on *her* Saturday, but such is life."

Devereaux colored slightly and looked away from her.

"Seriously, dude?" Bear asked. He stared at the man and shook his head. "If you want to make yourself look bad, do it when you're not on the clock or it reflects on all of us."

Jones spoke up. "We need to speak with her, Doctor."

She turned a disdainful eye on him. "No," Laine said flatly. "She's been sedated, so you'll have to wait." She nodded toward one of several chairs lining the corridor. "Have a seat, gentlemen, or you can use the waiting room. It's just down the hall."

Bear cupped Laine's elbow, and they started walking away from the other agents. "I have to get to the office before my superiors put out *another* APB on me. Take care of her, Laine."

"Bear," she began, "didn't you hear what I said? I said her symptoms are opposite of the classic indicators."

That spark of hope was struggling to flare to life, but he fought it. "I heard you," he replied, "and it doesn't matter."

"It *does* matter." Laine crossed her arms over her chest. "She's not euphoric, she's . . . sad. She knows how she feels about you, but she believes it's *completely* one-sided, and she's not saying anything. The sort of situation that triggers this emotional response makes people *careless* with what they say. They figure they don't have anything to lose because they may not make it out alive, so they just put everything out there." She put a hand on his arm. "They don't keep it to themselves, as she is."

Bear's insides twisted as he recalled her whispered declaration. "She told me she loved me," he said in a low voice. "I don't think she realized she'd said it out loud, not at first."

Laine's brows shot skyward. "Oh." She studied his face and Bear kept his expression impassive. "What did *you* say?"

Bear focused on the wall over her head, an ache throbbing beneath his sternum. "I said that once all of this was over, her feelings would go away." He sighed softly and rubbed his forehead. "That's the way it works."

"Not always." She eyed him speculatively. "But you have to be willing to risk something to find out, and you're not, are you?"

He shook his head once. "I learned my lesson the hard way."

Laine watched him carefully, and he had the feeling that regardless of the shields he erected, she saw right through him. He saw a flash of sadness in her eyes before she looked away. She patted his shoulder. "Well, I think you're in trouble, big guy. Regardless of whether *her* feelings are real, *yours* are, aren't they?" Her expression turned pensive. "I saw it that morning in my kitchen. You couldn't take your eyes off her."

"I was worried about her safety."

A soft sigh escaped her. "Keep telling yourself that if it makes you feel better. I know what I saw." She watched him carefully. "Y'know, Jack never told me he loved me until the night I killed Ripley."

Bear couldn't hide his surprise. "Seriously?"

Laine smiled sheepishly and looked at the floor. "Seriously. He told me he *fell* for me right before I met *you*, and just before the Marshals took me away, he said he would always love me, but, like you, I figured it was just an emotional response to the situation." Another sigh escaped her. "Neither of us said those three little words until that night." She lifted her golden-green eyes to his. "In the end it didn't matter because once he kicked Special Agent Vaughn to the curb I could read *Jack* like a book. We didn't need words because we just *knew* how the other felt."

Bear knew she was going somewhere with this, and he wasn't sure he liked it. "Your point?"

"My point is I hadn't seen *Bear* in a very long time, until that morning you and Beth showed up at my house." She pressed a hand to his cheek. "You need to remember how to clock out, or growing old alone won't be much of a concern because you won't *grow old*."

He glared at her and he wasn't sure why, other than she was right and he didn't like it. "Is that an official diagnosis, Dr. Vaughn?"

Her hand dropped to her side. "No, but when you see Bear would you tell him I miss him?" She turned. "Scowl at me all you want, Special Agent Bristol. It just means I'm right and you don't like it." Laine gave him a knowing look over her shoulder. "You have a nice day. I am going back to my patient."

Bear put his fists on his hips and stared at the ceiling as she walked back the way they'd come. He took a deep breath, held it, and then let it out. "Way to go. You are a world heavyweight asshole, you know that?" He watched the fluorescent light fixture for another few moments, before he turned and left the hospital.

He strode into the FBI's offices half an hour later. Since it was a Saturday, the place was mostly empty, but he heard voices toward the back, the Director's office. He recognized Jack's voice and Fellowes's, and walked down the familiar hallway. The door to the Director's office was open, and he tapped his knuckles lightly against the door frame.

Director Franklin Hume was a thirty-year veteran of the Bureau with three times more commendations than ex-wives, and the latter number currently stood at four. He was close to six feet tall and solidly built with brown hair, brown eyes, and heavy features. The man looked at him from his seat behind the wide, mahogany desk, brows drawn together, a frown pulling the corners of his mouth down. Jack and Fellowes sat in the two chairs facing the Director. Jack gave him a half-smile and Fellowes's face was blank.

"Nice of you to join us, Special Agent Bristol," Hume said. "Fellowes was just telling us that Sheriff Carter arrested that ranger, but the pilot is in the wind, no pun intended. His case has been handed off to the Marshals. Mind telling us what you've been up to since your visit to the mill this morning?"

"Sorry, sir," Bear said in a bland voice. He and Hume didn't always see eye to eye. In fact, they clashed on a fairly regular basis, but it would serve no purpose here. "I stopped by the hospital to check on my witness."

"She's not *your* witness," Hume corrected him. He narrowed his eyes on Bear and planted his elbows on the desk. "Both you and Miss Drummond belong to Fellowes now. This is *his* case."

Bear leaned against the door jamb. "Fine. I went by the hospital to check on *his* witness." He glanced at Fellowes. "She'll be fine, by the way, in case you were interested. Devereaux and Jones are there now."

"Good." Hume lifted one bushy eyebrow. "Now that you've no more *distractions*, you can give your statement and get back to work."

Bear bit back the snappy retort and crossed his arms over his chest. "I'd actually like to get back to my leave of absence, which I plan to do right after Fellowes explains *himself*."

Fellowes looked askance at him. "What are you talking about?"

Bear gave him a jaunty smile. "The bugs? The ones you or someone from your team planted in Special Agent Vaughn's house?"

Hume looked from Bear, to Fellowes, to Jack. "What is he talking about, Vaughn?"

Jack sighed and rubbed his eyes. "Several hours after Fellowes and his team left my house I found three bugs in the downstairs." He met Hume's eyes. "I believe that's how Perez found Miss Drummond's location."

"And he had to have help, sir," Bear added. "Jack didn't verbalize her specific location, so whoever was listening had the ability to access Special Agent Vaughn's personnel file and cross reference every detail of his professional and personal lives with dozens of data bases to make the connection." He gave Hume a pointed look. "Perez doesn't have that level of skill, or access."

Hume's brows drew together into a thick, black line on his forehead. "You're saying it was someone in house."

"I've been saying that since JC's death." Bear frowned. "But you and your superiors just thought I was being paranoid, sir."

"I swear I didn't have anything to do with the bugs, sir," Fellowes said.

Bear leaned against the door frame. "I already know that, Fellowes, but someone on your team did."

Hume laced his fingers and laid them on the desk. He stared at his hands for a moment then sighed. "All right, Bristol. I assume you have some sort of plan, you always do." He lifted his gaze to Bear's. "Lay it on me."

Chapter Twenty-Two

Bear stared across the table at Hector Perez. Perez looked bored and irritated to be handcuffed to the table, but Bear didn't really care. He flipped through the file folder, knowing that for each second that ticked off the clock, Perez grew more annoyed. After nearly thirty minutes, Perez finally snapped.

"Why am I here?"

Bear looked up from the file, both brows raised. "I'm sorry. Do you have somewhere more important to be?"

Perez ground his teeth together. "I've been here for more than half an hour, and you haven't said a word. You've just sat there, flipping through that file again and again." Perez leaned forward. "What do you want?"

Bear closed the file and allowed himself to feel the swirl of anger. It spun in his middle like a tornado in slow motion. "What do I want?" When Perez nodded, Bear scowled. "What I want is to go back in time so I can pull the trigger and end your worthless, miserable existence, instead of watching you murder a faithful, dedicated agent. That's what I *want*." He leaned forward and Perez shrank from him. "Since I can't have what I *want*, you're going to give me something else."

"What?"

Bear ignored the question and opened the file again. "We have you dead to rights on five counts of murder one." He whistled softly. "Wow. Those are capital crimes, and the jury will *adore* the photographs. I *love* living in a death penalty state, don't you?"

Perez spoke from between clenched teeth. "What do you want?"

"A name." Bear glared and leaned forward again. "And everything that goes with it. How you first made contact, how you convinced them to betray the Bureau, dates and times of meetings, how you passed information, how you compensated him for his betrayal, *all* of it."

"Wait." Perez's brows rose. "You're not going to ask me about the Don?"

Bear shook his head. "I'm not interested in the cartel. The DEA and the CIA can handle them." He flattened his hands on the table. "Now start talking, and if I like what I hear, maybe you *won't* get bail."

Perez stared at him for a moment and Bear could almost hear the wheels spinning. "I'm not telling you anything." The man shook his head. "There's no way any judge will grant me bail, not if I'm facing five capital murder charges."

"That's true, under *normal* circumstances." He gave Perez a small smile. "But, these aren't normal circumstances." He glanced at the file. *This is how a spider feels as it closes in on the fly.* "See, the State's Attorney owes me a few favors and you've drawn Judge . . . ooh, Abernathy." Bear glanced at Perez. "He's dismissed three of your last four indictments, so as long as the SA suggests an *outrageous* sum, say $50 to $100 million, and the surrender of your passport, chances are good that Abernathy will grant even *you* bail."

"You *want* me to get bail?" Perez stared at him in disbelief. "Why would you want that?" He sucked in a breath and sat up, absently pulling on his restraints. "You *want* me out, where the Don can get to me."

"Oh, I don't want that." Bear shook his head and looked out the window overlooking the offices toward a small alcove where the coffee maker was. A stately Hispanic gentleman in an expensive suit stood there, sipping from a Styrofoam cup and glancing their way. "But see that man?" He nodded out the window.

Perez's eyes turned that direction. "Yeah. Who's he?"

Bear's smile widened just a bit at the flicker of uncertainty in the other man's eyes. *The fly knows he's toast, but there isn't shit he can do about it.* "He's your attorney, courtesy of Diego Cárdenas. See, *I* don't want you out, but the Don is certainly anxious to see you, and *that* man has been authorized to pay whatever amount of bail the court deems suitable, even a *cash* bond." Bear leaned back in his chair and laced his fingers over his abdomen. "So, you either start singing like a canary, or I make *one* phone call to the State's Attorney, he suggests an *obscene* dollar amount of bail, Judge Abernathy *grants* you bail, and I'm forced to turn *you* over to *him*." He paused and glanced at the older, well-dressed gentleman, pulling hard on the surge of satisfaction that began to swell. He'd been doing this too long to be overconfident, even though he could practically smell victory. *And in goes the spider for the kill.* "Then I escort you and the counselor to the steps of the Federal Building where a limousine even now waits." He grinned at Perez. "Somehow, I doubt the chauffeur is the only one inside that vehicle."

Perez's face went red. "You're *blackmailing* me?"

"I'm not *blackmailing* you." Bear frowned. "I'm explaining your *options*. Be happy you have any given the number and types of crimes you've committed." He took a yellow legal pad, a pencil, and pushed them toward Perez. "Write it down, *all* of it."

"No. I want a lawyer . . . a *different* lawyer."

Perez had played the trump card but Bear had expected that. He sighed, stood, and picked up the folder. "Okay, but I doubt there's a lawyer this side of the Mississippi, any side of the Mississippi actually, the Don can't get to. I'm surprised you've already forgotten that's how the *last* witness scheduled to testify against your boss died. His court-appointed attorney came to visit him just before the trial, and the bailiffs found the witness in the holding area with his throat cut from ear to ear." Bear gave him a grim smile. "He was murdered by his own attorney while inside a locked cell in a Federal courthouse protected by metal detectors, monitored by state-of-the-art video cameras, and staffed with dozens of police personnel and bailiffs." He shrugged, pushed in his chair, and turned away from Perez. "But, if that's what you want, that *is* your right."

Bear walked toward the door. Just as he reached for the knob Perez spoke.

"Wait."

The fly fights back, but both victor and victim know it's only a token struggle. Bear grasped the doorknob and turned it. "You asked for a different lawyer which obligates me to get you one."

"Wait. Wait! I'll give you the name, just . . . wait."

Bear paused, looked over his shoulder, and watched as Perez picked up a pencil. He walked up to the felon and plucked the utensil from the man's hand. "Not yet." He opened the file and pulled out a form. He placed the single sheet of paper on the table in front of Perez, took a pen from his pocket, and put it next to the document. "Because you asked for a lawyer, before you put anything down on paper you have to sign this. It's a waiver acknowledging you have declined counsel at this time."

Perez gave him a mutinous look. "And if I don't sign?"

Bear shrugged. "Then I leave and get you a lawyer." Perez glared at him and then signed the waiver and started scribbling on the legal pad. Bear waited until Perez wrote the name he had expected. *And the fly is dead.* "Keep writing. I'll be back."

He left the room, doing an immediate U-turn into the observation area. Jack adjusted the focus on the camera and shook his head.

"You lucked out," Jack commented. "What if he hadn't signed, or he'd asked to represent himself?"

Bear stared through the one way glass, surprised at how little he felt. No matter what Perez had just done, it wouldn't bring JC back. He grunted. "Then he and I would still be discussing his *options*."

"You going to tell Jorge he can go home now?" Jack asked. "It was nice of him to come in on a Saturday just for us."

Bear glanced at the dignified man who stood near the coffee maker still sipping his drink. "Yes, it was." Monday through Friday Jorge Escobar wore a security guard's uniform and manned the desk in the lobby. Although this role was well outside of his work duties, Escobar hadn't hesitated at all when Bear had asked for his assistance. Bear tossed Jack a wry smile as he left the observation room and walked toward the coffee maker. He approached Jorge and the two shook hands. "Thanks again for coming in on Saturday wearing your Sunday best, Jorge."

"I still don't understand why you asked me to do this, Special Agent Bristol," Jorge Escobar said, his dark eyes twinkling, "and I probably don't want to know."

"Probably not." Bear glanced toward Perez and then fixed Escobar with a pointed look. "Now, I want you to look at me like you just caught me making love to your wife."

Escobar's brows rose. "I'm sorry?"

"I want you to look really pissed off, throw your coffee away, and storm out of here cursing in Spanish."

"But, I do not curse, Agent Bristol."

"I believe God will look the other way in this circumstance." Bear smiled. "It'll help bring Special Agent Acosta's killer to justice if that eases your mind."

Escobar's face darkened. "In that case . . . ." The older man glared at Bear, threw the half-empty coffee cup toward the trash can, splattering dark liquid on the wall and floor. Escobar stood toe to toe with him, cursing loudly and fluently, and even Bear was surprised at the vehemence behind Escobar's offensive. When he was finished, Escobar looked at Perez who had been watching the scene, transfixed. Escobar stormed through the office, knocking desk lamps and inboxes over as he went. Bear stared after him, brows raised. Jack appeared at his side.

"Wow." Jack crossed his arms over his chest. "That actually looked . . . *authentic.*"

Bear nodded. "And the Oscar goes to . . . Jorge Escobar, building security guard in the role of scumbag defense attorney. Bravo."

"What did you say to him?"

"I told him he would help bring JC's killer to justice." He chuckled. "That was all it took."

"Hmm." Jack looked at him. "Well, Phase One is done. What now?"

"Call your wife and have her bring Beth in." He glanced over Jack's shoulder. "Cyber-Crimes guys here?"

"Yep. They are even now looking into Fellowes's background."

"Good." Bear nodded. "We'll have everything we need to bring Fellowes down within an hour or so."

"But Fellowes isn't involved." Jack frowned. "Is he?"

"No." Bear fixed him with a pointed look. "But since we suggested Fellowes is dirty, the mole is going to go to extreme lengths to make it *look* like he is, especially since we didn't tell them exactly what we're looking for." He ran a hand over his hair. "What these guys don't know is that I spent three years in Cyber-Crimes myself. Most of *them* were still in middle school, but they're not the only ones who know how to set up a ghost network, organize and implement a bot-net, back-stop a cover story, or run a trace."

Jack laughed softly and shook his head. "So, the mole is digging his grave for us as we speak. Nice." He gave Bear a sidelong glance. "You bucking for Hume's job?"

Bear frowned. "Hell, no. I just enjoy the looks of amazement on everyone's faces when I pull this shit off." He shrugged. "Sometimes I impress myself."

Jack sat down on top of a nearby desk. "I'll be impressed when Phase Three gets started."

"Phase Three?" Bear kept his expression neutral, although he had a good idea where Jack was headed. "Sorry, hadn't planned that far out."

"Really? You should." A half-smile curved Jack's mouth. "Because once all this other shit is wrapped up, you're going to have to deal with what's going on between you and Beth."

Bear felt his shoulders tighten. *And, I'm right again.* "Nothing is going on between me and Beth." *At least, nothing I can do anything about. Damnit.*

"Bullshit." Jack shook his head. "You can shovel that for everyone else in this office, but don't try to sell it to me. The fact that you slept with her—"

"*Keep* your voice down."

Jack glanced around, but they were quite alone in the open space. The Cyber-Crimes division was housed in a separate area with extra cooling equipment for the massive computers, and the only other agent was Thornton who had taken over Perez-watch in the observation room. The door to that room was closed. Nevertheless, Jack lowered his voice.

"The Bear I know would *never* have done that unless he had some pretty strong feelings for the woman in question." Jack stood toe to toe with him. "Admit it. You're in love with her."

The warmth of that emotion expanded beneath Bear's heart for a split-second before the polar vortex of reality stormed in to extinguish it. He *did* love her, a fact that was scary enough on its own. Factor in the massive obstacles standing between them and a possible *happily-ever-after* and his brain threatened to shut down. He was the sort of man who took risks on an almost daily basis, but he wasn't the sort of man who behaved recklessly. Falling in love, however, required a certain amount of recklessness. Falling in love required that *he* be the fly, that he willingly fly into the web and hope the spider wanted to love him back rather than destroy him. The internal struggle nearly overwhelmed him and he ground his teeth together. "It doesn't really matter, now does it?"

Jack gaped at him. "Of *course* it matters. Do you *want* to spend the rest of your life alone?"

Bear narrowed his eyes on his best friend and grabbed hold of the frustration in his belly that threatened to blossom into something more. "You and Laine really have this tag-team thing down."

"I don't know what you're talking about." Jack glared at him. "I haven't spoken to Laine since we dropped her and Beth at the hospital this morning."

"Then you two are psychically linked or something," he growled. "She grilled me the same way you are."

Jack's brows rose. "That should tell you something."

A hot ball of anger roiled in Bear's midsection and he clenched his fists. "It tells me you should mind your own damn business."

"So, sue us for wanting you to be happy."

The heat inside him shrank back, crowded out by something cold and hard. "It doesn't matter what I feel for Beth," Bear said flatly, getting in Jack's face. "When all this is over and things return to normal, so will her feelings. We've both done this before. You and Laine ending up together is an anomaly and you *know* it."

Jack gaped at him. "That doesn't mean it can't happen to you."

"Statistically . . . it *does*."

"Bear . . . Beth is a remarkable woman."

Bear gaped at him. "*You're* telling *me* that?"

Jack continued as if he hadn't spoken. "Guys like us, we . . . we *need* remarkable women to put up with us, put up with the job, and everything that entails. You don't find women like that hanging out in dance clubs or at Starbucks."

Bear fought not to roll his eyes. "I suppose you find them on the side of a deserted highway in rural Montana."

Jack stared, his expression serious. "Yeah, or in the middle of Rocky Mountain National Park being chased by murderous cartel soldiers."

Bear leaned his head back and looked at the ceiling, his emotions twisting like a windsock in a tornado. The urge to punch Jack in the nose had his hands tightening into fists, but, as appealing as the idea was at the moment, he knew it would only be a temporary distraction. He had no desire to jeopardize their friendship, or piss Laine off, so he kept his expression impassive. At least, he *tried*. Obviously Beth wasn't the only one with the ability to get under his skin. It didn't help that Jack was right, he and Laine both. Beth *was* remarkable and so was the depth of his feelings for her. He wasn't the type who normally fell for someone before spending a considerable amount of time with them, but with Beth nothing had been normal.

"Give it a rest, Jack. It's *not* going to happen."

Jack's expression turned incredulous. He stared at Bear for

several long, silent seconds, and then narrowed his eyes and shook his head. "Wow. I never imagined falling in love would be the *one* thing that scares you more than dying." He huffed and turned on his heel.

Bear watched Jack walk away, his blank expression carefully in place. When Jack turned a corner, Bear exhaled sharply and tightened his abdominals against the invisible pummeling they were taking from the inside. Easing down on the edge of the nearest desk, he braced his arms at his sides and hung his head. *It's not falling in love that scares me, brother. What scares me is that she might not love me back.*

****

Beth stopped on the wide concrete slab and stared up at the multi-story building in front of her. Laine stood at her side and followed the direction of Beth's gaze.

"So, this is where Bear works." Beth took a deep breath. "I've driven by this building a thousand times, but I've never had cause to go inside."

"It's not so bad." Laine smiled at her. "C'mon. I'll be there with you, every step of the way."

That simple act of friendship broke through the terror clawing at her insides. Ever since Laine had told her the FBI needed to get her statement and they wanted to do it at their offices, she had been in a state of near panic. The only thing keeping her from totally losing it was the fact Bear would probably be there . . . somewhere.

"Will he be in there?"

"Perez? Probably."

"No." Beth shook her head. "Bear."

Laine's expression turned pensive. "Yes, but you won't get to see him." She put a hand on Beth's uninjured shoulder. "I'm sorry, Beth."

Beth smiled and sighed. "It's not your fault, Laine. And Bear already told me we wouldn't be able to see each other again." Saying the words made her stomach twist and started tears stinging behind her eyes. She blinked quickly and glanced at Laine. "It just makes me feel better to know he'll be close by."

"Oh, he'll be close by," Laine assured her. "And Jack will be doing your interview. I made it a condition of your release from the hospital." She squeezed Beth's shoulder lightly. "Let's get this over with. The sooner this is done, the sooner you can finish winning Bear over."

Beth wanted to hope she could do that, but she remembered the look in his eyes before he'd left her hospital room. It was the same expression he'd had when the helicopter lifted off, sad acceptance. Part of her was bothered that he seemed so willing to let go of what they shared, yet she understood his wariness. The closest she and Michael had come to marriage was to joke about it. Bear, on the other hand, had *wanted* to take that step. He had faced that risk the way he faced everything, with straightforward, unflinching resolve, only to be rejected. She could only imagine how deep and painful that wound had been. A lump formed in her throat, constricting her vocal chords, so instead of replying to Laine's confident statement, she just nodded and smiled.

She'd been too upset to pay any attention to him in the helicopter, but as soon as the elevator doors opened, she recognized Jack Vaughn. He was even better looking than in his photos. He leaned against the wall with the logo of the FBI emblazoned on it, arms crossed over his chest. Standing around 6'3", he had a beefy build, dark hair cut short, and stormy gray eyes. Beth had no trouble seeing what had attracted Laine to her husband. A grin lit his face and he walked toward them. Laine stepped forward and into her husband's embrace as he leaned in for a quick kiss. Then he draped an arm around his wife's shoulders and smiled at her.

"Miss Drummond." He extended his hand and they shook briefly. "We haven't been *formally* introduced, but any friend of Bear's is a friend of mine. Call me Jack."

"Well, Jack," Beth began, "I think we're a little past the formal introduction stage, but you can call me Beth." Nausea roiled but she took a deep breath. "Thanks for helping to save my life, by the way." A flush of embarrassment warmed her cheeks. "And I'm sorry about what I said to you in the helicopter. I was . . . upset."

He shook his head. "Don't apologize. It's all good." He released Laine. "All right, Beth. Let's get on with this." He gestured toward the open archway that led into the main office. "Now, here's what we're going to do. We'll go into an interview room, and then all you have to do is tell me what happened."

"Interview room?" She glanced at him as they walked. "Don't you mean interrogation room?"

"No." Jack grinned at her and she felt some of her apprehension recede. He wiggled his eyebrows. "Those are for suspects. For *you*, it's an interview room." He paused, glanced around, and lowered his voice. "By the way, for this interview you should leave out what happened between you and Bear at the cabin. No one needs to know about that."

Heat burned to her scalp. Beth blinked and nodded.

Past the reception area was a large open space filled with desks and cubicles. Laine followed behind and when Beth glanced over her shoulder at the woman, she gave a reassuring smile. Jack gently cupped her elbow and steered her between the utilitarian pieces of furniture and toward a series of rooms with windows that overlooked the workspaces. In those windows, hung Venetian blinds that were open. She saw a single table and two chairs facing each other in the center of each of the approximately twelve-foot square rooms.

Jack opened one of the doors and gestured for her to precede him inside. It looked like every "interview" room she'd ever seen on television or in the movies, nondescript tile floor, blank walls painted a pale grey, overhead fluorescent lights, and no windows other than the one that overlooked the office. In one corner a video camera hung, focused on the table, unmoving and unblinking. A large mirror, one-way glass she guessed, took up half of one wall, and she automatically sat down in the chair facing it. Jack sat down on the edge of the desk, and Laine leaned against the door frame.

"Once we start, I have to call you Miss Drummond." Jack rolled his eyes. "The State's Attorney wants us to be *professional.*" He shook his head, glanced at the mirror, and then looked at her warmly. "Would you like something to drink before we get started? Coffee, tea, water?"

Her stomach rolled again and this time her deep breath wasn't as effective. "Water would be nice, thank you."

He nodded. "You bet." He rose and approached his wife. "Stay with her? I'll be right back."

Laine gave him a smile. "No problem." After Jack had left the room, Laine sat down in the chair opposite and reached for her hand. "Don't worry, Beth. You're going to do great. It'll be painless and over before you know it."

Beth squeezed her fingers, drawing from Laine's calm. "When I went out taking pictures that day this is *not* where I imagined I'd end up." She closed her eyes briefly. "Although I know this is considerably better than where I'd be if Bear hadn't found me."

"At least you had the good luck to run into someone like him," Laine said softly. "But then, I've never been a big believer in luck."

Beth's brows drew together. "What do you mean?"

Laine looked pensive for a moment then smiled. "I just think the two of you meeting is more than simple chance. I mean, what are the odds that you would run into the one *perfect* person to rescue you from gun-toting thugs in the middle of the wilderness?"

Beth had already considered that. "Well, if it's true our meeting was more than coincidence, I'd like to tell whoever *is* responsible for it that I wish he or she had done it another place and time . . . obviously *before* this incident." She dropped her gaze, looked at their intertwined fingers, and lowered her voice. "Maybe then I'd get to keep him."

"Don't give up on him just yet, Beth," Laine whispered. "He's worth the fight."

The women had spoken softly, but Bear had heard every word. His insides went in two different directions at the same time, an odd sensation he wasn't sure he liked. Her words made something in him soar and drop at the same time. That shard of sadness he'd first felt at the motel grew until it felt like it was cutting through him from the inside. He looked at her and silently echoed her wish.

She wore jeans and a button-up shirt, her left arm in a sling. She looked battered, sad, and frightened, and he wished with everything inside him he could have spared her all of this. The door to the observation room opened. Bear dropped his expressionless shield in place, and without looking he knew who had joined him. He had sent for the man after all.

"Special Agent Bristol, you sent for me?"

Bear glanced at him and then looked again at Beth, crossing his arms over his chest. "I did, Special Agent Paulson. I need you to monitor the recording equipment while Special Agent Vaughn interviews this witness. As you can see we're a little short-staffed today."

Paulson chuckled. "Usually are on Saturdays ... thank goodness."

"Find anything interesting on Fellowes?" Bear asked absently.

"I did, sir. I put everything into a folder and gave it to Director Hume."

Bear nodded and then faced the man. Paulson was of average height and above-average looks, sandy blonde hair, blue eyes, and sculpted features. He had fair skin and Bear doubted the man ever set foot outside. Alexander Paulson had been at the Denver office for just over three and a half years and had spent his entire tour so far in the Cyber-Crimes unit. According to his file, he was a brilliant programmer and hacker, but no one seemed to know him very well on a personal level. Even after all this time, not one of his co-workers had ever seen the man outside of work, not even a casual run-in at a grocery store or coffee shop. Supposedly he was married, but apparently his wife also stayed off the radar. Rage bubbled inside Bear as he stared at the man who had given JC up. He gave Paulson a tight smile.

"Very good. After the interview is done and you forward the video feed to me, you can go. Shouldn't take too much longer."

Paulson looked surprised. "You're not staying?"

"No, I'm needed elsewhere." Bear walked toward the door. "But the Director is sitting in on this one, so you can't rest on your laurels."

Paulson straightened. "No worries, sir. I shall do my best."

"I know you will, Paulson." Bear nodded. "You can start recording whenever Special Agent Vaughn gives you the go ahead."

He glanced at Beth one last time before leaving the observation room and shutting the door. To avoid walking past the outside window of the interview room, he took the long way back to the Director's office, around the central area and down another hallway. Reaching the open door, he tapped on the frame and looked in.

"Come in, Bristol."

"We're getting started, sir." Bear glanced at the man seated across from the Director. "Are you ready for this, Special Agent Vargas?"

The head of the Cyber-Crimes Unit looked at him grimly, rose, and nodded. "You bet."

"Good." Bear's brows drew together. "Get in there and start ripping up Paulson's life." He fisted his hands at his sides. "Find my evidence. I want an iron-clad case for this one, and Perez's confession does *not* get me that. I'm counting on you."

"I know." Vargas scowled. "Paulson may be good, but I'm better. Rest assured, Special Agent Bristol, I'll find the proof you need. He's *not* getting away with this." He glanced at the Director, and when Hume nodded, Vargas walked past Bear and down the hallway towards the Cyber-Crimes Unit.

Bear looked at Hume. "Search warrant is being executed on the house as we speak. Ingram and Ahmadi are leading the teams."

Hume rose and approached him. "Good." The Director studied him for a moment. "When all this comes to a head, I hope I can count on you to keep your cool."

"When have I ever *not* kept my cool, sir?"

"Last time we had a traitor in house, you and Vaughn wound up with a body count almost in the double-digits in less than an hour."

"That wasn't me losing my cool." Bear lifted one brow. "That was just a hazard of the job, sir." He thought about it for a second. "Or a perk, depending on how you look at it."

"Well, not this time." Hume frowned. "Paulson isn't a cartel soldier or a domestic terrorist. He is . . . *was* . . . one of us. Keep your gun in its holster."

A chill of determination stiffened Bear's spine. "I will, unless he forces me to draw."

Hume rubbed his temples and sighed. "Son, I want Paulson as much as you do, but I want him to face his crimes. JC was a good agent, and the man who gave him up deserves more than the shot in the head you would give him."

"Don't worry, sir." Bear smiled grimly. "We'll get him, and if I have to . . . I'll just shoot him in the leg."

Chapter Twenty-Three

Jack strode in, handed Beth an icy bottle of water, and smiled at his wife. "You can go now, Doc. I'll call you when she's done."

"I think I'll hang out," Laine replied. "That way when you're finished, I can take her back to the hospital."

"Oh, I'm not going back to the hospital," Beth interjected. "I want to go home."

Laine frowned. "Beth, you need to go back to the hospital. Concussions can be tricky. Your brain got knocked around the inside of your skull pretty good, and I'd like to keep you at least overnight to make sure nothing more serious is happening in there."

Jack held up a hand. "We'll talk about this later. Right now, the State's Attorney is waiting for her testimony, so we need to get started." He cupped Laine's elbow as she walked, reluctantly, to the door. He smiled at her and brushed a kiss over her cheek. "Why don't you wait in Bear's office? He's got a great couch in there, and I'll come get you when we're done."

Laine looked at her once more before giving her husband a small smile and leaving the room. Jack watched his wife for a moment before he shut the door and sat down across from Beth.

"Okay, now before we start recording, I just want to go over it once more. All you have to do is tell me what happened. I may ask you a few clarifying questions, but this show is yours, Beth."

"Okay."

"So, remember everything I've told you up until now?" He gave her a meaningful look.

Beth nodded.

"We good to go?" he asked.

"We're good."

"All righty then." He turned toward the mirror. "Start recording please." He watched his reflection until there was a tap on the mirror and then faced her. He identified her, identified himself, announced the date and time, and smiled. "Okay, Miss Drummond. Start with what you were doing in the park and go from there."

Beth took a drink of water and the cool liquid helped to settle her stomach. She closed her eyes briefly and pictured Bear. Even his memory gave her strength, and she took a deep, cleansing breath as she looked at Jack. "All right, you asked for it."

****

Bear walked into his office and paused when he saw Laine standing at the window looking over the city. At any other time he'd be happy to see her, but the last thing he wanted was another cross-examination about him and Beth. He had always admired Laine's tenacity, but right now it was wearing thin for him.

He tossed the folder in his hand onto his desk and she turned at the sound. "What are you doing here?" He sat on the edge of the desk. "Aren't you still technically on your honeymoon?"

Laine moved to the couch and sat down. "Yeah, but once Jack finishes the interview, I'm going to try and convince Beth to go back to the hospital. She wants to go home, which I understand, but I'd feel better if she didn't, at least not tonight."

Bear's brows drew together. "Does she *need* to go back to the hospital?"

"She hit the dashboard so hard she broke her collarbone, Bear, and you saw the lump on her head." Laine sighed and rubbed her eyes. "I'd feel a lot better if she stayed overnight so I can make sure nothing else is going on inside her skull other than a concussion. We did a CT scan when she got to the hospital, but sometimes brain injuries don't show up on a CT scan right away."

Bear thought about it for a moment, then grabbed a small yellow pad, picked up a pencil, and scrawled a short note. He ripped the paper from the pad, folded it, and handed it to Laine. "Here. Give this to her after the interview is done. It may help you make your case."

Laine put the folded slip into her pocket without reading it. "Thanks." She met his eyes, and he saw the shadow of sadness before she dropped her gaze. "Bear, I owe you an apology."

"For what?"

"For giving you a hard time about Beth." She sighed and stretched out on the couch, kicking her feet up on the arm. "I just want you to be happy, and it seems like you haven't been happy for a while."

Bear approached the couch and motioned for her to move. She sat up, and after he had sat down, she put her head in his lap. Laine gave him a beseeching look and laced her fingers through his.

"Forgive me?" she asked.

"No need, but okay." He squeezed her hand. "And I know you want me to be happy, but pushing me and Beth isn't going to accomplish that."

"I know." She sighed. "I'll stop." Laine looked at him and smiled. "You two do look good together, though."

"Don't start."

"Sorry, but I like her. And I think you do, too." He scowled at her and she chuckled. "I'm not pushing. I'm just making an observation."

"Well, quit."

Her brows drew together. "You look tired, Bear. When was the last time you slept?"

"A while ago." He glanced at his watch. "Thirty plus hours ago. What about you?"

"I took a nap at the hospital after I got Beth situated." She sat up and leaned into his shoulder. "Why don't you lie down and try to catch some zees and I'll go wait at Jack's desk?"

Bear shook his head. "Can't. Jack's been in with Beth for over an hour now. I should be receiving my cue any moment."

"Cue?" Laine frowned. "What are you talking about?"

"It's time to clean house, sweetheart."

Laine stared at him for a few seconds, and then her brows drew down. "Are you using *her* as bait?" Her tone was sharp, disapproving, and Bear chuckled.

"No, Laine. She's not bait." He rubbed his chin. "She's more like . . . a catalyst."

"Sounds like you're walking that fine line again." Her expression told him she was unhappy with this turn of events.

Bear chucked her under the chin. "Relax. She's in no danger here."

Laine's brows rose. "You sure about that?"

"Absolutely." His cell phone chirped and he pulled it from his pocket. He glanced at the display, hit a few keys, and then slid it back into his pocket. "That's the signal. I have to go."

Bear got to his feet and paused when he felt Laine's hand on his arm. He looked down at her, the woman who he at one time thought he could fall in love with, and the realization of how he felt for Beth hit him square between the eyes. No longer did he feel the lingering envy for his best friend and the love Jack had found because his own heart had turned elsewhere. Laine must have seen something in his expression because she blinked and looked at him strangely.

"Bear, what is it?"

"Stay here."

"But—"

"No buts." He fixed her with a hard stare. "*Stay here*, and if you don't I swear, I will toss you over my shoulder and handcuff you to my desk. Are we clear?" He was absolutely serious and she seemed to sense it because she nodded once and sat back down. Bear gave her a small smile. "Thank you."

"You're welcome." She gave him a solemn look. "Be careful."

He wiggled his eyebrows at her. "You know me."

"I do. That's why I said it."

Bear chuckled and quickly made his way back toward the

interview rooms. The blinds on the room Beth was in were closed. He picked a desk directly opposite the door and sat down on the edge. After activating his earpiece that was tuned to the recording equipment, he braced his hands at his sides and waited. His pulse jumped a point when he heard Beth's voice.

". . . crash, I was in and out, but I remember Perez and his friend talking about someone named Alejandro." Beth paused for a few seconds and then continued. "Perez asked the other guy if he'd heard from Alejandro, and the other guy replied that he had."

"Did they give a last name?" It was Jack's voice.

"No, but the second man said Alejandro had their flight booked and their papers ready. This Alejandro was supposed to meet them at the terminal with their new passports."

"Did they say which airport?"

Bear clicked off his earpiece, rose, and walked toward the elevator bay. He stood in the lobby with his back against the FBI's logo wall. Only a couple of minutes passed before he heard footsteps, quick footsteps. He listened, judging the distance, and when the person grew closer, Bear did a one-eighty and moved quickly into the arch to block the person's exit. Alexander Paulson froze and his eyes went wide.

"Going somewhere?" Bear asked, keeping his expression neutral. Inside he was boiling but now was not the time. "They're not done with the interview yet."

Paulson backed up a few steps. "Um, my wife called. I need to get home."

"Why?" Bear crossed his arms over his chest. "Won't do any good. Search warrant has already been executed." He frowned. "At this moment my best forensics team is going over *every* inch of your home. They've seized *every* computer you own, and the Cyber-Crimes unit here is putting together the evidence of how *you* tried to frame *Fellowes* for *your* misdeeds." He let a little of the anger he felt manifest on his face. "And did I mention we have Hector Perez in custody? *You're* not going *anywhere*."

Paulson paled visibly and his eyes darted about, looking for an escape route. Bear had seen that expression before, on the face of every criminal he'd ever cornered. Paulson backed through the archway into the reception area. Bear kept pace with him, letting the man have his distance.

"You don't understand, Bear," Paulson said, a faint sheen of perspiration beading on his brow. He continued to back up, his hands held up in front of him. "They . . . they *knew* . . . about *everything*. The gambling, the debts, the money . . . all of it. I . . . I didn't *want* to do what I did, but I . . . I didn't have a choice."

Bear loosened his grip on his rage, and it exploded inside his chest like a bomb, heat and emotional shrapnel ripping through him. He was momentarily taken aback by the sensation, but instead of reeling it in, he let it go. In his mind flashed images of JC's death, the heart-wrenching moments after he'd broken the news to JC's wife, Marisol, the funeral, and scattered images of Beth's run from Perez. A boiling swell of anger, sorrow, and seething hostility crested inside him, and he tried to wrestle it back into control. It was harder to do than he'd imagined it would be. His pulse rose and his breathing quickened. When the adrenaline hit his bloodstream, he nearly lost it.

"Of course you had a choice," Bear said from between clenched teeth. "You could've said *no*."

"They threatened to tell the Director . . . they threatened me *and* my wife. I . . . I would've lost everything." Paulson retreated several more steps. "I would have gone to *prison*."

Bear took two long steps and closed the gap by several feet. "You took an oath!" He realized he was shouting, although the volume didn't register because all he could hear was the *whoosh-whoosh* of blood in his ears with every heartbeat. "JC is *dead* because of you!"

Paulson backed through the maze of cubicles and behind a half wall. Bear growled and toppled the barrier with a swipe of his hand.

"I didn't know!" Paulson skittered behind the desk and when Bear shoved that out of the way, Paulson practically leapt into the adjoining workspace.

Bear paused as what the man had said registered. He closed his eyes for a second and white hot rage erupted within him. With a roar he barreled through the metal and pressboard partition, and Paulson turned and ran until he found himself against a wall he couldn't push past or jump over. Bear closed in. "What did you *think* Perez was going to do when you told him he had an undercover FBI agent infiltrating his criminal organization?"

"They threatened to *kill* me." Paulson flattened himself against the wall and his eyes pleaded with Bear to understand. "They threatened to torture and kill my *wife*."

Bear stopped and fought to rein in his temper. The animal inside him was telling him to attack, invisible claws pawing at the ground in excited anticipation, while the human side of him knew he needed to throttle back. He was vaguely aware that he and Paulson were no longer alone in the main work area. He couldn't have taken his eyes from the other agent if he'd tried.

"You could've gone to any number of people if you were in trouble." Bear took a deep breath. "Director Hume, your supervisor, *me*." He took several more steps toward Paulson. "Instead you chose to switch sides and now, because of what you've done, a dedicated agent, a devoted husband, and a great father will never have the chance to see his children grow up." Two more steps. Now only about eight feet separated Bear from the man the beast inside him would kill without a second thought.

Bear hunched his shoulders. "You're facing accessory to the first degree murder of a Federal agent, which carries the same penalty as if you'd pulled the trigger yourself." He fixed Paulson with a scalding stare. "So I guess JC won't be the only one in a box. You'll be spending the rest of your natural life in a solitary cell after your conviction, because if they put you in general population . . . ? You'll be dead before the door closes behind you. That's *if* you don't get the death penalty." Bear allowed himself to feel the burst of immense satisfaction that mental image brought with it, and suddenly he was back in control again. However, he wasn't sure if Bear or Special Agent Bristol was in control. Oddly, it felt like neither as a smile curved his mouth. "I want you to think about that. What choice would you make *now*?"

Paulson drew his sidearm and aimed it at Bear's chest. His hand shook visibly, his eyes wide and shining with fear. Bear dropped his chin and glared at him, ignoring the shouts in the background.

"Really?" Bear narrowed his eyes on Paulson. "*You* are drawing down on *me*?" He clenched and unclenched his fists at his sides, vitriol coursing through him like powerful, poisonous venom, and now he *knew* he wasn't in control. The dark side of him, the one fed by all the anger and other emotions he'd bottled up was firmly in the driver's seat. He wasn't sure how to stop it, and when he spoke again, it was like having someone else's words forced from his mouth. He felt outside himself, as if he was watching a movie and couldn't turn it off. "When was the last time you fired a weapon, Paulson? *Quarterly training?*" He gave the agent a grim smile. "I shoot at least twice a week and I took out four people two days ago, so trust me when I say that before you can click off that safety, I *will* put a bullet in you."

The gun ticked back and forth in Paulson's trembling hand, sweat trickling down the sides of his face, his breathing sharp and ragged. Bear saw the panic set in, and when Paulson's hand moved, he knew what the man was going to do on an instinctual level before it registered intellectually. Bear automatically drew his weapon.

As Paulson swung the pistol toward his own head, Bear heard the shot and felt the recoil travel up through his wrist into his elbow. A red stain blossomed on the upper right shoulder of Paulson's button-up shirt, and the man was catapulted backwards by the force of the impact. Bear immediately rushed forward to kick the gun out of Paulson's reach and then stood over the fallen man.

He gazed down into those fear-filled eyes and pointed the pistol at Paulson's forehead. His pulse thrummed, his insides tight with red, seething rage. "You don't get to do that."

"Bristol!"

Bear continued, as if his boss hadn't just yelled his name. "If anyone's going to kill you, *Alejandro*, it's going to be *me*."

"Special Agent Bristol!"

Paulson blinked and Bear saw the two tears that ran down his face.

"So kill me already," Paulson said. "Do it!"

"Bear, don't!" It was Jack's voice. "Drop the gun, Bear. Drop it now!"

Bear flexed his fingers on the grip and moved his finger to the trigger.

Paulson's face went red, veins bulging in his forehead. "Do it!"

"Bear, don't make me shoot you, brother!"

Jack's threat barely registered. Bear paid him no heed. His eyes bored into Paulson's, and that monster inside him took a little bit tighter hold of his soul.

"Bear."

That voice registered. Bear moved only his eyes to look at Beth who stood half hidden behind Jack in the open doorway of the interview room.

"Bear, don't do this." Her golden eyes were bright with tears. "This isn't you."

Bear turned his gaze on Jack. "Get her out of here."

Beth scowled at him. "No." She tried to step around Jack, but he put an arm across her chest and kept her back. "If you're going to murder him, you're going to do it while I watch." Her chin trembled and her eyes pleaded with him. "Please, Bear. You're not like them. You *save* people, you don't hurt them, not unless you absolutely have to. This isn't one of those times."

She blinked and two silver tracks appeared on her cheeks. The anger in his chest cavity shrank a fraction.

"Bear, *please.*"

The soft, dulcet tones of her voice and those wide, amber eyes penetrated his rage and Bear felt the shift of gears as Special Agent Bristol kicked his dark side in the teeth and stepped back into his rightful place. The beast in him whimpered as it was locked back in its cage, and then fell silent.

His finger left the trigger and he looked down at Paulson. Sorrow flooded him, a heavy penetrating sensation oddly similar to drowning. He remembered the feeling from the time he'd almost drowned on a camping trip when he was eleven. His lungs struggled for a few seconds to draw air. He felt the weight pressing down on him as if he was underwater. He closed his eyes and imagined himself swimming back to the surface. When he was finally able to take a breath, he put his gun on the closest desk and stepped away from Paulson's prone figure. He heard Hume's voice, but it sounded hollow, like the man was speaking from inside a tin can.

"That's it, son. We'll take it from here." The Director clapped a hand on his shoulder and moved to look Bear in the face. A faint smile hovered on the man's mouth as he picked up Bear's gun. "I thought you said you were going to shoot him in the leg."

Hume's voice had been clear that time, and Bear blinked as the volume level returned to normal. He glanced at Paulson and wondered vaguely when Laine had appeared. Then again he had fired his weapon which, he realized as he looked around, had drawn every agent on the floor. He met Hume's eyes and shrugged. "I missed."

Hume's brows rose, but he said nothing else. After hearing from Laine that Paulson's wound was not life-threatening, the Director turned to him, met his gaze, and nodded once. Then the man made his way back toward his office. Bear watched for a moment as Laine tended Paulson's wound, the man's hands now cuffed in front of him. It was then he realized it was over. At least, until he remembered Beth was watching him.

Shame grated through him, leaving painful, bloody furrows on his heart, and he squeezed his eyes shut. He had lost control, something he *never* did, and he'd come within a breath of murdering someone. Killing in self-defense or the defense of another was one thing. Methodically putting a bullet in the brain of someone who wasn't a threat and couldn't defend themselves went against everything he believed in and stood for. And Beth had seen it all.

Bracing himself for the worst, he lifted his head and looked at her. He had expected at the very least disappointment, or possibly revulsion, but when he saw the warmth in her gaze, his heart did a back flip. She gave him a smile and mouthed the words, "Thank you."

Her acceptance did nothing to lessen his humiliation, but he was still relieved. Bear shook his head and said softly, "No, thank *you*." They stared at each other for another few seconds before he turned and walked back to his office. Once inside he closed the door, sat on the couch, and waited.

Beth watched him go, and her heart went with him. When he disappeared from sight, she felt hollow, empty, and alone. She moved back to the table in the interview room and sat down, exhaling sharply as tears slid slowly down her cheeks. Covering her face with her hands, she tried to get hold of herself. Jack put a hand gently on her shoulder. She wiped her face and looked up at him.

"Nicely done." He sat down on the edge of the desk, his expression solemn. "For a second there I thought . . . ." His voice trailed off and he dropped his gaze. "I've never seen him like that, and I've known him for more than ten years."

"Do you . . . do you really think he would have killed that man?" Beth watched his face carefully, but obviously Jack had trained at the Bear School of Emotionless Masks. "Do you think he's capable of that?"

Jack looked at her. "Oh, he's capable. We all are." He sighed. "JC's death hit him *hard*, and the fact Paulson is our second turncoat in three years only made it worse." He ran a hand over his brow. "When Bear told me he was taking an extended leave of absence, I had a feeling he wasn't going to come back. In fact, I firmly believe the only reason he is here at all," he gave her a sidelong glance, "is because of you."

Beth rubbed her eyes. "If not for me, he'd have no reason to be here." She sniffed. "He'd be sitting beside a campfire in the woods somewhere, decompressing and getting all of this out of his system."

"This is *not* your fault." Jack's brows drew together. "He listened to you. The Director was yelling at him, so was I, but yours was the only voice he heard. If not for you, he may very well have put a bullet in Paulson's brain, and now *he'd* be the one in handcuffs."

An invisible fist drilled into her midsection as that image came to life in her mind. For a moment she couldn't breathe. It was just too much, imagining Bear arrested, in jail, and then on trial for murder. Her throat constricted tightly and she dropped her chin, her vision wavering.

"What will happen to him now?" she whispered.

"He'll be put on administrative leave pending the outcome of the shooting investigation."

Her head snapped up. "But . . . Bear *had* to shoot that man, or he would have committed suicide. Everyone saw it."

A faint smile moved the corners of Jack's mouth, but just barely. "I know, Beth. It was a good shoot, but it still has to be reviewed. It's just procedure." He took her hand and squeezed her fingers. "Don't worry. He won't get in trouble for shooting Paulson. Everyone who witnessed the shooting will be questioned, and I have absolutely no doubt Bear will be fully exonerated of any wrongdoing."

Relief washed through her so completely she knew if she hadn't already been sitting, her legs would've given out. She crossed her arms on the table and rested her brow on the backs of her hands, suddenly exhausted. Jack squeezed her shoulder gently.

"Stay here. I'll be back in a few minutes, but I think we're done for the day."

Beth didn't bother to lift her head. She didn't have the strength. Nodding, she turned her head to the left and closed her eyes, weariness draping over her like a heavy blanket. Just as she started to doze off, the door to the interview room opened and she opened her eyes. Laine stood there, her expression somber.

Beth sighed. "Laine, I appreciate your concern, but please don't try to talk me into going back to the hospital." She lifted her head. "I just want to go *home*."

"I know." Laine nodded and sat opposite her. "I know, Beth, and I understand, but Bear asked me to give you this." She pulled a folded piece of yellow paper from her pocket and slid it across the table.

Beth stared at the note. "What is it?"

"I don't know, I didn't read it."

Beth looked at her for a moment, and then picked up the slip and opened it. She recognized Bear's sharp scrawl immediately, and as she read the words, tears obscured her vision.

Go back to the hospital. Please . . . .

She pressed shaking fingers to her mouth for a moment, closed her eyes and slipped the note into a pocket. It took her nearly a minute to find her voice, and when she did it was hardly more than a whisper. "I guess I'm going back to the hospital."

Laine's brows rose. "Wow. That was easier than expected." She studied Beth for a moment. "What did the note say?"

"Location joke," Beth replied with a tearful smile. "You had to be there."

Laine reached across the table and took her hand. "It's going to work out, Beth."

Beth closed her eyes and the tears fell. "I don't think so, Laine, but it's okay. I got what I asked for."

Chapter Twenty-Four

Beth looked at her reflection and adjusted the strap on the sling. The bruises were barely visible beneath the makeup Laine had helped her apply and the cuts and abrasions . . . those were a little harder to disguise, but they didn't totally mar her appearance. Thanks to the news coverage of her and Bear's adventure, the entire nation had heard the story, so if anyone was surprised by her less than perfect appearance, it just meant they lived in a cave and shouldn't be bothered with. She smoothed the skirt of the cranberry-colored, strapless cocktail dress and took a deep, cleansing breath. There was a light rap on the bathroom door.

"Beth?" Laine asked. "You okay?"

"I'm fine." She opened the door and gave Laine a smile. "I'm just a little nervous, that's all." She faced the mirror again and ran a hand over her carefully arranged hair. "How many people are there?"

Laine crossed her arms over her chest and leaned against the door frame. "I don't have an exact count, but the place is full and Andy is positively beaming. He kept most of the reporters and media people outside, thank goodness." Her eyes did a vertical scan. "You look stunning, by the way."

"Thanks to you." Beth glanced at her and smiled. "You look pretty hot yourself."

Laine chuckled and ran a hand over the black halter-style dress. "Well, Jack likes it, so I guess it works."

"Speaking of Jack, GQ called and they want their model back," Beth said with a chuckle. "Who'd have thought that putting him in a suit would have such dramatic results?"

Laine grinned. "Yeah, he's normally a jeans and button-up shirt kind of guy." Beth stepped into the hallway and linked arms with Laine. "I prefer him *out* of clothes, personally, but I don't think that would go over too well here."

Beth laughed as she and Laine walked down the darkened hallway toward the gallery. "You never know, although I would like to see that."

The two women paused at the weighted door that opened into

the rear of the gallery. Laine looked at her, her eyes twinkling, and she grasped Beth's hands.

"You ready for this?"

Beth met her gaze and took another breath. "No." She dropped her chin and stared at the toes of her slingback pumps. "I wish Bear was here."

"I know." Laine squeezed her fingers. "And he is, in spirit." She paused, and when she spoke again, her voice was hushed. "You know he'd be here if he could, don't you?"

"Of course." Beth closed her eyes. "Thanks for everything, Laine. My other girlfriends aren't quite sure what to do with me after what's happened." She chuckled softly and met Laine's eyes. "Somehow, getting a mani-pedi doesn't seem nearly as important as it used to."

Laine's expression was pensive. "I know what you mean. When you've come face to face with your own mortality, it kind of puts things in perspective." Then she grinned. "But, mani-pedis are still important. In fact, I think we should get one this weekend. What do you say?"

Beth looked at her and her eyes stung. Laine had become important to her in such a short time and had been a better friend than many of the friends she'd known for years. Between the FBI and the media coverage, most of her inner circle had run for the hills. Oddly, it didn't bother her as much as she'd thought it would. Beth put an arm around Laine's shoulders. "I think that's a great idea."

"It's a date then." Laine pressed against the bar to open the door. "But now, it's show time."

Laine opened the door and stood to the side as Beth walked into the gallery. The gallery's owner, Andrew Shaw, approached Beth and held out his arms.

Andrew Shaw had been a presence in her life since she'd won a photography contest he had sponsored when she was just fourteen. Ever since then he'd been her mentor, her biggest supporter, and one of her closest friends. He was one of the few people she knew who hadn't been spooked by the FBI investigation, the endless stream of reporters, and whispers of drug cartels. He stood just shy of six feet tall, and he was wonderfully fit with a sun-kissed glow that looked real but wasn't, and a British accent that seemed fake but was absolutely genuine. Regardless, it only added to his already inherent charm. His dark hair was graying at the temples, his features chiseled but not sharp, and his dark green eyes were full of life. Despite the fact he was in his early fifties, he attracted girls thirty years his junior who did their best, and worst, to snag him. Too bad for them he was gay and quite happy to let everyone believe otherwise.

"There's my girl," he said, closing in for an embrace. Beth smiled and leaned into him, kissing his cheek as she did so. After they hugged, he presented her with his arm and walked her to the center of the room. He released her, grabbed two champagne flutes from one of the many passing trays, and handed one to her. Then he pulled an expensive, silver pen from a pocket and tapped it against his glass. When the room went quiet and all eyes turned toward them, he faced her and lifted his drink. "Ladies and gentlemen, allow me to introduce the immense talent behind the amazing photographs you see here tonight. Miss Elizabeth Drummond."

Butterflies swooped inside her stomach and she felt mildly nauseous as the applause started. Flashbulbs glared and she heard the auto advances firing. Beth smiled and nodded several times, color heating her cheeks. She glanced at Laine who stood next to Jack and gave her a huge grin and a thumbs up. Beth continued to look around the room, her cheeks aching from smiling so widely. Finally the clapping died down and Andrew moved to stand behind her. They had rehearsed this, so she took a deep breath and tried to meet as many eyes in the room as she could.

"Thank you all for coming tonight. I am . . . overwhelmed and so very grateful. Not many people can say they love what they do for a living, but now that I can say photography is my living, *I* can." A chuckle went through the room and she faced Andrew. "I owe it all to you, Andrew. Without your unwavering support and belief in me, this would not be happening. Thank you . . . for everything."

The applause started again as she and Andrew embraced once more. Beth pulled back and pressed a hand to his cheek, blinking back tears. Andrew grinned unabashedly.

"You deserve this, love," he said softly. "It's about time the rest of the world knew how talented you are." He turned to the room and lifted his glass. "Thank you again for being here. Enjoy the party and drink up." The dull drone of conversation returned and Andrew drew close to her side. "I am so proud of you, Elizabeth." He looked her over from head to toe. "You look phenomenal, by the way."

"The sling doesn't clash with my dress?" Beth teased.

Andrew chuckled. "Not at all. The black looks quite fetching, actually." His brows drew together. "Where did your doctor friend find a black arm sling?"

Beth glanced at Laine, who was sipping champagne and chatting with Jack as they looked at an eight-by-eight-foot print of a cougar's face. The animal's distinctive golden eyes were looking directly into the camera with a penetrating sharpness that was arresting. It was one of her favorite shots.

"Apparently," she began, turning back to Andrew, "they make them in many colors now, so one can coordinate with their wardrobe."

"Hmm." Andrew took a sip of champagne. "The wonders of modern medicine." One of Andrew's assistants approached to whisper something in his ear and then retreated. Andrew smiled, framed her face, and kissed her soundly. "Mingle, darling. I have just been informed that the owner of the Weymar Gallery in San Francisco wants to discuss your West Coast showing. Fasten your seatbelt, love. This rocket is about to launch."

The next three hours were a blur of chit-chat, introductions, congratulations, and questions of how she'd managed to get such close up photographs of such deadly animals. As each minute ticked off, Beth acknowledged to herself that this was the part of her career she disliked the most. When the evening finally began to wind down, her cheeks ached and her feet were killing her. She'd just finished explaining the wonders of modern telephoto lenses to another amazed guest when she felt a tap on her shoulder. She turned and found herself looking into stormy silver eyes. Jack smiled at her.

"Jack. Are you and Laine heading out?" She looked around, but Laine was speaking with an older woman near a wall-sized print of a grizzly bear.

Jack's cell phone buzzed and he pulled it out of his pocket to give it a quick glance. "In a few." He put the phone away and met her gaze. "Night's not over quite yet. Laine and I don't get out that much, especially to shindigs like this. Thanks for the invite."

"You are very welcome." Beth smiled up at him and put a hand on his arm. "Thank *you* for being here. Your and Laine's support means the world to me. Just having the two of you in the room made all of this much easier. This whole . . . *marketing* thing really isn't my gig."

"Could've fooled me," Jack said with a quick grin. "You're a natural." He looked at her for a moment and his expression sobered. "The past week's been pretty tough on you, Beth, but you've been a real trooper."

"Didn't have much of a choice," she replied with a smile. "What doesn't kill you makes you stronger, right?"

"I suppose so." He stared at her for a few seconds, his expression inscrutable. "This is going to sound really weird, Beth, but . . . could you show me the back door?"

Beth blinked at him. "The back door?"

"Yeah, the one that exits into the alley behind the building." He leaned toward her and lowered his voice. "And don't ask me why, just trust me."

Her brows rose. "Okay. Give me a second." Jack nodded and she scanned the gallery for Andrew. When she caught sight of him, she walked over to him and put a hand on his arm. He turned and looked at her in silent question. "Andy, I'm going to step out for a bit if that's okay."

"Of course, love," he replied. "Take your time. I already have your next three showings booked and the party's winding down anyway."

"Thanks." She kissed Andrew on the cheek and walked back to where Jack stood. She gestured toward the back of the gallery. "This way."

Jack fell into step beside her as they made their way toward the weighted door that led to the gallery offices and storage space, the same one she had entered through mere hours before. When they reached the door, Jack pulled it open and let her precede him into the darkened hallway. Beth wondered what the hell was going on as they skirted stacks of packing crates, boxes, and frames during their trek to the exit, but she did as Jack requested and kept her mouth shut. Once she stood in front of the back door, she punched a code into the glowing keypad on the wall. When the light turned green, she pushed through the heavy panel. She stepped into the alley and faced Jack as he moved to her side.

"Okay, Jack. What's going on?"

Jack looked at her, a half smile curving his mouth. He glanced over his right shoulder and nodded in that direction. She peered down the darkened path. She didn't see anything, and when she turned toward Jack, he was just closing the gallery door behind himself. Beth stared, unable to believe that Jack had just walked her into the alley and left her there. She looked about and froze when she saw movement out of the corner of her eye. Her head snapped around and her heart hit the pavement as Bear stepped out of the shadows and walked toward her.

She stood motionless, rooted to the spot as he approached. Her pulse raced and her heart beat a brisk rhythm against her sternum. When they were toe to toe, Beth looked up into that sharply planed face, afraid to blink for fear he would be gone when she opened her eyes. He smiled and joy flooded her in a warm surge, tears welling.

"Hey, sweetheart."

If her collarbone hadn't been broken, she would have flung her arms around his neck. Instead, she wound her one good arm around his waist and laid her head on his chest. He chuckled softly and his embrace closed around her, his chin on top of her head. Beth bit her lip and squeezed her eyes shut as his strength enveloped her. He was so warm, the heat from his body penetrating their clothing and her. Suddenly nothing else mattered, not the gallery, not her showing, not the upcoming trial, none of it. *This* was what mattered, *he* was who mattered, and safe in his embrace was the only place she ever wanted to be.

He kissed the top of her head. "I shouldn't be here, but I had to see you, especially tonight."

Beth couldn't have replied even if she'd had something coherent to say. Her throat was tight with emotion, and it took every ounce of strength she had not to burst into tears.

His hands moved slowly over her back. "I am so happy for you, and I'm *so* proud." He pulled back slightly, curled one finger beneath her chin, and tipped her face up. "I told you you'd be beautiful."

She looked into those azure eyes and instantly recognized Bear. Apparently Special Agent Bristol was elsewhere, and that was fine with her. The warmth in his gaze sent her heart reeling. She was so happy to see him, and yet she knew it was only temporary. Without a word she put her head back on his chest and tightened her embrace, her fingers clutching the back of his shirt. Bear sighed softly and pressed his cheek to her hair.

"I've missed you," he whispered.

Beth fought back tears and took a ragged breath. Bear gently disentangled himself from her embrace and framed her face with his hands. His brows drew together as his eyes searched hers.

"Don't cry, please. Not tonight." His thumbs stroked lightly over her cheekbones. "This is your time to shine, Beth. You have *such* a gift, and judging by the crowd inside, I'm not the only one who thinks so."

"These are happy tears, Bear, and I don't care what they think."

He frowned. "Don't say that."

"Being a famous photographer isn't important to me." She covered his hand with hers. "The *only* thing missing in my life before this night was someone to share it with." Her hand fell back to her side and she chuckled ruefully. "Now my career is taking off, but nothing else has changed. I guess what they say is true . . . you can't have it all."

"Beth—"

"It's okay, Bear." She forced a smile. "I won't make you pay up for all that chicken-fried-steak you promised me until after the trial."

A shadow of sadness passed behind his eyes. "That could be a very long time."

Her insides wound tight and she dropped her chin. Tears fell and she swiped at her cheeks as she whispered, "I know."

There was a long pause. "I shouldn't have come here." He sighed heavily. "The last thing I wanted was to ruin your evening."

Beth's head came up and she laid her hand over his heart. "You didn't ruin my evening." Lifting onto her tiptoes, she tried to look him in the eye, but he focused on a spot over her head somewhere. She took his chin in her hand and forced him to look at her. "Bear, seeing you has *made* my evening." She smiled and released him. "I have been wishing *all* night that you were here. I got my wish." Tears blurred her vision. "This is the perfect way to end my night, but next time . . . next time I'm going to wish for you to never leave."

Bear pressed his forehead to hers. "I wish I could stay."

"Me too." She closed her eyes as an invisible hand squeezed her heart. "Before you leave, could you do something for me?"

"What?"

She hesitated, the words sticking in her throat. Beth gulped and took a shaky breath. "Kiss me?"

For a few moments he didn't move, his breath warm on her cheek. She thought he was going to pull away, but then he lowered his head and covered her mouth with his, softly, carefully. The movement of his lips against hers was delicate, tentative. Beth slid her hand up his chest and curled her fingers around the back of his neck. His skin was warm and smooth. The memory of their lovemaking sent heat through her like a desert wind. When she realized she might never again kiss him or touch him, jagged, cutting pains tore against her insides. But when he touched his tongue to hers, it didn't matter. She knew at that moment she could withstand anything to stay right where she was.

His arms tightened around her as he explored her mouth. Beth leaned into him and surrendered. He deepened the kiss and she moaned softly, her insides going molten. One hand moved to cup her head while the other settled in the small of her back. She felt the longing, the sorrow, the tightly restrained passion in him, and the ache in her soul sharpened.

She sensed his withdrawal before he actually pulled back and her heart wrenched. When he ended the kiss she took a deep, shuddering breath, anguish coursing through her like a cold, dark wave.

"Live your life, Beth," he whispered against her mouth. "Take the world by storm, fall in love, and *be happy*. Please." He cupped her head and pressed his lips against her brow for several long, poignant moments. "You deserve it."

Beth kept her eyes closed as she felt him turn, unable to watch him leave. She heard him rap lightly on the gallery's back door. The door creaked as it swung open, and then his footsteps retreated down the alley until she couldn't hear them anymore. Tears found a way out and slid slowly down her cheeks.

"I'm sorry, Beth," Jack said softly. He touched her arm. "Maybe I shouldn't have agreed to—"

"No," she interrupted. She looked up at him and smiled through her tears. "I'm glad you did."

His eyes narrowed and he ran the back of his finger over her wet cheek. "Doesn't look like it."

Her gaze was drawn down the alley. "No matter how much it hurt, before you and Laine were separated, would you have rather seen her, or not?"

Jack stared at her for a moment then put an arm around her shoulders. "Point taken. Now let's get back to the party before my coworkers watching the place realize you're gone and freak out."

****

Bear finished reading Beth's file and tossed it on the coffee table next to his half empty beer. Oddly enough he felt guilty for reading her official history. He would have preferred to learn about the major details of her life from her and not a background check, but rules were rules. Because he and Beth were both witnesses they could not see or speak to each other, and by the time court proceedings wrapped up, she very well may have moved on. It hurt to think of her going forward with her life, meeting someone else, falling in love, and forgetting about him. It hurt more to think of her stuck where she was, never able to move past what had happened. As much as he wanted her, he wanted her happiness more. With a sigh he leaned back against the couch and kicked his feet up on the coffee table. A glance at the clock told him it was after midnight, but he knew no matter what he did, it would be hours before he could sleep.

Every time he closed his eyes, hell, every time he *blinked* he saw Beth's image. If Hume found out he'd gone to the gallery, his week of administrative leave could turn into a suspension or worse. Oddly enough, at this point he really didn't care. He reached for his beer and took a long swig.

She had looked breathtaking. As he pictured her in the deep red dress, the familiar stirring started low in his abdomen. The faint scent of her perfume, the softness of her skin, and the lush curves of her mouth taunted him. Something in his chest constricted and an image of the two of them in the middle of Mason Lockhart's enormous bed flashed in his mind. Bear forced the thought aside with a low growl. After finishing his beer, he rose and walked to the window of his loft, staring at the street below without really seeing it.

He rubbed his eyes as he thought of the days, weeks, and possibly months to come. Perez had been arraigned and the State's Attorney planned to convene a Grand Jury before the end of the week. Once the Grand Jury handed down an indictment, the real circus would begin. He knew from experience a case of this nature could take six months to a year or longer just to get a verdict. The six days between when he had last seen her at the Bureau and the gallery showing had seemed like an eternity. He only hoped that time and distance would dull the ache inside him. Somehow, he doubted it.

"Way to go," he said softly, pinching the bridge of his nose. "You're going to pay for this one for a *while*."

A truck stopped in front of his building, and his eyes immediately focused on the vehicle. It was Jack's quad-cab, and he wasn't at all surprised when Jack got out, looked up at him, and then entered the building. Bear sighed and waited a minute before he walked over to the front door. He opened it just as Jack reached the landing, stepping back as his friend walked past him. Bear swung the door shut, walked to the couch, and sat down.

"What are you doing here, Jack? Shouldn't you be at home with your lovely wife?"

Jack sat down on a large armchair facing the couch and rested his elbows on his knees. "You okay?"

Bear fixed him with a bored look. "I'm fine. How am I supposed to be?"

Jack's brows drew together. "In case you've forgotten, I've been *exactly* where you are. I know what it feels like."

For some reason, the understanding in Jack's eyes made him

angry. Bear scowled. "No, you don't. What you and Laine went through was much worse."

"Which makes me even more qualified to help."

"I don't need *help*."

Jack sat up. "What do you need?"

The anger in his chest burned a little brighter, warming him, and not in a good way. He kept his face impassive. "What I *don't* need is another lecture about me and Beth."

"This isn't about *her*, it's about *you*." Jack stared at him. "You know, sometimes being your friend is a real bitch."

Bear glared at him. "Why is that?"

"Because you won't let anyone *be* a friend." He rose and stuffed his hands in his pockets. "I love you like a brother. I know that no matter what you've got my back, that you'd take a bullet for me, like I would for you. But outside of work . . . ?" His eyes narrowed. "Outside of work you hold everyone at arm's length, *including* me."

Bear had no reply for that. Normally he had no trouble arguing with his friend, but he knew better than to get into a debate he couldn't win. He merely remained silent and returned Jack's gaze.

"Trust me, Bear, you won't be any less formidable if you admit you're hurting."

Bear scowled. "I'm not worried about my intimidation index." He stood. "Besides, wounded animals are always more dangerous."

Jack's brows rose and his expression sobered. He watched Bear carefully and then said, "Well . . . that's a start."

They battled visually for several seconds before Bear broke eye contact and returned to his post by the window. "I could've lost my badge for what I did tonight."

Jack moved to his side. "I know." He chuckled. "You push the envelope a lot, Bear, but tonight you broke the sound barrier."

"And I'd do it again," Bear said in a low voice, "because for the first time in almost fifteen years I don't care." The anger sputtered out as a cold wave of sadness filled his chest cavity. "I finally met a woman who sees *me*, not my size, not my job, not the badge. She sees *me*, Jack." He sighed and pinched the bridge of his nose. "And I've already lost her."

"*No*, you *haven't.*"

"The trial could take months, even years. I don't expect her to put her life on hold until I'm free." He stared at the building across the street. "If she even feels the same by that time, which we both know may *not* be the case. Hell, whatever feelings she thinks she has for me could vanish before the trial even *starts*."

"I don't think you give her enough credit." Jack leaned a shoulder against the window frame. "She's not some twenty-something girl who doesn't know who she is or what she wants. She's a woman with a career, friends, and a life."

"Exactly." Bear glanced at him. "She has a life, and I want her to live it."

"Stop it."

"Stop what?"

"Stop being so damn self-sacrificing," Jack shot back. "Fight for yourself for a change. You deserve to be happy just as much as the next guy." He frowned. "Nothing ventured, nothing gained."

Bear thought about that for a moment. "Nothing ventured, nothing lost either."

"Seriously?" Jack gaped at him. "Knowing what you stand to lose or, more appropriately, *who* you stand to lose, are you really going to play it safe?"

"I don't have a choice right now, do I?" he asked dryly.

"And if you did?"

Bear lifted one brow and gave Jack a blasé look. "I sure as hell wouldn't be standing here talking to *you*."

Jack seemed surprised by that and then he smiled. "Oh. Outstanding." A mischievous twinkle entered his eyes. "I'll tell Laine that as soon as this trial wraps, we'll be double-dating. She'll *love* that."

"Throttle back, Cupid," Bear said. "By the time the trial wraps, Beth may have moved on." The very thought put a cloud of dark, damp melancholy square over his head, but he kept his expression neutral. He shrugged. "You'll still be able to double-date. It just won't be with me."

Jack put a hand on his shoulder. "Bear, I saw Beth's face after you left. That woman *loves* you. The only way that will change is if *you* kill it."

Chapter Twenty-Five

"Elizabeth."

Beth slid her blouse on. "Just a minute, Andy. I'm almost dressed."

"Elizabeth, open the door."

He sounded strange and Beth frowned. She buttoned the shirt as she crossed to the bedroom door and opened it. She stepped back as he walked past her. "What's the matter? I told you I was almost ready. We still have," she paused and looked at the clock on the nightstand, "an hour before I have to be at the courthouse. That's plenty of time." With a shake of her head she grinned and stepped into her heels. "Worried we'll be late for opening arguments? I know how you love your *Law and Order.*"

She walked to her dresser and picked up the strand of pearls laying there. As she went to fasten them, she glimpsed Andrew's face in the mirror and paused, a flutter of uneasiness brushing coldly against her skin. Beth put the necklace down and faced him. "Andy, what's going on? Why do you look like someone just shot your dog?"

Andrew blanched and took a deep breath. "You're not going to court today."

Beth rolled her eyes. "Another delay?" She turned and picked up the pearls. "What now? The defense can't find any character witnesses for their client? Big surprise." After fastening the necklace, she grabbed a brush and pulled it through her hair. "Perez's lawyers have been doing this for more than three months now. You'd think the judge would be sick to death of all these motions and requests for continuance."

Andrew approached her, took the brush from her, and gently clasped her hands, his expression solemn. Another chill went through her. He met her gaze, his dark green eyes filled with sadness. "There's been an incident at the courthouse."

Apprehension prickled over her skin. There had been an incident at the courthouse. Bear would be at the courthouse. That equation sent a chill straight through her. She swallowed hard against the fear worming up her throat. "What do you mean?"

Andrew opened his mouth to speak, but no words came out, and the fear crawling up her esophagus started to morph into panic. Andrew Shaw was *never* at a loss for words. *Never*. He looked down at their intertwined fingers and sighed. "Come with me, love."

Ever since she'd been discharged from the hospital after Perez's arrest, Beth had been living with Andrew in his lakeside mansion. The house was enormous and fully staffed, the grounds expansive, lush, and meticulously manicured, and the security system gave Fort Knox a run for its money. Armed guards patrolled the perimeter 24/7, and everywhere she went she had an armed escort. The only security measure Andrew *didn't* have in place, at least not to her knowledge, was an active minefield. Then again, he *had* told her to stay away from the freshly planted garden on the east side of the property . . . . She'd accused him of being paranoid, and his reply had been:

"Just because I'm paranoid doesn't mean they're not after me."

He was silent as they walked the wide, vaulted hallways toward the north side of the house where the massive, professionally appointed and fully staffed kitchen was. Hanging on the wall behind the breakfast nook was a sixty-four inch LCD TV, and her eyes were immediately drawn to the brilliant screen. The woman reporter for the local news on that screen was the stereotypical California blonde wearing a navy blue blazer, white blouse, modest jewelry, with perfect hair and makeup. The courthouse behind her was an impressive backdrop.

". . . are sketchy at this point. What we do know is two people were killed and several more injured after a gunman opened fire on law enforcement officers just outside the Federal Courthouse. The identities of the wounded have not been released at this time but . . . ."

It took a second for what the bottle-blonde had said to register, but when it did Beth's knees gave out and her heart dropped. Andrew quickly steered her into a chair. Her eyes welled and she looked at him. "No."

"I don't know, love," Andrew said softly. "All I know is one of the agents sent to pick you up got a call just after he arrived informing him of the shooting. He and his partner have been ordered to stay here and guard you."

Covering her mouth with one hand, Beth squeezed her eyes shut and tried not to panic. She knew Bear would be at the courthouse and knowing Bear, if there *was* a shootout he would be front and center regardless of the circumstances. And he wouldn't be alone. Jack would be right there with him. *Oh, God, no. Oh, please keep them safe.* Fear and despair raced through her, jockeying for the position of dominance, and neither was winning. She remembered the day Bear had shown up at the truck stop all cut up and bleeding with a bullet wound to the shoulder. Fear suddenly took the lead, leaving a cold trail in her veins. With a strangled sob, Beth jumped to her feet and ran for the front of the house.

"Elizabeth, wait!"

Beth sprinted out of the house and down the long driveway, heels be damned. The guard at the gate saw her coming and the heavy, wrought iron barrier started to roll slowly to the left. She shot through the opening. The agents tasked to escort her to the courthouse were sitting in their car parked a few feet away from the driveway, and when they saw her both of them exited the vehicle. She recognized Special Agents Devereaux and Jones from her stay at the hospital. Beth ran straight for Devereaux, who was closer.

"What happened?" she demanded, grasping the front of his jacket with both hands. Devereaux looked decidedly uncomfortable and his uneasiness only fed the fear reproducing like rabbits on steroids inside of her. She jerked on his jacket. "*What happened?*"

He gently pried her fingers loose and cradled her hands in his. He looked down at her, silent and unmoving, his dark brown eyes filled with sympathy and concern.

"We don't know, Miss Drummond." He glanced at Jones, who had both hands on the hood of the car, his expression grim. Devereaux met her gaze. "All we know is at least one agent and two deputies are down. We don't know how serious the injuries are or who's hurt." He sighed heavily. "They took the wounded to Memorial Hospital. That's all we know, I swear."

She glanced at Jones who nodded succinctly. Beth covered her face with her hands for a moment and tried to take a normal breath. "Thank you." Then it clicked. Memorial Hospital. Her head snapped up just as Andrew managed to reach her. "Laine."

Beth turned on her heel and raced toward the house.

"Elizabeth!"

She ran inside and down the hall to her room. Once inside the opulent suite, she grabbed for the cell phone charging on the nightstand, and jerked the phone and charger out of the wall. Tears blurred her vision and she cried out in frustration, her hands shaking so badly she couldn't dial. Andrew appeared and pried the phone from her fingers. He led her to the edge of the bed, sat her down, and crouched in front of her.

"What's the number, love?"

Beth stuttered out the number, emotion clogging her throat as Andrew calmly dialed. He listened for a few seconds and then handed the phone to her.

"Dr. Vaughn."

Beth took a great, gulping breath. "Laine . . . ?"

"Beth?"

"Laine, tell me he's okay. *Please* tell me they're both okay." The line was silent for a few seconds and Beth's heart dropped like a stone. She exhaled sharply and tears poured.

"Jack is fine, but Bear took one shot point blank to the chest," Laine finally said, her voice low and subdued.

Beth felt the floor open up beneath her and had the oddest sensation of floating in midair. The feeling was what she imagined a skydiver felt just after leaving the airplane, and then the realization that she was without a parachute sent panic clawing at her insides with sharp, ragged nails.

"He's okay, Beth. He was wearing a vest. In fact, he's already been discharged and Jack just took him home."

When Laine's statement finally registered, her lungs quite literally stopped functioning, refusing to either inhale or exhale. Beth dropped the phone as a wave of dizziness spun her. Leaning over and laying her chest on her thighs, she blinked slowly several times as the world spun crazily, images and shapes of the room wavering as if her retinas had been replaced with funhouse mirrors.

She saw Andrew pick up the phone and put it to his ear. His lips were moving, but all she heard was the sound of her own heartbeat whooshing in her ears. Tears fell, plopping onto the carpeted floor, but still she couldn't draw air. After Andrew hung up the phone, he knelt in front of her and took her in his arms.

"Breathe, darling. Breathe."

His voice sounded very far away, soft, and oddly muffled. As his hands moved slowly over her back, sheer survival instinct kicked in and she took a great, gasping gulp of air. A wave of nausea burgeoned sharply in her belly and she pushed him away. She barely made it to the toilet before her stomach rejected her earlier breakfast, but Andrew was right there, holding back her hair as she vomited. Sharp, stabbing pains cut through her abdomen and her stomach continued to curl in on itself, as if she was being kicked in the gut by a number of unseen opponents. When the spasms finally passed, her legs gave out. She sat on the cold, tile floor and leaned against the smooth wall.

The painted drywall was cool beneath her cheek, her breath coming in short gasps, her eyes closed. Behind her, she heard the faucet turn on briefly.

"Here."

Beth opened one eye and looked at the glass of water in Andrew's outstretched hand. He pressed it into her shaking fingers and wrapped his fingers around hers to steady them as she lifted the cup to her lips. She took several small sips and released the tumbler. Andrew put the glass on a shelf over the toilet and crouched at her side.

"Feel better?"

Her breathing finally back to normal, Beth nodded slowly.

"Then let's get you up and out of here." Andrew put a hand beneath her elbow. "The floor of the loo is for people who are sick or drunk. You, love, are neither."

Beth let him help her to her feet and was thankful for his

strength as her legs wobbled dangerously. He walked her back to the bed and sat her down. He knelt and slipped her pumps off her feet. After putting her heels aside, he sat next to her and tucked her hair behind one ear.

"You've had quite a shock, darling," he said softly. "Why don't you lay down, rest for a bit?"

"No." Beth shook her head. "I have to see him. I *need* to see him."

He rested a hand on her knee. "The FBI won't *let* you see him, love. You could try, but I doubt those agents sitting in front of my house will just let you drive off by yourself."

Beth turned toward him and wound her fingers through his. "Please, Andy. I just need a few minutes."

"They're not going to let me take you anywhere." His gaze wandered over her face. "They've already told me to keep you inside and away from any windows, whatever that means."

"So don't tell them." She held his hands to her chest. "You *do* have to go to the gallery today anyway, don't you?" When he nodded she shrugged. "I'll just . . . tag along and keep my head down. Who's to know?"

Andrew stared at her for a moment, then smiled and kissed her brow. "I think your FBI agent is rubbing off on you." He rose and held out a hand. "Come on. Let's get you to your Bear."

"I'll change and meet you in the garage." She placed her fingers in his. "And, let's take the Audi. That Q7 sits higher than the FBI's sedan."

Ten minutes later Beth was dressed, her hair pulled back into a ponytail. She made her way quickly through the house, careful to avoid the servants, and entered the attached five-car garage. Inside the large space were two Mercedes coupes, a Porsche 911 convertible, an Audi R8 sports car, and an Audi Q7 3.0 TDI, the top of the line SUV for Audi. The $90,000 vehicle was Andrew's favorite, and he gave Beth a quick grin as she opened the back door and draped herself across the rear floor. Andrew climbed into the driver's seat, started the engine, and activated the garage door. After backing out, he turned the wheel, put the engine in drive, and headed for the gate. Beth's heart started to thud as the vehicle slowed and then stopped.

"Morning, gentlemen," he said in a cheery voice. "Any news?"

"No," Special Agent Jones replied. "Where are you going?"

"As much as I would love to laze around my house all day long, I *do* have a business to run." Beth smiled as Andrew continued. "I'm going to the gallery."

"Where is Miss Drummond?"

"Resting. I gave her a Valium and put her to bed. Poor dear has had a rather difficult morning."

"I understand. We're all in shock."

"Yes, well, if you gents need anything, the staff has been

instructed to accommodate you. Just . . . let Elizabeth rest. The last thing she needs right now is to be interrogated or harassed."

"Of course, Mr. Shaw, and thanks."

"You're most welcome. Good day."

Beth held her breath and stayed put, unwilling to tempt fate as he drove away.

"How are you doing back there, love?"

"I'm fine." Her eyes stung and she reached between the front seats to touch his arm. "Thank you for doing this."

"Not at all." He tossed her a jaunty grin over his shoulder. "I find I'm rather enjoying myself."

"Last time I did this Bear was driving and I was scared out of my mind." She sighed. "I can't believe it's been more than three months since I've seen him." Her hand fell to her side. "I wonder if he ever thinks about me."

Andrew snorted derisively. "The man risked his career to see you on your opening night, love. I'd say that puts you pretty high on his priority list."

Beth blinked at him. "How did you . . . ?"

He glanced at her, a mischievous twinkle in his eyes. "Didn't I tell you I installed security cameras in the alley?"

Her brows rose. "Umm, *no.*"

He chuckled. "Well, I did. But don't worry." He wiggled his eyebrows. "The evidence has been erased. That was quite a passionate embrace, by the way. Wish I'd had audio to go with the video."

"Andy!" Heat rose in her cheeks and she covered her eyes with one hand. "Just . . . drive."

"I'm driving, love." He laughed softly. "I'm driving."

****

Bear stuffed another pillow behind his head and winced as pain radiated across his chest. He repositioned the icepack and closed his eyes. He could hear Jack rooting around in his refrigerator and a minute later a cold bottle was pressed into his hand. He looked at the Gatorade and snapped the lid off.

"Thanks, bud," he said.

"You bet, big guy." Jack stood at the side of the bed. "You sure you don't want any painkillers? Laine said she'd call in some of the good stuff for you, if you wanted."

"No." Bear took a long drink and leaned his head back. "There's some ibuprofen in that drawer behind you. That'll do."

Jack chuckled and the drawer opened and then closed. Bear listened to the rattle of pills as Jack shook the bottle, and he held out a hand. Jack dropped the capsules onto his palm.

Bear popped the pills into his mouth, drained the Gatorade, and handed the empty bottle to Jack. "Thanks, brother."

"Don't mention it. You *did* take a bullet for me earlier."

Bear smirked. "I wouldn't have had to if you had been paying more attention."

Jack laughed. "A thousand apologies for being shorter than you." He went quiet and his expression sobered. "Thanks, Bear. If you hadn't pushed me out of the way—"

Bear silenced him with a glare. "I *really* hate that fucking word," he growled. He stared at Jack for a moment and gave him a small smile. "You're welcome. You'd do the same for me. Enough said." He closed his eyes. "Get out. I want to take a nap."

Jack nodded. "Alright. I'll be in the living room if you need anything."

"You don't have to babysit me," Bear said. "I have some cracked ribs, that's it. I'm not crippled or immobile."

"Sorry, but Laine said if I leave you here alone, she'll skin me alive." He shrugged and stuffed his hands in his pockets as he walked toward the bedroom door. "She trumps you. After all, I have to sleep with her."

"Wow, you *have* to." Bear rolled his eyes. "How*ever* do you manage?"

Jack chuckled. "Get some rest, big guy. Holler if you need anything."

"All I need is to be alone for a while," he shot back. "And keep the volume on the TV down."

Once the door closed behind Jack, Bear started counting backwards from one hundred. He'd just reached seventy-two when he heard a knock on his front door. He opened his eyes and his brows drew together as he listened to Jack open the door and converse with someone in hushed tones. A second later the door closed. Good. He wasn't in the mood for company right now.

Bear closed his eyes and started counting backwards again, but before he even reached ninety-five, there was a soft knock on his bedroom door. Jack didn't wait for a response. He opened the door and stuck his head in.

"You have a visitor."

Bear scowled and closed his eyes. "I don't want to see anyone. I've answered enough questions for one morning. Tell them I'm asleep and to see me at the office when I go back."

Jack gave him a pointed look. "I think you're going to want to see this one." He stood to the side and pushed the door fully open.

Bear's heart leapt when he met those familiar, beautiful, golden eyes. He sat up and winced in pain.

"Hi," she said from the doorway, her voice hushed.

"Beth."

She took two steps into the room and hesitated, biting her lip as she did so. Jack glanced between them and smiled.

"I think I'll leave you two alone."

Bear looked at him. "Thanks, Jack."

He paused in the doorway. "Anytime." Then he was gone.

Bear closed his eyes briefly, and then focused on Beth and waved her forward. She blinked rapidly as she moved to his side, and her chin trembled briefly before she eased down onto the edge of the bed. He reached for her hand and wound her fingers through hers.

"What are you doing here?"

"I know I shouldn't be here." She sniffled. "But I had to see you."

"How did you find out where I lived?" Before she could say anything, the light bulb went on. "Laine." When she nodded he smiled inwardly. *Thank you, Laine.*

"Are you okay?" she asked in a whisper.

"I'm fine, sweetheart. Never better."

And he meant it. The cracked ribs, the bruises, the minor concussion, all of it melted away as the scent of her shampoo drifted to him. He had dreamt of seeing her again ever since he'd left her standing in the alley, and he was almost afraid to believe she was really here.

"What happened?" she asked.

His gaze wandered over her face. God, he loved looking at her. Because of all the media coverage regarding the murders, the links to Mexican cartels, and Beth's showing, she'd become quite the celebrity. She'd even made national news. Since the story had gone public, Laine had gathered every photograph, newspaper article, and interview done with Beth and put them into an album for him. He'd fought the urge at first, but after about a week of staring at the cover, he had opened it, and now he found himself looking through it every night before he went to bed. He even recorded her scheduled TV appearances, but seeing her in person was much better than seeing her on his LCD screen. He rememorized her features and tucked a fall of mahogany hair behind her ear. "Don't worry about it." Her brows drew together and the spark of anger in her eyes almost made him smile.

"Bear." She blinked rapidly and dropped her chin. "Tell me."

"Don't tell me what to do."

Her head snapped up and her mouth opened. She stared at him and the sadness he saw reflected in those golden pools nearly undid him.

"Please." Her eyes pleaded with him. "At least I know *you'll* tell me the truth."

Bear dragged his knuckles slowly over her cheek. "It was Montoya."

Her brows shot up and her eyes widened. He continued.

"Jack and I were talking with the State's Attorney and I thought I saw him out of the corner of my eye. With all the reporters and cameramen and trial groupies . . . I wasn't sure." He stared at the ceiling. "There were . . . *hundreds* of people in front of the courthouse, and by the time my line of sight cleared and I realized I hadn't imagined him . . . he had a bead on us." Bear looked at her out of the corner of his eye. "I pushed Jack and the State's Attorney out of the way, but he got off two shots before I even drew my weapon. One missed, one didn't. Thankfully, *he* wasn't wearing a vest, and I *don't* miss."

She closed her eyes and took a shaky breath. "Oh, my God."

He cupped her cheek. "I'm fine, sweetheart. Some fractured ribs, hit my head pretty hard on the courthouse steps, but I'm *fine.*"

"Would you tell me if you weren't?"

He studied her face for a few seconds and then moved over a bit and patted the mattress next to him. "Come here." Beth stretched out beside him, her head tucked into the crook of his neck, her hand flat on his belly. It was the same pose she'd assumed the first night they'd spent together. Bear closed his eyes and sighed as her body nestled against his. "Now, that's more like it."

"Bear—"

"Hush." He clasped his hands together, enclosing her in his arms. "I want to hold you for as long as I can." She sniffled again and he felt her tears on his neck.

"Okay," she whispered. Then she fell silent.

He wasn't sure how long they'd lain there, but her breathing had evened out and deepened, telling him she was asleep. He was half asleep himself, and was just falling into dreamland when there was another soft knock and the door to his room opened. His eyes narrowed on Jack.

"What?"

Jack smiled when he saw Beth and he leaned against the door frame. "Sorry to interrupt, but I just got off the phone with Hume and wanted to give you an update." He gave Bear a knowing look. "I would say I'm surprised she came, but I'm really not. It appears your theory was wrong, big guy. Doesn't look like she's moved on to me."

"Whatever." Bear scowled. "So give me this update and get out so I can get back to sleep."

Jack chuckled. "Roger that. Hume says the coroner found something very interesting." He paused and took a breath. "It looks like Montoya was tortured prior to his visit to the courthouse."

"Tortured?" He frowned. "What do you mean?"

"Somebody worked him over pretty hard. The bruises are fresh, he's got broken ribs, cigarette burns all over his body, *dozens* of them, and the only fingers that *weren't* broken were his thumb, index, and middle finger on his gun hand. Looks like someone . . . *creatively* persuaded Montoya to take you out." Jack's expression darkened. "He probably knew he had *one* chance. That's why he risked getting so close to you before firing."

"Cárdenas."

"It's a distinct possibility." Jack's brows rose. "So much for you being safe."

Bear's insides tightened like a spring. "Son of a bitch." He closed his eyes briefly and tightened his hold on Beth just a bit. "You need to get her out of here and into protective custody. Now."

"I really don't think that will be necessary."

"Why not?"

"Perez is dead."

Bear blinked and stared at Jack, uncertain if he'd heard correctly. "I'm sorry, what?"

Jack glanced at Beth. "About fifteen seconds after Montoya shot at us, a sniper got Perez as he was being led from the transport vehicle to the rear of the courthouse. Large caliber that almost took Perez's head completely off. Wounded two deputies, too." Jack crossed his arms over his chest. "I think Montoya was just a diversion, something to draw as many LEOs away from Perez as possible so the sniper would have a cleaner shot."

"Are the deputies okay?"

Jack sighed softly. "One will be fine. The other underwent emergency surgery and is currently in ICU. Only time will tell."

A phone ringing broke the quiet and Beth stirred. The noise came from the plastic bag from the hospital filled with Bear's belongings. Bear gave Jack a pointed look. Jack quickly fished the cell phone out of the bag and glanced at the display.

"Number is blocked." He held the phone out.

Bear took the cell, hit the button, and put it to his ear. "Bristol."

"Special Agent Bristol. I am happy to hear your voice."

Bear looked at Jack and mouthed, "Cárdenas." He eased out from under Beth and sat up, wincing when pain rippled across his chest and abdomen. She stirred, but didn't wake. "I'll bet, Don Cárdenas. Sorry your assassin wasn't successful in taking me out."

"So . . . you *were* involved. The news reports didn't say, but my *other* sources . . . ." The line was silent for a few seconds, and when the Don spoke again, his voice was low and level. "I can understand why you would think I sent Montoya after you, Special Agent Bristol, but I assure you I am deeply upset by today's events. I did not *anticipate* this, a truly regrettable lack of foresight on my part."

"Meaning?"

"Meaning, you were never the intended target."

"Tell that to Montoya," Bear shot back.

"I would," the Don said slowly, "but you killed him, did you not?"

"And you killed Perez. Or, more appropriately, you *had* him killed."

"You will never prove that."

Bear frowned. "You told me you wanted him dead."

"I'm a parent grieving the loss of my only son. Of course

my baser instincts want Ramon's killer dead, which is entirely understandable." Cárdenas sighed softly. "Were you not the one who said there might be a way we could both get what we wanted?" There was a brief pause. "My guess is Montoya simply took aim at the largest target he saw, and he is familiar with you, yes? We cannot ask the dead what was in their mind, now can we?"

"Why are you telling me this?" Bear growled.

"Because I said that you would be safe, for the time being, and I meant it," Cárdenas replied. "I do not give my word lightly, and while you may not hold my word in much esteem, there are those who do, even if it was given to a cop."

Bear lifted one brow. "So, in other words, this looks bad on your résumé."

The Don chuckled. "You have a way of cutting through the bullshit, Special Agent Bristol. I like that about you."

"And that's all, I'll wager."

"I would like you more if you worked for me."

Bear laughed derisively. "*Never* going to happen."

"I didn't think so."

"I know you didn't."

The man was quiet, and then he said, "I suppose this means I owe you some consideration the next time we meet."

Bear looked at Jack who was watching him closely. "I'll take it, but the chances of us meeting again are pretty small. The DEA has more interest in you than I, no offense."

Cárdenas chuckled. "No offense taken, although I am rather disappointed." He paused. "In a different world, I believe you and I could have become friends."

"It would have to be a *very* different world, Don Cárdenas, but I can't say I completely disagree with you."

The Don laughed. "Well, that is something. Good day, Special Agent Bristol, and again, my apologies. I wish you a full and speedy recovery."

The line clicked off and Bear looked at the phone for a moment before tossing it to Jack.

Jack stared at him expectantly. "Well?"

Bear lifted one brow. "According to the Don, I was never the target."

"Did he say who was?"

"Of course not, but I could infer from our conversation that you were right in your assessment. Montoya was just a diversion." He walked slowly back to the bed. "He wasn't *supposed* to shoot at me, he just did."

Jack watched as Bear slid in next to Beth and assumed his former position. "I guess I can understand that. If *I* only had three working fingers on my gun hand, I'd take aim at the largest target I could find." A grin twitched about Jack's mouth. "That's *always* going to be you, Bear."

Bear snorted. "What else is new?"

"*That* is," Jack said with a nod at Beth. Jack gave him an I-told-you-so smile. "Laine is right. You two *do* make a good looking couple."

Bear frowned. "Don't start."

Jack held up his hands in surrender, but the grin belied his passive gesture. "I'm not starting anything, but it looks like *you* are."

"Get out."

"No problem." Jack walked to the door. "Should I lock it behind me?"

"Get. Out."

Jack laughed softly and Bear scowled as the door closed behind him. Once he and Beth were alone, he pressed his lips to her brow and rested his chin atop her head as she snuggled closer. Bear closed his eyes with a sigh.

"Now . . . where were we?"

Chapter Twenty-Six

Beth felt something stroking over her right forearm and her eyelids fluttered open. For a moment she wasn't sure where she was and then the morning came back in a rush that made her suck in a breath. Her head snapped up and she sighed in relief when she saw Bear's face. He was looking at something, his brows drawn together. She glanced down at her inner forearm and the long, thin, red line that ran nearly from her elbow to her wrist. His fingers were lightly tracing the mark.

"Looks like a surgical scar," he commented.

Beth pulled away and dropped her chin. "It is." Her stomach twisted and vivid pictures flashed in her head. She took a deep breath and concentrated on willing those images back into the box where they couldn't hurt her. "How long . . . how long have I been asleep?"

"A couple of hours." He was quiet for a moment. "Are you ever going to tell me what happened?"

"I had . . . an accident." She tucked in beneath his chin. "Shattered my radius and ulna. Took three surgeries and a year of physical therapy, but now I'm all better." Closing her eyes, she relaxed against him. "I don't . . . talk about it. That was a really bad day."

"I imagine so."

"You wear a number of scars I could ask *you* about."

He chuckled. "Go ahead. Those were all bad days and almost all work related. No secrets there."

Beth opened her eyes. "Do you . . . do you ever think of doing something else, something . . . *less* dangerous?"

"Nope." He kissed her brow. "Sorry."

She sat up and looked at him. "Why are you sorry?"

He watched her for a few moments, his expression speculative. "When I meet a woman, the first thing she's usually attracted to is my size, and when she finds out what I do for a living she thinks it's exciting, at least in the beginning." He paused and looked at the wall. "But that's only temporary. It wears thin for most women really fast, because many times the job has to come first." He turned his head slightly and met her gaze. "That's not how I want it, that's just how it is."

She gave him a smile. "For the record, I can't imagine you doing anything else. I just wondered if *you* had." His brows rose and she turned her gaze to her lap. "You're *really* good at your job, Bear. It's what you were born to do."

"Well . . . ." He took a breath. "*That's* a first."

She looked at him through her lashes. "Sorry to screw up the curve."

He tucked her hair behind one ear and shook his head. "Don't be."

"Also for the record," she continued, "your size was *not* the first thing I was attracted to. It was your smile." He lifted one blonde brow and she looked away from him, heat crawling up her neck. "I remember the very first time you smiled at me. We were running through the woods, and I had a feeling you were pacing yourself so you didn't wear me out."

"You told me if you broke a leg I'd know."

Beth met his gaze and smiled, but before she could speak, there was a light tap on the door. She looked over her shoulder as Jack peeked in.

"Hey there," he said.

"What's up?" Bear asked.

He leaned against the jamb. "Since you're refusing to talk to anyone, Director Hume and the State's Attorney are on their way *here* to finish your debrief." He looked at Beth. "I need to get you out of here."

Her stomach dropped.

"Andy is on his way." Jack looked between the two of them and reached for the door handle. "I'll give you a couple of minutes."

"Thanks, Jack," Bear said softly.

Jack smiled. "Anytime."

When they were alone again, Beth exhaled sharply and closed her eyes as her stomach cramped. "I hate this." Bear said nothing and she glanced at him. His face was blank, as usual, and suddenly she wanted to yell at him. Instead, she looked away. "When will I see you again?"

"I don't know, sweetheart," he replied softly.

At least he was still calling her sweetheart. That was something. Beth sighed. "So, I guess . . . this is goodbye. Again."

"Hey." He pressed a hand to her cheek and turned her face to his. "We'll see each other sooner than you think."

She closed her eyes and covered his hand with hers. "The trial will take months, Bear. How is that sooner?"

"There's not going to be a trial."

Beth's lids snapped open and she stared at him. "What? Why?"

Bear's fingers moved slowly over her skin. "Perez is dead." Her brows rose and her mouth dropped open. He smiled grimly. "No defendant, no trial."

She blinked at him. "Then . . . I don't have to leave."

His expression sobered. "Yes, you do. It'll take the State's Attorney a few days to officially close the case. Until then, we still have to act as if there is going to be a trial. At least, *I* still have to act as if there is going to be a trial. Sorry, sweetheart, it's part of the job."

"Of course." She slid off the bed. "I'm sorry."

Bear grabbed her hand. "Stop apologizing," he said with a frown. "Save your apologies for when they're actually necessary."

Beth nodded and looked down at their intertwined fingers. Her eyes stung, but she blinked back the tears. "I'll miss you."

"Not half as much as I'll miss you."

She turned to leave, but he tugged on her hand and pulled her back. He sat up, cupped one hand behind her neck, and pulled her to him. He froze just before their lips touched. His eyes searched hers for a few moments, and then he kissed her. It was a warm, deep, leisurely kiss, and embers sparked to life inside her, sending heat fanning over her skin. Suddenly, she couldn't breathe. When he finally pulled back, her lungs were burning, but for some reason she still couldn't draw air. He pressed his brow to hers.

"I'll see you soon," he whispered.

Beth couldn't speak. She looked into his eyes, then brushed his lips with hers and nodded. Without a word, she turned and left the room.

****

Bear looked up from his laptop when there was a light rap on the frame of his open office door. He started to rise, but Director Hume waved a hand at him and walked over to one of the armchairs facing Bear's desk. Bear laced his fingers and flattened them on the blotter.

"It's done, Special Agent Bristol," Hume said as he seated himself. "The State's Attorney has officially closed the Perez case."

Bear nodded slowly and contemplated his desk blotter. "Does that mean I can go back to my leave of absence now, sir?"

Hume's expression was solemn. "Is that what you want?"

Bear closed his laptop. "Yes."

"The Paulson case is still pending."

"Doubt *that* will happen before Christmas." He rolled his eyes. "I'll be back *long* before then."

Hume looked at him speculatively for a few moments, and then straightened his tie and rose. "Then consider yourself back on leave."

Bear stood. "One thing, sir."

Hume's brows drew together. "What?"

"Now that the Perez case is done, I plan to start dating Beth Drummond."

"Are you sure about that, son?" He gave Bear an I-wouldn't-do-that-if-I-were-you look. "I was there when you got involved with Deirdre Franklin, and I remember what that did to you."

Bear took a breath. "I appreciate your concern, sir, but Beth Drummond is not Deirdre Franklin, and I am not the green rookie working his second case."

Hume's eyes narrowed and he pursed his lips. "True, you're definitely not a rookie, and I don't really think *veteran* is appropriate either."

"Sir?"

"Son, I've been with the Bureau for three decades." Hume fixed him with a pointed look. "Although you and I don't always agree, I consider you one of my best agents. During my career I have seen very few people with your level of inborn talent, skill, and instinct. If your gut tells you to go after Miss Drummond, then all I have to say is . . . go get her, Special Agent Bristol. Make us proud."

With that, Director Hume left his office and walked down the hall, whistling as he went.

****

Beth opened the door to her apartment, her arms laden with packages. She had her dress for that evening's showing over her shoulder in a plastic garment bag, and when she closed the door shut with her foot, it slid onto the floor. With a sigh of frustration Beth walked into the kitchen, put her other burdens down, then returned and picked the dress up from the floor. After hanging it on a rack near the door, she returned to the kitchen to put her groceries away.

It had been nearly a week since she'd last seen Bear, and she missed him every minute of every day. She glanced at the print she'd made from one of the pictures she'd taken of him at the cabin. She'd enlarged the image and it now hung on the wall next to her bedroom door. He was breathtaking, each muscle clearly defined, water glistening on his skin, that sharp gaze piercing her. Beth was transfixed. She closed her eyes as she remembered with vivid clarity the feel of his hard, muscular form pressed against hers. Desire flared to life inside her and a heaviness settled low in her belly.

Her cell phone rang, jerking her from her reverie. With a frown she pawed through her purse until she found the device. When she saw Bear's name on the caller ID, her heart somersaulted and she inhaled sharply. Beth pressed the button and put the phone to her ear.

"Hello?"

"Hi, sweetheart."

"Bear."

"How have you been?"

It took her a moment to find her voice. "Um, busy. You?"

"The same, but not anymore." He paused and her heart rate jumped. "The case has officially been closed, and that means . . . we need to talk."

He sounded serious, and a blade of uncertainty scored through her. The last time one of her boyfriends had said they 'needed to talk' she'd walked in on Michael having sex with her best friend. Beth blinked that image back and took a breath. "Okay. When?"

"You busy tonight?"

Beth swallowed the lump in her throat. "I . . . I have another showing at the gallery this evening. Just picked my dress up from the dry cleaners."

"Hmm."

"Come by," she suggested, not at all certain that was what she wanted. "We can talk there."

"I don't want to take you away from your work," he said, his voice carefully neutral.

His lack of inflection only intensified her uncertainty. Beth laughed, but it sounded forced even to her own ears. "It's Andy's work, not mine. I just have to make an appearance and then let him perform his magic." She took a breath and tried to calm the butterflies dive-bombing her insides. "We can talk in Andy's office, or there's a rooftop garden and terrace if you want something more private." He didn't say anything and it felt like a band of barbed wire was tightening around her chest. "Or, I can meet you somewhere once Andy releases me."

"No, I'll come by the gallery. I think Laine is going anyway, so I'll just tag along with her. See you about nine?"

She couldn't tell anything of his intentions from his voice and she pressed a hand to her brow. "Yeah, that's good. The showing starts at eight, so I should be done shaking the appropriate hands and smiling at all the right people by that time."

"Okay. I'll see you then."

"See you then."

Beth hung up the phone and sagged against the kitchen counter, anxiety tightening around her throat. She closed her eyes and tried to take slow, deep breaths. "Okay." She looked up at the ceiling. "Well, whoever arranged this, I have to believe you wouldn't have put Bear and I together only to rip us apart." She squeezed her eyes shut. "Please . . . don't let me be wrong."

****

Bear strode into Laine's kitchen at 8:15 p.m. and sent a wolf-whistle her way when she came downstairs, dressed in scrubs.

Laine rolled her eyes and pursed her lips. "Very funny."

"You didn't have to dress up for me," Bear said, unbuttoning his suit jacket. He leaned against the island. "What gives?"

Laine grabbed her purse from the table and plopped it on the island next to him. "Pile up on the Interstate." She started searching for something, her brow furrowed in frustration. "I got called in, so I can't go with you, big guy. Tell Beth I'm sorry, would you?"

"I have to go to this party alone?" Bear rubbed his chin. "Well *that* will kill my reputation."

Laine looked at him out of the corner of her eye and gave an unladylike snort. "Beth *will* be at the gallery." She continued to root around in her purse and smiled when she pulled out her keys. "I think your reputation will survive when they find out you're dating the hottest new photographer in the business."

"We're not dating . . . yet."

Laine froze and looked at him with brows raised. "Yet?" A smile started to form. "So you're going to risk it."

A flicker of uncertainty danced through him but he didn't let it show. "Should I not?"

"No," Laine said, "no, you *should*." Her smile deepened. "You *definitely* should."

He frowned. "So, why do you seem surprised?"

Laine looked at him for a few seconds and shook her head. She did a vertical scan. "Nice suit, Bear."

"Answer the question."

She fingered the sleeve. "Is that . . . Armani?"

Bear jerked away from her and scowled. "Yes."

Laine whistled. "You're really going all out for this, aren't you?"

He adjusted his tie. "I thought I should look . . . presentable."

"Oh, you look presentable." She gave him a wry grin. "You look *delicious*, and you're going to break the hearts of all the single women at the gallery. Some of the not-so-single women, too, I'll wager."

"*Why* do people keep saying that?" he asked, his brows drawing down.

Laine laughed and patted his arm. "Relax, big guy. As long as you don't break *Beth's* heart, you'll be just fine." She gave him a quick hug. "Now you should get going. And call me afterwards. I want to be kept in the loop."

The doubts he felt were a little harder to dismiss this time, settling coldly around his heart. "And if there's no loop?"

Laine grasped his hands. "Bear, you are one of the finest, best-looking, most charming men I know, aside from my hubby. Even if she *isn't* in love with you right now, as long as you leave Special Agent Bristol at home, you won't have to work very hard to change that." She squeezed his fingers and smiled up at him. "Now, do what you do best . . . and go get your girl."

****

Beth took a long sip of champagne and looked at the clock on the wall for the hundredth time it seemed. Soft music filled the gallery, setting an energetic yet relaxing ambiance. Uniformed wait-people flitted about in their white shirts and black bow-ties with champagne laden silver trays expertly balanced. Someone touched her arm and she jumped, spinning to face Andrew. His green eyes darkened with concern.

"Elizabeth, *what* is wrong with you? You've been like a cat on a hot plate all evening."

"I'm sorry, Andy." She dropped her chin and focused on the toes of her gold pumps.

"Don't be sorry, love. *Talk* to me."

Beth looked at her shoes for another moment, then lifted her head and drained her half full glass. After handing the empty flute to a passing waiter, she took a deep breath and faced her friend. "Bear called me today."

"Really?" Dark brows shot skyward. "Out of the blue?"

She nodded and leaned against the wall. "Yes. Apparently the Perez case is officially closed, and he said that meant we . . . *needed to talk.*"

"Isn't that *good* news?" Andrew asked, lightly grasping her upper arms. "I know how much you've missed him, and now that he's called, you're acting as if seeing him is the last thing on earth you want."

"No, I *want* to see him. It's just . . . ." Her voice trailed off and she dropped her chin. "He sounded so . . . *serious.* I'm not sure if I should be excited or apprehensive."

Andrew gently rubbed her arms. "I don't know your Special Agent Bristol, other than what you've told me and that scrumptious photograph, but he sounds like a serious chap." He moved to look her in the face. "Don't read anything into it, love. You will make yourself crazy for nothing."

Beth bit her lip and looked over Andrew's shoulder. "What . . . what if . . . ." The words stuck in her throat and she closed her eyes. "He said when this was over, my feelings for him would go away." Uneasiness coiled in her stomach, cold, heavy, and unyielding. "What if that's happened to him?"

Andrew curled a finger under her chin and tipped her face up. "Then he's not half as smart as you think he is." He smiled at her. "Is he a smart man?"

Beth took a deep breath and nodded. "He is, but since when does *love* involve *brains?*"

Andrew chuckled and moved to her side, his arm draping over her shoulders. "Your Federal agent sounds like the sort of man who considers *everything* he does *very* carefully." He searched her eyes. "Tell me if I'm wrong, Elizabeth."

She sighed heavily and ran a hand over her brow. "You're not wrong."

"All right then." He paused. "When is he supposed to arrive?"

"Nine o'clock."

Andrew glanced at his watch. "Well, that gives you about fifteen minutes to calm yourself down." He stepped away from her, grasped her shoulders, and turned her to face him. "Why don't you go up to my office, take your shoes off, get a glass of that *Grand Champagne* cognac you're so fond of, and *relax.*"

"But the showing?"

Andrew clucked his tongue in disapproval. "Don't worry about that, darling. You've already schmoozed the people I wanted you to, and they're just as impressed with you as I knew they would be. Now, it's my job to close the deals." He spun her away from him and gave her a light shove. "Cognac, my office, *now.*"

Beth had to admit a glass of cognac did sound pretty good. She nodded.

"Good." Andrew lightly smacked her backside. "I'll text you when I see him, that way you'll be ready."

Beth reached for his hand and squeezed his fingers lightly. "Thank you," she whispered.

He grinned at her and wiggled his perfectly shaped brows. "Anything for you, darling."

Beth walked toward the spiral staircase that led to Andrew's private office. His office was on the second floor, ran the length of the building, and overlooked the main gallery space. The upper half of the wall was thick Plexiglas so Andrew could oversee the gallery without having to be *in* the gallery. Beth carefully unfastened the chain hanging between the handrails with the sign that read "Authorized Personnel Only," stepped up two steps, and reattached the clip to the hook on the rail. Careful of her heels, she wound her way quickly up the narrow stairs and entered Andrew's private domain.

The door closed behind her and she inhaled deeply. She loved Andrew's office. It was tastefully decorated and always smelled like him, a mix of sandalwood and other exotic spices. The carpet was thick and expensive, the furnishings comfortable yet stylish, and even though it was obsessively neat and organized, it felt like a daddy's study, warm and inviting. The south end of the office was dominated by a large glass and metal desk. A wall of bookcases was filled with volumes on art, art history, and anything else having to do with the art world. In front of her was Andrew's liquor cabinet, and the other side of the office had an enormous leather couch and four large, comfortable, leather-covered chairs that formed an intimate seating area. Beth often napped on that couch. Next to the liquor cabinet was a door that led to the rooftop garden terrace. She tossed her clutch on a nearby table, kicked off her heels, found the cognac, and poured herself a liberal dose.

The walls of Andrew's office were covered in photographs and paintings, an odd and eclectic mix. Beth slowly sipped the cognac and the liquor warmed her throat and belly as she wandered slowly from frame to frame. In addition to collecting art, Andrew was an avid mountain-climber, and had done Everest twice before his fiftieth birthday. She smiled at the picture of him with his *Sherpa*, his arm around the tiny guide's shoulders, both men grinning as they stood on top of the world. Her toes sank into the plush carpeting, relieved to be out of her stilettos. With a sigh she moved to the couch, sat down, and picked up one of the many photo albums laying there.

She'd just gotten comfortable when her phone chirped, signaling an incoming text. Her heart stopped and she bolted upright, sending the photo album falling to the floor and splattering cognac on the table. Beth grabbed a handful of tissue from a nearby box to clean up the mess, then picked up the album and put it away.

The cognac soaked tissues went into a trash can and Beth ran a hand over her French twist. Taking several deep breaths, she walked over to the windows and rested her hands on the sill. Despite the crowd below, Bear was easy to spot.

A warm, bubbling sensation sprang up in her belly and filled her as she watched him enter the gallery. He looked amazing. The navy blue suit fit him perfectly, accentuating the great breadth of his shoulders and chest, narrowing sharply at the waist. She was pretty sure this was *not* one of his work suits. The fabric looked rich and had a faint sheen to it, which made it more suited to a formal affair than a day at the office. He looked like he belonged on a red carpet, and she noticed the appreciative female glances thrown his way as he walked toward the center of the room, his gaze searching.

As if sensing her perusal his eyes turned upward and met hers with the same striking, razor-sharp focus as they had the first day they'd met. In the next few seconds, Beth relived every moment she'd experienced since he'd saved her life: the adrenaline-filled runs, the terror, the quiet moments, the humor, and the passion. Her heart swelled and her eyes stung. She knew without a doubt that she loved this man with every fiber of her being. Once the admission was made, fear started whispering to her, soft and seductive, putting voice to the anxieties lurking inside her.

Apprehension burgeoned in dark, cold ripples as he stared at her, not a shred of emotion on his face. It was a look she was all too familiar with, and despite what Laine had said about him hiding something, her heart started to thump in a slow, painful rhythm against her sternum. She clenched her jaw and forced herself to maintain his gaze, but as each second ticked by the harder that became. Her throat tightened, sorrow seizing her lungs with vise-like fingers and squeezing. He neither moved nor blinked, and after nearly half a minute of staring at each other, Beth could stand no more. She took a deep breath, lifted her chin slightly, and gave him a short nod. Mustering what little dignity she had left, she turned on her heel and made her way to the roof, leaving the shattered remains of her heart on the floor of Andrew's office.

Chapter Twenty-Seven

Bear blinked when she disappeared from sight, snapped out of his reverie as the noise of the room returned to its normal volume. When he'd caught sight of her in the window, his heart had nearly stopped and all the sounds around him had faded into a hushed whisper. She was stunning. The shimmering gold cocktail dress was just a shade lighter than her eyes and reminded him vividly of the negligee from the cabin. He knew she'd mistaken his lack of response for something it wasn't and mentally kicked himself. He'd seen the flash of pain in her eyes before she'd turned away. He took a breath, held it for a second, and then exhaled as he made his way toward that spiral staircase. He reached for the chain with the APO sign, but before he could take hold of it, someone stepped in between him and the stairs. His brows drew together and he fixed the person with a scowl.

"Good evening, Special Agent Bristol."

The distinguished, tuxedoed gentleman was older, mid-to-late fifties, Bear guessed, with dark hair graying at the temples, a sun-kissed glow, and a distinctive British accent. His eyes were a dark green, his features chiseled but not sharp, and Bear knew he would turn the heads of just about any women no matter their age. The tuxedo fit him like a glove, perfectly tailored and probably very expensive, and the diamond pinky ring did not go unnoticed.

"I'm afraid I haven't had the pleasure," Bear said, his voice a low growl.

One dark brow rose and a half smile tipped one corner of the man's mouth. He looked Bear up and down once and extended his hand. His handshake was firm and sure.

"Andrew Shaw," he said.

Bear immediately recognized the name. As much as he wanted to push the man out of his way and go after what he really wanted, he knew Andrew Shaw was important to Beth. He had an obligation to at least be civil to the man. "So this is *your* party." He grabbed a glass of champagne from a passing waiter, took a sip, and tempered his impatience. "Nice turnout."

Shaw glanced about the room and nodded with a satisfied smile on his face. "Yes, it is. I knew it would be another successful showing, but this is beyond even what I imagined." He gave Bear a wry look. "The national headlines certainly didn't hurt. The best publicity is free publicity."

"I suppose so."

"Elizabeth will be very busy from here on out. In addition to interview requests and a movie studio wanting to make a film out of your run from the cartel, at least a dozen people have contacted me expressing the desire to show her work in galleries from New York to Rome."

Bear wasn't sure if he liked that or not, but he kept his feelings well hidden. "Good. She deserves the success."

Shaw looked at him out of the corner of his eye. "She deserves more than that . . . but I suppose that is not my business." The man looked at him thoughtfully. "May I show you something, Special Agent Bristol?"

Part of him didn't want to waste the time, but his sixth sense told him Andrew Shaw could be a valuable ally. Bear certainly didn't want to alienate the man, given his relationship with Beth. He studied the Brit for a moment, put his half-empty glass on the tray of a passing waiter and nodded curtly. The sooner he got this over with the sooner he could go after Beth.

Shaw smiled and turned on his heel. He strode toward a door on the back wall, opened it, and gestured for Bear to precede him. They entered a dark hallway and Shaw walked past him to another door. He opened it and ushered Bear inside the room.

"This is Elizabeth's studio," Shaw said as he flipped on the light. "She couldn't afford one of her own until recently, so I let her use this space. I know she's looking for a new space, but part of me hopes she stays here. I rather like having her around."

There was little in the average-sized room furniture wise other than a desk with a laptop, a large filing cabinet, several printers, a scanner, a light table, and various other pieces of computer equipment. On the far wall was a computer table with three large LCD monitors and several hard drives. On the wall above the screens were half dozen eight-by-ten-inch photographs arranged around an eleven-by-fourteen-inch print. Bear recognized the larger image immediately.

He remembered the first time he'd seen it, several years ago, and the visceral reaction he'd had. In the picture a woman knelt on the ground, her arms cradling the head of a dead U.S. Marine against her chest. Both she and the Marine were covered in blood and her head was thrown back, her face forever frozen in an anguished wail, her tears leaving clean tracks over her dirty, blood-spattered cheeks. Her fingers clutched the front of his flak jacket, and he could almost hear her sobs of grief. The image had completely captured the sorrow and devastating finality of the moment, and stunned a nation.

Shaw crossed the room and stood near the wall. "I take it you have seen this picture before."

"So have a hundred million other people." He moved to stand at Shaw's side. "It was AP's Photograph of the Year what . . . four, five years ago?" It was then he saw it: a camera on the ground at the woman's side as if it had been tossed there unheeded, housing shattered, lens broken, facing the sky, and covered in dust. The device wasn't immediately obvious, as if it had been put there as part of a "hidden-objects" drawing. Then he saw the woman's arm. He was all too familiar with bullet wounds and he exhaled sharply. He took another look at the woman's face and a stone dropped into the pit of his stomach, heavy and cold. "So that's how she got the scar."

"Yes." Shaw crossed his arms over his chest. "I wondered if you would recognize her."

His gut twisted as he gazed at the compelling image. He remembered the nightmare she'd had their first night together and knew she'd been reliving this incident. "Why does she keep this here?"

"To remind herself of what she left behind . . . and why."

Bear looked at him. "I don't understand."

"A man named Steven Schweikert took that photograph. He was with her in Afghanistan." A wistful smile softened Shaw's features. "She was so excited the day she called to tell me the Associated Press was sending her to Kandahar. One would never guess a woman would be so thrilled to go to a war zone."

Bear's gaze was drawn back to the photograph.

"She'd been vying for a spot as a war-correspondent, and they finally saw fit to grant her wish. It was more a fluff piece than actual war-time journalism, but she was happy. She and three of her fellow photojournalists were assigned to a Marine unit during the last month of their tour in Afghanistan. The reporters were supposed to document what the Marines did as they prepared to draw down and ship home, what their hopes and fears were about returning to the States, things like that. It was . . . *tripe* really, all things considered."

Bear clenched his jaw as the woman's — Beth's — tortured cries sprang to life and echoed inside his head.

"During her time there, she became quite close to a Lieutenant Cooper, Coop she called him. He was the Public Affairs Officer for the unit, and he had to approve every photograph and article before she sent them to the home office. He was thirty, married, one child he'd never met — a girl born while he was deployed. All the men were anxious to go home, but the military being the military, they still had to work. Three days before they were scheduled to ship out, the Lieutenant and his men had to perform a routine patrol of the local area, and he invited Elizabeth to go along. Mr. Schweikert, not to be outdone by a woman, insisted on accompanying them as well. The Lieutenant wasn't happy about it, but Elizabeth didn't care. She e-mailed me and wrote she was thrilled to be getting off base because things had been routine, even dull."

Bear took a deep breath. "The calm before the storm."

"Indeed." Shaw eased down on a nearby chair. "They left the base in a convoy of five Humvees. Elizabeth rode with the Lieutenant in the third vehicle and Steven was in the fourth. Everything seemed normal until they made their way through a small village a few miles from the base."

"Let me guess." Bear closed his eyes briefly, his stomach knotted. "Ambush."

Shaw glanced at him. "How did you know that? That information was not made public. The press reported the incident as a random IED. Did she tell you?"

"No." He shook his head. "Call it a hunch." He wanted to look away from that photograph because he didn't want to feel what it made him feel, but he couldn't. "What happened?"

"Well, the first vehicle *did* hit an IED, but there was nothing random about it. Three of the four Marines inside were killed instantly and the fourth received burns over 80% of his body. He's still at Walter Reed I believe."

Bear suddenly wished he hadn't relinquished his champagne glass.

"They started taking mortar fire from the rear. Obviously, the attack had been planned, but Marines are nothing if not prepared to fight. Lieutenant Cooper had pulled Elizabeth from the Humvee seconds before it was hit by an RPG, tossed her into a drainage ditch on the side of the road – saved her life."

The last man who saved my life . . . I watched him die. Bear exhaled slowly. "Jesus."

"After the Lieutenant had rejoined his comrades, Elizabeth tried to photograph what was going on, but the battle was too fierce. Each time she stuck her head up, bullets whizzed by. She set her camera to auto advance and just held it up, and received a bullet in the forearm and shattered bones for her efforts. I told her she had more courage than sense, but I'd suppose you'd know that as well as I now."

Bear scowled and Shaw chuckled. His gaze returned to the photo.

"Elizabeth's driver was lying a few feet away, wounded and unconscious, and without thinking she grabbed his rifle. She told me she just started shooting at anyone who wasn't wearing a military uniform, quite a feat with only one good arm. Eventually she ran out of ammunition, and she started crawling down the ditch, hoping to find more. That was when she saw Steven using the Marines as cover so he could take pictures. When the man he was hiding behind got shot, Steven just scurried on to the next Marine without even checking to see if the former was dead or alive. Elizabeth told me if she'd had any bullets at that point she would've shot *Steven.*"

A spark of anger burned hotly in his chest. "That's my girl."

Shaw blinked at that, and then continued. "She wasn't sure how much time passed before the Marines gained the upper hand, but she said it wasn't long." Shaw gave him a wry smile. "They *are* called Devil-Dogs for a reason, after all."

Bear chuckled mirthlessly. "Ooh rah."

Shaw turned his gaze back to the photograph. "When air support arrived the, battle was all but won. Once gunfire died down to a sporadic roar, Lieutenant Cooper came back for her. He leaned over, offered her his hand, and pulled her out of the ditch. As soon as she was on her feet he was shot in the neck by a sniper."

Bear ran a hand over his face as his insides dropped into his shoes. "God almighty."

"He bled out in seconds." Shaw's features hardened and his eyes took on a frosty glint. "As she knelt there, cradling his head and screaming for a medic, Schweikert stood a few feet off, smiling and taking pictures of it all. He didn't look for a corpsman, didn't even call for one. Then he had the audacity to thank her for giving him the 'shot of a lifetime.'"

"Bastard better pray we never run into each other, or they'll be pumping his stomach for his teeth," Bear said in a growl.

"Yes, well it gets better." Shaw pursed his lips and straightened his jacket. "When they finally got back to the home office, Steven was lauded for his accomplishments and Elizabeth was reprimanded."

Bear's gaze swung around and he didn't bother to hide his astonishment. "*Reprimanded?* For *what?*"

"For getting involved when she should have been impartially documenting what was happening. They told her she should have followed Steven's example."

Bear gaped at him. "Why didn't she say something?"

"Because she's better than that," Shaw said sharply, his gaze clearly saying Bear should know the answer to his own question. "She'd kill me if she knew I was telling *you* this. Technically, *I'm* not supposed to know." He glanced at the photo. "She quit, moved back to Denver, got a job at a local paper and didn't look back. I was never prouder of anyone than I was of her when she told me she'd left the AP and why."

"So, she's reprimanded and Schweikert becomes a star." Bear grunted. "Life really is a bitch sometimes." His brows drew down. "Maybe I should Google him, see if he's coming to Denver anytime soon and arrange a meet."

A malicious glint entered Shaw's eyes. "No need, Special Agent Bristol. What I'm doing to him is far more effective than a beating."

"What's that?"

Shaw set his jaw. "I've been in this business for more than thirty years. I know everyone who is anyone in the art world, and they know me. Trust me. *Photograph of the Year* is *all* Steven Schweikert will *ever* gain from his efforts in Afghanistan." He fixed Bear with a cold stare. "As soon as the presses stopped running, his fifteen minutes of fame were *over*."

"And is this part of your revenge . . . all these showings for Beth?"

Shaw stood. "I am showing Elizabeth's work because she is truly gifted and incredibly talented, and she's earned the recognition." One brow rose and he smiled. "And, because she's a close personal friend."

Bear kept his expression neutral. "How close?"

Shaw laughed softly, a mischievous light in his eyes. "Rest easy, Special Agent Bristol. Elizabeth is a beautiful woman, but . . . *you* are more my type than *she* is."

Bear gaped at him and Shaw gave him a shameless grin.

"If I didn't know you were hetero, I would have hit on you already. I have a *fondness* for large men."

Bear fought a smile. "Good to know."

"Now, I must return to my guests, but before I do, I have just one more thing to say."

Bear stood and faced him. "Fire away."

"Elizabeth is an extraordinary woman, Special Agent Bristol." Shaw rested a hand on Bear's shoulder. "The man who lets her get away from him is a fool." He looked at Bear for a moment before his hand dropped back to his side.

Bear narrowed his eyes on the man. "That's *two* things."

Shaw stared at him for a moment, then shook his head and laughed. "Indeed it is." He turned and walked toward the door. "I trust you can find your own way out?"

"I'm a big boy."

Shaw paused with his hand on the doorknob and gave him a look that reminded Bear of Emily Harper. "Yes . . . you *are*." The man sighed and opened the door. He stepped into the hall, but paused and turned back. "You should check the rooftop garden. Elizabeth often goes up there at night. There's a set of stairs," he paused and pointed, "at the end of the hall."

Bear watched the door close behind the man and turned his gaze back to Steven Schweikert's "Photograph of the Year." The surrounding photos had to be of Lieutenant Cooper, photos taken *before* he had been killed. He looked surprisingly young and handsome, with a boyish smile and laughing eyes. In one shot he was showing off a picture of a pretty young woman holding a baby, the woman's face beaming as she posed with the infant. Bear felt the tug of empathy and regret at what that woman and child had lost; what they had *all* lost. Another young Marine's life ended far too soon.

He looked at the photograph for another minute or so, then left the studio and closed the door behind him. Walking in the direction Shaw had indicated, he found the stairs and quickly ascended the four flights to the roof. The door at the top was unlocked, and he pushed it open with one hand.

The rooftop garden was actually that – a real garden. A brick path took a circuitous route through beds of flowering roses, camellias, and other blossoms he couldn't name. Soft, white Christmas-type lights hung from a wide, rough-hewn pergola, the wooden beams dripping with honeysuckle. Intimate seating areas were outlined with ferns and other delicate greenery, white wrought iron chaises and chairs invited lovers to come and stay a while. While Bear admired the romantic, whimsical effect, he wasn't interested in anything other than finding Beth.

He caught sight of her through the vines and paused, his eyes taking in the full measure of her beauty. She was barefoot, which he found oddly sexy, his eyes following the curve of her legs upward. The shimmery dress ended just above her knees and skimmed her figure rather than hugging it tightly, revealing the amazing curves while still being elegant and chic. His hands itched to cup that rounded bottom and pull her against him. Bear took a shaky breath as he remembered the night they had shared. She stood at the edge of the roof, her hands braced on the waist-high brick wall, her hair done up in a loose French twist. He wanted to kiss the graceful curve of her neck, pull the pins from the mahogany tresses, and watch as they tumbled down around her shoulders. He wanted to take that look of hurt and replace it with the smile that made his heart pound. He wanted her, all of her.

Beth had heard the door to the rooftop terrace open and close, but she didn't have the courage to turn around and face the person she knew stood there. His presence was bigger than life, and she sensed it from where she was nearly twenty feet away. Focusing on the city lights laid out before her, she tried to regulate her pulse and her breathing. A breeze curled around her briefly and only then did she feel the cool wetness of tears. She quickly ran a hand over her cheeks and wrapped her arms around herself.

"If I didn't know better, I'd say you were avoiding me."

His voice was low and silky and goose bumps prickled on her arms. Beth shook her head and closed her eyes briefly. "Why would I do that?"

"I don't know."

She gritted her teeth and tried to pull herself together, but the pain in her chest was as tangible as if the knife was still embedded in her sternum.

His footsteps approached, leisurely and unhurried. He stood at her back and she bit her lip. Part of her wanted to turn around and press her face into his chest, but she forced herself to remain aloof. She jumped when his jacket was draped over her shoulders and his scent wrapped around her. The knife in her chest twisted.

"Why are you up here instead of downstairs enjoying the spotlight?" he asked softly.

That sparked her temper, but not enough to give her the courage to face him. Beth focused on the dark windows of the building across the street, her fingers digging into her upper arms. "I don't *enjoy* the spotlight," she said from between clenched teeth, "but unfortunately it comes with the job."

She tensed when he put his hands on her shoulders but didn't resist when he turned her to him. The unreadable expression was firmly in place, but as each second passed it fell away and Beth recognized *Bear*. His expression was sad, pensive, and his gaze wandered slowly over her face.

"I almost didn't come here tonight." He met her eyes. "I wasn't sure I wanted to see you."

Beth blinked at him. She stared for several seconds and then focused on the neat double-Windsor. "Just what every girl wants to hear."

He cupped her chin and tipped her head up. He was scowling, his brows drawn together, anger glittering in those azure eyes. "Not because I didn't want to *see* you."

His nearness was too much and she pulled away from him. She tried to concentrate on slowing down her pulse. "Look, Bear, you don't have to explain anything to me. You can't force yourself to feel something you don't." The blade dug a little deeper and she dropped her chin. "Love can't be manufactured. It's either there or it isn't. Believe me, I understand."

His anger faded and she thought she saw a flicker of uncertainty . . . and fear. Her breath caught. She'd never seen Bear uncertain about or afraid of *anything*.

"I know what you're thinking, and you are so wrong." His fingers grazed her jaw. "I wasn't apprehensive because I was worried about breaking your heart. I'm more worried about *you* breaking *mine*." His eyes narrowed. "I didn't want to come here because I knew that once I looked at you . . . I'd have to acknowledge that, regardless of what you do or don't feel for *me*, *I* have feelings for *you*."

Beth stared at him. "You *know* how I feel about you."

"No, I *don't*." When she opened her mouth to argue, he pressed a finger to her lips. "I know what you said *then*, but the situation we were in can wreak havoc on a person's emotions." His eyes narrowed. "What about *now*?" Bear tucked a strand of hair behind her ear and trailed his fingers slowly down her neck. "I need to know how you feel *now*, Beth, because now . . . I'm in love with you."

For a moment she wasn't sure she'd heard correctly, but as she replayed it in her head, realization dawned and her heart thumped wildly against her ribs. "You are?" she whispered.

A small smile curved his mouth. "Don't sound so surprised."

Part of her was still unwilling to believe what he'd just said. She closed her eyes and tried to draw a breath. "Just in case nobody's ever told you, you're *really* good at hiding your feelings."

"I know, and I'm sorry." His knuckles brushed her cheek. "I've gotten so good at it that sometimes I'm not sure how to turn it off. But I don't want to hide anymore, not from you."

She met his gaze. "You don't have to hide from me, Bear. I see you. Not the job, not the badge, *you*. I see the man you are, a man who would lay down his life for his friends, or a stranger, without a second thought." Beth stepped closer. "I fell in love with *Bear*, not Special Agent Bristol."

"Special Agent Bristol is part of who I am."

"I know," she said with a small smile, "but there's so much more to you."

"There's more to you, too." He went silent as he gently traced the scar on her arm. After several moments he looked at her. "Mr. Shaw told me about Lieutenant Cooper."

Cold sorrow pierced her heart as the memory of Coop's laughing eyes flashed in her mind. The sporadic bursts of gunfire, the smell of dust and blood and gunpowder, the taste of terror and sheer chaos assaulted her in an eruption of disorganized mental pictures. Squeezing her eyes shut and fisting her hands at her sides, she forced the images back into the box. "He shouldn't have done that."

"Why not? What happened that day helped shape you into the woman you are." He took her hand and traced the scar. "I'm sorry for what happened, Beth."

Something cold and serpentine wound around her esophagus and squeezed as she met his gaze. "I don't want your pity."

His brows drew together. "I don't pity you. I feel empathy for Cooper's wife and child and family, and for what you went through, but that doesn't change how I feel about *you*." He laced his fingers through hers. "I made a decision before I came here tonight, and what your boss told me didn't influence that one way or the other."

"What decision?"

Bear took a deep breath and Beth watched the undisguised play of emotions on that sharply chiseled face: doubt, hope, anxiety, longing; a mirror for the chaos swirling inside her. Her breath caught.

"I'm not going to fight how I feel about you," he said softly. "Not anymore."

Beth blinked and exhaled sharply. Suddenly lightheaded, she walked over to the nearest chaise and sat down. She'd thought she would be overjoyed if Bear admitted to having feelings for her, but she realized now was the point where things became even more complicated. Part of her had been certain Bear would reject her. If she was entirely truthful, part of her had been hoping for that. She'd cry,

Andrew would hold her hand, and eventually she'd get over him and move on to someone who *didn't* intimidate the hell out of her. After all, it was far easier to never start a relationship than to crash and burn halfway through. When he crouched in front of her, she squeezed her eyes shut.

He seemed to sense her distress and rested his hands on her knees. "I don't know what you've been through, Beth, but I'm not *him*."

Her gaze flew to his face and she was caught off guard by the tenderness she saw there.

"Talk to me, sweetheart."

She looked into those beautiful azure eyes and her heart melted. "I am *such* an idiot."

"*No*, you're *not*. You're brilliant and you're beautiful." His brows drew together. "*Talk* to me."

Beth looked at her lap, unable to return the intensity of his gaze. Her throat was tight with anxiety, and it took her nearly half a minute to find her voice. "I mentioned my ex, Michael."

"You did, but only in the most flattering terms."

His humor couldn't parry the memory as it faded in from black, like the start of a movie. Beth sighed. "Well, when he and I parted ways . . . it wasn't your typical break-up."

"What was it?"

She chuckled darkly. "It was a mess."

He grasped her hands gently and kissed her fingers. "So tell me."

She was silent for several long seconds and the image brightened. "We'd been together about a year and a half, living together for four or five months, but it was over and we both knew it." Beth focused on the subtle geometric design of the navy blue tie around his neck. "He called me at work one day and said we *needed to talk*, asked me to come home for lunch. I said I'd be there by one and spent the next three hours bracing myself for the break-up I knew was coming."

"So, when I called this afternoon and said we needed to talk . . . ."

She nodded.

He pressed his lips gently to the back of her hand again, and suddenly the pain inside her, a pain she hadn't even realized she felt, faded. The concern in his eyes, the tender touch was like a balm to her soul.

"What happened?" he asked in a low, level voice.

Oddly, the memory didn't hurt her any longer. Beth let it rise, like a dead thing floating to the surface, and let it go. The ache evaporated like mist. "When I walked through the door of my apartment, I expected to see him at the kitchen table with his suitcase." She shook her head. "I did *not* expect to see him *on* the kitchen table, having sex with my best friend." She took a deep breath. "He timed it perfectly. In fact, he was checking the clock when I walked in."

Bear's brows rose and he rubbed her fingers absently. "Wow. He really *is* the world heavyweight champion asshole. How did *you* wind up with *him*?" She couldn't reply and his expression turned solemn. "You know why he did that, don't you?"

She'd never understood why Michael had gutted her that way, using her former best friend like a weapon, but Bear obviously did. "Why?"

"Because he didn't have the courage to do what you both knew needed to be done." Bear tucked a strand of hair behind her ear. "He did the *one* thing he knew would make you do what he couldn't."

"Well, it worked."

"Good." A pensive smile curved his mouth. "I guess we're both guilty of holding someone else's past sins against the other." His gaze wandered over her face and then a wicked gleam entered his eyes. "How about from now on . . . the only thing we hold against each other *is* each other."

Beth's pulse leapt and she gulped. He released her hands and brushed his fingertips over her jaw.

"I would *never* do what he did to you," he whispered, tracing her collarbone. "*Never*."

"I know." Her breathing quickened as warm tingles fanned over her skin. "I've always known."

"I have to warn you." Bear cupped her head and leaned forward until their brows touched. "I haven't done this in a long time, sweetheart. I may not be any good at it."

Beth grasped his forearms. "You're good at everything you do, Bear."

"Even you?"

He sounded like he was joking, but she saw the flash of trepidation in his eyes. "Especially me." She kissed him, pulling back sharply when unexpected heat seared through her. The look on his face told her he'd felt it, too. Her fears faded. She realized she'd rather run half a race with him than never leave the starting gate, and it didn't matter that somewhere deep inside her she still thought he was out of her league. He didn't think that or he wouldn't be here. She covered his hands with hers. "Give me forever, Bear."

His lips nearly touched hers, his gaze moving slowly over her face. "Forever may be all you get."

She smiled. "I'll take it."

Epilogue

Bear closed his eyes and listened to the sound of Beth's breathing. Her head nestled against his shoulder, her hand rested on his chest, and her naked body was pressed tight to his side. He trailed his fingers lightly over her arm and reveled in her closeness. Her hair lay draped over his arm, cool and soft, and her breath was warm on his neck. There was nowhere else on earth he wanted to be. Here, in his custom-made bed, in his converted loft, with her, was where he belonged. He knew it with as much certainty as he knew he was meant to be an FBI agent. Had Fate appeared to him and told him their love was written in the stars, he would have shrugged, smiled, and said, "Duh."

"What's so funny?" Beth asked in a soft, sleepy voice.

He hadn't realized he'd laughed. "Nothing."

"You chuckled."

Bear laced his fingers together, enclosing her completely in his embrace. "Just thinking amusing thoughts."

"About me?"

He tightened his hold on her. "No, funny doesn't figure into the thoughts I think about you." He pressed his lips to her brow. "Nope. No funny there."

She kissed his neck. "Mmm . . . good."

"So," he began, "when are you moving in?"

She was silent, and then she extricated herself from his arms to lean on one elbow. Her eyes were wide and incredulous. Bear wound a lock of hair around one finger, rubbing the mahogany strands absently as he returned her stare.

"Are you serious?" she finally asked.

He thought about it for a moment. "Yeah, I am."

She blinked at him. "Bear . . . we just . . . *started* this, and you're asking me to move in?"

"Technically, we started this almost four months ago, and you should know by now I'm an all or nothing kind of guy."

Beth's brows rose and she inhaled sharply. "I know that, but this is kind of like . . . jumping off the Golden Gate, all or nothing." She dropped her gaze. "Once you let go of the bridge, there's no going back."

Curling a finger under her chin, he turned her face to his. "I see you every time I go to sleep, Beth." He traced her cheekbone and the soft curves of her mouth. "I'd kind of like to see you when I'm awake, too."

The flash of trepidation in her vivid eyes was obvious to him and he fought a smile. She sat up and wrapped her arms around her knees. The gentle line of her back fascinated him, and he ran his hand over the satiny skin.

"Once Michael moved in with me, it was a straight shot downhill from that point." He saw the convulsive swallow as she squeezed her eyes shut. "I don't want to do *anything* that could make that happen with you . . . with *us*."

Bear sat up and kissed her bare shoulder. "I'm not Michael."

She turned toward him, her eyes filled with fear and dismay. "But I'm still *me*." Her gaze locked with his for a moment, and then she looked away. "What if it was *my* fault?"

He pushed a fall of hair away from her neck, his fingers lingering there. "Sweetheart, it takes two to make or break a relationship. No one person is ever totally at fault." He curled a hand around her neck and pulled her close. "I think the fact that Michael Ellison is a coward, more than anything else, is what doomed the two of you."

She rested her brow against his shoulder and took a shaky breath. "Do you really think so?"

Her fear was palpable and he wished he could take it from her, put it in a locked box aside his own misgivings and never look at it again. Not that he had many fears when it came to loving her. The way he felt for her only made him stronger. Bear wound his fingers through hers and held them to his chest.

"Love isn't easy, Beth." He kissed the back of her hand. "And maintaining it takes work, time, and . . . *dedication.* From what you've told me of him, I highly doubt Michael Ellison ever dedicated himself to *anything.*"

Her head came up slowly and the look she gave him made his throat tighten.

"I can't lose you, Bear," she whispered with a shake of her head. "Not again."

He framed her face and looked deeply into those golden eyes. "Sweetheart, as long as I'm breathing, I am *yours.*"

Before she could speak, he kissed her, and her surrender sent desire sparking inside him once more. Bear tasted her, explored her with slow, sensual purpose. Her body was taut with anxiety. He gently pushed her onto her back, easing down beside her, his mouth never leaving hers. She returned his kiss, but he sensed the uncertainty in her. He feathered kisses over her jaw to her ear.

"You don't *have* to move in," he whispered, nibbling her earlobe. "Just know the invitation is open. Here is where I want you, but only if you want that, too."

"I do," she replied, breathless. "Just . . . give me some time."

He slid his hand around her waist and over her back, slowly pressing her closer. "You take all the time you need, as long as you spend most of it here with me."

Capturing her lips again, he deepened the kiss. Her bare breasts brushed his chest and desire sizzled through him. Beth sighed softly, and he wanted to shout in triumph when her body relaxed against his. Her arms snaked around his neck, and she pressed her pelvis toward him. Bear ran a hand over her hip and down her leg, hooking his fingers behind her knee. He tugged and she wound her thigh around his waist. His groin throbbed and tightened and a low growl escaped him. Rolling onto his back, he pulled her on top of him. She looked at him with smoky eyes for a moment, moved her hips and took him inside her. Bear sucked in a breath. She braced her hands on his chest and looked down at him, her hair falling like a dark curtain around them.

"I love you, Bear," she said in a husky whisper, "and there's no place I'd rather be than with you."

✳✳✳✳

It took six months for Beth to make up her mind about moving in, but when she did, there was no discussion, no grand entrance, and no drama. She just showed up with her things, what little she had, and that was that. And Bear's loft still looked pretty much like his loft, with Beth touches here and there. Instead of bare walls he had rows upon rows of photographs of him, of her, of them together, of his family, of Laine and Jack, of the wildlife she spent her time chasing, and even Maverick and Andrew had shots in the mix. There were no throw pillows or frilly curtains, just the occasional lacy panty on the floor of the bedroom and the shampoo and body wash in the shower that reminded him of her. The combination of their respective homes had been almost as easy as falling in love . . . *almost.* He still didn't like having his picture taken.

THE END

About the author

Leslie McKelvey has been writing since she learned to write, and her mother still stores boxes of handwritten stories in the attic. Her debut novel, Accidental Affair, was published in 2012.

Leslie is a veteran of the Gulf War who served with the U.S. Navy, and she was among the first groups of women to work the flight deck of an aircraft carrier.

Leslie lives in California with her husband and has three sons.

Also by Leslie McKelvey

Accidental Affair

Jack Vaughn is sure his life is over as he tumbles down the wooded hillside onto the deserted two-lane stretch of asphalt. Years of work ended with a single gunshot. Yet, it's not over.

A good Samaritan stops to help him, despite the danger he poses to her.

Laine Wheeler knows better than to stop for strangers on the rural Montana highway near her home, but her conscience won't allow her to leave an injured man behind.

What she doesn't know is the man is an undercover ATF agent tasked with infiltrating a domestic terrorist group. His cover has been blown and helping him will put her life in danger.

Though there is an instant attraction, Jack knows that beginning a romantic relationship with Laine would be both unfair and unwise. Yet the farther they run, the harder it gets to ignore the feelings surging between them.

Coming soon from Leslie McKelvey

Her Sister's Keeper

Latest titles from Black Velvet Seductions

Playing for Keeps by Glenda Horsfall
The Love She Wants by Mila Winters
Holly's Big Bad Santa by Starla Kaye
Punished! by Richard Savage, Nadia Nautalia & Starla Kaye

See more of our titles at
www.blackvelvetseductions.com

Our titles are available from:
Amazon
Smashwords
LuLu
Nook
Blushing Books
All Romance eBooks
Bookstrand
and other retailers